Author of ove̶~~~~ ~~~~s
been married f̶~~~~ ~~~~
writer could ̶~~~~ ~~~~
books and has ̶~~~~ ~~~~ many other awards.
She blogs at the-twisted-sisters.com and can be found
at marilyn-pappano.com. She and her husband live in
Oklahoma with five rough-and-tumble dogs.

Carol Ericson lives in southern California, home of
state-of–the-art cosmetic surgery, wild motorway
chases, and a million amazing stories. These stories,
along with hordes of virile men and feisty women
clamour for release from Carol's head until she sets
them free to fulfil their destinies and her readers'
fantasies. To find out more about Carol and her current
books, please visit her website at carolericson.com,
'where romance flirts with danger'.

Cindy Myers became one of the most popular people
in eighth grade when she and her best friend wrote a
torrid historical romance and passed the manuscript
around among friends. Fame was short-lived, alas; the
English teacher confiscated the manuscript. Since then,
Cindy has written more than fifty published novels. Her
historical and contemporary romances and women's
fiction have garnered praise from reviewers and readers
alike.

Enemies to Lovers

Enemies to Lovers:
Trusting the Enemy

MARILYN PAPPANO

CAROL ERICSON

CINDI MYERS

MILLS & BOON

First Published in Great Britain 2022
By Mills & Boon, an imprint of HarperCollins*Publishers,* Ltd
1 London Bridge Street, London, SE1 9GF

www.harpercollins.co.uk

HarperCollins*Publishers*
1st Floor, Watermarque Building,
Ringsend Road, Dublin 4, Ireland

ENEMIES TO LOVERS: TRUSTING THE ENEMY
© 2022 Harlequin Enterprises ULC.

Detective Defender © 2017 Marilyn Pappano
Bulletproof SEAL © 2018 Carol Ericson
Danger on Dakota Ridge © 2018 Cynthia Myers

ISBN: 978-0-263-30458-9

MIX
Paper from
responsible sources
FSC™ C007454

This book is produced from independently certified FSC™ paper to ensure responsible forest management.

For more information visit: www.harpercollins.co.uk/green

Printed and Bound in Spain using 100% Renewable electricity at CPI Black Print, Barcelona

DETECTIVE DEFENDER

MARILYN PAPPANO

For the people who have loved New Orleans
with me:

Dale

Meg

Susan

And for the special cops in my life:

Brandon and Robert

I love you all!

Chapter 1

It was a strange winter. The sky hung heavy and gray, the clouds so dense that the sun hadn't managed to break through in days. Damp cold drifted through the French Quarter streets, spreading its chill with each bit of ground it covered. Martine Broussard had lived her entire life in southern Louisiana, and she couldn't recall any winter that been so relentlessly bleak for so shamelessly long.

Tugging her jacket tighter, she regretted not taking a few moments to run up the stairs from her shop to get a heavier coat before striking out for the river, but Paulina had been so insistent on the phone. *You have to come* now. *I really have to talk to you, Tine.*

When a ghost from your past broke twenty-four years of silence with both fear and anger in her voice, what could you do besides go *now*?

No one sat on the benches in Jackson Square or lounged on the grass, a rare emptiness that was as strange as the chill. The walkways along the four sides saw a bit more traffic, but people seemed eager to go from one place to another. Like them, Martine didn't linger but lengthened her stride instead. It was only a handful of blocks from her shop on Royal Street, and the walk to the river normally took ten minutes or so as she strolled and dawdled and exchanged hellos with fellow Quarter residents. This afternoon she cut the travel time in half, jogging across Decatur, crossing the trolley tracks, reaching the Moonwalk in record time. It was even colder here by the river, but that wasn't what caused the prickling of her nerves.

It was the sudden absolute sense of...*wrong*. This weather was wrong. The phone call from Paulina was wrong. The panic in her voice was wrong. The queasiness in Martine's gut was wrong. It was a normal Tuesday in a normal week in a normal January in a normal French Quarter, and the uneasiness, the nervousness, the weirdness, were all wrong.

But it *wasn't* a normal day, a normal week, a normal month.

The broad path stretching in both directions atop the riverside levee was empty. There were trees, benches and trash cans, all shrouded in swirling fog, but not a sign of life in either direction. Martine reached inside her jacket, touched her fingers lightly to the charm that lay beneath her shirt, then gripped it as a figure materialized a dozen feet ahead of her. A gasp escaped her before she recognized Paulina, but even recognition didn't slow the pounding of her heart.

"Never thought I could hide behind a little tree,

did you?" her old friend commented. Though she still looked very much like the girl Martine had grown up with, she was significantly different, too. Teenage Paulina had always carried an extra ten pounds that gave a soft roundedness to her beauty; she'd rarely been without a smile; her blond hair had gleamed and her blue eyes had glistened with life, love, anticipation and promise.

This woman needed an extra ten pounds to fill out the hollows in her face. Her hair hung dull and limp, and her eyes were hollow, too. She wore black pants that bagged on her skinny frame, a dingy white shirt and a gray fleece jacket that helped her blend into the steely day.

She would have been voted "the girl most likely to…" if their generation had done such things. Most likely to sleep with the boys. To talk back to the teachers. To flirt with the handsome football coach. To get suspended for being a wild child and named homecoming queen in the same year. To go to college, to live life loud, to run wild and travel far, to have the perfect career, marry the perfect man, birth perfect children.

Like the day, the weather and everything else, that title would have turned out to be wrong.

Realizing she was still clenching her charm, Martine let it drop and slowly closed the distance between them. "It's been a long time, Paulina."

"Not long enough. I'd hoped I'd never see you again."

Though the baldly spoken sentiment stung, Martine couldn't take offense because subconsciously she'd reached the same conclusion long ago. For fifteen years they'd been best friends—the two of them plus Callie

and Tallie, the Winchester twins, and Robin Railey—
but one June night had ended that. Robin had refused
anything to do with them starting the next day. The
twins had moved their summer visit to relatives in
England ahead by a month and left without a goodbye, and Paulina had escaped to college two months
early. As far as she knew, none of them had ever returned home.

"Why don't we get out of the cold? Get some coffee?" Martine gestured vaguely to her left, her wave
taking in Jax Brewery and Café du Monde.

Paulina shook her head and went straight to the
point. "Someone knows."

Without thought, Martine reached for the charm
again, caught herself and forced her hand away. A chill
swept through her, unsettling and eerie and totally ir-
rational. She knew that last part in her brain—had
tried to convince her friends of it twenty-four years
ago but never could. She gave herself a mental shake
and Paulina a faint smile. "Knows what, Paulina? That
five girls who'd had too much weed played some silly
games in the woods one night?"

Paulina's features looked as if they would crack if
she tried to return the smile. They were masklike, the
coloring off, the contours exaggerated, the eyes shallow and empty of any emotion that might come down
on the lighter side. A not-real mask of how a real Paulina might look if she were scared to death.

Scared to death? Because of something they'd done
when they were kids?

"They know what we did, Tine. I don't know how—
maybe they saw us, maybe Callie or Tallie or Robin
told someone—but they know, and they're…they're…"

Her gaze swept the area, her eyes wide. She hunched her shoulders and lowered her voice. "They're coming after us."

Martine shuddered, reminded of too many late girls' nights watching horror movies on TV or wandering the entire town after everyone else was in bed, snitching tomatoes from Mrs. Bush's plants, peaches from Mr. Everard's trees, sharing plans and jokes and stories to scare the pants off each other. Paulina had always been best at those, holding a flashlight so her face was mostly shadows, creating voices for every character, including low, growly, vicious ones for the villains. She'd never failed to make Martine shriek with good-natured fear, followed by laughter.

But a look at Paulina showed the great release of laughter wasn't on the agenda today.

Again, Martine gestured toward the more populated area a few dozen yards away. "Come with me, Paulina. I'll buy you a cup of coffee and some beignets. You always said they were God's dessert, and they're as good today as they were then." She even took a few steps before realizing that Paulina hadn't moved.

"Have you talked to Callie or Tallie or Robin?" the woman asked. "Heard anything about them from your family or on Facebook?"

Retracing her steps, Martine returned to her original spot. "No." The end of their friendships had come too fast, had been too hard. She'd moped around alone and lonely after they'd abandoned her, until finally she fled, too, though not far: only the fifty miles to New Orleans. She'd put them out of her head and eventually out of her heart, and she'd made new friends and built a new life with no room for them. The day she'd realized she could think of them dispassionately—*Oh, that blonde looks like Paulina* or *She reminds me of Robin with the way she walks*—had been a very long time coming.

"Well, you can't talk to Callie. She's dead. They tried to kill Tallie, but she got away. No one knows where she is. I haven't been able to find Robin, so I don't know if she's still alive. And that leaves you and me, Tine. Me, I don't stay in one place very long. You, though…you're living over there on Royal Street. Hell, you're even listed in the phone book. You need to leave. Run. Find a dark little hole and pull it in on top of you, because they're coming after us, and they're not going to stop until we're—we're…"

She said the last word in one of those scary-story voices, little more than a whisper but still loud enough to echo inside Martine's head: "Dead."

A passing ship chose that moment to blast its horn, both muffled and amplified by the heavy air. Martine gazed at it a moment, headed downriver. Once it reached the Gulf of Mexico, its crew could go any-place they wanted in the world. A tiny part of her wished herself on the deck, where soon the sun would shine and all of life's possibilities would open up before her again.

But she couldn't run away, wouldn't, especially from a problem that wasn't even really a problem. Those foolish kids from twenty-four years ago hadn't done anything deserving of punishment. Besides, she had a business here, a home and the best friends a woman could be blessed with. Who gave up perfect to run from unfounded fears?

Apparently Paulina. When Martine turned away

from the ship and back to her friend, Paulina was quickly disappearing into the mist ahead. "Paulina, wait!" Boots with three-inch heels weren't made for running, especially when the ground was damp, but she got close enough to snag the trailing hood of Paulina's jacket. "Paulina, please, let's talk about this. I'll get you a place to stay. You can get a good night's rest, tonight I'll cook your grandmother's gumbo, and in the morning we'll have beignets and coffee and straighten all this out."

Paulina's gaze took on a scornful cast as she spun around to face Martine. "You don't believe me, do you? You, with all your voodoo and charms and black-magic curses—you think I'm crazy. I knew Tallie would doubt me. She and Callie never had half a brain between them. And Robin…she always thought I didn't have half a brain, either. But you—you make your living off this stuff, you're surrounded by it all the time, and you think I'm crazy."

"I don't, Paulina, I don't think you're crazy at all. I just want—I want to understand it. I want to know what's happened. I want to wrap my head around it. We can do that together and maybe even find Robin. Just come back to the shop with me. Come on, we'll talk it all out and—and find some way to make things right, okay? We always made things right, didn't we?"

Stiffening, Paulina gave her a haughty stare. "You think I don't remember your lying-your-ass-off voice? So innocent and sincere that every adult you used it on believed every word you said?"

Heat flushed Martine's face. She hadn't realized when she slipped into the voice, but she'd recognized it by the end of her little speech. Her best friend Evie called it her dealing-with-psychos voice. A popular French Quarter psychic, Evie had her own version, the tourists-wanting-their-money's-worth voice.

"I'm sorry, I'm sorry. I didn't mean—" A screech rushed up from the fog that hid their feet, making them both jump. An instant later, an angry little dove flew up into view, hovered for a moment to chitter at them— they must have interrupted his dining on whatever scraps he'd found below—then darted off.

At the same moment, Paulina darted off, too. She moved fast and silent, either sure of her footing or not caring if she took a wrong step. Martine watched her go, tugged her coat even tighter and headed back to the shop.

Jimmy DiBiase didn't have the typical wanderlust. He had no desire to travel to every state in the union. He didn't like flying enough to want to spend hours in the air to tour Britain, France, Italy or Greece. He didn't care about China or India or Vietnam or any of hundreds of foreign places he'd never been. He'd been born and raised within spitting distance of the Mississippi River, and he was happy to stay within that same narrow range.

But he did like moving.

When he woke up, he knew automatically that it was Wednesday, and without looking at a clock, he knew it was too early for him to be awake, for which he could thank the person calling his cell. He knew it looked like another grim, dreary day, and he needed to take a leak, but he didn't know where the bathroom was because, not for the first time in his life—or even this year—he didn't know where he was.

First things first. He picked up the cell, setting it on the table next to the mattress. The mattress and the box spring were the only other furniture in the room, and the tile seemed to radiate out from them in dark shiny waves. Shoving his hair from his face, he answered the call as he sank back under the covers. "What time is it?"

"Five fifteen." The voice belonged to Jack Murphy, the homicide detective he worked with most often, and he sounded as unready to roll out of bed as Jimmy. Understandable when he had a beautiful wife curled up next to him. "Spare me the complaints, James. We got a case."

"How'd we get a case when our shift doesn't start for nearly two hours?" Jimmy sat up and swung his feet to the floor, then saw the wall of windows on the other side of the room. This was his new apartment. He'd seen it only once before and never in the dark, but there was no mistaking all that glass eight stories above the ground.

"Personal connection," Murphy said. "I'll pick you up in five."

"I'm at the new place."

"I'll be out front."

The call ended, and Jimmy thought for about ten seconds about stretching out again, but there was nothing in the world he loved as much as his job—not even sleep when his head was thick and his ass was dragging. Add in Murphy's personal connection to a homicide case, and he moved fast enough that he was standing on the sidewalk when Murphy pulled to the curb.

Jimmy slid into the passenger seat, angling the computer away to give himself some space. He fastened his seat belt and reached for the travel mug of steaming coffee in the holder nearest his seat. A carefully wrapped muffin sat on top of the cup—carrot and walnut, by the smell of it. Evie Murphy was a princess among wives. Murphy was damned lucky to have her.

Jimmy's behavior in his one and only marriage had proved he didn't deserve any kind of wife. The way he'd treated Alia must have seriously pissed off the gods; judging by the sorry state of his relationships since then, it seemed they were done with him.

With his dark hair standing on end and his tie looped around his neck instead of tied, Murphy was stoic and silent, not yet awake. He drove through the freaky, patchy fog, following empty streets past houses where outdoor lights cast dim halos. It wasn't raining, but everything was wet, and the dampness helped the cold penetrate deeper into a person's bones. Jimmy hadn't even begun to warm up until his muffin was gone, he'd downed half his coffee, and a swirl of ghostly blue and red emergency lights ahead announced their destination.

"A cemetery?" He glanced at Murphy. "You volunteered me for a case in the middle of the night at a cemetery that looks like a set for *Halloween 47: Everyone Dies*?" Then he realized he hadn't shown the courtesy of asking about the connection. "Do you know the victim? Does Evie?"

"No."

"Favor to family?"

"No."

"A former employee? A neighbor? Parents of one of your kids' friends?"

Murphy parked near the other vehicles and shut off the engine. He pulled on gloves before picking up his own coffee. "The only thing the victim had on her was a prepaid cell phone that had made only one call—to Charms, Notions and Potions."

Jimmy blinked. He was familiar with the business name. He'd worked half his life in the French Quarter and spent the other half partying, celebrating, crashing or living there. The cutesy name belonged to a shop owned by Martine Broussard, Evie's best friend, where up front she sold tourist stuff: good luck charms, candles, voodoo ritual kits, how-to books and worry dolls, along with the usual New Orleans T-shirts, coffee mugs and mass-produced voodoo dolls. In the back room she offered the serious practitioner stuff. Her market for that was mostly local. Tourists rarely ventured through the door separating the two rooms.

Family friendship aside, Jimmy wasn't sure he would have dragged himself out before dawn to *Halloween 47* just because the murder victim had called Martine's voodoo shop. Maybe she'd wanted directions. Maybe she'd been looking for a love potion or an Obatala candle for self-purification, or maybe she'd wanted to know if the bar across the street whose name she couldn't remember was open yet.

Not that it mattered. Murphy had wanted the case, and they had it. Now it was time to get out of the car, wander into the cemetery and start working it.

The cars belonging to the officers assigned the initial call and those of the crime scene technicians were parked along the street. Bright lights had been set up some fifty yards away among the graves, and a canopy had been erected to protect the body from the elements.

As Jimmy buttoned his overcoat, he noticed it was starting to rain, just small half-hearted drops, as if the fog had worn itself out and was liquefying in the sky.

He'd spent a lot of time in cemeteries—investigated a few murders that took place there, attended plenty of victims' funerals to see who else showed up and even gone to a few funerals for friends or distant relatives. Cemeteries didn't normally creep him out, but there was something about this scene…the weird weather, the unusual hush of the voices, the edginess that kept everyone focused on their duties. He wasn't the only one who'd rather be home in bed.

Yellow-and-black crime scene tape draped limply from crypt to crypt, cordoning off the area where the body lay. Uniformed cops stood outside the perimeter, detectives and crime scene investigators inside. Between them, he caught a glimpse of legs, ankles showing between sodden pants hiked to the calves and canvas sneakers, the skin unusually colorless under the bright lights.

"Detectives." A grim-faced patrolman lifted the tape so they could duck under, keeping his back to the scene. He looked so young that this was likely his first body, and he was doing his best to avoid it.

It was far from Jimmy's first, and probably just as far from his last.

"What do we know?" he asked, shoving his hands into his coat pockets.

It was a uniform who answered. "Neighbor out with his dog saw suspicious activity by the angel." He gestured behind him with one hand. "Myself and my partner didn't see anything from the street, but when we walked over here, we found…" He gave the body a quick nod that prevented any details from registering.

Everyone under the canopy mimicked his look at the victim, then turned to the angel. It adorned a spire atop the crypt twenty feet away, its gray marble turned dingy by time and weather. Her face was tilted to the sky, her wings stretched out. In prayer? Pleading? The promise of protection?

Had the victim seen the angel? Had she had a chance to pray? Or had she already been dead when she was brought here?

"She has no ID," Leland, the senior of the crime scene guys, said. He and Jimmy had started with the department at the same time, Jimmy an ambitious patrol officer, looking for arrests, wanting to make a meteoric rise through the ranks, and Leland a lab rat, perfectly content with handling corpses. The dead were so much less annoying than the living, he'd insisted. He'd risen through the ranks, too, to the point that he often had to deal with the living, as well. "No driver's license, no credit card, no jewelry, nothing. Just two hundred bucks cash in her jacket pocket and the cell phone with its one call."

"So it wasn't a robbery."

Jimmy didn't notice who'd stated the obvious—not him, not Murphy. He studied the woman instead: wet hair of dirty blond or light brown. Thin face, sunken cheeks, deep shadows under her eyes. Lines at the corners of her mouth and eyes, signs of worry or general unhappiness. Her T-shirt clung to her in wet folds, once white but now a vague shade of gray. She'd lost weight recently, judging from the long loop of drawstring that held her pants around her skinny hips and from the way her skin sat uncomfortably on her frame. Her clothes were cheap, maybe secondhand, but something about her didn't strike him as a secondhand-clothes person. There was a line on her left index finger where she'd long worn a ring, not a tan but a bit of shiny skin where the ring had rubbed back and forth, and all ten of her nails were bitten to the quick.

What there wasn't was an obvious cause of death. She didn't look like she was just sleeping, though Jimmy had seen his share of dead people who did. No, it was apparent with the quickest of glances that this woman was dead. The lights were out; the soul wasn't home.

Which meant the cause was on her back side. "Can you roll her over?" he asked, and the crime scene guys moved to comply. Something dark stained the back of her head. Blood, possibly from a blunt object, possibly the entry wound of a small-caliber bullet.

"There's something under her shirt," Leland said, and they returned her to her original position. He pulled up her T-shirt to reveal a large bandage, sticky clear film protecting some type of dressing. It was centered over her chest, crossing her breasts, extending above and below several inches.

"So she has surgery, someone kills her and dumps her in the cemetery?" It was the same voice that had stated the obvious earlier. This time Jimmy looked and identified its owner as one of the crime scene guys who'd so far managed to stay on the perimeter, not doing much of anything. Maybe one of their lab rats who'd thought working out in the field would be fun, or maybe a new guy who was destined to get on Jimmy's last nerve pretty quickly.

Ignoring his coworker, Leland began peeling back the edge of the dressing. He worked it loose carefully, teasing the adhesive from the skin, as gentle as if his patient were alive and watching, then abruptly he stopped. He looked a moment, then folded back the flap of bandage as his distraught gaze met Jimmy's. "I think we've found the cause of death."

Jimmy and Murphy both leaned forward, concentrating on the small area of chest that had been revealed—not pale smooth skin but a wickedly ugly wound and, inside, emptiness. Not real emptiness, of course, but the essence of something missing. Something important.

"Damn." Jimmy breathed the word the same time Murphy did, then looked to Leland for confirmation. Leland nodded.

"The killer removed her heart."

After a restless night, Martine gave up any hope for peaceful sleep, pulled her robe on and shuffled to the kitchen to make a cup of coffee. She'd had dreams all night—ugly, unsettling ones involving deep shadows, woods, birds screeching that had raised the hairs on her arms. If she were fanciful, she'd say the fog was keeping the happy dreams at bay. It didn't want her nights to be any more cheerful than her days had become since it moved in.

"It's just fog," she groused, pouring cream and sugar into her coffee. "A cloud of tiny water droplets hovering above the earth. It doesn't think or care or even know you exist, Tine."

The old, almost forgotten nickname made her pause before taking the first sip of coffee. Where was Paulina this morning? Had she checked into a motel or crawled into a hole and pulled it in after her? Had she stayed safe last night? Had she gotten anything hot to eat?

Was she crazy?

Martine had tried to put all the memories behind her when she got back to the shop yesterday, a task made easier by an influx of tourists. They'd worn a variety of N'Awlins T-shirts, a few had sported Mardi Gras beads or feather boas around their necks, and they'd done their best to project the carefree, good-time-in-the-Big-Easy air that most tourists came by naturally, but it had been a struggle for this group. Even inside the brightly lit shop, they'd huddled together in small numbers, their voices muted, lamenting the lack of sunshine and the mild weather they'd expected. They'd been worried without knowing why, and they had cleaned the shelves of every single good luck charm and candle in sight before leaving the way they'd come.

After the shop was closed, after Martine had finished off a po'boy from down the street and locked herself inside her cozy apartment, the memories had come knocking again. A search of the internet had proved true one of Paulina's claims: Callie Winchester had died three months ago in Seattle. The details reported by the news outlets were scarce, but the obituary confirmed it was their Callie. Her parents, who'd once lived two blocks from Martine's family, were now in Florida, and her twin, Tallie, made her home in London.

Callie…dead. Though Martine hadn't seen her in twenty-four years, though she hadn't thought about her much in twenty of those years, it hurt her heart to know she was dead. Callie had always been so vibrant, full of humor and wild ideas that usually ended in trouble for all of them. She'd been beautiful, with sleek black hair that reached down her back, olive skin and gray eyes, and she'd done a perfect imitation of her posh mother's British accent, but there had been nothing refined or elegant about her huge booming laugh. Tallie, identical in every way except the laugh, had compared it to a braying jackass, which merely made Callie laugh even harder.

And now she was gone. Someone had stolen her very life and discarded her for someone else to deal with, as if she were no more important than an empty burger wrapper.

That thought raised goose bumps on Martine's arms and stirred an ache in her gut. She was browsing through the pantry, looking for something to settle it, when the doorbell rang, echoing through the floorboards.

The clock on the microwave showed the time was 7:23. No one came to visit her before nine, and rarely without a phone call to alert her. Maybe it was just some punk, walking along the sidewalk and pressing doorbells. But no sooner had that thought cleared her brain, the bell rang again, seeming more impatient. Her nerves tightened, and apprehension throbbed behind her eyes. Whoever was downstairs on this ugly dreary morning after her ugly restless night couldn't possibly be good news for her.

Unless it was Paulina, come to take her up on her offer of coffee and beignets.

Hope rising over the dread, Martine hurried down the stairs as the bell rang a third time. Reaching the bottom, she jerked the security chain loose, undid the dead bolt lock and yanked the door open, prepared to meet her friend with a smile and a comforting hug—

But it wasn't Paulina. Jack Murphy stood on the stoop, dressed in the white shirt and dark suit that were his usual work clothes. He looked as if he'd slept in them, hadn't had time to shave and had forgotten to comb his hair, and his eyes were dark and somber with shadows.

Panic clutched Martine's chest, cutting off her breath. "Oh, God, please tell me nothing's happened to Evie or the kids."

His eyes widened, an instant of alarm followed by sudden regret. "No. No, God, no, they're fine."

Her knees going weak, she sagged against the doorjamb, one hand pressed to her chest. "Aw, jeez, you about gave me a heart attack! Don't do that again!" For emphasis, she poked him with one finger. "Not ever!"

"Is she always this ditzy?" a voice drawled from the curb, and Martine realized Jack wasn't alone. He'd brought along her least favorite police officer in the world—her least favorite *person*. It was too damn early in the morning—too damn early in the year—to face Jimmy DiBiase.

Especially when she was wearing what passed for pajamas and a robe: tank top, shorts, an old boyfriend's flannel shirt. She was exposed from the top of her thighs to her bare toes, to a letch like DiBiase with a freakishly cold fog silently creeping everywhere. No wonder her skin was crawling.

She was torn between slamming the door and fleeing upstairs to wrap up in her favorite quilt and inviting Jack inside while pointedly leaving DiBiase in the cold.

Neither action would surprise Jack; he knew DiBiase was an acquired taste for most women besides strippers, hookers and cop groupies.

Then the realization clicked in her brain: Evie and the kids were okay, but Jack was still here, still in work mode. That meant someone else... "Who is it? Anna Maria? Reece? Jones? Alia? Landry?" Her brain was spewing forth names faster than her mouth could get them out.

Paulina's voice sounded faintly through the mist, sending a bone-deep shiver through Martine: *They're coming after us, and they're not going to stop until we're dead.*

Dear God, could it be her?

"I'm sorry, Martine," Jack said. "I'm handling this badly. We've got a...victim." The grimness returned to his expression. "No ID, nothing but a call to your shop yesterday afternoon."

Martine thought longingly of the quilt, and of the coffee she'd left on the kitchen counter. She needed warmth. She needed a lot of it to melt the ice that suddenly coated everything inside her, slowing her heartbeat, making it difficult to breathe. Paulina had warned her, had told her they were in danger, and Martine had done nothing. Had let her walk away. Had let her die.

Because she knew in her heart Paulina was gone.

"Oh, God." She swayed forward, and a hand caught her arm, holding her steady. It was a big hand, strong, the skin olive-hued, the fingers bare, and the overcoat sleeve above it was gray. Jack's overcoat was black. She knew, because she'd helped Evie shop for it. Which meant this coat belonged to DiBiase.

The hand holding her up was DiBiase's hand. For

one brief moment, she let herself accept the warmth and comfort and strength that seeped from him, just one moment when she was too weak to do otherwise. Then, with the stubbornness she'd been legendary for back home, she tugged free, folded her arms over her chest and hid her fisted hands against the soft flannel.

"I guess you should come in." Her voice was flat and numb, a pretty good match for the dismay and sorrow building inside her. She'd been a fool for letting Paulina walk away. Paulina had obviously not been herself; she'd needed taking care of. Needed someone to pretend to believe her, to take her home and help her until she was better able to help herself.

Twenty-four years ago, Martine had been the person Paulina turned to first, before anyone else. *Oh, Tine, he broke up with me for good. Tine, I'm failing algebra, and my dad will take my car away for sure. Tine, my mom and dad are fighting again. Tine, I think I'm pregnant, but I'm too young to have a baby!*

They had been best friends—had had a bond that should have been unbreakable. But now, after all those years, when Paulina came to her again, Martine had let her down. She hadn't even tried. She'd just wanted to get out of the cold and go back to her shop and take care of business. She'd wanted to stuff the past back into its cramped little corner of her brain and never take it out again.

At the top of the stairs, she turned left into the kitchen. "I'll make coffee," she suggested with the same numbness.

"We'll do it." Jack touched her arm. "Go get some clothes on."

She glanced down. Her legs and feet were an unflattering shade of blue, thanks to the cold, and goose bumps covered every bit of skin. When she lifted her gaze again, it automatically went to DiBiase, who was also just lifting his gaze. *Jerk. Self-centered, unfaithful, two-timing, arrogant—*

Giving him a look of loathing, she went down the hall to her room, where she dressed in comfort clothes: fleece pants, a long-sleeved shirt, thick wool socks and cozy slippers. By the time she returned to the kitchen, the two men had their coffee, and Jack had reheated hers in the microwave until it steamed.

"You want to go into the living room?"

Martine paused, then shook her head. "In here."

Jimmy was the last to walk through the doorway she'd indicated. She went first, turning on lights, opening curtains, and Murphy followed. Jimmy stood at the threshold, taking in everything before invading it.

He would admit, he didn't know Martine well. That time he'd tried to get her to go home from Murphy's party with him had been only their second meeting, and since then she'd looked at him like he was some kind of bottom-feeder. He did know that he wished things had happened differently back then, that she and Evie Murphy were like sisters, that his ex-wife, Alia, had been welcomed into their group last year and that Martine ran the voodoo shop below: part good fun, part legitimate business. He knew she was serious and mysterious and superstitious and sometimes wild and worrisome.

This room didn't seem to go with any of that.

It had once been a dining room, he suspected, from the general size and shape, the proximity to the kitchen and the arched doorway into the living room. Now it looked like it belonged in a suburban house, reigned over by a crafter who indulged creativity in the lulls between being World's Best Soccer Mom and World's Best Cheer Mom. The woman belonging to this room drove an SUV, had a closet filled with conservative trendy clothes, was organized enough to keep complex schedules for four kids in her head, never missed a PTA meeting and terrorized any mother who did.

It looked nothing like the Martine he'd offended a few years ago.

It held a large rectangular table, the top etched with a one-inch grid, and four perfectly matched chairs. Every available inch of wall space was covered with white bookcases, and the shelves were filled with books, craft supplies, an array of tools, fabric and a lot of things he didn't recognize, all of it in color-coordinated hampers or boxes. The lamps in the room gave off bright white light; for the first time in a week or more, he could see clearly again. The fog had lifted, at least inside this small space.

Martine settled on one side of the table. Jimmy sat on the opposite side next to Murphy. She opened a white bin, neatly labeled with the years, and pulled out a photograph, laying it on the table in front of him and Murphy.

Jimmy leaned forward to study the shot of the smiling blonde in an off-the-shoulder gown. Gaudy decorations behind her suggested a high school prom, an innocent time. It was funny the things twenty-plus years could change and the things they couldn't. This pretty, smiling, well-nourished, blue-eyed blonde shouldn't have a thing in common with the underweight, hard-worn, weary woman they'd seen in the cemetery this morning, but he had no doubt they were one and the same.

Murphy knew, too, but he still offered his cell phone to Martine. She glanced at the picture—quickly the first time, as if afraid there might be damage she didn't want to have in her mind, then for a still quiet moment. Shivering, she held her hands to her coffee mug before lifting it for a drink.

"Her name is Paulina Adams. We grew up together in Marquitta. She called yesterday afternoon and asked to meet me by the river." Her voice sounded hollow and distant, making its way through a thick haze of shock and emotion and guilt and sorrow. Jimmy had heard that voice a hundred times from a hundred different people, when he broke the news that someone they loved had died. God, he hated that part of the job. Today, because it was Martine, he hated it even more.

"Did you meet her?" Murphy asked. Of course she did. Jimmy wouldn't even have asked.

"She, um…she looked like she'd been having a tough time. She was frightened. She said…" Her breath sounded loud in the room. "She thought someone was trying to kill her. I thought she was being paranoid. But I guess it's not paranoia if someone really is out to get you, right?" Her smile was faint and sickly and slid away faster than it had formed.

With prompting from Murphy—a lot of it; the hesitations and pauses started long and got longer—she related the conversation with Paulina. Paulie, she'd called her, and in return Paulina had called her Tine. After a time, she fell silent, locking gazes with Murphy. "How did she die?"

Death notifications were Jimmy's least favorite part of the job, and definitely the least favorite part of *that* job was answering questions like that. No one wanted to hear that their sixteen-year-old daughter was raped before she was murdered, or that their elderly father had been beaten with a baseball bat by the thugs who broke into his house. Certainly Martine did not want to know that her friend's heart had been cut from her chest.

"We're waiting for the autopsy report," Murphy said gently. All cops, no matter how tough or gruff or abrupt, had a gentle side—even Jimmy himself. Granted, the only people who ever saw his were the victims and the officers he worked with. Martine couldn't see anything when she pretty much pretended he didn't exist.

"Why would someone want to kill Paulina?" he asked, part curiosity, part to remind her that he did exist.

Martine breathed deeply, her fingers running along the edge of the storage bin in a slow back and forth pattern. Her nails were painted dark red, and heavy silver rings gave an elegant look to her hand. Those hands could perform magic. He'd felt it for himself that last night, when everything had been full of promise. He didn't know even now what he had expected at the time—a few hours, a few dates, maybe even something serious—but what he'd gotten was rejection and her never-ending scorn. Most of the time, he was okay with that. Most of the time, he provoked her just because he could. But sometimes he caught himself wondering *what if…*

Realizing he was watching her, she stopped the rubbing and clasped her hands. "I don't know. Before yesterday, I hadn't seen her in twenty-four years."

"But you were best friends."

"Were," she repeated for emphasis. "In school."

"What happened?"

Again she drew a deep breath. He wasn't sure if it was meant to imply her annoyance at being questioned by him or if she was using the time to figure out the right answer. Right answers never needed figuring. The truth came easier to most people than evasions or lies.

"We were kids. We went to the same school, the same church, had the same interests. Then we graduated and…things changed. We changed. The ones who went to college went elsewhere. The ones who didn't moved elsewhere, too. We wanted to see what the world had to offer, and we lost touch after a while." A narrow line creased her forehead. "Are you still in touch with your best bud from high school?"

"I am. I introduced him to his wife. His kids call me Uncle Jimmy."

The crease deepened into a scowl. "Of course they do." Snideness sharpened her tone. "Most of us move on after high school. We all found new lives and new friends."

"And yet when Paulina was having a tough time, when she thought someone was going to kill her, she came to you, someone she hadn't seen in twenty-four years. Doesn't that seem odd? That she wouldn't go to one of those new friends you all replaced each other with?"

Martine's face flushed, giving her the first real color he'd seen since she'd found them at her door.

Anger? Embarrassment that she didn't have an answer for a perfectly reasonable question? Guilt that if she wasn't outright lying, she was at least not being entirely truthful?

He had to give her credit: she didn't shove back from the table, pace around the room or throw him out of her house. He'd watched plenty of people do all three. He'd even been on the receiving end of a few punches in the process of being thrown out. No, Martine might have surpassed the limits of her tolerance for him, but she retained control.

"I don't know where Pauline's new life and new friends are," she said, a clenched sound to her words. "I don't know where she went after school, what she did, how she lived, whether she married or had children, if she kept in touch with her family or anyone else. No one could have been more surprised than I was when I heard her voice on the phone, or when I saw her, or when she ran off into the fog. We were friends a lifetime ago, but after twenty-four years, she's as much a stranger to me as she is to you. I'd have better luck coming up with suspects who want *you* dead than Paulina."

If the conversation hadn't been so serious, he might have laughed at that. He'd been a cop for eighteen years. Everyone could come up with a list of people who wanted him dead.

She slid her chair back and stood, replaced the picture in the bin and closed the lid. "I have to get ready to open the shop, and I need time to…"

Jimmy silently completed the sentence for her: grieve over a stranger who'd once meant the world to her. He needed time to figure out whether he believed everything—or even anything—she'd told them. His first two questions for himself after an interview were *Did she lie?* and *Why?* He wasn't looking forward to telling Murphy he believed his wife's best friend had lied.

Murphy made the small talk to get them out the door—*thanks, sorry, take care*—then they took the stairs in silence. The street was just as empty of life as it had been when they came.

Murphy started the engine and turned the heat to high before thoughtfully tapping his fingers on the steering wheel. "Notice how she just happened to have that box on the table? The yearbooks were inside there, too. A lot of pictures, souvenirs, old cards. Seeing Paulina yesterday upset her more than she wanted to show."

"Maybe she was wondering how Paulina went from that kid at the prom to that woman on your phone. Or maybe seeing her made her nostalgic for the good old days."

Murphy snorted. "I know you didn't miss the fact that she wasn't telling us everything, so don't make excuses. I love Martine, but I'm not here because she's my kids' godmother. My job is to find who killed Paulina and why."

"But you can't forget that she's your kids' godmother, can you, and that makes the job harder. Evie and the kids would never forgive you if you treated her like a suspect or an uncooperative witness."

"Hey, I can be tough," Murphy said in self-defense. "I once handcuffed Evie and took her to jail."

"Yeah, and you'll never do that again, will you?" That arrest had been the end of their relationship the first time around. Once Murphy realized he'd been duped, he'd had to solve a few murders, arrest a few corrupt feds and grovel like hell to get back into Evie's life. In Jimmy's opinion, that was a hell of a lot of work for one woman.

Which probably explained why he hadn't stuck with just one woman in a long, long time.

Chapter 2

Oh, God, she'd lied to the police—and not just to the police, but to Jack.

Groaning, Martine dragged her hair into a ponytail. Instead of being bouncy and perky like it should be, it just dangled limp and heavy—the way she felt, coincidentally. She'd put on makeup as soon as the detectives had left, but she'd had a hard time finding the balance between enough and too much. Even now, she couldn't tell whether she looked like someone who'd had a shock or someone trying to pass for a clown.

She hadn't actually lied to the police. She just hadn't volunteered a few things, like the fact that Paulina believed their voodoo curse was the reason for the threat against her. Or that one of their other best friends had been killed just a few months ago, allegedly because of the curse. Or that Tallie, Robin and Martine herself were on the supposed hit list, too.

Martine couldn't get past the cold hard fact that the others ignored: their voodoo curse wasn't real. It had been far more Dr. Seuss than Marie Laveau. They hadn't raised any spirits; they hadn't disturbed the peace between this world and the other; they hadn't done anything a million stupid kids before and after them hadn't done.

What had happened to William Fletcher had been a coincidence—not even a surprising one, according to gossip. He'd been warped in his tastes and careless in his pursuit of them, and Callie and Tallie's mom had often said that one day the consequences of his actions would catch up with him.

That Saturday night they had.

But it wasn't her fault, or Paulina's or the others'.

Heaving a sigh that echoed with restlessness and sadness, she pulled on a bright yellow-and-pink madras plaid rain slicker and a pair of boots and headed out. Back in the day when the shop was new and finding its way, she'd made time to bake goodies for her employees' breakfast and breaks, but business had luckily picked up about the time her baking interest waned. Now she visited Wild Berries, a small shop on Jackson Square, and bought treats far better than she could make.

The strange dampness made her pull the slicker hood over her head as she walked. It wasn't raining exactly. It was more as if the drops of water were suspended in air and broke only when a person bumped into them. The few that trickled down her face were ridiculously cold and sent shivers all the way to her feet.

And all the weather people could say was *Unusual weather patterns* or *Maybe a break this weekend.*

Anise, one of her employees, kept insisting the sun was never going to shine again, but then, Anise was a gloom-and-doom sort of person. With her distinctive Goth appearance, Martine hadn't decided whether she added to the ambiance of the shop or scared the customers instead.

When Martine stepped inside Wild Berries, a bell dinged overhead, and a small high voice sang out, "The sun will come out tomorrow..."

She slid her hood back to revel in the brilliant smile the shop owner, Shelley, gave her. Even on her worst day she summoned more optimism than Martine could even imagine at the moment. Shelley was happy, she'd once told Martine—truly, seriously, contented all the way down to her soul. Martine knew days of deep satisfaction, but she envied Shelley her pure unwavering light.

"How's business?" Martine asked as she strolled the length of display cases, her mouth watering with each new discovery. Lemon and brown sugar and chocolate perfumed the air, along with buttery pastry and cinnamon and coffee. If it was possible to absorb calories by osmosis, Wild Berries was the place to do it.

"My early birds are reliable. It's slow right now, but it'll pick up by lunch. How about your place?"

"People come, buy and go. Let me have twelve of your most decadent creations, would you? Make one lemon with a sign that says 'Hands off. For Martine's pleasure only.'"

With a laugh, Shelley folded a brightly decorated cardboard box and began filling it. "I thought I saw you pass by yesterday afternoon, but you were moving so fast, I wasn't sure."

Martine kept her smile in place by sheer will.
"Yeah, I—I had a—a meeting." With a woman who'd
been murdered twelve hours later. God, that sent a
chill through her soul. She wondered about Paulina's
parents: Where did they live now? When would they
be notified? How thoroughly would the loss of their
only daughter devastate them?

And more questions. Had she been married? Was
there a husband out there worrying where the hell his
wife had gone? God have mercy, what if there were
kids feeling the same?

And what about Tallie and Robin? They should
know, too, because they'd been Paulina's friends, too.
The five of them had shared a lot of history.

And they deserved a warning because, even if Martine didn't believe in the paying-for-their-curse business, it seemed someone else might.

Paulina had believed it, and she was dead. Callie had believed it, and she was dead, too. Martine
couldn't have helped Callie, and she hadn't helped Paulina, but if she at least contacted Tallie and Robin…at
least gave them a heads-up…

A flash of color wavered in front of her, and she
blinked hard, bringing the plastic bag holding the pastry box into focus. Shelley wore her usual smile, but
it was tinged with a bit of concern. "You okay, Martine?" she asked, and Martine was pretty sure it wasn't
the first time.

"Yeah, sure. Nothing a few days on a tropical beach
wouldn't cure."

"You and me both. Sun, sand, cabana boys…my
dearest dream. Maybe the lemon tart will take you
away for a few moments, at least."

Martine traded her debit card for the bag, then looked inside and located the tart underneath the box's cellophane lid. In fine print across the pastry, Shelley had written with frosting, *Reserved for Martine.* With a laugh, she pocketed the debit card again. "My employees are most grateful, and so am I."

"Have a good day. And don't let the weather get you down. No matter how dreary, it's still New Orleans, and that beats a sunny LA or New York or Chicago any day."

Martine waved as the bell dinged above her again. Shelley was right. A bad day in New Orleans was better than a good day anywhere else. She'd had a lot of dreams growing up, but in terms of distance, they'd ended fifty miles from her hometown. She enjoyed traveling, but at the end of every trip, she was happy to be home where she belonged.

Would always belong.

And no one—no old friend, no murderer, not even Detective Jimmy DiBiase—could take that from her.

She was halfway past Saint Louis Cathedral when the nerves between her shoulder blades prickled. The power of a look never failed to amaze her: this one was as physical as an actual touch, and it made shivers dash down her spine. She tried to casually glance over her shoulder to see who was watching her, but when she moved her head, the hood of the slicker stayed where it was, instead giving her a good look at the pink lining. Stopping and actually turning around was a bit obvious, but when she reached the intersection, that was exactly what she did.

It was truly raining now, so much more normal than the earlier damp that some pressure deep inside her eased. The few people around were intent on getting to their destination, except for a crowd of tourists huddled beneath a lime-green golf umbrella and conferring over a map. No one showed any interest in her. No one seemed to notice she existed, despite her yellow-and-pink slicker.

Nerves. She wasn't a person usually bothered by them, and they were making her jumpy. Bad weather, slow business, Paulina, DiBiase… It was all enough to give anyone a case of the creeps.

Satisfied that was it, she headed down the street again. Her path took her past the house where Evie and Jack lived, with its smaller entrance leading to her psychic shop. Guilt curling inside, Martine ducked her head and lengthened her stride. She would talk to Evie soon, but not yet.

Only half a block separated her from the dry warmth of her shop when footsteps sounded behind her and, too quickly for her to take evasive action, Detective DiBiase caught up with her and flashed that grin most women found so charming. She had once found it charming. If he ever caught her in a wildly weak moment, she feared she might find it so again. "Wild Berries. I like their stuff."

One of the lessons Callie and Tallie had taught her early on was that ignoring people who didn't want to be ignored was a waste of time. They had pestered her relentlessly until she gave in and dealt with them. She fell back on that now. "Think of more questions, Detective?"

"A few. You have one of those caramel bread puddings in there?"

Crossing the street between parked cars, she dug

in her pocket for her keys, unlocked the shop's old wooden door, jiggled it a bit and pushed it open. Rain made the wood swell and stick, but the door with its wavy glass was decades old. She hated to replace it with something new and inferior.

The lights that were always left on—one above the display window, others over the checkout counter in the middle of the room—banished some of the gloom but not enough for Martine. She flipped switches as she walked through the shop, pushed aside a curtain of beads and went into the storeroom/lounge, where she set down the pastries, then stripped off her slicker. She didn't need the slight squelching sounds behind her to know that DiBiase had followed. Just as she'd been aware of someone's attention at the square, she felt it now.

Damn, had he followed her all that way without her realizing it?

"What do you want?"

His gaze slid to the pastry box inside the wet bag, reminding her of a hopeful puppy. Grimacing, she shoved it across the table toward him, then started the coffee. The clock ticking loudly on the wall showed ten thirty, but it was still set to last summer's time so she had thirty minutes before opening the store, probably twenty minutes before Anise arrived. Wonderful. DiBiase could annoy her that long without even trying.

"You like lemon tarts, huh?" His deep Southern drawl scraped along her skin, an irritation she couldn't banish, like the cold, the fog and now the rain. "Appropriate."

Her gaze was narrowed when she faced him. "What does that mean?"

"Well, you are a bit sour."

He helped himself to a generous serving of cheese Danish, the ruffled white liner contrasting vividly against his dark skin. On a general scale of attractiveness, he ranked high. Even Martine couldn't deny that. With dark hair, devilish eyes, the grin and muscles that still impressed though his college football years were long behind, every woman she knew thought he was gorgeous. The problem was, he knew it and took advantage of it. Everywhere he went, he was waylaid by women wanting great sex, and he was happy to comply.

Even six years later, it still embarrassed Martine that she had almost been one of them.

It angered her that, on rare occasions, she even kind of regretted that she hadn't been.

"Consider the company," she said in response to his calling her sour. Then she turned her back on him and her thoughts, lifted a couple of boxes from the storage shelves and carried them to the front of the store.

Of course Jimmy followed her—not to the counter where she was ripping open the boxes with too much enthusiasm, but through the beaded curtains. He turned down the first aisle he came to and followed it around the perimeter of the shop. Despite living in Louisiana his whole life, he had little personal experience with voodoo. His parents had seen to it that the family was in church every Sunday—in their small town, it had been more a social event than a sacred one—and they had never encouraged questions about other beliefs. When he'd thought as a kid that he was so much smarter than them, he'd assumed it was because they were so tenuous about their own beliefs that they

didn't feel qualified to debate them. Later he'd realized that their unwillingness to debate had also been
more a social thing than religious. In a small town, it
was easier to go with the flow.

Most of the merchandise on the shelves could be
bought in a dozen places in the quarter. Some was
strictly fun, some for tourists, some for posers. But
in the room behind a door marked Private, that was
where the real stuff was, according to Jack—the stuff
that couldn't be picked up just anywhere. The stuff for
the practitioners, the true believers.

Jimmy watched Martine over a display of crudely
made dolls and wondered if she was either, or merely
a supplier of goods. Her mouth was set in a thin line,
and her brows were knitted together. She didn't want
him here, and that was okay. In his job, he was used to
people distrusting him. The prejudice against police
officers that had surged in the past few years made a
tough job a hell of a lot tougher. When it got bad, he
wondered why he spent his days wearing a gun, walking into dangerous situations, doing his damnedest to
protect communities that didn't appreciate it, but the
answer was simple. He was a cop. He'd saved a lot of
lives. He'd helped out a lot of people. He'd found justice for a lot of victims.

It was what he did best.

That, and piss off pretty shop owners who had a
thing about fidelity.

As he finally circled to the counter, Martine began
sliding small plastic bags onto rods extending from a
display case. "Don't you have better things to do this
morning than aggravate me? Like, I don't know, tell-

ing Paulina's parents what happened or, here's an idea, maybe even finding the person who did it?"

"Her parents live in Alabama. The police over there are making the notification. By the way, her name is Bradley now. Was Bradley."

Her fingers slowed, the tips tightening briefly around the plastic package that held an astrological charm. "Did she have children?"

"No." That always seemed a good thing to him with murder victims. Not having kids meant less damage, less grief. *But without children, what do they leave behind?* his father sometimes asked. Jimmy figured the old man didn't want the family name dying out. He was the only son his dad had, and neither of his sisters had been willing to hyphenate their married names. Poor Pops was stuck.

Jimmy picked up a worry stone from a dish filled with them, his thumb automatically rubbing the depression in the middle. "When Paulina called you yesterday, what did she say?"

"She wanted to meet me."

"No chitchat? Hey, long time, how are you?"

She glanced out the window, and Jimmy followed her gaze. The fog had risen high enough to cover a few inches of the glass. It was like being in a dream: the street disappeared from sight; a man walking his dog, both of them legless; a delivery truck driving by, its wheels invisible. There were going to be a lot of trips and falls and battered shins as long as this lasted.

"She said, 'Tine, it's Paulina. I need to see you. Meet at the river as quick as you can get there.' I told her I was busy. I had customers. She said, 'You have to come now. I really have to talk to you.' So I went."

Still rubbing the stone, he walked around to stand near her. "First contact in more than twenty years, and she demands you meet her on a day like yesterday, then tells you that someone's after her."

Martine paused a moment before nodding. After hanging the last of the charms, she stuffed one empty box inside the other, moved a few feet to a tall display of candles, guaranteed to bring a person health, riches, love or whatever else his heart desired, and started rearranging them.

"Did she ask you for money?"

"No."

"For help?"

"No."

"For advice? Sympathy? Directions? Did she want to say goodbye? Did she leave a message for her parents or her husband?" He watched each tiny shake of her head, then impatiently asked, "Then why the hell did she bother calling you, Martine? Just to say, 'I think someone wants me dead. Hey, I like your hair that way, and I hear your shop's doing pretty good. I'll probably die in the next twenty-four hours, so I won't be seeing you again. Have a good life'?"

"Stop it!" she demanded. "She's *dead*! Show a little respect."

"I'm not disrespecting *her*." It was part of the problem today: everyone wanted respect, even when they were lying, cheating, stealing, killing and telling the rest of the world to screw themselves. Martine didn't want to be questioned again, she didn't want any pressure even though she'd been less than forthcoming the first time around. Whatever she was hiding could be nothing. It could be personal, between her and Paulina.

Or it could be integral to solving the case. It wasn't up to her to decide.

Her face was pink, her breathing unsteady, when the rattle at the door announced a newcomer. A woman—early twenties, shiny black hair, pale face, dark makeup, black clothes—stepped inside, gave a shake like a great big dog, scattering rain everywhere, then looked up at them through water-splattered glasses. "The sun's never gonna shine again," she said in a doleful voice. She shuffled over, a huge black tote bag hanging from one shoulder, and stopped a few feet away. "I'm Anise."

Though he could feel hostility radiating from Martine—or maybe because of it—he grinned at the girl. "I'm Jimmy."

"Don't talk to him, Anise," Martine snapped before the girl could open her mouth again. "He's not welcome around here. In fact, if you could do a few wards to banish him from the premises, I would be most grateful."

Jimmy shifted his full attention to Anise. "You can banish me? Where, like, I wouldn't be able to walk in the door?"

"Maybe. I'm just a novice, but I'm pretty sure I can at least make it very uncomfortable for you to be here." She pushed her glasses higher on her nose.

He made a dismissive noise. "Your boss can do that with nothing more than a look." Once upon a time, she'd made him very uncomfortable with no more than a look…but in a most desirable way.

The color in Martine's face deepened. She murmured something—he saw her lips move but heard no words and figured it was a prayer of some kind—then with a deep breath faced him. "You should go now."

He good-naturedly shook his head. "You should tell me the truth now. All of it."

"I—"

"Have kept all the good parts to yourself, like why someone wanted Paulina dead, what happened to your friendship, why she came to you. You're a bad liar, Martine. I know it, and Jack knows it."

The look she gave him was defiant, with her jaw jutted out and her eyes darker than usual. A muscle quivered in her jaw, and her lips were thinned. He moved a few steps closer and lowered his voice for his last volley. "I intend to find out what you're holding back and why. So I'll be back, Martine, no matter how many wards Anise casts. I'll find out the truth, and God help you if anyone else gets hurt in the meantime."

For a long moment, their gazes locked. There was the usual annoyance and dislike in her eyes that sparked the usual regret in him, but along with them was fear. He hadn't thought she was even capable of the emotion.

It made him that much more determined to find out what the hell she was hiding.

Without enough customers to keep two employees busy, much less four, after a few hours, Martine gave up, said goodbye and went out the front door. The stoop to her apartment door was only a few feet away, just one big step when she could actually see it, but with the fog lingering, she went down the shop steps, up the other steps and let herself inside. The staircase was narrow and dimly lit, and she reminded herself for the tenth time to buy a couple of higher-wattage light bulbs for the top and the bottom.

As soon as she got to the top, though, the airy colors and tall windows that usually let in the sun made her forget about the stairs. They were just the gauntlet she had to run to reach the cozy comfort of her home.

Grabbing her laptop, she went into her workroom, curled in a chair next to the window and logged on to a search engine. There she paused. Paulina and Callie were dead. Tallie was in hiding, and Robin had long been lost, according to Paulina. Martine had zero idea how to find them, so she did what she used to do when she was stumped: she called her mother.

Bette Broussard still lived in the house where Martine had grown up, not that she spent a lot of time there. A few years after divorcing Martine's father, Bette had made herself over into a travel writer, taking advantage of everything the internet had to offer, and had become successful enough that these days, "vacation" meant staying at home for longer than a weekend. She'd finagled her travel-tip columns onto some very prestigious websites, had her own YouTube channel and boasted social media followers in the mid–six figures.

It had taken Martine five years just to get her shop's very simple website online.

After a couple of rings, her mother's husky voice greeted her. "Ha! When I got up this morning, I crossed my fingers and turned in a circle three times, chanting your name, and here you are!"

"You know, you could have picked up your phone and called me without risking getting dizzy and falling."

"I can't fall. I'm sixty-five years old. It could be dangerous."

"Just because you say you can't doesn't mean it can't happen anyway." Would that it were true. Martine would be spinning in circles and chanting her heart's desires until she passed out. *Paulina can't be dead. Callie can't be dead. Tallie and Robin and I can't be in danger. I can't have to see Detective DiBiase one more time.*

"In my world, it does." Bette said something in an aside, and Martine heard a British-sounding, *Yes, ma'am, of course, ma'am.* "Where are you?" she asked.

"Home. Where are you?"

"London. That was Chelsea. She's my translator on this trip."

"They speak English in London, Mom."

"Yes, but apparently they don't think *I* do. It was impossible to get anything done with them constantly asking me to repeat myself."

"Because they love your accent." Her mother sounded as if she'd stepped straight out of Southern belle charm school, her words all rounded and sweet and enchanting, gliding slowly one into the next and putting a person in mind of sultry afternoons on a veranda, sipping mint juleps and saying *y'all* a lot.

DiBiase's accent was pretty much the male version of Bette's.

Martine scowled hard until the thought disappeared from her mind.

"What's going on with you, Tine? You rarely call me in the middle of your workday."

Too late, of course, Martine rethought the call. Did she really want to deliver sad news to her mother while she was on a business trip? Bette had adored her daughter's friends, and they'd felt the same about her.

But her mom was always on a trip. She could handle news, and she would want to know.

"You remember Paulina? And Callie?"

Bette snickered. "That's like asking if I remember your father. Those girls practically lived in our house. I never really knew what happened between you all, but you know, it was like losing part of the family. One day I had all five of you underfoot, and the next you were all gone. Moved on. I knew it was inevitable, of course, but I wasn't prepared for it. Then your father left, and I..."

Martine remembered her mother's shock as well as her own when Mark Broussard had packed his bags and moved into his fishing cabin ten miles outside town. He hadn't had an affair. He hadn't wanted a divorce. He'd sworn he was happy and loved Bette and Martine as much as ever. He'd just needed some time alone.

Bette had given him time—six months, a year, two, her life effectively put on hold—and then she'd given him an ultimatum: life together or divorce. He'd refused to choose, so she had.

Twenty-plus years he'd lived in that cabin, working when he had to, fishing when he could, communing with nature and his own spirit and still insisting that he loved Bette and Martine as much as ever. It was strange, but Martine believed he was genuinely happy.

Bette's sigh was long and blue, then her voice brightened. "Have you heard from the girls? Is that why they're on your mind after all this time?"

"Sort of. I saw Paulina for a few minutes yesterday. She was, uh..." Martine had to stop, had to close her eyes to push back the tears that threatened. When she thought it safe to continue, her words wobbled with emotion. "She was murdered last night, Mom."

For an instant, the silence on the line was thick, then her mother's own voice wobbled. "Oh, honey… Good Lord, how awful. Her poor parents… Was it a mugging or a robbery or what?"

Her fingers aching, Martine switched her phone to the other hand. "I don't know. Just…her body was found this morning, and Jack is assigned to the case."

"Well, it's good to know New Orleans has their finest on the case. Still…so sad. Heavens, I can't imagine what Paulina's parents are feeling right now."

"Not just Paulina's parents. It's weird, Mom, but she told me Callie had been murdered a few months ago."

That bombshell rendered Bette speechless. Martine worked her boots off, then drew her feet onto the chair and gazed forlornly out the window. The tiny courtyard below that never failed to make her smile failed now. The fountain was turned off, the bright-colored cushions for the chairs stored downstairs. The plants drooped as if they might collapse under one more drop of rain, and everything looked sallow and depressed, in need of a dose of brilliant sunshine.

"Poor Callie," her mother said at last. "And poor Paulina. What a sad, sad coincidence."

A lot of people didn't believe in coincidence. They insisted there was a great plan, that everything happened as it must. Her mom wasn't among them. She thought coincidence was a lovely wrinkle that delighted her more often than not.

Could it be coincidence? Martine really wanted to believe it. Life was dangerous. Some people were willing to kill for a pair of shoes, a handful of change or because they felt slighted. It could be just really bad luck that first Callie, then her old friend Paulina had become victims. Just because their lives had been connected didn't mean that their deaths were.

But she couldn't quite convince herself of that.

"Mom, I wanted to get in touch with Tallie and Robin to let them know about Paulina, but I don't have any idea where they are. Do you have phone numbers or addresses for their parents?"

"I'm not sure, but I do know their mothers follow me on Facebook. I'll look them up and email their info to you right away, okay?" There was a brief pause with the faint sound of typing in the background. "And Tine? Be careful, honey. It would rip my heart right out of my chest if anything happened to you. I love you more than my life."

Martine swallowed hard. "I love you, too, Mama."

After disconnecting the call, she gazed down at the courtyard again. The barren branches of the crape myrtles faded into the brick wall behind them. The fog lifted here, swirled there, but thanks to the protection of four walls, it mostly just hovered.

It made Martine feel cold and damp and heavy.

Her gaze went distant as her mind shifted back to the conversation. She'd never imagined she would be contacting Paulina's or Callie's parents. Never imagined she would be offering condolences on their daughters' deaths. Never imagined two of her four former best friends would be murdered. Never imagined for even an instant that Tallie's or Robin's or her own life might be in danger.

Movement in the courtyard caught her attention, drawing her to her feet and closer to the window. Nothing was there, just the fog bumping into the walls that constricted it, then slowly settling back into its lazy ramble. Still, a shiver passed through her, leaving her ice cold as she sank back into the chair.

Danger or coincidence: Did it matter? Either way, it didn't change what she had to do.

Resolutely she typed a message on her phone, drew a deep breath and hit Send.

Now all she could do was wait.

Jimmy had a hundred favorite hangouts in New Orleans. Today it was a bar on Bourbon Street, relatively small, with wood floors, tables closely spaced and tall French doors usually open to the sounds, sights and smells of the Quarter. Today the cold kept all but the main entry closed, but he didn't mind. There was blues on the sound system, he had takeout from his favorite Cajun restaurant and his ex-wife was seated across from him.

Alia had provided the takeout, easily enough for four people and most of it for herself. She had a passion for food that few people he'd ever met could match. Luckily, she was also blessed with a passion for working out and a metabolism that favored her.

She buttered a piece of corn bread but paused before taking a bite. "So this new case of yours…the victim was a friend of Martine's."

"Yeah, best friend from high school." He didn't ask how she knew. She was a special agent with the Naval Criminal Investigative Service. She was also friends with Evie and Jack, and her husband, Landry, was co-owner of the place and tending bar at the moment. She had a lot of sources.

"I bet she's thrilled with you," Alia said with a smirk.

"She likes to pretend I don't exist."

"A lot of people like to pretend you don't exist, Jimmy." There was no bitterness in Alia's voice or her smile. She liked him a lot better now that she wasn't married to him, which was only fair. He'd been a crappy husband. He just hadn't…cared.

Oh, he'd loved her. He still did, in different ways. But he'd been younger, stupider, more reckless, less understanding. Marriage had been more about taking a chance than making a commitment. Practically everyone in his circle of friends had been married and divorced at least once; it was no big deal. You tried it; if it didn't work out, you moved on.

Now he knew—years too late—how idiotic that attitude had been. He'd hurt Alia, hadn't done himself any favors and had convinced a lot of people that he was a complete jackass.

Alia had gotten over him and was much happier with Landry than she ever would have been with him. Jimmy had gotten over himself, too. But a lot of people still thought he was a jackass.

He didn't often admit it, but on occasion he found himself wishing Martine wasn't among them. After the way things had ended between them before they'd even really started, he should have forgotten her—written her off as one of the few women he couldn't seduce. But she was a damn hard woman to forget.

"I also heard the killer removed her heart," Alia went on. "Is that true?"

This time Jimmy scowled at her. "Did Evie tell you that?"

"Ew, Jack would never tell Evie anything that gross. Isn't that a voodoo thing? The heart of your enemy makes you strong?"

"I think around here it's more of a movie thing. I'd have to ask someone who knows more about voodoo than me."

"Ooh, and Martine is just such a person."

He scowled again. "Yeah, we'll let Jack handle that. I'll stick to digging through the victim's life and finding out all her secrets." That part of the job was both interesting and off-putting. Cops were curious; it was part of the job. But wasn't Paulina Bradley entitled to a bit of privacy after her death? Wasn't it bad enough that she'd died violently, alone and afraid? Did it have to come to light now that she was a lousy housekeeper, that she read porn, that she daydreamed about things she would never accomplish? Did it matter now that she kept chocolate stuffed in her underwear drawer, that she had a crush on her neighbor or that she drank too much when her husband was gone?

"It's kind of like a car wreck," Alia said sympathetically. "You know you should look away, but you have to see what happens. There's so little dignity after a violent death."

"I do my best." His phone buzzed with an incoming text message, and he finished his last bite of gumbo before picking it up. "Crap. Jack's out of town—"

"Since when?"

"Don't know. He got me out of bed two hours early this morning to take this case, then he headed to the coroner's while I interviewed the guy who called 911. Let's see… Lincoln, Nebraska, PD picked up his double-homicide suspect that jumped bail last month, and he's on his way to get him. And Martine's decided to share some information with him that she didn't give earlier."

Alia grinned. "She's going to be disappointed when you show up instead of Jack. Maybe you should politely remind her that the sooner she tells you everything, the sooner she'll be rid of you."

"Yeah. Though I don't think she's gonna fall for anything polite after I called her a liar a couple hours ago." He stood and shrugged into his overcoat. He hated the coat; it was constrictive and awkward when he was running or needed to draw his pistol or Taser. He could dress down, like most of his fellow detectives, but he shared one quirk with Jack: work clothes meant shirt, coat and tie. Old-fashioned but respectful of the job and the victims and the families they dealt with.

"Aw, Jimmy." Alia stood and straightened his collar for him. "I'd chastise you, but you've seen me do worse with an uncooperative witness. Just remember, she's also our friend."

Not *his* friend, he thought as he waved to Landry, then walked out onto the street. At the time they'd met and almost made it to bed together, he hadn't cared about having female friends. But, like he said, he'd gotten over himself since then. He had more than a few female friends now. It said an awful lot for Alia that she was one of them.

When he reached Martine's store, he wiggled and jiggled the swollen door to open it, stepped inside and reached back to close it. When his fingers wrapped around the knob, electricity jolted through them, minor, little more than static but enough to make him jerk his hand away and swear softly.

"What happened?"

He glanced from his hand to Anise, still looking as gloomy as the weather, even though a spark of interest lit her black-rimmed eyes. "I got shocked."

"Hmm. That wasn't the effect I was going for. I'll have to try again." Turning without a sound, she disappeared into the depths of the store as if he was no longer there. A lesson she'd learned from her boss, probably.

His nose wrinkling against the particularly strong odors of the incense on the shelf beside him, he headed for the central counter. The kid slumped over a textbook there straightened to his full height of six foot four, maybe five. He was thin, long-necked, long-armed, long-legged, long-haired and apparently short on words. No *Can I help you?* or *How are you today?* He just stood there, giving Jimmy a long steady owl-like gaze, and waited.

Jimmy showed the kid his badge. "Martine?"

The kid lifted his gaze to the ceiling, then accompanied it with one long thin finger pointing straight up.

"Niles, we're not supposed to talk to that guy," Anise called from the back. "Don't tell him where Martine is."

Niles, poor guy, turned red and very slowly folded that finger back down, then hid his hands behind his back for good measure.

Jimmy grinned at him and went back out the front door. Once again, when he touched the knob to close the door, a shock fired through his fingers. It might not be painful, but it was going to become annoying pretty damn quickly.

He stepped across from one stoop to the other and

was about to ring the doorbell when the door opened with a haunted-house-worthy creak. The hair on his neck stood on end, and his hand was already sliding beneath his coat to the .40 holstered on his belt before the thought even crossed his mind. He stilled when a woman with wild hair and pink glasses popped out from behind the door.

"Did I startle you? I'm Ramona." She squeezed by, then patted his arm. "Go on up, Detective Murphy. She's waiting."

She was definitely expecting Jack. Jimmy was going to piss her off this time just by walking into the room. But that was okay, because this time he wasn't leaving without some answers.

Chapter 3

Customers sometimes thought that because Martine knew something about voodoo, she must know all the other woowoo stuff. They asked if she was a witch, a psychic, a medicine woman, if she could talk to the dead or read auras or throw the bones. She patiently explained that she had knowledge but no powers. She never knew who was calling before looking at caller ID. If she met a premonition, she wouldn't recognize it, and all she ever knew about a person was what anyone else with eyes could see.

But as the footsteps reached the top of the stairs and turned automatically to the right, a shiver ran through her. She didn't need supernatural powers to know that Jack had stood her up, the rat, and sent DiBiase in his place. Anyone who shared her dislike for the detective could have told the same thing just based on instinct, pheromones or the hairs dancing on their nape. There was nothing special about it.

Nothing special about instincts or hairs dancing on her nape. But pheromones, those man/woman chemicals that signaled interest and attraction and desire … those were pretty damn special.

But not in play here. Not between her and DiBiase.

He stopped in the workroom doorway, slid off his damp coat, looked around, then hung it on the corner of the door. His hair was damp, too, the bright overhead lights glinting off it. He raised both hands as if to stall whatever criticism she might offer. "Jack had to go out of town to pick up a prisoner."

"A fact he failed to mention when he texted that he would be over soon." But as she said the words, she acknowledged that wasn't exactly what he'd said. She'd said she wanted to give him information about Paulina, and he'd sent back three words: Be there soon. He couldn't be held responsible, he would argue, if she wrongly assumed he meant *he* would be there soon, could he?

Blowing out her breath, she gestured to the chair across from her. The plastic bin was out again, this time sitting on the seat beside her. She wished she'd thrown out this stuff years ago, that she'd run farther than New Orleans and changed her name and never, ever heard from her one-time friends again, because then maybe Callie and Paulina would be alive, and even if they weren't, she wouldn't know about it.

But maybe something in this bin or some bit of information in her memories would help lead the police to their killers…or killer. Maybe it would save Tallie and Robin from the same fate.

Maybe it would save Martine, and then she truly could bury the past.

DiBiase sat across from her and pulled a notebook, small and scruffy, from his jacket pocket. Silently she slid a paper across to him. "Those are the names of Paulina's and my best friends when we were kids. I don't know anything current about them, except that Tallie lives in London. The names underneath—that's their mothers' Facebook accounts. They follow my mother. Paulina had been looking for Robin and Tallie for a while, and she couldn't find them, and Callie…"

"Callie?" DiBiase's gaze was razor-sharp. She wasn't the only one in the room with instincts, and she would wager his were far better developed than her own. He'd known from the start that she was holding something back. He hadn't been happy then, and he would be even less so when she told him.

Sighing, she slid another piece of paper to him. It was a printout of Callie's bare-bones obituary. "She was murdered three months ago in Seattle. Paulina told me about it."

Hands trembling, she folded them together and waited for the explosion of anger that was sure to come. DiBiase read the obituary, his mouth thinning, his eyes going dark and hard. Taking out his cell phone, he placed a call, withdrew an ink pen from his pocket and began making notes in tiny neat lines on the paper. "Hey, this is Jimmy. I need the short version on a homicide in Seattle three months ago… Yeah, the eighteenth. Victim's name was Callista Jane Winchester. Can I hold while you get it for me?"

His stern gaze cut back to Martine. "She went by Callie?"

She nodded, and he made a note on the obituary page. "And her sister. Tali...whatever?"

"Taliesin. It was the name of Frank Lloyd Wright's house. Their father was an architect." She caught herself before rambling further afield and mumbled, "We called her Tallie."

He noted that, then a distant voice came from his phone. He started writing again, murmuring *Okay* at appropriate times. If Martine had to compare his writing with the fonts on her computer, she would guess his font size was slightly less than eight points, which was as small as her fonts went. From her vantage point, across the table and upside down, it looked like an incredibly detailed pattern rather than words.

Abruptly his pen stopped, and everything about him went cold. Martine shuddered, reached to pull a quilted throw from one of the shelves and wrapped it around herself. Obviously, he'd learned something that surprised or sickened or angered him. *Please don't let it be proof that Paulina and Callie were killed by the same guy.*

His conversation lasted a few more minutes, and when he laid the phone aside, he sat back and looked at her. She couldn't recall ever seeing him so serious. Despite his job, or maybe because of it, he was usually looking at the bright side of life, quick with a grin, a joke or, if there was an available woman, a pickup line. He didn't take much seriously, she sometimes thought, beyond annoying her.

He was taking whatever information he'd just gotten very seriously. "What do you know about Callie's death?" His accent was less noticeable when he was this intense. He sounded businesslike, no-nonsense. Life might be a joking matter to him, but death wasn't.

"Just what's there. I—I don't even know if I believed Paulina when she told me. She was...melodramatic."

He stared at her a long time, making her shift positions awkwardly, sending a rush of heat through her. She felt like the bug pinned underneath the microscope, and he was the scientist unsympathetic to her plight.

After a moment, he broke the eye contact. "Okay, let's pick up where you started withholding information this morning. You met Paulina at the river. She'd been having a tough time, she was frightened, she thought someone was trying to kill her."

A childhood memory flashed through her brain: her mom and dad sitting her down after some minor infraction at school. *Always tell the truth*, her father had said, and when she'd asked why, he'd explained: *It's easier than remembering a lie.* Her mom had swatted him on the shoulder and corrected him: *It's the right thing to do.*

She'd pretty much lived by that rule, for both reasons, but this afternoon, nothing was easy, and she wasn't sure which actions were right. But she'd committed herself to telling everything, and although it irritated her that DiBiase thought her a liar, and embarrassed her that he had reason to think so, she was going to take the route that was neither easier nor guaranteed to be right.

"What was the first thing she said to you?"

"That she'd hoped she would never see me again."

A slow blink was the only emotion he showed. Not

quite what he'd expected, she guessed, given how close she and Paulina had once been. "And you said?"

"I offered to buy her some coffee, to get out of the cold. I thought she looked underfed."

"And?"

Ducking her head, Martine pressed the bridge of her nose to ease the tension gathered behind her eyes. She was tired and blue and melancholy and sickened by the recent events. She wasn't sure she could bear one more day of the nerves that had been stretched taut ever since hearing Paulina's voice on the phone or the creepy bleak weather or the sensation that something terribly wrong was connected to it. She didn't want to know what had happened to her former friends, wanted to erase them from her memory, wanted to jump on to the first plane heading to London and ask her mom to cuddle and pamper and coddle her into a brighter, sunnier, safer place.

As if London didn't have fog and rain.

"Martine." DiBiase's voice came from nearby, and she looked up. He'd moved around the room, transferred the plastic bin to the table and seated himself beside her, all without her hearing a thing. The intensity was still etched in the lines of his face, but it wasn't so harsh now. She couldn't have blamed him if it was. She'd been less than helpful so far with his investigation.

"Did you go for coffee?"

She shook her head. "Paulina—Paulina said, 'Someone knows.' She didn't know who or how, but they knew, and they were coming after us. She said Callie was already dead, that Tallie and Robin had disappeared and might be dead, and that they—this someone—wouldn't stop until they had also killed us."

It took every bit of air in her lungs to get the words out, and for one awful moment she couldn't replace it. Her chest was tight, her brain too dazed to give the command to breathe, so that when her body couldn't wait one instant more, her lungs dragged in oxygen with a terrible, broken wheezing sound.

DiBiase laid his hand on hers where it curled tightly around the quilt. His skin was warm against the ice of her own, his palm large enough to cover her fisted hand, his fingers closing tightly around hers in a way that made her feel safe. It allowed her to breathe evenly, regularly, and chased away the panic.

It took a few heartbeats for her to realize that for the first time in years, hostility wasn't foremost among her emotions toward him. She was grateful for his steadiness and solidness and for the sense of security he gave her.

Many deep breaths later, the moment passed. She wiggled her fingers free of his, found a tissue to wipe at her eyes, then searched wildly to find even the slightest sarcasm. "Do they teach you that in detective school? Calming Hysterical Females 101?"

He didn't move back to his original seat, but he did lean back, putting some precious space between them. "I have two younger sisters. I had advanced training in how to make females hysterical by the time I was ten. Calming them is sort of the same stuff in reverse."

"Huh. I never thought of you as having sisters to torment."

"Or be tormented by."

"Then you probably also have a mother and a father."

His look was wry. "And grandparents, three nieces and two nephews. No, I didn't magically come to life as the perfect guy. I had to work to get where I am."

She smiled very faintly, then looked past him at the stark-white pieces of paper on the table. Grimness settled over her like a cloak, icy and awful, and it echoed in her sigh.

"You ready to go on?" DiBiase asked.

If she said no, would he give her more time? Or would he try to wheedle, cajole or charm her into continuing? Ten minutes ago, she would have said he couldn't have done it, but he'd just proved her wrong.

She nodded.

"What was Paulina talking about? What did this someone know?"

She opened her mouth, then closed it again. Her dad had been wrong. Telling the truth wasn't always easiest. She could think of at least a hundred lies that she could tell with far more polish than the truth would get. Her mom had probably been correct that it was the right thing, but Martine would give anything to keep their foolishness from that long-ago night to herself.

Anything except someone else's life.

Jimmy listened to the creaks of the old building, the occasional vehicle sounds from outside and not much of anything else. Any pedestrians out there weren't lingering; the residents weren't walking their dogs; no one's windows or doors were open to share their music. It was quiet in a city that was rarely quiet, a strange-enough occurrence to set a vague unease niggling between his shoulder blades. New Orleans was a city of magic and myth—the unexplained often happened in this town—but this weird combination of cold and fog and murder carried a sense of menace he couldn't recall experiencing.

It was just coincidence. The logical part of his brain knew that, but it felt like…more.

"Martine." He liked the sound of her name. Liked the feel of her. The smell and the taste of her. It had been a long time since their night-gone-bust, but a man didn't just forget the feel of a woman like her in his arms.

This time when she opened her mouth, words came out, determination dragging them one by one. "Our last year in high school, we had a new teacher, Mr. Fletcher. We called him Fletcher the Letcher. He was about our fathers' ages, and he was creepy. It wasn't anything hugely overt. He looked at girls when he thought no one noticed him. If we got caught in a crowded hallway with him, he was always accidentally bumping into us, brushing against our boobs, fondling us but, of course, never on purpose. He was just a jerk. As far as we knew, he never took it any further, never did anything that he couldn't *claim* was an accident, but it was gross. We really hated him."

Jimmy reached for the printouts she'd given him and wrote a couple of lines. Maybe Fletcher the Letcher *had* gone further, with his victim too embarrassed to confide even in her best friends. That kind of betrayal of authority could certainly cause a teenage girl who otherwise had everything she needed to succeed to wind up terrified, paranoid, on the run and then murdered.

"The Saturday night after graduation," Martine went on, "the five of us went out in the woods near our houses. Someone brought some weed, and someone sneaked a bottle of booze from their house. We decided it would be fun to put a curse on Mr. Fletcher, to—to stop him from being such a perv. We put together a crude voodoo doll out of a bandanna and twigs and Spanish moss, and I made up a chant, something really juvenile about making him stop bothering the girls. At the end, we stuck a stick through its chest, and Paulina skewered its crotch with a metal nail file. It was just… silly. A game. None of us knew anything about voodoo. We were high and tipsy and stupid. That's all it was."

Using the lid from the storage box as a table, Jimmy used his own shorthand to document the story while waiting for her to go on. In his experience, there was always more, and he had the patience of Job when it came to waiting.

Martine pushed back the quilt and stood, pacing to the nearest window, then to the next one, then flipping the switch on a space heater tucked into the corner. She'd changed the loose pants she'd worn this morning for faded jeans that clung to her hips and every inch of her long legs, and added a chambray shirt over the long-sleeved T-shirt. With all that, she was still pale, her skin still bearing the faintest tinge of blue. She'd always been so confident, so capable, that he wouldn't have thought her afraid of anything.

But, of course, she was. She feared the one thing everyone did, even him: something happening to the people she loved. Hadn't her initial response to seeing Jack this morning been fear that trouble had befallen Evie and the kids?

Arms folded across her chest, she paced the length of the room on the opposite side of the table, making a neat little turn at each end. "We did our moronic ritual, stayed until the weed was gone and the booze was gone and it was late and we were sure we could get into our houses and into our rooms without our parents catching us, and then we went home. The next morning…" Her voice faltered, and so did her steps. She stood at the window, staring out, but Jimmy knew for damn sure it wasn't the courtyard or the building next door she was seeing.

"The next morning we heard Mr. Fletcher had been found dead. He'd been shot in the chest and in the groin. A day or two later, his wife was arrested. She confessed, said she didn't want a trial and went to prison."

"But you were convinced—" He considered it a moment, then changed tacks. "Your friends were convinced that somehow your ritual had caused his death. Had made her kill him."

Still staring out, she nodded. "It ended everything. Our entire lives' worth of friendship. I tried to tell them it was ridiculous. We had no power, no experience, no knowledge. We'd been playing a dumb game, and it was just a coincidence that he'd died, but they felt so guilty. They left town, put as much distance between all of us as quickly as they could. As far as I know, other than the twins, none of us had any contact until Paulina showed up yesterday."

Like Jimmy had told Alia, he didn't know much about voodoo, despite a lifetime in Louisiana. He respected it for the religion it was, but as for the curses, the gris-gris, the powerful magic… Maybe he was skeptical, but he didn't believe the most skilled voodoo priestess could kill a man using nothing more than a doll and words. And Martine and her friends had been, by her own admission, far more stupid kids than skilled medicine women. Young, easily influenced and gullible enough to believe they had unleashed forces that cost a man his life.

"He wouldn't be the first philandering husband whose wife took her revenge on the family jewels," he remarked.

She glanced over her shoulder at him, a faint movement that might have been a smile tugging at her mouth, then sat down again.

"I take it you never told anyone about this."

She shook her head.

"And they probably never did, either."

"I don't believe so. They were too scared and ashamed."

"So who did Paulina think had discovered the secret?"

"She didn't say."

He tapped his ink pen but didn't quite let it touch the pad. The noise when it did tended to annoy the hell out of Jack, Alia or anyone else he was working with. They preferred not trying to think with the relentless *tap-tap-tap* for accompaniment, so he'd learned to be satisfied with just the movement.

"She obviously thought it was tied to Fletcher's death. Maybe because of Callie's death? Do you know how she found out about that?"

"No."

"Other than thinking someone was out to kill her, how did she seem to you? Like someone going through a bad time that would pass or maybe someone with real long-term problems?"

"Someone *was* out to kill her."

"Yeah. I'm just trying to figure out what her mental status was before you saw her, before she took off from home in the middle of the day and disappeared for the next three months. Her husband's driving over from Alabama, so I'm meeting him tomorrow, find out what he knows."

Martine shrugged, her features sad. "She was troubled. She looked like she wasn't sleeping at all, like she'd lost a lot of weight. Her clothes didn't fit. Her skin didn't fit. I remember thinking she looked...scared to death. And she accused me of thinking she was crazy."

"Did it cross your mind?"

She was reluctant to answer. It always surprised him how many people took to heart the bit about not talking badly of the dead, when it was usually the bad parts he needed to solve a crime. Once a person was dead, there were no more consequences. Secrets didn't help anyone.

Finally she nodded. "It did. You can't imagine the difference from that night in the woods and yesterday. She used to be so bright and happy and full of life, and then she looked like an escapee from a horror movie set."

A pretty good comparison, Jimmy thought, remembering his first impression of the graveyard where the body had been found. *Halloween 47: Everyone Dies.*

If it turned out that Paulina hadn't been unnecessarily paranoid, *everyone* could—would—logically include Martine.

Every muscle in his body knotted. He would be damned if he would let that happen. Even with the grudge she nursed against him, life wouldn't be the same without her in it.

"So…can I ask a question?"

His gaze flicked up to her face, and she seemed taken aback by the ferocity of it. He blinked, swallowed hard and worked to substitute something bland and far less intimidating. "I can't promise I'll answer."

"How was Paulina killed?"

Damn, he'd been expecting that. People who cooperated usually felt entitled to a little information in return, and they usually asked one of two questions: *Why?* Or *How?* There was never a satisfactory answer to the first; even if the victim was a lying, thieving, murdering thug, there was always someone in his world who'd loved him and didn't believe he'd deserved to die.

As for the *how*, Jimmy didn't believe it brought comfort, except along the lines of died-too-quickly-to-feel-any-pain. Shot, stabbed, beaten, run down in the street, drug overdose, bomb, burned alive, torture, ritual, poison…dead was dead. But families felt compelled to ask.

He carefully lined the edges of the papers she'd given him and folded them in half. "She had blunt-force trauma to the back of her head." Enough to render her unconscious, according to the preliminary autopsy reports, but not the cause of death. That appeared to be, as Leland had suggested at the scene, the removal of her heart.

The same manner of death as Callista Jane Winchester.

"There's something else."

"Yeah, but I can't…"

"Was it… Is it connected to Callie's death?"

Suddenly Jimmy felt tired. He couldn't count the number of times he'd talked to families about the horrible things done to their loved ones. No one outside of a coroner should know as much about the ends of strangers' lives as he did. It just wasn't natural.

But it was the career he'd chosen—or maybe it had chosen him. He was always too late to save the victim, but he usually managed to get justice for them and, often enough, saved another life or two along the way.

He fully intended to save Martine's life.

"Yes. I'm pretty sure it was. The…other details of the cases match." Exhaling heavily, he stood. "I've got a lot of files to read, a lot of people to talk to, but finding Tallie and Robin are at the top of my list. If they're alive, we'll keep them that way. You, too. Don't go out alone. Don't meet any other old friends who happen to call. Don't forget there's a killer out there."

For a long time, still pale, still looking as fragile as spun glass, she held his gaze. When she finally looked away to open the storage bin, her hands trembled. "I picked out some pictures of the girls in case…" She brought out an envelope and offered it, but when he took hold of one end, she had trouble letting go of the other.

"Thanks. It helps to put faces to names."

"I also have…" This time she pulled out the yearbook from her senior year. The girls, their friends and any possible rivals and Fletcher the Letcher, all in one book. He'd meant to ask for it but got distracted. She'd saved him a trip.

He accepted it, along with the plastic shopping bag she plucked from a box meant for the store, and slid everything inside to keep it dry. He needed only one more thing before he went back to the office: a source to talk to about the possible voodoo aspects of the case. He'd intended to ask Martine a few questions but not now. She was freaked out enough already. Asking *Who can tell me about the ritual taking of human body parts?* would send her over the edge. He would find his source another way. That was what he got paid the big bucks for.

"Look, Martine—"

"Please don't tell me not to worry."

"Oh, hell, no. Two of your friends have been murdered half a country apart. You'd damn well better worry." He shoved his fingers through his hair. "I just wanted to say… I'm sorry."

She didn't ask what he was sorry for—Paulina's and Callie's deaths, being a jackass, leading her on, pissing her off. Any of it. All of it. She just nodded grimly.

"If anything out of the ordinary happens, call me." He offered his business card. "Anything—a hang-up, a customer who seems vaguely familiar or overly friendly, anything at all. Okay?"

Her face was as colorless as before. "Okay," she said in little more than a whisper. "Thank you."

"Now come downstairs and lock the door behind me."

She obeyed, moving so lightly on the stairs that he felt her presence rather than heard it. When they reached the dimly lit foyer, he hesitated, his hand on the doorknob, then faced her. "It'll be okay." They were meaningless words—*okay* might come in a few weeks, a few months, a few years or not at all, because no matter what happened in the end, Paulina Bradley and Callie Winchester were still dead—but people seemed to appreciate hearing them, and it filled some need in him to say them.

She drew a deep breath, squared her shoulders and straightened her spine. Her chin lifted a notch, and a smile touched her mouth. "My mama says everything will always be okay, because even though we can't change what's happened, we can change the way we deal with it. If the human race wasn't adaptable, it would have ceased to exist before it ever got started."

"Your mama's a smart woman." He opened the door, and the air in the small space turned cold and damp. After stepping outside, he gave her his usual grin. "You'll be hearing from me."

He closed the door and waited until he heard the lock engage before going down the steps. In the instant before the *snick* of metal sinking into metal, he heard her murmured response.

"Lucky me."

After rattling around her apartment for half an hour, Martine realized that DiBiase's instruction not to go out alone wasn't as simple as it sounded. She had excess energy to burn, and the best way to do that was to bundle up and head out for a rapid-paced tour of the Quarter. But she'd learned this morning how easily someone could follow her when her senses were hampered by her rain slicker, she didn't own an umbrella and she didn't find that physical misery made anything better.

Instead, she fell back on her number two energy-eater: she went back to the shop. Ramona had left for the day, Niles was out for lunch—literally this time, as well as figuratively—and Anise was ringing up a customer's selection of candles, oils and charms. Martine gave her own charm a gentle touch as she greeted both women with a nod, then went into the storeroom.

She was checking inventory when the clerk came into the room. "Is he gone?"

He… "Detective DiBiase? Yes." Martine didn't point out that he obviously wasn't in the shop, and she wouldn't have left him alone in her apartment. She loved her employees and counted on them quite a lot, but all of them were a little oblivious. Evie said the customers liked it, that it was part of the shop's mysterious, illusive air that some tourists expected.

"He got shocked both times he closed the front door." Anise's tone was distant, dreamy. "When he came in and when he left. Like static electricity, only not. That wasn't what I expected from the spell, but it's a start."

"Spell? What—" Oh, yeah, the comment Martine had made earlier about banishing him from the premises. Now who was being oblivious? Then she suppressed a shudder. The thought that Anise might actually have some power rather than mere interest in the paranormal was a little bit scary.

The clerk perched on the edge of the counter. "Why is he coming around anyway? Are you in trouble?"

Martine wished she could truthfully answer no to the question, but wishes were nothing more than hopes sent up into the ether. Some came true, but the rest evaporated into the mist, breaking into a thousand wistful pieces that never fit back together again.

"An old friend of mine from back home was murdered last night," she finally said. "I was apparently the last person to see her." She failed at suppressing this shudder. How sad for Paulina that her last conversation in life with a friend was the unsatisfying, borderline hostile exchange they'd shared.

"Wow. I've never known anyone who was murdered."

Martine had known Paulina. And Callie. And Fletcher the Letcher. What kind of normal law-abiding citizen knew three murder victims? Dear God, she hoped the list ended there. She wasn't afraid of death for herself. It was part of the cycle of life. But she wanted to go peacefully, naturally, not in a fit of someone else's rage.

"Evie's here," Anise announced, hopping to the floor a moment before the usual wiggle-rattle started at the front door. Again Martine wondered if her assistant truly might have power, but then she realized Anise could actually see the front door from where she'd sat.

Giving herself a figurative eye roll, Martine made a note to call a carpenter to repair the door. Some of the old building's quirks were charming. Her customers and friends having to wrestle the door to get inside wasn't one of them.

"I'll finish the inventory," Anise offered. "Or at least work on it until Niles gets back."

Thanking her, Martine walked through the bead curtain and met her best friend at the checkout. As was normal on Evie's visits, she laid a bag of baked goodies on the counter. Outside of normal was the big embrace she gave Martine. They were besties, but not usually the touchy-feely kind. Even so, the only thing that could have possibly felt better at that moment would have been a hug from her mom.

"I'm so sorry about Paulina," Evie murmured, squeezing extra tightly before releasing her. "And I'm sorry Jack sent Jimmy over in his place."

"It's okay." Martine sat on a stool next to the counter and watched Evie do the same. She'd been working today—she wore her fortune-teller look, with its long flowing skirt, snug shirt, lots of jewelry and mystique. Today it was part of her shtick, but truth was, she'd always loved long flowy clothes and scarves and wearing her weight in silver.

"Where are the kids?"

Evie replied cheerfully, "Nursery school, preschool and school. I know they're on their way home when I feel the shock waves disturbing the atmosphere."

"And Jack? Did he really go out of town?"

"Really. He called a few hours ago, asked me to pack a bag and picked it up on his way to the airport. How was Jimmy?"

Martine considered it. "Surprisingly not-Jimmy for the most part."

"You didn't think he had a mode that wasn't arrogant bastard? Come on, Martine, NOPD wouldn't keep him on nearly twenty years if he wasn't good at what he does."

"I knew. I just thought being charming and obnoxious and smarmy were the only things he was good at."

"Well, yeah, there's that, too. He's multitalented." Evie reached inside her bag and pulled out two bottles of water from an insulated bag, then set a small plastic dish between them, filling it with fresh raisin oatmeal cookies from the bag. "You haven't eaten lunch, have you?"

"I'm not hungry." That was a hard thing to say when Evie's cookies were sitting inches away. To appease the sudden gnawing in her stomach, Martine broke off a tiny piece, mostly raisin, and ate it. "I'm sorry I wasn't very cooperative with Jack."

"Ooh, he didn't tell me that." Evie smiled. "You know Jack. After our case, he doesn't tell me much about the job, and frankly I don't usually want to know much. The only way he would have brought me into this would have been so I could give you a smack or two and make you tell him everything."

Martine snorted. "Like you could make me do anything."

"Ha, I am so much more persuasive than you are. Remember my job—I talk money out of customers' hands every day."

She snorted again. Evie was an honest-to-God psychic who pretended to be a fraud. She gave the casual tourists value for their money, scattering tidbits of truth in the generic readings. Her serious talents, though, were saved for her serious customers.

Suddenly morose, Martine asked, "If I ask you a question, will you give me the truth?"

"You know I don't read you well, but yes. Of course I'll tell you if I know it."

"Don't you want to know the question first?"

"I know the question. You want to ask if you're going to die. And the answer is yes."

Martine's nerves tightened and her breath caught raggedly in her chest in the half instant it took Evie to go on.

"We're all going to die, sweetie. The only variables are when and how. But are you going to die now, the same way your friend did? No. And you know why? Because I don't even have to know Paulina to know that you're not like her. You won't run away. You won't try to deal with it on your own. You're wise enough to know when you need help and to accept it when it's offered."

"I'm not feeling very wise today," Martine murmured. Hadn't she just apologized for not cooperating with Jack? Hadn't she kept back important information during her interview with him and DiBiase this morning? Hadn't she wasted precious breaths wishing she could make this whole awful situation go away so she wouldn't have to deal with it?

"Eat another cookie," Evie said, pushing the plate closer. "I have it on good authority that cookies make everything better."

Realizing she'd consumed one cookie bits at a time, Martine picked up another. "Whose authority? Jackson or Jack?"

"Both, and Isabella and Evangelina." Evie's smile was a glorious thing to see. They made up the perfect happy family: handsome dad, beautiful mom, three gorgeous, smart, funny kids. No one would ever guess by looking at them the trouble she and Jack had gone through to get where they were. They deserved every bit of the light in their lives.

Martine rarely envied anyone anything. She loved her shop, her home, her family and her friends. She didn't earn a fortune, but she met all her needs and most of her wants and still had money in the bank.

While there was no great love in her life, there'd been more than one or two men who'd been great for those moments in time. As far as kids, she'd never known if she'd truly wanted to be a mother. For a long time, she'd expected it to just happen. It was how things worked in her experience: a woman fell in love, got married, had kids and lived out the rest of her life. She'd done the falling in love, the getting married, but kids/no kids had been an issue for them.

She loved Evie's kids. She loved their friend Reece's kids, too, but as for children in general, not so much. At some point, she'd accepted they weren't part of the plan for her, and she was all right with that.

She'd also mostly accepted that a good man wasn't part of her plan, either. But when she saw Evie's expression while talking about Jack, or Reece whenever she talked about Jones, she felt a little bit of jealousy. A whole lot of loneliness. Just not enough to settle for less than perfect.

How fitting that when she thought those last three words, it was Jimmy DiBiase's image that came to mind. If any man she'd ever met was so perfectly less than perfect, it was him.

"What are you thinking about?" Evie asked.

Because her friend really, truly liked DiBiase, Martine fudged her answer. "Just wondering how you got so lucky in the It's-a-Wonderful-Life jackpot."

Evie dithered over picking a cookie as if it were the most momentous decision of her day before sneaking a glance to Martine. "Do you still have dreams about Jake?"

The question startled her. She could honestly say

Jake Lassiter had popped into her mind only twice in
the last four or five years, both times in the past minute. He was another blast from the past, even more unwelcome than Paulina had been. When she and Jake
had married about a million years ago, she'd believed
she'd won the jackpot, but her ambitious politician husband had been even less a believer of things that went
bump in the night than Jack had started out, and he'd
been entirely too convinced of his abilities to manage,
maneuver and manipulate things—namely, Martine
and the shop—to his advantage.

They'd had two good years together, then three
stormy years followed by a divorce. So quick that by
the time he'd informed Martine about it, it was all over
but the signing of the papers. He'd agreed that she
should keep everything she'd brought into the marriage, and she'd agreed that if she couldn't have him,
she sure as hell didn't want anything of his, and *bang*,
they were done. He'd remarried, this time a suitable
up-and-coming politician's wife, before Martine had
even caught her breath.

"I haven't thought of Jake in years," she said honestly. "It's funny. He was such a huge deal in my life
for so long, and then suddenly he wasn't. Probably the
last time his name crossed my mind was when he last
ran for reelection. Wow." She sighed easily. "I tried so
hard to forget him—"

"After you put a dozen curses on him."

"Two dozen, at least. And then I forgot him so completely that I forgot I was even trying."

"Hmm, if you can pinpoint exactly when you put
him out of your head, and whatever else was going
on in your life at the time, you could make a fortune

in forgetting candles. They could be shaped like the groom half of the cake toppers people use at weddings, and they could melt down to nothing by the time the conscribed burning period is over."

"I like that. Just a goop of black wax, with the face the last part to melt, of course. In a grisly, eyes-wide-open scream." Behind Martine, the front door banged and rattled, then the bell announced a visitor.

"Just me," Tee, the mail carrier, called before she could rise from the stool. He wore the bulky slicker that covered the mailbags he carried, a knitted cap under the hood and navy blue shorts that reached his knees, with black socks and walking shoes. He joined them at the counter and counted out a half-dozen pieces for the shop: a utility bill, an invoice, three catalogs and a manila envelope.

"Have a cookie, Tee," Evie offered. "Take two or three."

The young man flashed her a grin. "Thanks, Miss Evie."

"And for heaven's sake, get some long pants," Martine added. "Your legs are turning blue."

"You know my motto. Neither snow nor rain nor heat nor gloom of night can make me give up my shorts." He kept one cookie to eat, wrapped the others in a paper towel Evie provided from beneath the counter and left again, as quickly and as noisily as he'd come.

Evie stood and stretched. "I guess I should head out, too. The kids will be home soon. The other day they locked Anna Maria in the reading room but forgot about the door leading into the house, so they were wildly disappointed when she got out that way and sneaked up behind them. I fully expect them to keep trying until they succeed, and then heaven knows what they'll try for an encore."

Yeah, loving her godchildren was best done from a safe distance. Though she wouldn't have to worry about a similar fate. Anna Maria's mistake was letting them know she was an instantly forgiving pushover. Martine kept them guessing about just how many lines they could cross before suffering the consequences.

"Thank you for the cookies and the conversation." Martine pushed the plate of cookies toward Evie, but Evie pushed them right back.

"Keep them. Give them to Jimmy next time you see him." Oh, she said it so casually, as if it happened all the time and was a choice on both their parts, but the look in her eyes was wickedly teasing.

A shudder ricocheted through Martine, one she greatly exaggerated to express her displeasure. "I should have just shot him at that party. I blame you, you know, for inviting me and Jack for inviting him and for not warning me in advance."

"Sweetie, you'd been married to a politician. I figured you'd recognize a good-for-nothing, sweet-talking charmer from a mile away with a blindfold on. Besides, Alia's forgiven him for all that. Why can't you?"

"She's a better woman than me. Besides, when Alia looks at Jimmy, then at Landry, she gets on her knees and thanks God for kicking Jimmy to the curb for her so she would be free for Landry."

Again, uncharacteristically, Evie hugged her. "No one's better than you. That's why I love you." Weaving around the counter, then the displays, she called back,

"If you don't have anything to cook tonight, order in. Don't go out by yourself. Better yet, don't go out at all. Don't answer your door without your baseball bat, and don't take any calls from numbers you don't know."

"What? Did DiBiase think I need reminding?"

"Oh, no. That's what Jack tells me every single time he has to work late. Love you."

"Love you, too." Martine watched Evie go, feeling a bit lost as she disappeared down the street. She delivered the bills to the desk where Anise was still working and left the rest of the mail in a basket on a shelf behind the front door to go through when she got home.

With even more on her mind than before Evie had come, she got cleaning supplies from beneath the counter and went to the front plate-glass windows. When she'd gone home for a visit one fall weekend during her parents' divorce, she'd found her mother cleaning with a vengeance. *You can never start spring cleaning too early,* Bette had said in what she'd obviously thought was a cheery manner that had struck Martine as far more manic than happy. Like a good daughter, she hadn't pointed it out, or mentioned that the only things she was cleaning belonged to Mark, or that her notion of cleaning was swiping with a cloth, then tossing the item into one box for trash, one for giveaway or one to return to him. Virtually everything had gone into the trash box.

Other than her small bin of high school memories, Martine didn't have anything to dispose of to clear her mind, but she could throw her energy into cleaning. Spring was the season of promise. When spring came, this week would be a distant memory and getting more so every day. The sun would be shining, the tourists would be happy, business would be booming and her life would be back to normal.

She would make it so.

Chapter 4

By the time Jimmy left his desk, the sun had already set, though it hadn't been visible to anyone within a hundred-mile radius of New Orleans. He thought about dinner, well aware that the refrigerator, cupboards and pantry in his new place were as empty as the day they'd arrived for installation. Some of his buddies had gone to a bar they favored that served damn good greasy hamburgers and crispy fries, but while the food sounded good, the company didn't. He'd left the station; he hadn't left work. There were things he wanted to read, notes to organize, thoughts to get down in some rational form.

He settled for picking up a pizza and going home. The apartment had a mostly open layout: living room, dining room, kitchen, office and gym sharing one large space, each area designated by its own carpet laid over black tiles and/or ceiling-to-floor drapes that opened and closed soundlessly at a push of a button. The bedroom and bathrooms actually had four walls and doors, so he didn't care much about the rest of it.

He changed into a pair of jeans and a sweatshirt from his long-ago college days, set his paperwork on one end of the island, the pizza on the other, and picked a stool in the middle. For the worst part of the eating, he would thumb through Martine's yearbook, which he could do with one-handed ease. With a small memo pad and a handful of paper clips, he opened the book.

He'd gathered recent photos of four of the five women. Robin Railey had been living in Illinois, a suburb of Chicago, the last time she'd renewed her driver's license. That had been the middle of last summer, but in early November, she'd moved from her condo, quit her job and apparently fled. No cell phone records, no credit card use, no social media activity, nothing going on with her social security number. She was like an illusion: here, then gone. The coworkers and friends he'd spoken to had worried about her for a while, but her absence from their lives meant she'd eventually faded from their thoughts.

Her parents should have been even easier to locate than Robin. They were in their sixties, an age when people tended to be more deeply rooted in their lives. A month after Robin left Illinois, Vince and Melissa Railey left their retirement community in Arizona. They'd told neighbors they were going where it "never got cold" and the cost of living was cheap. They told family they were taking a luxury round-the-world cruise and leaving their cell phones behind. They said they would be back in eight months, ten months, a year, or they might take up residence on the prettiest deserted island they passed. Their credit cards and social media, likewise, had gone unused.

In her senior picture, Robin had looked like your typical eighteen-year-old. Her hair was short, straight, her features were bland, and her occasional comments were those of a protected teenager. She didn't look like Martine's choice for a best friend, though to be truthful, that observation was based mostly on the fact that Robin wasn't Evie. Some people had been together too long and fit together too well to ever imagine anyone else in their places.

He finished his first piece of pizza, washed it down with bottled water, then sprinkled hot red pepper flakes over the next piece. After taking a large bite that left cheese stringing from his mouth to the slice, he turned a few pages to the Winchester girls' pictures. Beneath their photos were their proper names, Callista and Taliesin, both scratched out and replaced with their nicknames, one in hot pink ink, one in lime green, both in a very girlie style. The girls were mostly identical: Callie's lips a little thinner, the tip of Tallie's nose a little sharper. They wore their hair the same, the same makeup colors, but Callie wore a shirt left undone one button too low, while Tallie's denim jacket showed little of the modestly rounded neckline of her shirt.

He'd tried to contact Tallie and Callie's parents a half-dozen times and got nothing but voice mail. He'd requested a copy of Tallie's passport picture from the State Department and gotten that back, along with the information that the passport had last been scanned in London back in November—a few weeks after Callie's funeral, Jimmy guessed. His IT guy hadn't been able to find much of an internet presence for Tallie: no Facebook, Twitter, Instagram, Snapchat, LinkedIn or any of the other countless outlets. There were a few cached references to her on the website of the investment firm she'd worked for, but nothing whatsoever since her sister's obituary.

Wiping his hands, he rooted through his stuff for the email he'd gotten from the Seattle detective investigating Callie's murder, with all its attachments. Her cell phone hadn't been recovered, but her social media accounts boasted a lot of selfies, usually surrounded by a crowd, in clubs, restaurants, theaters, sometimes alone, often in lingerie or a bikini. Alone, she mostly wore a sly, secretive smile, staring straight at the camera as if she could see into the eyes of the person viewing the pictures. In a few, she looked pensive.

Then he came to the last picture in the file. Callista Jane Winchester, lying on her back in a cemetery, clothes damp, a wound to the back of her head, a large waterproof dressing hiding the brutal attack on her chest.

Related? the detective had echoed when Jimmy brought up the fact. *In what way?*

Mother of God, he said after Jimmy told him, and he could easily imagine the man making the sign of the cross. He was tempted himself, and he wasn't even Catholic. *I'll help however I can, but it's hardly even an active case here. No clues, no suspects, nothing.*

How could a person do that kind of damage to another human being and no one else know? It should be tattooed on their foreheads, the evil in their souls forcing its way out to warn anyone they met. To have the dead-cold ability to mutilate a person like that and the even deader, even colder ability to hide it from everyone who saw him... A person like that was too dangerous to walk free.

And their guy was not only free, he had likely set his sights on Martine. Of the remaining three, she was the easiest to find, the only one living right out there in public, not fifty miles from where they'd grown up. She was the only one who had never bought into the blame game for William Fletcher's death.

Good thing Jimmy was more determined to keep Martine safe than the killer could possibly be to claim her.

Flipping through the yearbook pages, he stopped at the faculty section. There he was, Fletcher the Letcher. Probably about forty, light hair going a little thin on top, dark eyes, white shirt, sport coat, printed tie. He could have sold insurance or used cars, kept books or managed personnel; he had that sort of remarkably average look.

But none of those other jobs would have provided him pretty much unlimited access to teenage girls.

Jimmy found the list he'd been adding to all day and wrote Fletcher's name at the bottom. Where had he taught before coming to Marquitta? Why had he left his last job? How long had he been married, and why had his wife chosen to go to prison without presenting some sort of defense? If he'd been abusive—always a possibility in domestic cases—she might have gotten off, depending on the degree of abuse, but she hadn't even tried.

The early start to his day was making itself felt. He rubbed his eyes, then stood and stretched out the kinks before putting the leftover pizza in the refrigerator, its empty gleaming surfaces reminding him to go grocery shopping the next day. He didn't cook much, but he knew from experience he could live on cheese and crackers, tortilla chips and salsa, and peanut butter sandwiches, and he always appreciated a cold beer from time to time.

Or maybe, as rain suddenly pounded the windows, a hot buttered rum.

The rain blurred the city lights that stretched as far as he could see and made him sigh. New Orleans, with its subtropical climate, was always a damp place, and he actually preferred humidity to drier weather, but this was too much. He had four or five pairs of wet shoes drying along the bedroom wall. Every day for the past week, he'd had the option of changing clothes when he got a chance or spending the day in some degree of wetness. He wanted to put away the overcoat and feel the sunshine on his face, the sooner, the better.

Besides, there was a hell of a difference between rain with subtropical temperatures and rain with the midthirty degrees they were having tonight. Another couple of bumps down on the thermometer, and New Orleans could wake up to snow and/or ice in the morning, and that would be the icing on a truly bad weather cake.

He was shutting off lights when his cell phone rang. He didn't glance at caller ID before answering it. He gave his number to so many people—suspects, witnesses, families and friends, lawyers, district attorneys—that the majority of calls came from people whose names he didn't always recognize.

"DiBiase," he said, heading past the kitchen into

the short hallway that connected to the bathroom and bedroom.

"Um…" The caller cleared his or her throat. With the next word, Jimmy recognized the voice. "Detective…"

His muscles tightened. "Martine. Is something wrong?"

"I'm sorry to bother you, but I, uh, got an envelope in the mail today. I just got around to opening it, and… It's a note that says… It says, *I know what you did.*" Her voice quavered on the last word, and she drew in a noisy breath. "There's something else in the envelope. It's stuck to the glue on the flap, and I didn't want to tear the envelope to get it out since I thought you might want it intact, but… It looks like a piece of fabric."

"Fabric?" he echoed. Executing a sharp turn, he went back to the island, switching on the lights overhead, shuffling through the papers there. He found the report from the Seattle detective, scanned through it until he reached the inventory of items found on Callie Winchester's body, and then he cursed softly. "About an inch square? Some sort of blue pattern?"

For a long time, she was still. He wasn't. He headed to the bedroom, shoved his feet into running shoes, threaded his belt and holstered weapon through the denim loops of his jeans, then grabbed his Taser in its holster and clipped it onto his waistband in back. "Martine? Are you there?"

After another moment of nothingness, she whispered, "Oh, God. It's part of the bandanna we used to make the voodoo doll, isn't it? And you found it on Paulina, too, or Callie."

"Callie." He opened the coat closet in the entry,

yanking on a rain slicker, shoving a canister of pepper spray into one of its oversize pockets. "I'm coming over now. Is everything locked up? All the doors, windows, the gate to the courtyard?"

"Yes, yes."

Tension came over the line in waves, tightening the knots in his neck, jaw and shoulder muscles. He was tempted to run down the stairs to the garage, but the elevator would be quicker. Its bell dinged and the door opened only seconds after he punched the button. "Stay on the phone with me. I'm not far away, and I don't have to worry about breaking any traffic laws."

"One of the perks of the job, huh?" She sounded a little more relaxed or, at least, as if she was trying.

"That, and parking illegally. That really comes in handy when you're picking up takeout." He stepped out of the elevator onto the bottom level of the garage and jogged to his car. "That's what I did when I picked up my dinner tonight."

"Of course you did. While we law-abiding citizens circle endlessly."

Though they'd never discussed it, he'd just known she would frown on any perks he got because of the job—free or discounted meals, a pass on traffic infractions, whatever else, but especially the easy parking. Grinning because he knew she would hear it in his voice, he pulled out of the garage, made a sharp turn and headed her way. "Aw, come on. Do you know what we get paid?"

"I hear you don't work for the city because you love the pay."

"You've been asking about me?"

For the first time in hours, she was back to her usual

scornful self. "I don't have to ask. You give everyone so much to gossip about that it's hard, when we know the same people, not to hear at least some of it."

There'd been plenty of gossip over the years, mostly about his ways with women, some about how an honest cop could afford his lifestyle. He doubted Martine cared about the money situation—though over the years, there had been plenty of people outranking him who did—but if she'd heard any of the talk about him and women before their second meeting, she never would have let him within arm's length of her. "Yeah, okay. I work for the city because I love the job. And I happen to have a bit of family money that helps smooth over the rough places." Like the apartment he'd just leased. The mountain cabin he rented once a year in Wyoming. The cars he swapped out for new ones every few years.

Before she could respond to that, he went on. "I just turned onto your block. Don't open the door until I ring the bell."

"Okay." The word sounded flat, the lighter moment gone. As he pulled into the empty space beside her car, he added his usual professional encouragement. "It'll be okay, Martine."

Martine listened to the bell, immediately followed by DiBiase's gruff voice. "Open up. It's pouring." She undid the locks, then backstepped to avoid the water running from him to puddle on the mat. She wasn't at all surprised that just one glimpse of his face sent her personal security rating zooming from *no one can save me* to *the big strong man will protect me* in half a nanosecond. It wasn't all Jimmy, either, she reminded herself. Any woman who was feeling vulnerable would gain strength from a man in uniform, even when he didn't actually wear a uniform. Being with Jack made her feel safe. Ditto for navy cop Alia, Jimmy's ex-wife. People who swore to serve and protect—and who carried big guns—always got two big thumbs-up from Martine.

But she couldn't honestly admit that if Jack or Alia was standing in her entry she would be thinking about how easily they filled the space, or about the warmth that just sort of radiated off them, or that they smelled incredibly fresh and green and musky.

She shook her head as she turned and started up the stairs. Shadows fell over her, one looming ahead, long and threatening, another sneaking along behind. New light bulbs, she reminded herself. At least three hundred watts each. She wanted this staircase to be visible from outer space.

When they reached the kitchen, he hung his slicker over the back of a dining chair while she took a clean towel from a drawer and handed it to him to dry his face.

"One of my homeless guys says the city's going to float away if this keeps up. They'll find us floating somewhere in the gulf, and the state will have to decide whether it wants us back. If not, we'll all be learning Spanish."

Maybe Martine was shallow, but she appreciated every moment she could think of something besides her own troubles. "Does he sleep out on nights like this?"

"He's got places. Back when I was in Patrol, I'd pick him up on bad nights and take him to a shelter.

He'd be all grateful—*Thank you, young James, you've saved my life*—and three or four hours later, I'd find him sneaking back to one of his hiding places." He shook his head, and a bead of water fell from his hair to his temple. He wiped it away with the towel before spreading it over the lip of the sink. "Some people really can't handle the shelters—the crowding, the rules, the conformity. Darrell's the nicest guy you'd want to meet under a bridge or in an abandoned warehouse, but put him in a shelter..." He shook his head.

Martine knew Jack helped homeless people and runaways and prostitutes and budding juvenile offenders beyond the scope of his job—she supposed she knew rationally that a lot of cops did. But to find out the same about DiBiase... She'd been quite happy believing the worst of him for practically the entire time she'd known him. She wasn't sure she was comfortable with giving up one of the constants in her normally comfortable life.

"You want coffee?" She gestured toward the counter as she picked up her own mug. She'd brewed two while on the phone, after he'd said he was coming over. Everything needed for the perfect cup was on the counter in easy reach: sugar, sweetener packets and cream, along with bottles of Bailey's, Frangelico, Kahlúa, bourbon, whiskey and rum. Every spirit she had in the house, in fact.

"I like variety in coffee," he said, a teasing note lightening his words.

"Yeah, well, the plain stuff wasn't making the chill go away." Wrapping her hands around her mug, she took a sip, and the rum fanned a tiny flame to life deep in her stomach. She wasn't much of a drinker, in part because booze always made her flush uncomfortably. Now that was her goal.

He added sugar and cream to his, bypassing the liquor as he faced her. "You okay?"

"Oh, sure. When my friend said someone was trying to kill her, I thought she was crazy. When she said someone wanted me dead, I thought she was freaking crazy, and now she's dead and some lunatic is threatening me." She held the cup tighter as she went down the hall to the living room and plopped in the chair closest to the gas fireplace, its flames dancing as they released heat into the air.

The second floor of her building had originally been a single-family home, then divided into two apartments before she bought it. She'd rented the other space occasionally, though Reece, then her employee, had been the last to live there. After she'd moved into her own place with Jones a few years ago, Martine had opened hers up again, knocking out walls, turning numerous small rooms into fewer larger rooms, exposing brick walls and ancient wood floors along the way.

DiBiase took a seat on the couch, set his cup down, and opened a small black bag that she hadn't noticed before. Or his truly disreputable running shoes, way overdue for a trip to the landfill. Or his sweatshirt, the angry wave logo faded but still proclaiming his loyalty to Tulane.

In the last twenty minutes, she hadn't noticed anything but the intense desire to break down into a sobbing, terrified heap.

From the bag he removed latex gloves, evidence bags and a marker, then turned his attention to the elephant in the room, sitting in the middle of the coffee table. The envelope was a regular business size, made of heavyweight kraft paper, and there were faded spots on it, likely splatters from the rain. The note, in contrast, was written on the cheapest of white paper, almost as flimsy as tissue. She'd slit the envelope along one short end, and when she'd turned it over, the note had fallen out. It had taken her a few minutes and a whole range of emotions to realize that something remained inside the envelope.

Despite the gloves, DiBiase handled the paper gently. "We'll need your fingerprints for exclusionary purposes. We can do that in the morning." He sounded intense even though he looked as if nothing else existed at the moment but the note. "'I know what you did.' Didn't put much thought into it, did he?"

Her hands began to tremble again, and she took a large drink of coffee and rum and decided her next cup would be mostly rum. "Enough to make my heart stop, which, I'm guessing, was the purpose."

He glanced sharply at her, then slid the note into an evidence bag and picked up the envelope. "No return address. Postmarked three weeks ago in Jackson, Mississippi. You know anyone there?"

"No." She was still having trouble believing she knew anyone capable of murder. Sure, she thought most people, herself included, could kill to protect themselves or someone else, but cold-blooded premeditated murder...to track down someone like Paulina or Callie, to terrorize them, kill them and discard their bodies in a cemetery...

Squeezing the top and bottom of the envelope made the sides push out, and DiBiase squinted inside, leaning closer to the lamp at the end of the sofa. "Blue bandanna. It's faded, looks old but not worn. Like someone's been saving it all these years." His gaze shifted to her again. "That's what you used to make the doll."

Sick deep inside, she nodded. "I told you, it was really crude. Callie, I think, or maybe Tallie, had her hair tied back with it. She said she would sacrifice it to the cause." Hearing the word *sacrifice* out loud made her cringe. They'd been so stupid and insensitive and naive.

But no one deserved to die for it.

Letting the envelope close again, he put it, too, in an evidence bag and labeled both before stripping off the gloves and turning toward her. "So either one of your friends told someone the details of what you'd done, or someone was watching you in the woods that night."

Lord, she was tired of shivers racing down her spine. Was it possible someone had followed them and spied on them that entire evening, two, three hours or more? That while they laughed and passed a joint and a bottle and acted their silly selves, someone who was truly evil had waited near enough to hear what they said and see what they did? Had he intended to confront them, hurt them, maybe kidnap or even kill them, or had he been satisfied at that time with being a simple peeping pervert instead of a murderous one?

"I can't imagine they told anyone. Like I said, it destroyed our friendships. It changed our entire lives." She worried the edge of her lip between her teeth for a moment before sighing. "I guess someone could have followed us. We weren't the smartest kids around. We thought the world pretty much revolved around us."

"Did you have any enemies?"

Though she'd watched enough TV shows to expect the question, it still seemed totally surreal to her. They'd been seventeen and eighteen years old—*kids*. Shouldn't developing enemies capable of murder have to wait at least until they were grown up? "I don't think Sybil Merchant waited twenty-four years to kill Callie for stealing her boyfriend."

DiBiase reached for his coffee. "You were pretty girls who liked to have fun. I'm guessing the guys liked you, and the girls wanted to be part of your group."

She'd really never given it much thought, but yes, they'd been popular. They'd all made friends easily, and boyfriends had come even more easily. And their little clique had been exclusive but not by design. They'd been best friends forever. They hadn't deliberately shut anyone out; they'd just had no reason to let anyone in.

"We weren't mean girls," Martine said at last. "Callie didn't really steal Sybil's boyfriend. He'd already broken up with her, and Callie only went out with him once. We were nice…enough."

"But you were the cool girls, and other girls wanted to be one of you. Other guys, besides Sybil's ex, wanted to be chosen by one of you."

"I guess. Yeah. But it was just high school. It wasn't the best years of our lives. It wasn't the wonder years that we would look back on with great fondness and relive at every reunion that came along. It just wasn't that important."

He grinned. "Maybe not to you, and definitely not in the greater scheme of things. But you'd be surprised how many people do consider it the best time, the wonder years. A lot of people are just older versions of who they were then. Life hasn't lived up to their expectations, so they live in the past. They still hold the same petty grudges and jealousies. They still envy the cool kids and are intimidated by the smart kids and scared of the tough kids. It made them who they are today, and they can't let go. So…any enemies besides Sybil?"

"Who went to college in Los Angeles, by the way, married and divorced a very successful movie producer and now lives on the beach in Malibu when she's not at her Paris flat. The boyfriend who broke her heart sells cars in Shreveport."

The liquor was doing its job. At least, she hoped it was the reason the chills had finally left her and at least some of the tension had drained from her body. She dearly hoped it had nothing to do with the fact that the biggest womanizer—heartbreaker—charmer—of the New Orleans Police Department was focusing all his attention on her.

Suddenly even warmer than before, she shifted away from the fire to get more comfortable. "Honestly, none that I can recall. The aftermath of our dabbling in voodoo was the only traumatic thing that had happened. Our parents were all still together, our families were close, we had friends and boyfriends, we made good grades, we were looking forward to college or moving away. Most people liked us. Some didn't, but even with the ones who didn't, it was no big deal. It was just normal life."

The humor that had lit DiBiase's face a moment ago faded, leaving the intensity back in place. "Callie and Paulina are dead, Martine, and their deaths are somehow connected to that night. It was a very big deal to someone."

* * *

Jimmy drained the last of his coffee. "I'm going to get this stuff to the lab—" or maybe have a patrol officer meet him somewhere and deliver it for him; his bed was still calling his name "—then I need to get to sleep. I'm going to Marquitta tomorrow to look around, talk to some people. You think you could go? Show me where you did the ritual if it still exists?"

As he stood up, so did she. "Okay. When will Jack be back?"

Hoping that if he got back overnight, he could be the one taking her for a drive tomorrow? Jimmy kept his sigh to himself. Whenever Jack did get back, he would defer to Jimmy on pretty much everything about this case. They may have started out sharing it, but his leaving made it primarily Jimmy's case. He wouldn't tell her that, though, not now. "He doesn't know. Bad weather, and the guy's lawyer is trying to keep him in Nebraska. Here he faces two first-degree murder charges. They've only got him on armed robbery there. Is your Jimmy fun-meter on overload?"

She didn't make the kind of caustic remark he'd come to expect. Instead, her mouth curved, nowhere near enough to suggest a smile, but it was a start. "Evie doesn't like for him to be gone."

"Why don't you spend the night over there? She'd be happy to see you, and the kids would scare away most of your basic stalker types."

For a moment, she looked tempted, but then the look faded. "If someone's watching me, I couldn't possibly lead them to Evie's door. When she and Jack were getting back together and she got caught up in that case of his, we agreed to keep our potential killers away from each other." Her face screwed up into part frown, part bewilderment. "Of course, at the time, I didn't think I would ever have a potential killer."

"And your killer doesn't know you've got me." She'd had him for a long time in one way or another: interested, attracted, intrigued. In the beginning, he'd considered her a possible friend with benefits, then an enemy whom he could surely convert if he made the effort, an acquaintance, a thorn in his side, an annoyance and, still, someone who drew him in a way no one else ever had. But that was his secret.

He forced what Evie called his crap-eating grin: big, broad and confident. "In fact, if he knew I had this case, he would probably just mark you off the list and move on out of town. I have a reputation, you know."

His words and action made her expression go dry. "I know your reputation. I doubt there's a woman in the city who doesn't."

"I'm talking about my reputation as a damn good detective." He went into the kitchen, rummaged through the slicker pocket and pulled out the pepper spray. "You know what this is?"

She nodded from the doorway.

"You ever used it?"

As she shook her head, she slowly closed the distance between them.

"It's small enough to carry in your pocket. Don't put it in your purse, then have to dig it out. Shake it up really good before you go out, and if you need it, make sure you're upwind and slide your finger right in here and press."

He held it out, but she didn't take it right away.

"Does the police chief know you go around arming citizens?"

"Who do you think put the idea in my head?" He pushed the can a little closer, and finally she wrapped her fingers loosely around the bottom part of it. "Hold it firmly. You don't want someone grabbing it out of your hand. Up here." He loosened her fingers, then slid them higher. "There's no safety, no on/off switch. You slide your finger under this little flap, you point and you spray, then run like hell the other way."

Her fingers were cool and unsteady beneath his. He guided her index finger along the length of the can, until the tip was resting lightly on the button. If she wanted, she would need only two seconds to tilt the can upward and blast him in the face. He'd seen her a time or two when she might have been angry enough to do it. That passion had surprised him. He'd figured a woman her age, not married, as independent as anyone he knew and open to a one-night stand wouldn't give a damn about that one-night stand's marital status.

He'd figured wrong. Vows, fidelity, infidelity— hers, his, anyone else's—were important to her. She believed they said an awful lot about a person—in his case, an awful lot that was bad.

And his attitude hadn't helped any. The next time they'd met, this time out to dinner with Evie and Jack, Jimmy, surprised by her disdain, had remarked, *So you almost slept with a married man. If it's okay with me, and I'm the one who's actually married, why is it such a problem for you?*

He should have kept his mouth shut and his hands off her and definitely his mouth off her. He should have thought, *Damn, she's gorgeous, and when I'm divorced and not with anyone else, I'm going to ask her out.*

And now he should keep his mind on what he was doing.

Slowly she removed her hand, and the pepper spray, from his. "Will you get in trouble loaning this to me?"

"It's mine, not the department's. No one will care. Same with this." Reaching behind him, he unclipped the Taser holster and set it on the table.

"I've never used a gun." Martine backed away, a bit of panic in her voice.

"It's a Taser. Less-lethal force. You shock the hell out of someone, knock 'em to the ground for a bit, and you run like hell. It's got a laser sight, so wherever you put the dot is where the barbs are going to go. You can shoot it from as far as fifteen feet, and the shock lasts thirty seconds, which gives you time to escape." He removed the weapon from the holster and showed her the power button, the safety, the flashlight and the laser. He removed the cartridge and showed her that, and how to reinsert it, and how to use the Taser without the barbs as a stun gun. Then he offered the black-and-yellow weapon to her.

"I'm not asking you to go around armed all the time. I don't believe people should carry weapons for self-protection unless they're absolutely committed to using them. A gun does no good if the bad guy takes it away and uses it on you." He shifted his gaze from the barrel of the Taser to her face.

"But you've got some wingnut out there who wants to hurt you for something you didn't do. He knows where you work and where you live. Now that Paulina's out of the way, he's probably watching you. Neither the pepper spray nor the Taser are going to kill him, but they will give you an advantage, and when your life is at stake, Martine, you take every advantage you can get."

He watched the emotion flicker through her eyes, from a clear desire to refuse to some degree of interest, from distaste to fear to resignation to relief. He rarely felt physically vulnerable; he'd always been big, strong, fast, more than capable of holding his own. He'd learned to fight in school and honed it on the job, and a pistol on his hip or in his hand was as natural as a cup of coffee to someone else.

But he understood how vulnerable people could feel, just going about their everyday life, and Martine was in a much worse situation than that. No one knew how the killer had gotten his hands on Callie or Paulina. They had no clue just how much he had known about their daily activities. Had they been safe at home when he took them? Had he persuaded them to meet him? Had he grabbed them off the street?

"When this is over, when we catch this guy, you can give them back. You'll never have to pick up a weapon again…unless you decide you like being prepared to defend yourself. But for now, Martine…please. I don't want anything to happen to you."

Again, emotion flickered through her eyes. Surprise at how serious his last words had sounded? Before she could give it too much thought, before *he* could give it too much thought, he grinned. "If you get hurt on my watch, Evie and Jack will give me hell every day of my life."

She took a breath, wrapped her fingers around the Taser grip and blew out a deep breath. "Okay. Run through this with me again."

* * *

Martine went to bed Wednesday night convinced she wouldn't sleep, but fatigue won out...maybe, with a little help from the pepper spray and the Taser hidden beneath the extra pillow on her bed. Less-lethal force, DiBiase had called them. She didn't want to kill anyone, but she didn't want to die, either. If his weapons could get her out of a life-or-death situation without having to kill someone else, she was happy to hoard them close.

He'd said he would be by around ten to pick her up for the trip to Marquitta. She didn't want to spend hours in a car with him. Didn't want to show him that spot out by Twins' Landing where she and the girls had their last big hurrah. Didn't want to see the town and the familiar faces, familiar places, that would remind her of them. She just didn't want to go, period.

But she owed it to her girls, to herself and to DiBiase. And who knew? The life she helped him save might be her own.

She'd called Anise, asking her to come in early to open, eaten a small breakfast, inhaled three cups of coffee and changed pants four times. She wasn't looking for the pair that flattered her most, she reminded herself with a scowl in the mirror. She needed pants with a pocket big enough for the pepper spray and with a substantial enough waistband to make wearing the Taser as comfortable as she was ever going to be with something stuck inside her pants. She settled on olive-drab cargo pants and, to go with them, sturdy boots and a white shirt with a khaki sweater over it. With the heavy sweater tugged over her hips, no one would notice the weapons adding bulk where she didn't have it.

When she saw DiBiase's car pull to the curb, she grabbed her purse and slicker and trotted down the stairs. The bell rang before she reached the halfway point, and she called, "I'm coming."

Hurry, Tine, Paulina used to shout, and she'd shouted back, *I'm coming!* All those years, constantly coming and going, never more than a phone call apart, so close they could finish each other's sentences.

All gone. All those good times, all the potential, all the promises. Vanished.

She undid the locks and stepped outside. Her breath misted in front of her face, but for once there was no fog, no rain. Still no sun.

From where he stood at the bottom of the steps, DiBiase said, "Anise says this is a temporary break. The fog will be back today, and we may see some snow before it's all over."

Martine wrinkled her nose. "I hope she's not dabbling in weather control."

"Nope." He opened the passenger door for her, then grinned. "She's watching the Weather Channel."

"Did you go inside the shop?"

"No, she was turning over the Open signs when I got here. She opened the door to speak."

Martine was faintly relieved that he hadn't gone into the shop. It just really wasn't a good time to find out that he'd gotten another static shock from the doorknob.

"I called the police department in Marquitta," he said as he pulled away from the curb. "I want to talk to the detective who investigated Fletcher's murder. Find out what their case looked like before the wife confessed."

"What does that matter? She admitted she did it. Case closed."

"You'd be surprised how many false confessions have resulted in convictions. People trying to protect somebody else, people trying to take credit for someone else's actions, people who have mental issues that cause them to confess to just about anything. And that's not including the ones who are coerced into a false confession by cops."

"You could never make me confess to something I didn't do."

"Of course I could. It's called the Reid technique." DiBiase glanced at her from the corner of his eyes. "Given enough time, I could get you to confess to killing Paulina and Callie yourself. It's trickery, deception and psychological manipulation at its finest. You break down your suspect and build them back into someone who believes you'll help them if they just tell you what you want to hear."

"It sounds unethical."

"It can be with the wrong cop."

She hesitated, then asked, "You ever settle for a confession you knew wasn't true?"

"No."

He said it simply, normally, and she believed him. He might not grasp the meaning of things like *forsaking all others* and *until death do us part*, but her problems with him were with the man, not the cop.

A man she hadn't seen much of the past two days.

A cop who'd impressed her with his dedication to the job, with his patience with her, with his need to protect people and find justice for people he'd never known.

A cop who'd come out last night after a hellishly long day, in pouring rain, to pick up evidence and to make her feel safer. Who'd brought her ways to negate her overwhelming sense of helplessness.

They drove a few miles in silence, those last thoughts replaying in her mind: impress, dedication, patience, need to protect. A few days ago, she would have claimed Jimmy DiBiase could never impress her on more than a superficial he's-damn-hot level, and she wouldn't have believed he could even define the other things.

What a difference a murder made.

As he merged onto the interstate, he glanced her away. "Did you ever meet Fletcher's wife?"

Eyes narrowed, Martine focused on the past. In elementary school, she'd adored her teachers and cried each time she'd passed to the next grade and a new teacher. By senior year, all she had cared about was the easiest classes that would fulfill her graduation requirements, going to the dances and staying out of Fletcher's reach. "If I did, I don't remember."

"Did they have any kids?"

Their school hadn't been huge; she'd known either names or faces for pretty much everyone, but she couldn't recall a Fletcher son or daughter. "Not that I can think of. Maybe a younger kid?"

"How much do you remember about the case?"

A shudder rocketed through her, and she moved uneasily to hide it, shifting her weight and tugging at her seat belt. There wasn't much room in the passenger seat with the computer extending into her space, and she felt she needed it right now.

"I was the last one to leave town. Robin and the

twins were gone practically before the police started
their investigation. Paulina took off next. At first Mrs.
Fletcher denied having anything to do with it. She
swore she hadn't seen him since the night before, that
she'd fallen asleep on the couch. Then, after a couple days, she stopped crying, got all stiff-backed and
stony-eyed—that was how my mom described her—
and apologized for lying. She said he'd made a fool of
her one time too many, that she'd snapped and shot
him while he slept. She said that wasn't the life he'd
promised her, and people had to pay when they broke
their promises."

She considered that a moment. "I don't understand... When my dad decided he didn't want my mom
anymore, she hired a lawyer and made sure she was
taken care of. She didn't for a minute think about taking out his rifle and killing him. I didn't consider killing my ex. Alia didn't consider killing you."

"Sure, she did," he said with a grin. "Granted, she's
a highly capable federal agent. She probably could
have gotten away with it easier than you or your mom
could."

Martine appreciated the smile his response brought
her. Alia often said things to or about DiBiase that
seemed really harsh on the surface, but it didn't take
anyone long to see that they still shared an affection
few divorced couples managed. It was probably because they *were* divorced. They hadn't dragged the
marriage out long enough for Alia's love to turn to
hatred.

Jimmy's infidelity probably meant more to Martine
at the moment than it did to the woman he'd cheated

on. There was a lesson in that, but not one that Martine wanted to look closely at now.

And she wasn't going to start calling him Jimmy. *DiBiase* had worked just fine for years. It would continue to do so now.

The drive to Marquitta would always be familiar, not that she'd made it very often since her mom started her travel career. When they visited, it was usually Bette stopping in New Orleans on her way someplace else, and visits with her father... Well, she'd always been more of a mama's girl. She saw Mark at Christmas, on both their birthdays and Father's Day but not very regularly other than that. He'd changed from the father she'd grown up with, and she didn't have much in common with the man he'd become.

"Did you grow up dreaming of leaving your hick hometown in the dust?"

The question drew her glance across the car. DiBiase sat in a comfortable slouch behind the wheel, one hand resting at the top. His suit today was dark gray, the shirt white, the tie black-and-silver stripes. Evie had once shown her Jack's half of the closet, and they'd snickered together over the seven dark suits, seven lighter suits, seven white shirts and the rack of similarly dark ties. Now she wondered if DiBiase's closet looked the same. As far as contents, probably, though she didn't imagine his would be nearly as neat as Jack's. Jack was always more put-together, while Jimmy, no matter how squared away he was, always gave a bit of a tousled impression. It was too easy for comfort to imagine him in a looser, more relaxed setting.

A more intimate setting.

Even, if she relaxed her guard, in no clothes at all.

Martine scowled. Apparently, her brain *was* going to start calling him Jimmy, with her permission or without, and thinking all sorts of things about him that she'd sworn off that night she found he was married. Damn.

She forced herself to concentrate on his question. "Aw, I wouldn't call Marquitta a hick town. It's got at least eighteen thousand people." Then she shrugged. "I loved New Orleans from the first time I saw it. I was convinced God had intended for me to live there but dropped me in Marquitta by mistake. Getting there was the goal for the first part of my life, and staying there has been the goal since. What about you? Could you not wait to get out of your hick hometown?"

"I would have moved away in seventh grade if I could have. My hick town is Cypress Hill. Back that way." He gestured vaguely toward the west.

"I've been there. When my mom first started her travel blog, she mostly focused on local places. She did a story about the plantation the town is named for, and I went along. Gorgeous place." A *Gone with the Wind*–type place, huge, white, gracious—a real step back in time. Massive columns, immense live oak trees, regimented gardens, lush velvety grass and more antiques than all the shops in the Quarter could hold. A tribute to a time long past. Lovely to visit, but she wouldn't want to live there. "Have you toured it?"

He didn't meet her gaze. "Yeah, I've, uh, seen it."

"Of course. You live that close to a historic site, you probably see more of it than you want, between school field trips and showing family guests around town."

"Uh-huh."

Still he didn't look at her, and her gaze narrowed as she identified discomfort in the set of his jaw. His fingers were tighter on the steering wheel than they'd been moments ago, and his slouch didn't look so comfortable now.

I work for the city because I love the job, he'd said last night, then added, *And I happen to have a bit of family money that helps smooth over the rough places.*

Cypress Hill was a decent enough little town, though dusty and sleepy, one of those rural places where the population dropped steadily every decade as the young people went off looking for jobs and careers. Not the sort of place that attracted a lot of businesses or families of a lot of wealth. In fact, all its wealth, if she recalled her mom's research correctly, pretty much belonged to the family that owned the plantation. She was certain they had been mentioned in the article, as well—when Bette did a story, she did it justice—but all Martine remembered was that the property had come down through the wife's family so there were two surnames involved.

A bit of family money... "I don't remember Cypress Hill having much in the way of opportunities. A couple of convenience stores, some churches, a bank, a few bars." She couldn't be sure of any that, but she knew from Bette's travels that the description covered a great many small towns.

"Yeah. We went to school in the next town over. And to the doctor, the dentist, the grocery store..."

She was enjoying being the one asking questions that he hadn't expected. Turnabout was always fair play, even when it was on a much less important subject. "Did you ever ask your parents to move to the next town?"

"They couldn't do that."

"Why not?"

Finally he looked at her and lifted one shoulder in a careless shrug. "Their income was kind of tied to Cypress Hill."

"Cypress Hill the town? Or Cypress Hill the plantation?"

He slowed to take the next exit, the signal light blinking, then came to a stop at the highway where he needed to turn. "Okay. My DiBiase father married my Ravenel mother, whose family built Cypress Hill back in 1820. She grew up in the house. So did my sisters and I. After my sisters left home, my parents had a smaller place built way out back and opened the house up for tours, weddings, overnight stays, etcetera. It's been very successful for them."

"Wait a minute. I'm trying to picture this." Martine closed her eyes, imagining a beautiful, refined, beloved mansion and Jimmy at eight, twelve and sixteen, sitting on furniture fit for a castle and eating off dishes fit for a king. Jimmy, being polite, well-mannered and behaved, as generations of Ravenels before him had always been.

Opening her eyes again, she smiled smugly. "The image just won't form."

The look he gave her was grumpy. "Where did you think I grew up? In a home for juvenile delinquents? On a farm, with the animals?"

"Don't get annoyed with me. I didn't know you even had parents until last night." She pointed helpfully to the right. "Marquitta's that way. Just follow the road to the middle of nowhere."

Her mood significantly better, she returned to gazing out ahead of them, this time with a smile easing the tension on her face.

After a moment, she caught a tiny glimpse of a smile on Jimmy's face, as well.

Chapter 5

Marquitta had so much more to offer than Cypress Hill that if Jimmy had grown up there, he might have gone back after college. It had all the businesses he needed to survive: grocery stores, convenience stores, liquor stores and restaurants. Its police department was of a decent size, around thirty-five officers, and there was enough crime to keep them busy, though homicides were rare. For a homicide detective, that could be good or bad, depending on the week.

"I've got an appointment with the detective in charge of the Fletcher case in fifteen minutes at a coffee shop up here," he said as he drove along the main drag downtown. "I'll ask if he minds you listening in, but if he says yes, you'll have to have your coffee alone."

"Or I could walk around downtown."

"Or you can sit at another table and have your coffee alone. Come on, Martine, this guy who's very upset with you and your friends probably lived here when you did. He knows your face, and he knows his way around if he followed you into the woods, so you don't get to go off anywhere without me."

"Okay."

Her easy acceptance made him shake his head. Just a few days ago, the idea of her agreeing to something he suggested would have seemed impossible. All she'd seen when she looked at him was the cheater, the betrayer, the liar who had almost seduced her.

Damn, he regretted that he'd failed. Regretted that he'd even tried. Wondered what would have happened if he'd waited until he was single again.

And while she was cooperating at the moment, he wondered what it would take to make her forget that guy completely. To convince her that he'd changed.

Yeah, he heard that line a lot from people he'd arrested, and he rarely believed it from them. He'd gotten cynical enough over the years that he wasn't sure he would believe himself.

The coffee shop was located on the corner across the street from the police department. Jimmy found a parking space on the adjacent street, met Martine on the sidewalk, and they headed back to the corner. "Are you armed?"

She held her arms out from her sides. "Can you tell?"

He gave her a long, attentive look, from her shoulders to her knees, then back again, even though he knew exactly where the pepper spray and the Taser would be. "With all those clothes, you could be packing an AR-15 under there for all I know. Are you comfortable wearing them?"

"They don't seem as weird as I thought they would."

"Hopefully we'll get this guy before they become second nature." He opened the coffee shop door, and heat rushed out, carrying the aromas of coffee, sugar and cream on the air.

A white-haired man stood up at a table in the center, surrounded by other older gentlemen, with enough empty sugar packets and creamer tubs to indicate that they'd been at it awhile. "You DiBiase?"

"Yes, sir, I am." *You'll recognize me*, the guy had said, *because I'll be sitting at the old cop farts' table. Bunch of retirees that have nothing better to do than relive their glory days.*

Much as Jimmy appreciated a hot cup of coffee or three in the morning and swapping stories with other cops, when he retired, he sincerely hoped he didn't find himself hanging out in a cop coffee shop or bar, rehashing old cases. He intended to have more in his life than getting old and nostalgic.

The older guy met him in the aisle, a brown expandable folder tucked under his arm, shook hands, then smiled at Martine. "Do you know we didn't get our first female officer until eight years ago? I bet you brighten up the office. I'm Carl Taylor."

"Nice to meet you, Carl. I'm Martine Broussard."

"Martine's not an officer, Detective," Jimmy said. "I wanted her to sit in because she knows some of the victims involved in my case, but if you'd prefer she didn't, that's fine."

Taylor's gaze shifted back to Martine, shrewd and evaluating, before he smiled again. "If DiBiase trusts you, who am I to object? It's his case. And it's Carl, son. If I get used to being called Detective again, my wife's gonna pitch a fit. She says it took the first ten years of retirement for me to remember what my first name is."

They took a table for four in the back, Jimmy sliding out the chair in the corner for Martine. He hadn't realized exactly how uncomfortable he was going to be with her visiting her hometown until they'd crossed the city limits. He didn't know enough about the suspect's pattern to know whether bringing her here increased the danger or provided a bit of safety over leaving her in the shop and the home that the guy already knew about.

At least they were in a room with a bunch of retired cops, and the police station was only a ten-second run away.

Taylor waved to a waitress who took their orders for coffee, then set the folder on the table. "So you were asking about the Fletcher case. Easiest murder case we ever closed. Not that we have very many murders around here. Do you mind if I ask why you're looking at it now? It's been over twenty years."

"I have a new case that appears to be tied to that one."

"Tied how?"

Jimmy had been debating how to answer that question since making the appointment. In general, he didn't like sharing with outside agencies, but sometimes there wasn't much choice. Other cops didn't like it when he asked all the questions and gave them nothing in return, even if it was only to satisfy their curiosity.

"Can I get into that later?" he asked as the waitress brought three steaming cups of coffee.

"Sure," Taylor agreed. "I won't forget. So… I'll just start at the beginning. Police got a call around eight fifteen on a Sunday morning. Katie Jo Fletcher, in hysterics, screaming that her husband was dead. She was so shaken, she couldn't even get her address right. We found him in bed, shot once in the chest and once in the groin. No sign of a break-in, no struggle and no weapon."

"Any neighbors hear the shots?"

"Nah. They lived back a good ways off the road. Katie Jo, she was wailing and keening, going on about how he didn't deserve that, that he'd been a good husband and a good father—"

"Father?" Jimmy glanced at Martine. "How many kids did he have?"

"Just the one, Irena. Stepdaughter, really. Used her daddy's name—Young."

Martine's brows narrowed in the way that meant she was concentrating. "I think… Do you have a picture of her, Carl?"

Taylor thumbed through the files in the thick folder and pulled out a thinner one. All it held was a school photo and a single sheet of paper with minimal information.

When Martine took it, Jimmy leaned close to see it better. A strand of her hair brushed against his cheek, and the scent of her perfume drifted on the air. Not the time to think how good she smelled or how good she'd felt all that time ago.

He barely managed to keep himself from rolling his eyes. *Any time* was a good time to think those kinds of things. Life was too short and uncertain to limit pleasures to certain times or places.

Irena Young was a pretty enough girl, though her hair was overstyled, her makeup overdone, her outfit overmatched. The effect was desperation—to fit in, to be accepted—and the fear that it wasn't going to happen shadowed her eyes.

Resettling in his chair, Jimmy asked, "You remember her, Martine?"

"I... I do. She was new that year, and she didn't seem to like it. We felt bad for her, having to start her senior year at a brand-new school. But we had no clue she was Mr. Fletcher's stepdaughter."

"Would you have wanted anyone to know if you were her?"

"No, of course not." Her fingers trembled slightly as she returned the folder to Taylor.

"So you're from here." Taylor's gaze narrowed. "Are you Bette and Mark Broussard's daughter?"

"Yes, sir."

"You look like your mom, but you've got your daddy's coloring. What remote part of the world is she in now?"

"London. Not too remote."

"Our hometown girl made good. Not that we see much of her anymore. She tells my wife life's too short to waste."

"Smart woman," Jimmy said, grinning at the coincidence before returning to the subject. "You said this was the easiest murder case you ever had. Did you suspect Katie Jo from the beginning?"

"She was the wife. We always suspect them. But no more than usual. They seemed to get along fine, though there were rumors that he ran around on her. Also rumors about what went on behind closed doors. They didn't socialize, didn't go to church, he wouldn't let her get a job. According to her, he was pretty controlling. But she was truly grief-stricken. I've seen a lot of people at the worst times of their lives. I can usually tell if they're playing a part or if they're sincere, and that woman was sincerely in shock at her husband's death."

"But?"

Taylor tore open three packets of sugar, dumped them into his coffee and stirred it, the spoon clinking against the porcelain. "But the next day, she was all calmed down, like she'd cried every tear she had. She walked into the police station, quiet, head held high, told us she'd shot him and where she'd hidden the gun."

"Did you believe her?"

Again, Taylor took a moment before answering. Jimmy knew from his own experience that the detective was replaying the scene in his head, looking at it from every angle. Finally, he shrugged. "No reason not to. She knew where Fletcher kept the gun. He'd taught her how to use it in case she ever needed to defend herself. He'd moved them around an awful lot— never stayed at a job more than a year. He took her and the daughter away from their family and friends, the girl had trouble fitting in at new schools over and over, they had money problems, and there were those rumors. Plus the gun, and her prints were on it and the bullets still loaded. We couldn't ask for more."

With that evidence, Jimmy would have believed her, too. "Why did he change jobs so often?"

"We checked with the schools where he used to work. Never fired, just resigned at the end of each year. Wife said he wanted to experience life elsewhere. Not something she was aware of when she met him." Taylor shrugged again. "I got the impression she wouldn't have married him if she'd known he was going to up-root them every year."

Wouldn't have married him. Not the sign of a happy marriage.

And never fired meant nothing. Jimmy had heard of too many problem teachers who'd never been fired—just forced into resigning by a school district willing to keep silent as long as they got to pass the problem on to someone else. Thieves, dopers, philanderers, abusers, pedophiles. Fletcher appeared to qualify on at least two counts.

What better motivation for killing a husband than his messing with her kid? Whether Fletcher had gotten too friendly with Irena, like he did with the girls at school, or had just made her life miserable because of his choices, Katie Jo might have felt drastic action was necessary.

Beside him, Martine spoke up. "Why didn't she want a trial? It seems she might have gotten some sympathy from a jury."

Taylor shifted in his chair, crossing one ankle over his knee. He didn't have to consult his notes. He'd probably refreshed his memory after Jimmy's call yesterday, but a lot of cases stuck with a cop, and this was probably one of Taylor's never-forgets. "She didn't want her girl to have to go through that. She'd done the crime, and she was willing to do the time. She said the sooner it was over, the sooner Irena could get on with her life. I suspect she also didn't want anything coming out at trial that would tarnish Irena's memory of her stepfather, or maybe she didn't want her to hear the details of what she'd done herself."

"Maybe she was a killer with a conscience. I've run

into a few of those over the years." Jimmy hesitated, glanced at Martine, then quietly asked, "Did you know the victim's nickname at the local high school was Fletcher the Letcher?"

The detective had not known that. An hour later, back in the car and buckling her seat belt, Martine marveled over the fact. As Jimmy stowed the detective's folder—including Taylor's own personal investigative notes—in the back seat, then fastened his own seat belt, she sighed. "Every girl in high school that year knew about Fletcher. It was about as far from being a secret as anything could be. With that many people who knew, how is it possible that not one of them ever said anything to a mother, a sister, another teacher or a counselor?"

He gave her a steady look. "You were one of those girls. Did you tell your mom?"

Slowly, regretfully, she shook her head. "I never considered it."

"Your parents would have been upset. They would have wanted to know if he'd touched you, and when and where. They would have made a big deal of it, invading your privacy, making you feel guilty or dirty or somehow responsible. And you didn't want anyone thinking, even for a minute, that you might have been Fletcher the Letcher's victim. So you stayed quiet. So did your friends, for the same reasons. So did all the girls, and the boys who knew."

She pressed her fingertips to her temples, rubbing to lessen the tension gathered there. "Poor Irena knew."

"And she stayed quiet, too. That's how these guys get away with it. In the beginning, no one wants to believe they're capable of it. No one wants to believe it's serious, that it wasn't just a bump or an accident, and when they figure out it is serious, no one wants to be the one to complain. No one wants to be labeled a victim. No one wants to face the scrutiny and the questions and the gossip that come with speaking out."

He was right on every point—he had a good grasp of the way teenage girls thought—but she couldn't help but feel ashamed. "It was a really crappy thing for us to do." If they'd come forward, told their parents, made complaints, how different would Katie Jo's and Irena's lives have been? How many girls would have escaped the letch's attention?

Jimmy twisted in the seat to face her. That intensity had returned to his face and his voice, strong with emotion and understanding and an expression she was beginning to think of as his driven-to-get-justice look. "Would it have been nice if you'd all stormed the principal's office the first time he touched one of you? Sure. Are you somehow culpable for what he did because you didn't? Of course not. You were kids. You'd be surprised how many adults can't or won't speak up. I can't count how many murders I've investigated that took place in restaurants, bars, crowded places, and nobody saw nothin'. I work months to solve cases where all the victims' families and friends know who killed them, but they won't tell me a damn thing. That's the job."

"Sounds frustrating."

"It can be."

"So why do you do it?"

His grin came unexpectedly, lightening the tension in his face, making his eyes dance with smug macho arrogant sweet-talking pretty-boy satisfaction. "It's not what I do. It's who I am."

Last week she would have scoffed at that. He was a legend in his own mind, she would have said. Pity the people of New Orleans, she would have added.

This afternoon, she took it at face value. He was a dedicated cop with a better understanding of people than she'd ever given him credit for. And not just understanding but acceptance, too. He knew what motivated people, what scared them, what drove them and what held them back, when she'd thought he was just a complete and total jerk.

Now she was coming to realize that he was just a partial jerk, and since the same could be said of her...

He started the engine, then pulled out of the parking space. "How do we find these woods of yours?"

"Go straight." She gazed out the side window at familiar old buildings, most occupied by unfamiliar businesses. The dress shop on the corner was now a bookstore; the mom-and-pop pharmacy that still had a soda fountain into her teens was an insurance office; and the shop where her dad had gotten his hair trimmed every few weeks was empty, the striped barber pole still in place outside, its glass cracked.

But the diner where the Broussards had eaten breakfast every Sunday was still in the same spot with the same specials advertised on the windows. She looked longingly at it even after they'd passed, wishing they were going there instead of to the woods.

"I don't know if the woods are even there anymore," she said as the diner faded from sight. "The property was owned by the Winchesters. They might have sold it when they moved away. It had waterfront access, sort

of. There's a creek that leads to the lake where they'd
built a dock, and Mr. Winchester took his boat out
from there. We used to picnic and play and swim there,
though as we got older, we mostly just laid in the sun.
They called it Twins' Landing after Callie and Tallie."

Her chest burned, and she realized she'd run out of
air. She filled her lungs, then let the breath out slowly.
The burning from the lack of oxygen eased but moved
instead to her throat and made her eyes go damp. It
was one thing knowing that Paulina and Callie were
dead, to even see the picture of Paulina, pale and still,
but being in Marquitta made it worse. Made it more
real. She'd ridden bikes down these streets with them;
they'd gone to movies at the theater just ahead; they'd
attended that elementary school together and played
in that park. They'd learned to drive here, had their
first dates, first kisses, first sex here.

They'd *lived* here—still lived here in her memories,
a little fuzzy and distant but here.

Would it still be the five of them here after she returned to New Orleans today, or would only three of
them remain in those fuzzy, distant images?

When Jimmy's hand took hold of hers, she startled,
her eyes jerking open, her breath catching. For just an
instant she'd forgotten him, had been so lost in the past
and the sadness and the regrets. He didn't say a word
but curled his fingers, warm and strong, over hers,
and held on tightly.

She held back just as tightly.

When their turn appeared ahead, she had to clear
her throat to speak. "Turn right at the light." That
would take them to the neighborhood where her and
Paulina's families had lived since before they were

born, where the other three families had moved in and completed their tight-knit little circle.

Jimmy made the turn before he began talking in an idle manner that struck her more as thinking out loud than actual conversation. She was happy for the distraction, though.

"So...as far as Taylor knows, Katie Jo is still in prison, and Irena went to live with her mother's sister in Idaho. Irena probably wasn't crazy about her stepfather, given that he created so much disruption in her life and that she managed to hide the fact that he *was* her stepfather for the entire school year. She probably came back to Louisiana to visit her mom—maybe even moved here when she was able, so I'll check on her and Katie Jo when we get back. I'll go through Taylor's notes, too, see if there was any evidence of the affairs."

"Turn left here," Martine said absently. Katie Jo Fletcher had gotten a life sentence, according to Detective Taylor. She hadn't negotiated, hadn't tried to get herself any kind of deal whatsoever. Martine couldn't imagine giving in so completely.

But it was even harder to imagine being in a marriage so bad that murder seemed the only way out.

"Do you think she planned it? Practiced her grief-stricken widow routine until it came naturally? Waited until graduation so Irena wouldn't have to change schools again? Slept on the couch because she couldn't bear to lie in bed with him one more night? Got up and checked on her daughter to make sure she was still asleep and wouldn't see anything? Walked into the bedroom and shot her husband, went out into the woods to hide the gun, then came back and called the police?"

"Maybe. Probably. Though the grief-stricken part might not have been such a stretch. Some people don't realize the impact of killing someone until they've done it. They've been exposed to so much violence on the streets, in the news, on TV shows and in movies, and they think it's no big deal. You point the gun, pull the trigger, and boom, it's over. But once it's done, once they see the blood, once they realize that person is truly dead and is never coming back, it can haunt them.

"I suspect Katie Jo falls into that group. Whether it was one moment of rage or a calculated plan, it changed her whole life. It changed Irena's whole life. Katie Jo didn't want that much out of life, and all she got was prison. The sad fact is that if she believed murder was her only option—and she must have, since that's the one she chose—then prison was probably better than what she had before."

It was way beyond sad, but Martine didn't want to focus on that now. "Stop here," she said, leaning forward to look past him at the house across the street. "That's my house. My mom's house. I grew up there."

He glanced at her, then the house. It was a great place, big and white with deep green trim, new enough to lack the headaches of a truly old home but built to look as if it had been there a hundred years. She'd spent entire chunks of her life on that broad front porch with her girlfriends, her boyfriends, her mom's cats, her parents and other family when they visited. This house had been the center of her life.

A life she wanted desperately to distance herself from.

She pointed out the four other houses as they followed the winding streets to the back of the neighborhood. The Winchesters' house was last, set in the middle of a lot twice the size of the others, a mini-mansion, bordered on three sides with woods.

"We'll have to walk from here," she murmured, huddling deeper into her jacket. Jimmy pulled to the curb and shut off the engine. She got the impression he would let her linger if she wanted, but she opened the door immediately. Any lingering she did today would be at home, in the comfort of her secure little apartment, herself locked in and the world locked out.

The idea of Martine Broussard going into hiding would make most people who knew her snort…but most people who knew her knew nothing about the voodoo ritual or Fletcher's death or Katie Jo's life sentence or the harshness of Irena's life. They didn't know about Callie or Paulina. They didn't know that for the first time in her entire life, Martine was scared. If it wasn't for Jimmy, she would be too scared to set foot outside her apartment.

Jimmy DiBiase making her feel safe. Now, that was a thought worthy of all the snorts in the world.

Maybe it was the cold, the gray, the surrounding dampness, but the clearing Martine led Jimmy to in the woods seemed an unlikely haunt for five teenage girls. The thick carpet of pine needles dampened sound, and there were enough leafy trees and shrubs to provide a barrier outside of which anyone could hide, especially after dark, and spy on them. A thought that had likely never crossed their minds.

Had Katie Jo done just that? Had she come upon them out here and watched, listened, wished for her daughter to have that kind of friendship? She'd wanted a happy, normal life for Irena, for herself, and thanks to her husband, neither of them had it.

"Do you think he molested Irena?" Martine asked.

Jimmy turned to her, standing at the edge of the clearing, huddled in her slicker. She looked cold and miserable, and neither had to do with the weather. A drop of rain plopped on her forehead, and she looked at the sky with annoyance before pulling the hood into place.

"He could have married Katie Jo with the idea of having his own little victim in-house. Or he could have discovered the joys of perversion after they married and turned to the girls he had easy access to at school rather than the one who lived in his house. Some guys like to keep it in the family. Some don't take it anywhere near them."

But Katie Jo's willingness to give up her right to a trial… Protecting Irena from knowing ugly stuff about her parents, Taylor had thought. It could just as easily have been protecting Irena from having to divulge ugly stuff about how her stepfather had abused her.

"Do you know where the Fletcher house was from here? Pickering Road?"

Martine's brow furrowed, then she pointed downstream. "A mile or so that way. You can't get there from this neighborhood. You have to go back to the main road, turn left, then turn left again after a ways. It's a dirt road, maybe a thousand feet before it dead-ends."

An easy enough walk for Katie Jo if she'd needed to get out of the house for a while. She could have stumbled on the girls here and stayed hidden, making silent wishes for her daughter. She could have heard them talk about her husband's behavior at school with shock, if she hadn't known before, or disgust if she had. It could have been the breaking point for her, and the ritual could have inspired her.

Jimmy wasn't about to share that last thought with Martine. The other four had believed all along that they were somehow responsible for Fletcher's death. If Martine thought Katie Jo might have gotten the idea from their game, the guilt would embrace her as surely as it had the others.

And it would be so much crap. You could put an idea into a person's head, but the responsibility for acting on it belonged entirely to that person. *The teenage girls down the street made me do it* just wouldn't fly as an excuse.

He looked around one last time. There was really nothing to see, just a spot where for years kids had sneaked off to do the things kids did: Martine and her friends two decades ago, the current neighborhood kids today if the small collection of empty beer cans and used condoms behind a fallen tree was anything to judge by. Kids who had friends and drinking buddies and hookup partners.

He started to turn, but something held him there, his gaze shifting over the live oak that sheltered the clearing. Its branches were huge, some dipping down to rest on the ground before arching back up into the sky, all of them capable of bearing the weight of anyone who wanted to spy.

Any teenager not invited to the party. Any jealous, lonely misfit who wanted desperately to have just one friend. Any awkward, shy kid who couldn't imagine much better than being welcomed into the coolest group of girls at the school. Anyone who knew they hung out here, who lived near enough to walk along the creek under cover of darkness and watch and wish and want.

Maybe Katie Jo Fletcher hadn't killed her husband. Maybe she had been genuinely horrified by his death. Maybe she'd known where to find the gun because someone had told her. Maybe she'd been willing to go to prison because she hadn't wanted to ruin her daughter's life any more than William Fletcher already had.

Maybe it had been Irena Young standing next to her parents' bed, gun in hand, guided by the ritual she'd just witnessed, killing the bastard who'd made her life so hard.

Justification, Jimmy thought again. It would have been easier for Katie Jo to spend her life in prison—her punishment for bringing Fletcher into their lives—than to stand by and let her daughter go. The best of Irena's life could still be ahead, while the worst of Katie Jo's would end.

Jimmy blew out a deep breath, then refilled his lungs, the air heavy with the smells of the creek, the trees, the decay. If Katie Jo had gone to prison for the crime her daughter committed, the guilt must have eaten at Irena every single day. Had she honored her mother's sacrifice by living the absolute best life she could live? Or had she let resentment and anger slowly destroy her until she latched on to someone else, anyone else, to blame for losing Katie Jo?

"I'm going back to the car to wait."

By the time Martine's words registered in his brain, she had a fifty-yard head start, enough that her pink-and-yellow slicker was starting to fade into the gloom. He jogged to catch up to her, wondering if anything he could say would take the edge off her emotions. Not likely, so instead he concentrated on ignoring the cold and damp that had seeped into his clothes and the fact that when he breathed out again in a sigh, his breath formed a little cloud. This crap wouldn't be so bad if it would just get cold enough to snow. He liked snow, and New Orleans had had precious little of it in the city's history.

But as long as the wet stayed in liquid form, it was just damn dreary.

Neither of them spoke until they were in the car, heater running on high, windshield wipers working rhythmically, and he was turning the car around to leave the neighborhood. His stomach grumbled, reminding him breakfast had been a long time ago. "You want to get something to eat?"

"Not in this town."

"Okay." There were plenty of places on the way back to the city, and he wasn't particular. Though he wouldn't have minded hitting that diner she'd looked so longingly at downtown. He had a fondness for diners, strong coffee and fried eggs. But New Orleans had plenty of places like that, and he couldn't blame her for not wanting to spend any more time here than necessary.

"You mind talking?" he asked after a while, once they'd left the city limits and were traveling along the highway.

Though her head was turned so she could stare out the side window, he saw her lift one hand to rub her eyes before grimly asking, "Any chance it could be about anything in the world besides this case?"

He grinned. "A couple of days ago, you wouldn't have talked to me about anything in the world *except* a case." A couple of days. Less than two days ago, he'd still thought of Martine primarily as the one he hadn't been able to charm and she'd still looked at him as if she'd caught a whiff of something particularly nasty. He could have easily imagined spending this much time with her but for damn sure not in this way, and she would have been horrified by the idea of spending time with him, much less letting him into her apartment and her life.

Big changes. And all it had taken was for Paulina to give up her life.

"What do you want to talk about?" Feeling the need to draw her out of the funk she'd sunk into, he injected the smug note into his voice that had always driven her crazy. Better to have her crazy than so lowdown blue. "How about how much you regret not sleeping with me that night?"

Slowly her head turned, and on her face was the scathing look he'd come to know so well. "Thank you for reminding me you're a jerk." That was better, that spark that flared in her eyes.

"I'm a good cop," he protested.

"Who's a jerk."

"But not on the job."

She opened her mouth as if to debate that, then closed it again. It was a source of pride to him that his reputation was for solving ugly cases while being relatively fair and courteous to everyone involved. Suspect, person of interest, family or witness—cooperating or not—he treated them the way people deserved to be treated. Granted, he didn't have huge amounts of patience with people who lied to him, but that was one of his people qualities, not a cop quality.

Though Martine's dislike for him stemmed from the fact that she considered him a liar, because he had come on to her without telling her he was married. At the time, he'd defended himself by pointing out that he hadn't said he wasn't married; he just hadn't said he was. It hadn't been much of an excuse, not in her eyes, not even in his own. *Of course* he shouldn't have been flirting with any woman other than Alia. *Of course* he shouldn't have tried to seduce Martine. *Of course* being an unfaithful bastard had been wrong, and he didn't blame her for holding it against him.

But that was a long time ago. He'd learned since then. He'd changed.

She moistened her lips. "You're actually not as… You're a better…detective…a better per-per—" With her cheeks flushed deep red and her inability to finish *person*, she rolled her eyes, shook her head and looked away again.

Jimmy's impulse was to make light of it. To tease that, along with New Orleans, hell must have frozen over because Martine Broussard was actually complimenting him. To grin his crap-eating grin and make another over-the-top, guaranteed-to-piss-her-off comment. But he didn't. That was the stupid Jimmy from before. The Jimmy he was today didn't even want to.

Instead he swallowed hard and quietly, sincerely said, "Thank you, Martine. You don't know how much I appreciate that."

Then stupid Jimmy just couldn't resist it. His most

obnoxious smile stretching across his face, he added, "Hell has officially frozen over."

After burgers at a little hole-in-the-wall place just off the interstate and more rain, dear Lord, than Martine could bear, they were finally back in the French Quarter, driving slowly along Royal Street. Water rushed along the street, some diverted into the city's overtaxed drainage system, the rest running where it could, puddling where it couldn't. When her building came into view ahead, a great sense of relief flooded through her, easing the muscles cramping in her neck, her shoulders and her back. Funny, that after spending part of the day in her hometown, she felt as if she was finally home, but that was exactly the feeling warming and brightening her.

They'd been gone not quite four and a half hours, but she felt as if she'd risen with the nonexistent sun and trekked the whole way on foot. All she wanted was to crawl into bed, turn the TV on to something frivolous and funny and not come out until morning to bright sunlight, fabulous early-spring weather and the last few days erased from her memory.

Hey, if she was going to wish, she would wish big.

Jimmy stopped in his usual spot. "You okay?"

"I'm adapting."

He nodded, apparently remembering her mother's words about that. "I have an appointment at five with Mr. Bradley."

"Mister— Oh." Paulina's husband. "I don't envy you."

"Yeah, if Jack were here, I'd be passing it on to

him. Bradley got in about an hour ago. He has paperwork to take care of to transfer his wife's body home
for the funeral as soon as the coroner releases it." He
drummed his fingers on the steering wheel, gazing
past her. "Everything look okay?"

She turned, saw nothing suspicious at her front
door, then saw Ramona and Anise watching from behind a display of T-shirts. Ramona, as always, was
smiling; Anise, as often enough, was glowering. Martine might have to clarify her comments to the girl
about Jimmy so she didn't try any new methods of
keeping him out.

"It looks the same. Except…" She'd just flitted a
look over her car in the driveway, but now she studied it closer. Climbing out of Jimmy's car, she crossed
the sidewalk to walk inside the arch that covered her
parking space. His footsteps sounded right behind her.

A few pieces of trash had blown inside; she picked
those up and dropped them into the can in the corner.
As long as she was at the front of the car, next to the
tall wrought iron gate that led into the courtyard, she
rattled it to make sure it was secure. The chain jangled
before uncoiling and landing on the bricks below, the
still-closed padlock making a *thunk*.

Jimmy took her hand from the gate and began pulling her backward. "Someone cut the chain instead of
the padlock to make it less noticeable that they'd tampered with it. When was the last time you checked it?"

Weariness made her eyes ache. "I don't know. I always look when I get in my car, but as far as actually
touching it…"

Still holding on, he steered her back to the sidewalk and up the stoop. He found her keys in her jacket pocket, unlocked the door and ushered her inside. "I'll call someone and have them check it out. I'll get someone to replace it, too. Right now we'll take a quick look at this, then go from there."

This was the reason she'd gone to the car in the first place; she'd just gotten totally distracted. It was the same kind of kraft envelope she'd received in the mail the day before, and it had been tucked under the windshield wiper on her car. It looked heavier than the other, and whatever was inside, she didn't want to see.

But how could she *not* look?

On the way up the stairs, Jimmy called in and requested a patrol officer. Once he was off the phone, he seemed quite at home in her apartment. He turned her in the direction of her workroom, flipped on the lights and switched on the space heater. After pulling on a pair of thin gloves from his coat pocket—"I never leave home without 'em"—he took a seat and carefully cut open one end of the envelope.

Inside was a piece of typing paper, folded in thirds, with photographs taped to it, the folds made to avoid bending the pictures. Martine stood behind him, looking over his shoulder, vaguely detailing things she shouldn't be noticing, like the dark sheen to his damp hair, the scent of his cologne, the breadth of his shoulders. Other things, too: the silence in the apartment, the loud hollow whoosh of her breathing, the awareness that if someone had trespassed in her courtyard without her knowledge, they could have trespassed in her apartment, too. Maybe they were just that good, that there were no visible signs.

Maybe she wasn't so safe here, after all.

Jimmy cautiously unfolded the paper, resting his gloved hands on either side to hold it flat. Across the top in thick black print, someone had written *Actions have consequences*.

Underneath that was Callie's senior picture, cut from the yearbook, the slashes careless and including portions of the pictures around her. A thick black X blocked most of her face. Beneath it was Paulina's picture, again including portions of the nearby shots and another X. On the bottom row were pictures of Tallie, Robin and Martine. A question mark was scrawled onto the paper above each of them.

"Actions have consequences." Martine sank into the chair next to Jimmy. "Actions have… That was something Fletcher said all the time. He got a kick out of enforcing the rules. He was rigid about it. I think he just liked having the kids plead with him not to get them into trouble, plus it gave him a chance to get alone with the girls to discuss their infractions."

"So pretty much anyone in one of his classes would know he said that a lot." Jimmy folded the paper again and slid it into the envelope. "Katie Jo and Irena would have known, too."

"But Katie Jo's in prison—"

"Maybe."

"And Irena… She was just a kid."

"You were all just kids then. If Paulina and Callie could be killed for what they did as kids, then the killer could be the kid they did it to, loosely speaking."

Martine recalled Irena's image, a scared teenage girl trying too hard and having a tough time of it. Being a high school student wasn't supposed to be so hard, but it was for so many, and they took it so very seriously.

But she couldn't imagine Irena, or anyone truthfully, resorting to violence twenty-four years later. That was a long time to nurse wounded feelings and letdowns, time where there had been so much more important stuff going on in life: college or a job, a career, falling in love, marrying, having children, travel.

Unless the consequences of their actions had robbed her of all that.

Martine stubbornly shook her head. "I've just got it in my mind that it's a man. A man would find it so much easier to grab a woman off the street, to contain and control her, to bash her skull in and dump her body in a cemetery."

"But a woman doesn't need physical strength. Typically, women aren't seen as threatening, and people don't expect them to be armed. A skinny little girl could walk into your store, chat you up when you're alone, pull a gun and do whatever she wanted with you. Take you where she wanted. Dump you where she wanted." He looked up at her, his expression grim. "Women are resourceful, Martine. Don't ever underestimate them."

To think that a woman, a girl they'd gone to school with, was capable of murder…

A girl they'd gone to school with for an entire year and Martine had barely remembered. She must have had classes with Irena Young, must have passed her in the hall, must have seen her on an almost daily basis, and she'd completely forgotten her. Couldn't recall a single conversation with her, not one friendly exchange.

She pulled a chair to the heater, where she could absorb most of the warmth it put out, and sank down. Wishing her voice sounded more like a capable adult's and not a frightened girl's, she wistfully asked, "Do you really think it could be Irena? Blaming us for breaking up her family, getting even because we weren't friendly enough?"

Jimmy pulled a plastic shopping bag from the box on the shelf and put the envelope inside. He definitely felt at home there.

The odd thing—as if that wasn't odd enough—was that she didn't mind. She had no desire to drag the table and chairs and sofa into the street, douse them with gasoline and burn the DiBiase cooties until not even ash remained. She didn't want to do a cleansing ritual to rid the space of his germs and scents or to meditate the memory of him within these walls right out of her mind.

"I have a list of suspects," he said after tying the bag's handles into a loose knot. "Katie Jo might have gotten an early release. Twenty-four years is a long time to think about the choices she made. Irena might have gone on with her life, or she might have spent those same twenty-four years wondering why the hell you and the others were so special that you got to be pretty and popular and have best friends and parents who loved you and normal lives while she was stuck with her nightmare.

"Fletcher might have had a friend who shared his tastes—another teacher, a neighbor, someone at his church. Irena's father might have resented Fletcher for taking his place in his daughter's life, taking her away from him. Fletcher could have gone a lot further than just touching with some girl, who would resent everyone who knew what he was doing and didn't tell, or that girl's father could be playing the avenging angel. Or one of your friends could have told someone who felt compelled for whatever reason to punish whoever they could."

His smile was tight-lipped, not showing his teeth, and disappeared quickly. "There's no shortage of people on my list, Martine. The only thing I'm sure of right now is that you're not on it."

Relief seeped into her, thawing some of the ice that had settled in her stomach. And more: gratitude. A little bit of security. Comfort.

And a little too much of the desire that had almost led her to break her number-one relationship rule and jump into bed with a married man.

Who wasn't married now and hadn't been for a long time.

He crouched in front of her. "I've got to drop this off for the lab guys and make a couple calls before I meet with Mr. Bradley. Don't answer the door unless it's someone from your life here." He emphasized that with a tap of his fingers on the wooden arm of her chair. "Don't go out. Don't talk to any old friends or acquaintances. If you go to the shop, don't stay there alone. When the others leave, you leave, too, and ask them to wait outside until you get yourself locked in here. Don't open any windows, don't unlock any doors. Just pretend you're a bear and hibernate."

The obstinate part of her wanted to argue with him, even though she intended to do exactly as he said, but she didn't have the energy. Instead she nodded mutely, then roused herself enough to say, "So when the officer comes to look at my gate?"

"I'll talk to him. Don't open the door even to a cop unless it's Jack or me."

Again she nodded.

He pushed to his feet, reached for her hand as if it was the most natural thing in his world, and she let him take it as if it was the most natural thing in hers. Together they walked down the stairs to the entry, where he squinted up at the light bulb, then gazed down at her. "We'll get this guy."

"Or girl."

He acknowledged that with a grimace that she privately echoed. What did it matter whether it was a man or a woman? Dead was dead, no matter whose hand accomplished it.

Shaking off the thought, she focused on Jimmy. "I can't say it's been a fun day, but…thank you, Jimmy."

The look that flashed across his face was…sweet. Not his sweet-talker look, either; that was always smug. No, this was just plain sweet, and it hurt her heart just a little. She'd spent a lot of time wishing she'd never met this man, and here he was now, trying to save her life. No matter what happened, she would always be grateful for that.

Unless, of course, he failed. Then she would haunt him.

Ah, there was the old Martine.

And with his grin, the old Jimmy appeared in front of her. "Like I said, hell has officially frozen over. I'll see you."

After locking the dead bolt behind him—and the chain lock—and shoving the concrete planter in the corner over to block the door—Martine headed back up the stairs. It wasn't until she reached the top that she realized she was still smiling.

Chapter 6

Jimmy didn't have an office, just a desk in a room shared with other desks, so he met Shawn Bradley in one of the interview rooms. The man was about his age, his skin sallow, his face hollowed, the last few months having worn hard on him. His tone varied from quavering to flat and blank, as if he just didn't have the emotional reserves to keep up the inflection.

Jimmy offered his condolences, asked about the transfer arrangements and if he needed anything while he was in town, then, hiding his reluctance, went straight to his main interest. "You filed a missing person report on your wife three months ago. What happened?"

Bradley drew a deep breath and held it, his shoulders shaking when he released it. "Everything was fine. Honestly, I'm not stupid. I didn't see anything unusual. Her job was normal, my job was normal, money was good, we were getting along fine with family, she doted on the cats like she always did. We were even planning a vacation—a few days after Christmas in Bermuda. Then one day I kissed her, told her I loved her and left for work, and…I never saw her again."

Even after all this time, his tone was bewildered. He still couldn't understand how everything could change so drastically in a single moment. Jimmy had never experienced it, but he'd spent a lot of time with people who had. Some of them never understood it. Some never accepted it.

"She didn't leave a note?"

Bradley shook his head. "Her purse was gone, her keys, her car. So was a suitcase of clothes—jeans, T-shirts— and her personal savings account was cleaned out. She left her cell phone, her wallet, all her jewelry. Video from the bank showed she was alone when she got the money. Traffic camera videos showed her alone in her car, which was found the next day in Montgomery. There was no sign of her."

"Was there anything unusual on her computer? Anything personal in the mail? Text messages or phone calls?"

"No. I tore the house apart a dozen times, looking for something that seemed wrong or out of place. Her parents and I even hired private investigators, but there was nothing."

Jimmy found it easier to look at his notes than to see the loss and grief on Bradley's face. He would bet this month's rent that Paulina had gotten an envelope in the mail, maybe at work, like Martine, so her husband wouldn't have been aware of it. Already suscep-

tible to the guilt from their teenage prank, the note and
the small bit of voodoo doll/bandanna had certainly
freaked her out. Had that made her flee, or had she
held out until the second letter arrived?

Actions have consequences. A marked-out photo of
Callie. Maybe an internet search to find out that Callie
was indeed dead, and at some point Paulina had made
the effort to contact Tallie and Robin, either before her
flight or while on the run.

"Did she talk much about high school?"

Bradley's frown tightened. "High... That was a long
time ago."

Jimmy waited.

"Uh, not much. She grew up somewhere around
here. Moved to Mobile first chance she got. That's
where we met, at the University of South Alabama."

"Did she stay in touch with any of her high school
friends?"

His brows arched, his gaze lifting toward the ceiling, while he considered it. "There were a couple—
sisters, I think. Sometimes they traded Christmas
cards, not every year but from time to time. Paulina
never said much about them. 'Just someone I used to
know.'"

Jimmy made a note of that, wondering more defen-
sively than he should why those three had maintained
any contact while cutting Martine off cold. She had
been one of them. She and Paulina had been the first
friends, the best.

And she had been the odd one out at the end, the
only one who didn't accept any blame for Fletcher's
murder.

"Did your wife ever mention William Fletcher? He was a teacher her senior year."

Bradley thought about it, looking as if he'd just about exhausted his supply of answers. "No, she never talked about school. She never kept any yearbooks, pictures, dried corsages, nothing. She never even casually said anything like, 'Oh, yeah, back when I was in school…' That time didn't exist for her anymore. I never asked why. It was just the way she was."

"One last question. Did she ever mention Tine or Martine Broussard?"

"No. Who was she?"

"Her best friend through high school." Jimmy hesitated, then went on. "She came to New Orleans to see Martine. She met with her for a few minutes Tuesday afternoon."

For a moment Bradley was unmoving. Finally, with a deep exhale, he slumped back in his chair. "My wife just disappears like she never existed, then pops up three months later in a city she refused to ever set foot in to visit her best friend I never heard of and is murdered that night. Why? Where was she in the meantime? What was she running from? What the hell was going on? Is this Martine person involved? Do you think she killed Paulina?"

"No, absolutely not," Jimmy said firmly. "As for the rest of it, we're trying to find out, Mr. Bradley. We'll find this person and see that he pays for Paulina's death." He didn't promise; he knew promises could be impossible to keep, but he did have every intention of stopping Irena/Katie Jo/Mr. Young/whoever the hell was responsible for this man's sorrow.

He damn well intended to keep them from hurting Martine.

After getting an officer to take Mr. Bradley back to his hotel, Jimmy returned to the computer on his desk, working his way through the questions in his notes. Police work was so very different with the internet and computers. He still did a lot of legwork, but a lot of information that in the past would have required visits to various offices and endless phone calls or faxes was often quick and easy to access.

It took only a couple of minutes to strike one suspect off his list: Katie Jo Fletcher had died of natural causes—complications of pneumonia—at the Louisiana Correctional Institute for Women in St. Gabriel last September. The news made him sad for a woman he'd never met, a woman who'd spent half her life in prison for a crime his gut instincts insisted she didn't commit. All she'd wanted was a normal life for her daughter, and all she'd gotten was disappointment.

Jimmy took a break to get a fresh cup of coffee, then returned to his computer. It took longer to get information on Irena Young, and it was no help at all. The address on her driver's license came back to a Baton Rouge apartment, but a phone call to the manager said she'd moved the year before. The woman who answered at the work number she'd given said she'd quit her job as a salesclerk about the same time, and the cell phone Irena had listed went to a generic voice mail message. He would have to get in touch with the provider to find out if the number was still hers.

"You're working late."

Jimmy glanced up, a smile forming automatically. The petite blonde standing there worked with Alia over at NCIS, and they'd met a number of times over the past year for dinner or drinks—not dates, just evenings out with Alia and Landry. She was smart, pretty, had too nice a body to hide in plain gray pants and a matching jacket over a black shirt, and her name was Delaney, but damned if he could remember whether that was her first name or last.

Holy crap, Jimmy, you never forget a woman's name.

Hey, he'd been insisting he'd changed, hadn't he?

"I'm a dedicated officer of the law," he replied, gesturing toward an empty chair nearby. "Why aren't you home where it's warm and dry?"

"That's where I'm headed. I needed to talk to one of your fellow detectives first." Delaney—first name, he was pretty sure—sat down, crossed her legs and clasped her hands. "Alia tells me you're looking for a lonely heart. Any idea where it got off to?"

He rolled his eyes at her teasing note, but not at the subject. The heart's location was a question that had stayed in the back of his mind. He could too easily imagine it in the killer's home, wrapped in foil in the freezer or floating in liquid in a glass jar on a shelf, ghastly and creepy and giving the killer a jolt of pleasure every time he or she saw it. "I hope it's buried somewhere."

"Or eaten. 'The heart of your enemy...' Maybe used in medicine or offered as a gift to the spirits."

He grimaced at her matter-of-fact response. He could stomach a lot, but some things he would really prefer to remain uninformed about. Nevertheless, he flipped open his notebook and picked up a pen. Finding someone knowledgeable about such things was still on his to-do list, and he was never one to turn his back on freely offered information. "You familiar with human sacrifice?"

"It's an interest of mine. I can probably answer your questions, and if I can't, I know people who can."

"Okay, the heart of your enemy…people really do that?"

"Since the beginning of time. It's been reliably reported that it's happened recently in the Middle East. People believe it's the ultimate revenge on their enemy but also that they gain whatever power or strengths the enemy had. The fresher the heart is, the more power it holds."

"So they like it still beating?" His stomach flipped at her nod. He'd been thinking a rare steak and baked potato sounded pretty good for dinner, but he could forget that for a week…or two or three. "Is it a thing in voodoo?"

"No. Not legitimately. One of the central beliefs of voodoo is reincarnation. They believe that a person will be brought back in the same body, the same form, and so if the body has been mutilated, the mutilations remain, so it's taboo."

"But in every group there are extremists who twist the religion or the beliefs to fit their own needs."

She nodded. "Voodoo has been misappropriated by some practitioners not out of deep devotion but to frighten off competitors, to gain fame, to build a fortune or just out of a sense of fanaticism, and those people tend to do things their religion forbids. Medicine murder is one of those things. Practitioners of a lot of religions, not just voodoo, believe that the sacrifice of a living creature empowers and protects them. Animal sacrifice is common, but among the extremists, humans are believed to give the most power. Their organs are used to make medicine. Some body parts— eyes, fingers, genitals—become charms, and heads are buried to keep evil spirits from the house."

"Damn," he muttered, wincing at the thought.

"It's more common in Africa, though there have been cases worldwide. It most likely has absolutely nothing to do with your murder." Delaney smiled the way only a cop could, as if she hadn't just talked about cutting off private bits and stringing them up to wear. "Are there any other ritual aspects to your case? Any other body parts missing? Any sign of a ceremony taking place?"

He shook his head.

"Then three possibilities come to mind. First, a healthy heart is worth around one hundred and fifty thousand dollars on the black market for transplant. It would be a pretty sophisticated process, though, removing it, transporting it, keeping it usable, and if you're going to kill someone to steal a heart, why not take the liver and a kidney or two? Why settle for a hundred fifty grand when you could get nearly seven fifty?"

She raised her hand, ticking off another finger. "Second, taking the heart could have been an attempt to throw your investigation off track, to make you think voodoo or witchcraft was involved, but the guy didn't know enough about either to make it look realistic. Third and most likely, taking the heart was symbolic. You've got a really angry person, holding a hell of a grudge, believing the victim was coldhearted or heartless in her treatment of him. Not only did he kill her, but now she really is heartless. In that case, he probably threw it in the river, tossed it in a Dumpster or, who knows, fed it to a gator. It wouldn't have any real value to him."

"Isn't that a lot of work to punish someone who's dead?"

Delaney shrugged. "I'm no doctor. I would imagine, though, that getting through the rib cage is the hardest part, and a pair of bolt cutters would do the trick. Maybe even garden loppers."

"Holding a grudge fits with my theory. You know there's a second victim in Seattle? And the two women grew up together."

She rolled her blue eyes. "Gee, Jimmy, if I'd known that, I could have saved myself climbing a flight of stairs to see you." Her smile softened the words. "But you have to cover all the bases, don't you? I know it hasn't been long, but are you making any progress?"

"I've managed to take one person off the suspect list."

"You do have other cases, don't you? Or are you NOPD guys so pampered that you only take one case at a time?"

"Hey, at least we don't need a TV show for people to know who we are. If it wasn't for that, the average citizen wouldn't have a clue what NCIS is."

She stood, adjusted her jacket over the gun on her hip and gave him a recruitment poster–worthy smile. "The people I put in prison know what it is, and that's all that matters to me. Good seeing you, Jimmy. Get home before the temperature drops another degree and that wet stuff turns to ice."

"Thanks, Delaney." He watched her walk away, admiring the way she sashayed, then dropped his gaze to his battered notebook. He always had multiple cases going, but it was typical of the job: the most recent case took precedence. The longer an investigation dragged out, the slower the leads developed and the less active work it got. Keeping Martine and her friends alive was more important at the moment than finding out who killed the victims in his other cases, and not just because he had a thing for Martine. Even if she was a total stranger who didn't spark a bit of interest in him, the living still counted for more than the dead.

Besides, his other open cases were all of the *I didn't see nothing, I didn't hear nothing, I didn't do nothing, I'm not saying nothing* variety. The witnesses would still be just as uncooperative in a few days or a few weeks as they'd been so far.

His priority now was keeping Martine alive, not for a few days or a few weeks but for good.

There was nothing like being stuck somewhere to make Martine want to go elsewhere, even if she had no destination in mind. After closing up the shop with Anise and Niles, she'd had a long soak in a hot bath filled with her favorite scented bubbles, drunk a glass of wine and spent a little time on the internet before edginess made her set the computer aside. She'd been wandering the apartment for the past hour, the television turned on for background noise. A trip downstairs reassured her that the front door remained secure, and a few rounds of the apartment confirmed that every window, along with the rear door that led to the court-yard, was also locked.

She stood at the kitchen sink, gazing down into the

dimly lit square, envisioning it in summer when the color and fragrance of the flowers were almost overwhelming. At the first sign of spring, she would drag out her patio furniture and prepare for eight months or more of sitting by the fountain, sipping tea, chatting with Evie and Reece and watching their kids play. The store staff would eat lunches there, and she would have dinners there, too, in her own private little paradise.

That someone had invaded.

Even now, safe inside, she shivered as the sound of the chain and padlock falling echoed in her memory. Now she wondered if she would ever feel as safe in the courtyard as she had before—if she would feel as safe in her life as she had before.

Distantly through the floor, she heard a clang, similar to the chain falling but stronger, more menacing. She was standing directly above the gate. Had someone bumped it? Opened it the wrong way and hit her car or opened it the right way and banged the giant cast-iron urn at the edge of the garden?

Her heart pounded, and her chest grew tight, making a deep breath impossible. A shudder raced through her, momentarily leaving her unable to think, to reason, to figure out what to do. The Taser was on her belt, the pepper spray in her left jeans pocket, the cell phone in the right, but she didn't reach for any of them, not until the cell rang, its jangle making her gasp and literally jump, her toes clearing the floor by a fraction of an inch.

With trembling hands, she pulled it from her pocket, clutched it tightly and stabbed at the screen. Her *hello* was tiny and shaky, barely more than a squeak.

"Hey, Martine, it's me." It was Jimmy, and he sounded concerned. "Are you okay?"

"That depends. Are you downstairs?"

"Yeah, I am, putting a new chain on the gate."

Oh, thank God. Knees wobbling, she leaned against the counter and pressed her free hand to her face. "Then I'm fine. Just—" She filled her lungs with air. "Just overreacting to everything."

"Sorry. The end of the chain slipped when I was pushing it through the gate. I'm locking it from inside the courtyard, so can I come in the back?"

"Yeah, sure." Trying a slow-breathing exercise to calm her heart, she fumbled the few feet to the door and undid the locks. A moment later, heavy footsteps sounded on the stairs.

"I'm coming in now. No force, please, less-lethal or otherwise, okay?"

"Okay." As she put away her phone, the door opened with a slow creak, letting in cold damp air and the scents she was starting to associate with him: cologne, shampoo, *man*. They were accompanied by amazing aromas emanating from the bag he carried.

"Are you hungry?" he asked as he set the bag on the counter, then shrugged out of his overcoat.

Two minutes ago, she hadn't been. She hadn't even thought about food since lunch. Now her stomach rumbled as gracelessly as possible, and her mouth began to water. "I'm starved. What did you bring?"

As he unpacked the bag, her stress washed away. Sure, there was still some of that *I'm the target of a crazed killer* fear knotted in her stomach that wasn't going away, but at this moment, Jimmy was here, and if anyone could keep the crazed killer away, it was him.

If anyone could make her feel safe, it was him.

And all that aside, she was glad to see him.

He'd brought comfort food, exactly what she would have chosen herself if she'd remembered she was hungry: fried chicken, potato salad, macaroni and cheese, coleslaw and, sweet mercy, yes, two slices of apple pie and a pint of vanilla ice cream.

Her mood improving 100 percent, she began gathering dishes, napkins, utensils and sodas. Without much discussion, they each filled their own plate and went into the living room, where she unfolded two TV trays from the corner. "They may be old-fashioned, but it beats spilling good food in your lap." She settled in her favorite chair, leaned forward to inhale deeply of the aromas, then sighed happily. "You've got good taste."

"You know, for the last however many years," he warned, "I've only gotten insults from you. If you stop being hostile *and* start paying compliments, I won't know how to act."

Though her cheeks flushed, her mouth was too full of hot, tender, juicy chicken with the perfect amount of crispy crust. When she swallowed it, she wiped her fingers delicately. "You can't deny you trolled for women while you were married."

"I'm not proud of it, but I don't deny it." His eyes twinkled. "You were much nicer before you knew."

"You weren't a cheat before I knew."

"Did one of your ex-boyfriends cheat on you?"

"Not that I'm aware of. Not my ex-husband, either, and not my dad on my mom or vice versa. I just grew up believing that there were certain things you honored, and marriage vows were high on that list. I know people get married for a lot of reasons, but done right, it's supposed to be a commitment, a partnership, giving and taking and growing together." She chewed a bite of potato salad, savoring the sweet mayo, the tang of the mustard and the bite of the pickle juice in the dressing. "I sound really old-fashioned, don't I?"

"You sound like my sisters." He waited a beat before continuing. "Who are really old-fashioned." After a moment, though, with a drumstick in his hand, he gestured. "You were right, Martine. It was a really crappy thing to do. I knew it then. I know it better now. I can't change what I did then, but I can say I wouldn't do it now."

Martine found herself entirely too tempted to believe his words. She managed a smile, but it wasn't as light as she'd hoped for. "Aw, Jack tells me that your fellow detectives rate the odds of you and monogamy ever being mentioned in the same sentence at somewhere around one in a billion."

His smile was designed for sarcasm. "Jack should keep his mouth shut. I believe in monogamy. I really do. I think people who claim it's an unnatural state just use that as an excuse for their own behavior."

"I think you're right," Martine said, and his brows arched as he leaned closer.

"What was that? Could you repeat it?"

She laughed. She actually felt good enough to laugh. Oh, how she'd missed it.

Before the thought of asking what he'd learned about the case could even fully form in her brain, she said, "Tell me how you terrorized your sisters growing up."

"Why does everyone think that? I was their favorite brother."

"And only brother. You told me you had advanced training in making them hysterical by the time you were ten."

"Oh, yeah, I did." He finished his chicken and picked up a spoonful of macaroni and cheese. "Imagine the kind of things you and your girls got into, only ten times more complicated. That's Dani and Rebecca. They were regular little generals of chaos, enlisting all the kids in town and half the adults in their mischief. And they always looked so innocent, with pigtails or braids, big eyes and the sweetest, most adorable smiles. They were a menace to the parish, only no one really believed they were capable of the pranks they pulled. People always thought I was behind most of them, but truthfully, no one could get you like Dani and Becca could."

Discovering that her plate was clean, Martine considered getting a refill, then decided she was good. Tucking her feet into the seat, she held her glass in both hands and settled in. "What about now? Are they still master manipulators?"

"Pretty much. Dani runs marketing at Cypress Hill, and Becca's in charge of everything else. They've got five kids between them who are being homeschooled and get to do things that are cool and actually make school look fun. The kids also help out at the big house. Everyone's got chores, even me, and the conse—" he hesitated so briefly over the word that she doubted anyone else would have noticed "—um, consequences of not doing them can be severe."

That was the way to handle it: just let the word and its ugliness slide away, out of her mind. There would always be time to face up to her situation, but pleasant, easy moments like this had been hard to find lately.

"It's funny to think that I might have met your parents or your sisters when my mom and I toured the place."

"You might even have met me. I haven't lived there since high school, but I've gone back for plenty of visits."

She might have seen him—younger, less polished, still too damn good-looking for his own good, charming and brash—but she doubted she could have met him and forgotten. She'd always had a fine appreciation for handsome, sexy men.

Then he said, "Nah. I would have remembered meeting you." Adding with unshakable confidence, "And you would have remembered meeting me."

She smiled sweetly. "I love modest men." She studied her glass, shaking it just enough to make the ice cubes clink, before lifting her gaze back to Jimmy. She didn't want to ask, didn't want to leave this comfortable moment for the darkness that her life had become, but the question slipped out despite her best intentions. "How did your meeting with Paulina's husband go?"

His humor giving way to seriousness, he gave what she was sure was an abbreviated version. She wondered what kind of guy Paulina had chosen to marry—her tastes in high school boys had varied widely—and sadly recalled their old promises that they would each be maid of honor to the other. But that night had happened, and Martine's maid of honor had been a roommate she'd lost touch with before her first anniversary rolled around. Who had been there for Paulina? Had the other three girls been invited, or had she left out everyone from the first eighteen years of her life on the big day?

"I haven't located Irena Young yet, but I did find out that Katie Jo Fletcher died in prison last fall."

The news gave her a bit of a jolt. "I'm sorry, for both her and Irena. She had a sad life." After a moment, she gestured to her laptop on the coffee table. "People say you can find anyone and anything on the internet, but it's not true, is it? I've Googled and Binged and searched every other way I could think of for Tallie and Robin, but I haven't found anything of use."

Finished with his meal, he settled more comfortably, too. Even sprawled back on the couch as he was, there was no mistaking the fine quality of his suit or the high price of his shoes. A public servant with a private fortune—or, at least, enough for occasional splurges.

But he looked just as good in jeans and a T-shirt.

Probably even better in nothing at all.

"Internet or not, if someone doesn't want to be found and is reasonably intelligent, they can hide as easily as ever. You ditch your credit cards, your cell phone, your email and your vehicle, you use public transportation, you pay cash, and you're officially off the grid. Look at Paulina. Three months on the run, police and private investigators looking for her, and they couldn't trace her beyond the first twenty-four hours. All we know about the time she was missing is that she bought a burner phone and used cash."

"And that she came here. And she was scared." Martine did her best to ignore the shiver of her own fear. It was futile when Jimmy, his voice grim, finished.

"And now she's dead."

* * *

After taking their dishes into the kitchen, Martine cleaned up quickly, brewed coffee for Jimmy and poured another glass of wine for herself, then glanced out the kitchen window. The rain shimmered in the air, falling in slow flat drops…that were actually snowflakes. For an instant, she brightened inside with just a hint of the wonder she'd always felt as a child when they'd been blessed with snow. Now she liked it mostly when it disappeared overnight, but it was gorgeous in its pristine falling state. Tourists didn't like snow in New Orleans, either, and business had been off enough the past week.

She used a small plate to make a tray for Jimmy, holding coffee, cream and sugar, and carried that and her wine to the living room. "It's snowing."

"Oh, boy," he said sourly. "Police work is so much fun when you add slick roads and ice and inexperienced drivers."

Martine sat, sipped her wine, then returned to their earlier conversation. "Why didn't Paulina tell her husband? Why not call the police? She had resources. Why didn't she use them?"

Jimmy tilted his head to one side, then the other, as if releasing the tension gathered there, before lifting both shoulders in a weary shrug. "Maybe she thought running away would protect her family from the danger. Maybe she was too ashamed to admit what you guys had done, or maybe she'd lived with the secret so long, she believed it more than ever and just couldn't face the con—"

Consequences. It wasn't as easy this time to just let the word slide away.

"I don't know if I showed good sense in not believing we were responsible for Fletcher's death or if I've just been selfishly going along in my own little world, refusing to acknowledge the impact of what we did."

His dark eyes narrowing, Jimmy patted the sofa cushion beside him. "Come here."

Something warm and promising curled in her stomach, even as some smidgen of lingering wariness warned her against it. He was here only because of his job; she was a subject in his investigation, nothing more. It wasn't supposed to be anything more. How could it ever be? As he'd pointed out, she hadn't spoken a civil word to him since that party, in a quiet dark nook in Evie's garden, his arms wrapped around her, his tongue halfway down her throat, his hands doing incredible things to her body and her willpower, when his phone had rung. Her dazed brain had been stunned when he pulled away to check the screen, then put it away again. *My wife*, he'd murmured carelessly. *I'll call her later.*

Even now, she felt a flare of that old dismay, disgust, scorn…and disappointment, because up to that point, she'd been thoroughly captivated by him. She would have followed him anywhere, would have plastered herself so firmly against him that she might have absorbed at least parts of him into her soul. She'd thought he might be…*special*.

That had happened six years ago, but since then he'd never made any secret of his attraction to her, even when she'd found it annoying rather than flattering. He was waiting, he'd told her once after the divorce, for her to give up her grudge so they could pick up where they'd left off. She'd suggested he would burn in hell first.

The wary voice in her head wasn't trying hard enough to warn her away. Without permission from her brain, her feet slid to the floor, her hands gripped the chair arms to push herself up, and she eased around the corner of the coffee table to sit down, half a cushion between her and Jimmy.

"Big step," he teased as she turned to face him. "No kitchen knife handy, my dinner fork is out of your reach, nothing to crack my skull with."

Her smile felt steadier than she'd thought it would be. "I still have your Taser and pepper spray. Having watched a few episodes of *Cops*, I've always wondered how much fun it would be to Tase someone in a non-dangerous situation."

"I'm not volunteering. Though on a busy night on Bourbon Street, offer fifteen bucks, and I bet you'll get plenty of takers, especially if you video it and promise to put it on YouTube."

She smiled, thinking of the foolish and reckless young men she'd known. Some outgrew it in their twenties; some took until their thirties; and some, she supposed, never outgrew it at all. Jimmy, she was pretty convinced, was a bit of a mix. He took his job seriously as hell, the rest of life not so much. He could be grown up when the situation required it, but he enjoyed the rest of his life as if he didn't have a care in the world.

Could he enjoy the rest of his life with the restrictions imposed by a monogamous relationship?

The question faded away when he moved, and her heart increased its steady beat. This close, she could better smell his cologne, could see the stubble of beard dotting his jaw and the tired lines etching the corners of his eyes and mouth. He'd had a couple of long days and was planning to have a few more, she suspected, until he caught the killer or at least scared him—or her—off.

His strong, comforting hand claimed hers, his fingers lacing with hers, the pad of his thumb rubbing firmly back and forth over the heel of her palm. "Fletcher's death wasn't your fault, Martine, and there's nothing selfish about acknowledging that. The fact that the other girls believed it didn't make them right. The fact that the killer might have gotten a couple ideas from you still doesn't make you responsible. You didn't know you were being spied on. You didn't put the thought of murder or the capacity for it into Katie Jo or Irena or anyone else. You know human nature. People don't become violent because they overhear girls playing. William Fletcher died because he was a lousy husband and stepfather and a teacher with a fondness for doing God knows what to kids. Period."

She must not have looked convinced, because he squeezed her fingers lightly. "You ever see a movie where a woman fakes her own death to get away from an abusive husband, he finds her and she kills him? What if someone else who sees it uses that as a blueprint to escape her own abuser, right down to the murder at the end? Does that make the screenwriter or the producer or the actress responsible?"

"Of course not," she murmured.

"And you're not, either. There's nothing original, Martine—not one single action in the history of mankind that hasn't been done before. Every good thing you can think of, every bad thing, millions of other people have already thought of them. And in my experience, most murderers don't need inspiration. They just need opportunity."

She sighed, tilted her head to one side to study him and bumped his arm, resting on the back of the sofa. Automatically, he wrapped his arm around her shoulders, scooted her closer and guided her head to his own shoulder.

Damn. The closer she got, the better he smelled. The better she felt. And oh, hell, yes, the better *he* felt. Hard muscle, soft skin, power, courage. He was a protector—her protector, for the moment—and she reveled in it in a way she never would have thought possible. Even the *crazed-killer* fear was calmer, almost dormant. For the first time in two days, she could relax, close her eyes, turn off the worries and feel normal again.

She would never undervalue feeling normal again.

She lost track of how long they sat there, warmed by his body and his presence, feeling a sense of ease seep through her with each breath, thinking that grudges became burdens after a while and when the wronged person—in this case, Alia—didn't hold a grudge, wasn't it presumptuous of Martine to?

You just want to have sex with him, her wariness pointed out. *Just like you wanted that night and practically every time you've seen him since.*

A faint smile curved her lips. Her wary nature knew her well, probably because they'd kept such close company all this time.

"What are you smiling about?" His voice was soft, his mouth close enough that she felt his breath on her cheek.

She fibbed. "You smell like apple pie."

"Nah, you smell the apple pie in the kitchen." After a pause, he shifted his shoulder, gently nudging her cheek, and repeated, "Hey, there's apple pie in the kitchen."

His boyish tone made her laugh. "Dessert coming right up. I'm guessing you like it warm with ice cream melting over the top."

"Hell, yeah."

She started to push up from the couch, but his hand stopped her. His eyes were dark, the familiar intensity back in place, but this time it wasn't for the case. It was for *her*, and the same sharp awareness sliced through her. His lips parted, and she wondered—anticipated—what he would say, but she would never know because, after a moment, they curved into a smile. His fingers stroked hers gently, lightly, before he stood up, then pulled her to her feet.

"I'll help you."

He'd been doing that all along—helping her to feel secure, helping her deal with Paulina's death, helping her find the answers to the million questions that plagued her. Given the way things had been between them before, she was impressed. And grateful. And regretful. And hopeful.

Her work and her friends had exposed her to a lot of mysteries in life, but this might be the biggest surprise of all.

Jimmy DiBiase had become the light in her life.

By the time Jimmy motivated himself enough to get off the couch one last time to go home, the snow was falling harder, accumulating thickly on all the flat surfaces except the middle of the street. Only a few tourists were on the sidewalks, warmed by spirits, he would bet, and traffic was almost nonexistent. His car gleamed white in the light from the street lamps, with enough of the cold stuff piled on it that he wished for gloves. And a heavier coat.

Martine wasn't wearing any coat at all. Just jeans that fitted snugly to every curve and a long-sleeved touristy shirt paying homage to New Orleans's chicory coffee that did the same. She hugged her arms across her middle as they watched the snow in companionable silence from the doorway. Comfortable silence. The only thing that would make it better was if they were watching from her window upstairs, where the air was warm and the bedroom was only a few yards away.

"You like snow?" she asked after a moment.

"Nope. But when it's like this, all fat and thick and nothing's turned to ice yet, it's damn pretty to watch." He knew he should leave: tell her good-night, wait to hear the locks click and the planter scrape as she dragged it back into place, then clear enough of the car windows to get himself home. He was tired. She was cold. Standing here would just make him more tired and her colder.

But it was hard to take that first step over the threshold.

He shoved his hands into his pockets, felt the keys there held together with a small wire loop and remembered one of his reasons for coming over tonight. "Here are the keys to your new lock." He pressed them into her hand, her fingers already cold. "I know it's a hassle, but for right now you need to open it from inside the courtyard. The chain is looped around that cast-iron planter, and the lock is against the planter, so no one can reach it to cut it."

"Can't they just cut the chain again?"

Thinking of the chain he'd damn near had to drag across the driveway, he grinned. "They could, but not without being noticed."

She gave him a skeptical look, then stepped outside. His first impulse was to catch her hand, pull her back inside out of sight of whoever happened to be looking. But considering how reasonably she'd cooperated with his requests to restrict her movements, he let her go, instead closing the door, following her down the steps, into the covered driveway and back to the gate.

Her laugh upon seeing the tow chain that made the old chain look like a length of twine was fresh and sweet and normal. He appreciated the sound of it, and the feel, and couldn't wait for the day it came naturally and often.

If she let him come around again once the case was closed.

The lines across her forehead eased, revealing more relief than he suspected she knew. "Thank you, Jimmy. I'll reimburse you for it tomorrow."

The old Jimmy could give her a list of various types of reimbursement he would prefer over money. The new Jimmy—the smarter Jimmy—kept his mouth shut, because after a long time of trying, Martine was starting to like him again, and he wasn't about to risk that for a sly, flirty, maybe sleazy remark.

"You'd better get back inside before you turn into an icicle." His voice was quiet, the sound hollow as the brick arch reflected the words back.

But she didn't move. "I'm not that cold." Also quiet, hollow. Her gaze locked on his.

He reminded himself to breathe, but his lungs wouldn't fill, not with the tightness around his chest that came from nowhere. Her own breaths were shallow, causing the slightest lift and fall of her chest, and her cheeks were red, her lips tinged blue, belying her comment.

Slowly he lifted his hand to feather back a strand of hair that had fallen across her forehead. "The first time I saw you…"

She'd been with Evie, who had come by the station to see Jack, and he'd thought a lot of things: she was gorgeous. She had killer long legs, and the curves of her breasts, waist and hips gave her exactly the lush type of body that he preferred. Her smile was incredibly easy and passionate. She wasn't his usual sort of woman, but they would be great in bed, and at the time all he'd been interested in was a great time in bed.

Instead of choosing one of those things to tell her, he changed the subject, sort of. "I haven't dated anyone since before Alia and Landry got married." Did Martine remember scowling at him through the ceremony or deliberately spilling champagne on him after the cake was cut? She had snubbed his every attempt to talk to her—talk, when he'd really wanted to take her in his arms, dance with her, touch her and persuade her that he was deserving of another chance. Her iceberg act had made him the butt of jokes for the other cops in attendance. Not the first time, not the last, and he'd deserved it.

Her deepening flush suggested she did remember.

It passed quickly, though, and her gaze narrowed on his. "Define *date*."

"Gone out with. Had a meal or drinks with. Spent time with a woman with the intention of starting or building a relationship."

The corners of her mouth twitched. "Wasn't there an exotic dancer you were serious about?"

He'd been working a series of murders with Alia at the time, murders that had brought Landry into her life. Nina had been a sweet girl but temporary. She'd been ten years younger by age, double that in life experience. For a stripper, she'd held on to her naïveté pretty fiercely. By the time the murders had been solved, the relationship had been over.

"We were a mutually agreed-upon short-term thing." His fingers were still in her hair. He slid them over icy black silk to her shoulder and gave the taut muscles there a squeeze. "Does it bother you that she was a stripper?" He knew what a lot of people thought of exotic dancers—and the people who got involved with them. Alia, wiser than most, had been amused. Would Martine, or would she fall back on her judgmental attitude?

"Does it bother you that I dated a stripper?"

His gaze widened, and so did her smile.

"His name was Nico, and we were together about six weeks before he moved on to Dallas. He was a nice guy—had a degree in engineering but found out he could make more money dancing—and he taught me some *mo-oves*…"

She swung her hips in a sensual shimmy that ended with her chilled body skimming across the front of his. Again Jimmy's breath caught in his chest, and for one long moment he couldn't remember how to let it go, how to replace it with fresh oxygen to feed his starving brain cells.

"Does not dating mean not having sex?" she asked, and what little bit of breath he'd caught rushed out again.

"You don't pull punches, do you?" he asked wryly.

"What's the point?"

"Yes, not dating means not having sex."

"Wow. In…" Silently she counted up the months since Alia and Landry's wedding. "I'm impressed."

"Wow," he echoed. "I've been trying to impress you for six years, and all it took was giving up sex for a year? You're not an easy woman, Martine." Something about his words surprised her—the trying-to-impress part? Her mouth formed a small *oh* of surprise, and because it was too tempting, and because his body was still tingling where she'd barely touched him, he cupped his hands to her face and bent over her. "Lucky for me, I like a challenge."

His mouth covered hers, cold lips, hot breath, eager tongues. When her arms wrapped around his neck and she rose onto her toes to press her body against his, his hands moved without thought, sliding from her face to her shoulders to her spine, gliding downward to cup her butt and pull her hips against his erection. The cold didn't matter anymore, or the snow or the case or the murders. Nothing mattered but getting closer to her, touching, seeing, tasting, needing every bit of her, satisfying the hunger she'd stirred six years ago that had never gone away.

Her moan echoed in the small space, given strength by the unusually quiet night and by the need that scraped across his nerves with a painful sting. He'd heard that sound from her before, had made that sound with her before, and welcomed it again. The first time—last time—had been ruined by the ring of his cell phone and his mention of his wife. At the time, he'd thought it was the stupidest thing he'd ever done, but now he knew better. Just being with her then, kissing her, wanting her, had been wrong in ways he hadn't comprehended then.

He did now.

Anything more that happened between them now would have to be a rational, clearheaded decision on both their parts, or he would lose another chance with her, and this one would likely be the last.

That would be the stupidest thing he'd ever done.

Reluctantly he ended the kiss—the hardest thing he'd ever done—and nuzzled her throat, her jaw, her ear, before murmuring, "I should go."

Part of him hoped she would say, *No, you should stay.* The weaker part hoped she wouldn't.

Her breath was slow, audible, forming a tiny cloud in the air. "You probably should."

"It's not that I don't want you."

Her lips quirking into a smirk very much like his own fallback expression, she shifted her body against his, making his breath catch, his nerves tingle, his muscles damn near spasm with pleasure. "I know that. But we should be sure."

I'm damn sure. "Rational," he agreed.

She nodded. "Reasonable."

"Certain we can set aside the past."

"Make a calm decision not based on emotions of the moment."

The need inside him that wasn't about to go away anytime soon snickered. If any decision should be based on emotion, it was this one. But he ignored it. "Certain you can trust me."

She stilled, then her gaze sought his in the dim light. For a long time, she looked at him, her expression all serious and complex and intense, making his breath catch once more. When it eased, so did the tension inside him, and when the corners of her mouth turned up in the smallest of smiles, the tightness in his body eased, too.

"I do trust you, Jimmy," she said, and the honesty in her voice humbled him. "I trust you with my life."

And he would protect her with his life. And maybe, when all of this was over, she would trust him with her heart, too.

Chapter 7

After a surprisingly peaceful night, Martine woke to find a mostly pure blanket of white coating everything. Cradling a cup of coffee between her palms, she looked down on the courtyard, undeniably a magical fairyland with all the snow, and grunted with a distinct lack of appreciation. Sunshine. She wanted sunshine and warm breezes and no more of this winter crap.

In the living room, the morning news anchors were talking about nothing but the snow and its complications. Lists of schools closed for the day scrolled across the bottom of the screen while lists of areas to avoid due to traffic accidents were updated every few minutes. *Stay home unless you really need to go out*, the cheery blonde said with exaggerated sincerity.

Between sips of coffee, Martine texted Niles and Ramona and told them not to come in today, then gave

Anise a choice. She usually needed the money more than the other two. If she could get to the shop safely, Martine would open and work beside her today. She could use some company.

Niles replied K. Ramona said, Thnx. Regretting the slow disappearance of the written language as Martine knew it, she was rewarded with Anise's message: I'll be there before ten and will bring lunch.

Mention of lunch made Martine's stomach rumble. She got a chicken drumstick and the last few scoops of potato salad from the refrigerator and took it with her coffee into the crafts room. With the lights on, the heater running and the curtains open, it was the least claustrophobic place in her apartment. If she ever needed to defend herself there, she had plenty of sharp or heavy objects, from scissors to paper cutters, in addition to the Taser and the pepper spray.

She was in the process of selecting a new project to start or an old one to finish when her cell phone rang. Spying Evie's name, she put it on speakerphone and forced the happiest greeting she'd managed in a while.

"Hey, the kids haven't seen you in nearly a week. You want to come and have an early lunch with us?"

"Hmm, when the kids invite me somewhere, there's usually a hook, like the waiters are six-foot-tall rats."

"They were mice. You've seen enough rats down by the river to recognize the difference. But you will need a coat. Maybe two of them. And a hat. A scarf, gloves, boots, maybe earmuffs if you have any."

Evie's amused voice was interrupted by Jackson's shout. "Aunt Martine, we're having a picnic in the snow. Please come!" A second later, Isabella added her pleas, and a garbled message from little Evangelina suggested she was doing the same.

Evie wrestled the phone back from her children. "Now it's my turn to talk."

"It's always your turn," Isabella said archly.

"When you have your own phone—"

Martine interrupted. "Which will probably be for their next birthdays so Jack can keep track of them."

Evie snorted. "He would have the vet plant tracking chips in them if he could."

"Is he back yet?"

"No. He's snowed in in Omaha."

Martine felt a niggle of guilt because she hadn't even given Jack more than a thought or two since he'd left. She hadn't spent much more attention on Evie, home alone with the three kids who were definitely Daddy's boy and girls. Ordinarily, she'd be helping Evie distract them in the evenings, but this wasn't an ordinary week.

"I appreciate the invite," she said, grateful she had a legitimate reason for turning it down. Sitting outside to eat and drink in the snow didn't make the happy girl inside her jump and cheer.

"But you've got more sense than I do."

"No. You know I'd do it, but… I'm not supposed to go anywhere where someone might see me, and I wouldn't want to risk anyone following me to your house, scaring the kids or—or hurting…" She couldn't think beyond that. Her brain just refused to.

"I'm sorry, Martine. I didn't forget. I just didn't realize. Without Jack here to keep me updated, I just thought things were the same as Tuesday. Are you in danger?"

Martine's gut clenched. She didn't want to tell her best friend that Paulina's killer knew her address, had been to her house and sent her messages, but she also didn't want Evie showing up at the apartment or the shop to keep her company, either. "Enough that you should forget you know me for a while."

Evie gasped. "I can't—I won't—"

"For the kids' sake, Evie." Martine could actually feel the moment Evie relented. Her friend was a strong woman, loyal to the friends who made up her family and fiercely protective. She also understood thoroughly that having kids changed the dynamics of that family. In matters of safety, the kids always, always came first.

"Tell the little monsters that I'm sorry I can't join them on their snow picnic, but send me pictures."

"I will. We will." A tremor shook Evie's voice. "You be careful, Martine. And tell Jimmy if he doesn't do his absolute best on this case and keep you safe, I will put a curse on him that will make his dangly bits shrivel up and ruin him for any other woman the rest of his life."

Martine winced at the threat. Evie's powers were of the foretelling-the-future variety, but if anyone knew someone who could do what she'd threatened, it was her. Martine decided to give her good news—or, at least, interesting news—to offset the bad. "Oh, no, don't do that," she said, a little bit of slyness working its way into her voice. "*I* intend to ruin him for any other woman for the rest of his life."

There was a moment of stunned silence, then Evie squealed. "Are you being bad with NOPD's baddest boy? Jack said if you didn't kill him in the first twelve hours, he'd probably be okay, but this sounds like way more than okay. Give me details, Martine. I need gossip."

"Oops, I think I hear Anise downstairs," Martine lied. "Gotta go. Love to the kids and love you, too. Don't freeze on your picnic."

Though she knew she'd frustrated Evie—exactly as she'd intended—her friend's laughter pealed before the call disconnected. Smiling, she wiped her fingers on a wet wipe from the box on the bookcase, shook out an inexpensive vinyl tablecloth to cover the table, then began taking items from the shelves. She had ninety minutes before Anise would arrive downstairs and no desire to spend it being idle, where her mind could wander wherever it wanted.

Painting fabric was one of her many hobbies, one that helped justify having an entire room just for crafts. She'd made gorgeous watercolor cushions for her patio furniture last year and had bought a plain white hammock on closeout last fall with the intent of doing it to match. She already loved her courtyard and was sure she would love it more with the hammock tucked near the niches built into the brick wall that held candles inside hurricane glasses. With plenty of soft pillows, it would be the perfect place to relax on a lazy evening, and with the double-sized hammock, there would be plenty of room to share it with Jimmy.

Or some other guy, she reminded herself. Just because they both wanted to give this thing a chance didn't mean it would work out. Yeah, it could be another guy. Maybe Nico would come back through town, or maybe someone she hadn't yet met.

Or Jimmy, the stubborn part of her repeated. Maybe it wouldn't work out for the long term, but for a few months, enough for the evenings to get warm enough to laze outside, yeah, it could last that long. Long enough to surprise everyone who knew him. Maybe long enough to surprise everyone who knew her, too.

Maybe even...

She rolled her eyes, not willing to go there, and focused on her task. After taking her breakfast dishes to the kitchen, she returned with two cups of water, one for the paint medium and the other to wet the watercolors. The pigments were strong, vibrant colors that spread across her canvas in swirls and swoops, seeping into the fabric as the water helped move it along and toned down the hues to a dozen shades of gorgeous pastels that made her happy just to look at them.

By the time the phone interrupted her again, she was applying the last swipes of paint medium. Pleased with her efforts, she traded the brush for the phone, arched her back in a stretch and answered without looking at the caller ID. "Hey, Anise, perfect timing. I'll be down in a few minutes."

There was no response. No, that wasn't true. She could hear something in the background—a rustle, a whisper, really just a sense of a sound—then the bell downstairs buzzed. Jumping, she almost dropped the phone before calming her heart and her nerves and jogging down the stairs.

Anise stood on the stoop, bundled up as if the worst blizzard in the history of the world was raging. Only her eyes and the bridge of her nose were visible, and ice crystals decorated her yellow ski mask where it covered her mouth. Martine undid the locks and pushed the planter to the side so she could open the door. "Too cold to even say, 'Hey, I'm here,' before you hang up?" she teased.

"If I didn't already suffer from seasonal depression, this weather would do it to me," Anise said flatly. "Hey, I'm here."

Martine's smile faltered. "Didn't you just call my cell to let me know…"

Anise shook her head.

A shiver seeped through the open collar of Martine's shirt and raced along her skin, trailing up her spine and down into her suddenly queasy stomach. "Oh. Okay. Um, why don't you come in? I just need to grab a few things. Coat. Bag."

"Shoes." Anise looked pointedly at her socked feet. "Go on. I'll wait here." Though she walked the ten blocks between home and the shop twice a day, Anise didn't do stairs unless they were unavoidable. That, she insisted, was why God invented elevators.

Turning, Martine dashed back up the stairs. As soon as she rounded the corner out of her assistant's sight, she yanked the phone from her pocket and checked caller ID. Her heart stopped, giving a stutter or two before it managed to find a rhythm again, and stone-cold ice spread through her. Unable to depend on her legs, she sagged against the wall, and her gaze went unfocused, scanning the room without making sense of anything until it reached the kitchen window, then the back door.

The apartment was filled with windows and doors, entries and exits, window glass easy to break, doors easy to kick. Even with locks, even with Jimmy's weapons, even with her sense of security—false sense?— she wasn't safe here. The killer had found Callie. He'd found Paulina in a strange city that no one knew she was even in besides Martine. He'd already proved he knew where to find her.

It was just a matter of time.

"Don't hurry on my account," Anise called up the stairs. "Just because it's twenty degrees colder down here than it is up there."

The girl's voice was enough to shake Martine from her shock. She hustled into the bedroom, pulled on a pair of comfortable boots, grabbed her purse from the kitchen table and a coat from the coat tree. Before she reached the stairs again, she drew a deep, deep breath to control the panic inside her. She forced herself to walk down the steps at a sane pace, to follow Anise outside, to lock the door securely, then tiptoe through the snow to the shop's stoop.

The weather-sensitive door creaked and groaned, but within seconds they were inside, where she made a beeline for the storeroom. "I'll start the coffee," she called, not entirely a lie since she intended to do that, too. First, though, she had a phone call to make.

"DiBiase." Jimmy's voice was warm and confident and would have done tingly girlie things to her inside if she wasn't too chilled to tingle.

"Hey, Jimmy, it's Martine."

His voice went softer, sweeter. "It's not even ten o'clock. Miss me?"

More than you know. "Um, listen, Jimmy, I just got a phone call."

"Yeah?" Interest and concern in one syllable.

"Yeah." Her fingers clenched tighter, and she had to force air into her lungs before she could get the words out.

"Caller ID said it was from Callie Winchester's phone."

When Jimmy was a kid, swearing was strictly prohibited in the DiBiase household. Convinced that his

parents would somehow find out he was breaking the
rule, he abided by it until he was about twelve, when
he wrecked his bike and skidded twenty feet along the
pavement, shredding the skin exposed on his arms and
legs. *Damn*, he'd muttered, and it had lessened his pain
a little, so he'd repeated it, like a mantra, until he'd
vented all his frustration and hurt. Now the word kept
running through his brain. *Damn damn damn damn.*

It wasn't lessening anything this time.

It took too long to get a warrant to Callie's cell service provider, then too long to get back the location of
her phone when the call was made—though instantly
would have been too long—and finding out made the
hairs on the back of his neck prickle. He rose from
his desk, too edgy to sit still, pulled on his coat and
headed out to his car.

Whoever had called Martine had been in Jackson Square, specifically in the corner nearest Café du
Monde. Far too close for comfort, but not as close as
earlier. One of the towers the phone had pinged before the call placed it on Royal Street less than ten
minutes before.

The killer had walked past Martine's apartment,
had possibly stood outside and watched the building
while she was oblivious inside, going about her pre-
work routine. Then she—his gut was leaning heavily
toward a woman, and although he remained open to
all possibilities, he didn't argue with gut instinct—had
gone to Jackson Square and placed the call, frightening Martine without saying a word. Then, according
to the service provider, the phone's signal had disappeared, meaning either the phone was turned off or
the battery went dead.

He was pretty sure this woman, this person responsible for two murders, hadn't been careless enough to let the battery die.

Which meant she could be back on Royal Street, watching Martine's place. Hell, she could be in the shop posing as a customer.

Dread shuddered through him. He was generally well acquainted with the feeling—that came from going to too many crime scenes, from investigating too many victims—but this dread was different. It was sharp edged and left him in some odd limbo before numbness and angry raw fear.

Head ducked against the cold, he got into his car and started the engine, shuddering as cold air blew out the defroster vents, fogging the windows.

When he pulled away from the curb, he automatically headed in the direction of Royal. Martine had to close the shop. Had to get out of her apartment. Had to go into hiding someplace where she couldn't be found.

Like Tallie Winchester. Robin Railey. Irena Young.

He knew exactly where he wanted Martine to go.

And it wasn't going to be easy to get her there.

Like most Southern cities, New Orleans's policy for dealing with snow was simple: wait it out. Eventually the sun would come out and the air would warm and the snow would go away on its own. It was a good time to hibernate. He just wished he could.

Parking next to Martine's car, he stepped out, and the snow crunched beneath his feet. Trails were worn in the white stuff, including a mess of prints going up and then down Martine's steps. The same prints marked the shop's steps, though his own bigger footprints obliterated them. He jiggled the knob and pushed at the door until it gave, stomped his feet to clean his shoes, then went inside. When he closed the door, a mild shock shot through his fingers. "Damn," he muttered, and a dozen feet away, Anise gave him a curious look.

"How was it?" She cocked her head to one side. "The same as before? Stronger? Weaker?"

Remembering her comment the first time it happened—*That wasn't the effect I was going for*—he scowled at her. "Where's Martine?"

"In there." She cocked her head toward the door marked Private.

Jimmy went that way, but before opening the door, he turned back. "A little stronger than before. Is that the effect you were going for?"

Smiling serenely, she shrugged and returned her attention to the shelves she was rearranging.

The door opened into a medium-sized room with display counters, shelves, cabinets and tall jars and bins holding who knew what. There were no windows, the only lighting artificial and not nearly substantial enough. Though no candles or incense burned, an exotic, acrid smell drifted on the air.

Goose bumps raised along his arms. This was the real stuff, the merchandise she sold to real practitioners.

"Are you looking for me or just looking?"

The voice came from the right and shifted Jimmy's heart into overdrive. His hand had already shoved past his overcoat and jacket to his pistol before it registered as Martine's. After sucking in a sharp breath through his teeth, he turned to find her standing a few feet from him, her dark clothes and black hair blending with the shadows in the corner. "Holy crap, Martine, don't you know better than to sneak up on an armed man?"

She raised both hands palm out. "I didn't sneak. I didn't move at all." Then she did move, coming into the light, resting her hands on the glass countertop. "You must have bad news."

"Why do you say that?"

"Fabulous news gets delivered in person. Good or so-so news can be passed over the phone. Bad news usually requires a face-to-face visit." Her gaze raked over him, and a thin smile turned up the corners of her mouth. "You don't look like you've got fabulous news."

Lines furrowed around her eyes, her forehead and tagged the smile as less than authentic. She looked soul weary, as if the call from her dead friend's phone had been the very last straw. It made him want to wrap his arms around her, to hold her until she remembered that she wasn't alone in this, to give her some bit of strength to help her through.

By God, she *would* get through.

"The cell towers show the call came from Jackson Square, but they put the phone on this street just before then," he said grimly.

Even in the dim light, he saw the color blanch from her face. "*My* street?"

"Yes."

"While I was making coffee, I went to the living room window and looked out to see how much snow we'd gotten. I saw a few people on the street and thought they were more suckers for punishment than me. They just seemed normal, people on their way to work. None of them stood out." Her gaze scanned the room as if danger might lurk in every shadow before coming back to him. Fear darkened her irises, but she was making an obvious effort to contain it. "But that's the problem, isn't it? Whoever killed Callie and Paulina, whoever left that envelope on my car and cut the chain to my gate, they just looked normal, too, didn't they? The kind of person you'd smile at and say hello to on the street. Not some crazed psychopath who might drag you around the corner and crack your skull open."

He moved his hand to her shoulder, rubbing away the shivers there. "You're a wise woman to be scared, Martine, but—"

"I think I should close the shop for a few days."

The comment surprised him. He'd figured she would give him an argument about closing, about hiding and letting someone else control her life. He'd thought he would have to persuade her, pointing out that it was just temporary, that it was safer for everyone if she avoided the shop, that being smart and alive was better than being independent and dead. It took him a moment to catch up with her and nod. "I agree."

Again her gaze skimmed the room, stopping on the door he'd left open behind him, focusing on the world outside. A dangerous world. "The thing is…" Once more the pretend smile touched her mouth. "I don't feel safe in my apartment. This morning, after that call, it just really hit that the murd—" She swallowed hard, corrected herself. "The person who killed Paulina and Callie is here, waiting for me. I lock myself in my apartment, but there are ways in. He or she could walk into the store at any time, and I wouldn't know, I wouldn't suspect, until it was too late. They could be watching outside when I leave with you, they could follow us, they could have a tracking device on your car, and the minute you turn your back—"

When he'd first walked into the room, he'd wanted to hold her—just as he'd wanted to keep holding her when he'd walked away last night—but he'd waited. Now he took a step to reach her and pulled her close to him. She was so slender and insubstantial, a shaky mass of emotions dominated by fear. "Hey, don't insult my cop intellect," he lightly teased. "I check my car every day. No one's gonna follow me unless I want them to. And I'm the best at ID'ing vehicles driving the same route I am, sticking too close or taking too many of the same turns."

Bless her, Martine made an effort, even with her face pressed to the soft wool of his coat. "Huh. Jack says he's the best at all that stuff."

"Well, Jack may say it, but with me, it's really true. You would be amazed, Tine, at all the things I'm best at. You come stay at my place, and I'll show you. Or tell you." He hesitated, then returned to his original word choice. "No, show you."

Tension ratcheted through her body as she lifted her head, staring at him. Was she thinking that in a tourist destination like New Orleans, there were a thousand better places to stay than with him? Wondering what people would think? Wondering what *he* would think?

Or wondering what *she* would think. Feel. Do.

Or not do.

"I've got room," he went on. "It's safe. There's a security system. A doorman. No one will know you're there. Seriously, of all the places you could hide out, who in this city would ever believe you'd choose mine?"

She stared a moment longer before a real smile came to her face. Among their friends and acquaintances, it was well known—and a source of amusement for most—that the mere sight of him pushed her irritation level to the max. The closest she ever came to a smile around him was the baring of her teeth, and anything she had to say, she said in a fearsome growl. He figured all that was going through her mind, too, because curiosity and possibility both seeped into her expression.

"They say you always go to your lady friends' homes so you don't have to meet the minimum standards of cleanliness in your own."

"Or so I can leave the next morning pretty much when I want to."

She was relaxing a little in his arms, warming to the subject of what he was sure had been many conversations about his failings and shortcomings. "And that you prefer crappy apartments in crappy areas so women don't feel safe going there alone. That way no one ever shows up without an invitation and an escort."

"Aw, that's not true. But sometimes," he said drily, "I do try to live within my salary, and cheap apartments are often crappy ones. It also has the advantage of putting me close to the calls I work."

"They also say—"

"Wow, they talk an awful lot about me when my back is turned, don't they? And you listen to an awful lot of it for someone who professes to hate me."

She smiled innocently. "Have I ever actually used the word *hate*?"

He was too lost in looking at her to answer right away. She was beautiful and sexy, and she had this way of gazing at a man that made him feel she was giving him everything—every bit of her attention, emotion, desire, need. She had another way of looking that could make a man go weak, pretty sure she might leave him a boneless, brainless puddle and grateful for it. But add innocence to the sexiness and sensuality, and he was a goner.

He lost track of the conversation, instead maneuvering her even closer against him, bending to kiss her ear, to make her shiver. "I'm more interested in words you might actually use in the future," he murmured even as a rattle sounded outside the room. Anise's voice filtered in the air, along with a stranger's, their words impossible to make out. Jimmy didn't know if he went taut first or if Martine did, but he put her away and pivoted toward the door.

It was an older woman talking to the clerk, wearing a coat too thin for the day, silvery hair peeking out under a knitted New Orleans Saints cap. Not Irena. Not Tallie or Robin. Neither predator nor prey.

Nope, not exactly right. Irena might be his favorite choice for the killer, but that didn't mean he could rule out anyone else. A sweet lined face and pure white hair weren't enough to take that stranger out of the running for anything. When he didn't have a clue who his suspect was, then it could be anyone. Good reason to get Martine out of sight and keep her there.

Martine, moving soundlessly, eased the door shut and sighed. "At least we won't lose much money. The whole week's been a bust. Please, God, may the sun shine again Monday."

"As soon as Anise's finished, we'll lock up and give her a ride home. Don't tell her or anyone else where you're going. Oh, and I'll need your phone." When he held out his hand, she gave it to him with just a little reluctance. He powered it down and slid it into his pocket, heard the doorbell ring and sneaked a peek to find Anise alone. "Come on, Tine. Let's go."

Martine had lived in her apartment nearly twenty years and she loved it more than the day she'd moved in, but a heavy sense of unease prickled through her as she climbed the stairs. Even with Jimmy two steps behind her, she was afraid to reach the top, to notice a window cracked open, the back door unsecured, signs of an intruder soiling her space and spoiling its aura.

There weren't any windows cracked open, and the back door was still locked, and not a single thing had changed from the last time she was there, but the unease didn't go away. She grabbed a backpack from the coat tree and a cardboard box from the workroom, along with a handful of the shop's logoed bags. She filled the backpack and the box with clothing and shoes, with toiletries and makeup going into the shopping bags. She didn't want anyone who saw her to think she was running away but maybe making a delivery for the store.

"I do have luggage," she said to Jimmy, leaning against the doorjamb, arms crossed, just in case he thought she was one of those people who really did pack in cardboard and plastic.

"Luggage says 'I'm going somewhere.' Boxes and bags say 'But I'll be back in a few hours.'" He grinned. "Didn't think I caught the subtle nuances of that, did you?"

"I didn't know you knew a thing about 'subtle' or 'nuances.'" But there was no sting to her words. She glanced around the room, thinking of nothing else she wanted besides the laptop in the living room and a heavier coat from the rack. "I guess I'm ready."

She swung one strap of the backpack over her shoulder while Jimmy picked up the box and the bags. When she scooped up her computer, he shook his head. "No."

"No?" she echoed.

"You can't send email, use social media or surf the net. Providers are too easy to follow. You can use mine, but you still can't do email or social media. Okay?"

Swallowing a sigh, she put the computer in a desk drawer as she passed, then started down the stairs. She hadn't brought any projects, any books, any music. She would probably go stark-raving mad within twenty-four hours.

Unless Jimmy found a way to entertain her.

Had he noticed the condoms she'd sneaked into the bag with her hand lotion and other stuff? Smart women were never caught unprepared, right? Neither were smart men—or easy men—but given that he'd been celibate for a year, she thought it best to provide recently purchased protection.

Even if she didn't get to use it.

She waited inside the door while he put her bags in the trunk of his car. Then they returned to the shop and helped Anise close up. If the girl thought something was wrong, she kept it to herself. All the way to her house, she spoke only in partial sentences to give Jimmy directions.

There she swung her legs out the rear door, then paused. "You want me to let Ramona and Niles know?"

"Yes, please. Tell them I'll still pay you guys."

Anise fixed a grim look on her. "It's not just the

money. We're responsible. We could keep the shop open."

"I know you could, sweetie, but…" Martine didn't want to even hint that the store could be a dangerous place right now. If the killer was frustrated by Martine's disappearance, what revenge might he take on her employees?

"I really think it's best if we just all take a break. If you need anything, call my cell, okay?" Martine assumed Jimmy would be keeping it at work, in case the killer called again, and he could keep her updated on any other calls.

"Okay." Anise stood up, then ducked down inside again. "You'd better not let anything happen to her," she said to Jimmy, "or those shocks are just the beginning."

He acknowledged her with a relatively serious nod. She straightened, slammed the door and picked her way carefully through the snow to the porch of the small house she shared with her father.

"Are you still getting shocked by the doorknob?"

He gave the fingers of his left hand a rueful look. "Yeah. I think they're getting stronger."

Martine frowned. "I adore Anise, but…that's a little scary."

"You doubted her powers?"

"Well…yes. Anise's a dabbler. So is Niles, only he's not much of a believer. Creating a ward that shocks only one person, and the same person every time… who knows what she might do if she finds a talented mentor willing to work with her?"

"Like you?"

She shook her head. "I'm not talented. I can put together protection bags and charms and make cleansing potions and healing potions, but the difference between, say, me and Auntie Katrine—you know her, right?"

An eye roll accompanied Jimmy's nod, as if to say *everyone* in the NOPD knew Auntie Katrine. She was a fixture in the French Quarter, her business set up in good weather or bad on the sidewalk in front of her small shotgun house, painted hot pink and lime green. She was short and fat—she'd *tsk* if you used any other word—and she came from Trinidad, or maybe it was Antigua or West Caicos. She'd been here forty years going on seventy, and she'd birthed fourteen children and buried five husbands…or was it ten children and seven husbands? With Auntie Katrine, details always varied, but one thing didn't. She was on better terms with the spirits than anyone Martine had ever known.

"Take the executive chef at the best five-star restaurant in the entire world, and that would be Auntie Katrine. I would be the perpetually stained, sweaty, steamy peon in the back washing dishes. We'd both be in the restaurant business, but that's where the similarities end."

He squeezed her fingers lightly. "I'd like to see you sweaty and steamy for the right reasons."

This time it was her eyes rolling, but she wasn't annoyed. Some of his lines, his practiced smiles, his flippant comments, could still set her hair on fire, but her ticked off–meter wasn't nearly as sensitive as it used to be with him.

You need to get to know him, Evie always said. *When you figure out what's real and what isn't, he's a good guy.*

Of course, Evie was already happily married to the love of her life at the time she met Jimmy, so she was never the target of his over-the-top charming smiles or his sweet-talking ways.

In an attempt to distract herself, Martine gazed out the window. "Where do you live?"

"You'll be surprised."

Acknowledging that she likely would, she changed the subject. "Did the killer take Paulina's cell phone?"

"She left it at home when she ran away. The one she used to call you was a burner phone. It didn't have anything personal on it."

"So he took Callie's because it did have stuff on it—names, pictures. So she had no clue what was about to happen. She was going about her life as usual, and one night she died." She considered that for a moment. "I think I might prefer it that way—the surprise, you know. Poor Paulina looked like she'd been living in hell. She was afraid to stay in one place, to look over her shoulder, terrified of what she might see. But it didn't help her. She knew death was coming. Her only surprise was when, and maybe who."

"Paulina didn't get help," Jimmy said quietly. "She could have gone to the police. Her family could have hired bodyguards. They could have spirited her away to some isolated place on another continent or put her on a yacht in the middle of the ocean."

"Maybe she thought she didn't deserve any of that. Maybe she thought death was what she deserved."

Or maybe not. Her last known act had been to warn Martine. Without that, the killer could have grabbed Martine the very next day or anytime since. She would have been vulnerable and helpless and most likely have ended up like Callie and Paulina.

She didn't focus back into the present until the clicking of the turn signal pulled her there. Jimmy was turning into the parking garage of a tall building just a short distance from the river, stopping, waiting for the security guard to step out of the shack, give him a wave, then activate the iron gate. There were expensive shops on the ground floor of the building, the kind outside her budget except for very special events—which were pretty much outside her lifestyle—and she vaguely remembered hearing about condos upstairs.

Jimmy DiBiase, who according to legend had never cared one bit about the places he called home, lived in a sky-high condo in the Central Business District of the city. He had been right. She was surprised.

He parked in one of two spaces marked 805. Silently, they gathered her belongings from the trunk and hustled to the elevator fifty feet away. It was marked Residents Only and required a swipe card to operate, and it took them quickly to the eighth floor.

The condo had great bones, easy to tell because it had very little in it: a sofa that had seen better days. A television mounted to the wall above the fireplace. Stools at the counter that separated the kitchen, which didn't hold a single one of the usual items that tended to clutter counters. No dishes, no soap, no can opener, no sugar or coffee, nothing but half a roll of paper towels. Through an open door down the hall, she saw the corner of a mattress set, resting directly on the floor.

He set her stuff on the counter, and she added the backpack to the pile. "Are you planning to finish moving in soon?" she asked pleasantly, drawing a growl from him as she walked to the tall windows that looked out over the city. "Somehow, I didn't picture you living in an actual apartment—with a living room, kitchen and everything. I figured all you needed was a bedroom and a bathroom. You know, like a motel."

He looked as if he didn't know whether to be annoyed or to agree with her. Finally, with a grin, he opened his arms to encompass the mostly empty space. "I'm finished moving in. What you see is all I've got."

"Are there dishes in the cabinets?"

"Nope. No food, either. I *have* dishes. They're in boxes down the hall. I haven't had time to unpack them. And I'll get groceries today. I've just been a little preoccupied."

With this case, Martine knew. With her. "I appreciate your preoccupation."

His grin appeared again before he gestured toward the hall. "Want the five-second tour?"

It actually took about ten seconds. There was the master bedroom: the mattress set, a lamp sitting on a box, a closet, a bathroom and a wall of windows. The hall circled around behind the kitchen, leading to another bedroom, smaller in all senses, including the windows, then went back into the living room, passing the guest bath on the way. Neatly labeled boxes were stacked in the hall, and there was no furniture—zip, zilch, nada—in the guest room.

"So I'm sleeping on the couch." The idea tickled her: after practically jumping his bones the second time they met, and regretting not doing it on more than one occasion, the first time they spent the night in the same space, she'd be passing it on an old, worn, comfy sofa.

He gave her a long, serious, tantalizing look. "You're always welcome in my bed, Martine. I made that clear a long time ago."

"Yes, but you were *married*, Jimmy."

After another moment, he slowly smiled. "I have to admit, I admire the fact that it mattered to you. I even admire your unwillingness to let it go. I like that kind of commitment to your beliefs."

She believed him, especially when he touched her so gently, his fingers stroking along her jaw. The contact made her all warm and melty inside, made her forget all the ugliness and let her just be a woman with desires and needs and uncertainties.

"What are you committed to, Jimmy?" Her voice was barely a whisper, and the sound was unsteady, shaky, like her legs that didn't want to support her, like her fingers that trembled when they cupped his hand where it rested on her cheek.

He moved closer, brushed his mouth across her forehead, kissed a trail to her ear, then glided down to the corner of her lips. He toyed with her, sliding his mouth back and forth, teasing her lips apart, briefly tasting her, giving her a taste of him, before he lifted his head and met her gaze. His was fiercely protective and possessive and hot.

"You, Tine," he answered gruffly. "I'm committed to you."

Chapter 8

In all his years with the department, Jimmy couldn't recall ever not wanting to work as much as he did when he had to leave the apartment and Martine. It was a strange feeling. From the time he'd graduated the academy and started his first day with his training officer, he'd counted himself lucky for loving the job. From doing traffic stops to refereeing domestic disputes to drug arrests, he'd never gotten up in the morning and thought *I don't want to do this today.*

Right now, though, he didn't want to return to work. Two thoughts kept running through his mind, one that knotted his gut and another that could make him a believer in spontaneous combustion: Martine was in danger, and damn, the things they could do if he didn't leave. God knew, he'd worked enough long hours over the years to justify taking an afternoon off, but that wasn't the way he did things.

Instead, he kissed her again and left the apartment, arranging with the building's concierge service to take care of the shopping, and returned to the station.

When he got to his desk, he called Paulina's husband, back home in Alabama with the unenviable job of planning his wife's funeral. Shawn Bradley didn't sound as if he had gotten past the shock of her death.

"Your wife left her cell phone behind when she left. Is that right?" Jimmy asked after apologizing for bothering the man.

"Yes, she did."

"Did any calls come in on the phone after her disappearance?"

"A lot of text messages. Most of the calls were from me. At first I didn't know she was gone, and then I just... I wanted to hear her voice on the outgoing message." Bradley's voice cracked, and he took a deep breath to steady it. "In the first few days, there were calls from friends and coworkers who didn't know she'd disappeared. Those dropped off for a while, then it was like something jogged their memory and they called to see if she was back. Now it's down to her parents and me."

"Did you know most of the callers?"

"By name if not personally. Paulina liked to share the details of her day—who made her laugh, who ticked her off, who she had lunch with. The rest seemed to be just acquaintances, not part of her regular life. People who heard that a Paulina Bradley was missing and wanted to make sure it wasn't her."

He fell silent, so still that Jimmy thought they might have lost their connection. He was about to speak when Bradley did.

"Then there were the hang-ups. Though if I recall, one of them..." His tone turned thoughtful, and the rustling of papers sounded in the background. "Paulina *hated* missing a call—we used to joke that the phone was glued to her hand—so in the beginning, I kept track of them all since the phone would only store so many numbers. Okay, here it is. Two weeks after she went missing, she got a call from one of the Christmas-card friends I told you about—the sisters. Callie Winchester, from the 206 area code. No message, just a hang-up."

So the killer hadn't been watching Paulina, hadn't known she'd run away. Why the change with Martine?

Because the killer had found Paulina in New Orleans, and it was convenient to take care of her and Martine at the same time. Because Paulina had warned Martine. Because with Tallie and Robin already in hiding, Martine had been the only one the killer could easily locate.

"Does that help, Detective?"

"Yes, Mr. Bradley, it does." He got the cell carrier's name and Paulina's number so he could confirm the call through the company, said goodbye, then tapped his pen in the air above the notebook.

He'd been blessed with some cases so easy to close that a monkey could have done it: an angry avenger still holding the weapon, a remorseful spouse covered with the victim's blood and gunshot residue, a rival proud to have put the competition out of business. But there was no challenge to those kinds of cases, and he did love a challenge.

"Uncle Jimmy!" The cry came from the doorway an instant before Isabella and Jackson Murphy charged around his desk, each determined to reach him first. He slid his chair back in time for Isabella, ducking nimbly around her brother, to leap into his lap and press her cold cheek to his. "I won," she said with a dazzling smile.

"She cheated," Jackson complained as he climbed up, too.

"I don't think she cheated, buddy. She was just a little bit faster."

"Because Mom says I can't shove her out of the way."

Evie, carrying Evangelina, slid into the chair that faced Jimmy's desk. "She doesn't get to shove you, either, Jackson." As soon as the admonishment was spoken, she turned her gaze on Jimmy. "What have you done with Martine?"

Grinning, he pressed his hands over Isabella's ears. "I can't answer that in front of the kids."

Evie's gaze narrowed. "We went by the store, and it's closed, and she's not answering her door or her phone. Even if you were *n-a-k-e-d* in *b-e-d*, she wouldn't leave me standing in the snow frantic about her."

Picking up a pen and finding a piece of paper, Jackson carefully started writing. *N-a-k.* "What comes after the *k*, Uncle Jimmy?"

He deliberately misunderstood. "What comes after *k*? *H-i-j-k-l-m-n-o*—"

"*P!*" the older two shouted before dissolving into giggles.

Jimmy took advantage of their distraction. "She's someplace safe."

Evie's scowl spoke to her dissatisfaction. "I know that. I want to know where. Your apartment?"

Holding on to both kids, he shifted position. "You think she'd consent to that?"

Tilting her head to one side, Evie studied him before smiling slyly. "I think she'd consent to that and a whole lot more."

Images of the things Martine might consent to, and with him, thickened his brain and notched up the temperature a few uncomfortable degrees. If he let them linger at all, he would embarrass himself with the kids and give the other detectives one more thing to joke about. Deliberately he changed the subject. "Any idea when Jack will be back?"

"Tomorrow, if God takes mercy on my sanity. You'd think Omaha would have been better prepared for snow. They live up north, for heaven's sake."

"I bet people up north say things like that about New Orleans and hurricanes."

"Yes, but when I say it, it makes sense." Evie nudged Evangelina, sitting quietly. "Sweetie, give Uncle Jimmy the goodies we brought."

For the first time he noticed the paper bag Jack's youngest was clutching, the same pink as her jacket. Eyes wide and two fingers stuck in her mouth, she shook her head and held it tighter.

"We made you cookies," Isabella said, and Jackson prodded, "Give it to him, Vangie."

Evangelina shook her head again. Evie whispered something in her ear. After considering it, the girl took her fingers from her mouth and thrust it at him. "Here, Uncle Jimmy."

He accepted the bag, still faintly warm and smelling

of chocolate chips and oatmeal and raisins, and thanked each of the kids. "What did you tell her? Maybe I can use it next time I'm questioning a suspect."

"She's a little girl, not a suspect." Lips thinned, Evie added in a murmur, "At least, not yet. Kids, are you ready to get back out in the snow?"

Jackson wiggled to the floor, then held up his hand to high-five Jimmy. Isabella pressed her cheek to his once again before sliding down, and in a blur of movement and noise, the Murphy clan disappeared down the hall.

It wasn't until quiet had settled again that Jimmy realized Evie had left his question about her tactics unanswered.

But with the comment about Martine, she'd given him more than enough to think about.

There were no food or dishes in the kitchen, Jimmy had said, but by three o'clock, Martine's hunger pangs had led her to snooping. He was almost totally correct: the cabinets and drawers were empty. But the big gleaming silver refrigerator... Everything else might be bare, but occupying the top shelf was a large pizza box, and inside the box were two pieces of pie. It was from one of her favorite places, and the order tag still clung to the box, indicating he'd bought the pizza on Wednesday. Good enough for her.

Using paper towels as both plate and napkin, she warmed the slices just enough to soften the cheese, then climbed onto a barstool and took a ravenous bite. The flavors of the sauce, the meats, the cheeses, and especially the onions and peppers, settled and soothed the grumbling in her stomach. Too soon the pizza was gone. She washed her hands, then carried her stuff into the guest room.

Unpacking was simple: her folded clothes went on the shelves in the closet, her shoes on the floor underneath and her toiletries in the guest bath cabinet. She wandered back into the hall and around to the other bedroom and stood in the doorway. The bed was queen-size—she'd seen so many massive beds that she'd doubted anyone but her owned a smaller size— and the sheets were light blue. A blue blanket covered them, and a shades-of-blue quilt was pushed to one side. It was handmade, with perfectly aligned corners and tiny stitches.

So this was where the infamous Jimmy DiBiase laid his head at night.

This was where she could lay her head at night. For a while. Maybe a long while.

I'm committed to you, Tine.

Maybe for the rest—the best—of her life.

When a loud buzz sounded, she shrieked and whirled around, then sagged against the door. Intercom. Alarm system. Doorman. Concierge service. Jimmy had told her about them before he'd left. He hadn't told her someone might be calling, but that was okay. As soon as she stopped shaking, she would answer like a normal adult.

"This is Stefan from the concierge desk." The voice was young, male, the accent distinctly not Southern. "We have Mr. DiBiase's grocery delivery. Shall we bring it up now?"

Martine told him yes, then smiled faintly on her way to the door. So that was how people with money did their grocery shopping. It was a perk she could get accustomed to.

Within minutes, Stefan was at the door, pushing a trolley loaded with canvas shopping bags. He made polite small talk while unloading everything onto the kitchen counters, and bless his heart, his smile never wavered when it became clear that no tip was forthcoming. With a pleasant reminder to reset the alarm, he left, and she returned to the kitchen, regretting her habit of never carrying cash.

"Yeah, like you woke up this morning thinking you'd be tipping the concierge for a delivery," she murmured as she began unpacking. She wasn't sure she'd ever even stayed at a place with a concierge before, much less used their services.

There were a lot of shopping bags—natural, she supposed, for someone who was starting from scratch. All the staples were there: flour, sugar, spices, oil, condiments. A selection of canned, frozen and fresh vegetables. Shrimp, beef, chicken and pork. Rice, pasta, bread, deli meats and cheeses. Lots of cheeses, and three boxes of crackers. So Jimmy was a cheese-and-cracker guy.

Smiling at the image of him hunkered on a barstool, making a dinner of that and one of the sodas or beers, she opened the last bags and found two large cartons of ice cream, an apple caramel pie fresh from the bakery, an assortment of chocolates and coffee. The final bag, one Stefan had placed carefully in a corner of the counter, held tall paper sleeves, each cushioning a bottle of liquor: Bailey's, Kahlúa, bourbon and rum. Four of the spirits she'd offered him at the apartment.

It touched her that he'd remembered.

It seemed odd, deciding where food would go in someone else's kitchen. Once she'd taken care of that, she folded the empty shopping bags, stored them in a drawer, then retrieved a box of dishes from the hall. Now that she had dish soap and had discovered a stash of kitchen towels, she might as well unpack some of his supplies so they could make use of the groceries. Besides, she doubted Jimmy was going to be letting her out of the apartment every time a meal rolled around. That seemed to defeat the point of hiding.

With the television turned on for company, she washed and dried insulated glasses, plastic giveaway cups, logoed coffee cups and cereal bowls. There was a set of dishes so artfully mismatched that they seemed beyond Jimmy's ability to choose. A leftover from Alia? No, Alia loved food, but she didn't give a damn what it was served on, and she wasn't into subtleties of tones and variations any more than Jimmy.

Maybe another former girlfriend had chosen the vintage floral-pattern dishes. Heaven knew, he'd had plenty of them. It was a fact of his life, part of how he'd become the man he was. He'd made mistakes, and he said he'd learned from them.

She believed him.

Never get involved with a man with the intention of changing him, her mother's lifelong best friend and serial divorcée, Rona, liked to say. *Accept him the way he is, or move on down the road, honey, because that ride you're on is gonna get real bumpy.*

Bette had said Rona's ride was never going to smooth out until she swore off either marriage or divorce. Going on ten years single, it seemed she'd made the right choice.

After unpacking, washing, drying and putting away six boxes of kitchenware, Martine walked into the hall for a seventh, stopped and stretched, feet apart, arms high in the air, then slowly bent at the waist to ease the kinks out of her spine. As her fingertips brushed the floor, a key turned in the front door lock, and an instant later, the door swung open to reveal an upside-down version of Jimmy in the hallway. Immediately her face flushed deeper than could be blamed on the position, and just as immediately a grin spread across his face.

She stood more quickly than she should have, hair tumbling back into her face, heat rushing through her but not from embarrassment. The way he'd looked at her, the hungry, needy glaze in his eyes, the memories of their kiss and of his quiet declaration—*I'm committed to you*... They all combined to make her feel warm and quivery and nervous and excited and very, very girlie.

Summoning a normal voice from somewhere, she said, "You should give a person warning."

He stepped inside, shrugged out of his overcoat and hung it in the closet. "I figured using the intercom or ringing the bell might startle you, and if you tried to use the Taser or the pepper spray, I could duck back out and close the door really fast." He removed his jacket, too, and loosened the tie around his neck as he approached her. A whiff of cold, fresh air came off him, and an aura of satisfaction surrounded him.

"You have a good day?"

He shrugged. "In between. I learned a little. Not enough." He glanced at the stack of empty boxes teetering on one side of the hallway. "Wow. You got a lot done."

"I know I should have asked, but I had no way to get hold of you, and what good is food without dishes?"

"You didn't need to ask." He shoved one hand in his pocket and pulled out a cell phone. "I got this for you. It's prepaid, and with the number blocked, no one you call can press Redial and get you. It doesn't have all the bells and whistles, but it'll do what you need. Don't give the number to anyone, not even Evie. Not even your mom. I'll let you know if you get calls to return, and you can do those from my phone, okay?"

She reached for the phone, and he caught her fingers, pulling her closer. She didn't even pretend to resist. "Keep this with you all the time," he said, pressing the cell into her hand. "I've got a few numbers programmed already—mine, Jack's—he should be back tomorrow—and Gus. He's head of security here. His office is on the second floor. If anything happens, call all three of us. You know how to use it?"

She pulled her hand free and studied the phone. It was simpler than her smartphone—a good thing since she'd discovered she wasn't as clearheaded in a panic as she'd always thought she would be. "Yeah, I can figure it out."

"Good. Let me change clothes, and I'll help you in here."

Martine made sure she did understand the workings of the phone before sliding it into her pocket and going back to work. She hung the damp dish towel over an empty box, took a new one from its drawer and filled the sink again with hot sudsy water. The next box she opened held mixing and storage bowls, along with lids. Surely in one of the remaining cartons, she would find some cookware. She could easily see Jimmy preferring standing over a smoky grill with a beer in hand, but the only thing the apartment lacked was a balcony to hold said grill.

He returned from the bedroom wearing jeans, a snug-fitting T-shirt and socks. Even though, in deference to the situation, his gun was still holstered on his belt, something about him without shoes struck her as so…homey. So ridiculously right and cozy. He smelled good enough to wake her girlie hormones if they hadn't gone on high alert just at the sight of him, spicy and woodsy and rich.

"You know, I washed the dishes before I packed them." He lifted a milky-green bowl from the second sink, rinsed and began to dry it.

"I suspected as much. But who knows how long they've been in these boxes, or where the packing paper came from?" She gave him a sidelong look. "I do like your dishes, though."

He opened cabinet doors, looking for a place to set the bowl, then frowned. "You haven't seen them yet."

"Those pretty floral plates?"

"Oh. My sister made those. Running the family business and homeschooling the kids don't keep her busy enough, so she also dabbles in stuff. She made 'em, painted 'em, glazed 'em, fired 'em…whatever all it takes. She said I should use those instead of my real dishes."

"What's wrong with your real dishes?" Martine could make a pretty good guess, considering the other surprises she'd gotten about him this week.

He dropped the towel, brought in another box, lifted out a dinner plate and handed it to her. It felt as delicate as a fine sheet of ice, as if she dropped it, God forbid, it would float rather than fall to the floor. The colors were delicate, pale flowers on a creamy background, and the whole glowed with a lovely translucency.

She very carefully handed it back. "You were eating off those?"

He set it back in its nest in the box. "They're dishes. That's what they're meant for."

"No, by the time they get that old, they're meant for display and *maybe* a once-in-a-lifetime celebration." She narrowed her gaze. "I bet your mother's holding on to any other family heirlooms you've inherited, isn't she?"

He grinned, not the least bit embarrassed. "I tell her I could use the dining table because I don't have a desk and that the cabinet that goes with the dishes would make a great place to store stuff like files, footballs, shoes, but she just turns pale and pretends she doesn't hear me."

Martine appreciated the affection in his voice when he talked about his mother. She knew so many adults who had little to no relationship with their parents—Evie, Jack, Landry, Reece and Jones. Even, when it came to her father, herself. Jimmy, though, seemed on good terms with all of his family, and she admired that.

Admired him.

More than admired him.

The sun had abandoned New Orleans, there was snow on the ground, and Martine Broussard was falling in love with Jimmy DiBiase. Had stranger things ever happened?

Jimmy hadn't spent enough time in the apartment to have gotten accustomed to being there alone—he'd moved in only on Sunday—but he did wonder, after a while, why it didn't seem odd that Martine was there. He'd never been the sort to entertain at home. From the time his social life had begun, dinner with a date had always meant going out; quiet evenings at home were at *her* home; his bed was best for sleeping in alone. Even Alia, in the months before they got married, hadn't been to his place more than a handful of times and had never spent the night there. Though, to be honest, that was her choice as much as his.

But it felt right to have Martine here. She made it feel really and truly like home, and that was a sensation he hadn't had in longer than he could remember.

They had fixed dinner and eaten it, washed the dishes and returned the kitchen to its neat state. In her unpacking, Martine had found the coffee maker, and now they each had a cup, dosed with enough Irish cream to warm from the inside out, and the gas logs in the fireplace crackled and popped without the hassle—or the charm—of the real thing.

"So." Martine shifted at the other end of the couch, kicking off her shoes and turning to face him with her feet tucked underneath the cushion separating them. "The places you've chosen to live in the past are legendary for their undesirability. Why make such a drastic change?"

"I don't know. Maybe subconsciously I knew I would meet a damsel in distress who would need a safe place to stay."

The look she gave him was skeptical. "You already knew me."

"Not really. We'd already *met*. There's a difference."

She acknowledged that with a nod, then her eyebrows drew together. "A damsel in distress?"

"Hey, if it weren't for the saying, I wouldn't even know what a damsel is. I would just say 'a white female, five feet eight inches, one hundred and thirty pounds with black hair and brown eyes.'" And nice breasts. A narrow waist. Sweet hips, an incredible butt and legs that stretched all the way up to her eyebrows.

He wondered if she would object to the weight he'd guessed—he'd learned a long time ago on the job that little was more dangerous than guessing a woman's weight and getting it wrong—but any dissatisfaction she might have felt didn't stop her from smiling.

She was so damn beautiful when she smiled.

"You ever forget you're a cop?"

He didn't need to follow her gaze to the pistol on his hip. After so many years, it was second nature. Its absence would be more unusual than its presence. "No. I'm always prepared."

That earned him another smile. "Sometimes I think you like to play the stereotypical jock. Big, dumb, likes to party, all about easy sex and lots of it, not the sharpest knife in the drawer."

"Play?" He drank from his mug, watching her over the rim.

"Yeah, *play*. As in 'pretend to be.' You're a lot smarter, a lot more mature and empathetic, than you want people to believe. You cultivate this image, and not very many people get past it."

What did it say for a forty-year-old man that being called mature and empathetic was one of the best compliments he'd ever been given? And considering its source... Sweet damnation, Martine considered him mature. Nothing she could have said—not even *Let's get out of these clothes and into bed*—could have made him feel better.

"It's not an image so much," he admitted, dragging his fingers through his hair, "as who I really was. It took me a while to grow up. I'm an only son in a family that loves its daughters but really loves its sons. I was top ranked in football in high school. I played college ball for four years. I've been a cop for eighteen years, and just like football, the job has its groupies. Things have always come pretty easy, and I've always been... shallow, except when it comes to my job."

That wasn't as easy to admit as he'd thought it would be. It wasn't as if she didn't already *know* he'd had about as much emotional depth as a puddle after a rainstorm. She'd spent six years hating him because of it. Still, the words were tougher to say out loud than he'd expected. If things didn't feel so damn right between them, he wasn't sure he could have gotten them out.

She leaned over to set her coffee on the floor, then rested one arm on the back of the sofa, her cheek pressed against her fist. Her hair fell forward over one shoulder, catching and reflecting the light from the fire. "What did you major in in college?"

"Football and sex." It was a flippant answer that came as naturally to him as breathing. Immediately, though, he relented. "General studies. Liberal arts. Not that I'm particularly liberal about anything."

"Except sex." There was a lightness to her voice, like none of that mattered anymore. It stirred something in his gut, hard and hot, and sent a flush through his body as if the temperature in the room had soared.

He set his own coffee down, too, not trusting his hands to remain steady. Not wanting them busy doing anything else. "I used to be. Not anymore." His voice was husky and thick and no steadier than his nerves that had gone tingly. Like the shock touching the doorknob of the shop gave him, only magnified a million times.

"I believe you."

"I'm honored." He was, too. He'd wanted her, been intrigued by her, for so long, but after that disastrous night, he'd thought he didn't stand a snowflake's chance in hell. He was sorry it had taken two murders and death threats against her to undo the damage he'd done back then, but he believed something good always came out of the bad. Martine could be his good, and he could be hers.

"Did you ever want to play pro ball?"

"Nah. Football's too hard on the body after a time, and I didn't want to spend half my year living, playing or practicing someplace else. New Orleans is home. And I wanted to be a cop. I just had to get a degree to make my parents happy first."

"And making your parents happy was important?"

"They deserved a little payback for all the time, money and frustration I cost them."

Had she moved a little closer? It seemed so, but he couldn't say for sure because somehow, he was closer, too, and he couldn't remember leaning away from the sofa arm behind him. But there was definitely less than a full cushion between them now, and even that distance disappeared as she shifted onto her knees, then leaned over him.

She wrapped her arms around his neck and touched

her mouth to his with no hesitation, no slow buildup, no uncertainty at all. Her tongue slid along between his lips, then dipped inside his mouth and stroked. Hell, yes, it had definitely gotten warmer in the room, like closing-in-on-the-sun at supersonic speed, and his clothes had turned heavy, trapping heat and constraining everything flowing through him all at the same time.

He wasn't dumb, she'd told him, but for an instant, he felt it. His muscles were taut, his synapses firing constantly, and his brain was so overwhelmed, its orders were muddled. Hold her? Touch her? Kiss her? Tear her clothes off? Carry her off into the bedroom or just trade places with her on the couch?

Or relax and enjoy?

Oh, yeah, that sounded good. Relax as much as he could with a raging hard-on and enjoy it even when the pleasure left him broken into a whole lot of pieces of happy nothingness.

His hands shifted to rest on her spine, one at the base of her neck, the other low on her back. Even through her clothing, the contact felt unreasonably intimate. When they got undressed, when he could touch her bare skin, nothing between them anymore, no anger, no smugness, no misunderstandings...

Finally she made the last small move he'd been waiting for, sinking down, taking her weight from her knees, her body stretching the length of his, her hips cradling his erection, her breasts pressed against his chest, the pleasure of her desire crashing hard against the pain of his.

Sliding his hands upward, he skimmed them beneath her shirt, over the soft skin of her back, higher to the barrier of her bra, then back down again. They resumed their upward movement on the outside of her shirt, not stopping until he'd reached her ponytail. Even with his eyes closed, he didn't fumble over the clasp that held it, tossing it aside and letting her hair fall, long and silken over his hands. He stroked it, caressed it, then laid his palms flat against her head, held her still and took control of the kiss, plunging in his tongue to fill her mouth.

She whimpered softly, not in complaint or protest, and when she glided her hands along his body to his groin, he groaned far less softly.

Wriggling together, they were working their way into a prone position on the sofa when his cell phone rang. Martine's breath caught—hard to miss when his tongue was in her mouth—and her body, for an instant, was as rigid as his own before she pushed herself up onto her arms. The intrusion, both of the phone and the unwelcome memories it brought, washed over him like an ice bath, stopping his heart midbeat, making his hands shake. No, damn it, not this time... He'd waited so long...

The phone rang again, and suddenly her body went all soft again, pressing against him in the most sensitive places. A smile that was part frustration and part sly touched her lips before she pressed a chaste kiss to his mouth, then pushed herself off the couch. "See if you need to answer that," she said, raising her hands to the buttons of her black shirt. She undid one, then two, then three, head ducked, hair falling across her face, before catching his stunned gaze and smiling. "I'll wait for you in the bedroom."

Skimming through the rest of the buttons, she

slid the shirt off her arms, let it fall to the floor and walked—sauntered—sashayed—away before he had a chance to notice much more than the bright orange of her bra and the smooth brown of all that skin.

He had to roll onto his side to work his cell from his pocket and to grind out a nongreeting. "This better be important."

"Some information came in on your missing heart case." It was Steve Lawson, one of the detectives on shift.

Jimmy rubbed the back of his neck, his frustration subsiding. Nothing else was, thankfully. "Text it or email it to me, will you? Just don't call me the rest of the night."

"Aw, DiBiase's committing assault with a friendly weapon," Lawson said in an aside, and in the background a couple of people snickered.

"You guys ever gonna grow up?"

"That's rich, coming from Detective Peter Pan. Check your email when you're done. What'll that be? Five minutes?"

"Screw you, Lawson." He hung up before any of the guys could respond and left the phone on the kitchen counter on his way to the bedroom.

The only light in the room came through the windows, dampened by the screen that kept peepers from seeing in while still allowing a view out, and it all seemed to gather on Martine, standing beside the bed.

All those years ago, she'd been sort of a challenge: something he'd wanted and expected to get. Like he'd told her, everything had come easily...until her. His untrustworthiness had turned her into an opportunity missed, one that he'd regretted ever since. But here she was. With him. Wearing jeans and socks and frilly bits of silly orange lace that would soon be gone.

Here she was, giving him another chance, not just for great sex but everything he'd wanted...and some things he hadn't even known he wanted.

God help him, he wouldn't screw it up this time.

Warm air drifted over Martine's bare skin—so much of it—as the central heat kicked on, chasing away the goose bumps on her arms but doing nothing to settle the butterflies in her stomach. She wasn't new to standing naked, or partly so, in front of a man— her sex life was a healthy one—but something about this felt new.

It wasn't the gorgeous apartment. She'd dated men with money before. It wasn't the fact that her body wasn't quite as toned and firm now as it had been ten or even five years ago. She was growing older as graciously as she could. It wasn't even all those years of hostility and yearning and anger she'd harbored for Jimmy.

It was this moment. The yearning now. The need. The intensity. The seriousness of it. The not-just-sexness of it. The he-was-getting-too-important-ness of it. It was wanting to please him and wanting to please herself and being oh, so grateful that doing one would naturally accomplish the other.

She let her gaze slide over him: his dark hair still mussed from running his hand through it; the familiar devilish and sly and boyish and charming gleam in his eyes; the stubble on his jaw that indicated a long day; the navy T-shirt, bearing a large gold star and crescent of the New Orleans Police Department's badge, that stretched broad across his chest but clung to his flat stomach; the faded jeans that clung everywhere, and quite impressively. "No phone?"

He shook his head. "I left it out there. I told them if they called back, I'd shoot 'em." As he spoke, he lifted his shirt on the right side and removed his pistol from the holster, skirting around her to lay it on the night table next to a Taser and a canister of pepper spray.

She reined in her smile but couldn't help the easy, light tone to her voice. "Is that it on the weapons?"

"Depends on your definition of 'weapon.'"

"You are ready for everything," she teased. "You happen to have any condoms?"

"Somewhere."

"Don't bother looking." She took off her own Taser and pepper spray, added them to his, then reached into her hip pocket to remove a sleeve of condoms. "I come prepared, too."

Finally he moved toward her, and all the warmth she'd felt a few moments ago disappeared, chased away by the shivers racing through her. These were good shivers, though, the kind that promised delight and satisfaction, the kind she would never grow tired of.

He reached her with four steps, but instead of pulling her close for a hard kiss, as she expected, he stood a bit away, raised his hand and touched her cheek with a gentleness that humbled her. "You're an amazing woman, Tine."

She forced back the lump rising in her throat, blinked back sudden moisture in her eyes and, when his fingertips skimmed close to her mouth, she caught his hand, guided it to her mouth and pressed a long, slow damp kiss to his palm.

His free hand cradled her nape and pulled her against him, while his right hand reached lower on her spine, to the thin closure of her bra. With her hips pressed to his, his arousal seemed even more impressive, and she couldn't deny that the silly woman who still peeked out from her brain from time to time was amused by his one-handed dexterity with bra closures. A moment of subtle movements, and the garment fluttered, shifted downward until the straps caught on her shoulders.

"Oh, you're good at that," she murmured before he took her mouth. She slid the straps off and let it fall, nibbled at his tongue, then began exploring his still fully clothed body. The shirt was soft, like an old favorite, but not as soft as the skin it covered. Living art, an expansive canvas that invited her to touch rigid muscles, sensitive nerves, the network of bone that drew her hands downward. *The collarbone connected to the rib bone, the rib bone connected to the hip bone, the hip bone connected to the pelvic bone* and… Hallelujah. She was a happy girl.

Groaning, he shifted his hips out of her reach, so she grabbed handfuls of his shirt and began peeling it upward, forcing them both to break the kiss or be strangled in the process. She stared at him, her thoughts too chaotic with emotion, at the small knot of scars on his right shoulder, at another scar that ran across his biceps, at the gorgeous even tint of his skin and the way it stretched across his rib cage and dipped low over his abs.

"You forgot to say that you're handsome as sin," she murmured, her hands touching here, gliding there, savoring over there. "That's the biggest reason women were so easy. The money helped, the football and the badge, too, but being so damn gorgeous with that naughty-boy grin was the icing on the cake."

He rested his forehead against hers, his gaze heavy and all-seeing at such proximity. "It truly surprised me to find out that not all women—namely you—found my naughty-boy grin charming."

"At this moment…" Her voice was fading as drawing air into her constricted lungs became harder. "…I'm sure I would find everything about you totally charming if we could just get out of these clothes."

It was if she'd unknowingly discovered the magic words to send him from languidly touching and kissing and looking to stripping off his own clothes with breathtaking speed. He took a moment longer with hers, undoing the button and the zipper on her jeans, pulling the flaps of denim away from her body to glimpse inside, then yanking everything off as efficiently as he'd done with his own.

"I've never been with a woman wearing orange panties," he said with a broad grin as said panties sailed across the room inside her jeans. "Come Mardi Gras, we'll have a private party—you in those panties and bra and me in nothing. I'll even give you beads if you show me your breasts."

Mardi Gras. That was the end of February, not even two months away. Would they be together then?

Not the time to think about it, her rational mind decided. Damn sure not the time to wonder if she would even be alive then. This was now, and she was going to make the absolute best of it.

Without a frame, the bed sat lower to the floor, and when Jimmy took hold of her shoulders to lower her back, her breath caught at the falling sensation. A foot above the mattress, he let go and let her fall, and she bounced on the shades-of-blue quilt with a laugh. The mattress bounced again as he joined her, but his mouth on hers stopped her laughter, and his body over hers sent shivers and need rushing through her. In bed, there was always time for play, but right now, with fire dancing in her stomach, with hunger long too unsatisfied burning through her and his dark eyes stark with that nothing-matters-but-you look, playtime was over.

When he knelt between her knees, plastic crinkled beneath her hip. She groped blindly for the string of condoms, tore off one packet before throwing the others aside, then smiled her sweetest, most innocent smile. She pushed up, and he obligingly rolled until he was on his back and she was kneeling just a few inches below where she needed to be. "Let me put this where it goes—" she drew her fingers over the length of his erection "—and then I've got a promise to keep."

She was going to ruin him for other women.

And herself for other men.

For the rest of their lives.

Nothing could wear a man out like a long week at work, days spent mostly with Martine and nights spent mostly worrying, thinking, wanting her, besides a couple of hours of impressively good sex. Jimmy lay on his stomach, the pillow he hugged underneath his head nothing compared with the silky skin he'd been touching and tasting and just looking his fill of. He was pretty sure, if he had a bit of artistic talent, he could draw a perfect replica of her perfect body, with every bump, birthmark and pore exactly in place. That was how intently he'd studied her.

She lay on her back, her hair spread over the other pillow, her cheeks flushed, her smile radiant. Sex was a great pastime—no one would ever get an argument on that from him—but sex with someone special was... well, special.

So much for Martine thinking he was smarter than he let on. Blame it on his oxygen- and blood-deprived brain. That part of him was still processing the fact that Martine had actually had sex with him, that she'd given him a second chance, that she was looking at him as if third and fourth and endless chances might be forthcoming.

Don't get too ambitious, buddy. You might act like a kid, but you're still forty. Those all-night workouts are a thing of the past. Though if anyone could bring them back into the present, it would be Martine.

She turned onto her side, bunching the pillow under her head, and gazed at him. "If I'd known you had a thing for orange lingerie, I would have worn it sooner."

"If *I'd* known I had a thing for it. For what it's worth, pink works, too. Red. Yellow. Green. Purple. Brown. Black. White. Beige."

"So, basically, every color known to man."

He wrapped a tendril of her hair around his finger, taking care to not pull. "Every color known to this man. And all the millions I have no clue about."

"So...was it worth the wait?"

Letting her hair uncurl, he moved his hand to her stomach, caressing with just the tips of his fingers across her concave belly, up to her breasts with their sensitive nipples, over her hip bones and lightly, just

barely, between her legs. "Haven't I stroked your...
ego enough tonight?"

With the pause, he penetrated the damp curls and
made her breath catch, sending hundreds of little quiv-
ers along her nerves. She caught his hand, lifted it
away and pressed a kiss to his wrist. "That wasn't the
reward I had in mind."

"Reward?" He grinned. "I like rewards."

"Was it worth a piece of warm apple pie with vanilla ice cream in bed?"

His grin gave way to laughter. Martine had a weak-
ness for apple pie. That was going to make life easy
when he needed a quick apology, a little persuasion or
just a little treat to give. A man could find good apple
pie anywhere.

"It deserves the whole damn pie. Stay here, and
I'll get it." He kissed her and swung his feet over the
side of the bed just as his cell phone rang. He sighed.

"At least their timing is better." Martine slid up to
lean against the headboard, the sheet tucked under her
arms. She was the prettiest sight he'd ever seen.

He tugged on his boxers, then headed down the
hall, snatching up the phone as the next ring started.
"Didn't I say don't call me again tonight?"

Lawson responded, "Hey, we gave you a couple
hours. Even you can get laid in that amount of time.
Besides, we're working. Why shouldn't you?"

He glanced down the hall, where he'd pulled the
bedroom door until it was almost closed. The sound
of water came faintly from behind it. Martine was
in the master bath. He turned on the speaker, set the
phone on the counter next to the stove and got the ice
cream from the freezer. "Oh, I don't know. Because

I put in all my hours for the week and already made a good start on next week's hours?" After peeling off the plastic lid from the pie, he plated two large pieces and popped them into the microwave. "What's up?"

"We got something new on your lonely heart case."

"Don't call it that."

"That NCIS agent—"

"The cute one," another voice chimed in. Detective Petitjohn.

"The cute one that you didn't used to be married to," Lawson clarified. "She called it the lonely heart case, and you know it fits. Poor heart out there, wondering where the hell its body got off to. Besides, all good serial killers need a name of some sort."

The microwave dinged, and Jimmy removed the hot bowls and started spooning up ice cream. "Forget the name. What about the case?"

"A woman took her dog out for a walk a little bit ago. He ran off into the woods and came back chewing on something."

Petitjohn took over. Jimmy had never met a detective, himself included, who didn't like having his say in a conversation. "This woman's a surgical nurse, and she recognized it right away as a human heart. Your victim's, we assume. We got no shortage of heartless killers around here, but yours is the only heartless victim at the moment."

A soft rustle came from behind him, a sound Jimmy couldn't identify. He spun around and saw Martine, wearing the white button-down shirt he'd tossed on the bathroom counter after work and leaning heavily against the doorjamb where her legs had apparently given way. Grief and revulsion etched deep lines into her face, and the blood that had drained left her so pale, he thought she might faint.

Damn it. Dropping the spoon, he took a step toward her, but she backed away.

"They cut out her heart? Her *heart*?" Horror echoed through the words and showed on her face and in the crumpling lines of her body. She sagged, and he lunged for her, catching her on the way to the floor, sinking with her the last few inches.

As he lifted her into his lap and wrapped his arms around her, Lawson's voice came distantly. "Uh, look, sounds like you have your hands full. We just, uh, thought you'd want to know. Later, man."

He assumed the phone went silent, but he couldn't tell because Martine's panicked attempts to draw a full breath were too painful to separate out any other sounds. He held her snugly and stroked her tousled hair back from her face. "Breathe, darlin'. Just focus on that, one slow breath... That's good, Tine, now take one more... Breathe a little deeper this time... That's it, sweetheart."

Unlike most men, he had a natural talent for dealing with distraught women. Being big brother to two drama princesses had given him a good start, and his job had taught him the rest. He'd never been the sort of cop who stood by stoically while a victim or family member broke down and wished for a female officer to deal with them. He knew the value of a touch, a hug, a hand to hold and a few quiet words.

The floor was hard and cold, and the air was still, carrying a hint of cooling apple pie. After a few minutes of rasping breaths, Martine grew quieter, but shudders racked through her. Somehow, the fact that he felt her sobs more than heard them made them that much worse, as if she couldn't find the strength inside to give them voice.

He couldn't guess how long she cried. Long enough for his butt to go numb, for the muscles in his arms and legs to get stiff from the awkward position. Long enough to drain whatever energy she had, but nowhere near long enough to find any real comfort.

When her body grew still and her tears subsided, he continued to stroke her hair. "I didn't intend to tell you. It's information the public doesn't need to know, and I knew it would..." *Break your heart*, he'd been about to say. "It would be too much to hear about someone you loved. I'm sorry you found out, and I'm sorry you found out this way."

She lifted her head an inch or two so she could see him. Exhaustion and revulsion etched lines into her face. "Is there any good way—" a hiccup interrupted her "—to find out your friend's heart was cut from her body after she died?"

By sheer will, Jimmy kept his muscles from contracting. *Don't ask, don't ask, please, God, don't let her ask.* He didn't think he could tell her that Paulina hadn't been dead when the killer started carving. She was too shaken. Learning that her friend didn't die a relatively easy death from blunt force trauma to the head but instead was butchered alive was too much for her to take in at one time.

Was there ever a good time?

Her head sagged against his shoulder again. She shifted, wiping away dampness from her cheeks, then switched her focus again to breathing. The tremors slowly faded, and her muscles very slowly relaxed.

For a long time, she was so quiet that he thought she might have fallen asleep. Her week had been as long and stressful as his, her evening as energetic and cathartic. Now all he had to figure out was how to get his feet under him and stand up without jarring her too much, then carry her to bed.

Ten years ago, he could have done it without much effort. Tonight, just thinking about it made him consider the possibility of sleeping on the tile floor, uncomfortable as it was.

Before he'd moved, she pressed her cheek harder against him. "When I asked you if Paulina's death was related to Callie's, you said yes. That the details of the cases matched. Does that mean Callie also...?"

Her voice was soft and weary, and it fueled the rage deep inside him. He hated people so bitter, so angry with the world, that they thought they had the right to destroy other people's lives. No parent or spouse or child should ever have to know that someone took their loved one's life for any reason. If Irena Young or whoever the hell had committed these murders couldn't bear to live as long as her victims did, then she should have damn well killed herself. Problem solved.

"Yes."

"So this person who wants me dead...he intends to remove my heart, too." She raised her hand protectively to her chest, as if she were saluting a flag. "Promise me you won't let that happen. I'm very attached to this heart, and I really don't think I could bear losing it. I know I'd be dead and wouldn't know it, but please, Jimmy..." Her tone edging closer to hysterical with each word she spoke, she clamped her jaws shut, keeping any other plea inside.

He laid his own hand over hers. "I won't, Tine. I swear on my life."

She breathed, then nodded, but it was clear she didn't entirely believe him. He couldn't even take offense. He could promise her anything, and he could mean it with his heart and soul and even his life.

But that didn't mean he could force it to come true.

He would do his damnedest, though. Or die trying.

Chapter 9

The rest of the night and Saturday morning passed in a blur for Martine. She woke to a dark gray sky, rolled over and went back to sleep, snuggling against Jimmy's body. The next time she woke, the sky was light but still dreary and Jimmy was gone from the bed. She slid into the depression where he had lain, faintly warm and smelling of his cologne, and fell asleep again with her head on his pillow.

The third time she woke, she felt thickheaded, as if she'd closed down a few Bourbon Street bars all on her own. Her body ached, and her stomach was so empty that it was distressing her brain. Her eyes were too puffy and sore to make out the numbers on the bedside clock, but she thought there were only three, so it was past noon, not yet night.

She needed a shower. A toothbrushing. A delete

button on her brain to clear out ugly memories she would never forget.

Paulina, Callie, I'm so sorry. I never should have let things end the way they did.

They *walked away from* you, her internal voice reminded her. They *forgot* you.

Sliding to the edge of the bed, she rubbed her empty stomach and decided the one thing she needed most of all: Jimmy. She didn't care that she looked like she'd tested her hair in hurricane-force winds or that yesterday's makeup was smeared and clumped or wiped off completely. She just wanted to feel his presence. Just wanted to feel safe.

Leaving his bedroom, she tiptoed around to the guest room for warm socks and fuzzy slippers. On impulse, she grabbed a pair of leggings and squirmed into them, then proceeded to the living room. The logs were ablaze again in the fireplace, and the central heat spread warmth to the spaces too far for its reach. But being this cold from the inside out, she wasn't likely to warm up very fast.

Jimmy had pulled three empty boxes over to form a table in front of the couch and was studying papers, notes, photographs and such from the files spread out. She was careful not to look at any of them. She didn't want to see anything her brain wasn't ready for.

He sat back and watched her circle the boxes to join him. She would have sat at the opposite end, but when he extended his hand, she grasped it tightly and let him pull her down next to him. For a long time he just looked at her, then he gently combed his fingers through her hair, undoing some tangles. "You okay?"

"I'll survive." It was the most hopeful answer she

could give and had the added benefit of being true. She *was* going to survive this thing. She might never be the same person again, but she would, at least, *be*.

Jimmy maneuvered them until he was leaning back against the sofa arm and she was tucked up close. She liked being so close.

"The temperature is in the forties today, so the rest of the snow should be gone soon. Jack's back in town and grumpy after spending so much time with his fugitive. I saved you a piece of apple pie, but first you've got to eat something. Breakfast, lunch, your choice."

Even though her first thought was to turn down food, her stomach growled so loudly, it would have been a refusal nobody believed. "How about toast?" She could keep dry white toast down, right?

"How do you want your egg? Scrambled or fried? Over-medium or -hard? I'll warn you, I don't do over-easy. The goop on top is just gross."

"Toast will be fine."

"I'll make it over-hard so the yolk doesn't drip. What kind of cheese do you want? We have Swiss, cheddar, gruyere, pepper jack, provolone..." His expression was innocent, as if he wasn't ignoring every word coming out of her mouth.

Since he was sweet enough to care, and she would like to see if he could actually fry an egg properly, and she really was hungry, she relented. "You choose, and I'll eat it."

He kissed her forehead, then brushed his mouth across hers before standing. "While you wait, you might want to..." One hand circled in the general area of her face, which she took to mean *Wash your face, brush your teeth, get your hair under control.*

Okay, so when she returned to the bathroom, she looked all ready for Halloween. She took a shower, scrubbed her face and brushed her teeth twice before dressing in the leggings again and a red sweater. Underneath she wore a matched set of violet lace lingerie.

Wonderful aromas filled the air when she went back to the living room: fried eggs, melted cheese, artisanal bread and coffee. Jimmy was on the couch again, and he'd cleared a space on the boxes for her meal. She sat on the hearth instead, savoring the heat of the fire, the buttery warmth of the toasted egg-and-cheese sandwich and the sight of him, in disreputable jeans and another NOPD T-shirt. Even though he hadn't shaved, even though his hair stood on end, he was the most beautiful man she'd ever known.

The first bite of sandwich made her moan softly. "The man can cook," she murmured to herself, but his grin showed he didn't need to hear the words to understand the compliment. She polished off the sandwich far too quickly for good manners and drained half her coffee before wiping her hands on a napkin and gazing at him. He was sorting through papers, making notes in that cramped little style of his.

After a moment, he looked up. "Are you ready for the apple pie?"

"Not yet." With her backside blazing warm, she shifted along the hearth, propping her feet on the stone so they could get warm, too. "Is there anything new you can tell me?"

He put his ratty notebook down and raised his arms high above his head in a tension-relieving stretch. Lacing his fingers together, he rested both hands on the back of his head, propped his feet on the corner of a box and sighed. "Everything I've got on Irena Young is a dead end. If she's worked since her mother's death, it's been under a different social security number or she's gotten paid off the books. She still has the same cell phone, according to the provider, but hasn't made a single call since the week after her mother's death, and it's rarely turned on. Those calls went to family back in Idaho, but they say they haven't talked to her since and don't know where she is or what she's doing. She hasn't updated the address on her Louisiana driver's license, but she doesn't have a license from any other state, either."

That was a sad way to live: having no contact with her family, no friends, apparently no one who mattered in her life beyond her mother. Martine loved her mom dearly, but even Bette, with her larger-than-life personality, wasn't enough to fill up all that space. Where would she be without friends, coworkers, acquaintances and lovers?

"Her father's out of the picture, too. He moved down south—way south, like Panama or Colombia—when he retired and hasn't been back to the States since. The Marquitta police can't find anyone there who maintained contact with Irena or Katie Jo after the murder. There were no identifiable fingerprints on the letters or the pictures, no saliva from licking the envelopes, no spores or microbes or anything." He loosed his hands and shrugged. "We've got a lot of nothing."

Warm enough at last, Martine left the hearth to curl up on the sofa. "What—" Nausea rose in her stomach, but she forced it down again and steadied her voice the best she could. "What will they do with—with Paulina's—her—"

Compassion and tenderness—two things she'd never thought the superficial Jimmy capable of—softened his gaze. "Her heart?"

She nodded.

"DNA will confirm that it's hers. Then her husband will have the option of having the coroner's office dispose of it, or it can be returned to her body for burial, or he can have it cremated. Her funeral is scheduled for the early part of next week, and the results probably won't be back by then. I don't know if he'll delay it or have the heart placed later or what."

Logically, Martine knew Paulina was beyond caring that her heart was gone. Emotionally, she couldn't imagine her friend's spirit feeling anything but distress. How could she rest in peace without her heart?

Wrapping her arms around her knees, she contained the tiny shivers passing through her before they could grow in intensity. Forcing her thoughts away from that one terrible point, she quietly said, "I can't go, can I?"

Jimmy shook his head. "A lot of killers attend their victims' services. The local police will be there. They'll photograph everyone at the church and the cemetery. You'll have to look at the pictures to see if you recognize anyone."

Her smile was sad. "I barely recognized Paulina herself. Tallie, of course, will look a lot like Callie. Robin... Irena... Only as long as they haven't changed very much."

Or they could be looking for someone else. Someone she would never expect to find in the photos. Someone she'd forgotten or hardly known, someone she might not have known at all. If she had known him, he couldn't possibly be the same. Surely whatever led him to such horrific actions against girls he'd known would have left some sort of mark on his spirit and his soul, if not his face. And if she didn't know him, she would be worse than useless to Jimmy.

It was a good thing he wanted more than just information from her.

She hoped he wanted everything she had to give.

It was shortly after three when the doorman called up to announce a visitor. Jimmy cleared him, and a few minutes later, Jack rang the bell. Proving the meteorologists right, his only jacket was a hoodie, and he carried a stack of files and a folding chair, kept handy in his vehicle for cookouts and the kids' soccer games.

"Look, he hasn't even seen the place and he brings along his own chair," Martine teased.

Jack snorted. "He hasn't had enough furniture since that time we were moving him when two patrol officers tried to stack the armchairs and make it down the steps in one trip, and they dropped them from the third-floor landing."

"Would it have killed them to climb the stairs twice?" Jimmy asked.

"In that neighborhood, quite possibly." Jack tossed the files on the table, unfolded the chair nearby, then bent to hug Martine. "You haven't hurt him yet. I'm proud of your restraint. How are you?"

"I'm okay."

It wasn't a ringing endorsement, with a sort of woefulness to it, but Jimmy knew Jack would accept it as the best they could expect. Being an intended victim wasn't easy. Jimmy was proud of her for managing that much.

"I'll get some coffee—"

Martine interrupted. "I'll do that. You guys do all your ugly-part discussion while I'm out of the room." She rose, squeezed his hand as she passed as casually as if Jack's presence didn't change anything. Being just one more of Jimmy's girlfriends, especially in front of his cop friends, wasn't always easy, either. Expectations for them were usually pretty low.

Jack made only one dry comment. "You know, if you hurt her, you're going to have my wife to answer to."

"I'm not afraid of your wife."

"You should be."

Reclaiming his seat on the couch, Jimmy glanced at Martine, her back to them in the kitchen, lowered his voice and caught Jack up on everything they'd learned—or not learned—during his absence.

Jack hadn't been idle, either. Snowed in in Nebraska, he'd had plenty of time for phone calls, internet searches and records requests, and he'd taken on Jimmy's least favorite task: investigating the subjects' financial backgrounds. He had a lot of printouts, but nothing that grabbed for attention. They might still miss information that would make sense of it all. They might have it and just not got the pieces together properly. Or they might never get it all.

That was an outcome Jimmy couldn't accept.

"I kept trying to get hold of Callie Winchester's parents, and their lawyer finally called last night," Jack started. "The Winchesters are grieving the loss of their daughter. They have nothing to tell us that could possibly help in our investigation, and the subject of their daughter Tallie is strictly off-limits, for her own protection. She's somewhere safe. On what continent, he wouldn't say. He has no clue whether her parents have been in contact with any of the other parents, and he has no intention of asking them."

That seemed about right for the people who'd lived in the pretentious house at the end of the Broussards' street. "I've never understood families who won't do everything they possibly can to find their child's murderer."

"If everyone did things the way a reasonable person expects, we'd be out of a job, James. Unlike you, most of us need it."

"I need it," Jimmy protested. "If I was phased out, I'd have to move back home, where they'd probably make me handyman and security guard for the house. The kids would make me a badge from cardboard covered with aluminum foil, and my parents would drive me stark-raving mad urging me to get married, have kids and carry on the family name."

"There's a lot to be said for marriage and kids."

Jimmy resisted the urge to look in Martine's direction or give any hint that he was even vaguely interested in how their future looked. It was a long-standing joke at work that certain words had never been in his vocabulary, like *forever. Commitment. Monogamy. Fidelity.* When he and Alia had gotten married, his fellow officers had started a pool on how long it would last, and not one of them had given it more than a year.

He regretted that he'd been so immature and easy to read.

"Is it safe to come back?" Martine asked from the kitchen.

"Sure." Jimmy murmured, "She's a little squeamish about the heart."

"Who the hell isn't?"

Martine carried a sterling tray, ornately decorated and heavy enough to give a fifteen-year-old boy a concussion, as Dani and Becca had found out in a practical joke gone wrong. Jimmy had been the one injured, and also the one punished since the joke had been his. He'd never again sneaked up on the girls late at night when there was metalware within reach.

After they'd fixed their coffees, she asked, "Are you done with the ugly stuff, or do I need to leave the room?"

Jimmy didn't want her to go. Though she couldn't possibly be safer than she was at the moment, he felt more comfortable being able to see her. "You already know pretty much everything." Except that both hearts had been removed while the victims were still alive, and he'd already warned Jack of that.

Jack gave her a moment to get settled on the couch before he started. "I did a lot of checking into finances while I was in Omaha. What do you remember about the different families' money status when you were kids?"

Martine blinked blankly. "I don't know I ever thought about it. We all lived in the same neighborhood, though the Winchesters' house was definitely the biggest and nicest and Robin's house was kind of small. We couldn't have sleepovers there because it was too crowded, and she didn't really ever invite us. Her parents were nice enough, but they didn't socialize much with our parents except holidays or parties. Mom and Paulina's and the twins' moms had lunch every other Tuesday, and our dads played golf every weekend, but not the Raileys."

"Was she ever left out of your activities because of money issues?"

Jimmy looked up from his notebook—he was the dedicated note taker in this partnership—and watched Martine's gaze go thoughtful. Were Jack's instincts pointing to Robin? Jimmy was open to any suspect, preferably one they could stop, and Robin was as good a candidate as any, though she needed a motive. Maybe she'd never felt as much a member of the group as the others had. Maybe she still harbored some jealousy or anger toward them.

It was scary to think how little things that happened as kids could have such profound effects on people twenty or thirty years later, but he'd seen enough examples of it himself. Jealousy turned to envy turned to resentment turned to bitterness turned to rage, and rage trumped everything, even love.

"There were times she couldn't spend the afternoons with us because she had to work—she had a part-time job to pay for her cheerleading costs—but we did the same things all the time. It wasn't really missing out." Martine hesitated, as if she wanted to say something, even took a breath and opened her mouth, but closed it again right away.

Do you think Robin is the killer? Jimmy would bet that was what she wanted—and didn't want—to know. It was hard to accept that two of her friends had been brutally murdered. Harder still to know the killer wanted to do the same to her. It just might be impossible to believe it was another of her friends who hated them so.

"The Winchesters had a lot of money, didn't they?" Jack asked.

She smiled drily. "When the twins turned sixteen, their parents gave them each a brand-shiny-new convertible. Paulina and Robin and me—we were blown away, but their dad just grinned. He couldn't expect them to share a car, now, could he? What was another forty thousand dollars when his girls' happiness was at stake?"

"Damn," Jack muttered. "Jackson and my girls will be lucky if I allow them to leave the house by themselves when they're sixteen."

One of the downsides of police work: a cop knew better than anyone the danger lurking in the outside world. A cop who was a parent couldn't help but make some of it personal: *What if that was my kid?* And it extended beyond that. Too often the last couple of days, when Jimmy remembered the sight of Paulina lying dead in the cemetery, he wondered, *What if that becomes Martine?*

It wouldn't. Couldn't. Jimmy DiBiase didn't fail, and Jack Murphy didn't fail, and between the two of them, they *would* keep her safe.

Jack had more questions about Tallie and Callie— their relationship, their spending, their habits, their attitudes. Martine found the conversation surreal. He actually suspected Robin or Tallie of killing Paulina and Callie. She had great admiration for him as a detective, but this time he was wrong. She was certain of it.

Closing her eyes, she called up images of her old friends. Except for the end, their years together had been good times with so much laughter. They were peas in a pod, her father had teased, one personality split between five girls. They had shared meals, clothes, classes, activities, friends, families, experiences. They'd had a sort of conversational shorthand that allowed them to communicate with no more than a look, a word or two, and had led them into adventures and disasters. They had lived such *fun* lives.

Could either of them have become a killer?

It was unfathomable. Even trying to consider it made her stomach clench with revulsion. It had to be Irena Young. Irena didn't know Martine and the others, didn't love them. Or someone else, someone who'd thought he had reason to kill Callie, then had gone after Paulina to misdirect the investigation. Someone who'd never met Paulina or Martine or Robin or even Tallie.

It would still break her heart that Callie and Paulina were dead, but it would be easier to deal with if the real reason had nothing to do with the teenage bond they'd shared.

Was that selfish of her?

Before she could find the answer to that question inside her, she was startled back to the present when Jimmy and Jack both stood. Her knees were drawn up, her hands clasped around her now cold coffee. Jimmy's notebook lay open on the boxes, the one page visible filled with his tiny printing, and Jack's chair was folded, tucked under his arm.

"Give Evie and the kids a hug for me," she said wanly.

He said he would before walking to the door with Jimmy. They talked a moment longer while she gazed into the fire. Uneasiness crept through her like the past week's fog, filling all the empty spaces inside, worse than it had been before Jack's arrival. Sure, Jimmy had considered everyone a suspect but her, but actually being questioned about Robin and Tallie gave the situation a reality she wasn't prepared to accept.

She didn't know if she ever would be.

Jimmy returned, tugging her coffee cup from her hands. He took the empty mugs into the kitchen, then came back a moment later with a bottle of water for each of them. He circled behind the couch, pressing a kiss to the top of her head, then took his seat again at the other end of the couch. "Let's talk."

In her experience, when men said, *Let's talk*, it didn't bode well for the relationship. Either they wanted more than she was willing to give, or they wanted out. Intuitively, she knew Jimmy wanted her to talk, and he would listen, and then he would offer what comfort he could. Gratitude warmed her to her core, but it didn't shake the edginess.

She drank from the bottle, then fiddled with the cap before finally meeting his gaze. "Tallie wouldn't kill Callie." She infused the words with all the certainty in her heart, but a few beats later, more words escaped. "Would she?"

"Tallie's lived in London for twelve years. According to the State Department, Callie hasn't been there for more than fifteen years, and Tallie's trips to the US have been few and far between. There wasn't much in the way of phone calls, emails or texts between them, either."

"They're *identical twins*. Two halves of a whole. My mom used to say they lived in each other's back pocket."

"Or each other's shadow."

Martine was an only child who had longed for a sibling until she'd met Paulina, then the others. It was hard for her to think that sisters could be *too* close. And despite the two-halves-of-a-whole bit, they were still people with their own personalities, quirks, weaknesses and passions. Individuals who had been treated as one for the first eighteen years of their lives.

All four of them had cut Martine off without a word. Was it so unlikely that the sisters had had a falling-out, as well?

And what about Robin? Had she felt like she was in the shadows, too? That somehow she didn't measure up to the rest of them because her parents didn't have as much money? Had she resented them without their even knowing it?

Her head ached from the rounds of no-she-couldn't and maybe-she-could-have. Switching the water to her other hand, she pressed her palm to her forehead, letting the cool dampness left from the bottle ease her heated skin.

Her sigh was soft and tired. "You know what? I'd like to have one hour where I don't have to think about anything from the past."

Jimmy's grin was smug and sweet. "Take those clothes off, and I'll give you two."

"You're so charming."

"Hey, I think that's a pretty good offer. You get naked, and I give you two hours of fun and forgetfulness."

"Sadly, I think the forgetfulness is the more appealing of the two right now."

He set his water aside and made room for her—a

very small bit of room—beside him. She shifted around and settled between his hard warm body and the back cushions of the couch, and he wrapped his arms around her. For a long time, he just held her and she just savored it, letting her eyes close, her memories shut down, her brain concentrate on nothing but how good he felt and how good she felt with him.

"It'll be okay, Tine." The softness of his voice slid over her, easing muscles and soothing fluttering nerves.

"How do you do it?" Peering through her lashes, she watched him cock his head in question. "How do you spend every single workday with people at the worst time of their lives without letting hopelessness and despair take over your own life?"

He didn't have a pat answer, as she'd expected. Instead, he gave it a few moments' thought. "I have an occasional drink. I have good friends. I have great sex. From time to time, I go a little bit crazy for a few days. Then I get back to it." His shrug flowed through his body and into hers. "Someone's got to do it, Tine. It might as well be me. I'm good at it."

"You see so much ugliness."

"And a lot of good. And I do some good."

She rested her cheek against his chest, absorbing the quiet *thud-thud* of his heart. *Someone* had to do every tough job: care for babies whose lives were destined to be short; hold the hands of elderly patients as they passed from this world; fight fires and wars; advocate for abused children; counsel victims who lived; autopsy those who died, and find the persons responsible.

She couldn't be that *someone*. Put her in the shop, with its tourist- and voodoo-related items, and she was great. Ask her to do something so vital as heal, touch, love, grieve, protect, defend and find justice for those who couldn't do it for themselves, she would get lost in the darkness and never find her way out again.

"I'm impressed."

"By what?"

She lifted her head to see if he was serious. He was. "You. Your commitment. Your passion."

Surprise flitted through his eyes, then his expression softened. He raised her hand to his mouth and kissed it in such a gentlemanly fashion that she almost didn't notice the swelling of his erection as he turned onto his side to face her. "Contrary to popular belief, I do know how to commit to something." He settled her hand on his hip, then tilted her face so he could nuzzle her jaw. "And to someone. I may be a jerk, Tine, but I'm trainable, if you'll just give me the chance."

She cradled his cheeks in her hands and kissed him thoroughly before making a show of checking her watch. "It's four forty-five. My two hours start..." The old-fashioned second hand swept, *tick-tick-tick*, around the watch face before finally reaching the twelve.

She gave him a greedy, hungry, needy look and slid her hand down his flat stomach to his groin, making his breath catch, before she said the magic word.

"Now."

She jumped up and dashed away from the couch. "Hey," Jimmy called, scrambling to follow her, catching hold of her narrow waist just as she dived onto the bed. They landed in a tangle of limbs and covers, laughing, pulling at their clothes, struggling to get naked and to get him suited up before the need burned through them like a wildfire. It was fast and hard and funny and touching, and it led to a slower, lazier, easier, harder, damn more intimate second time. It left him feeling...

The Jimmy he'd been most of his life couldn't find words to describe what he felt. The Jimmy he'd been slowly evolving into wasn't sure, either, but was willing to give it a try.

Connected. Lucky. Tender. Protective.
Blessed.

In a culture where *Bless your heart* was an insult as often than not, *blessed* was in his vocabulary, just not used much. His family said the blessing before meals. His sisters' kids sang a song about counting their blessings, and he was on the receiving end of plenty of *bless-yous* when he sneezed.

Looking at Martine, though, lying quiet in his arms, the sweat drying from her body, her hair covering the pillow, her hand lightly resting on his chest, he was definitely feeling blessed.

Her eyes closed, her face sleepy, she murmured, "I heard you tell Jack you aren't afraid of Evie. He was right. You should be. She threatened to put a curse on you that would make your dangly bits shrivel away and ruin you for any other woman."

"Ouch. I hope you asked her not to."

Her eyes opened to bare slits, and a womanly smile curved her mouth. "I told her *I* intend to ruin you for other women."

He kissed her forehead. "You've accomplished that, sweetheart."

She closed her eyes again, but the smile widened as she resettled in silence.

He liked Evie, he thought as he stroked Martine's

silken skin. Even loved her in a sister-who-could-kick-his-ass way. She was fiercely protective of the people in her world. She gave Jack unfailing support, gave the kids unconditional love, gave Jimmy unasked-for but always appropriate advice, and she was the best friend that Martine deserved. The other four had let her down, but not Evie. Jimmy loved her more for that.

Dusk had settled, followed by dark, though it was never really dark in downtown New Orleans. A small snore from his side indicated that Martine had drifted off, and if he closed his eyes for a few minutes, he was pretty sure he could, too. Why not? Security was at their posts downstairs, the door was locked, the alarm was set, and the nightstand was crowded with their weapons. Nothing was going to happen tonight, besides snuggling with Martine and maybe a few more rounds of forgetting, or at least dreaming about it...

The ringing of the cell phone was harsh, out of place. He was dreaming, in the mountains where he vacationed, with tall trees, crisp air, the sun shining brightly, the water of a snow-fed creek tumbling across rocks, and Martine. Why would he take his phone there and leave it turned on? Most days he didn't even have reception there.

Dream-Martine turned to look at him, brows raised questioningly, and real-Martine thumped him with her elbow as she rolled away. "Answer the phone."

Slowly he came out of the dream, saw the lit screen of his cell phone on the table and picked it up. Groggy, much preferring the sunny Colorado mountains over reality, he grunted a greeting.

"Detective DiBiase?"

The voice was familiar. Clearheaded, he would have

no problem putting a face and a name to it, but clear-headed, he was not. "Yeah."

"Sorry for waking you, sir. This is Chaz Jordan."

A patrol officer in the Quarter. Tall, broad shouldered, weight lifter. He would come in handy on Jimmy's next move, and he wouldn't be dropping anything from a third-floor landing. "It's okay, Jordan. What's up?"

"We got a call about a disturbance on Royal Street." He gave the number, and Jimmy's heart missed two or three beats before starting again. "It's nothing big, but someone started a fire on the stoop. The person who called it in poured bottled water on it before it got really going. There are a few scorch marks on the door but nothing a coat of paint can't cover."

"Can you tell what was burned?"

"Pictures. Old ones. I know you've got a case involving the woman who lives here, and she's not answering the door, so I figured I'd let you know."

"Listen, Jordan, can you stay until I get there? It won't be ten minutes."

"Sure. I'll see you."

Jimmy spotted his jeans as he stood, yanked them on, then grabbed his shirt, socks, shoes. The mattress shifted behind him while he pulled on his socks, and Martine bent close. "What happened?"

Damn, he hated that fear in her voice. She couldn't have figured out from his side of the conversation that the call involved her, but she worried anyway.

"It's not a big deal. Someone set a fire on your doorstep. Guy put it out and called the police, and the cop's waiting for me to pick up what's left over." He shoved his feet into running shoes without untying them, tugged his shirt over his head, then started threading his belt through the loops on his jeans.

"I want to go with you."

"Martine—"

"I won't get out of the car. I won't talk to anyone. No one will even notice me. I just… I need to see that everything's okay. Please, Jimmy."

He tried to stand his ground, but it was a losing battle. "It's not fair to ask favors when you're sitting there naked," he grumbled. "You'll stay in the back seat, and I'm locking you in. Give me any trouble, and I'll take you to jail. We've got cells for people like you."

She dressed more quickly than he did, grabbed the Taser and the pepper spray as if she'd been doing it for years, and was in the hallway heading for the door before he finished securing his own weapons. Shaking his head, wishing he could just handcuff her to the bedframe—not that he had a bedframe—he caught up with her at the door where she was putting on her jacket.

He pulled on his own jacket, then grabbed a hoodie from its hanger. It was black, big enough that she could wear it over her coat, bulky enough to add a little camouflage to her slender body. She didn't argue, just slid her arms into the sleeves and stood impatiently while he zipped it, then pulled the hood over her hair, casting her face into shadow.

"If you tie it, I'm going to look like that cartoon kid on TV."

"Kenny. You watch *South Park*? You don't seem the smart-ass bratty-kid type."

Her smile was sarcastic. "My best friends have kids. I pick up popular culture by osmosis."

Holding on to the edges of the hood on both sides, he ducked his head to give her an intense look. "We're taking my department car, and you're seriously riding in the back seat, out of sight, and I really am locking you in when we get there. You good with that?"

She nodded firmly. "I'm good."

The elevator was empty, and no one lingered in the garage, either. The air was cold and muffled sounds from the nearby streets, but it was warmer than it had been that morning. Maybe a normal winter was on its way back to New Orleans. Maybe everything would be back to normal soon.

Except him and Martine. He intended to make these last few days their new normal.

And keep it forever.

His gaze constantly scanning, he opened the rear door of the vehicle so she could slide into the seat, closed it and got behind the wheel. Glancing into the rearview mirror, he cautioned, "Stay out of sight. I don't want the security guards to see you."

Silently she disappeared from view.

Only one guard was at the entrance, the other one probably making rounds. Jimmy acknowledged him with a wave, then turned toward Royal Street.

Jordan's patrol unit was parked in front of Martine's apartment. Jimmy stopped on the opposite side of the street in front of the shop, where shadows would help hide her. This late at night on this particular block, he wasn't concerned about impeding traffic, not that he cared much. "I'll be back."

She didn't reply, move or even, as far as he could tell, take a breath. She was, for all intents and purposes, a ghost.

No. Not a ghost. Just invisible.

Jordan climbed out of his car and met Jimmy at the stoop, carrying a large evidence bag and a pair of gloves. The smell of charred paper lingered in the air, thin and acrid, made sour by the water poured on it.

"Thanks for waiting."

"No problem, Detective."

"Aw, you can call me Jimmy." Rank didn't mean a lot to him. He preferred to be on good terms with everyone, best terms with the officers on the street. They saw things, knew things, that came in damn useful to him. He wasn't about to stand on formalities with someone who would eventually make him look good.

Jimmy pulled on the gloves and felt the top of the pile. The uppermost layers had burned, but beneath were intact photographs, some areas turned to ash, others scorched, edges curling. They were cool to the touch, no dormant flames smoldering underneath.

"Thanks, Detec—Jimmy." Jordan held the bag open. "Is the woman who lives here okay?"

"Yeah. She's staying elsewhere." Jimmy flipped through the top few layers carefully, making note that the pictures appeared older, faded, the subjects young and unaware of what was to come. His brain registered a couple of shots of a teenaged Martine before he carefully scooped up the pile and slid them into the bag. He didn't bother to seal or initial it. Ordinarily, he would take them to the office and study them before logging them in as evidence, but it was the middle of the night. He would take them home, examine them and spread them out so the damp pages could dry thoroughly before he rebagged them. First thing in the morning, he would deliver them to Evidence.

With his hands free, Jordan shined his flashlight on the door. "You can see where a few flames got it, and it looks the paint bubbled a bit, but it's not much. I checked the lock, and it's secure. I also checked the gate to the courtyard and the door to the shop, and they're okay, too." Jordan looked up and down the street, then lowered his voice. "Isn't this part of that murder case—the woman found in the graveyard?"

"Yeah, it is."

"Cool." Immediately an abashed look came over his face. "I mean, damn. Too bad."

Jimmy grinned, remembering a time when he would have traded his next fifty routine calls for just one with a little depth and excitement to it. He followed Jordan's lead and looked from one corner to the other, from one side of the street to the other. When the killer had called Martine Friday morning, she'd stood out here first. Not the first time she'd come there, not the last. But he and Jordan were the only people out. A hundred people could be watching from the windows and doors of the buildings across the way, but the premises concealed them.

The back of his neck prickled as he turned toward the cars. "Thanks a lot, Jordan. I really appreciate it." He crossed the damp pavement in long strides, got in his car and started the engine. When he took a calming breath, he smelled Martine in the light flowery perfume that clung to her skin, in the honey scent of her shampoo and in the faint, barely there essence of fear.

As he drove, his gaze shifted from the street ahead to the rearview mirror, back to the street. He made a series of random turns, circling the block, making absolutely certain no one was following them.

"I assume you don't see any crazies."

Martine's voice came from lower in the back—not the seat itself but the floorboards. He grinned. She'd taken his don't-be-seen admonition to heart.

"Just the one driving this car. We're coming up on the garage entrance." Not only were they not being followed, he had seen very few cars. It seemed everyone was giving the city one more night to get over the snow and cold before they flooded the streets again.

At the gate, he stopped. "Hey, Travers, if you see anything odd—car keeps driving by, someone paying too much attention—let me know, will you?"

The guard, standing in the open doorway of the guard shack, blew on a cup of steaming coffee. "Always, Detective. They got you working late, huh?"

"At least it was a short trip this time." Smiling, listening to the even tenor of Martine's breathing, he drove through the gate and to his space.

Martine stood near the counter, watching as Jimmy, wearing gloves again, meticulously separated the top pictures on the stack, reduced to ash, from half-burned photos in the middle and, at the bottom of the pile, mostly undamaged shots.

When he finished, she counted thirty-five pictures, filled with familiar faces and memories. There were only four of the girls in most of the photos, except for the ones where the camera was handed off to a bystander—usually a boyfriend, a friend or someone eager to be a friend.

Jimmy pulled out his cell phone and took his own pictures of the pictures, no doubt to add to his growing pile of folders. Unlike Jack, who was pretty much all digital, Jimmy liked his evidence the old-fashioned way, in hard-copy form that he could look at, touch, highlight, process in his own way.

He slid onto a stool, then gestured her nearer. "Have you seen them before?"

"I've probably got copies in my storage bin."

"Who's the photographer?"

It was mostly a rhetorical question. It was easy enough to see from the array who was missing from most of the shots. "The camera..." Her hands started to tremble. She clasped them tightly. "It was before cell phone cameras. We all had little dinky versions, of course, but this was a thirty-five-millimeter SLR film camera. Pricey, fun to use, took great pictures. It was... It was Tallie's."

The name hung there in the air as invisible bands tightened around her chest. She forced out the next words with too little air to give them substance. "It doesn't mean it was her. She always got multiple copies and gave them out. Those could be anybody's— Callie's or Robin's or even mine."

"If the killer had stolen them."

But her place was secure; nothing was missing from Paulina's house; and there had been no report of a theft before or after Callie's death. Which left Tallie or Robin.

Martine's knees buckled, and Jimmy grabbed her, lifting her onto the stool next to his. She bent forward, pressing her forehead against her knees, taking rapid breaths that left her feeling light-headed and confused. She needed another hour of forgetfulness—an entire day of it. She was tired of knowing the worst about people she'd loved, suspecting the worst about other people she'd loved. Tired and sick and disillusioned.

Jimmy patted her back until her breathing was under control again, but she could tell when his attention wandered back to the evidence. His shadow shifted over her as he picked up one photo, turned it over and examined it. "This one's thicker than the others. Maybe it's two stuck together or..."

Martine straightened and watched as he pulled the knife from his pocket and gently worked the blade point into one corner, separating one piece of paper from the other. With that start, they came apart easily, each bearing the same wrinkles where they'd connected, but the second piece wasn't a photo.

Thick black letters, like the first message she'd received, were centered on a file card: *It's too late to hide, Tine.*

Jimmy slid to his feet, crossed the living room and rooted through the piles on the makeshift coffee table. He came back with the yearbook, open to the twins' senior pictures, set the notecard on the opposite page and looked at Martine.

The yearbook adviser had insisted on labeling their pictures Callista and Taliesin, and the girls had insisted on inking those names out and writing in Callie and Tallie. The *t*, the *a*, the *l*, *i* and *e* from the card bore an eerie resemblance to Tallie's handwriting in the yearbook.

"How could this happen?" Her voice was small and weak, the same way she felt. "How could so much love turn to that much hate?"

Jimmy didn't answer. What could he say? *I don't know. It just happens. Life gets screwed up.* She could come up with those answers on her own. The only one who might know the truth was Tallie, and it was too late for her to share. The other half of her whole was dead.

Don't meet any other old friends who happen to call, Jimmy had warned Martine a few days earlier. At the time, she'd taken it to mean that the killer might be watching. She much preferred that to the knowledge that the old friend was likely the killer.

Jimmy left the counter again, going to the fireplace. A moment later, blues music drifted into the air from speakers hidden around the apartment. There were no lyrics, just sexy, sweet instrumentals that made her muscles relax and stretch and long to move.

He came back, pulled her to her feet and shut off the light over the pictures, leaving the room illuminated only by the city's lights spilling through the glass wall. She half expected him to lead her toward the bedroom, but instead he wrapped his arms around her, drew her near and slowly, sensuously danced her toward the center of the living room.

"Not too sad for you?" he murmured in her ear.

The raspy sexy sound of his voice drew a smile she couldn't have summoned on her own. "My mother says if dancing to the blues makes you sad, then you're not doing it right."

"I'd like to meet your mother."

Martine rested her head on his shoulder, let him lead her in languorous steps around the gleaming tile floor. Comfort was slowly seeping into her body from his body, from the rustle of the air, from the lament of the saxophones. "You would like her, and she would like you. But I have to warn you, Jack is her favorite man in the entire world."

"Only because she hasn't met me yet. Does she come to town often?"

"When she's stopping off between trips. I'm going to ask her to come soon. While this is incredible—" she nodded to him, then herself "—sometimes…"

"A girl needs her mother."

"Yes." Just the thought of Bette in her bigger-than-life mama-lion mode was enough to bring a tear or two to Martine's eyes. "She'll charm you. She charms the whole world."

"And I'll charm her right back."

Another smile worked its way out. "That'll be a nice change. She hated my ex-husband."

"Parents are supposed to hate their kids' exes. Every time I see Alia's grandparents, they say rude things to me in Vietnamese."

"Do you speak Vietnamese?"

"No. But some things don't need translation."

And there it was—a laugh, when she'd begun to think she might never laugh again. She slid her arms around his neck and left a trail of kisses along his throat before brushing her mouth to his, sighing softly. "I've known you for six years—"

"Five days," he corrected her, and in a very real sense, he was right.

"And I never imagined I'd say this, but… You're good for me, Jimmy DiBiase."

And with that, she kissed him.

Chapter 10

In cases of emergency or convenience, cell phones were a wondrous thing. There ought to be times, though, Martine was convinced, when people should be unreachable, and this early on a Sunday morning was one of those times. She burrowed deeper under the covers, trying to block the ringing of Jimmy's phone, but once it had penetrated her sleep, she couldn't shut it out.

Thankfully, it went quiet after a moment…until the message alert sounded. A few seconds after that, the ringing began again.

Shoving back the covers, she looked at him, sprawled on his back, dead to the world, then slid out of bed. The tile floor was cold on her bare feet, making her do a little dance around the bed to the phone. All she intended to do was mute the ringer, then wake him up in case it was police business he needed to deal with. The number displayed on the screen stopped her.

The call was coming from her shop. The only people in the world with a key to her shop were her and Anise. Had her employee gone by there and seen something wrong? Encountered some problem? Found another message from Tallie?

She answered with a quiet "Hello" as she shrugged into Jimmy's shirt from last night, then left the room. The music still played in the living room, the same sort of sexy, sad songs she and Jimmy had danced to, made love to, fallen asleep to. She found the remote on the mantel and shut it off, then checked out the window to see that the fog had returned. From this vantage point, it looked as if the buildings were floating atop a drab colorless cloud.

"Hello," she repeated.

Anise's response, somewhere between relief and a whimper, came suddenly. "Oh, thank God, Martine, it's you! I've called and called, and I was so afraid, I didn't know what to do!"

The hairs on Martine's nape stood on end, and goose bumps covered her entire body. It was just that the room was cold, she told herself, and the tile floor even colder, but she couldn't even pretend to believe it. Something was horribly wrong. She felt it in the nausea sweeping over her, the trembling that made her clutch the phone, the roiling in her stomach. Even so, she managed an even, reasonable tone when she spoke. "Take a deep breath, Anise, then tell me why you're at the shop this early when you know we're closed today."

Anise obeyed, her first breath ragged and painful, the next a little less so. "Niles left some stuff here, and I'm meeting him this morning for breakfast so I said I'd pick it up for him, but when I got here— Oh, God,

Martine, I'm so sorry I did this! I just didn't think—I didn't really believe—"

Martine padded to the couch, curled into a small ball and gripped the phone tighter. "What happened when you got there, Anise?" *Please let it be nothing, just some silly thing that she's overreacting to, God, please.*

There was a rustle of noise in the background—nothing she could identify, just a sense of sound, activity— then Anise spoke again. This time, the panic was mostly gone, her tone dull and heavy with regret. "I've got a message for you, Martine."

Another hesitation, another rustling, then… "Actions have consequences."

The call disconnected.

Dear God, Tallie was at the shop, and she had Anise. If Martine wasn't already sitting, her legs would have given way beneath her. "Anise?" she whispered, even though she knew her friend couldn't hear. "Anise, please…oh, please…"

She had to wake Jimmy, had to tell him, to take him with her when she went to the shop so he could arrest Tallie, so he could free Anise and bring an end to this entire awful mess. He would need time to call Jack and maybe some other officers, to make a plan, to get people in place and to keep Martine safe—

Halfway to her feet, she sank down again. Tallie wanted to deal with *her*, not the police. She had killed Paulina. God help her, she had killed her own twin sister. She wouldn't hesitate to kill Anise, too, if Martine sent the police in her stead.

Jimmy won't let you walk through that door. It's too dangerous.

But what about the danger to Anise if she didn't? She trusted Jimmy with her life. She had faith in his abilities to do his job better than anyone could, but she couldn't bear it if her young employee suffered because of her.

Grimly, she stood, hardly noticing the chill from the floor. She went to the guest room, dressed in jeans, a sweater and running shoes, got her slicker, then slipped into Jimmy's room to leave his phone where she'd found it. After sliding the weapons into her jacket pockets, adding his knife just in case, she couldn't resist stopping a moment, touching her hand to his arm and whispering without sound, "I love you, Jimmy."

Then, before her courage fled, she left the room, the apartment, the building. Shivering inside her slicker, she greeted the security guard as if she were just any resident out for a stroll. Once she turned the corner out of his sight, she began running.

She hadn't been anywhere alone in days, and she should have been relishing the freedom: the people she passed who paid her no mind; the eeriness of the fog, cool and damp where it touched her skin; the unusual quiet for a Sunday morning. She wasn't, though. All she could think about was the shop. If Anise was okay. What she would do when she got there. Whether she was a fool for sneaking out on Jimmy. If she would pay for it with her life.

Her fingers clenched around the pepper spray in one pocket, the Taser in the other. Maybe she would die, but Tallie wouldn't get away unscathed.

By the time she reached her block, deep breaths were impossible to come by and pain throbbed in her side. She slowed to a walk, gaze locked on her destination, mind racing to come up with a plan.

She had nothing. She sold T-shirts and postcards, anointing oil and John the Conqueror root, for God's sake. She didn't know the first thing about confronting psychotic killers who were holding someone she loved hostage. She was totally unprepared.

But she had no choice.

As she reached the edge of the plate-glass windows, she slowed her steps and peered inside. Only the lights over the checkout counter were on, not enough to dispel the gloom on a dreary day. She saw no sign of Anise or Tallie.

The sign on the door was still turned to Closed. It was impossible to make a stealthy entrance, given the door's habit of sticking, so she wrapped her fingers around the knob, took a deep breath and turned and jiggled and forced her way in with all the accompanying noise. It made more noise as she closed it, then all went silent.

Martine believed in evil, but her experience with it had been extremely limited. She read about it, saw it on the news, heard stories about it. But this morning she felt it in the air, smelled it in the overpowering scents of the incense display, heard it with every thud of her heart. She wanted to yank the door open and run screaming down the street. She wanted to race up the stairs next door to her apartment and hide under her bed. She wanted to be anywhere but here, doing anything but this.

Instead, she walked farther into the room. "Anise?"

Another silence, another rustle, then... "In here."

The door marked Private was open, a faint light coming out, too little to dispel the heavy darkness of the main room. Martine slowly walked that way, circling shelves that blocked her path, coming to a stop in the doorway.

Anise huddled on the stool behind the counter, her face a stark contrast to her black hair and clothing. She was trying to make herself look as small as possible, but no matter how small she got, it was hard to ignore the tremors rocketing through her. Her gaze was moving constantly in silent warning, from Martine's face to the shadows against the wall on her left.

Martine eased into the room to the other side, intending to stay as far from Tallie as the U-shaped counter would allow, but hardly five steps into the room, she tripped and fell against the glass. Thankfully, the counter was sturdy, the wood frame absorbing the force of her stumble. She regained her balance quickly, looked to see what had tripped her and gasped.

There, her dark clothes blending into the shadows, motionless—*dear God, please not lifeless, too*—lay Tallie.

Relief washed over Martine. They'd been wrong. Tallie hadn't killed their friends. She hadn't grown into some kind of homicidal maniac. Just like her sister, Paulina and Martine, she was an innocent victim.

So who…

A whisper of movement interrupted the question as a slender figure stepped out of the shadows into the light. "It's nice to see you again, Martine."

Unable to draw a deep breath, Martine stared across the room into the face of her tormentor, her one-time friend and now her would-be killer. "I'd rather see you burning in hell, Robin."

* * *

Between the steady beeps of his cell phone, Jimmy surrendered, rolled onto his side and picked up the phone. He rarely turned it off, though he could, of course. Even in a job filled with emergencies, no one could legitimately expect him to be available twenty-four hours a day. It had just always been a thing with him. He'd rarely had any real reason to *not* be available.

According to the cell, he'd missed two calls and two messages. He squinted at the information on the screen, hoping it was just the sudden awakening that made it hard to bring the caller ID into focus and not his age. He also hoped the calls didn't have anything to do with this case, weren't anything that might call him away from home. It was Sunday, dreary and gray outside, a perfect day for a decadent meal, a game or two on TV and lazing in bed with—

He glanced behind him. Martine was already up— had been long enough for the sheets to cool. He didn't hear any noises from the bathroom, living room or kitchen, but she was the sort to stay quiet and let him sleep. She'd probably slipped out of the room for coffee and breakfast…though he swore he could smell fresh coffee from a hundred yards and no aroma lingered in the air.

"Martine?" He sat up, still grasping the phone. His call got no reply, and deep inside, he knew why: she was gone. There was a feel to the silence, an emptiness, that meant he was alone.

Swearing, he jumped from the bed and did a quick walk-through of the apartment, confirming his gut instinct. When he wound up back in the bedroom, he checked caller ID, better able to see now that he was wide-awake. His muscles went taut at the name of the shop. "Damn it, Martine—"

Hands shaking, he listened to the message. He needed a moment to identify the panicky voice talking double her usual speed and half an octave higher. *Detective, I need to talk to Martine. I know you know where she is, I know you can get in touch with her, and I know you won't want to, but it's an emergency. I have to talk to her right away. Call her right now and tell her to call me. This isn't one of those times you get to decide what everybody else does. Call her! Right now! It's important.*

The second call came as soon Anise finished the message. The anxiety in her voice was palpable, crawling along his skin as she left a message more of the same. Then, according to the call log, a third call was received—and answered. The conversation lasted just under ninety seconds. Long enough for Anise to report a problem, one significant enough to make Martine sneak out to meet her.

It wasn't hard to guess the nature of the problem. Martine had been so compliant with his requests and restrictions up to this point. The only thing that could lure her out in the open now would be a threat to someone close to her. They knew Tallie had been watching the shop and her apartment. It was a fair guess that she'd realized Martine wasn't coming back until the danger had passed—also a fair guess that if Anise had gone to the shop this morning, Tallie could have seen her arrive. It was far too easy to guess that she knew Martine would put her own life at risk to protect Anise's.

Fear spread through him, leaving fine crystals of

ice in its wake, freezing his blood, his heart, even his brain. This couldn't happen. He'd just gotten this second chance with her. He'd just fallen in love with her. He couldn't lose her now. He wouldn't.

His gaze shifted to the night table, its weapons looking lonely with the others gone. She'd taken his knife, too—a weapon of last resort. Pepper spraying or Tasing someone—that could be done from a distance, maybe ten feet for the spray, up to fifteen for the Taser. But a knife…that was up close and personal. That could give a person nightmares.

Most mornings, he needed a hot shower and steaming coffee to reach his mental best. This morning, panic was a pretty good substitute. He put the phone on speaker, then called Jack while he dressed. His partner wasn't very happy about being awake at such an unholy hour on a Sunday morning—it wasn't even eight yet—but at least he was used to it; his kids woke him early every Sunday.

Jimmy related the conversation, and Jack's grumpiness disappeared. "What do we do now?"

"We stop Tallie."

Jack snorted at the obvious answer. "We're assuming she's already got one hostage. Martine'll make two. We're going in? Just you and me?"

"Call Lawson and Petitjohn."

"Aw, man, they're idiots."

"Not when they're on the job." Then they were fearless. "Have them meet us on Dumaine at the intersection with Royal."

"We'll be there."

Jimmy was well aware as he left the apartment that they were violating department policy. He should re-

port a suspected hostage situation higher up the chain
of command, let them call the Special Operations Di-
vision, let the negotiator take the lead. Fine as they
were, though, the tactical platoon didn't know Martine.
Being emotionally involved with a subject definitely
could have its downside, but there were advantages,
too, one of them being that he would do *anything* to
get her back safe. Besides, going through official channels took time, and he wasn't sure how much of that
Martine and Anise had.

Stopping at the gate, he asked the security guard if
he'd seen Martine. She'd left five or ten minutes earlier, on foot, friendly but not chatty, a woman with a
purpose. Probably, the guard joked, of enjoying this
wonderful sunny morning.

Jimmy parked his car nearer Jack's house than Martine's, grabbed binoculars from the trunk and jogged
to the intersection nearest the shop. It wasn't the finest
view he could have asked for, but it was enough to see
no one was in the main room. Next he checked the car
parked in Martine's driveway, calling in the tag number to dispatch. When footsteps sounded behind him,
he didn't look around. Jack always walked like a man
with a purpose. He had an aura of authority Jimmy
would like to have when he was finished growing up.

A moment later, Petitjohn and Lawson arrived.
They worked together, hung out together, vacationed
together and showed up together any time they were
summoned, so much that people wondered whether
they were partners just on the job or in life, too. Jimmy
didn't give a damn. Like he'd said, they were fearless,
and that was what he needed.

Sliding back around the corner, out of sight of the

shop, Jimmy looked at his backup: alert, clearheaded, bulletproof vests under dark hoodies or windbreakers. He didn't need to see to know each of them was more heavily armed than he was. Good. Because Tallie Winchester wasn't walking out of here free.

"The car parked out front comes back to Phillip Malloy in Chicago," he said. "I don't know whether Malloy's somehow involved or just another victim."

Jack pulled a couple of papers from inside his jacket. "This is a sketch Evie did of the shop. Here's the front door. The back goes into the courtyard. The apartment has a courtyard door, too, on the second floor, and there's a gate here, but it's secure. There's no indoor access from the shop to the apartment."

Petitjohn pointed at the three smaller rooms inside the shop. "What are these?"

"Bathroom, break and storeroom," Jack answered, "and this is where she sells supplies to serious voodoo practitioners. Only one door into each of these spaces and no windows."

"So we need to find out which floor they're on." Lawson grinned. "I don't suppose your pretty wife sent a spare key to the apartment to help out with that?"

Jack let a ring with a lone key dangle from his finger. "I also brought pictures. They're not current, but they're all within the last five years. Martine—she's ours. Anise works for Martine. Tallie Winchester—we think she's the killer. Robin Railey—we think she's another intended victim. Railey may be halfway around the world, but just in case..."

Something clicked in Jimmy's mind. "She lived in Chicago. Robin Railey. She disappeared there after the first murder. Went into hiding, according to the second victim. Either she or Tallie could have stolen the car to get away."

Petitjohn took the key from Jack. "So we're gonna check the apartment and make sure they're not there," he said as Lawson took the sketch, which also included the layout of the apartment. All the time Jimmy had spent there, and there were three rooms he hadn't seen.

"I'm going with you," Jack added. "I'll take the courtyard stairs to the rear door of the shop."

"I don't suppose you have the spare key for that."

Jack shook his head.

"So you and I go in loud." If they all survived this, Jimmy hoped Anise would be grateful enough to remove her curse from the doorknob so he could come and go without absorbing ever-increasing voltage.

"One last thing…" This time it was Petitjohn handing something around: earbuds so they could stay in touch. One of the perks of working with a tech geek.

Jimmy tucked the earbud in, then the other three took off back the way they'd come. They would circle the block and come in from the opposite end. No one inside the shop would be able to see them without pressing right up to the window, which would allow Jimmy to see *them*.

Martine was in the shop. He knew it in his bones. He was hoping she'd left the front door unlocked, unless Tallie had ordered otherwise. A simple thing like that probably wouldn't cross her mind when Anise was in danger. And Tallie would want a quick escape, no dealing with locks and creaky sticking doors.

When Jack, Lawson and Petitjohn reached the apartment stoop, Petitjohn unlocked the door while the others ducked behind the car—letting the air out of the tires, Jimmy realized. A moment later, the three of them disappeared inside. He listened to the quiet, heavy and ominous, that came over the buds, his gut roiling, holding his breath so he didn't miss the faintest sound.

Sticking the binoculars in his pocket, he strode across the street and down the sidewalk. Halfway to the shop, a heavy exhale sounded over the link. "Nothing here but us cops," Lawson murmured. "Petitjohn's going out the back. I'm coming to you."

All right. Martine was just a few yards away and presumably safe for the moment. Big emphasis on *presumably*. Tallie could have met Martine at the door with a gun and walked her and Anise out of the area. Could have taken Martine and left Anise behind. Could be on her way right now to the place where she'd cut Paulina's heart from her chest. Could…could…could…

"You wait here," he murmured to Lawson. "Anyone who comes out, put 'em in cuffs."

When the detective nodded, Jimmy climbed the steps to the door and prepared to wrestle it open, announcing his arrival to everyone inside. His Taser drawn, he wrapped his fingers around the knob and got a hell of a shock, enough to make him spit out a silent curse and make his fingers twitch. "You'll hear me come in," he said to Jack, then pushed the door.

It opened as smoothly and silently as a well-oiled high-tech marvel. Stunned at his good luck, Jimmy headed toward the room marked Private. The door was open, a light was on inside, and the faint sound of voices drifted on the air. Though he neither recognized the voices nor understood the words, a jolt through his chest told him which one was Martine's. His knees damn near went weak with the proof that she was still alive.

Now, God help them, they had to make sure she stayed that way.

"Burning in hell?" Robin echoed the words with a serious helping of disbelief. "Really, Martine, twenty-four years since you've seen me, and the first words out of your mouth consign me to hell? So much for old friendships being the best."

"I didn't end the friendship. You guys did when you scattered like frightened little mice. You abandoned me, and you think you have the right to come back now and turn my life inside out?"

Martine listened to herself and wondered where the words were coming from. Certainly not from her own little frightened mouse, quaking in the corner of her brain. She'd assumed she would come in here, calm and in control, and reason with Tal—Robin until an opportunity to use her weapons arose. Apparently, calm, control and reason were hiding in the corner with mouse. Instead, Martine was angry—about Callie's and Paulina's deaths, about whatever Robin had done to Tallie, about the threat she'd made against Anise. She was furious about the past week, the fear, the grief, the sorrow, the guilt, the sadness and the regret, and she for damn sure wasn't going to make it any easier for Robin to kill her.

"Hey, I'm the one holding the gun here." Robin waved it in the air for a moment. "I have a right to do whatever I damn well please."

Martine's fingers flexed around her weapons. She would use the Taser, effective and with the least chance of hurting herself. Pepper spray could drift on the air and burn innocent eyes as well as evil ones, and the knife… Only if it was a choice between it and death. She did not want Robin's blood on her.

Martine moved a few steps deeper into the room. "Anise, leave."

Surprise emphasized the paleness of Anise's face. She slid from the stool to her feet, but her knees sagged before catching her weight. "I—I can go?"

"No!" Robin slammed her free hand onto the glass, and Anise hopped like a frog back onto the stool. "You can't give orders here, Martine. *I'm* in charge."

Calm, control and reason knew that, but anger and frustration had the direct line to Martine's mouth. She wasn't about to let Robin terrorize or kill an innocent young woman who hadn't even been born when their problems started. She continued to move toward the opening of the counter. "Go, Anise. This is between Robin and me."

This time Anise was prepared. She didn't ask permission, didn't walk to the pass-through but boosted herself onto the counter, spun around, hopped off on the other side and darted through the shadows to the door. Just as Martine had done, she tripped over Tallie, shrieked and said, "Sorry, sorry, I forgot. Sorry."

Shock held Robin rigid. "You—you—I can't believe you—" A laugh escaped her, as chilling as the fog. Then, requiring a great deal of control, she forced herself to relax. "It's okay. She was just bait. All I really need, I've got. Tallie's not dead, by the way. Not yet."

Her gaze locked on Robin, Martine strained to hear the sounds of Anise's passing through the shop. She tried so hard she wasn't sure whether the sounds she picked up were real or imagined: a shuffle of feet, a gasp, a whimper, a creak of wood and the reassuring rumble of what might have been a male voice. Hope surged inside her. Jimmy was here, or Jack, or...*oh, please don't let it be Niles*. Panic was his usual state of affairs.

Martine eased back in the direction of the door. "So all you need to be a happy woman is to kill Tallie and me." A bit of fresh air wafted through the doorway—because the front door had opened?—and barely detectable on the cold air was a dear scent. Jimmy's cologne, fresh and near and full of hope. He was out there, somewhere within screaming distance. She was going to be okay.

Robin followed on the opposite side of the room. She may have let Anise go, but Martine was sure if she tried to walk out, her old friend would use that gun.

She stopped a distance from the door to lessen the chances that Robin might look into the main room. Sadly, she couldn't see, either. "Why?"

Robin gestured with both hands, still holding that damn gun. "It's Callie's fault. I never would have come up with the idea on my own."

"Callie wanted you to kill us, starting with her?"

"Of course not." Robin backed into the shadows again. When this was over, Martine swore she would have new bright lights installed all through the shop. She didn't care how much her customers liked atmosphere. No one would ever be able to hide in here again.

"Did I tell you I got engaged? Of course not, because we haven't spoken for twenty-four years." Robin drifted into the light again to reveal a massive diamond on her left hand. Under normal circumstances, it would have taken Martine's breath away, but now, knowing that those hands cut their friends' hearts out of their chests, all she could see was the stone bathed in blood.

"First," Robin began conversationally, "let me catch you up on the years since we last spoke. I went to college—had to work my way through that, just like high school. Had a couple of decent jobs—too little pay for too much work. Got married—twice. Got cheated on and divorced—twice. Moved to Chicago for a new job. Pay wasn't great, but I met a lot of important people. Including Philip Malloy."

She paused, obviously expecting a response. "You don't know who he is, do you? Damn, Martine, you always thought the sun rose and set on this stupid city. Small-town Louisiana girl never could imagine anything bigger or better than New Orleans. Philip owns half of Chicago and a good chunk of the Midwest. He's got more money than Mr. Winchester ever dreamed of, and he wants to spend it all on me."

Robin gazed at the ring a moment, her smile sweet, the affection in it sincere. For her fiancé? Or for the millions he could give her?

"I told Callie. She and Tallie sent me Christmas and birthday cards sometimes. And you know what she did? She asked me for money. Can you believe it? *Money.* When I had to work for everything I ever got. Seems Daddy's generosity ended when she turned forty and still had her hand out all the time."

Martine wished she could be surprised by Callie's request, but the twins had been raised that way. They'd only had to ask, no matter how outrageous the desire, and they got it. Had anyone truly expected them to become self-sufficient adults?

"I knew better than to think it would be a one-time deal. If I paid her, she'd be back in a year or six months or a few weeks, wanting more. So I told her no, and she said she would tell Philip about the curse we put on Fletcher."

The slightest blur of movement flickered outside the door. Martine glanced that way, as if checking on Tallie, and saw Jimmy on his hands and knees. Her heart squeezing painfully, she wished she'd awakened him to tell him she loved him. What if she didn't get another chance?

He gestured toward Tallie, making a pulling motion, and Martine walked back along the aisle. Robin followed her on the opposite side.

"You have to understand that Philip is a very private, almost reclusive man. He avoids the media and shuns the spotlight. His good name is sacred to him. When Callie threatened to tell him… If I hadn't silenced her, I would have lost everything."

Martine's stomach clenched at her casual, reasonable tone, as if reputation and money were perfectly logical reasons for murder. "So you killed her and made it look like a ritual murder to throw suspicion on…who? Fletcher's family? One of us?" When Robin shrugged, Martine pointed out, "Ritual murder isn't a voodoo thing."

"Oh, for God's sake, Martine, how many people know that? I needed a distraction, and it worked. Then I realized that Callie couldn't talk, but you, Paulina and

Tallie could. If I was going to keep my secret safe…
Benjamin Franklin said, 'Three can keep a secret, if
two of them are dead.' Who am I to argue with one of
our founding fathers? Though, of course, four shared
my secret."

Two of them were dead, and one lay injured and
possibly dying. Finally, it became too much for Martine to resist a look toward Tallie. With the cabinets
and merchandise in the way, she couldn't see her, and
though she'd listened hard, she hadn't heard a sound.

"So…" Robin gestured with the gun. "Time to go.
I had planned on you and Goth Girl carrying Tallie to
the car, but now I suppose I'll have to help you. Then
we'll go to the same place I took Paulina, and…" She
let her shrug finish the sentence.

Martine didn't move. "You expect me to just go
along quietly?"

"Yes, because I'll shoot Tallie if you don't." With
another sweet smile, this time tinged with regret, Robin
sighed. "That's where we're different, Martine. You
still care about us. All I care about is Philip and me
and how incredibly happy we're going to be. So *move*.
Before Goth Girl comes back with the police."

Still Martine didn't move. Had Jimmy had enough
time to get Tallie out and reposition himself? What
if he could hear but not understand them? What if he
was vulnerable when Robin walked through the door?
What if she shot him instead?

That image forced her into motion, long strides
leading to the end of the counter. When Robin rounded
the corner and saw nothing but bare floor where Tallie
had lain, a keening sound escaped her, full of anger and

making the hairs on Martine's neck stand on end. Furiously, she charged through the doorway, screaming, the pistol up and ready to fire, and Martine charged after her.

Jimmy and Jack were near the shop's entry, Tallie cradled in Jimmy's arms, his back to them as he handed the woman over to Jack. Jack shouted a warning and Jimmy spun, but he'd holstered his weapon to pick up Tallie. Even as he grabbed for it, Martine knew it would be too late.

Her actions were pure instinct: she'd yanked the Taser from her pocket as she ran, had activated it and flipped off the safety. Now she centered the laser on Robin's back and pulled the trigger. It crackled and popped and, an instant later, Robin's body went rigid as she fell to the floor, her body convulsing from the electrical shock, her screams turning to curses.

Then reaction hit. Like Robin, Martine's muscles locked in place. She couldn't lower the Taser, couldn't control the shudders racking her body, couldn't breathe or speak or stop the tears filling her eyes. She stared at Robin as she twitched, the longest thirty seconds of her life, both horrified and perversely satisfied by the knowledge that *she* had dealt that punishment. Even more perversely, when the charge ended, she wanted to trigger it again: thirty seconds for each life she'd destroyed or tried to.

"Tine? It's okay, Tine."

Jimmy's soft, anxious voice came from nearby, and he tugged until her cramped fingers let go of the Taser. It clattered when he set it on a shelf beside them, then he wrapped his arms around her and held her so tight she could scarcely breathe. She wanted him to never let go.

His breathing was rapid and shallow, and he was shaking, too, but slowly he calmed, and so did she, breathing deeply of all his scents. Voices sounded behind them, and sirens wailed outside, but right there in his embrace, everything *was* okay. He'd kept his promise.

After a moment, he tilted her face back to stare into her eyes. "You saved my life."

It took a moment for the words to process, then she slowly smiled. "Yes, I did."

"There's an old saying that if you save a man's life, you're responsible for him ever after. Want to spend the rest of your life looking out for me, Tine?"

It was a serious moment, serious words, serious intent, and she couldn't stop the laughter bubbling inside her. "Really, DiBiase? You ask that now, surrounded by cops and paramedics and gawkers and a crazy psychotic killer who tried to shoot you?"

And there it was—the grin she loved with all her heart, smug and brash and overconfident and sexy and sweet, aw, damn, so sweet it made her ache. "If I wait until everything's back to normal, you might come to your senses and turn me down. I love you, Tine. I always will."

After years of nurturing her hostility toward him, she *had* come to her senses. She knew him. Wanted him. Loved him. Trusted him. Forever.

In reply, she cupped her hands to his face and kissed him, sliding her mouth from one end of his to the other before parting his lips with her tongue, dipping inside, tasting him, teasing him. "I love you, Jimmy," she murmured, "and I always will. Just one question."

When his brow quirked, she smiled innocently. "Will you let me keep the Taser?"

* * * * *

BULLETPROOF SEAL

CAROL ERICSON

Prologue

The sweat stung Quinn's eyes and he squeezed them shut for a second—just a second before he refocused on his target. Rikki's beautiful face swam before him in his scope, her red hair standing out like a burst of flame against the emerald green landscape. Quinn's hand trembled.

He shifted his sniper rifle to the two North Korean soldiers walking behind Rikki, prodding her forward. They had rifles pointed at her back. Quinn spit the sour taste out of his mouth, along with the mud from the hillside in the DMZ between North and South Korea.

Someone had misinformed the CIA. Rikki Taylor was no rogue operative working with the North Koreans. She was their captive…unless she'd set up this whole scene for cover.

Quinn knew better than anyone about Rikki's duplicitous nature. But this? Working with the enemy to damage her own government and put her fellow CIA agents at risk?

He had a hard time believing Rikki would endanger agents in the field. Quinn lowered his sniper rifle and swiped the back of his hand across his mouth.

The trio below him stopped, and one of the soldiers pulled out a bottle of water.

Squinting, Quinn scanned the lush land where the borders of North and South Korea met—a no-man's-land where hostility and mistrust haunted the verdant beauty—not to mention the scattered land mines. This mistrust permeated his pores, had him doubting his mission, a mission he should've refused once he'd discovered the target.

He would've had to have come up with a good reason to refuse an assignment from the navy—even after that untraceable text he'd received. He could've tried the truth, but then he would've come under suspicion. Then his pride had taken over and he had to prove that he could carry out the assignment, prove his professionalism and dedication.

He snorted softly, and the leaves on the branch tickling his nose stirred. Prove to whom? His old man?

The group on the ground was on the move again, and Quinn took up his position. His rifle weighed on his shoulder like a lead block. His breath came out in short spurts.

Usually before he dropped a target, a deadly calm descended on him. Now, his heart raced and his trigger finger twitched. In this condition he'd be lucky to hit that boulder twenty feet away.

He closed his eyes and took a deep, steadying breath through his nose and blew it out through puckered lips. He swallowed. He shifted. He braced the toes of his boots against the rock behind him.

Then he refocused. He put Rikki Taylor in his crosshairs for the last time.

Rikki licked her lips, and Quinn could almost taste their sweet honey on his own tongue. She tossed her fiery hair over one shoulder.

Quinn blinked and, in the split second of that one

blink, Rikki attacked one of the guards, going for his weapon.

Quinn needed no other proof. He tracked his rifle to the other guard, lined him up and took the shot. The soldier jerked once and dropped to the ground.

Quinn swung his scope back to Rikki's struggle with her captor, and his heart stuttered. The soldier had possession of his gun, and Rikki had fallen to the ground, out of sight behind a clump of bushes.

As Quinn watched through his scope, blood pounding in his ears, the North Korean soldier shot his weapon into the bushes.

In a fury, Quinn zeroed in on the man who'd just shot Rikki, but before he could even take aim, Quinn came under attack from a hail of bullets.

Taking down the other soldier had revealed his position, and now he was outnumbered and outgunned. He rolled to his back and scrambled down the hillside like a forward-moving crab. He scuttled behind a row of trees and started breaking down his rifle.

Dragging himself up and wedging his back against a tree trunk, he stuffed his gear into his bag and then swung it onto his back.

He lunged forward onto his belly and army-crawled his way through the forest to the tunnel that would take him back to South Korea and the designated pickup point.

What would he tell his superiors? He did end up with mission success. Although it wasn't his bullet that had done the job, he *had* neutralized the target—Rikki Taylor.

They'd been wrong. They'd all been wrong. Rikki had not been working with the enemy.

And now that Quinn was responsible for her death, his life wasn't worth living.

Chapter One

Sixteen months later

The footsteps echoed behind her on the rain-slicked pavement. Rikki stopped and spun around. Silence greeted her as she peered down the dark, narrow street.

With her muscles coiled tightly, she continued, and her tag-along followed suit. As she began to turn again, the footsteps, two sets, quickened and two bodies rushed her.

The glint from a knife flashed in the night, and Rikki finished her turn with her feet flying. She kicked the assailant with the knife in the gut, and he doubled over, his weapon clattering to the cobblestones.

The other man yelped in surprise and before he could recover, Rikki swept up the knife from the ground and wielded it toward her attacker's face.

"Get lost, or I'll slice you from chin to navel. Yu done know?"

The man's eyes widened so that the whites gleamed like two orbs. His friend groaned from the ground.

Rikki growled, "And take him with you."

He held up one hand and grabbed his buddy by the arm with the other, dragging him to his feet. "Eazy, nuh."

"You take it easy and get moving or I'll call the police."

The two hapless muggers took off, and Rikki pocketed the knife. The streets of Jamaica, even in the tourist trap of Montego Bay, turned deadly after dark, but Rikki had more to fear in her own country right now.

She slipped into the alley where an orange light swayed in the breeze, sidling along the walls of the ramshackle building. She ducked under a tattered blue-and-white-striped awning and rapped at the window.

A curtain stirred. Rikki stepped sideways into the weak light to identify herself.

A wiry man opened the door and hustled her inside as he poked his head into the alley and looked both ways. "Where's your ride?"

"I walked from the main street."

He shook his head. "Dangerous place for anyone to be walking, especially a girl like you."

Rikki hid her smile behind a covered cough. "I'm okay. Are you Baily?"

"The one and only." He double-locked the door behind them and twitched the curtain back in place.

"Do you have everything ready?"

"Come with me." He crooked one long finger in her direction.

Rikki followed him through a single room where an old woman sat in front of an older TV, the blue light flickering across her lined face. She didn't acknowledge Rikki's presence or even move a muscle.

Baily shoved a dark curtain aside and waved Rikki into a small room. He pointed to a green screen and said, "Stand in front of that. I'll get your picture first. Everything else is ready to go."

As she took a step toward the screen, Baily tugged on her sleeve. "Business first."

Rikki pulled a wad of cash from her pocket. Those thieves on the street would've hit pay dirt with her—well, except for the fact that they'd picked a CIA operative, trained in self-defense and street fighting, as their target.

She counted out the agreed-upon sum, and Baily got to work.

Thirty minutes later, Rikki had a Canadian passport and a birth certificate for one April Thompson. She studied the passport with the Jamaican stamp. "I heard you were good, Baily. These better not let me down."

"Never had a problem yet." He cocked his head in a bird-like fashion. "Girl like you in trouble with the Babylon?"

"Babylon?" She stuffed the documents into the manila envelope he'd handed to her.

"De law." He waved his hands in a big circle. "De system."

"You could say that." She stuck out her hand. "Pleasure doing business with you."

He shook her hand and then yelled, "Darien!"

Rikki jumped, jerking her hand from his grip and placing it over the newly acquired knife in her waistband.

Baily placed one finger against the side of his nose. "No worries. Darien just my boy. He'll take you back."

A skinny young man poked his head into the room, his dreadlocks bobbing and swaying. "Yeah, Daddy?"

"Take this young woman wherever she wants to go. Don't stop anywhere."

Darien grinned. "Sure ting."

After thanking Baily, Rikki followed Darien outside.

He turned sideways and scooted between two of the houses along the alley. A chain clinked and rattled, and

Darien pushed a scooter out in front of him. "Hop on de back."

Clutching her fake documents to her chest, Rikki climbed on the back of Darien's scooter. He zoomed through the streets of Montego Bay as she shouted directions in his ear over the buzzing sound of the bike.

A block away from the resort, she tapped Darien's shoulder and pointed to the side of the street.

The bike sputtered to a stop, and he leaned it to one side as if it were a mammoth Harley instead of a putt-putt scooter. Rikki slid off the back and handed Darien a folded bill.

His gaze darted from the outstretched money to her face. "Daddy would smack me in da head if I took that."

"Daddy doesn't have to know." She tucked the cash beneath his fingers curled around the handlebar of his scooter and twirled away. She made a beeline for the resort and didn't slow her pace until she walked through the front entrance.

"Good evening, Miss Rikki."

"Hey, George." She waved her manila envelope and scurried out the side door and across the pool deck, where drunken tourists had gathered for one last nightcap.

The damp foliage brushed her skin, and she inhaled the sweet, heavy fragrance of the white bellflower as she tromped down the path to the cottage. When she was inside, she leaned against the front door, closing her eyes and hugging the fake documents to her chest.

"Did you get what you needed, Rikki?"

Rikki opened one eye and dipped her chin to her chest. "I did. Thanks, Chaz."

Her stepfather winked. "I've been on this island a long time. I know important people in low places."

Her mother floated into the room behind Chaz, her

long gray braid hanging over one shoulder. "Are you sure you want to do this, Rikki? You don't owe them anything, and as far as they know, you're dead. You and Bella could live here with us for as long as you like."

Rikki rolled her eyes. "I would go stir-crazy here, Mom. Besides, I have to do this. I have important information."

"They don't deserve it." Mom sniffed.

Bella cooed and gurgled from the other room, and Rikki dropped the manila envelope on a table and hurried toward the bedroom. She leaned over the crib and scooped up her baby girl, holding her close and breathing in her baby-powder scent.

"She's going to miss you."

Rikki glanced at her mom, who stood with her shoulder wedged against the doorjamb, and blinked the sudden tears from her eyes. "I'm doing it for her, Mom. I have to get my life back for both of us."

"Does that mean seeing *him*?"

"I have to start with him, see what he knows, maybe use his contacts."

"You don't have to tell him about Bella. She'll be safe with us until you can return and reclaim her, reclaim your life."

Rikki bounced her daughter in her arms, burying her face in Bella's soft ginger hair. "I'll see how it goes. I plan to use him to get what I want, and if that means telling him we have a daughter, I'll do it."

"He doesn't have a right to know about her."

"Lizzie." Chaz had come up behind his wife and placed a hand on her shoulder. "Let Rikki handle this herself…and let her have some time alone with the baby before she has to leave."

Chaz ushered Mom out of the room and blew Rikki a kiss before shutting the door.

Rikki collapsed in the rocking chair, cuddling Bella in the crook of her arm. As she sang softly to her baby, Rikki let the tears spill onto her cheeks.

She didn't know what she'd do when she came face-to-face with Quinn McBride—the man who'd tried to kill her and had gotten her locked up in a North Korean labor camp.

The man she still loved.

QUINN STUMBLED INTO his apartment and made his way to the kitchen, rubbing his eyes. He banged his shin on the coffee table and scowled at it. "Who put you there?"

He yanked open the fridge door and studied the sparse contents as he swayed on his feet. Giving up, he slammed the door, and the condiment bottles rattled and clinked against the beer bottles.

His stomach growled. The taxi driver had refused to wait for him outside the restaurant where he'd wanted to pick up some food, and Quinn didn't want to get stuck walking home through the streets of New Orleans lugging a bag of food, especially without a weapon at his side.

And he didn't trust himself with a weapon right now—not in his condition.

He fumbled in his back pocket for his cell phone and scrolled through his contacts. If he couldn't get to the food, he'd make the food come to him.

His thumb swept past Rinaldi's Pizza and he backed up. Rikki's name jumped out at him, grabbing him by the throat. As he hovered over her name, his finger shook, and it had nothing to do with the booze coursing through his veins.

He'd kept her number on his phone and had even called it once or twice just to hear her low, sultry voice caress his ear. But the last time he'd tried to call it, the harsh tones of an automated operator told him the cell number was out of service, and he had no business trying to contact the woman he'd sent to her death.

Dropping his chin to his chest, Quinn smacked the cell phone against his temple. If only he'd shown more restraint out there on the DMZ. He could've taken out both of the soldiers holding Rikki. She would've responded in an instant, would've been able to take appropriate evasive action.

She'd been one of the best damned operatives in the field.

The CIA and navy had clouded his judgment, had accused Rikki of being a double agent, had sent him there to take her out. If he hadn't been so damned eager to please his superiors, he would've gone in with a backup plan.

He always had something to prove.

He wiped the back of his hand across his mouth. He needed to stop playing back the incident in his head over and over every day. Rikki was gone. The CIA was happy. The navy had sent him out on another assignment, which had allowed him to stuff everything away as he'd concentrated on the mission, and now that he was home on leave, he could erase it from his mind another way—the old-fashioned McBride way.

He hunched over the kitchen counter, bringing the phone close to his face. Avoiding Rikki's number, he placed a call to Rinaldi's and ordered an extralarge pizza with everything on it.

When he ended the call, he smacked the phone on the counter and yelled out to the empty apartment, "That calls for another beer."

His stomach rumbled again as he stared at the fridge, and suddenly the effort required to grab a bottle and twist off the top overwhelmed him. He went into the living room instead and crashed onto the sofa, grabbing the TV remote on his way down.

He clicked through the channels, settling on a true crime show about some cold-case murder, and stuffed a throw pillow beneath his head.

The doorbell startled him awake, and the remote fell from his fingers, which had been dangling off the sofa. He ran his tongue around his parched mouth and swept his wallet from the coffee table.

He peered out the peephole at the pimply-faced kid on his doorstep and swung open the door.

The delivery guy's eyes popped open as he held out the pizza box. "Your pizza, sir."

God, he must look even worse than he felt. He handed the kid more money than he should've just to compensate for scaring the hell out of him.

When he collapsed back down on the sofa, Quinn rewound the show, since he'd dozed off during most of it—*dozing off* being a polite term for passing out stinking drunk.

Before digging into the pizza, he retrieved a bottle of water from the fridge and downed half of it before making it back to the sofa. Three slices later and no closer to figuring out whodunit, Quinn closed his eyes and tipped his head back against the sofa cushion.

This time, the click of a gun near his temple woke him up.

Other than blinking once, Quinn didn't move one muscle. Then he spread his hands in front of him and said, "Take what you want, man. Wallet's on the table. Anything you can carry out is yours."

The gunman behind him huffed out a breath and then purred in the low, husky voice that haunted his dreams, "You sure have gotten soft since trying to kill me, McBride."

Chapter Two

Quinn jerked forward and cranked his head around. He choked as he stared at Rikki—but not Rikki—behind the Glock. She always did prefer a Glock.

Her blue eyes had been replaced by a pair of dark brown ones, narrowed in rage. Long, straight strands of brown hair framed her face instead of the thick, wavy red locks that used to dance on her shoulders like tongues of flame, tickling his body when they made love.

"Rikki?" He held out a trembling hand and then clenched it, cursing his drunken state. Maybe this was all an alcohol-infused hallucination. "Is it really you?"

She stepped back, wrinkling her nose. "You smell like a brewery."

Then it hit him. Her presence two feet away sobered him up like a cold shower and a pot of coffee, and his blood hummed through his veins with elation. "How are you here? I—we thought you were dead."

She took another step back, her aim at his head never faltering. "Yeah, too bad for you the North Koreans wanted me more alive than dead. That shot the soldier took grazed me, nothing fatal, but at least it protected me from the bullet waiting up on that hill—a bullet from a deadly navy SEAL sniper."

"I wasn't going to do it. Why do you think I took out

the other soldier? I realized you hadn't turned traitor the minute I saw you make a grab for your guard's gun. I couldn't get a clean shot at the soldier holding you, but I thought you might be able to take care of him yourself."

Her lashes dipped over her eyes once. Her mouth softened, and for a crazy minute he almost took that as a sign to kiss her. *Yeah, if he wanted a bullet between the eyes.*

"That's a good story. At what point during your prep for the assignment did you realize the CIA *spy* you were supposed to eliminate was your former lover?"

"Not right away."

"But even if you had known immediately, you never would've turned down the mission, would you?"

He lifted a shoulder. "I received an order. The CIA had proof."

His words, spoken aloud now to Rikki's face, sounded tinny and paltry to his own ears. How would they sound to hers?

She snorted. "And of course you would've had to reveal that you'd carried on a fling with a CIA operative while we were both on assignment in the Middle East."

"If I had doubted the evidence against you in any way, not only would I have owned up to our...affair, but I would've tried to convince them to call off the hit."

"Instead you charged right in like the good little soldier you are, all honor and duty." Her dark gaze flickered to the half-empty pizza box and the two bottles of beer on their sides at the base of the coffee table.

"All I needed to see was one shred of proof contradicting the CIA's story—and you gave it to me when you charged that soldier. That's why I shot the other one. I was trying to give you a chance."

"Are you sure you didn't kill him because you were afraid I'd already passed along secrets to him?"

"They were low-level grunts marching you along the DMZ. I didn't figure that was the time and place you were going to spill intel. Besides—" Quinn kicked the pizza box out of the way and braced his foot on the edge of the coffee table "—if I'd wanted to take everyone out, including you, I would've started with you first and then dealt with the two soldiers."

She flipped back her dark hair with a shrug of her shoulder. "Maybe."

"I had you in my crosshairs, Rikki. Had you there for a while. I could've dropped you at any time. I couldn't do it."

The corner of her eye twitched. "What does the CIA think? I know my name's not cleared, so whatever you told them, it didn't have much of an impact. Unless you told them nothing and took credit for eliminating a CIA spy."

He scratched his unshaven jaw. How did she know her name hadn't been cleared? How did she get out of North Korea? "I told the CIA and my commanding officers in the navy exactly what happened. Told them their intel must've been wrong, that the North Koreans had you as a captive."

"They didn't believe you?"

"They didn't care. I also told them the North Korean soldier had shot you dead. Case closed."

"Except it's not closed, is it? Here I am."

At least the gun had slipped a little from her grip. Even in his current muddled state, he probably could disarm her. Then again, nobody ever benefited from mistaking Rikki Taylor for an easy target.

"How'd you get out of North Korea? How'd you get

here? Where have you been the past—" he counted on his fingers "—sixteen months? And can you get that gun out of my face?"

"If I do, will you take me down? Call the CIA and turn me in?"

He rubbed his eyes and pinched the bridge of his nose. "Do I look like I'm in any condition to do that?"

She cocked her head. "You do look pretty bad, but I'm not stupid enough to underestimate a navy SEAL sniper—even one I shared a bed with. Or maybe that should be *especially* one I shared my bed with."

"Ouch." He held his hands in front of him, wrists pinned together. "You can tie me up or cuff me if you want."

A light sparked in her eyes, and her nostrils flared, the heat between them still palpable.

Desire and need surged through his body, making him hard.

"Drop your pants." She waved the gun.

He swallowed. He'd been kidding, but he should've known better than to kid with Rikki—not in her current frame of mind. "You're serious?"

"Damn right. I can't check you for weapons, but at least if you're naked I can make sure you're unarmed."

"Rikki…"

"The last time we were together, if you want to call it that, you had me in the crosshairs of your sniper rifle ready to take me out." She steadied her Glock. "What's changed since then except I had the good fortune to escape from the labor camp?"

A knot twisted in his gut. He knew those North Korean labor camps, and the thought of Rikki confined to one of them made him sick.

"Drop 'em."

"Okay, okay." He pushed himself to his feet, feeling completely sober. He unbuttoned the fly on his shorts and yanked them down. The flip-flops he'd been wearing earlier were wedged beneath the coffee table, so the shorts dropped to his bare feet.

"Kick them off and stand away from the sofa where I can see you."

He rolled his eyes but complied, stepping out of his shorts and kicking them across the room. He could get into a tussle with her right now, but she did have the upper hand.

He stepped away from the sofa and the table and held his arms out to the side. "Nothing on me."

Except the raging erection she could clearly see bulging in his black briefs.

Rikki's gaze dropped from his face to his crotch, and her cheeks flushed. "Now the T-shirt."

Patting his chest, he said, "Do you really believe I have a holster on underneath this shirt? A knife strapped to my back?"

"I'm not taking any chances. Off."

He grabbed the hem of his T-shirt and peeled it off his body. He dropped it to the floor. "Happy?"

"Turn around."

Turning around for her inspection only made him harder. Maybe that would be enough to prove to Rikki that he was on her side—would always be on her side.

When he faced her again, he shoved his thumbs in the waistband of his briefs. "You want the rest off?"

"Don't be ridiculous." She reached behind her back and pulled out a pair of open handcuffs, dangling them from her fingers.

Quinn's mouth dropped open. "No way."

"I know you. I know who you are and what you're

capable of. I've come this far, and I'm not taking any chances." She jingled the cuffs. "If you want any more information out of me, hold out your arm—your right arm."

He stretched his arm in front of him. Two more inches and he could touch her soft cheek, tell her everything he'd thought about this past year.

She snapped the cuff around his wrist and yanked on it, the metal cutting into his flesh. "Over here, by the radiator."

He would've preferred the bedroom, but he followed in her wake as she pulled him toward the window.

"Sit down and link the other cuff around this pipe."

He slid to the floor and hooked himself up to the pipe on the radiator. He crouched on his haunches.

Rikki let out a long sigh and placed her weapon on the counter that separated the kitchen from the living room. She dragged a stool from the kitchen and straddled it. "That's better."

"Rikki, I'd never hurt you."

"You were singing a different tune sixteen months ago."

"I explained all that to you. Now that I'm—" he rattled his cuffs against the pipe "—contained, are you going to tell me what happened? What were you doing in North Korea?"

"You mind if I have a beer? Scratch the request. What are you going to do about it?" She hopped off the stool, and he watched the sway of her hips in those tight jeans as she walked around the counter into the kitchen.

Before Rikki sat back down, she tipped the neck of the beer bottle at him. "You keep drinking like you were tonight, and you're gonna trade one six-pack for another...and wind up just like your old man."

He clenched his stomach muscles. She'd been checking him out despite all the tough talk. "North Korea?"

"My partner, David Dawson, got intel that Vlad was meeting with the North Koreans."

Quinn raised his eyebrows. "Vlad?"

"I knew that would get your attention." She took a sip of beer. "David had a way into the country across the DMZ and tagged me to go with him."

"Under the radar of the CIA. They didn't know why you were there."

"David didn't trust anyone, and it turns out he was right." Rikki sniffled and wiped the hand holding the beer bottle across her nose.

"The CIA didn't kill David. They thought you had a hand in his death."

"I know, but they were wrong. The North Koreans killed David and captured me. I had already been their…guest for several days before you spotted me marching along."

"They killed David and were sending you to a labor camp." Quinn bumped his manacled hands against his forehead. "If I had been faster, had taken out the soldier holding you first, you might've had a chance."

"I had no chance, not there. I figured I was a dead woman when I went for the soldier's gun anyway. The area was crawling with North Koreans. You saw that after you took your shot." She dragged her fingernail down the bottle's damp label, ripping a line through it. "I-I thought the person out there was trying to save me and I didn't even know it was you—not until later. And then I found out it was you and you were trying to assassinate me."

He clanged the bracelets against the radiator. "Not when I killed that soldier. I'd changed my mind already.

I was trying to help you, Rikki, but I failed, and I've been punishing myself ever since."

Her gaze swept over his unkempt apartment, his tousled hair, the stubble on his face. "Maybe the navy punished you for failing in your duty, for failing to take out the rogue CIA operative."

"They didn't. They figured you were dead and one way or the other, I was the cause of your death." Closing his eyes, he lowered his backside to the floor and drew his knees to his chest. "I'd figured the same thing."

"That's why neither the CIA nor the navy can know I'm still alive." She pinged her fingernail against the bottle. "Not until I can sort all of this out."

"How did you escape from the labor camp?"

"The kindness of strangers."

"The kindness of strangers and a will to survive. I know you, too, Rikki."

"I had a lot to live for."

"Because you got information on Vlad?"

"Yeah, Vlad." Her eyelashes fluttered. "And now I'm going to bring him down and clear my name."

"I'll help you."

She chugged some beer, eyeing him over the bottle. "How do I know I can trust you? How do I know you're not going to run back to your commanding officers and tell them I'm still alive?"

Quinn lifted his hands. "Do you really think I couldn't get out of these if I wanted?"

She sputtered and slammed her bottle on the counter. "Try it."

"I don't want to." He hunched his shoulders. "That's the point. I want you to feel secure. I'm no threat to you, Rikki. I wanna help you."

Someone banged on the front door, and Rikki jumped from the stool, grabbing her weapon. "Who'd you call?"

"Nobody."

"Quinn? Quinn, buddy? You alive in there?"

Rikki took three steps toward the radiator, raising her brows and her gun in his direction.

Quinn whispered, "It's just a friend, an acquaintance from the bar."

Leaning over him, Rikki pushed open the window. As she clambered onto the sill above him, she said over her shoulder, "Get rid of him."

"You're crazy." Quinn tried to grab her ankle with his manacled hand, but she slipped out the window and onto the ledge outside the building.

"Quinn? I know you're in there, buddy. You left your hat at the bar."

A knock followed his words, and a woman's voice came through the door. "C'mon, sugar. Open up, and we can continue the party."

His hat. Damn it. He didn't care about the hat.

Alice's singsong voice continued. "Little pig, little pig, let me in, or I'll huff and puff and blow."

The doorknob rattled, and Quinn's stomach sank when the door started to ease open. He'd forgotten to lock it. He rose from the floor and stuck his head out the window. "Rikki. Give me those keys."

In response, she slid the window half-closed and left him to his fate.

Chapter Three

Rikki heard the door bang open all the way, and the woman with the Southern accent let out a whoop.

"Whatcha doin' there, sugar?"

The man, who seemed a bit more sober, said, "This isn't a burglary or anything, is it?"

Quinn rattled the handcuffs. "Just a little…fun that got out of hand."

The man swore and chuckled. "Is the little lady still here?"

Rikki held her breath as she pressed the palms of her hands against the rough siding of Quinn's apartment building.

"Long gone. Can I get some help here, Elvin?"

"I don't know about that, sugar. I like what I'm seein'."

Rikki didn't blame Ms. Southern Belle. She'd liked what she'd seen of Quinn, too. His slide into despair over her supposed death couldn't have been that dire, given the condition of his hard body. Hard all over. Hard for her.

Elvin grunted. "Alice, if you think I'm going to hang around while you torture Quinn here, you've been drinkin' too many Hurricanes."

"Who said anything about torture, and who said anything about you hanging around?" Alice must've walked toward Quinn, as her words carried right out the gap in the window.

Rikki shuffled a few steps on the ledge to the left.

"I finally got Quinn right where I want him, as soon as he loses that underwear."

Quinn cleared his throat. "Yeah, well, I think I've had enough fun and games for the night. Thanks anyway, Alice."

Elvin interrupted Alice's foreplay. "Do you have the keys, man?"

Rikki traced the outline of the cuff keys in her front pocket. At least Elvin seemed to be in a hurry to get out of there. A nearly naked man in handcuffs would probably give this good ol' boy nightmares.

The handcuffs jangled against the radiator. "She took the keys. Must've thought it was pretty funny."

"You want me to call a locksmith or something? Go home and get my saw?"

"God, no."

Quinn practically shouted, and Rikki couldn't help the smile that curved her lips. Served him right for leaving her for dead in the DMZ.

"Grab a paper clip from the drawer by the dishwasher. There should be a bunch of loose ones in there. That'll do it."

Rikki heard heavy footsteps and then heavy breathing near the open window.

Alice asked in a low, hoarse voice, "You sure you don't wanna give me a whirl, sugar? I know I could do you better than the girl who left you here."

"No offense, Alice, but I'm not sure you could. She wore me out."

Rikki clapped a hand over the laugh bubbling on her lips and teetered forward.

Finally, Elvin came to the rescue. "Will this work?"

"That'll do it. Right there."

A scrape and a click later and Quinn said, "That's better. Thanks, man, and thanks for picking up my hat. I could've lived without it."

"We'll get out of here. Maybe that little firebrand will return."

Quinn raised his voice. "I hope so."

"Can we at least take the pizza?"

Quinn answered, "Go for it, Alice. I'll see you guys around."

"Maybe another time, sugar, when you're not so… tired."

Quinn mumbled something incoherent, and Rikki closed her eyes and took a deep breath, thankful she didn't have to listen to some other woman having her way with a naked and chained-up Quinn.

The front door shut, and Rikki's eyelids flew open. Now Quinn was free, probably armed and most likely pissed off.

The window beside her slid open the rest of the way, and Quinn stuck his head out. "Are you okay out here? God, I had visions of you tumbling off my building."

Rikki tossed her head. "It's a wide ledge and it's so humid out here, I'm practically stuck to the side of the apartment."

"Come here." He stretched out his arms. "And for God's sake, be careful."

She sidled along the wall and ignored his help when she got to the window. "I got this."

When Quinn stepped back, Rikki swung into the room, her gun in the waistband of her jeans. She drank him in, still in his briefs, a light sheen of sweat dampening his chest.

"Why did you do that? Why'd you leave me hooked up to the radiator?"

"How was I supposed to know your front door was unlocked? If I'd known that, I wouldn't have gone through all the trouble of breaking into your place through your bathroom window."

"You left me exposed to that...man-eater." He hooked a finger around one bracelet of the cuffs and dangled them in the air. "I should've taken her up on her offer and left you out on that ledge until morning."

"Why didn't you?"

Her question wiped the smile from his face. "Because you're here, standing in front of me, fulfilling every one of my wishes over the past year, and now I don't ever want to let you go."

Before she had a chance to blink, Quinn had her in his arms, and hers curled around his neck in a traitorous response.

His head dipped, and his mouth sought hers. The kiss he pressed against her lips tasted like booze and... desperation. Her muscles tensed. She wasn't here to be Quinn McBride's salvation.

The desire that pumped through her veins and clouded her brain began to lift. As if waking from a dream, she planted her hands against the flat, smooth planes of muscle shifting across his chest. She pulled away from his demanding mouth, backed away from the prodding erection that promised a night of heaven and a morass of hell.

"Quinn. We're not doing this." And how much of "this" was a trick to lure her into trusting him?

Quinn's large frame shuddered. He dropped his

hands from her shoulders and clenched his fists at his sides.

Rikki felt the loss of his touch like a cold wave washing over her. Tears ached in her throat. While she'd been locked up, she found out it had been Quinn behind that sniper rifle, and her hatred of him had kept her alive in the labor camp—that and his baby in her belly.

Without her anger, what did she have left but love? And loving Quinn McBride had only ever brought her heartache. That's all love ever brought.

Flexing his fingers, he turned away from her and plucked his shorts from the floor. He stepped into them and ran a hand through his messy hair. "I just hope you believe me, that I'd changed my mind about the assignment. You can't stand there and tell me that if the CIA had given you orders to take me down, you wouldn't have done it."

"I guess we'll never know." She shoved her hands in her front pockets to stop herself from reaching for him again and smoothing her palms against the muscles that bulged and dipped beneath his flesh. "It's not like we were…together at the time of your mission, anyway."

He sliced a hand through the air. "Don't put that on me. I tried to follow up with you, but you'd disappeared and wouldn't respond to my messages."

"I had my own assignment going on. That's when David told me about Vlad and the North Koreans. At the end of our affair, I thought we'd decided to call it what it was."

"And what was it, Rikki?" He crossed his arms over his broad chest, the skin across his biceps tight.

She flipped the unfamiliar dark hair over her shoulder. "A fling—a dangerous, ill-conceived fling that defied all the rules of the navy and the CIA. A fling

that would've gotten both of us written up and reprimanded."

"You really believe that shooting you offered me
a way out, a way to keep our affair secret?" His dark
eyes narrowed to dangerous slits. "What we did wasn't
the brightest move on either of our parts, but it wasn't
enough to get me court-martialed or ruin my career.
And you spooks break the rules all the time to justify
the means in the end."

Licking her lips, she took a step back. "I've never
slept with someone to get intel."

"Neither have I."

"I didn't mean…" She waved one arm over his shirtless body. "I didn't think that's what you were doing here."

"Really? 'Cause you sure pulled away fast. The
Rikki I knew wouldn't have been able to turn off her
desire like that. The Rikki I knew ran as hot as blazes."

A pulse beat at the base of her throat, and tingles
ran up the insides of her thighs. Their need for each
other had been undeniable and unquenchable. Whenever
he'd touched her, she'd responded like a feral creature,
her hunger not satisfied until he'd taken control of her
body and mind in every way, slaked her thirst, tamed
her wild cravings. He'd been the only man in her life
who'd understood what she needed—before she'd understood it herself.

Her nipples crinkled under her T-shirt, and the familiar wanting throbbed between her legs. Beneath
half-closed lids, her gaze wandered to the handcuffs
Quinn had let slide to the floor.

If he didn't ask now, if he didn't wait for her consent,
if he restrained and ravished her body like he used to,
he'd fill the need she'd carried with her since the day
she left him in Dubai.

She cleared her throat and stuck out her hand. "Truce? You don't get in my way, and I won't kill you."

He ignored her outstretched hand. "I can help you. Someone must already be giving you information, since you seem to know a lot of what went down. One of David's guys?"

"You're right. Someone else is already helping me, so I don't need your assistance." She swept her weapon from the counter and shoved it into the back of her waistband. "I just needed to hear a few things from your own lips."

Her cell phone buzzed, and she pulled it from her pocket. She entered her code and swiped her finger across the text message that had come through. She read the words *Gator Lounge* and then shoved the phone back in her pocket.

When she raised her head, she almost bumped Quinn's chin. He'd moved in on her again, and the heat coming from his body seemed to find its way into her pores.

She stumbled back, crossing her arms over her chest.

He held up his hands. "Since you wanted to talk to me, does that mean you already suspected I'd changed my mind about assassinating you?"

She'd been hoping like hell he could convince her, and he had done so, but she still didn't think she could tell him about Bella—not yet.

"I was blinded by rage when I found out you were the sniper on that hill, but I'd already figured any navy SEAL sniper worth his salt would've been able to take me out before dropping those soldiers—especially you." She held up one finger. "But the fact that you took the assignment enraged me just the same."

"I'm sorry, Rikki. If I had to do it all over again…"

"You'd do the exact same thing. Duty and country."
She crouched down and picked up the handcuffs, then
snapped them in their holder on her belt. She had no
intention of leaving them here for Alice.

"I won't be staying in New Orleans long, and you can
get back to doing whatever it was you were doing." She
wrapped her fingers around the neck of her beer bottle on the kitchen counter and tipped it back and forth.
"But if you're getting deployed again soon, I suggest
you clean up your act, sailor."

"Where are you off to next? You can stay here until
you leave."

She snorted. "Not a good idea. Take care of yourself, Quinn."

She held out her hand for a shake again. This time he
took it, but instead of squeezing her hand, he cinched
his fingers around her wrist and rotated her hand
around. He pressed his lips against the center of her
palm. "I'm glad you're alive, Rikki. Makes the world a
whole helluva lot more bearable."

She pulled away from him and crossed the room to
the front door. As she grasped the handle, she tried to
think of some flip, clever way to say goodbye, but her
throat closed and her bottom lip trembled.

In the end, Rikki slipped out the door without another word or backward glance.

The sultry night air pressed against her as she loped
along the streets not far from the French Quarter. She
ducked into a clump of bushes in a park a few blocks
from Quinn's apartment and pulled out her scooter.

Just after midnight, the bars would still be open, and
Rikki had another appointment at the Gator Lounge be-
fore she settled her business in this city. Before she left
Quinn—maybe for good this time.

She hopped on the electric scooter and motored back toward the lights and action of downtown.

One quick glance over her shoulder, and she let out a sigh of relief. Nobody had followed her. Why would anyone be following her? As far as the CIA knew, a North Korean soldier had shot her dead in the DMZ and a trustworthy navy SEAL had witnessed her death.

She could trust Quinn not to out her. Besides, if he did and the CIA brought her in, he'd be going down with her. She'd make sure of that.

Traffic got heavier as she got closer to the French Quarter. She kept her eye on the side mirror to monitor anything unusual behind her, and would slip between cars if someone seemed to be following too closely or for too long.

When she reached the streets of the French Quarter, still teeming with tourists, she located the bar and then stashed the scooter on a side street. She slid from the seat and ran her fingers through her hair. Her contact had indicated the bar had a casual atmosphere, but she didn't want to look like she'd just come in from a horse ride.

She ducked to peer into the side-view mirror and pulled a lipstick from the purse strapped across her body. She hadn't thought to primp before accosting Quinn in his apartment, but then she hadn't thought much at all about what she wanted to accomplish by seeing him.

To make sure the heat still blazed between them? Check. To see if he still had a body that could weaken her knees? Check. To find out if her presence would make him happy? Check.

She had to admit to herself that seeing him...disheveled had given her a small, petty sense of pleasure. It had also backed up his claim that he'd had a change of heart about shooting her. Quinn wouldn't be drinking if something weren't troubling him.

Now that she'd confirmed that, she'd have to tell him about Bella. He deserved to know about his daughter, even though he'd never mentioned wanting children to her.

She straightened up and pulled her blouse over the gun in her waistband. She didn't expect trouble from her contact, but she had to be prepared for anything. Ariel had vouched for him, and that was good enough for Rikki.

She'd know her guy by his blue Dodgers cap in a city with no pro baseball team. Rikki joined the throng of tourists still crowding Bourbon Street after midnight, and quickened her pace when she saw the street for the bar up ahead.

Someone plowed into her and she spun around, her hand hovering at her waist. The drunk who'd bumped her gave her a sloppy smile and raised his drink. She stepped to the side and rounded the next corner. A green neon sign announced the Gator Lounge, and Rikki surveyed the pedestrians behind her before ducking inside the darkness.

She shivered as the air-conditioning hit her warm skin. She'd overdressed for the heat and humidity in jeans, a blouse and tennies, but shorts and a T wouldn't have worked for breaking into Quinn's place and carrying a weapon and cuffs.

Her gaze flickered across the small cocktail tables and then rested on the back of a man seated at the bar, a blue baseball cap on his head.

Rikki scooped in a breath and threaded her way

through the tables. As she hopped onto the stool next to her contact, she waved at the bartender.

"What can I getcha?" The bartender slapped a napkin on the bar in front of her.

"Light beer, no glass." She slid a glance to her right to see if her words registered with the man in the Dodgers hat.

She waited for his prearranged response—a folding of all four corners of his napkin.

He picked at the label on his beer bottle with his fingernail.

She held her breath.

The bartender placed her beer on the napkin. "Three dollars. Running a tab?"

"No." Her eyes glued to her contact's cocktail napkin, she unzipped the front compartment of her purse and pulled out a five.

Finally the man beside her dipped his head. "I have what you want, but who are you?"

The question had her convulsively clenching her fist around the bill in her hand. That was not part of the deal. He wasn't supposed to ask any questions. He was supposed to hand over a flash drive with information— after folding the damned corners of his napkin.

She turned toward him and smiled sweetly. "You can't possibly have what I want...sugar. And who the hell are you?"

He jerked his thumb upward, hitting the bill of his cap.

Rikki's heart stuttered. None of this made sense. He had half of the plan right, and it couldn't be just a coincidence. Who else would be wearing a Dodgers cap in this particular bar in New Orleans at this exact time?

Her laugh tinkled as she creased her money and

tucked it beneath a candle. "Sorry, I'm no Dodgers fan. In fact, I don't even like baseball."

Wedging one foot on the floor, she took a quick gulp of her beer. She needed to abandon this rendezvous—and fast.

As she shoved herself to her feet, the man grabbed her wrist and growled in her ear, "I have a gun pointed at your ribs. Make a move, and I'll take you down."

Chapter Four

Quinn plowed through the crowd of people on Bourbon Street, stepping on a few toes and upsetting a few drinks. The Gator Lounge occupied a side street, and he made for the corner of that street like a heat-seeking missile.

Before he stepped through the front door of the bar, he tugged his baseball cap low on his forehead. If Rikki made him as soon as he walked into the bar, he'd lose his chance to find out what business she had in New Orleans. He might lose his chance of ever seeing her again.

Shoving his hands in his pockets, he hunched his shoulders and dipped his head. Two steps into the bar, he scanned it quickly, and his heart jumped in his chest.

His gaze locked onto Rikki and a man in a blue cap heading for the back of the bar. Quinn had frequented enough bars in the past few months to know this one led to an alley running behind it. Rikki and her companion were headed either for the restrooms or out the back door. Either way, he'd be in the vicinity to intercept them.

He backed out of the Gator Lounge and jogged through a small courtyard between buildings. He hugged the side of the bar and poked his head around the corner into the alley.

The blood in his veins ran cold as he watched the man propel Rikki in front of him—by force. Every line in her body screamed that she didn't want to be in his company or be going anywhere with him.

Plenty of people had seeped into this alley off the main street, and Quinn joined their ranks, edging closer to Rikki and her abductor.

The guy in the cap seemed distracted. He didn't notice the pedestrians who passed by him and Rikki, wasn't expecting any kind of intervention—and that was the way Quinn liked it.

Quinn joined a trio of late-night revelers and as they walked past Rikki and the man, Quinn dropped back. He reached out and grabbed the man's arm, twisting it behind him before he could use the weapon gripped in his hand.

Rikki made a muffled cry and dropped to the ground.

Quinn gave the man's arm a quick yank and heard the crack of his bone.

The man howled, his legs buckling beneath him.

Quinn heard a shout behind him. "Hey, hey. What are you doing?"

Plucking the gun from the man's useless arm, Quinn kicked him in the gut for good measure.

Someone came up behind Quinn and grabbed his arm. "What are you doing?"

As Quinn shrugged off the stranger's hand, he slid the man's weapon beneath his shirt. "Dude was taking off with my girl. You're comin' home with me, Lila."

Rikki grabbed the sleeve of Quinn's T-shirt, glanced over her shoulder at the concerned onlooker and shrugged. "Jealousy."

Quinn hustled Rikki out of the alley before someone called the cops or an ambulance. When they hit Bourbon Street, Quinn whipped the hat from his head and clasped it against his side with his arm. "Are you okay?"

"I'm fine. How the hell did you know where I was?"

"Car?"

"Scooter a few blocks away."

"You wear a helmet with that thing?"

She poked him in the side. "You're concerned about helmet safety at a time like this?"

"Let's get that helmet from your scooter, and then we'll hop on my bike."

"If you see me to my scooter, I'll be fine."

"Oh, no, you don't." He gripped her upper arm. "I'm not letting you out of my sight. Some guy with a gun almost took you away—again. I wanna know what kind of danger you're in, and I wanna help. I owe you that."

"Really..." She tripped as he pinched her arm tighter. "Okay. My scooter's around the next corner."

Quinn loosened his hold on her and smoothed his fingers over the bunched material of her blouse. If he'd learned anything about Rikki during their short affair, he knew she didn't respond to halfhearted attempts at persuasion—or lovemaking.

She pointed to a small electric job with a white helmet locked to the back. "That's it."

"Let's grab it and go. You don't know if they ID'd your vehicle or followed you."

"No." She bent over the scooter and released her helmet. "I was not followed from your place—unless it was by you. How'd you know where I was?"

"Later. My motorcycle is back toward the bar." He patted his waistband. "I got the guy's gun, so unless he has a backup he's not going to be taking any shots at you."

"The way his bone cracked when you twisted his

arm behind his back, I don't think he could handle any weapon right now." She crossed her arms over her helmet, hugging it to her midsection.

"When I saw him hustling you away at gunpoint, I wanted to do worse than break his arm, but I don't need to be charged with murder or even questioned at this point. Who was he?" He placed his hand at the small of her back and propelled her across the street.

"Later."

As they reached the other side of the street, Quinn ran his hand along the waistband of Rikki's jeans, sitting low on the curve of her hips.

She stiffened beneath his touch. "I don't think it's the time or place to be groping me."

"I'm not groping you, unless you want me to." He briefly cupped her derriere through the tight denim. "What happened to your gun and handcuffs?"

"He relieved me of them and dropped them in a Dumpster right outside the club."

Quinn muttered an expletive. "Maybe we can retrieve them tomorrow."

"We?"

"Here's my bike. Get that helmet on and hop on the back."

She placed a hand on his shoulder. "Are you okay to drive this thing? You were sleeping off a bender when I sneaked into your apartment."

"The events since that time have gone a long way to sober me up."

She held out her hand. "Doesn't matter how you feel, Quinn. Your blood alcohol level is probably still over the legal limit. You don't want to get arrested for murder *or* driving while under the influence."

He jingled the keys and glanced down at his Honda.

"Can you manage a bike this size? It's not your little scooter."

She snorted. "Hop on the back."

Rikki handled the bike like she handled everything else—with confidence and ease. He did have to help her hoist the bike onto its kickstand, but she'd been right about taking the wheel—or the handlebars. He'd been an idiot to take a chance like that on the bike, no matter how sober he felt, but he couldn't stand to see her waltz right out of his life just after he'd discovered she'd survived the ordeal in North Korea.

How the hell had she escaped that torture?

As they approached his front door, Rikki hung back. "You didn't leave your place unlocked again, did you? We're not going to find Alice waiting in your bed, are we? Or worse?"

"I can dispense with Alice easily enough, but if that man who had you at gunpoint has any friends, we want to make sure he hasn't ID'd me and dispatched one of his cohorts to wait for us."

Rikki's brown eyes widened as if the thought had never occurred to her. If it hadn't, her spy skills needed some refreshment.

Where had she been since escaping from North Korea?

He tucked her behind him. "Wait here while I give it a quick check."

Her hand grabbed his side, and she lifted her abductor's gun from his waistband. "Now I'm armed, too. We'll take 'em on together."

"I forgot who I was dealing with." He unlocked his door and pushed it open slowly with his foot. When it stood wide, he entered his apartment with his weapon sweeping the room.

Rikki closed and locked the door behind them and crept in beside him, peeling off to check out the back rooms. She called out, "All clear."

Quinn peered over the counter into the kitchen. "All clear here."

Rikki joined him and blew out a breath. "How would that guy have ID'd you? He barely got a look at you before you took him down."

"If he knows who you are, he might make the connection from New Orleans to me and me to you."

"There aren't many people who knew what we did in Dubai." Her lashes fluttered, and she got busy putting away the spare gun. "I mean, that we…hooked up. I don't think some random person from intelligence is going to make that link between me and you."

"Intelligence? Is that who that was? You said it yourself earlier. The CIA thinks you're dead."

She raised her shoulders to her ears. "I don't know who he was, and more important, he didn't know who I was."

"Are you telling me that was some kind of random abduction?" Quinn shook his head. "No common street thug is going to get over on you, Rikki, especially when you have a gun and cuffs on you."

"I didn't say he was a common criminal. The guy had mad skills himself and I'm not downplaying your heroic rescue, but he'd let his guard down by the time he got me outside the Gator Lounge. He wasn't expecting anyone to come riding to my defense."

"You think he was from the Company?"

"I don't know. We didn't get that far in our acquaintance, but he did not know who I was. He asked me."

"Maybe I am still drunk." Quinn massaged his temple with two fingers. "If he didn't know who you were and he was some kind of spy, why was he abducting you and why were you meeting him?"

Rikki hopped on a stool, straddling it, knees wide. "First, you. How did you know I was going to the Gator Lounge when I left here?"

"I didn't know you were going straight there when you took off, but I saw the text message come through." He clicked his tongue. "Careless, Rikki. I was looking straight down at your phone, but then maybe you wanted me to see that message."

She shot up on the stool, her back ramrod straight. "That's ridiculous."

"Now you. Who were you meeting at the Gator and why?" He held up one finger. "And don't even try lying to me."

She slumped, her shoulders rounding, her hands on her knees. "I don't know exactly who I was meeting. We had a series of clues for each other, a back-and-forth, starting with his Dodgers cap."

"That guy was wearing a Dodgers cap. What happened?"

"I spotted him at the bar, everything on track. I ordered a beer, using the agreed-upon language, but he didn't reciprocate. He went off script. My contact didn't know who I was and wasn't supposed to ask, but this guy…" She waved one hand in the air.

"You figured he wasn't your guy or maybe your guy had been replaced? What did you do?"

"I admitted nothing to him and was getting ready to abandon the mission. I must've telegraphed that because the next thing I knew, he had his gun poking me in the side."

Quinn crossed his arms, curling his fingers into his biceps. "Did he ask you any more questions at that point?"

"Nope. Started marching me away to God-knows-where." She captured the unfamiliar brown hair in one hand and curled it around her fist.

Quinn's gaze locked onto the dark, silky strands. Even without her wavy red hair and bright blue eyes, he'd recognized Rikki in a flash. Why wouldn't he? She'd been in his dreams nightly.

He tugged on a lock of his own hair, which he'd grown out since his previous deployment. "Is that a wig? It's so…different."

Her mouth formed an *O* and released a little puff of air. "I thought we were talking about my abductor."

"We are, we will, just wondering about the transformation." The warmth from his chest began creeping up his neck.

Even discussing a violent incident and a mystery, Quinn couldn't tamp down his attraction to Rikki. He could take her right now, across that kitchen counter, bent over that stool, and not give another thought to her mysterious meeting or the man he'd beaten down in the alley.

What did any of it matter with this woman back in his life, sitting right in front of him, inches away?

She tossed her head, and the dark hair flowed over one shoulder. "It's not a wig. I had my hair straightened when I had it colored. It'll last for several weeks—as long as I need."

Quinn ran both hands over his face as if waking from a long, drugged sleep. "As long as you need to do what, Rikki? What are you doing in New Orleans? What was that meeting all about?"

"The man I was supposed to meet had something for me, something that might help me clear my name. I need that. I need something before I can go to the CIA and reveal that I'm still alive—and no traitor." She blinked and rubbed her nose with the back of her hand.

The Rikki he knew, the woman who'd dumped him in Dubai, never cried. But that woman had been a trusted CIA operative at the top of her game and still on the rise.

When she'd succumbed to him, knowing her superiors would frown on her conduct, knowing she could be reprimanded, she'd spun out of control. Their desire for each other had been so great they'd both thrown caution to the wind. They'd made love in glass elevators high above the glittering city, coupled in the warm waters of the Persian Gulf in a place that frowned upon spouses holding hands in public.

And during all of it, the kick-ass CIA operative who could disarm a man without breaking a sweat and interrogate a suspected terrorist for twenty-four hours straight had relinquished control to him in every way. She'd waited for his commands, done his bidding, which was really her own. She could pretend to herself that he'd mastered her mind and body, but in reality he'd been the captive. She'd enthralled him. Still did.

Quinn launched forward and crouched beside her. His thumb swept her bottom lashes where a single teardrop trembled, although she'd willed it not to fall.

"You deserve that life back, and I'm going to help you reclaim it. What did your contact have for you?"

"A-a flash drive containing some information. I don't think he even knew what the info meant, but he was going to pass it along to me."

"On whose authority? Who's your contact at the agency? Who sent him?"

Rikki swept her tongue along her bottom lip. "Maybe

it was all a setup. Maybe the goal of the plan all along included my capture. The flash drive a ruse to lure me out."

"Who sent him? Not some anonymous source? You didn't trust some anonymous CIA drone, did you?"

"It was Ariel." She hunched forward, her nose almost touching his. "You know Ariel, don't you?"

"The head of the Vlad task force. Several of my SEAL team members have been on assignments controlled by Ariel—and they trust her, or him."

"Her. Ariel is definitely female."

"How do you know that? I think one of my team members actually spoke to her, but we're not even sure it was the real Ariel." Quinn's eyes narrowed. "You know her?"

"Ariel was my mentor at the CIA when I started. You know, one female spy to another in a department dominated by men."

Quinn sat back on his heels. "You mean, you know the *real* Ariel? The actual woman behind the clever pseudonym? From what I understand, the Vlad task force is controlled by Prospero, Jack Coburn's black ops organization. Ariel, Prospero—from the Shakespeare play."

"Yeah, I remember my Shakespeare and yeah, Ariel is with Prospero now, recruited from the CIA several years ago."

"Her real name?"

Rikki ran her fingertip along the seam of her lips. "Ariel."

Quinn jumped to his feet and paced in front of the window. "You don't owe her anything if she set you up."

"I can't be sure she did. She's the one who discovered I was in the labor camp and not dead. She's the one who helped me escape, get back to…get out."

"Maybe she did all that so she could dial in the CIA and have them recapture you. Maybe she didn't want you hobnobbing with the North Koreans, possibly passing them intel."

"I don't believe that, not... Ariel. If that's what she wanted, my contact at the bar would've followed through with our assignment without alarming me, and then she could've sent the FBI to pick me up and arrest me." Rikki slid from the stool and edged around the counter into the kitchen. "That's not how this went down."

"Maybe the contact himself went rogue. Maybe he recognized you."

She made a half turn from the fridge, a bottle of water in her hand. She raised it. "In this getup? Just because you had me figured out immediately doesn't mean some CIA agent is going to recognize me from a photo in a briefing on spies within the Agency. Dark hair, dark eyes..." She patted her hip. "A few extra pounds. This is a damned good disguise."

When she touched her body, Quinn's gaze followed her hand. Rikki had always been long and lean. He tracked up the curve of her hip to the loose blouse draped over her form, brushing the ample swell of her breasts.

He swallowed hard. He'd always enjoyed Rikki's slim, athletic build—especially given their marathon lovemaking sessions in...unusual places and circumstances. But for the first time this crazy evening, he noticed the new softness of her body—the way her jeans hugged her derriere and thighs, the seductive sway of her hips when she walked, the way her blouse pulled tight across her breasts when she spread her arms or gestured. His erection pulsed again.

Then he blinked. Rikki hadn't just escaped from a North Korean labor camp. She'd been recuperating somewhere.

Quinn cleared his throat. "God, it's late. You're bunking here tonight, and I don't want to hear any arguments."

She snapped her mouth closed and chugged some water from the bottle. "Okay, but just so we're clear you're sleeping in the bed and I'm taking the couch."

Quinn's erection ached for relief, and he tugged on the hem of his cargo shorts. "Yeah, of course, but I have a sofa bed in my office and you can have that." He opened his mouth in a pretend yawn. "We can try to figure out what happened to your contact tomorrow. If you still trust her, get in touch with Ariel."

Rikki sloshed some water in her mouth before swallowing. "Do you happen to have an extra toothbrush?"

"I'm on leave, and you're in luck because I just went to my dentist two weeks ago. I think he's under some misconception that the navy supplies me with one toothbrush every two years, because he loaded me up. They're in the second drawer on the right. This place has two bathrooms, so you're welcome to the other one."

"I'll take the water with me to bed." She swept her small purse from the counter. "This is good. I'll get a good night's sleep and regroup in the morning. I'm sure Ariel will have an explanation for me."

"If you think you can trust her."

"I do." She turned at the entrance to the hallway. "Thanks for your assistance tonight, Quinn. Maybe I *did* want you to see that text after all."

"You can always ask me, Rikki. You can ask me for anything."

A smile trembled on her lips, and then she disappeared down the hallway.

Cocking his head to the side, Quinn listened as she got a toothbrush from his bathroom and then shut herself in the other one.

He sprinted down the hall and ducked into the second bedroom. He pulled out the sofa bed, darted to his bedroom, snagged a pillow from his bed and tossed it onto the sofa bed. Despite his best efforts at a quick assembly, Rikki hovered at the door of the office as he dragged a blanket across the bed.

"Just making up the sofa bed. Did you find the toothbrush and toothpaste okay?"

"Yep." She ran her tongue along her teeth.

"Okay, then. Tomorrow." His gaze darted to Rikki still propping up the doorjamb. She didn't expect him to squeeze past her, did she? He couldn't handle that.

A few seconds later that seemed like minutes, Rikki pushed herself off the door. "Nice apartment. I had memorized your address from…before. I was hoping you still lived here."

He spread his arms. "Still here. Sleep tight."

He practically ran from the room, slamming the door behind him. Sleep tight? What did that even mean, anyway?

He brushed his own teeth and studied his reflection in the mirror. He needed a shave—and an attitude adjustment. Rikki didn't want him anymore. She'd made that clear before. And after he'd gone on a mission to assassinate her? Yeah, pretty much killed any thread of a chance he had left with her. Now if he could only send that message to his body.

He yanked the covers back from his bed and pulled off his T-shirt. He unzipped the fly on his shorts and

hooked his thumbs in the band of his briefs as he started
to take them down with his shorts. He usually slept
naked, but maybe leaving on his underwear would protect him from lustful thoughts about Rikki.

He crawled between the sheets, rolled on his side,
then the other side, and then flopped onto his back,
one arm flung across his face. Briefs, no briefs, fully
clothed, suit of armor—didn't matter. Rikki Taylor was
in his blood, and now she was back in his life.

About an hour later on the edge of another feverish
dream, Quinn bolted upright in bed, his heart racing.
He paused and heard the noise that had awakened him.

Someone pounded on the door again.

Quinn rolled out of bed and grabbed the gun on his
nightstand. He crept toward the front door and paused,
holding his breath.

The pounding resumed, following by a groan and a
shout. "Quinn? Quinn, you there?"

Quinn drew his brows over his nose and released the
locks. He eased open the door, and a man fell across the
threshold, bruised and bloody.

"Quinn, you gotta help me. They're gonna kill me."

Chapter Five

With her blouse pulled on over her panties, Rikki tip-toed to the office door, the gun Quinn had taken from her abductor clutched in her hand.

She opened the door a crack and sucked in a breath as the men's voices, Quinn's and someone else's, carried down the hallway.

Had he called someone to take her in?

She rubbed her eyes. If that were the case, the guy wouldn't be banging on the front door in the wee morning hours. She pressed her ear to the gap in the door, wrinkling her nose. She couldn't hear a damned thing.

With the gun leading the way, she edged down the hallway and tripped to a stop.

Quinn looked up from tending to a badly beaten man stretched out on his living room floor. "Put down that gun and soak some towels with water."

The authoritative tone of his voice had her jumping into action. She placed the weapon on the kitchen counter and scurried back to the hallway, where she rummaged through a few shelves, sweeping towels into her arms.

In the kitchen, she ran two of the towels beneath the faucet until they were soaked and dropped next to Quinn attending to the injured man.

As Quinn checked the man's injuries, Rikki dabbed

the cuts on his face with the corner of a damp towel. "Who is he?"

"CIA."

Rikki dropped the towel and jerked back. "You called him?"

Quinn spit out between clenched teeth, "I did not. He just showed up on my doorstep like this. I don't know what the hell he's doing here, but he's a friend, and I'm not turning him away."

"O-of course not." Rikki grabbed the towel and continued cleaning the man's facial wounds. "What happened to him?"

"I don't have a clue. He appeared and collapsed."

The man moaned, and Quinn leaned in close. "Jeff, Jeff. What happened?"

Jeff peeled open one puffy eye, caked with blood. "Got the jump on me. Beat me up."

"Who? Street robbery? Do you want me to call the cops?"

"No." Jeff dug his fingers into the flesh of Quinn's arms. "On the job."

Quinn's eyes met Rikki's for a split second, and her heart flip-flopped. The CIA on the job in New Orleans? She couldn't stay here. Couldn't stay with Quinn any longer.

Quinn tugged Jeff's shirt back down over his stomach. "I don't see any weapon wounds."

"No weapons." Jeff closed his eyes. "Unless you count the guy's fists."

"You need some ice." Rikki dabbed the last of the blood from Jeff's face. She gathered the bloodstained towels and wrapped them in a plastic bag. She loaded another plastic bag with ice.

When she returned to the living room, Quinn had

helped Jeff onto the sofa. Without the blood smearing his face, Jeff no longer looked half-dead.

Rikki perched on the edge of the coffee table, facing Jeff. She thrust the bag of ice at him. "Here. Can you manage?"

"Yeah, thanks." Jeff grabbed the impromptu ice pack and pressed it against the lump forming around his eye.

Quinn started for the hallway. "I'll get you some ibuprofen and water."

As Quinn walked away, Rikki scooted off the table. "I'll get the water."

She and Quinn returned to Jeff's side at about the same time, and Rikki noticed Quinn had pulled on his shorts. That made two times she'd seen the man almost naked in one night, and she didn't have to use her imagination for the rest. They'd spent two whole days together in his hotel room sans clothing. Answering the door for room service had been the only times either of them had slipped into something to cover their nakedness.

Rikki tucked her hair behind one ear and held out the bottle to Jeff. "Here you go. Feeling better?"

She just hoped to God her disguise would see her through and Jeff wouldn't recognize her, but then nobody in the CIA would be expecting to run into Rikki Taylor—the dead double agent.

"I feel a lot better." Jeff tapped his jaw and winced. "I'm really sorry about intruding here."

Heat prickled Rikki's cheeks. *If only.* "Oh, no, we…"

Quinn shrugged and dragged Rikki against his side with one arm, his hand resting perilously close to the under-curve of her breast, his warm skin soaking through the thin material of her blouse.

In her haste, Rikki had yanked on her top but hadn't

bothered with a bra and Quinn seemed to be taking full advantage of that fact.

"Yeah, man, bad timing."

Rikki bit her bottom lip. Definitely taking advantage.

"I'll be out of your way tomorrow morning. If I can just stay the night, I think can get back on track."

"Are you sure you don't need medical care?"

"I could use some, but there's nothing urgent. Nothing that can't wait for tomorrow. I'm really sorry, Quinn."

"Don't worry about it. I'm just glad I was here. Can you tell me what you were doing in New Orleans?"

"Can't do that, man, not even for a badass navy SEAL, and especially not in front of your girl here."

"Me?" Rikki tried to wriggle out of Quinn's grasp, but he wasn't having it.

His fingers curled into the curve of her hip. "She can go into the other room."

Rikki nodded, anxious to escape Quinn's realm where she had zero discipline and even less self-control.

"Sworn to secrecy. You know the drill."

"I do know the drill. I wouldn't tell you about my next mission, either." Quinn jerked his thumb over his shoulder. "I've got a spare room with a sofa bed all made up. I even have a few extra toothbrushes."

Rikki bumped Quinn's hip with her own. "Maybe Jeff would be more comfortable out here."

Jeff tilted his head from side to side, stretching his neck. "Honestly? Stretching out on a bed sounds like a sure cure for me right now."

"Make sure that bed's made up for Jeff, honey." Quinn gave her a little shove from behind, and Rikki clenched her fist at her side. He was milking this situation to the max.

She could raise a fuss in front of this CIA agent,

someone who would recognize the name Rikki Taylor immediately, but why tempt fate on this crazy night? "Sure, of course. Why don't you find him a toothbrush and clean towel?"

"I owe you one, McBride, more than one."

Rikki scurried down the hallway and slipped into the office. She smoothed out the covers on the sofa bed and grabbed the rest of her clothes and her purse. Then she crossed the hall to Quinn's bedroom.

As long as he'd invited her into his inner sanctum, she'd make herself at home. She swung open the walk-in closet and dragged a T-shirt off its hanger. Still inside the closet, she pulled the blouse over her head and replaced it with Quinn's T-shirt.

Beneath the T-shirt, she skimmed her hands over her body. Would he be able to tell she'd given birth nine months ago? She cupped her breasts, which still felt heavy although she'd given up breastfeeding a month ago in anticipation of her journey.

Reaching around outside the closet, she flicked off the light. Quinn McBride would not be getting a look at her naked body.

The bedroom door clicked softly as she stepped out of the closet.

Quinn's head jerked up. "Where'd you come from? I thought maybe you'd slipped out onto the ledge again."

She tugged at the hem of the T-shirt. "Thought I'd find some proper sleepwear."

His dark gaze scorched her head to toe, making her feel as if she were standing in front of him without a stitch on instead of in a baggy shirt.

"Sorry about that. Jeff deserved my full hospitality after what he'd been through. I had to offer him that bed."

She wedged a hand on her hip. "You're not sorry. You jumped at the chance to kick me out of that bed and lure me into this one."

A slow smile claimed Quinn's wide mouth. "I saw it as a win-win."

He crossed to the other side of the king-size bed and flipped down the messy covers. "Be my guest."

Rikki folded her arms, grabbing handfuls of the cotton material of the T-shirt, her gaze darting around the room. She leveled a finger at the floor. "You can sleep there for just one night. I'm sure you've slept on harder surfaces than that in your illustrious career as a navy SEAL sniper."

"Not happening." He set his jaw in a hard line. "The bed's big enough for the two of us. You stay on your side, and I'll stay on mine."

She looked him up and down—all six feet three inches of rippling muscle. "This bed is barely big enough for you."

"On my honor—" he drew a cross over his heart "—I'm not gonna lay a finger on you, Rikki. What kind of caveman do you take me for?"

Her eyes flickered across his broad shoulders. *The thoroughly delicious kind.* "Okay, okay. We both need our rest anyway."

Quinn returned to his side of the bed and dropped his shorts.

Holding her breath, she watched him out of the corner of her eye. Those shorts had better be the only piece of clothing he planned to shed. She eased out that captive breath when he slid between the sheets in his briefs.

As she positioned herself at the very edge of her side of the bed, Quinn punched a pillow and said, "At least we know your identity is still safe."

Her eyes flew open. "What do you mean?"

"Rikki."

The mattress dipped and she knew he'd turned toward her. "What? What does that mean, I'm safe?"

"You didn't figure it out?"

"Figure what out?" She rolled onto her back, her head falling to the side.

"Jeff was your contact person."

She hoisted herself up abruptly, banging her head against the soaring headboard. "No."

"Of course he was. Instead of meeting you at the Gator Lounge, he met up with someone who wanted to replace him. The man you saw in the bar, the man who marched you out at gunpoint, is the same man who beat up Jeff and stole his baseball cap."

Rikki covered her face with her hands. *Of course.* How could she be so stupid? Had she really believed two CIA covert ops were going on in New Orleans at the same time?

Motherhood had affected her brain in more ways than one. Or maybe she could chalk it up to the distracting presence of Quinn.

"You see that, right?"

"I-I-I do now. Of course, that's clear. I'm an idiot."

"Don't beat yourself up. You've had a rough night, a rough year." He smoothed his palm up her thigh, froze and then snatched his hand away. "Sorry."

His touch had sent goose bumps racing up her inner thighs. "You're right. I didn't register for Jeff at all except as your late-night booty call."

A laugh rumbled in Quinn's chest. "You say that like it's a bad thing. Look, Jeff doesn't know who he was supposed to meet or why. You were smart to stick to code words and exchanges instead of descriptions."

She wriggled up higher against the pillow. "But where's that flash drive? Do you think he has it on him?"

"Do you really think the guy who beat him up and stole his hat didn't search him? Maybe he didn't want to have the flash drive on him when he met you. Maybe he left it somewhere in case the meeting didn't come off—which it didn't."

"If he takes a shower tomorrow morning, I'm not above searching through his clothes."

"I'll strongly advise him to take a shower."

"Wait." She sat up straight, crossing her legs beneath her, under the covers. "Why did he come here?"

"For help. Jeff and I go way back. He knows I live in New Orleans. He's been to my place a few times. He came to me for help." A muscle ticked in Quinn's jaw. "You don't think I had anything to do with his coming here, do you? I hope we're past that suspicion. If I'd wanted to turn you over to the Agency, I could've done it hours ago."

"We're past that." She grabbed the pillow and slid down again, pulling it beneath her head.

"Good. Get some sleep."

Still on her back, Rikki shifted her gaze to the right, taking in Quinn's large frame, positioned on his side, facing her. He'd pushed the covers down to his waist, although the air-conditioning had cooled the room down to a comfortable temperature.

Her eyes had adjusted to the darkness and she drank in the lines of his body, the hard muscles, even in repose, still etched beneath his smooth flesh.

Before she knew what she was doing, before she could stop herself, her hand shot out and she traced her fingertips around one of his brown nipples.

He sucked in a breath. "You don't want this, remember? Don't tease me, Rikki."

She snatched her hand back and rolled to her side, away from him and his irresistible body. "You're right."

Quinn released a long, shuddering breath.

She had teased him with her light touch, had made him hard. Sighing, she drew her knees to her chest, thrusting out her backside, the heat of Quinn's body inches away. Just inches.

She yawned and wriggled into place, her toes skimming his shin, the hair on his leg tickling her.

"Rikki."

She edged toward him, curling one arm around his waist. "Maybe just once, for old times' sake."

He hissed through his teeth. "You're sure about this?"

She pulled her body closer to his, her front flush against his, and breathed into his ear. "I'm sure."

She edged her fingers between the elastic of his briefs and the flat, hard muscles of his abdomen, dragging her nails along the tip of his erection, barely contained by the thin cotton of his underwear.

He shivered. "I've been imagining that all night, but nothing tops the real thing."

She plunged her hand deeper and cupped him with her palm while stroking his tight flesh with her thumb. Her voice, rough with desire, rasped in his ear. "Take me like only you can."

His erection throbbed in her hand, and she could feel her bones melt and her breasts soften in anticipation of his fiery touch.

Quinn hesitated for just a second until Rikki squeezed him and bit the back of his neck.

In one motion, Quinn rose to his knees and ripped the covers from them both. Towering over her, bulging from the confines of his briefs, he growled, "Take them off."

Tingles rushed through her body at his gruff tone of voice, and she started the game. Leaning forward, she took the band of his briefs between her teeth and dragged them down, over his erection. She continued pulling down his underwear with her mouth, past the flaring muscles of his thighs, down to his knees, buried in the mattress of the bed.

Closing his eyes, he plowed his fingers through her hair. "I can pretend it's the fiery red I love."

"Shh." She pressed the pad of her thumb to his lips.

His fingers dug into her scalp as he urged her down. "Take me in your mouth. Taste me."

She closed her lips around his girth, and he moaned in rhythm as she drew him in and out of her mouth.

He pulled away from her, sitting back on his heels. "It's been too long. I can't last like that."

She caressed his shoulders and kissed the spot right above his left nipple. "Tell me what to do next."

He grabbed a fistful of T-shirt. "You can take this off for starters. Why are you still covered?"

She clutched the edge of the shirt, suddenly shy. Would he notice the differences in her body? Would he know what they meant?

She'd been rail-thin when she escaped from the labor camp, four months pregnant. Undernourished and overworked, she'd feared for the life of her baby. If she'd been captive any more than the two months she'd endured, she would've lost Bella for sure.

Instead, she'd wound up in Jamaica with her mother and Chaz, and Mom had coddled her through the duration of her pregnancy, kept her in bed the first two months, well fed and stationary.

Rikki had put on more than enough weight for her pregnancy, and Bella, although born a few weeks early, had posted a healthy weight and length.

During the pregnancy and after, Rikki's breasts had increased in size and softened, her hips had widened, too, and she presented a much different figure than the taut, tight athlete Quinn had first bedded in Dubai.

Impatient with her reluctance, Quinn dragged the T-shirt from her body and yanked down her panties. "That's much better."

With her bottom lip caught between her teeth, Rikki watched Quinn study her new body. His eyes darkened to unfathomable depths.

Then he reached out and cupped her breasts. The thrill of his touch shot down to her belly and lower, creating an aching need. She arched her back, thrusting her chest forward.

He juggled her breasts in his hands as if testing their heft. "I like this new development."

He molded her waist with his palms and reached back to stroke her derriere. "And this. When you get your job back with the Agency, you should let them know you wanna lay off the PT because someone likes your new curves."

One side of her mouth crooked into a smile. He approved of her appearance, and more important, he'd dismissed it as the lack of rigorous physical training on her part. Not that she planned to keep Bella a secret from him forever. She just needed to get through this, get her life back, and then she'd tell Quinn everything—no strings attached.

He kissed her mouth. "What are you smiling about?"

"I'm just glad you like the difference."

"You're kidding. I wouldn't think you'd give a damn one way or the other." He eased her back onto the bed and straddled her on his knees. He lowered his body and squeezed her breasts around the tip of his erection. "But just in case you do give a damn and need proof? Here it is, baby."

He skimmed his tip down the length of her body, prodding between her legs.

Her knees fell open, inviting him in, inviting him home.

He stretched out on the bed on his stomach, between her legs, his own hanging off the foot of the bed. He placed his hands against her inner thighs and spread them apart.

Butterflies swirled in her stomach, and her legs shook.

Quinn dragged his scruffy chin over her soft flesh, drawing a gasp from her lips. Then he probed her with the tip of his tongue, searching out all her secret places.

She stretched her arms over her head, crossing them at the wrists, in total supplication and surrender. Raising her hips off the bed, she choked out, "More, please don't stop."

"Oh, I won't stop, my little Buttercup, but you wanted to play this game, didn't you?"

The teasing glint in his eye had her desperate laugh ending on a hiccup. Her job demanded that she be strong, in control, tough as nails, and she'd delivered. When she first met Quinn, he'd joked that she could scare the buttercups off their stems. So when she became soft and vulnerable for him, just for him, he'd started calling her Buttercup. It still made her weak in the knees.

But he hadn't forgotten the game they played, and he began in earnest. He removed his tongue from her throbbing, swollen flesh and nibbled on the insides of her thighs. He touched her everywhere in every way, except for the pleasure spot between her legs.

He set every nerve ending on fire, had her thrashing her head from side to side, digging her fingernails into his buttocks, wrapping her legs around his hips—until she quivered and begged beneath him.

"Please, Quinn. Please. I'm aching."

He sat back, his erection bobbing in front of him, his skin flushed, obviously experiencing the same frustrated, agonizing pleasure she was—but that wasn't their game.

"I need you. Only you. I'm begging you."

He gave her burning nipple one more tweak. "Since you asked so nicely, Buttercup."

He buried his head between her thighs, and two flicks from his tongue sent her over the edge.

Her orgasm roared through her, wringing the strength from every inch of her body, draining her, releasing her from every expectation, every responsibility, the sensations of her body taking over her mind, flooding it with pleasure.

She whimpered beneath him as he plowed into her, his hard desire eager and hungry.

Rikki wrapped her arms and legs around Quinn as he spent himself inside her.

After, he shifted from her body and pulled her back against his front, nuzzling the hollow of her neck. "I'm glad you're among the living. It's like I just had Christmas, my birthday and Mardi Gras all on the same day."

"Me, too." She pressed a hand against her stomach to calm the butterflies. Quinn wasn't the bad guy. He needed to know about Bella, however he felt about having a child.

"Quinn?"

"Mmm?"

"I have something to tell you. I-I hope, well, I hope you'll be happy about it." She paused and swallowed. In a hoarse whisper, she said, "I had a baby—your baby."

She waited several seconds while Quinn's breathing deepened and slowed. Twisting her head over her shoulder, she scooted onto her back.

She sighed as she took in Quinn, sound asleep, still blissfully ignorant that he was a father.

THE FOLLOWING MORNING, Quinn woke her up by holding a mug of coffee beneath her nose. "He's in the shower."

"Who? What?" She rubbed her eyes. "Jeff?"

Quinn nodded, and she nearly upset the coffee as she bounded out of bed.

"Relax. I already searched his clothes, which he left on the bedroom floor. I didn't find a thing."

She tripped to a stop and pulled the T-shirt she'd been clutching to her chest over her head. "Do you think you can devise some story to get him to tell you about the flash drive without revealing who I am? Maybe I can just admit I'm the person he was supposed to meet."

"If you do, that'll connect you to me. He's gonna wonder what our relationship is all about."

She grabbed the edge of her T-shirt and twisted it into knots with her fingers. "Jeff didn't know why he was meeting me. Didn't know who I was. I'm sure he still thinks Rikki Taylor is dead, if he thinks about her at all. He sure as hell doesn't know you had a fling with Rikki once upon a time." She narrowed her eyes. "Does he?"

"It's getting cold." He held out the mug to her. "And no, Jeff doesn't know anything about my personal life."

"Then let's just tell him I was his intended contact last night." She took the mug from him and curled both hands around it.

"I don't like that idea, Rikki. The lower you keep your profile, the better. What if Jeff talks?"

"Doesn't seem like much of a talker. Pretty tight-lipped if you ask me." She took a sip of the black brew and rolled it in her mouth before swallowing it.

"He's discreet, a good agent, but what if he hears

something about us from someone and puts two and two together? You've been doing a good job of keeping under the radar."

"We're going to have to reconnect anyway. I'm not letting that flash drive slip out of my clutches if it's something that can help me. He's going to see me then."

"Not necessarily. You can arrange a drop where you don't meet face-to-face. That'll be easy for you to insist on, since Jeff has already been compromised."

Rikki sank to the foot of the bed. What Quinn said made a lot of sense. She didn't want to reveal any clues to her identity to anyone.

"You're right. I'll arrange a drop with him." She curled one leg beneath her. "Who do you think ambushed him, us or them?"

"Since he's still alive, I'm betting on one of ours— FBI maybe. They could suspect him of being a double agent. The good news is that they were following Jeff and not you."

"All Jeff needs to do is get Ariel to vouch for him without revealing anything else. She's doing stuff not even the CIA knows about."

"Obviously, if she's helping you. Why is she helping you?"

"Let's just say Ariel is a kindred spirit."

"You mean another woman in a male-dominated field. You mentioned that before."

"Something like that." She pulled the T-shirt away from her body. "I'm going to take a shower."

As she brushed past Quinn, he grabbed a handful of her T-shirt and pulled her toward him. "Any regrets about last night?"

"None at all." She kissed the edge of his chin. "You?"

"No, except that I feel like I kinda tricked you, I mean by inviting Jeff to take the extra room."

She snorted. "You didn't have me fooled for one minute, Quinn McBride."

Showered and dressed in the jeans and blouse from last night, Rikki joined the men in the kitchen with her empty coffee cup.

Jeff raised a piece of toast in her direction. "I was just telling Quinn how sorry I am that I barged in on you two."

Rikki squinted at Jeff's black eye and puffy jaw. "I'm glad Quinn was home. Do you need to see a doctor?"

"I might need some stitches." He brushed aside the lock of hair drooping over a bandage on his forehead. "But I'm okay."

Hopping up on a stool at the kitchen counter, Rikki placed her cell phone in front of her. "Then we don't mind at all, do we, Quinn?"

"Happy to help, bro." Quinn held up the coffeepot. "Refills?"

Rikki shoved her cup across the counter, and Jeff nodded as he pulled his cell phone from his pocket.

"Do you want something else to eat, Jeff?" He pointed to the fridge. "Eggs?"

"Nothing fancy. Toast is okay."

Her phone buzzed on the counter, and Rikki grabbed it. Jeff had sent her a text.

Slowly she raised her gaze to meet his. Understanding and acknowledgment flashed between them.

She'd been outed.

Chapter Six

A charged silence descended on the kitchen. Rikki held her breath as Quinn looked up from pulling slices of bread from a bag. His gaze darted from Jeff to her, understanding dawning in his eyes.

Rikki locked eyes with Jeff, his color high. Her chest rose and fell with each breath, her fight-or-flight instinct in high gear.

Jeff ventured first, turning his cell phone outward. "You're my contact, aren't you?"

She ignored the question. "What happened to you last night? You can tell me."

Jeff shifted his gaze to Quinn, his head down, busy with a bag of bread, whistling like an idiot—as if she and Jeff didn't know he was listening to every word they said.

Rikki waved her hand in Quinn's direction. "You can trust him."

Jeff tipped his head at Quinn. "Are you involved in this?"

"Who, me? I'm just making toast." Quinn held up two pieces of bread.

"Quinn's not involved." Rikki circled the edge of her coffee cup with the tip of her finger. "I know him, knew he lived here. Just like you, I went to him for help after things fell apart last night."

Jeff dropped his shoulders as if dropping his guard. "I'm glad to see you're okay. I didn't know what happened after that guy attacked me and took my cap. He was trying to get info out of me, but a cop came by and he took off. He knew where we were meeting but none of the details."

"That became obvious pretty quickly, since he didn't have the sequence of codes down."

"I'm sorry. I would've stayed around to warn you, but the cops wanted to question me. I had to get out of there, and then I passed out in a churchyard." Jeff traced the lump beneath his eye. "He didn't get anything out of you? Didn't hurt you?"

"I-I was able to get away, and that's when I called this guy." She leveled a finger at Quinn.

Quinn shrugged and snatched the toast from the toaster. "I guess I'm the go-to guy in New Orleans."

Rikki crossed her arms on the counter and leaned forward. "Do you have it?"

"Not on me." Jeff patted his pockets. "Thank God. That man would've snatched it in a second."

Quinn slid a plate in front of Rikki. "Do you have any idea who he was, Jeff? Was he one of yours?"

"CIA coming after one of its own? Maybe."

"Let's face it." Rikki pinged her cup with her fingernail. "You were not on official CIA business. You were on Ariel's business, and she flies under the CIA radar. Maybe someone at the Company picked up your actions and figured you for a double agent."

Jeff leaned against the kitchen counter for support. "I hope not. I don't want to have to do any explaining.

After that whole Rikki Taylor thing with North Korea, our agency is on high alert."

Rikki's eye twitched and she rubbed it. "Rikki Taylor is dead."

"Yeah, but not forgotten." Jeff wiped his mouth with the back of his hand and then dumped his coffee into the sink.

She wanted to ask Jeff the meaning of those words but didn't want to show too much interest in Rikki Taylor. Quinn had been right. He wasn't one to kiss and tell, and Jeff didn't know of the connection between her and Quinn.

Now this second chance had fallen into her lap, and she had no intention of letting it slip by.

"Where is it?" Rikki had broken up her toast into several pieces but hadn't taken one bite yet.

Jeff narrowed his eyes. "Why didn't you tell me who you were last night when I staggered across Quinn's threshold? You must've made me right away as your contact."

"Quinn's a friend. I didn't want to expose him—not to you, not to the CIA. He's on leave trying to relax. Just because we both chose to drag him into our business doesn't give us the right to put a target on his back."

"Hey, what are friends for?" Quinn raised one hand.

Jeff nodded. "I get it. I wouldn't have come here if I thought I could get back to my hotel safely."

Rikki's heart flip-flopped. "Nobody followed you here, right?"

"I was careful."

Rikki pressed her lips together. Not that careful if he'd been found out before. "Anyway, I didn't want to pull Quinn into this and didn't want you linking me to him. I figured I could get you to drop the flash drive for me somewhere, and I'd pick it up and be on my way. Less exposure for you, too—you don't know who you met, what she looked like or why you were dropping the flash drive."

Jeff coughed. "I didn't even know it was a flash drive. All I have is a small padded envelope."

"My bad." She exchanged a quick glance with Quinn, who was pretending to clean up the kitchen. Rikki should've known Ariel would keep things as anonymous as possible. "So, can you get it for me now?"

"I'll do you one better. I'll give you the same information I meant to give you at our meeting."

"I'm ready."

"It's in the St. Louis Cemetery Number One."

Rikki's mouth dropped open. "You couldn't leave it in a safe-deposit box?"

"Who's going to suspect a cemetery?" Jeff lifted one shoulder. "It's in the entrance to one of those family mausoleums—the St. Germaines. Two steps down, loose stone six in on the right. Pull that out, and you'll find your flash drive...or whatever."

"Kind of a public place, and it's summertime with lots of tourists. Hope nobody stole it." Quinn crossed his arms, feigning disinterest no more.

"Honestly, I wasn't expecting it to be there overnight." Jeff pushed himself off the counter. "Now I'd like to get out of this city."

Quinn didn't budge from his position, and with his arms crossed and his biceps bulging, he looked large and in charge. "How and where do you think that guy picked up your trail?"

"I don't have a clue." Jeff licked his lips. "Nobody knew I was out here. I was thinking it must've been

Ariel. Maybe someone is tracking her communications."

"Why would that be?" Rikki tried to keep the panic from her voice, and she slipped her hands beneath the counter where she twisted her fingers into knots.

"I'm not sure. Have you ever met her?"

Rikki relaxed the lines of her face into a smooth mask. "No."

"Nobody has. Do we even know if she's male or female? Ariel's a pseudonym."

"I'm assuming Ariel is she." Rikki lifted and dropped her shoulders quickly.

"She's a woman."

Rikki held her breath and swiveled her head around toward Quinn. He'd better not out Ariel. Rikki asked, "How do you know that?"

"One of my teammates actually spoke to her. She was going to help him out with an ambush but didn't have to in the end."

"If that's who he was really speaking to. All I know is Ariel is the head of the Vlad task force, and she has a lot leeway, including employing navy SEALs stateside in her efforts to stop him." Jeff wagged his finger at Quinn. "You'd better lie low, or she'll get you, too."

Quinn held up his hands. "I'm trying to, but you never answered my question. Do you know when this guy picked you up?"

"I'm ashamed to say, I don't. He wasn't in a talkative mood while he was punching me in the face."

Quinn stepped aside, clearing the way for Jeff to leave the kitchen. "Take it easy, man, and get those stitches, and, Jeff?"

Jeff glanced down at the hand Quinn had placed on his shoulder. "Yeah?"

"You never came here, never saw me, never saw her here, never saw her period, right?"

"Yeah, yeah. Of course, man." Jeff ducked away from Quinn and nodded once to Rikki. "Good luck."

Rikki let out a long sigh when Jeff closed the door behind him. "What do you think?"

"I don't know." Quinn rubbed his knuckles across the dark stubble on his jaw. "I think Ariel could've picked a better agent to make the drop. Someone obviously followed Jeff from his hotel, from the airport, who knows? And Jeff didn't have a clue."

Rikki slid from the stool and stretched. "At least that guy last night hadn't been following *me*. It seems as if Jeff was the focus of that whole mess. Someone suspects him of double-crossing the Agency. Hopefully, once it's cleared through Ariel, he'll be off the hook."

"Ariel is currently not answerable to anyone in the CIA. I know guys who have been on her assignments. You're lucky she can act at will." He swept her plate with its crumbled toast from the counter and dumped it in the sink. "Why is she looking out for you?"

"I told you. It has to do with Vlad."

"And we know Ariel would move heaven and earth to bring down Vlad. Do you know why?"

Rikki shoved her hands in her pockets. She had no intention of outing Ariel. The woman had her back, and Rikki would do everything in her power to keep Ariel's secrets. "That's a dumb question. Vlad is building a terrorist network across the globe. He's involved in drugs, weapons, assassinations. He's the CIA's public enemy number one. Why *wouldn't* Ariel be hot to bring him down?"

"From what I've heard, it seems...obsessive."

"I don't know. All I can tell you is that David was

on Vlad's tail when he proposed that North Korea trip to me."

"Talk about dumb." Quinn slammed his fist into his palm, and Rikki jumped. "David should never have dragged you along on that assignment."

"Why? Because I'm a girl?" Rikki wedged her hands on her hips.

"No, damn it." In two steps, he ate up the distance between them and grabbed her by the shoulders. "Because I was falling in love with you, and David took you away from me."

Rikki pressed a hand to her chest, above her fluttering heart. "That wasn't going to work, Quinn. It was hot and heavy sex in the heat of Dubai. I left because of my job, a job I couldn't do tangled up in the sheets with you."

He pinched her shoulders, his fingers digging into her flesh. "Don't pretend that's all it was between us. I'll admit, the sex was exciting, crazy—just like last night—but you know there was more than that."

She stroked his wrist. "Your libido can play tricks on you sometimes."

"I'm a man, not a boy." He softened his hold on her, smoothing this thumbs across her clavicles. "I know the difference between sex and love. When you left me—" he thumped a fist against his chest "—I felt it here, not farther south."

"And when you got the assignment to kill me?"

"God, Rikki." He spun away from her. "Didn't we go through this yesterday? I didn't know it was you until it was too late to back out. They'd already convinced me of your guilt before I got the name and picture of my target. If it had been so easy to prove your innocence and call off the hit, where was your precious Ariel? How come she didn't do anything about it?"

"Like you said, the proof was there, but someone manufactured that proof against me and David. That's what I hope to discover from the flash drive—information about who double-crossed us. That's my starting point."

She backed up from the heat emanating from Quinn's body. She wanted to get on safe ground and away from Quinn's feelings. Had he really just mentioned love?

She'd always been afraid of hearing that word from any man. For her mother, it had been a magic spell, and she'd dragged Rikki around from man to man, giving up everything for that one little word. Rikki had a mission, a career, or at least she'd had one. Even if she did clear her name, she had Bella now.

Her stomach sank. She had to tell Quinn about his daughter. If she really did want to push him away, keeping his daughter from him would cement that. She couldn't do that. For all Quinn's sexy manhood, he had a big heart. He'd fallen for her, foolishly and disastrously, and here he was admitting it. Any other man whose lover had left him would never fess up, never make himself vulnerable to that woman again. And yet here he was.

Of course, he'd had a sniper rifle trained on her last year.

He dragged both hands through his hair. "Okay, your starting point is that flash drive. Let's go get it."

"You know where this cemetery is?"

"Of course I do. Every good N'awlins boy does. I'm not sure how we're going to march up there and remove a stone from a mausoleum in the middle of the day with tour groups wandering around."

"I am not going to a New Orleans cemetery at night."

"It's not deserted. There are tours at night, too. Those might be the more popular tours."

Rikki cocked her head. "Should we join one of those? Just two tourists on a cemetery tour at night? We could break off from the group to examine the St. Germaine mausoleum more thoroughly. That way, if anyone tracked Jeff there, we wouldn't stick out."

"You had the same thought I did." He swung his leg over the barstool, straddling it. "How long had Jeff's attacker been following him?"

"That's exactly what I thought. Maybe he hadn't been tailing Jeff closely enough to see him stash something at the cemetery, but he could've seen him go there." Rikki bumped her forehead with the heel of her hand. "I can't believe some of Jeff's actions."

"He would pick a cemetery." Quinn raised one eyebrow. "Sounds like Jeff was watching too many spy films."

"I guess he just never figured he was being followed. This wasn't a regular assignment for him. He probably jumped at the chance to do a favor for Ariel and the Vlad task force."

"Maybe." Quinn strode into the living room and slid his laptop in front of him on the coffee table.

"What are you doing?"

He looked up. "We're gonna book a tour of St. Louis Number One tonight."

THEY'D DECIDED AGAINST the midnight ghost tour. The one after dinner in the dark would be creepy enough.

Rikki had wanted to get the grand tour of New Orleans with Quinn as her guide. She'd been to the city just twice before, but Quinn had a love of his hometown and would've been able to do it justice.

He'd put a stop to that idea, however. Although the chances were low, Quinn didn't want to run into Rikki's attacker from last night. They took a quick trip to Rikki's run-down motel to collect her possessions and check her out of the room, and then reclaimed her scooter from the French Quarter.

Quinn had insisted he could protect her better at his place, and Rikki didn't doubt that, but they both knew they'd wind up in bed together for as many nights as she stayed.

She needed to use one of those opportunities to break the news about Bella. Quinn hadn't wanted children, as his own mother had abandoned him, and his father never let him forget it. Even though Quinn's dad was an alcoholic and the adult Quinn knew his mother had run from him, the child within Quinn never stopped blaming himself. Then he somehow figured if both his father and mother had been uncaring parents, how could he possibly be any better?

Rikki couldn't imagine Quinn as anything but a loving, doting father. It was one of the things about him that had scared her off—his ability to feel deeply.

She thought she'd been getting into a relationship marked by kinky sex and a shallow appreciation of each other's bodies. But Quinn was right. It had started developing into so much more—and had scared the hell out of her. David's call had come just in time.

Later that night, Quinn emerged from the back rooms with his freshly washed hair slicked back and a towel around his neck. He eyed the sundress she'd changed into when they went to her hotel. "You're not going to change into all black for the occasion?"

"In this heat?" She fanned herself with her hand. "No, thanks. Maybe my floral dress will keep the ghosts at bay."

"Or maybe it will bring them out to force you to have some respect for their final resting place."

She pointed at his light-colored shorts. "I see you're dressing more for the weather than the occasion."

"It's almost July. I'm not crazy."

She combined the remains of their Chinese food into a couple of containers. "Thanks for dinner, but take-out Chinese is not exactly what I was expecting in New Orleans with all the fantastic restaurants here."

"We're not on vacation, despite the tour. We don't know where that guy is or even who he is. He could be lurking around waiting for you."

"Unless Jeff has already reported back to Ariel and gotten the all-clear."

"Nobody told you yet, so you're gonna lie low."

She poked her head around the refrigerator door while putting away the leftovers. "This is your dream come true, isn't it? To keep me captive in your apartment?"

He widened his eyes. "You're making me sound like a perv. I just wanna keep you safe."

"I know that." She slammed the fridge door. "I can't stay hiding out here forever, can I?"

"No. I don't expect that. I meant what I said that first night. I want to help you get your life back—even if that life doesn't include me."

She turned her back on him and dumped their dishes in the sink. That life would have to include him once she told him about Bella.

Thirty minutes later, Rikki climbed onto the back of Quinn's motorcycle and pulled on her helmet. Quinn had a small car he used while in town, but he always used his bike downtown for parking purposes. That was why she'd rented a scooter—she'd needed to get in and around the city quickly.

Quinn claimed a parking spot for his motorcycle at the edge of a small lot about a block from the cemetery.

Rikki slid from the back of the bike as Quinn tipped it to the side. She pulled the helmet from her head and shook out her hair.

"I'll take that." Quinn took her helmet from her and locked it on the back of the motorcycle along with his.

He took her hand, and they jogged across the street toward the rambling cemetery behind a wrought iron fence. He led her to a group of people hanging out by the entrance gates, and they joined the rest of the tourists, taking pictures with their phones and peeking through the gate.

Several minutes later, a tall African-American woman with long braids and a gauzy skirt floated up to the group. "Everyone here for the tour? I'm Aida, your guide. We'll take care of earthly matters first if you'll hand me your printed ticket or show me the ticket on your phone. Then we'll get to the unearthly matters."

One of the tour members, who'd had a few too many Hurricanes to drink, let loose with a ghoulish laugh.

Aida raised her brows at him. "Taunt the spirits at your own risk."

Despite the real ghouls Rikki had encountered over the past year, she sidled up next to Quinn and tucked her hand in the crook of his elbow.

Once Aida had checked all their tickets, she led them into the cemetery and stopped at a small grave site with an ornate cherub guarding it. She rested one hand on the cherub's chubby winged foot. "This is the sad resting place of AnaBella Lafleur. She died at the tender age of five, but her wealthy father forbade her burial in the family mausoleum because he never accepted her as his daughter. He had suspected his wife of cheating on him, and even after the child's death, he never got over it and ended up murdering his wife."

The warmth of the evening couldn't suppress the little chill that ran up Rikki's back. She tugged on Quinn's arm and whispered, "Jeff and his morbid ideas."

As the group moved past AnaBella's grave, Quinn brushed his hand over the headstone. "Poor Bella."

Rikki tripped over a crack, and Quinn steadied her. "Whoa."

She pulled him away from the group. "Once we find the St. Germaines, let's get out of here. I don't want to hear about any more dead children."

He cocked his head at her. "You okay?"

"Nervous."

"I don't blame you. It's gonna be okay."

He draped an arm over her shoulder, and she welcomed the heavy pressure of it. Why had he called that girl Bella? It must have been a sign.

Aida delivered the history and the atmosphere as the group moved from grave site to grave site, and Rikki might've enjoyed this tour another time.

A half hour into the tour, Aida stopped at a Baroque-style mausoleum with heralding angels on either side of the entrance and a profusion of flowers carved in stone and trailing down the columns.

Aida folded her hands in front of her. "This is the St. Germaine mausoleum, notable for its Baroque style and detailed stonework."

As Aida's smooth voice hummed in the background, Rikki elbowed Quinn, her mouth dry. She scooted closer to the steps, and someone asked if they were going inside.

Aida replied, "Not this one. There's a smaller one toward the end of the tour, and a few people at a time can duck inside."

Aida continued talking about the stone carvings as Rikki took one step down, pretending to study the writing on the side of the mausoleum.

The group began to shuffle off, and Rikki took the next step down, running her fingers over the rough stone on the right—six in, loose stone. Aida had better not catch her and Quinn defacing a crypt.

Aida's voice grew fainter, and Quinn joined her on the second step. "Did you find it?"

"Not—" her fingers scrabbled over the stone, looking for a gap or a give "—yet."

She crouched down and flashed the light from her phone on the wall.

Quinn crouched beside her, bumping her shoulder. "Is it loose right here?"

She shoved the heel of her hand against the spot he'd indicated with his middle finger, and the stone seemed to rock.

A scrape and a shuffle had her spinning around, knocking into Quinn as he straightened up, reacting to the noise.

Rikki's throat tightened as she looked up at the drunken man, not looking so drunk now, his face lit from below, his eyes narrowed.

"What are you two doing down here? And why don't you let me in on it?"

Chapter Seven

Quinn instinctively stepped in front of Rikki. "Just doing a little historical investigation."

"Yeah, right." The man pulled a gun from his waistband, a silencer attached to the barrel.

Quinn's own weapon burned against his back, useless. He held up his hands. "Look, man. We don't want any trouble. We were just looking around."

"Looking around for something that spook left you?" The man laughed. "The CIA needs to do a better job of screening its applicants."

Rikki squeaked next to Quinn. "CIA? What are you talking about? I thought you were a cemetery ranger or whatever and thought we were defacing the mausoleum. You really are drunk."

The man glanced quickly to his side as laughter rose from the group. "Who are you?"

Quinn raised his hands higher, hoping Rikki might see the gun stuck in the back of his waistband, beneath his shirt, and hoping she might be able to get her hands on it. "Buddy, we're a couple of tourists on a cemetery tour. I don't know what your game is, but we don't have any money on us and you're not going to get too far with our credit cards."

Another laugh from the group had the man licking his lips and sliding one foot off the top step.

That was all Quinn needed. With the man off balance, Quinn charged him, knocking him backward. The gun tipped up and Quinn made sure it stayed that way by slamming his fist against the man's elbow.

The force and placement of the blow caused the man to drop the gun, and Quinn kicked it away. As the man came at him again, Quinn grabbed him by the throat.

"Now it's your turn. Who the hell are you?"

"Is there a problem?" The tour guide hovered several feet away. "Are you two fighting?"

Under the cover of the shadows, Quinn put the man in a sleeper hold. He slumped, and Quinn lowered him to the ground.

"I think this guy had a little too much to drink. He was bothering us, but no harm done." He jerked his thumb over his shoulder at Rikki, who'd been no help at all. "My wife's done with the tour, though."

Rikki stepped over the prone body and brushed off the skirt of her dress. "Yeah, I've had enough."

Aida put her hand to her heart. "Do I need to call the police?"

"If you want to report a drunk in public." Quinn slipped the tour guide a twenty. "Thanks. Great tour."

Putting his hand at the small of Rikki's back, he propelled her through the cemetery as if they had a couple of ghosts on their tail.

When they escaped through the gate, Quinn let out a breathy whistle. "How the hell did he pick us up? And what the hell were you doing back there? Didn't you see the gun in my waistband?"

"I saw it, but I was attending to more important business."

"Really? There's more important business than saving my life?"

She plunged her hand into her purse and pulled out a folded envelope. "I got the stone loose and grabbed the envelope Jeff left for me."

He pinched her cheek. "Smart girl, but I guess you answered my question."

"Your question?" She took one skipping step next to him.

"That envelope is more important than my life."

She gave him a shove from behind. "I knew you could handle that guy."

"Thanks for the vote of confidence." He pulled out his weapon. "Still didn't answer the first question, though. How'd that guy make us? He walked up a little later, after we met the group out front."

Rikki took a step back and wrapped her fingers around the bars of the cemetery fence. "There are at least two of them. The drunk in the cemetery and the guy who beat up Jeff and tried to hustle me out of the bar last night."

"There could be more." Quinn dangled his gun at his side as they started down the street. "The good news is that they don't seem to have a clue who you are."

"And they might not be CIA. Sure didn't sound like he worked for the Agency, did it? If they did, wouldn't Jeff had already cleared himself through Ariel? The CIA must know by now that Jeff wasn't involved in any counterespionage. So why would they still be after the flash drive?"

He pulled her close to him. "Let's get home right now. We'll talk about this later. I'm worried that dude in the cemetery has a partner out here."

"We already know what his partner looks like. He tried to kidnap me last night."

"If it's just the two of them."

"Who the hell are they if not CIA? Why were they following Jeff?"

"I think we need to talk to Jeff again."

Quinn didn't let out the breath he'd been holding until they reached his motorcycle. Once on board, Quinn gunned the engine and took a different route back to his place, keeping an eye on his mirror.

They returned to his apartment unnoticed, and Quinn let Rikki off the bike before tucking it into his parking space next to his car.

They walked inside his place, and he fired up his laptop. "Let's see what's on this flash drive, and it better be worth all the trouble."

Rikki dug into her purse, pulling out the envelope. She ripped it open and dumped the flash drive into her palm. "Okay. I'm ready."

She sat next to him on the sofa and scooted in close as she reached past him to insert the flash drive into the side of his computer.

Quinn double-clicked on the device when it appeared on his display. He ran the cursor down the list of files. "Emails. Is that what you were expecting?"

"I didn't know what to expect. Ariel indicated she'd run across some files that might be useful to me."

Quinn opened the first email, and Rikki gasped beside him.

"They're David's emails."

"To you?" Quinn hunched forward and squinted at the addresses at the top of the message. "No. Who's Frederick Von?"

"I have no clue." Rikki grabbed the laptop with both

hands and brought it close to her face, as if that would help her identify the recipient of David's email.

"It sounds like he's discussing his trip to South Korea."

"It does, but that's strange." She placed the computer back on the coffee table. "I thought the two of us, David and I, were the only ones in on that trip."

"He probably had to get approval from someone."

"That someone was Ariel." She tapped the keyboard. "Let's see the next one."

After Rikki opened four emails in a row, Quinn whistled. "Looks like David was two-timing you. He sent all these messages to Freddy, and they all seem to be referencing the trip to South Korea that he took with you."

"Frederick Von." Rikki drummed her fingers on the edge of the laptop. "That name sounds familiar to me."

"Another agent?"

"Not sure." Rikki clicked back through the emails, and then slumped against the sofa. "This doesn't tell me anything. These are mundane messages about a trip I was on. They make no sense to me. Why would Ariel think these would be useful, and why would those men following Jeff go to such great lengths to get them?"

Quinn squeezed Rikki's thigh. "Maybe there's something in the simplicity of the messages. Why would David be relaying insignificant details about his trip to someone—unless the details mean something else?"

She shot up. "Like a code?"

"That makes more sense to me than these emails."

She opened the first email again and read it aloud. "'Frederick, the trip to South Korea is on. We have intel about our man. I'll follow up with time and location.'"

"Time and location for what? Did the two of you meet anyone in South Korea before you crossed over?"

"Just our guide. I'm not sure what happened to him after David was murdered and I was captured."

"I'm assuming your guide wasn't Frederick Von."

"No. His name was Buddy Song."

He bumped her knee with his. "Let me have a look."

Jabbing his finger at the next open email, he said, "This email, which is the next one in the sequence, doesn't have any more information about the promised time and location. This one discusses car rental details."

"We didn't rent a car." She tilted her head to the side and caught her long hair with one hand. "Buddy picked us up and drove us around. This email doesn't even make sense."

"None of them do." He'd clicked open several more and bounced among the messages. "These are in order by date, but the subject matter isn't sequential."

"A code." She tossed her hair over her shoulder. "The emails are significant in another way, a way only Frederick understands."

"How'd you do in secret code class?"

"Secret code class?" She snorted softly. "No such thing."

"Yeah, right. I know you agents learn stuff like that. Hell, we reviewed it ourselves. Were you an A student in deciphering like everything else?"

She sucked in her bottom lip, clamping it between her teeth. "Something like this? It could be anything— position of letters, single words, and the entire message might be run across all the emails with different rules for different messages."

"But there are people at Langley who specialize in this, aren't there?"

Spreading her arms, Rikki kicked her feet up on the coffee table next to the computer. "Do I look like I'm in with Langley? They think I'm dead, and good riddance. Do you think Langley would appreciate learning that Ariel from a black ops organization got into one of their dead agents' emails? That ain't gonna happen, McBride."

He tapped one finger on the laptop. "That's all right. I have my sources, and they're not connected to the Agency."

"Like Jeff? No, thanks."

"I said my source is *not* with the Agency." He put his feet up next to hers and tapped them with the ball of his foot. "Are you giving up? You went through a lot to get this flash drive. Ariel must've understood the significance of finding a set of David's emails, and she went through a lot to get them to you."

"Who said I was giving up?" She draped her leg over his and wiggled her toes against his ankle. "I'll give it a try. I just don't understand why David was sending coded messages to someone about our trip."

"Maybe he had a different reason for taking that trip, one he didn't reveal to you."

Closing her eyes, she tipped her head back against the sofa, but she was anything but relaxed. Her hands curled into fists in her lap, and her eyelids flickered and twitched.

"What is it? He told you he had info about Vlad, right? Maybe that wasn't it at all. Maybe he just said that to get Ariel's support…and funds."

"Yes, he said we were on Vlad's trail, but that's not what I'm thinking of. David was…different on this trip. I thought about it after he died, and figured I was reading too much into his behavior because it was the last assignment we'd do together, but he was definitely in a different place."

"In what way? Do you think he was lying to you? Had he ever lied to you before?"

"Once." She opened one eye. "And it wasn't about work."

"What then?"

"Love."

Quinn raised his eyebrows. "He lied to you about love?"

"Yesss." The word came out like a hiss.

Quinn waited. If Rikki wanted to tell him, she'd tell him. She'd found the perfect profession for her temperament. She kept secrets like nobody else he knew…had kept secrets from him.

Rikki sighed and sat up, drilling him with her gaze so that he clenched the muscles in his stomach and prepared himself.

"David was in love with me…or at least he thought he was."

A muscle flickered at the corner of Quinn's jaw. What man in his right mind *wouldn't* be in love with Rikki? "I thought David Dawson was a married man."

"He is…was. That was the problem, or at least one of them. I told him in no uncertain terms I didn't fool around with married men, and of course I felt guilty that maybe I'd led him on."

"You didn't. You're no tease." Quinn ran a hand over his mouth. "How'd he take it?"

"Not well—at first. He gave me all the old excuses married guys trot out—Belinda didn't understand him, the marriage was in name only, he thought she might be having an affair of her own, they were on the verge of divorce." She squeezed the back of her neck. "Then I dropped the other shoe."

"Which was?"

"Even if all those things were true, I wasn't in love with him, and I apologized for suggesting otherwise."

"How'd he take *that*?" Quinn didn't even have to imagine David's despair at the news, as he'd felt it himself when he woke up in that empty hotel room in Dubai with a white sheet of paper on the pillow next to him.

"Better than I expected. He didn't rant or rave or protest or even try to convince me I felt differently. Although it pained me, I suggested we work apart for a while, but he wouldn't hear of it. Insisted he could cope and keep our relationship on a purely business level— and that's when he lied to me."

"He kept up his protestations of love?" He could almost feel sorry for the poor sap, but at least Quinn had taken it like a man and never had contact with Rikki again—until it came time to kill her.

"David never mentioned it to me again, but I knew he still had feelings for me." She ran her hand down Quinn's arm and threaded her fingers through his. "I could tell he did when you came onto the scene."

"Me?"

"David knew about us in Dubai, of course. David and I knew each other so well, he could tell. He got all fatherly on me and played the role of the mentor, which of course he was. He warned me about what having a fling while on assignment could do to my career." She pulled his hand to her lips and kissed his knuckles. "As if I could've stopped that wildfire between us even if I'd wanted to—and I didn't."

"Until the end." He disentangled his fingers from hers so that he could think straight. "Is that what happened? Is that why you left me high and dry? David's sage advice?"

Now he felt no sympathy for the man, but had an itching desire to punch him in the face—except he was dead.

"No." She brushed the hair from his forehead to torture him some more. "I realized our relationship belonged in the short and combustible category."

"You realized that without discussing it with me, then. I could've combusted like that forever."

A low chuckle vibrated in her throat, and he swallowed. The damnedest things about her could make him hard.

"Anyway, David's cautionary words didn't have any influence on my leaving you and Dubai."

"Maybe his cautionary words didn't, but his actions did." Quinn sat up on the edge of the sofa, making a half turn toward Rikki. "If you don't think he pulled you out of Dubai to go on this wild-goose chase in South Korea to separate us, you're naive—and I've never considered you naive before."

"I suppose there was that element to it, but David was hot for this mission and wanted me along." She shrugged.

Quinn snorted. "David was hot for you. He never did leave his wife, did he? That horrible, half-baked, failing marriage."

"No."

"So, that was the one time David lied to you. Said he'd accepted you two would never be more than colleagues but all the while harboring that fire down below."

She held up her finger. "Careful, you're talking about a dead man and a damned good agent who died for his country."

"You're right." He grabbed her finger and kissed the tip. "If he lied about that, how do you know he wasn't lying to you about other things, like this trip to South Korea?"

"Because he wasn't a very good liar, was he? He couldn't hide his feelings for me."

"A CIA agent who's not a good liar? He should've found another career."

Rikki cocked her head. "I mean, he was a good liar. If you could've seen him in action with our contacts… masterful."

"Then he could've been masterfully lying to you about Korea."

"Not to me." She shook her head, and her dark hair slipped over her shoulder.

Quinn wrapped his finger around one silky lock, missing her red curls. "Overconfident much?"

She bit her lip. "Pretty smug, huh? You're right. He could've totally been playing me, but why?"

"I can't tell you, but it sounds like David used you as a cover and put both of you in danger. Stupid move." Quinn stretched and then pointed to his laptop. "Are you going to look at these anymore?"

"I'm calling it a night." She pushed herself up from the sofa. "At least we have one thing to be grateful for."

He snapped the lid of his laptop closed and stood up next to her, resting a hand on her hip. He was just grateful Rikki was alive and back in his life—sort of. "I know what I'm grateful for."

Her lips formed an *O*, and a blush washed over her cheeks. "I-I meant that those people out there who were following Jeff don't seem to know who I am or what they're looking for."

"Yeah, of course." He pinched her hip. He didn't want to put Rikki on the spot. If she chose to fly away once she found whatever it was she was looking for, he'd let her go.

She'd gutted him the first time she left him, but her supposed death and rebirth had given him perspective. As long as Rikki Taylor was living and breathing in this world, he'd take that as a win.

Twisting his T-shirt between her fingers, Rikki leaned into him and kissed his chin. "Meet you in bed."

"You go ahead and get ready. I'll lock up."

Quinn checked his doors and windows and stopped to stare down at the dark street. Rikki had been right. They hadn't been on anyone's radar until Jeff had been compromised. One of those two men or both had been following Jeff before they even accosted him. They'd tracked him to the cemetery but hadn't been able to see what he'd done there.

The one guy had already ID'd Rikki as Jeff's contact, and the other man must've been keeping watch on that cemetery and spotted Rikki.

But they didn't know who she was, and if they weren't working for the CIA, maybe they didn't care. As far as the Agency knew, Rikki was dead. Did they want to keep her that way?

Quinn twitched the curtains closed and secured his apartment before sailing through the master bedroom to Rikki snug in his bed. "I'm just gonna brush my teeth. Don't steal all the covers before I can make it in there."

She looked up from some papers in her lap. "What is this Quinn, a book?"

He took a detour from his beeline to the bathroom and snatched the papers out of her hand. "Nosy."

"You're writing a book?"

"Nothing definite, just telling some stories—with the

names and places changed. Just a collection of ideas at this point. Don't make a big deal out of it."

"It *is* a big deal. You'll have to run it by the navy, won't you?"

"Of course." He waved the papers. "It's in its infancy."

"Had me hooked right away."

He dumped the papers on his nightstand. "Definitely not bedtime reading, especially after the day we had."

Quinn went into the bathroom to brush his teeth and splash some water on his face. When he returned to the bedroom, Rikki had his notes clutched in her hands again, sitting cross-legged on top of the covers.

"Oh, come on. It's not that good."

"I think you've got something here, Quinn. I'd read this."

"Yeah, because you live it." He snatched the papers from her hands again and tossed them on the floor. "I'm looking at something a lot more interesting."

On his knees, he straddled her and buried one hand in her hair, pulling her close.

Her body, usually so pliant and willing beneath his touch, stiffened.

He kissed her mouth, but her soft lips didn't return the kiss. He opened his eyes and ran the pad of his thumb over the crease between her eyebrows. "Too wound up? I can fix that."

"Frederick Von."

"What? David's email recipient? Did you remember who he is?"

"Oh, yeah. I remember now."

Quinn shifted his body and lay on his side, propping up his head with one hand. "Who is he?"

"Frederick Von is a character in David's spy novel."

"That's not what I expected to hear. David wrote a spy novel?"

"He was working on one, and he shared it with me— yours is much better."

"That's a relief to hear, but mine's nonfiction. Why would David be sending emails to a fictional character—his own?"

Rikki crossed her arms and hunched her shoulders. "Frederick Von was the bad guy in David's book."

"I'm not following you, Rikki."

"Frederick Von was the bad guy—a traitor."

Quinn blinked.

"A trai-tor."

Rikki strung out the two syllables as if speaking to someone with a tenuous hold on the English language, and right now he felt as if she *were* speaking in a different tongue.

He shook his head. "You need to give me a break here. One minute I was ready to ravish you, and the next you're staring at me speaking gibberish about some fictional character in a bad spy novel—and it would have to be bad if it's worse than my drivel."

"I think David was being clever for the sake of being clever in those emails, just because he could and nobody would catch on…nobody but me."

"David *is* clever because I still don't understand the significance."

"Von is a traitor, Quinn—just like David."

Chapter Eight

"Whoa, whoa." Quinn held up his hands. "How did you jump to that conclusion?"

"Why the secret emails? Ariel discovered these on a different server, a nonclassified server that wouldn't be under intense scrutiny after his death. There would've been no reason for David to send these emails. The only people who knew about the trip besides David were me and Ariel. David and I communicated in person about the trip. And what do those emails even mean? You said it yourself. They appeared to be cover for a code."

"A code. It doesn't mean David was a traitor just because he used the name of his character, who happens to be a traitor." Quinn slid back under the covers. "If it is true, what do you think David was doing in South Korea if not tracking down a lead on Vlad?"

"I'm not sure, but it all went horribly wrong. David was killed, and I was captured by the North Koreans." She stretched out beside Quinn and rested her head on his shoulder. "The whole assignment was off. I saw the red flags but didn't trust my instincts, like David had always taught me."

"That's convenient. David taught you to go with your gut…until your gut was warning you against him."

"I never thought I'd see the day when I had to look into David Dawson."

"Look into him? How do you propose to do that?"

Draping her arm around Quinn's waist, Rikki nuzzled his neck. "I'm going to pay a visit to Belinda, David's widow."

"That's a dangerous idea. You want to stay anonymous for as long as you can."

"Belinda and I never met. She doesn't have a clue what I look like. She'd know the name, but I'm no longer Rikki Taylor, remember?"

"I think you'd better let me check in on the widow."

"You'd come along?" She fluttered her eyelashes against his face. "You don't even know where I'm going."

"Doesn't matter. If you're going to be doing any investigating, I'm coming with you." He combed his fingers through her hair. "Where *are* we going?"

"I'll have to check for sure, but they lived in Georgia—Savannah. She's from there, so I can't imagine she'd want to leave after David's death."

"We can drive, but I'm not sure what you hope to find out from her."

"It's a start. Besides, most agents confide in their spouses, whether or not they're supposed to. That's why…" She broke off and buried her face in the hollow between Quinn's neck and shoulder. That's why she'd never wanted to get married or have a serious relationship with someone. That's why she'd run out on Quinn without a backward glance. Her career always had to come first. She never wanted to follow in the footsteps of a man.

But now she and Quinn had a child together, and the longer she waited to tell him, the harder it was going to be to spit it out. What was she afraid of? Quinn would welcome the news, despite his own fears of being a bad father.

"Yeah, yeah." He wrapped her in his arms. "That's why you never wanted to get married. We don't have to get married, Rikki, but we can pretend for a few nights."

Then he made love to her in a way that no married man had a right to make love to his wife.

THE FOLLOWING MORNING, Rikki searched for Belinda Dawson and found her in Savannah. She poked at the monitor displaying the address and said, "I think this is a different address from the one she shared with David, but at least she's still in Savannah."

"Then it's on to Georgia today. Map it out and see how far we have to go. It's about a ten-hour drive, if you're up to it. I think it's safer than flying right now, even though you have your fake ID."

"Driving is fine." She entered Belinda's address on the computer. "Will your car make it?"

"It's sturdier than it looks, and I just changed the oil. Let's get some breakfast, throw a few things in a bag and hit the road."

She tapped the print key and heard the printer in the other room gear up. "That car may be sturdier than it looks, but I know it doesn't have a GPS."

"I'll use my phone's GPS, but we need a plan beyond showing up on her doorstep, especially if you're not going to out yourself."

"We have ten hours to think up a plan." Rikki hopped off the stool and circled into the kitchen. "Besides, we need to get out of New Orleans. You just disabled those two guys. You didn't eliminate them."

"Yeah, can you imagine me explaining two dead bodies in my hometown?"

"At least those two dead bodies aren't ours." She grabbed the coffeepot and raised it. "Eggs or pancakes?"

Two hours later, Quinn aimed his little junker car across the Pontchartrain bridge and they headed out of New Orleans.

Rikki dozed while Quinn drove the first few hours, and she woke up trying to hold on to the last wisps of dreams about Bella. Her heart ached, and she wanted nothing more than to call Mom in Jamaica and hear her daughter's coos and babbles.

She slid a sidelong glance at Quinn. He'd probably want to hear his daughter, too. She had to tell him, sooner rather than later. If she waited for the perfect time, she'd never tell him. There would never be a perfect time to tell him that she'd discovered her pregnancy while on assignment in South Korea and had spent the next few months of that pregnancy locked up in a North Korean labor camp, and then believing the father of her child had tried to assassinate her. Yeah, never a perfect time for that.

"Everything okay?"

"Sure, why?"

"You sighed like you meant it. Are you having second thoughts?"

"About this trip?" *About telling him about his child?* "No. I know this is the right thing to do."

He cocked an eyebrow while drilling the road ahead with his gaze. "The right thing to do? You make it sound like a moral decision. It's just a chance we're taking that Belinda knows something about David's activities before his death."

"I know that." She covered his hand clenching the steering wheel with her own. "It's nice being on the road with you. Do you want me to drive for a while?"

"I can go for another few hours. Then we'll stop for gas, get something to eat, and you can take the wheel."

"Just let me know." She stretched her arms to the roof of the car and wiggled her fingers. "A big guy like you needs a bigger car than this."

"Not the best for long trips, but when I'm home I don't drive it much. I stick with my bike."

"How much more leave do you have?"

"Less than a month, and I intend to help you wrap this up before my next deployment."

"I appreciate it, but that's not why I contacted you."

"I know." He turned up the air. "You looked me up to find out if I was really going to kill you. How did you find out it was me behind that sniper rifle?"

"Not telling." She clapped a hand over her mouth.

"Ariel. It had to be Ariel. What can you tell me about her? Are you close to her?"

With her hand still over her mouth, Rikki shook her head.

Quinn puffed out a breath. "Whatever. I know you female spies stick together. She's risking a lot by keeping your secret and giving you classified information."

"David's emails aren't classified, and Ariel doesn't work for the CIA. She's Prospero and doesn't report to anyone."

"Yeah, Jack Coburn's black ops agency, but I didn't realize she had such free reign."

"Oops, then I guess I did reveal something about her. See how that works?" She snapped her fingers. "That's why we're paying a visit to David's widow."

"About that, now that you've had a nap, let's brainstorm. Who are we and why are we there?"

Rikki drummed her fingers on the dashboard. "We're with the Agency. If she tried to check up on our story, she won't be surprised if the CIA denies our existence. She and David had been married for twenty years. She knows the drill."

"Okay, we're with the Agency. How about from human resources? We're following up on some benefits? Or we're collecting some equipment."

"The second scenario is more likely, since HR would just call or send an email. If we were checking up on equipment, that would explain our in-person visit."

Quinn skimmed his hands over the steering wheel, warming to the task. "Maybe someone already confirmed that she had David's equipment for pickup. The fact that she doesn't know what we're talking about can be written off as bureaucratic red tape."

"Plenty of that, and your story might give us an excuse to look around."

He let out a short laugh and hit the steering wheel with the palm of his hand. "Would you let two goons from the CIA search your place?"

"After what they did to me?" She rolled her eyes. "I wouldn't let them set foot on my porch."

Quinn took a swig from the bottle of water in the cup holder. "I thought that was the point of this whole exercise. I thought you wanted back in at the Agency."

"I want my life back, my reputation. I want to be able to return to the States as Rikki Taylor without getting taken down at gunpoint."

"And you wouldn't go back to the CIA if they'd have you? Does that mean you're done with the spy business?"

"I don't know." She flicked the air vent away from her and rubbed the goose bumps from her arms.

They'd veered onto dangerous ground here. She didn't want to talk to Quinn about the future—hers, theirs. Right now she just wanted to clear her name and be with Bella without worry. And Quinn? She'd never wanted him more, but she had to tell him about Bella.

"Kids?"

She choked on the water she'd just sipped. "What?"

"Kids. Do David and Belinda have children?"

"They don't."

"Good. I mean, that makes things a little easier, and it makes sense."

"Does it?"

"Why would someone in David's line of work…or yours…want children? Just a complication."

Rikki stuffed her hands beneath her thighs. From the frying pan to the fire. "People do."

"Selfish people."

She reached forward and twisted the knob for the air. "It's cold in here. So, we're CIA paper pushers looking for government equipment. I'm going to use a different name from the one on my current ID. No need for anyone to link up April Thompson from Canada with a CIA agent. Who are you?"

"I'll think about it, but we'll probably need some badges in case she asks for ID."

"You're right." She pressed her fist against her forehead. "I'm sure David taught her to be cautious."

"Do you think you could have someone re-create that badge?"

"To pass someone's brief glance? Sure. Do you know Savannah? I don't. Where would we get these badges?"

"You know as well as I do, there are people in every city across the country who provide these services—for a price."

She patted her purse, thinking about Baily in Jamaica. "I sure do, but we're not going to have much time."

"Since you can't exactly call one of your former contacts, I can ask one of my teammates to look up something in Savannah for us."

"Your navy SEAL teammates? Would they know?"

"You'd be surprised what they know about covert operations, especially now. Your BFF, Ariel, has been dragging them in from deployment to do her bidding."

"Really?" Rikki folded her arms across her stomach. Had Ariel had an ulterior motive in directing her to stop in on Quinn when she arrived stateside? She hadn't needed much encouragement, as she'd wanted to square things with Quinn first…and tell him about Bella, but Ariel had initiated the idea.

"Why is Ariel using your sniper teammates for these assignments?"

"Because of Vlad. Because we know him. Because he knows us."

She whipped her head to the side. "Vlad knows you?"

"Who do you think nicknamed him Vlad?" He jabbed a thumb against his chest. "That was us, or more specifically I think it was my teammate Alexei Ivanov, the moody Russian."

"Why Vlad? He's not Russian, is he?"

"We don't know what he is. He's a man of many disguises. Just when we think we know what he looks like, he appears as someone else."

"So if he's not Russian, that you know of, why'd Alexei start calling him Vlad?"

"Because of his Russian sniper rifle—the Dragunov. Alexei uses the same rifle. Vlad was a sniper for the opposition forces, any opposition forces, before he started amassing his terrorist network. We came up against him many times. Sometimes we bested him, sometimes he bested us, but we never killed each other. Make no mistake about it, Vlad knows my entire team. I think he even reached out to the Russian mobster who killed Alexei's father just for that reason."

A chill claimed her body, and she'd turned off the air conditioner ten miles ago. "That's scary."

"Yeah, it's personal, so Ariel fights fire with fire. She's involved us in the battle to bring him down. I think I'm the only one who's escaped—and here I am."

"Yeah, here you are." Rikki nibbled on the end of her finger.

Quinn glanced her way and flexed his fingers on the steering wheel "What are you saying? Are you telling me it wasn't your idea to look me up?"

"It was my idea, but…"

"But Ariel was on board." Quinn twisted his head to the side and pinned her with a questioning gaze. "Ariel knows about us?"

Rikki dipped her chin to her chest. "She does. Sh-she knew before, before I even went on that assignment in Korea with David."

Quinn whistled. "I wonder if she knew you were my target before I did."

"I don't know why she would." Rikki traced the pattern on her skirt with her fingertip. "She's not CIA. Why would the Agency give Prospero a heads-up on their…assassinations? Especially of one of their own."

"C'mon. Prospero has ways of discovering things, even about other intelligence agencies. They're the best in the business."

He picked up his bottle and swirled the water inside.

"I can't believe Ariel knew about our relationship

and knew about your assignment and did nothing to warn you."

"She did." Quinn slammed the bottle back in the cup holder. "She did, damn it."

"What are you talking about?"

"After the navy revealed my target to me, along with the evidence of your betrayal, I was sick. I didn't think I could go through with it."

"But the evidence was irrefutable." She twirled her finger in the air. "I believe you."

"When I was already in South Korea preparing for the assignment, I received an anonymous text on my secure phone. Just two words—*she's innocent*."

Rikki gasped and smacked her hand against her chest. "Ariel?"

"Who else? Of course, the text sent me into a tailspin, planted doubts in my head. I couldn't call off the mission based on an anonymous text. It could've been from the enemy. But it was enough. When I saw those soldiers marching you along, guns at your back, and saw your last, desperate attempt to get away from the very people you were supposed to be conspiring with, I knew the truth."

"You're here because Ariel wanted you here with me—looking into who set me up, looking into Vlad."

"Since it wasn't your own idea to contact me, I'm grateful to Ariel for intervening." His lips twisted into a bitter smile.

"She didn't have to do much convincing, Quinn. I wanted to see you. After the initial shock and anger and much reflection, I knew you'd changed your mind about that mission, about me." She rubbed her hand down his bare thigh.

"Where did you do all this reflecting? You haven't

even told me where you were after the escape from North Korea."

She owed him. "Jamaica."

"Jamaica?" His thigh muscles tensed beneath her touch. "What's there?"

"My mother and stepfather."

"Ah, the former hippie, right?"

"They've been there for years. My stepfather runs the rental shop out of one of the resorts there—snorkeling equipment, skimboards, parasails. My mother met him there and stayed, which is no surprise. She'd follow any man anywhere, always did."

"I'm assuming the Agency knows about them?"

"Of course, but the CIA thinks I'm dead. No reason to question my mom. I felt safe there."

"If Ariel knew about us, knew you were alive and knew I hadn't gone through with the assassination, why didn't she tell me about you?" Quinn clenched his hands on the wheel, his knuckles turning white.

"She didn't know if she could trust you, Quinn. I didn't know if I could trust you." She ran her fingers over the ridges of his knuckles. "Someone had been actively working against me, planting false evidence. I didn't know how much of that you believed."

"I suppose I don't have room to complain. I *was* stationed on that hillside, ready to take you out." He rolled his shoulders. "I wish it had been someone else."

"I don't."

"You're happy a former lover had you in his crosshairs?"

"If it had been anyone else, I'd be dead."

Chapter Nine

When they reached the outskirts of Montgomery, Quinn eased off the gas pedal. "Keep an eye out for a gas station and a few fast-food joints."

Rikki jerked her thumb over her shoulder. "I saw a sign back there listing a bunch of places. Should be right off the highway, convenient for travelers."

"We're making good time and should be in Savannah before eleven o'clock if we keep moving."

She eyed him up and down, and he felt the familiar ache under her gaze, even after five hours of driving, cramped in the same position. His attraction to Rikki knew no bounds.

"Are you sure you don't need to get out and walk around? We can wait for a rest stop."

"I'm used to hunching in the same position for long periods of time. Doesn't bother me."

"I'm still taking the wheel. You can nap, if you like. Your phone's GPS has gotten us this far, so I'm sure I'll be okay."

"I can sleep anytime, anywhere, even standing up."

"Like a horse." She rapped one knuckle on the window. "Two miles until services."

Two miles later, Quinn took an exit toward a clump

of gas stations and restaurants. "Do you have a preference for food?"

"Chicken."

"I think we'll be able to find chicken in Georgia." He made a hard right turn into a gas station. "Let's fill up first. Bathroom?"

"I'd rather wait and use the restroom in one of the restaurants. I don't trust these gas station restrooms."

Quinn filled the tank while Rikki walked around the car with a squeegee, washing splattered bugs from the windows.

"Ugh, these bugs in the south are supersize."

"That's right. You've never spent much time down here, have you?"

"Back in Dubai, you promised to show me around New Orleans sometime." She dropped the squeegee in the soapy water and grabbed a couple of paper towels.

"What do you mean? I showed you a good time on Bourbon Street and we had a helluva cemetery tour."

She bunched the paper towels into a ball and threw it at his head. "You've got a sick sense of humor, McBride."

The nozzle clicked, and he pulled it from the gas tank. "Let's get you some chicken and get back on the road."

Rikki opted for a crispy chicken sandwich so she could eat and drive at the same time.

Quinn lowered the back of his seat and stretched his legs as far as they would go. He grabbed a sweatshirt from the backseat and bunched it between his head and the window. "I'm gonna catch a few hours of shut-eye if you think you'll be okay. You're going to head toward Atlanta and then veer east."

"Don't worry. I'm good at directions, especially when the nice computer lady spits them out."

"I trust you. You made it out of North Korea." Quinn adjusted his seat again and closed his eyes. At least he trusted her to get them to Savannah in one piece, but he didn't quite trust her to leave his heart in one piece.

Rikki woke him up twice along the way to pull into a rest area to use the bathroom. After the second time, he stayed awake for their arrival into Savannah. He pointed out a small motel outside the historic district where Belinda Dawson had a house. "Looks like there's a vacancy here."

"We should pay cash."

"Nobody's tracking me. I'm on leave, and I can do what I damn well please."

"But you're here under an assumed name, which you haven't chosen, by the way. What if Belinda checks you out?"

"You really think she's going to ask us where we're staying and call to confirm our names?"

"Humor me." She jerked her head toward her purse in the backseat. "I have enough cash in there to cover it."

"I'll humor you, and I've got it."

If the motel clerk thought it was strange that they paid for two nights up front with cash, her bored face didn't show it.

When they got to the room, Quinn picked up a card on the desk. "Free Wi-Fi. Can you get on my laptop and re-create a CIA badge? That'll make it easier when we ask someone to produce a badge for us."

"Did you hear from your friends yet?"

He held up his phone. "Two suggestions from two different sources. It's gonna mean a trip to one of the seedier areas of Savannah."

"That kind of stuff always does."

"Yeah, you should know, Ms. Thompson."

"I'm going to use a different name for this identity." Her gaze tracked to the digital clock on the bedside table. "Not tonight?"

"We'll save it for tomorrow. Do you know if Belinda works?"

"She did. I don't know about now, since David's death."

"Nine-to-five job?"

"She's in marketing, and I think she went into an office. So we should pay her a visit at the end of the workday."

"Exactly, but not too late. We don't want to scare her by showing up on her doorstep in the dead of night."

"Poor woman has had enough to deal with. I almost feel guilty nosing around."

Quinn threw himself across the bed and toed off his shoes. "We're just there to look around and assess. We're not gonna accuse her husband of anything, but if we see anything that needs closer examination, I'm not gonna rule out making a return visit—while she's not there."

"I agree." Rikki yawned. "I'm tired."

He patted the bed. "Come on over here and I'll give you a massage."

"I know how your massages end." She put her hands on her curvy hips. "I said I was tired."

"I missed you, Rikki. I missed us, but I think I can control myself if you're too tired for sex. Hell, I'm just happy holding you in my arms." And as insincere as that sounded, he'd meant it. "Go brush your teeth and do whatever it is you do to get so beautiful and then I'll deliver a no-strings-attached massage to your aching body."

"Sounds like heaven."

When she returned to the bedroom, an above-the-knee cotton nightgown floating around her body, Quinn turned off the TV and jumped from the bed. "Stretch out. I'll brush my teeth and be right back."

While in the bathroom, Quinn washed his hands with warm water and plucked a little bottle of lotion from the counter. Squeezing the lotion into his hands, he walked back into the bedroom and winked at Rikki. "I was afraid you'd be sound asleep."

"Close to it, but I'm curious to witness this self-control of yours as I've never seen it."

"That's cold." He perched on the edge of the bed, rubbing his hands together. "No massage oils, but I found some lotion."

"That'll work." She stretched like a cat, pointing her toes off the foot of the bed.

"Um." He tugged at the hem of her nightgown. "Do you want to remove this?"

She twisted around. "I knew it."

"Come on. Even massage therapists who are complete strangers have you disrobe for a massage."

As she pulled the nightgown over her head, she said in a muffled voice, "But they usually have a towel or sheet for the naughty bits."

"Do you really want me to cover you with a towel?"

She tossed the nightgown over her shoulder, and he made a concerted effort to keep his gaze off her luscious breasts.

"Nope. Have your way with me, McBride. You always do." She lay back down on her stomach, her arms at her sides.

He started with her shoulders, digging his thumbs into the sides of her neck.

She let out a long breath of air between her teeth in a hiss. "That feels good."

"Did you forget about these magic fingers?"

"I remember the magic fingers. I just don't remember them plowing into the sore muscles of my neck."

"Shh. You talk too much."

She wasn't kidding about those sore muscles. He worked at the tight knots at the base of her neck until they disappeared, and then he squeezed her shoulders and pressed the heels of his hands into her shoulder blades.

Rikki's breathing had deepened, and Quinn continued massaging the smooth flesh of her back. He expected another sarcastic comment from her when he reached her buttocks, but she moaned softly as he kneaded her glutes.

Her new womanly shape enticed him as much as her fit, athletic build had, but he knew now his attraction to Rikki ran more than skin deep. He'd known it all along, from the moment he met her at that hotel bar in Dubai. He'd known it the minute he awakened in that same hotel all alone.

His loss had punched him in the gut then and had nearly brought him to his knees months after that when he watched that North Korean guard shoot her.

He'd had his next assignment to distract him after his second, more permanent loss of Rikki, but his leave had sent him spiraling out of control. How much longer he could've gone on like that if Rikki hadn't shown up on his doorstep two nights ago, he hadn't a clue.

This time, as he faced his third abandonment by Rikki, he'd be ready. She'd survived. That was all that mattered to him.

He caressed her outer thighs and whispered, "Do

you want me to go on? I can do a mean foot massage that could put any pedicurist to shame."

Her only response was a long, drawn-out sigh.

He stopped, his hands hovering above her legs. He slid off the bed and crouched beside it, his face close to Rikki's, nose to nose.

Her long lashes fluttered, and her lips parted on a minty breath.

That was the first time he'd ever put Rikki Taylor to sleep...and it gave him a good feeling. He drew the sheet up to her shoulders and climbed into bed next to her.

She shifted onto her side, facing him, and he stroked the side of her full breast.

He murmured the words he'd never say to her out loud. "Love you."

She mumbled something, and Quinn's heart skipped a beat. Had she heard him and responded in kind?

"What?" He held his breath until he realized she was fast asleep.

She spoke in her sleep again, and this time he heard the word and repeated it. "Bell?"

Her mouth curved into a soft, sweet smile, and he kissed the tip of his finger and touched her bottom lip.

He didn't hear any bells, but he didn't have to. He knew how he felt about Rikki...even if she wanted to keep denying her own feelings for him.

And he'd do whatever it took to make her happy—with or without him.

THEY SPENT THE following day getting two credible CIA badges and a handful of matching business cards with Quinn's temp cell phone number, shopping for some convincing clothes to wear and holing up in the air-conditioned motel room.

Watching TV from the bed, Rikki crossed her legs at her ankles and tapped her bare feet together. "The small glimpses I'm getting of the city make me want to see more of it. The architecture is incredible, and I'm itching to tour some of those homes."

"We'll put Savannah on your list the next time you come out to New Orleans and do a two-for-one. I'll even throw in Nashville."

"I'll take you up on it." She drew her knees to her chest and wrapped one arm around her legs. "That was some massage last night. Totally relaxing."

"I aim to please." He touched two fingers to his forehead.

"I'm sorry I fell asleep. I mean…"

"Proved you wrong, didn't I?"

"You did?"

"You didn't think I could give you a massage without jumping your bones."

She balanced her chin on her knees. "I didn't mean to imply you were a caveman with no self-control. It's that our relationship before…"

"Was purely physical?" He shrugged. "Maybe for you."

Her eyes widened. "We didn't have that much time in Dubai."

"It was enough time for me, Rikki. You don't think I know what I want in a woman? What qualities are important to me?"

The panicked look on her face stopped him cold.

"You know what? We should start getting ready if we want to greet Belinda Dawson when she gets home from work. We don't want to give her too much time to go out again."

"You're right, although I dread putting on that suit." She rolled from the bed and grabbed a jacket from the back of the chair.

"You and me both." He ripped the plastic from the cheap, off-the-rack suit he'd bought earlier that day. "Do you know you talk in your sleep?"

"I do?" She froze and clutched the jacket to her chest, her pale face a shade lighter than the light beige of the suit. "What did I say?"

"I honestly don't remember." He just knew it hadn't been his name or any form of endearment for him. "Okay, I'm gonna put this thing on—if you think you can control yourself while I change."

She laughed a little too loudly. "That's fair."

He dropped his shorts to the floor and pulled on the polyester slacks. "Are you nervous about this?"

"David and I used to do stuff like this all the time. It's a snap."

"I'm not David. Are you afraid I'm going to screw it up?"

"You'll be fine. You're a quick learner."

Forty minutes later as Quinn drove his car, which had developed a rattle, down the gracious streets of Savannah's historic district, Rikki poked him in the side.

"You're going to have to park this jalopy a few blocks away. There is no way David's wife is going to believe the CIA is paying her an official visit in this little death trap."

Quinn ducked his head and peered at the palatial homes behind the live oaks dripping with Spanish moss. He whistled through his teeth. "Either David was making a lot more money than you at the Agency or he had a ton of life insurance. Did you say this was a new address for Belinda?"

"Yeah." Rikki rolled down the window and took a deep breath. "Smells lovely out here."

"Where did they live before?"

"Not in this neighborhood. I looked up David's old address and it wasn't near here, so the widow purchased some new digs after her husband's untimely death."

Glancing at the GPS, Quinn said, "Her house is up ahead on the right. I'm going to pull up alongside this park. Can you check the signs?"

"Slow down." Rikki stuck her head out the window. "It's okay to park here."

Quinn pulled up to the curb and unfolded himself from the car. "Can you please grab my jacket from the back?"

Rikki joined him on the sidewalk, jacket in hand. "Here you go."

They walked the two blocks to Belinda Dawson's house. Quinn's hand swung at his side so close to Rikki's, they kept brushing knuckles. He resisted the urge to grab her hand.

What would they do after this dead end? What would Rikki do? Where else would she go to find answers? He wanted to send her back to Jamaica and continue the investigation on his own. He had sources at the CIA— better sources than the hapless Jeff. He might be able to track this down for her. It might even be a good idea for Rikki to turn herself in and cooperate with the investigation.

He slid a glance at her firm jaw and long stride. No way. She wouldn't go down that road, and he didn't blame her. If the powers that be at the CIA thought they had their woman a year ago, what would change their mind this time? The fact that she'd spent time in a North Korean labor camp wouldn't convince them.

"There it is." Rikki tugged on his sleeve. "And there's a Lexus in the driveway, so she's probably home."

"Home and livin' large."

She drove a knuckle into his back. "You act like she's happy her husband's dead and would rather have the money."

"David Dawson was a snake. You should know that better than anyone. He wanted to cheat on his wife... with you. You don't really believe that garbage he was spewing about how Belinda didn't understand him. That's the oldest line in the book."

"I know that."

"And if you were so quick to peg David as a traitor based on the flimsy evidence of a fictional character, deep down you knew David was a snake."

"All right, all right." She put her finger to her lips as they approached the wrought iron gate ringing the house. "It's time to keep your thoughts to yourself."

Quinn pushed down on the handle of the gate. "Whew, not locked. Ready, Agent Reid?"

"Copy, Agent Miller."

Once on the broad porch, Quinn rang the doorbell, which resounded somewhere deep in the house. "I wouldn't be surprised if a maid in a frilly apron answered the door."

"Or a butler."

A soft voice with a honeyed Southern accent floated out to the porch over an intercom. "Who is it? Press the white button, please."

Quinn reached for the speaker to the right of the doorbell and jabbed the button with his thumb. He laid his own Nawlins accent on thick. "Good evening, ma'am. I'm Agent Miller and this is Agent Reid. We've come to collect Agent Dawson's equipment."

At first Quinn thought she was going to ignore them and shut them out. Then the soft drawl responded, "Equipment?"

"I'm sorry, ma'am. The Agency contacted you about some equipment of Agent Dawson's and you indicated you had it at home?"

"I don't remember that." The locks on the door clicked, and it inched open.

A petite woman with fluffy blond hair appeared in the doorway.

Rikki stuck out her hand. "Mrs. Dawson? I'm Agent Reid. Sorry for any confusion. We were sent to pick up some equipment."

Belinda released a measured sigh. "Sometimes I wonder how the government functions. Please come in."

Quinn took the attractive woman's soft hand in his. "Sorry for your loss, ma'am, and sorry for the red tape."

"It's been over a year. I'm used to it." She closed the door and folded her hands in front of her. "Can I get you some tea? Lemonade?"

"I'd love some tea, ma'am." Quinn slathered on the Southern charm. A woman like Belinda Dawson would expect it. A quick glance around the lavishly appointed living room marked Belinda as a woman who spared herself no comfort or reward.

Rikki shook her head. "Nothing for me, thank you. You have a beautiful home."

"Thank you." Belinda started for the kitchen and glanced over her shoulder. "I'll get it for you myself. The help has gone home for the day."

When she entered the vast kitchen, Quinn exchanged a quick look with Rikki, who raised her eyebrows.

Belinda returned to the room, carrying two glasses of tea, the ice clinking softly. As she handed one glass to Quinn, she said, "Equipment, you say?"

"Yes, when we…lose an agent, we do an inventory of his equipment. A few pieces were missing from Agent Dawson's effects. Agent Reid and I received notification that you'd been contacted and had located the missing equipment."

"You know, it's completely possible." Belinda aimed her big blue eyes at Quinn over the rim of her glass as she took a sip of the very sweet tea. "There was so much…red tape when David died. Did you know him?"

"I did not have the pleasure, ma'am." At least Quinn could be truthful about something.

"Agent Reid?" Belinda had approached Rikki from behind, hovering over her shoulder as Rikki studied a vast array of framed photographs on a shelf.

Rikki cranked her head over her shoulder. "No, I never met Agent Dawson, but then our paths wouldn't have crossed. I'd heard he was an incredible agent, though. A real treasure to the Agency."

Belinda bowed her head. "That's nice to hear. It's too bad he was betrayed by the one person he trusted the most."

Quinn's heart hammered as he watched Rikki across the room. *C'mon, Agent Reid, keep it together.*

"Oh?" Rikki tipped her head and her dark ponytail swung behind her. "I'd heard he was killed by the North Koreans."

"He was, but his partner made that happen. Rikki Taylor." She spit out the name as if it were poison on her tongue. "They were partners. He was her mentor. He taught her everything. She tried to seduce him first, and when that didn't work she betrayed him to the North

Koreans. But she got hers. I heard she died, too. I don't know how or when, but it gave me some measure of satisfaction."

Rikki blinked. "I can imagine it would. We didn't hear that story."

Quinn ground his back teeth together. Dawson was worse than a snake if he told his wife Rikki had been trying to seduce him. Belinda probably found some evidence of David's infatuation with his partner, and he turned it around on Rikki.

Rikki picked up a picture from the shelf. "Is this Agent Dawson?"

Quinn had uncoiled his muscles enough to move toward the two women. He wanted a firsthand look at the snake himself. He'd only ever seen him at a distance when he first met Rikki in Dubai.

Belinda took the framed photo from Rikki's hands and traced a finger over the form of a fit, compact man in his midforties, with the build of a long-distance runner, shirtless and standing in knee-deep water.

Belinda almost whispered. "This is Davey. This is the last picture I have of him. We'd taken a brief vacation to the Bahamas before he left for Dubai, and then North Korea."

Rikki sniffed. "I'm so sorry, Mrs. Dawson. We didn't come here to bring up painful memories. If you don't have Agent Dawson's equipment, we can write it off as a misunderstanding."

"I can pretty much confirm I don't have any of Davey's work equipment here. I moved into this house about nine months ago—too many memories in the old place—and I would've remembered seeing anything of Davey's from work and moving it over with me."

"We'll report that, ma'am. Don't concern yourself."

Quinn raised his glass before finishing off the tea. "That sure hit the spot."

Belinda placed Dawson's picture back on the shelf, caressing the edges of the frame. "If I do find something, is there a number where I can reach you?"

Quinn reached into his front pocket for his newly minted business cards and pulled one out. He pinched it between his fingers. "Here you go, ma'am. It's best to call my cell phone number."

"Well, I will certainly take a look." She made a half turn toward Rikki. "Are you sure you don't want some refreshment before you leave?"

"No, thank you. I feel bad that we troubled you on this wild-goose chase."

Belinda waved her hands. "Oh, Davey and I were married for over twenty years. I know how the Agency works."

A bead of sweat rolled down Quinn's back in his cheap suit, despite the chilly air in Belinda Dawson's house. Not only did this turn out to be a wild-goose chase for Rikki, she'd had to listen to David's slights and lies.

As Belinda walked them to the front door, she asked, "Are you taking any time to see the city? I do volunteer work at the Savannah Historical Society every weekday morning, and we have an incredible selection of artifacts and can give you some good sightseeing suggestions."

Rikki shook her head, her ponytail waving from side to side. "I'm afraid it's business only for us."

Quinn smiled. "Thanks again, ma'am."

Belinda opened the front door and turned to shake their hands again. "Have a nice trip back to... Washington."

They didn't say a word to each other as they walked down the pathway to the front gate and into the still night, light from the setting sun playing peekaboo between the trailing tails of Spanish moss.

When they hit the sidewalk out of sight of the house, Quinn took Rikki's arm. "Sorry about that."

"Sorry?" She turned toward him, her eyes alight with sparks. "I couldn't be happier with the results."

He tripped to a stop. "You enjoy getting trashed and vilified?"

"Small price to pay for the truth and the first big break in my investigation."

"You lost me."

"Quinn." She grabbed his lapels. "David Dawson is still alive."

Chapter Ten

Quinn's eyes popped open. "What are you talking about? How did you come to that conclusion?"

Rikki looked over his shoulder. She didn't trust Belinda Dawson one iota. "Let's keep moving. She could be calling the CIA or your cell phone number as we speak."

Quinn continued on the sidewalk, excitement lengthening his stride so that she had to hold on to his arm to keep up with him.

With a slight pant, she said, "It was that picture."

"The vacation picture from the Bahamas?"

"That wasn't the Bahamas. Did you get a load of that water? Looked like some muddy rice paddy in Southeast Asia."

"You're saying that's a recent picture of David? One taken after his supposed death in North Korea?"

"That's exactly what I'm saying."

"How could you possibly know that? Because of an imagined rice paddy?"

"Wait for the car. I'm not blabbing this on the sidewalk, even if there is nobody else around."

By the time they reached the car, sweat was dampening Rikki's back. She ripped off her jacket, and Quinn did the same.

Once in the car with the engine and the air running, Rikki bounced in her seat and turned toward Quinn. "It's not the place. It's the man and more specifically the tattoo."

"That tattoo on his chest? He didn't have that before?"

"Nope. The last time I saw David, right before I witnessed his so-called murder at the hands of the North Koreans, he most definitely did not have a big tattoo on his chest—a tattoo of a phoenix, I might add."

"You've seen David Dawson's chest?"

Her cough turned into a laugh. "That's all you can focus on? Of course I've seen David's chest. You know how scorching it gets in Korea, and all the other hot spots we've been in around the world. You've been in some of the same hot spots. I've seen him without his shirt several times, and I can say unequivocally the man never had a tattoo. Why Belinda keeps that picture around is beyond me. Beyond stupid."

"You don't think it could've been one of those temporary tattoos, do you?"

Compressing her lips into a thin line, Rikki tilted her head. "Really? The man is forty-four, not eight."

Quinn pulled away from the curb, his brows creating a vee over his nose. "David set up this Korea trip for the two of you with the cover that he had a line on Vlad. That got him money and support from Ariel. He engineered his own death, while fingering you as a traitor at the same time. Why you?"

Rikki's knees bounced. "Because of just that—the Vlad story was a cover and if nothing came of it, I'd be a witness."

"If nothing came of it, he could claim his sources fell through. Happens all the time."

Quinn snapped his fingers several times. "This trip was David's opportunity to turn, to go over to the other side. He fakes his death so nobody is looking for him, and he sets up his partner so she takes the fall for being the traitor…and he gets his revenge."

"Revenge?" Rikki's stomach dropped. "What do you mean by that?"

"Because you rejected him, Rikki. He kills a lot of birds with those stones."

"Oh my God." She wrapped her ponytail around her hand. "It was David all along. He set me up. Why? Who is he working for?"

"This has Vlad's fingerprints all over it. This wouldn't be the first time he turned an agent or someone on the inside. My buddy Miguel Estrada had to deal with that. He was betrayed in Afghanistan and captured. Vlad is a master of manipulation. It wouldn't surprise me at all if he'd worked on David. Did you get the full effect of Belinda's house? Do you really think life insurance money and a government pension are paying for that? It sounds like she quit her marketing job, too, and is volunteering her time."

"She knows. Of course she knows her husband's alive. He sent her that picture—maybe as proof." Rikki smacked her hand against her knee. "I should've taken that photo. I need to provide proof that David's still alive—not in a North Korean labor camp, not held captive, not suffering from amnesia and wandering around South Korea—but alive and well and functioning as a traitor to his country."

"Taking that picture would've been risky. Belinda would've known it was missing and would've known it was us."

"I need to get some proof."

"The decoding. Let me get my guy, Donovan Chan, to work on David's emails. I think we can take it to the bank that those messages contain some incriminating information." Quinn wheeled into a parking lot and squealed to a stop. "And if Dawson's betrayal has anything to do with Vlad, we're going to nail them both."

"I want that picture, Quinn. I'm sure I'm not the only person who can testify to the fact that David Dawson didn't have a tattoo when he went to North Korea. If I can plant some doubt that he perished in North Korea, maybe the CIA can start looking into Belinda Dawson's finances. There might be an offshore account or some other irregularities, but it starts with that photo."

"We can't just steal the picture. We'll have to stage it as a break-in, and we'll have to do it at night. God knows how many butlers, housekeepers and gardeners Belinda has around the house during the day."

"Tonight. We do it tonight."

"She'll know it's us."

"I don't care. Let her suspect. I'm only too happy to strike some fear into her heart—and David's." Crossing her arms, she hunched her shoulders. "I can't believe he turned on me, after everything we went through together."

"You know what I think?" Quinn put the car in gear and drove out of the parking lot. "I think if he had been successful in seducing you, he would've tried to lure you to the dark side with him. As devastated as I'm sure he was when you rejected him, that's not what pushed him over the edge. Guys like that are bad seeds. He would've turned anyway if the price was right."

"You're probably right." She tapped on the window. "Where are we going?"

"I'm starving. We're going to get something to eat

before returning to the motel and changing into something more comfortable for breaking and entering."

"Can we please go out? I doubt we're going to run into Belinda Dawson at dinner, since she seemed to have something simmering on her stove when we were there. Nobody else knows we're here. Nobody knows I'm anywhere…just like David."

"I'll meet you halfway. We'll pick up some soul food and eat at the hotel pool."

"I guess it's better than fast food in the room." She turned toward him with a tilt to her head. "What exactly is soul food?"

Quinn quirked his eyebrows up and down. "Allow me to introduce you to its delights."

THE DELIGHTS OF soul food included lots of deep frying and lots of carbs. Rikki sucked down a big gulp of disgustingly sweet tea and curled her legs beneath her on the chaise longue by the pool. She yawned. "So, soul food is a sleep aid, because the only thing I want to do right now is close my eyes and drift off."

Quinn rubbed and then patted his flat stomach. "Pretty good, huh?"

"Delish." Rikki eyed his trim waistline.

How did he manage to put away all that food and still look like a Greek god? She'd pay him the compliment, but she didn't want to get caught up in a discussion of food and weight and start Quinn wondering about all her new soft spots. He seemed to like them, anyway.

She pressed her hands against her own belly and the butterflies taking wing there. She'd tell Quinn about Bella as soon as she got the proof on David. Maybe she'd even let someone else take over the investigation, as long as the CIA didn't want to take her into custody.

Rikki swept up the used napkins on the table between them and shoved them into one of the plastic bags. "I have my clothes all picked out—black leggings, black T-shirt and a pair of sneakers for a quick getaway."

"And I have all my burglar tools. Should be a cinch to break in there—as long as she doesn't have an alarm system. If she has one of those, it'll take a little longer."

Rikki clambered out of the chaise longue and dumped their trash in the bin by the gate. "I should be able to tell if she does have an alarm system and if it's armed."

"If it is, I got that covered." He held up a deep-fried ball of something. "Do you want the last one?"

"Knock yourself out."

They returned to the room and changed into their night-crawler outfits.

Standing before the mirror, Rikki wound the elastic holder around her ponytail once more. "Wish we had your motorcycle for this little assignment, or better yet, my silent electric scooter."

"We'll be fine. I'll leave the car by the park again. We'll get in there, swipe the picture and get out. Who knows? Belinda may not even notice it's missing for a day or two."

"Wait." Rikki spun around from the mirror. "I thought we were going to steal a few more things to make it look like a break-in."

"Do you really want to steal some woman's jewelry and small electronics?"

"You don't seriously expect me to feel some sympathy for a traitor and his wife, do you?"

"I'm not a thief."

"It would be extremely odd for a burglar to steal a framed photograph only. You're the one who made this point earlier." She wedged a hand on her hip. "Why are you having an attack of conscience now?"

"Okay, we'll take a few other things and then return them to…someone."

"Whatever you want to do. We should return them to the CIA for the secrets David probably stole."

"We'll figure it out." Quinn hitched a small backpack over one shoulder. "Are you ready?"

"Oh, yeah."

They didn't say much on the way over, and Rikki focused her private thoughts on David and his behavior their last year together. He had changed, had become less open with her. She'd written this change off to the awkwardness after his declaration of love for her and his anger when he found out about her and Quinn. Because he had been angry. Had that set him on this course?

No. He had to have arranged the North Korea trip prior to Dubai. Quinn was right. David already had the inclination to betray his country; whether that came from greed or disagreements with the country's policies, she couldn't tell, and it didn't matter anyway. There could be no valid excuse.

Quinn parked the car and cut the engine. "Do you think we should give it another hour? It's not much past midnight. What if she's a night owl?"

"She's not. She turns in early. I remember David telling me that—it was supposedly another point of contention between them, since he liked to stay up late and sleep in when he wasn't working, and Belinda preferred the opposite."

Quinn snorted. "Yeah, because that's a good reason to cheat on someone and end a marriage."

"That was probably all a lie. He probably just wanted to compromise me to use me. I'm sure he never loved me. If Belinda is okay with his deceit and is happy to spend his blood money, they're made for each other."

He clasped the back of her neck and squeezed it gently. "It's not you. Dawson would've betrayed any partner."

"Okay, let's do this." She dropped her head to the side and kissed his wrist.

The night air was heavy with the scent of magnolias from the park, and the sweet smell reminded her of the fragrant blooms in Jamaica and nights spent cradling Bella in the rocking chair in Mom's garden.

What was she doing here? She yearned to be back with her baby. She yearned to tell Quinn all about their daughter.

But she couldn't live her life as a dead woman.

It didn't take long for Quinn to break into Belinda's house. In an odd stroke of luck, Belinda hadn't enabled her alarm system.

They stepped through the side door and Rikki held her breath as she looked around the living room where they'd been earlier this evening. Low lights from beneath the kitchen counters gave a soft glow to the room, and they didn't even have to use their flashlights. What a nice welcome.

Rikki made a beeline for the built-in bookshelf and tripped to a stop. With her gloved fingers, she tapped the empty space that David's picture had occupied.

She gestured to Quinn, still hovering by the door.

He ducked next to her, and she whispered in his ear, "The picture is gone."

He swept the light from his phone across the photos on the shelves and swore softly under his breath. "I don't like this, Rikki. We need to get out."

Her heart jumped, mimicking the urgency in his voice. "Wh-why?"

"It's all too convenient for us—the alarm system, the lights and now the missing picture. It's almost like she expected us."

"Then why would she make it easy for us?"

"To lure us in." He grabbed her arm. "We're done here."

Rikki twisted her head around for one last, longing look at that bookshelf as Quinn pulled her toward the side door—the door that hadn't been double-locked.

What had Belinda done with that incriminating picture? Had she realized the stupidity of showing it to a couple of CIA agents? Belinda had probably figured nobody would do a before-and-after comparison of her dead husband's chest.

Quinn hustled Rikki through the side door, and eased it closed. As soon as the door clicked, Rikki heard another click.

"Get your hands up where I can see them."

Chapter Eleven

A shot of adrenaline pumped through Quinn's body and he dropped to the ground, making a grab for Rikki's legs to take her down with him. But Rikki was two steps ahead of him, already on the ground and army-crawling toward the back of the house.

A beam of light swept the space above them, bouncing off the door they'd just passed through.

Staying low, Quinn lunged around the same corner where Rikki had just disappeared. His gun dug into his ribs. He left it there. Although any cop worth his salt would've lit up the scene by now with more than just a flashlight, Quinn couldn't be sure that the Savannah PD *didn't* have them at gunpoint. It could very well be some rookie cop on the other side of that click.

Whoever it was hadn't given them a second order. He probably couldn't see them with the clouds wafting across the crescent moon and no lights illuminating the side of the house. That was another convenience Belinda had afforded them. She might have lured them to the dark side of the house, but she'd also just given them an advantage.

Neither of them spoke, but Quinn could hear Rikki's short spurts of breath as she dragged herself up to a crouching position.

She jabbed his shoulder and pointed to the fence.

A semicircle of light awaited them on their way to that fence, but Quinn didn't want to give their pursuer a shot at them once he rounded the corner.

He shook his head at Rikki and jerked his thumb over his shoulder at the stealthy rustle behind them. A seasoned cop would've called backup by now, but Quinn couldn't be 100 percent sure that Belinda hadn't called the police, and he didn't want to risk tangling with a member of law enforcement—especially since he and Rikki had been caught red-handed breaking and entering.

A body of water to his left caught a glimmer of light from the slice of moon as it emerged from a rolling cloud cover. Quinn tugged on Rikki's pant leg and tipped his chin toward the pond. Even if they made a splash going into the water, the man with the gun wouldn't be able to get a clear line of sight on them— not like he would once he came around that corner with his flashlight.

Rikki didn't need any encouragement from him. On her hands and knees, she crawled to the edge of the pond and slipped in headfirst.

Quinn rolled in after her and kept his body flat. The pond had enough water to cover them, but only if they stretched out their bodies and kept low. Now all they needed was a couple of reeds to poke up above the surface of the water to breathe.

He and Rikki floated and bobbed side by side, submerged in the murky water until they reached the far end of the pond.

They'd have to head over the back fence and make a run for it if they hoped to get out of this situation. He squeezed Rikki's arm.

Again, she knew what had to be done.

She breached the surface first, emerging from the water like some slinky, primordial creature, and he scrambled over the slippery edge behind her. The noise of their escape broke the silence of the night, and the light from the flashlight made a jerky survey above the pond.

By the time the beam of light found Quinn, Rikki had launched herself over the fence. As Quinn grabbed the slats of wood to freedom, their assailant fired his first shot—from a silencer.

The bullet cracked the fence inches from Quinn's right hand. That was all the incentive he needed. He hoisted himself over and landed on the ground.

Rikki grabbed the back of his shirt at the collar. "Run."

"No kidding."

They'd landed in someone else's backyard, but Quinn couldn't even see the house from their position. Belinda had bought herself a place on a large lot, alongside other homes on equally large lots. The size of these yards would save their necks.

In a crouch, they ran for the fence to their left. The clouds cooperated with them and drifted across the slice of moon again.

Rikki hit the fence with both hands. "I can't get over this without a boost. Can you?"

"Piece of cake, Buttercup." He laced his fingers together, and Rikki wedged the sole of her tennis shoe against his palms. "Ready?"

"Just hurry it up."

He launched her up, and she hoisted herself over.

His height gave him an advantage, and he swung over the fence with ease.

They made their way through a couple more lawns like that before hitting the street. Their shoes squishing with water, they kept to the shadows until they reached the park.

Rikki was panting by the time she grabbed the door handle of his vehicle. "It's a good thing we left the car down here."

"Yep, but I'm surprised Belinda Dawson didn't provide a getaway car for us."

Quinn started the engine before he fully sat down or closed the door. He left the lights off as he crawled into the street, checking his rearview mirror.

The cars on the streets of Savannah were few and far between until they emerged from the quiet residential streets into a boulevard dotted with bars and nightspots.

Quinn finally let out a pent-up breath, but still kept watch on his mirrors.

Rikki slumped in her seat, pressing a hand over her heart and the wet T-shirt that stuck to her chest. "That was close. He was no cop, was he? Did you get a look at him?"

"I didn't see him at all, but you're right. I don't think Belinda called the cops on us." Quinn sluiced his wet hair back from his forehead and combed out a piece of moss.

"Then who did she call? Who was that? He had a silencer." Rikki crossed her arms over her midsection. "It must've been CIA. She called the Agency to check on us and discovered nobody had been sent for David's equipment."

"Maybe, but how did someone get here so quickly and why the subterfuge?" Quinn rubbed his palms, which the fence had abraded, against the steering wheel. "If she called the CIA, found out we were impostors and then reported us, why would she collude with the Agency to catch us in the act? The CIA would never use a spouse like that to lure impostors out of the woodwork. Especially a widow. Can you imagine the liability if the Agency did that and a spouse wound up dead?"

"It could've been someone from the Agency but not sanctioned by the Agency. Is that what you mean? Someone already out here looking after Belinda. Someone who's in on the joke and knows that David is alive and well and getting tattooed in Thailand, or wherever." Rikki grabbed her ponytail and twisted it to wring out the pond water.

"That's what I'm thinking, someone with the Agency—or not, but nobody official."

Rikki tucked a wet strand of hair behind her ear. "That's a scarier scenario than having an on-duty agent after us."

"Except—" Quinn wheeled into the parking lot of their motel and parked in front of their room "—if an agent had captured us, taken us down at gunpoint, the Agency would've wasted no time identifying you, unless you erased your fingerprints with acid, but I recall your fingertips being intact."

She wiggled her fingers in front of her. "The hair and the eyes are as far as I'll go for a disguise. I'm going to agree with you and bet our shooter was either a rogue agent working with David or someone involved in this traitorous network of David's jumping on any hint that someone believes he's still alive."

Quinn cut the engine and lights but didn't make a move to leave the car. "Which brings us back to Belinda."

"It sure seemed like she trusted us while we were there. What do you think set off her alarm bells?"

"Maybe the interest in the photo. She realized after we left that the picture was of David post-death and started to get worried."

Rikki leveled a finger at him, seemingly in no hurry to get out of the car and her wet clothing. "Or she called the number on your fake card."

He tapped the burner phone in his cup holder. "Except I didn't get any calls on this phone."

"Either I showed too much interest in that picture or she had orders from David to be wary of any outreach from the Agency. She called the CIA to check out our story."

"Our story didn't pass the test. She brushed it off with the Agency and then made a call to her henchman."

"And set us up." Rikki rubbed her chin. "How did she know we'd be back?"

"She didn't know for sure, or Dawson is so paranoid he orchestrated the setup just to be on the safe side."

"Do you think she called David after we left?"

"Makes sense, doesn't it? Isn't that something David would do? Disable the alarm system, leave off the lights on one side of the house, disengage one set of locks on the door and have Belinda call in backup when we showed up. Hell—" he yanked the door handle "—she might've had a camera watching our every move down there."

Back in the room, Rikki peeled off her wet T-shirt and shimmied out of the jeans sticking to her thighs. "Ugh, that pond water was disgusting. I hope you didn't swallow any of it."

"My lips were sealed. I'm just glad we left our phones in the car. I would've had a lot of explaining to do to get my encrypted phone replaced."

Rikki kicked her wet clothes into a corner. "We need

to get David's emails to Chan and decoded. I want to know what he was up to and what he was doing in South Korea."

"Other than setting up his own death and your entrapment? I'd say Dawson was a busy boy—and I already sent the emails to Chan."

"Why South Korea? There must've been a reason for him to pick that area instead of staging all this in Dubai, for example."

"That's a mystery those messages might solve." Quinn pulled his own damp T-shirt over his head and tossed it into Rikki's wet pile of clothes. "Right now I want to get this pond scum off my body. Do you want to help me?"

"I'd like nothing more than to rub pond scum from your body."

Quinn sprinted past Rikki to the bathroom before she could change her mind. He ran a warm bath and dumped some body wash in the water to create bubbles. Then he stripped off the rest of his clothes and sank into the tub, as much as his six-foot-three frame could sink.

"That was fast—bubbles and everything." Rikki hung on the door frame in her underwear.

"Technically it's body wash, but it worked." He scooped up a handful of bubbles and blew on them.

"I knew navy SEALs were resourceful. I just didn't realize in how many ways." She stepped out of her panties and unhooked her bra.

Quinn opened his legs, patting the water between them. "I have a place for you right here."

Rikki dipped a toe in the water before stepping in and lowering herself into the tub. Leaning back against his chest, she said, "Don't get any ideas in here, McBride. We might both end up drowning."

"Ideas?" He cupped her breasts from behind and nuzzled her neck. "What ideas do you think I might have?"

She put one arm behind her, winding it around his neck. "The kinds of ideas you have every time we're within two feet of each other."

"Can I help it if I find you irresistible?"

And then he used all his resourcefulness to show her.

THE FOLLOWING MORNING, Quinn got back to business. While Rikki looked through her old emails from David, Quinn contacted Donovan Chan again. If Chan wondered why Quinn was asking about a dead agent, he kept his questions to himself.

Rikki looked up from Quinn's laptop. "I don't see anything suspicious in David's communications, nothing to suggest that our mission to Korea was anything other than what he claimed—a lead on Vlad."

"Did he ever disclose how he got this intel?" Quinn tossed his phone on the cushion beside him.

Rikki wedged the tip of her finger between her teeth. "Not in the emails, but he mentioned a name when we were in Dubai, and it was the same guy we met in South Korea—Buddy Song."

"Was this Song in intelligence in South Korea? Why wouldn't Song go straight to the CIA or to Ariel and the Vlad task force?"

"I don't know." Rikki shrugged. "I didn't ask him. David had his contacts outside of our partnership, relationships he'd cultivated over the years before I even became an agent and started working with him."

"Do you know how to contact Song? Did anyone ever reach out to him after David's supposed murder and your capture?"

"My supposed murder, too." She raised her eyebrows. "You know that better than anyone."

Quinn clasped the back of his neck and squeezed. "Do you have to keep reminding me?"

"Like I said before, if it hadn't been you I'd be dead." She tipped the computer from her lap onto the bed and crossed her legs. "Ariel didn't tell me what kind of investigation was done into David's murder, but I doubt anyone knows about Song. David didn't even put his name in an email to me. We only ever spoke about him."

"I think Song is a good place to start. What do you remember about him? Where did you meet?"

"We met in Seoul, at a park. He spoke English very well. He helped us cross the border, and I got the feeling it wasn't his first rodeo."

"He was probably someone who facilitated border crossings between North and South Korea. Maybe that was his insight into Vlad. He probably helped him cross the border, too."

"Could be. Song got us to a tunnel between the two countries and said goodbye there. The rest is history. David and I crossed over and hadn't traveled five miles before I was taken and David killed—or so I thought."

"But now we know Song didn't set up David. David manipulated the entire scenario, with or without Song's knowledge."

"And definitely without mine."

Rikki rubbed her nose, and Quinn knew David's betrayal of her stung. He couldn't imagine any of his sniper teammates turning on him like that. For a while, the navy had tried to tell them Miguel Estrada had been working with the enemy, but he and the rest of the guys hadn't believed that for one second.

But Rikki had proof.

Quinn stood up and stretched his arms, almost brushing his fingertips on the ceiling. "Do you think Ariel can track down Song? Would she? She's deep undercover enough that nobody's following her movements."

"I can ask her. I never thought about him before, but that's when I believed our mission to Korea was something straightforward, or at least as straightforward as our missions ever were. Now that I know David pulled a scam on me—" she flicked her fingers in the air "—everything and everyone is fair game."

Quinn peered through the curtains on the window. "We can do all this on computers and on my trusty phone. We don't need to stay in Savannah."

"When do you have to report back for duty?"

"Three weeks." A sudden fear gripped Quinn's heart. "If we can't clear you before then, you need to go back to Jamaica where you'll be safe."

Rikki's lashes dropped over her eyes. "Maybe. I vowed I wouldn't return there until my name was cleared."

"I can continue our sleuthing."

She widened her eyes. "From Afghanistan or Pakistan or Libya or wherever you're going? I don't think so, Quinn."

In two steps, he was at the bed and sitting on the edge. "Then we'll figure it out, and then maybe you don't have to go back to Jamaica. You can go back to your job and I can do mine and maybe we can be together—freewheeling and fancy-free, no strings, nothing to tie us down except each other."

Rikki sucked in her lower lip. "That's what you want?"

"That's what I always wanted. I don't understand why I scared you off in Dubai to the point you felt you had to run away. Yeah, I felt something deep for you, maybe deeper than you felt yourself, but that never meant I wanted to restrict you, make you give up the job you love. Hell, my job isn't exactly a nine-to-five, white-picket-fence deal."

"We have to talk this through first." Rikki twisted her fingers. "There's a lot I have to tell you."

"About your time in the labor camp and your escape?" He cupped his hand over one of her knees. "I do want to hear about that, Rikki. It'll only make me think you're more amazing than I already do."

"It's not just that, Quinn. Jamaica…"

"You're not going to tell me you have a boyfriend in Jamaica, are you?" He curled his fingers into her leg. "I don't even care. I know I love you more than anyone else could."

She pressed her fingers against her bottom lip and whispered, "Quinn."

"So whatever it is…" He jerked his head toward the ringing phone on the table by the window. "That's not my regular phone. That's the burner, and nobody has that number except Belinda."

"Or random telemarketers."

Quinn pushed himself off the bed and lunged for the phone. "It's her."

He jabbed the button to answer and to put the phone on speaker at the same time. "Hello? Agent Miller."

"Agent Miller, this is Belinda Dawson."

"Mrs. Dawson, did you find some of your husband's equipment after all?" He rolled his eyes at Rikki, who'd followed him off the bed and had her hip wedged against the table.

"Let's cut to the chase, Miller, if that's really your name."

Quinn swallowed. "Pardon me, ma'am?"

"You can cut the Southern boy charm, too. I'm immune."

"I'm afraid you lost me, Mrs. Dawson."

"I almost lost you last night to that thug watching my house night and day."

Rikki grabbed his wrist, her eyes taking up half her face.

"You're going to have to explain yourself, Mrs. Dawson."

"You and I both know my husband is alive, Agent Miller, and I can give you the proof you need."

Chapter Twelve

Rikki clapped a hand over her mouth. Why was Belinda doing this? Why was she outing David?

Quinn braced his hands on the table and hunched over the phone. "Why would you give me proof that your husband is alive?"

"That's what you were sniffing around here for, wasn't it? You and your...partner seemed awfully interested in that photo of David—the one taken after his supposed death. When you zeroed in on that picture, I finally felt a glimmer of hope."

Quinn raised his eyebrows at Rikki, but all she could do was shrug. She had no idea where Belinda was going with this.

Quinn cleared his throat. "What do you mean by hope? Hope for what?"

"David swore me to secrecy about his betrayal. He warned me that I'd lose everything if the CIA found out he'd been spying for the enemy. He sent people to watch me, to keep tabs on me."

"How do you know my partner and I aren't just two more watchdogs?"

Rikki nodded at Quinn. He knew all the right questions—the same ones she'd be asking.

"You were fishing. They don't fish. Your unexpected

appearance on my doorstep yesterday told me that the CIA has doubts about David's story."

Rikki scribbled a question on a napkin and shoved it toward Quinn.

He gave her a thumbs-up. "Why didn't you just call the CIA yourself and report this?"

"You're kidding." Belinda gave a soft snort. "You work for the Agency, so you should understand. I don't know whom to trust over there. I didn't know who was in on it, or even if his fake death had been sanctioned by someone over there. I wasn't about to step out of line, but you two…"

Quinn cut her off and with a gruff voice asked, "If you trusted us so much, why did you call the dogs on us last night?"

Belinda released a long sigh. "That wasn't me."

"The alarm system, the lights, the door? You even took the picture."

"They ordered me to do all that. They knew you'd been there." She sobbed. "They bugged my house."

Quinn's gaze locked on to Rikki's. "And now? How do you know you're not being bugged now?"

"I bought a throwaway phone, and I'm at a restaurant waiting to have brunch with my friend. David taught me well."

Rikki couldn't contain herself anymore. "Why are you turning on your husband now, Mrs. Dawson?"

Belinda sucked in a quick breath over the line. "I'm tired of living this way. David was supposed to send for me, but he hasn't. I can't trust anyone. I don't want to get on the bad side of the CIA and be tried as a traitor. I'd be willing to…you know, testify against him to save myself."

Rikki avoided Quinn's warning looks and plunged

ahead. "At the beginning of the call, you said you had proof that David is alive. Is that the picture?"

"That and other things. I'll turn them over to you so you can go after him and I can be protected. I *will* be protected, won't I?"

Clamping a hand on Rikki's shoulder, Quinn answered the desperate wife. "I think we can work something out. How do you propose to get us this proof if you're under such close watch?"

"There are ways. I have a lot of old friends in this town, and I socialize quite frequently. In fact, I'm meeting old friends tonight for cocktails. If Agent Reid were to stop by our table, just another Savannah socialite… or friend of my husband's, who would question that?"

Quinn shook his head at her, and Rikki put her finger to her lips. "Let's hear the plan, Mrs. Dawson."

As Belinda laid out her scheme to pass off proof that David had faked his death, Quinn peppered her with questions and Rikki took a few notes.

When she finished, Belinda said, with a hitch in her voice, "I really want to do this. I need to think about myself now."

"I'll be there, Mrs. Dawson."

Quinn ended the call and tapped the edge of the phone against his chin. "Why should we trust her?"

"Because her reasoning sounds plausible."

"What if it's a trick to get us on someone's radar?"

"If it is, we can outmaneuver them. We did it last night when we weren't even expecting a trap. This time we'll be even more on our guard and on our game. Besides—" she ran a hand down his tense back "—why would Belinda admit the truth about David being alive if she weren't on the up-and-up?"

Quinn's back got even stiffer. "It wouldn't matter... if she planned to have us killed."

Rikki's hand stopped midcircle where she was rubbing Quinn's back. "I need this proof, Quinn. Nobody is going to believe me, or worse yet, some anonymous tip that Agent David Dawson is a traitor who faked his own death."

"Ariel will believe you. Take this to her and let her launch an investigation."

"There's no denying Ariel is pretty untouchable in the intelligence community, but she has her hands full running the Vlad task force."

"You said it yourself, Rikki. We could make a good case that this *is* about Vlad."

"A good case? A string of undeciphered, coded emails and the word of a disgraced CIA agent, presumed dead?" She slid her hand down his arm and entwined her fingers with his. "I have to do this, Quinn. I won't be by myself, right? You'll be there to look out for me."

"I don't like it, Rikki. I know better than anyone that a sniper can pick you off at a distance and we wouldn't realize it until it was too late."

"Then you also know better than anyone that I can get in and out of that restaurant undercover. With you on my side, no sniper or shooter is going to get a chance at me."

"I think you're exaggerating my talents." He turned and wedged a knuckle beneath her chin. "I'll get you inside that bar, and then you have one drink or whatever Belinda has planned, get the proof and get out of there."

"I think it'll work, and it's not possible for me to exaggerate your talents."

"I'm just glad you decided to forgive me so that I

could help you with all this. Not that you're not a kick-ass agent, but at least two people need to be doing this job and I think we make a great team." He raised her hand to his lips and kissed the back of it.

She rested her head against his shoulder. They *did* make a good team, and she planned to tell him just how much they were going to be a team to raise their daughter—as soon as they got past this danger.

A FEW HOURS after dinner, Rikki slipped on taupe sling-back heels and smoothed her beige skirt over her thighs. "What do you think? Do I look like a Southern belle born to privilege and debutante balls?"

"I don't know about all that, but you look beautiful." Quinn came up behind her and ran a hand through her hair. "I miss those riotous red curls, though, and how the sun would set them on fire. The last time I saw you…"

His fingers tightened in her hair, sending a tingle down her thighs.

Tipping her head into the curve of his palm, she whispered, "But that wasn't the last time you saw me. I'm here now. We both are."

He pressed a kiss against her temple. "Let's keep it that way. Are you sure you want to meet Belinda? It could be a trap. She could have someone waiting for us."

"I have to get my hands on this proof." She placed a finger over his lips. "Why would she want us out of the picture? She knows we don't have any other evidence that David is alive."

"Why did the guy last night taking shots at us want us out of the way?"

"Because if he's working with David, he doesn't know what we have. He doesn't know what Belinda told us. He was trying to eliminate a possible threat."

"Let's get this over with. I can see there's no talking you out of it. You might as well have that red hair on your head, because you're just as stubborn as a brunette."

"Red hair does not make you stubborn." She gave Quinn a playful push while a smile curved her lips as she thought about little red-haired Bella already trying to assert herself at nine months old.

Rikki grabbed a light sweater from the back of the chair and held it up. "Just in case they're blasting the air in the bar."

Before they left the hotel, Quinn called a car for her and saw her safely inside before heading for his own vehicle.

Rikki waved to him out the back window and settled in her seat with a sense of excitement buzzing through her veins. She'd been made for this work. If she could clear her name, how would she reconcile her career with motherhood? Bella meant more to her than anything in the world, more to her than a career—even this career.

And Quinn? How would he fit into it all? He'd been the one talking about forever when they were in Dubai, and that had rattled her. Now he'd changed his tune and had suggested they could both pursue their careers and meet up all over the world when they could. Now she had to break it to him that they had a child together.

She sighed and pressed her fingers against the window. "Almost there?"

"Just about. Ever been to Savannah Joe's before?"

"Nope."

"Nice place. You gotta try the mint juleps—best in the city."

"I'll do that. Thanks for the tip."

The driver pulled up in front of the restaurant-bar,

and Rikki thanked him and slipped out of the back-seat. As Quinn had instructed, she ducked her head and made a beeline for the entrance. If someone had a rifle trained on the entrance to the restaurant, he'd have to recognize her first and set up a shot. She'd given him no time for that at all.

Stepping through the front door, she let out a breath. Belinda had explained the layout—a restaurant in front with tables behind large screened windows, and a busy bar in the back on the river.

As the hostess approached her, Rikki pointed to the back and then made her way to the large bar that separated the dining area from the cocktail lounge.

She rubbed her lips together, moistening her lipstick, and squared her shoulders as she stepped down into the bar area. She scanned the room, and Belinda's subtle wave caught her attention.

Quinn didn't have to worry about the setup. This bar, packed with people, didn't exactly lend itself to ambush and murder at the end of a sniper's rifle.

Rikki plastered a smile on her face and wended her way through the tables to reach Belinda and her two friends, crowded around a cocktail table.

Belinda half rose from her seat. "Here she is. Peyton, this is Melissa and Jordan. Ladies, Peyton, a friend of David's family."

"So nice to meet you." Rikki shared limp handshakes with the other two women and sat next to Belinda. "This is a great place. I heard the mint juleps are to die for."

"Have this one." Belinda shoved a tall glass with a spray of mint in front of Rikki. "I've already had one, and these two already ordered another round."

"Thank you." Rikki smoothed out the napkin beneath the sweating glass. She wanted to keep her wits about her tonight, get the photo and whatever else Belinda had, and get out. Quinn was supposed to be waiting at the back door of the restaurant to whisk her away once Belinda had handed off the proof in the ladies' room.

She'd let Belinda call the shots and make the move to the ladies' room, but this had to look like a legit social interaction in case anyone was watching Belinda.

"Looks refreshing." Rikki swirled the straw in her glass as the waitress delivered three more drinks.

The waitress raised her eyebrows at Rikki. "Can I get you something?"

"I'm good, thanks." Rikki tapped the glass and then almost choked when she glanced over the waitress's shoulder and saw Quinn sitting at the bar.

He had to see that she'd be safe here. She'd rather have him keeping watch outside, and she hoped Belinda hadn't noticed him.

"To friendships." Belinda raised her glass in the center of the table and the other two women held up their glasses, as well.

Rikki clinked her glass with theirs. "To friendships."

The women immediately launched into a discussion of some mutual acquaintance, ripping apart her parenting skills.

Rikki smirked. So much for friendships. She pulled the straw from the glass and sucked some liquid from the bottom of the straw—just a drop or two.

Rikki puckered her lips. She'd never had a mint julep before, and the tartness of the drink surprised her. The garnish on the drink didn't even include a slice of lime.

She stuck the straw back in the glass and took a tentative sip.

Rikki rolled the liquid on the surface of her tongue,

and her nostrils flared as the sour smell reached her nose. The drink dribbled down the back of her throat, but Rikki froze, refusing to swallow.

David's voice floated across her consciousness, and she could picture him in the hotel room in Bangkok pinching a small vial between his fingers. "I discovered this here, Rikki, and it's very useful because it has an immediate impact but proceeds to incapacitate slowly and gradually. It also has a tart taste and smell that could pass for a citrus garnish on a cocktail."

Rikki convulsively clutched the hem of the tablecloth. The liquid had traveled too far for her to stop it unless she made a scene coughing it up.

So she allowed the poison to slide down her throat.

Chapter Thirteen

Quinn studied the four women over the rim of his beer mug. Rikki seemed to be doing a good job of acting like the long-lost friend. She laughed, chattered and sipped her mint julep along with the rest.

Did she forget this wasn't a social call? She needed to nudge Belinda along for their meeting in the john—if Belinda planned to stick with the scheme. He didn't trust the woman for a second.

"Another beer, sir?"

He waved off the bartender and plucked some bills from his pocket. Then from the corner of his eye, he sensed a commotion.

He jerked his head to the side to see Rikki stagger to her feet, almost upsetting her chair. His muscles coiled. His head swiveled from side to side. Nobody else had noticed.

Belinda rose from the table and placed a hand on Rikki's arm. Maybe this was the ruse to get them to the ladies' room.

Rikki leaned against Belinda while Belinda laughed with the other women and curled an arm around Rikki's waist.

Quinn let out a breath. For a minute he thought Rikki

might be injured, but the demeanor of the other two women didn't support this.

Belinda would take Rikki to the ladies' room, hand over the proof, and then they could get the hell out of here.

Quinn narrowed his eyes and followed their progress to the hallway at the back. His gaze shifted to Belinda's friends, still at the table.

He'd give Rikki and Belinda exactly thirty seconds before he went back there himself and hustled Rikki out of the bar. Just because she'd gotten in here without incident didn't mean they'd let her leave. Belinda could have someone waiting for them in the alley.

Quinn shoved himself off his barstool and strode to the back of the room. Turning the corner to the restrooms, he grazed shoulders with a man coming out of the men's room, and the hair on the back of his neck quivered.

Knots formed in his gut and he crashed into the ladies' room.

A woman washing her hands at the sink smirked. "Wrong place."

Quinn ignored her and peered under the first stall. Rikki hadn't been wearing short boots.

He pushed in the door of the next stall. "Rikki?"

A groan from the third stall answered him and he gave the door a shove. The door just missed Rikki propped up against the stall, her face white and twisted with pain.

"What happened? Where's Belinda?"

"Follow her. Just left. Get her."

"I'm not going anywhere. What the hell happened?"

"I'm okay. I'll be okay." She pressed her purse into his hands, her own shaking. "Get the ipecac."

He dumped the contents of her purse on the tile floor and grabbed a small brown bottle. "This stuff?"

She nodded. "Open."

He twisted off the cap and handed it to her. She placed it at her lips and threw some back. Almost immediately, she heaved.

"Out." She pushed him out of the stall.

Another woman had come in and hovered by the first stall. "Is she okay?"

The sound of vomiting came from Rikki's stall, and Quinn shrugged. "She's sick."

The woman wrinkled her nose. "Probably too many of those mint juleps."

Several minutes later, Rikki emerged from the stall, shoving her hair back from her face. She gave the woman at the sink a weak smile. "Sorry about that."

"Oh, honey, it was those mint juleps, wasn't it? Bourbon, powdered sugar." She stuck out her tongue. "Vile."

"You could say that." Rikki ran water over her hands in the sink and splashed her face and rinsed her mouth.

Quinn yanked several paper towels from the dispenser and handed them to her. "Feeling better?"

"Lots." She dabbed her face and neck with the paper towels and ducked back into the stall, ripping off a length of toilet paper. While she blew her nose and did another round of hand-washing, Quinn gathered the items from her purse off the floor and stuffed them back into her bag, including the bottle of ipecac. How the hell did she happen to have that? He studied the sharpened nail file, a bit of rope and another bottle of a clear substance before dropping each into her purse. Travel kit for a CIA agent on assignment?

Two other women had come into the restroom and Quinn apologized, explaining that his wife had been ill, but the women's presence didn't give him and Rikki a chance to talk. And they needed to talk.

Quinn took her arm and hunched over her as they exited the ladies' room. He placed a hand on the silver bar of the back door. "Stay down, crouch forward, stay next to the building."

Rikki cleared her throat. "I don't think we have to worry about anyone else. Belinda was lying about being followed. Besides, I'm supposed to be dead—again."

"Don't argue."

Quinn sneaked Rikki out the back door of the restaurant as if they had a team of snipers taking aim from all four corners of the alley.

He'd wedged his car behind a waitress's after paying her forty bucks for the privilege to get as close as possible to the restaurant. When he handed Rikki into the passenger seat, he said, "Stay down."

She complied, arms folded over her stomach, and he hoped she wouldn't have another episode in his car.

Checking all mirrors, he pulled out of the alley and drove for several blocks.

Rikki finally piped up. "We need to go after Belinda, Quinn."

"Can you tell me what happened now?"

"She poisoned me, slipped it in my mint julep. As soon as I figured out what I was drinking, I stopped drinking it. I wiped my mouth several times and spit the drink into a napkin. One time, I was able to pour out a bit on the floor."

His hands gripped the steering wheel. And he'd been worried about shooters outside the restaurant. "So that and the syrup of ipecac saved you. How'd you know to bring it, or is it standard operating procedure for you spooks?"

"Actually, David saved me."

"What?"

"I'd never had a mint julep before, but this one tasted nothing like I expected. It had a tart taste and smell, and then I remembered David showing me a poison he'd discovered in Thailand. Fast-acting to incapacitate the victim, but slow enough to delay actual death for a few days. Belinda didn't want me dropping dead at the table, but she also had no intention of giving me David's picture or any other proof."

"Did she tell you this as she led you away to the bathroom?"

"She didn't say much of anything. She kept up appearances to the end, soothing me and sympathizing—up until the moment she abandoned me in the bathroom stall and took off."

"She admitted David was alive because she planned to kill you and never turn over any evidence. But why go through all this to kill you? Why not call out one of David's henchmen, like she did at her house?"

"That didn't work because you were there."

"And why just you and not me? Unless she has something else planned for me."

"She probably does."

"But now I'm on my guard."

Rikki smacked the dashboard with both hands. "It's time to strike. She thinks I'm dead and you're running scared."

"This makes no sense to me, Rikki." Quinn plowed a hand through his hair. "If she had called in one of David's associates to take us out in the parking lot, or even if she never contacted us at all after the failed attempt at her house, both of those scenarios would compute better. Admitting David was alive? Luring you out to kill you with poison? I don't get it."

She pressed her hands against her bubbling tummy. "We don't have to get it. We just have to get her. She thinks I'm dead. Part of my stumbling and staggering with her was an act to convince her of that fact. She's going to pass on the news of my demise to the men she has coming after us."

"I'm very much alive, and wouldn't I be coming right at the woman who killed my partner?"

"We'll take her by surprise, at her house."

Quinn tugged on his ear. "You're after the photo again. She's probably destroyed it by now. Maybe it's better if I set up a meeting with her. She knows I'm still alive."

"Then what? A meeting is not going to do any good if she doesn't bring proof that David is alive."

"Instead of a meeting—" Quinn drummed his thumbs against the steering wheel as he made the last turn to their motel "—I'll take her by surprise. I'll escort her someplace where we can have a private...conversation. You stay out of sight until the interrogation. I want to get to the bottom of this. I want her to explain her actions."

"I want that picture."

"I know you do." He rubbed her arm. "But we have to expect she destroyed it. Let's get some answers from her first."

"Where are you going to catch her off guard?"

Quinn parked the car and released his seat belt. "Despite her subterfuge on behalf of David, Belinda seems to go on with her life. We know she volunteers at the Savannah Historical Society in the mornings. I'll catch her when she's leaving her shift tomorrow morning. Just a friendly little talk."

"You don't believe someone's watching her?"

"Why would they? She's on David's side. She proved that tonight by trying to poison you." As that fact hit him all over again, he reached out to grab Rikki's hand. "I think she has an associate or two of David's close by that she can call out when she needs help, like setting us up last night, but I don't think they're keeping tabs on her. I doubt there was anyone there tonight."

"Just her and her little vial of poison." She pounded her knee with her fist. "I can't believe I fell for the oldest trick in the book."

"You didn't fall for it. You recognized the smell and taste of the poison and you took action. Your instincts are still good, kid."

She smiled at him before opening the door and slipping out of the car.

When they got to the motel room, Quinn checked his laptop. "Hey, I got a message from Chan on the decoding."

Rikki leaned over him, her hair fluttering against his cheek. "Can he do it?"

"He's going to try. He has some programs he's going to use."

"Fingers crossed." And then she crossed them.

He closed his hand around her crossed fingers and kissed the tips. "We're going to solve this and get you back into action—where you belong."

Rikki's eyes flooded with tears. "Back where I belong."

As one of those tears slid down Rikki's cheek, Quinn kissed it away, tasting the salt on his lips.

Were those tears for him? If she didn't think she belonged with him by now, he'd have to up his game to convince her otherwise. And he'd start tonight.

THE NEXT MORNING, Quinn pulled on a pair of cargo shorts with big side pockets as he watched Rikki tuck her gun into a purse.

"It's times like these I wish I had a purse." Quinn grabbed his own weapon and slipped it into a pocket of his shorts where it banged against his thigh. "I'd like to carry bigger, but I don't want to be obvious."

Rikki held up her purse, swinging it from her fingertips. "I'd like to carry bigger, too, but I'm not going to lug around a suitcase."

"Remember—" he took her by the shoulders, his thumb nestling beneath the strap of her purse "—stay out of sight, even when I get her alone. She doesn't need to know you're still alive."

"Got it."

"Nobody knows Rikki Taylor is alive. There's no reason for anyone to know April Thompson is alive, either, or Agent Reid, or whoever you were for Belinda's friends."

He released her, and she adjusted the straps of her sundress. Then she crossed to the bed and swept up a big hat. "I'll be wearing this for cover, too."

"Once I make contact with her and show her my gun, I'll walk her to the park in the opposite direction of the coffeehouse where you'll be waiting. Stay there until I text you or come and get you. I'll only come and get you when I'm sure Belinda is on her way home and can't see you."

"But if she still has the picture of David, you'll be going back home with her to get it, right?"

"I'm hoping for even better proof he's alive, so don't hold your breath on that picture."

"Just don't drink anything she offers."

"Don't worry about that."

They would be arriving to the area separately, so Quinn left first with the car. Rikki would be taking a taxi later. He didn't want her anywhere near Belinda Dawson after what Belinda had tried last night, but trying to keep Rikki away would take more patience than he had. Also, he'd discovered that keeping Rikki away was not in his DNA.

Quinn parked a few blocks away from the Savannah Historical Society and waited in his car for almost thirty minutes. They'd checked the volunteer shifts for that morning, and five minutes before he figured Belinda would be leaving, he walked to the block that housed the building and sat on a park bench facing the front entrance. She couldn't exit to the rear, and if she came out a side door, she'd be forced to this street anyway. He had it all sussed out—but the best-laid plans had a way of taking a twist.

He glanced casually to his right at the coffeehouse with its umbrellaed tables spilling onto the sidewalk, and his heart jumped when he spied a big white hat with a black-and-white polka-dot band around it—as long as she stayed out of sight.

Quinn shifted his focus back to the building that housed the Historical Society and his eyes narrowed as he picked out Belinda skipping down the two steps, her arm tucked around the arm of another woman.

Quinn shook his head. As far as Belinda knew, she'd poisoned a woman last night, and she looked like a sorority sister going to lunch.

He held his breath as he watched the two women. He hadn't planned on dealing with a second person.

When the other woman peeled off in another direction, Quinn let out his breath and pushed himself up from the bench. Go time.

Quinn ripped back the Velcro on his shorts' pocket and gripped his gun inside—not that he planned to use it, but he wouldn't mind putting a little fear into the woman who'd poisoned Rikki.

Belinda kept her eyes glued to her phone as she strode down the sidewalk.

Quinn moved behind her and quickened his pace. He lost the element of surprise as she swung her head around and then tripped to a stop.

"You."

He slowed his gait as he continued to approach her, his hand curled around the gun in his pocket. "You killed my partner, and I wanna know why. I wanna know where your husband is."

Belinda's eyes widened and she licked her lips, her gaze dropping to his pocket. "I-I..."

A zipping sound ripped through the air. Belinda's eyes bugged out of their sockets one second before she collapsed in front of him.

Chapter Fourteen

Rikki squinted through the small binoculars she cupped in the palm of her hand. As Belinda turned to confront Quinn, Rikki whispered, "Shoot. You gotta have more stealth than that, sailor."

Then Belinda's body jerked, and she fell to the ground.

With her heart pounding in her chest and a voice screaming in her head, Rikki jumped up from the table, knocking over her glass of water. Clutching her purse against her body, she ran across the street toward the Historical Society.

Her vision blurred as she ran, and she could no longer see Quinn standing on the sidewalk. She panted and bumped into someone running from the scene.

Someone shouted, "Active shooter."

Rikki jogged toward the downed figure and as she got close, a hand shot out from behind a tree and grabbed her.

Quinn pulled her back behind the tree with him. "Someone shot her. He might still be active. I don't think she's dead."

"I need to talk to her." She broke away from Quinn and dropped to the ground. Sirens wailed in the distance, and most people had hit the pavement or had taken cover behind trees.

Rikki crawled toward Belinda, her hand stretched out and her fingers curled. She grabbed Belinda's hand and scooted toward her, nose to nose.

Quinn had followed her and crouched beside her, blocking her from the direction of the sniper.

Blood seeped out from beneath Belinda's body, but her eyes were open and she'd zeroed in on Rikki's face. Her lips parted and she croaked.

Rikki squeezed her hand. "I need to know where David is."

Belinda gasped and mumbled, and Rikki put her ear close to her lips.

"Not telling you. Did you think I didn't know you when I saw you? David's beloved Rikki."

Rikki's mouth fell open.

"Wasn't sure. Then you saw picture. You knew. 'Course you knew David's body. You were his lover."

"That never happened. He turned on me. Set me up." Rikki rushed her words as the sirens from the ambulance sounded louder.

"Revenge, you broke it off. When I told him you were alive, it gave him…life." Belinda's lips twisted, whether in pain or bitterness, Rikki couldn't tell.

"So I wanted to take your life again. Away from him."

"Who did this to you? Where's David now?"

"Davey did it. You don't cross David."

An EMT's voice shouted above them. "Ma'am, ma'am. I need you to get out of the way now."

"Tell me. We'll take him down together." Rikki gripped Belinda's wrist. "Where is he?"

The EMT physically pulled Rikki away from Belinda, but not before she choked out one word. "Song."

Quinn took her arm, and his head swiveled back and forth like a weather vane in a hurricane. "You put yourself in extreme danger. Was it worth it?"

"Her last word to me? *Song.* Buddy Song knows where David is. I'd say that's worth it. The sniper was long gone anyway."

He cocked one eyebrow in her direction as he practically dragged her across the street. "Because you're an expert on snipers?"

"Well, he wasn't a very good one, was he? He didn't kill Belinda."

"Not yet."

"She seemed pretty lucid for someone on death's doorstep. She could very well recover from this."

"Maybe that sniper didn't want to kill her. Maybe he just wanted to interrupt her conversation with me or teach her a lesson about going rogue and murdering random CIA agents."

"Wasn't he ready to murder random CIA agents the other night at Belinda's house?"

"We don't know what his intentions were that night. He could've just wanted to trap and question, like I planned to do with Belinda." He took her hand and led her into a small public parking lot. "I'm in here."

She ducked into the car and slumped in the seat. "At least we can now start with Buddy Song."

"We knew about him anyway, and Belinda could've been lying." He cranked on the engine and squealed out of the parking lot. "What else was she telling you? That conversation lasted longer than one name."

"Oh, yeah." Rikki slumped farther in the seat. "She knew who I was."

"What?" Quinn stomped on the brakes at the stop sign, and her body strained against the shoulder strap and then thumped back.

"She made me." Rikki twisted her fingers in her lap. "She suspected who I was when we first got to her house, and when I showed interest in the picture, that confirmed it for her."

"Maybe she won't recover."

"Quinn." She jerked her head around.

"I'm supposed to be rooting for a woman who called out a gunman on us, tried to poison you and now knows your identity?" He lifted his shoulders. "I'm sorry. I don't have much sympathy for her. I don't want her blabbing to anyone in the CIA about you before we're ready, and we won't be ready until someone talks to Buddy Song or Chan decodes David's emails."

"It's too late." Rikki pressed her hands against her stomach. In the shock of Belinda's shooting and getting info about David out of her, Rikki hadn't dwelled on the fact that Belinda had known who she was from the get-go. Now the truth of it punched her in the gut.

"She already told someone, and it's the reason why she tried to kill me."

"Back up. Who'd she tell? Did that person order her to poison you?"

"She told David."

Quinn uttered an expletive. "And David ordered your death a second time? I can't wait to get my hands on him."

"I'm not sure it went down like that." Rikki dug her fingers in her hair. "Belinda told David I was alive, and apparently, he was a little too happy about it for Belinda's liking. She always thought David and I were lovers, and his reaction to her news seemed to confirm that for her."

Quinn's jaw tightened. "David lied to her, told her you came onto him. She told us as much."

"Probably." Rikki rolled her shoulders, but the stress just clawed its way up her neck. "His reaction to my being alive wasn't what she'd hoped for, so she decided to take me out—it sounds like to spite him."

He swung the car into a parking space at their motel and threw it into Park. "She thinks her own husband ordered this hit on her today because she tried to kill you? Does David really think you're going to forgive him for setting you up as a traitor?"

"I don't know what David thinks. It sounds like he's gone completely off the deep end, but it gave me a little leverage with her to give up some intel on David."

"Buddy Song's name is hardly intel. If David knows you're still alive, it won't be long before the CIA knows."

"He's not exactly going to call them from the dead, is he?"

"He'll use other methods to get the news out. You know he will." He stroked her arm from shoulder to wrist. "Do you want to take what we have now and go to the Agency? Do you want to turn yourself in?"

"Take what we have?" She snapped off her seat belt. "We have nothing. No proof. I don't even have that picture of David with the tattoo he never had before his supposed death."

Quinn lifted his hips from the seat of the car and dug into his voluminous pocket. He pulled out a cell phone and held it in front of her face. "I have this."

"Belinda's?" Her heart skipped in her chest and she pounced on the phone, snatching it from Quinn's hand.

"She was holding it when I approached her. When the bullet hit her, she dropped it and I scooped it up."

Rikki pressed the phone to her chest. "Quick thinking."

"Let's regroup and get your life back."

When they returned to the motel room, Rikki huddled in a chair by the window and tapped Belinda's phone to wake it up. "Ugh, it's password-protected."

"You know how to get around that, right? Isn't that CIA 101?"

"There are a couple of ways I can get in, although every time the manufacturers hear about another trick to bypass security codes, they change things up." Rikki tapped through several key sequences and let out a pent-up breath when Belinda's home screen popped up. "I'm in. This looks like her real phone and not the temp she used to call you."

"And which she probably used to contact her husband." Quinn circled his finger in the air. "She'll have her personal stuff on this one, though."

Rikki swept her finger through Belinda's photos. "Lots of pics of Savannah and her house. She must've done some remodeling lately."

"That's not gonna help."

"Wait." With a shaking finger, Rikki tapped an image of a shirtless man. "It's here. The picture of David with that tattoo that he never had before he died."

"All right!" Quinn pumped his fist in the air. "Now, who can verify that the tattoo is a new acquisition besides you?"

"Anyone who did PT with David. If they changed in the locker room with him or even if he wore a tank top during PT, his chest would've been on display, and I'm telling you he never had that giant phoenix tattoo."

"You're going to send that to Ariel." Quinn leveled a finger at the phone. "What's your answer if someone tries to claim he got it in Korea?"

"Not enough time—and look at it." She jabbed her finger at the serious face in the picture, the face she used to trust. "It's not a brand-new tattoo. We weren't in Korea long enough for something like that to heal up. Hell, we weren't in Korea long enough before we were captured for him to even get a tattoo like that. Don't those tattoo artists take several days to create a work of art like that?"

"It could take more than one sitting. It looks like we might have Dawson dead to rights on this." Quinn rubbed his chin and gazed over her right shoulder.

"What? I don't like that look."

His gaze snapped back to her face. "Dawson knows you're alive."

"Y-yes?" She squared Belinda's phone on the table and clasped her hands between her knees.

"He might try to get word to the CIA—anonymously, of course."

"Why would the Agency believe a man who faked his own death in North Korea and set up his partner to take the fall as a traitor?"

"What if he already beat us to the punch? What if the CIA already got a tip that Rikki Taylor is alive and well and skulking around Savannah, and is taking action?" Quinn paced to the window and back to the TV, his long stride eating up the space in a few steps.

Rikki's eyes wandered to the window of their dumpy motel and fixed on a road sign across the street. "You mean like right now?"

"We need to get out of this town and back to New

Orleans." Quinn stopped in midturn. "Does Dawson know much about me? Where I live?"

"I never told him anything. He knew we were...together in Dubai, and he probably knew your name and knew that you were a SEAL from asking around, but I doubt if he got any personal info on you, and I certainly didn't tell him anything like that."

"Navy's not going to give him any details about me, but then he's CIA. He can get those details his own way."

Rikki shook her head. "I don't think he would've done that, and he can't do it now."

"Let's head back tonight." He grabbed the remote from the bed. "You up for an all-night drive?"

"To get out of Savannah? Hell, yeah."

Quinn clicked on the TV. "We don't even know if Belinda made it or not."

"I'm sure she did. From the blood pooling, it looked like she got hit in the back. Although she was losing a lot of blood, she was conscious and the EMTs got right to work on her."

Quinn flipped through the channels until he settled on some local news. "We may have missed the story. It must've been the lead."

"The hospital won't tell us anything." Rikki pushed herself up from the chair and stood in front of the TV with her arms crossed. Even though Belinda Dawson had tried to poison her, Rikki couldn't help feeling sorry for her. She must really love David to keep his secrets, secrets that could get her charged with espionage, and then to believe the man you loved, the man you'd protected, was obsessed with someone else must be torture.

Rikki had watched her mother bounce from man to man, putting her faith in love time after time only to have her heart broken. No man was worth that kind of pain.

Rikki's gaze slid to Quinn, perched on the foot of the bed, hunched forward. He was different from any man her mom had followed around the world. Sincere. Loyal. Family-oriented.

And he didn't know he had one.

His head jerked to the side. "What?"

"Just thinking about Belinda." Rikki gathered her hair into a ponytail. "When do we get out of here?"

"As soon as you can throw your stuff together. We can eat on the road."

"Have you heard anything more from Chan about David's emails?"

"Not yet. Did you send that picture of Dawson to your phone?"

As she reached for Belinda's phone on the table, Quinn said, "Wait. Better yet. Send that picture to my phone, and I'll send it along to Ariel. My phone is untraceable and won't come up on anyone's radar. We don't want that photo leaking out. Dawson's not going to know we have it, and we don't want to clue him in."

Rikki cupped Belinda's phone in her palm. "David knows I'm alive, but does he realize that I know he's alive?"

"I'm assuming Belinda told him, right?" He grabbed his phone and aimed it at her. "Send it."

"She didn't really say one way or the other. I guess if she told him about my seeing the picture, he'd know that I figured it out." She tapped the phone to text the picture to Quinn's number. "Why?"

"Just wondering if Dawson would try to contact you."

Heat prickled across her skin, and she dropped the phone. It clattered on the table. "Why would he?"

Quinn lifted one shoulder. "To make some kind of overture."

"Overture?" Rikki's eye twitched and she rubbed it. "What kind of overture could he make with me now after setting me up as a traitor to the CIA and arranging to have me killed? How do you start that conversation?"

He joined her at the table and rubbed her back. "I hope you don't have to find out."

"Let's get out of here." She held up Belinda's phone. "I'm taking this with me. Who knows what else I can discover on here?"

Quinn dragged his bag from the closet floor. "Any texts?"

"Just a couple with some girl talk." Rikki pocketed Belinda's phone. "I wonder what all of Belinda's good, good friends would think about her if they knew she ran around poisoning drinks and covering for her traitor husband."

"They're going to find out soon enough once we get this investigation in official hands. That woman's going to get hers for trying to kill you."

Rikki pressed her lips together as she started packing. Having Quinn on her side gave her a warm glow in her belly.

Quinn had given her something else in her belly eighteen months ago, and she planned to tell him all about that little miracle when they got back to New Orleans.

AS THEY HEADED out of Savannah, Rikki dug Belinda's phone from her pocket. "I'm going to look through this while it's still working. Once Belinda realizes her phone is missing, she'll have it deactivated."

"We don't even know if she's dead or alive. The most

recent report I saw on my phone was that someone had been critically injured in that shooting, nothing about a fatality."

"I think if she'd died it would've made the news. Nothing about a suspect?"

"He's not going to be caught, and if she survives, Belinda's not going to implicate anyone."

Rikki rolled back the seat and wedged her bare feet against the glove compartment. "Do you mind?"

"You can put your feet anywhere." Quinn reached forward and caressed her ankle.

She curled her toes and almost purred. Instead, she thumbed through Belinda's pictures. "No more suspicious photos. Either that's the only one David sent her, or she deleted the rest."

"We lucked out with that one."

"Yep." She squinted at the text messages as she scrolled through each set. "No new messages, either. It's creepy that there's a text here to one of her friends about drinks the other night. Funny she doesn't mention the poison."

"Yeah, that's just what you want to tell your old friends. Meeting for drinks, and by the way, don't mind the dead chick at the table."

Rikki tapped Belinda's contacts and swept her finger down the list. One name flew by, and she gasped.

"What?"

"One of her contacts." Rikki dragged her finger back up the names and stopped on the most important one. "Frederick Von."

"You're kidding." Quinn flexed his fingers on the wheel of the car. "Dawson should've trained his wife better in the rules of espionage."

"Who would know the name of David's villain in an

unpublished work of fiction? Besides, I'm sure he believed Belinda would never come under suspicion, that *he'd* never come under suspicion."

"And yet here they are—under suspicion." Quinn cranked his head to the side. "What are you going to do about it?"

She held the phone between both of her hands as if in prayer. "You think I should call him?"

"I do."

"If I do, I'm going to play nice." She tapped her steepled fingers against her chin. "I'm going to pretend I don't know he set me up."

Quinn raised his eyebrows as he studied the road in front of him. "Do you think he's gonna believe that?"

"I'll make him believe it. Why would I think he set me up? I thought he'd been killed, I was captured by the North Koreans, and I don't know anything about the CIA trying to take me down as a traitor."

"Devil's advocate here." He tapped his chest. "If you don't know he set you up, why haven't you gone straight to the Agency? Why are you floundering around Louisiana and Georgia?"

She held up one finger. "I didn't say the CIA didn't think I was a traitor. I just don't know *why* they think I'm one."

"He's gonna be suspicious as to why you don't believe it's him. He faked his death, you were captured, there was no Vlad."

"I just *thought* he died and we were both played."

"Do you think he'll believe you?"

Rikki dipped her head to hide her warm cheeks behind a veil of hair. "I think I can make David Dawson believe anything if I put my mind to it."

The silence stretched between them, and Rikki peeked at Quinn's hard profile.

He cleared his throat. "Then do it."

She wiped the back of her hand across her forehead despite the air-conditioning blasting her face. With an unsteady finger, she tapped Frederick Von and then put the phone on Speaker, even though she really didn't want Quinn listening to this conversation.

The phone rang, and Rikki clutched the seat's armrest. It rang several more times before a pleasant recording told her the phone's owner didn't have voice mail set up.

Rikki snorted. "I'd like to hear that voice mail greeting."

"Try again later. We have no idea where he is or what time zone he's in." He hunched forward and rapped a knuckle against the windshield. "Let's stop for some food and knock out the rest of this trip."

Four hours later and halfway through the drive, Rikki poked through one of the bags from the fast-food restaurant they'd driven through for dinner. "Do you want the rest of these French fries?"

"Are you hungry again? We can stop. We're making good time."

"Not really." She stuffed one of the fries in her mouth and licked the salt from her fingers. "Just bored."

"Do you feel like driving?"

"Too tired."

"Take a nap."

Belinda's cell, which Rikki had tucked beneath her right thigh, buzzed to life. She grabbed the phone and felt the blood drain from her face. "It's him."

"Are you ready?" Quinn put on his signal to pull into a rest area.

Rikki licked her lips and nodded. "Hello?"

The man's voice, David's voice from the grave, started before the first word left Rikki's lips.

"Belinda, what the hell are you doing calling me on this phone? I don't care if you have me listed as Dr. Seuss. You don't use this phone, especially not now."

"David, it's Rikki."

He sucked in a breath across the miles. "Rikki? My God. It sounds like you. What was the name of the bartender our first night in Athens?"

"Gypsy Rose."

A noisy rush of air gushed over the line. "Wh-when Belinda told me you were alive, I couldn't believe it."

Rikki met Quinn's gaze and dipped her chin once. David would admit nothing, whether he thought she believed him or not. She could do this.

Squaring her shoulders, she pinned them against the seat back. "I felt the same way when I discovered you were alive."

"From the picture. You saw the picture. That's what Belinda said. You knew. You knew me so well, you could tell it was recent."

Quinn made a sharp movement in the driver's seat, and Rikki placed a hand on his thigh.

They'd have to both get through this. "It was the tattoo, David."

"Of course." He coughed. "What did Belinda tell you?"

"Tell me? She told me nothing, but I saw the picture."

"Who was the man with you when you came to the house?"

"A paid associate." She squeezed Quinn's knee. "He doesn't know anything about what I'm doing."

David paused for two beats. "What are you trying

to do, Rikki? Why aren't you with the Agency…or are you?"

"As far as I can tell, the Agency thinks I'm a traitor. That debacle in North Korea pretty much torpedoed both of our careers." She paused herself. "Why aren't you with the Agency? Where are you?"

"Deep undercover. The Agency thinks I'm dead, and I want to keep it that way. But what happened to you? I'd heard from my guy in South Korea that you'd been killed."

David's voice actually broke, and Rikki had to grip the phone harder to keep from throwing it out the window.

"The North Koreans captured me."

"Oh my God. We both know what that means. How'd you escape?"

"I had some help and some good luck. Seems like we both did." For just a moment, the knots in Rikki's stomach had loosened and it felt like old times talking with David about an assignment.

She only had to glance at Quinn's tight jaw to remember it wasn't.

"What have you been doing, David? Where are you? What happened to your lead on Vlad? Was it all counterintelligence?"

"That's the thing, Rikki. I'm hot on Vlad's trail right now. This will be my ticket back to the Agency—mine and yours."

Quinn poked her in the ribs, but he didn't have to prod her to encourage David in this line of thinking.

"Your intel panned out?"

"Once I escaped from the North Koreans, I buckled down and burrowed in. I'm getting ready to bring down Vlad and I couldn't be happier that you're alive to help me do it." He cleared his throat. "Just like old times, Rikki, right? You want to do this with me, right?"

Quinn jabbed her again, and she didn't know if he approved or not, but Rikki refused to look at him—just in case he wanted to dissuade her.

"O-of course, David. I'm in."

"You sound hesitant. You believe me, don't you, Rikki? You believe I never meant our operation to go down like that—you captured, us split up."

"I… Yes."

"Of course things are a little different now, but we can work around all that."

"Different? You mean because we're rogue agents instead of official ones with support from the CIA?"

"There's that…and the other matter. Your personal issue."

Quinn jerked in the seat beside her, and Rikki's heart began to hammer painfully in her chest.

"My personal issue?"

"You know—the fact that you have a daughter now. You can't try to tell me that little redheaded baby in Jamaica with your mother isn't yours."

Chapter Fifteen

The roaring in Quinn's ears sounded like a Mack truck coming up behind them in the rest stop. His gaze flew to Rikki's face, a white oval in the darkness of the car.

Quinn waited for the eye roll. The laugh. The denial.

She stammered. "Wh-what are you talking about? You're in Jamaica?"

The bastard's voice lowered, silky smooth. "I'm not in this alone, Rikki. As soon as Belinda told me the good news that you were alive and well and...snooping around Savannah with a big bodyguard type, I sent one of my associates out to Jamaica. You see how well we know each other? I remembered your mother was out there. I thought maybe we could get some information about you out of her, and my associate discovered something even better."

The only response Rikki could muster was a small gurgle, and Quinn clenched his jaw so hard he thought his teeth would break.

No denial. It had to be true. A child? A baby? Did it happen in Korea? Good God, it couldn't be David's.

David's voice continued, and Quinn just wanted to punch the phone.

"Don't try to deny she's yours, Rikki. I've only ever seen that hair color on one other person." Dawson's voice had an almost dreamy quality, and Quinn clenched his fists. "That, and we asked around. The locals are talkative, especially when cash is involved."

Rikki's lips emitted small bursts of air, as if she couldn't take in enough air to breathe. "Better?"

"What?"

"You said better. Why is discovering my…daughter better?"

Quinn wanted to shake Rikki, but she hadn't even looked at him since Dawson dropped the bombshell. Had she been raped in the labor camp? Quinn's blood boiled in his veins.

David sucked in a breath. "Having a child is a happy occasion, and she's not a small infant. Although I don't know much about babies, I do know yours must've been conceived before we left for Korea."

A shaft of pain pierced the back of Quinn's head. He wanted to grab the phone and end the call. He wanted Rikki to look at him. He wanted her to explain.

"Of course it's happy." Rikki leaned her head against the window. "I just don't understand your interest in my child."

"Everything about you interests me, Rikki. Let's just say, I need your help on this Vlad assignment. I've always needed you, Rikki."

"I'll help you. Where are you?"

"We'll talk again later…partner."

"D-don't you want to hear about Belinda? How I happen to have her phone?"

"I don't really care. Just keep it."

Quinn had been building to the boiling point during that call and wanted to pounce on Rikki with a million questions and accusations. But when Dawson ended the call, he sat there, staring out the window at the Alabama trees guarding the rest area, feeling like he'd been steamrollered.

Rikki didn't move, but mewling noises started coming from the other side of the car where she was huddled against the window.

Quinn opened his mouth, but he couldn't form any words, would probably sound like Rikki right now.

He swallowed and tried again. "What's going on? Whose baby?"

Rikki sniffled, and Belinda's phone slid from her hand and dropped to the floor of the car. "She's yours, Quinn. Ours."

Quinn covered his face with his hands. He had a baby with Rikki. How did she manage to keep it from him all this time? She lied for a living.

Cool fingers encircled his wrist. "I'm sorry. I was going to tell you. I'd planned to tell you all along, but—" she waved one arm in the small confines of the car "—this all got in the way."

Rikki's voice had a tone he'd never heard from her before—pleading, unsure, frightened—and it shocked him out of his trance.

He dropped his hands from his face and rounded on her, grabbing her shoulder. "You were pregnant before you were in Korea."

"Y-yes. Of course. Bella is yours."

"Oh God, Rikki." He cupped the side of her face, his thumb caressing her wet cheek. "You were pregnant while you were in that labor camp."

She dropped her lashes, sticky with her tears. "I was."

"You must've been terrified, not only for yourself but for the baby."

"I just assumed I was going to lose her, and even after I escaped, I was concerned she might suffer."

A fist squeezed Quinn's heart and his breath caught in his throat. "Did she? Is she…?"

Rikki met his eyes for the first time, and a soft smile hovered on her lips. "Oh, Quinn. She's perfect in every way. You understand, don't you? You do understand why I had to keep her a secret, even from you?"

"I'm sure it didn't help my case for fatherhood when you found out I was the one behind that sniper rifle."

Her eyes widened, and fresh tears began a path down her face. "But she's not a secret anymore. David knows. He has someone in Jamaica."

"He's not going to do anything." He threaded his fingers through Rikki's hair and pulled her in for a quick kiss. "The guy still loves you."

She choked. "He set me up to be killed or captured, ruined my career, and just threatened my daughter. That's love?"

"The twisted, obsessive, delusional kind." He took both her hands in his. "The kind that you can use. You're not above using David Dawson, are you?"

"Who, me?" She lifted her shoulder and wiped her nose on her sleeve. "Hell no."

Quinn chuckled. "That's my Rikki Taylor. Now you've got another four hours on the road to tell me all about our daughter, Bella, but first you need to call your mother in Jamaica and give her a heads-up. Do she and your stepfather have people they can trust out there? People to look after them?"

"Oh, yeah. Chaz, my stepfather, has been down there for years. The locals have adopted him, adopted Bella."

"Good. She needs everyone looking out for her." He reached into his front pocket and pulled out his phone. "Use this one. Will your mom be alarmed?"

"My mom is accustomed to my work, and Chaz

will make sure she stays calm. She takes all her cues from him."

"That's a good thing right now."

As Quinn got back on the road, he half listened as Rikki explained to her mother the need to keep Bella safe.

She ended the call and heaved a sigh. "Mom had already noticed a couple of tourists eyeing Bella at the hotel."

"Maybe you got the spy gene from your mom. Did you scare her?"

"A little, but she got Chaz right on the phone and he assured me they'd take care of Bella. I trust him... and the locals."

Quinn rolled his shoulders. "When did you find out you were pregnant?"

Rikki's posture stiffened. "I swear, Quinn. I had no idea until I was in South Korea. I thought the food didn't agree with me."

"You don't have to defend your decisions, Rikki."

"Why not? I figured the longer I waited to tell you, the more furious you'd be with me for keeping it from you, and now...you don't seem furious at all."

"What right do I have to be mad? When were you supposed to tell me? The moment you discovered it was me on the other end of that sniper rifle waiting and willing to take you down?"

"You didn't."

"You've been through hell and back, Rikki, keeping our daughter safe through it all. I owe you nothing but gratitude. But you know what this means, right?"

She folded her hands and clasped them between her knees. "What?"

"You're never leaving me high and dry again."

"I don't want to, Quinn, ever."

He might be a fool, but he believed her.

"Now tell me all about our daughter."

BY THE TIME they reached New Orleans, Quinn had already carved out a place in his heart for his little Bella, a girl with her mother's ginger curls and her father's stubbornness, although he secretly thought that trait came from Mom, too.

As Quinn inserted his key in the lock of his front door, Rikki put her hand over his. "Do you think your place could've been compromised?"

"Dawson wouldn't be able to get any information on me."

Rikki chewed on her bottom lip. "I don't know. He found out your name in Dubai and knew you were a navy SEAL."

"Navy's not going to give him anything." He held up his hand. "And before you tell me Dawson's some kind of CIA superagent, the CIA isn't going to give him anything, either."

He studied Rikki's face—eyebrows drawn over her nose, lips twisted into a frown—and pulled out his weapon. "Stay back."

He pushed open his front door and swept his gun from side to side as he scanned the living room and kitchen. "Everything looks in order."

Following him over the threshold, Rikki took out her own weapon and crouched behind him as he moved toward the back of the apartment. They searched through both of the rooms and found nothing out of place.

Quinn double-locked his front door. "Feel better?"

Rikki sagged against the doorjamb of the bedroom. "Not really. David knows about you. He must know

Bella is yours, and maybe he even figured out you paid a visit to Belinda with me."

"Then it's your job—" he touched Rikki's nose with the tip of his finger "—to convince him he's the only man in your life."

"He's not a fool, Quinn."

"When a man has feelings about a woman like Dawson has about you, he'll be only too eager to believe what you're puttin' down."

She quirked an eyebrow at him. "Speaking from experience?"

"One of many differences between me and Dawson." Quinn held up a finger. "I'm in love with you, not obsessed with you. That allows me to look at you realistically. That's why I let you go when you hightailed it out of Dubai and left me holding the sheets. For whatever reason, you couldn't handle the feelings between us. It cut me to the core, but you had to do what worked for you. If you could figure it out and come back to me, I would be there with open arms."

"I figured it out, sailor." She wrapped her arms around his waist and rested her head against his chest.

He stroked her hair. "Dawson doesn't want to let you go. He pissed off his own wife, the woman keeping his secrets, with his reaction to the news that you weren't dead. Then he probably tried to have her killed for attempting to poison you."

"We don't know if that was David behind the shooting. He answered that phone call from me as if he thought it was Belinda."

"Maybe the order was to shoot his wife, but not to kill her. When he saw the call from her cell, of course he'd act like he didn't know anything about the attempt on her life."

"That's so cold."

"He doesn't want Belinda. He wants you, Rikki, and you're going to give him what he wants." He squeezed the back of her neck. "Are you okay with that? We can do it a different way—bring in Dawson and find out his connection with Vlad."

"If you think I'm going to let this opportunity pass me by, there are a few more things I need to teach you about myself before you start professing your love for me again."

"I'm sure there are a lot of things you can still teach me about yourself, but none of that's going to change how I feel." He wrapped her in a bear hug and rested his chin on top of her head.

She spoke into his chest. "And I'm ready to give David what he wants."

Quinn tightened his hold on her. "But first you're gonna give me what I want."

"Always, Quinn McBride."

He swept her up in his arms to carry her to his bedroom, but his lust couldn't blot out the twinge of uneasiness in his heart.

She still hadn't told him she loved him. He wanted more than her body. He wanted more than Bella to bind them together.

He wanted her love, unconditional and unreserved.

THE FOLLOWING MORNING, they worked on a plan over breakfast.

Quinn stabbed a clump of scrambled eggs and shook it at Rikki. "Dawson wants to bring you into his scheme. He always wanted that. Whether he believes you're game because he has someone watching Bella or because you've realized you can't live without him, doesn't matter. But he'll be more open with you if he believes the latter."

"I think I can pull it off, but if he knows I'm with you, that's going to put a serious crimp in my game. He was so jealous of you."

Quinn squirted some ketchup on his plate. "You've got an ace in the hole."

"I do?"

"I was the sniper who tried to take you out. Everyone believes I did the job. Dawson has to know that." He swept a forkful of eggs through the ketchup and held it over his plate as a red drop fell into the pile of eggs. "How could a woman ever forgive that, even if the sniper is the father of her baby?"

Hunching forward, Rikki broke a piece of toast in two. "That's believable. I can make a story out of that."

"Make that case to Dawson. And you need to tell Ariel what's going down."

"I will. Maybe she can send reinforcements for whatever David has planned."

"I forgot to mention." Quinn wiped his hands on a napkin and pulled his phone toward him with one finger. "Chan is making progress on Dawson's emails to Frederick Von, thinks he found a pattern, one he can enter into his computer program."

"The more evidence I can present to Ariel, the better. I'll let her take it to the CIA. I'm not going to the Agency directly."

"Good idea." Quinn stacked his plate on top of Rikki's. "Does Belinda's cell phone still work?"

"It does. She doesn't realize yet that it's missing, she's too injured to care or…she's dead."

Quinn tapped his phone. "Latest story I could find on the incident still lists one critically injured, no fatalities. Unless the CIA is hiding her condition from the press, it looks like she survived."

"Then David wanted her to survive."

"If it was David who ordered the hit." Quinn took their dishes to the sink. "I hope he plans to contact you soon, before Belinda turns that phone off."

"I did write down the number for Von, so I can always contact him if he doesn't get back to me."

"Yeah, but we want him reaching out to you first. He needs to make the first move." Quinn ran some water over the dishes and it hit him all over again that he was a father. He grinned. "When do I get to see some pictures of my little girl?"

"As soon as we get past this and we know Bella is safe, I'll have Mom text me some pictures to my temp phone."

"I can't wait." Quinn crossed the room to yank open the drapes. "I'm picturing those red curls and big blue eyes just like her—"

Rikki screamed, "Get down!"

Instinct had him dropping his head and jerking to the side. He hit the floor—but not before he felt the searing pain of the bullet slam into his body. And all this time he'd thought he was bulletproof.

Chapter Sixteen

Her heart thundering in her chest, Rikki crawled toward Quinn bleeding on the floor. "Please, God. Please, God."

When she reached him, he groaned and spit out an expletive.

"Quinn, you're hit." She cupped his head with both hands, her fingers searching every inch of his scalp.

"It's not my head, damn it. It's my shoulder."

Quinn lay on his side, his knees to his chest, blood pooling beneath him.

"Thank God."

"Really? Because it hurts like hell."

A laugh bubbled to her lips, and she kissed the side of his intact head. "I thought… I thought, when I saw the blood… I thought…"

He rolled to his back with a low moan. "You need to come back to planet earth and tell me what it looks like."

She ripped off what was left of his shredded, blood-soaked sleeve and peered at the damaged flesh. "Hang on. This is going to hurt."

She probed the wound and tucked her hand beneath his shoulder. "Went clean through, Quinn. Stay right here. I'll get some towels to stop the bleeding."

He grabbed her ankle as she started to crawl away. "No 911. We'll handle this."

Cranking her head over her shoulder, she said, "No 911, but you're going to have to see a doctor at some point. You need that properly cleaned, maybe some stitches, and you'll need some antibiotics for infection."

"I have some old antibiotics in the bathroom and ibuprofen. I need something to dull this pain."

Rikki didn't stand upright until she got to his hallway, away from that window. David. It had to have been David. They had both underestimated David's obsession with her. While still in good standing with the CIA, David had probably gotten a complete dossier on Quinn McBride once he learned about her affair with him.

She gathered several towels, wet down a few of them, and then snatched bottles of ibuprofen and expired antibiotics from a drawer in the bathroom.

She crawled back into the living room, pushing her medical supplies ahead of her. A few feet away from Quinn, she came to a dead halt and gagged.

He peeled open one eye where it gleamed from his bloody face. "Does it look bad?"

"What did you do? What happened? Why is that blood all over your face?"

"Because I'm a dead man. I just got shot in the head and you're going to take a picture of me for proof."

"For David."

"That's right. That bullet was meant for me, to get me out of the picture and out of your life."

"Why am I not crazy with grief?"

He scooped a little more blood from his shoulder wound and dragged it through his hair. "Because I'm the sniper the navy and the CIA sent to take you out. You always knew that. You were using me to get information and to help protect you against the CIA. Now you have Dawson."

Rikki left the towels and bottles on the floor and scooted toward the kitchen to retrieve her phone. She yanked on the charger to bring down her phone and made her way back to Quinn.

He positioned himself to resemble a man who'd been shot in the head, and as a navy SEAL sniper with plenty of kills under his belt, he knew exactly what that would look like.

"Take the pictures."

Rikki swallowed, almost believing the proof before her eyes and imagining how destroyed she would've been if the sniper had hit his mark.

She loved this man. He hadn't even been angry that she'd kept Bella's existence from him. His only concern had been how she'd begun her pregnancy in a North Korean labor camp and its effects on their baby.

She could give herself completely to Quinn and he'd never use or abuse her devotion. He'd only return it tenfold.

She clicked several pictures of him and his bloody head, and then grabbed the towels.

Quinn rolled to his stomach. "Not yet. Get back on that phone and call Dawson. He'll expect it, either way. His guy is probably still watching the apartment building. He's gonna wonder where the lights and sirens are."

"David would know I'm not in any position to talk to the police and then the navy."

"Whatever. You need to make contact now. What reason would you have to keep silent, other than a desire to hide from him and hide the fact that his mission failed?"

"I hate him."

"Use that passion." He wiped his hand across his bloody mouth. "And hand me a towel so I can stop gushing blood on the floor."

She threw him a wet towel and a dry towel. "Bunch that dry towel under your shoulder and get on your back to apply pressure."

Taking a deep breath, she grabbed her phone and tapped the number she'd saved for David.

He must've been waiting, because he picked up on the first ring. "Yes?"

"It's Rikki."

"I figured as much. You okay?"

"Oh, I'm just fine, but Quinn McBride is dead, shot in the head right through his window. Are you crazy?" Her fingers got busy texting him Quinn's death shots.

"Do you care that much about him? The father of your baby? I could tell you a thing or two about your heroic Quinn McBride."

"Nothing I don't already know, like he was the navy SEAL sniper sent to eliminate me, the traitor."

David choked. "You knew that already?"

"Why do you think I came to see him right out of Jamaica? I wanted to take care of business. You taught me that, David."

Rikki glanced at Quinn, who'd paused from stanching his blood flow to stick his finger in his mouth. She scowled at him.

"But you didn't take care of business. You stayed with him, took him with you to visit Belinda."

"I needed him as a protector. He's all muscle and brawn, but not too much brain."

Quinn kicked her foot, and she stuck out her tongue at him.

"I knew the two of you weren't meant for each other,

Rikki. I'm sorry I had him taken out right in front of you, but he has to be out of the picture for us to move forward."

"Oh, he's out of the picture." She tapped her phone several times and sent the last of Quinn's death pictures to David. "Am I safe now?"

"The sniper? He's long gone." David clicked his tongue. "Got the pictures. Once he saw McBride fall, he disassembled and took off—just in case you went ballistic and called in the authorities."

Rikki snorted. "No chance of that. Do you think I want to talk to a bunch of cops? Once they found out Quinn's identity, they'd call in the navy. No, thanks. His death needs to remain a secret for as long as possible."

"Any chance of discovery there?"

"Nobody heard the shot. There's a bullet hole in the window, but the velocity of the bullet was such that the window didn't shatter. McBride's deploying in another few weeks, and I'm assuming that's when his body will be discovered. He has no family to speak of. Nobody's going to miss him."

Quinn kicked her again.

"Good. There's someone very important I want you to meet. Plenty of people have already switched to his side. He pays well and he's loyal—unlike the Agency."

"Y-you don't mean who I think you mean, do you? I thought we were going out to Korea to provide information that would lead to his capture. Can't we still do that?"

"There's no need for it, Rikki. What he does is no different from what we were doing, but he's supporting different countries than we are. That's all. He's not interested in taking down the US, but he wants us to think twice before sticking our noses in other countries' business—countries he wants to control."

"I'm not saying I'm in, David, but I also won't betray you. I'm done with the Agency. Y-you were always my first loyalty anyway."

"We could do this together, Rikki—partners. I could provide your daughter riches beyond belief, and with those riches, safety and security."

Rikki pressed a hand to her chest. Hearing David talk about her daughter struck fear in her heart. His threats against Bella always simmered beneath the surface. "When is this meeting? Where are you, David?"

"I'm where it all began for him, Rikki. I'm in Berlin."

Her gaze flew to Quinn's face, and he lifted his good shoulder.

"You want me in Berlin?"

"You must have an ID that you're using or you never would've made it to the US from Jamaica undetected. Besides, nobody knows you're alive except me and Belinda. We don't have to worry about McBride anymore."

"What about Belinda? Did you have her…shot?"

"I did. I had no intention of killing her, or she'd be dead." David made a strange hissing sound before speaking again. "I found out she tried to kill you, Rikki. She knew I was always in love with you. I couldn't allow that to stand. I wanted to let her know I could get to her anytime, anywhere. And now that you and I are going to be together, we don't have to give her another thought."

Rikki rubbed the sick feeling in her stomach. "Who is he? Who is Vlad?"

"You'll see."

David spent the rest of the phone call giving her instructions for getting to Berlin, but wouldn't give her the meeting place with Vlad.

After his precise orders, David's voice softened. "I know you don't love me...yet. I know you're not on board with joining forces with the other side...yet. But I think you're halfway there on both, aren't you?"

"I think I've always been half in love with you, David." She glanced at Quinn, but he avoided her gaze in favor of tending to his wound. "The other... I don't know."

"I knew it, but I hope you understand, Rikki."

"Understand what?"

"If you don't join forces with our friend and do a really, really good job of pretending you love me, we'll take your daughter."

Chapter Seventeen

A white-hot fury coursed through Quinn's veins. His head felt light. Two seconds later, Rikki's cool hand fluttered about his face.

"You passed out." She folded a clean towel and applied pressure against his gunshot wound. "Enough of this nonsense. You need a doctor."

Quinn blinked and squeezed his eyes. "I need to find out where David is taking you to meet Vlad. This is our chance, maybe our one and only chance."

"You heard David. He's not going to tell me in advance. He's meeting me at the airport and taking me directly to the meeting. If he gets a hint that anyone has come with me or is following us, it's over, and it could be over for Bella. I'm not going to risk that."

"I'm not either." He winced as Rikki got aggressive with the pressure. "Following you is not good enough. We need to know the meeting place in advance so that we can set up."

Once she secured the towel against his arm and finished cleaning up his blood, Rikki scrambled to her feet and closed the drapes over the glass with the bullet hole.

"Let's get you up." She took his arm and helped him up.

He collapsed on the sofa, clutching the pill bottles in his hand. "Can you get me some water to down these?"

She took away the bloody towels and stuffed them into plastic garbage bags. She banged through his cupboards and returned with a bottle of water and a bottle of whiskey.

"Now that's a good idea, even at ten in the morning."

She shook the water bottle. "This first and then a shot of whiskey just so you won't pass out on me again."

"Yes, ma'am."

She twisted off the water bottle cap and handed the bottle to him.

He downed a couple of antibiotics and three ibuprofens. "You need to call Ariel now."

Rikki poured him a shot in a juice glass and thrust it at him. "Drink this first."

"You don't have to twist my arm." He threw back the whiskey, and the burning down his throat made his eyes water but cleared his senses. "Ariel."

Rikki got through to the head of the Vlad task force almost immediately, and Ariel's smooth voice almost purred over the line. "What do you have for me, Rikki?"

"Quinn McBride is listening in."

"I would expect that. Did David reach out to you?"

"You could say that. David hired someone to take out Quinn."

"Since Quinn's listening in on this call, I'm guessing the hit wasn't successful."

"Only because Rikki saw the laser and saved my life." Quinn laced his fingers through Rikki's. "Did I ever thank you for that?"

"You were in shock. I don't hold it against you."

Ariel sighed. "If you two are finished with your cute banter, what's the upshot?"

Rikki explained to Ariel how they faked Quinn's death and told her about David's proposal.

The pause from Ariel dragged on so long, Quinn exchanged a glance with Rikki. He thought Ariel would be all over this.

Finally she spoke, her voice strained and thin. "You're meeting with Vlad?"

"I am. I have to go through with it."

"And we need to be there to make sure it's the last meeting he ever has."

"Agreed." Quinn squeezed Rikki's hand before releasing her. "David Dawson is never going to fall for any surveillance. We have to know in advance and we have to be ready."

"It's yours, Quinn, yours and your teammates', all of them. I'm calling them all into Berlin right now, today."

Patting his shoulder, Quinn winced. "I'm not sure how much use I'm going to be with a sniper rifle right now. That shooter missed my head, but a bullet went clean through my shoulder."

"We have five other sniper rifles to back you up."

"Wait, wait." Rikki waved her hands in the air. "This all sounds wonderful, but we can't have six navy SEAL snipers roaming around Berlin looking for a meeting place."

Quinn rubbed his knuckles down Rikki's thigh. "I've been thinking about this. We have Dawson's phone number, Ariel."

"That's a start."

Rikki threw up another roadblock. "If you think you're going to put a trace on David's phone, he'll be way ahead of you. He's not going to take it with him."

Ariel said, "No, but he'll need to communicate with Vlad, and we can track those communications."

No wonder Ariel was leading this task force. Quinn snapped his fingers. "Exactly."

"Again." Rikki pushed the hair from her face and scooted to the edge of the sofa as if ready to do battle. "David and Vlad are not going to communicate in plain English or any other plain language."

"They'll use code." Quinn tapped her knee. "Like the code in those emails."

Ariel spoke up. "We're working on those."

"Ariel, I have a guy working them as well, and he's getting close."

"Berlin, huh?" Ariel's voice had a dreamy, far-away quality and Quinn raised his eyebrows at Rikki, who shrugged.

"I know Berlin is a big city, but this meeting won't be in a public place. Vlad would be too worried about plants among the crowd."

"The forest." Ariel's voice rose with excitement. "The Grunewald forest is in Berlin."

Rikki scrunched up her nose. "I suppose that would be a good place for him. They would notice any people wandering around, wouldn't they? I know there are some schlosses there that attract tourists, but it's a big forest. Why did that come to mind, Ariel?"

She coughed. "Seems like it would work for him, but we need to do our research. When do you leave, Rikki?"

"I have a flight out tomorrow, and the meeting is the following day."

"That's not much time, but I can get Quinn's sniper team into Berlin tonight. I think Alexei Ivanov is still in LA. Miguel Estrada is in San Diego at Coronado. Josh Elliott is already back in Europe, as is Slade Gallagher, and Austin Foley is in the Middle East. I'll get them moving today, military transport."

"Whew." Quinn raised his eyes to the ceiling. "You're way ahead of me."

Ariel cut him off. "The number. Rikki, give me Dawson's number. We have to start intercepting now and hope we're not already too late."

When they finished their plans with Ariel and ended the call, Quinn drummed his fingers on the coffee table. "She's a dynamo for sure. Why is she so invested in bringing down Vlad, and what made her think of the Grunewald forest?"

"It's her job." Rikki bounded up from the sofa. "I'm going to check in with Mom, and then I'm going to pack. You'd better start thinking about a disguise to get out of this apartment house in case it's being watched."

"Don't worry about me. I have a way out of here, and nobody ever has to know I left." He reached for his phone. "I need to get on Chan and tell him to expedite the decoding."

After sending a message to Chan, Quinn got on his own laptop and brought up Dawson's email exchanges with Vlad—he had to have been communicating with Vlad and Dawson had childishly given Vlad his own villain's name from his book. Hubris was one quality that usually brought people down, and Dawson was no different. He couldn't really believe that Rikki would fall in love with him, and yet here he was, making plans.

A sudden, piercing pain gripped Quinn's shoulder, and he grabbed it. He hoped he wasn't suffering from the same delusions as David Dawson.

Rikki charged in from the back rooms. "Bella's doing fine. Mom says there's a twenty-four-hour watch on their place by some tough dudes from Montego Bay. Nobody's going to get to her." She held up her phone. "And I just got off the phone with Ariel again. She's sending a doc around for a house call. I have his number. Maybe you can sneak him in."

"Better yet. We're sneaking out of here, or at least I am. You go out the regular way in case someone's watching my place."

"Where are we going?"

"I have a buddy who manages a hotel just off Rue Royale. I did him a...favor once and he lets me have a suite at the hotel whenever I want."

"The Fourth of July weekend is coming up. Is he going to have anything available?"

"He usually has a high-end suite up for grabs that they use for upgrades. I'm calling in my chips."

Two HOURS LATER, Quinn had sneaked out of his apartment through the basement and into a penthouse suite overlooking the French Quarter, and Rikki had followed him out the front door of his apartment and assured him nobody had followed her.

She stood next to him on the balcony, resting her head against his good shoulder. "This is going to work, Quinn."

"I have a backup plan in case we can't get your location in advance."

She folded her arms on the railing of the balcony and bent forward, surveying the street. "Shoot—or maybe I shouldn't be telling a sniper to shoot."

His lips twisted as he pointed to his bum shoulder. "I don't know when I'll be able to hoist my rifle again."

"There will be five other ones there to do the job, but what's the backup?"

"You're CIA, or you were. You must know about the internal GPS."

She dipped her head. "You mean the one that's swallowed?"

"That's the one. It's undetectable if they scan and search you, but we'll have your location."

"I can do that. I will do that, but it might be too late once I'm there. Vlad probably has lookouts. Hell, he's a sniper himself, isn't he?"

"That's the problem, but it's better than nothing. Even if we miss Vlad, we might be able to go in and get Dawson."

"Don't miss Vlad." She dug her fingernails into his arm. "Whatever you do, whatever happens to me, don't let Vlad get away."

He cradled her jaw in his palm. "Do you think nailing Vlad is more important to me than you are? I'm not risking your life to get Vlad—and I'm not going to let anyone else do it, either."

She turned her head to kiss his hand. "You know we'll never be safe as long as he's alive. He has a personal vendetta against you guys. That's probably how David knew where you lived in New Orleans. Vlad may be distracted now because you've disrupted his plans so many times, but he'll come back at you and the others again and again."

"Let him." Quinn spread out his arms and faced the Mississippi, feeling invincible—until an ache claimed his shoulder.

"It's not just you, tough guy." She traced the outline of his bandage. "You have Bella now. You told me Miguel has a little boy, and Josh's girlfriend has a son. Austin Foley's girlfriend is not going to live on his parents' ranch forever, and Slade's new love puts herself in danger all over the world. And if you think that crazy, intense Russian, Alexei Ivanov is ever going to give up on Vlad, you're as crazy as he is. It has to end now—in Berlin, where according to David it all started for Vlad."

"Point taken. I shouldn't have updated you on all my teammates." Quinn scratched his jaw. "Dawson did say that, didn't he?"

"What?"

"That it all began in Berlin for Vlad."

"Y-yes." She dropped her lashes and shifted away from him.

"I'd heard that when Ariel was with the CIA, she spent time in Berlin."

"I think so." Rikki pointed across the rooftops to the river. "Are those barges always there?"

"Not usually. They're getting ready for the fireworks." He cocked his head at her, and she pushed herself off the balcony and spun around to the room.

"The doctor should be here soon."

Quinn wiped a bead of sweat from his forehead and followed her back into the air-conditioned room.

Ten minutes later the doc showed up, and he must've come from Ariel's special list, but Rikki still made herself scarce.

Dr. Smith, as he called himself, peeled back the homemade bandage from Quinn's shoulder and slipped his glasses to the edge of his nose. "Clean gunshot wound right there. You're lucky."

With very little further conversation, the doctor thoroughly cleaned the wound, replaced the bandage with something more secure, and gave Quinn a new bottle of antibiotics and some painkillers.

Dr. Smith shook the bottle of painkillers. "These will make you sleepy, so you might want to stick with the ibuprofen."

Quinn picked up a sling and dangled it from his fingertips. "And this?"

"You'll want to hold your arm still and pressed

against your body. That will help, but your shoulder is going to be stiff as hell if it isn't already."

Quinn rolled his shoulder back in a test and winced. "It's getting there."

"That's all I got for you." The doc snapped his black medical bag closed. "Take the antibiotics as prescribed. In the unlikely event the wound starts to fester, you'll need additional treatment. If you're still here, that'll probably be me, but I have a feeling—" Dr. Smith shot a glance at Rikki's bag in the corner "—you won't be here much longer."

Quinn got up and extended his hand. "I hope you mean I won't be in New Orleans much longer and not on this Earth."

The doctor chuckled. "With you guys, it's always a crapshoot."

When Dr. Smith left, Rikki sauntered in from the back bedroom. "Everything okay? You gonna live?"

"According to the cheerful doctor Ariel sent, that's debatable."

"What?" Rikki flew to his side and grabbed his hand.

"I'm kidding. He was referring to something other than the bullet hole in my shoulder. That's going to be just fine." He kissed the inside of her wrist. "How about you? Are you just fine with all this?"

"I've been fine with all this for almost ten years. It's my job, Quinn. I can handle David Dawson *and* Vlad."

"The stakes have never been higher, Rikki. You never had this much to lose—Bella."

"You." She brushed her knuckles across his cheek. "We're going to do this, Quinn. And then I'll introduce you to your daughter."

He squeezed the top of his shoulder. "I'm not sure

I can do anything with this shoulder. How am I going to fire my rifle?"

"Your whole team will be there. It doesn't have to be you who takes out Vlad."

"After what we've been through with him, it would be a gold star for any of us. It might not just be Vlad. We might have to take down Dawson, too, although Ariel might prefer we bring him in for interrogation. Are you okay with that?"

"David is already dead to me. He turned, and he didn't even do it for ideology. He did it for money."

"And because he could—pride." Quinn toyed with the edge of his bandage. "You said you read his book, right?"

"Yeah, the whole thing." She rolled her eyes. "It was painful, and that was when I still liked the guy."

"Do you have it somewhere so I can read it?"

"You're not going to pick up any tips from it."

"Maybe not about writing, but there could be lots of tips about Dawson in there."

"I can get you to it." She stepped away from him and sat at the table with his laptop in front of her. "He put it up on a document-sharing platform for me to read. It's over a year old. I read it before we went to Dubai, so if he's made any changes they won't be in this draft."

"That's okay. Bring it up for me. I'll need something to read on my flight to Berlin. My military transport is not going to be as comfortable as your first class on a commercial airline."

Rikki spent several minutes at his laptop navigating to the shared document site. She scribbled something on a slip of hotel stationery and propped it up on his laptop's keyboard. "Here's my user name and password for this site."

Quinn stretched his arms over his head. "I'd better get packing. I leave tonight."

Rikki rose from the desk and returned to his side. She skimmed her hand down the front of his body and curled her fingers into the waistband of his shorts. "You didn't take any of those painkillers, did you?"

"No." When she touched him like that, he felt no pain at all.

"Because if you're leaving tonight, that means I have to spend the night in this giant suite in that giant bed all by myself."

His breathing grew shallow, and prickles of desire raced across his skin. "That would be a damned waste."

Sliding his hands down her back, he slanted his mouth across hers and kissed her hard and possessively. If she had to pretend to love Dawson, he didn't want her to forget what true love felt like.

She took his hand and led him into the suite's master bedroom.

Sometime later, with their legs and arms entwined around each other, when he didn't know where he ended and Rikki began, she kissed the edge of his jaw.

"I want you to know, Quinn McBride, before we go into this battle and risk everything, I love you. I loved you in Dubai. I loved you when I found out you'd had orders to kill me. I loved you when I found you again in New Orleans. And I love you now. I'm not afraid of love anymore, not your love."

He smoothed her hair back from her face. "That's all I ever wanted to hear from you."

Later that night, Dawson's words bounced on the screen as the C-5 hit an air pocket over the Atlantic. Quinn steadied his laptop.

The story dragged and Dawson's prose reeked, but

Quinn couldn't shake the feeling that if Dawson used his villain's name for Vlad, there might be other hints in his work of fiction. Dawson must've been working with Vlad already when he penned this mess. In fact, Frederick Von seemed to be a thinly veiled reincarnation of Vlad.

Quinn plowed through the rest of the book, his eyelids drooping until a passage gave him a shot of adrenaline, a passage about Von's hideaway—a schloss in the Grunewald forest outside Berlin.

Chapter Eighteen

Ariel's team had a full day to set up at Grunewald before Rikki's meeting with Dawson and Vlad. They'd located a schloss in the forest owned by a blind trust.

In case Vlad had his people in the area, the sniper team came in as construction workers, tourists and locals out for a stroll. But if Vlad's people were counting, they'd know not everyone who'd entered the area for work or play left.

That first night with his brothers, his sniper team, had been like a homecoming for Quinn. They'd been scattered for so long, but the teamwork and comradery returned like second nature.

Alexei stroked his rifle like he would a beautiful woman. "Who's going to get the final shot at Vlad?"

"If there is a final shot." Austin Foley, gung ho and still a little green, looked up from his laptop. "We don't even know if this is the place."

"It's the place." Quinn formed his fingers into a gun and aimed at Austin.

Austin tapped the keyboard. "Rikki's in the hotel. Are you sure Dawson won't be able to detect the GPS in her system?"

Slade Gallagher waved him off. "You worry too much, Austin. Dawson's not going to know, and if he suspects, he'll be confident that Vlad's people are not going to allow anyone to follow him and Rikki."

"We know who's *not* going to take the shot." Josh Elliott tipped his head toward Quinn. "You got yourself a bum shoulder, son. You're out of the running."

Quinn snorted. "I'm almost sure I still have better aim with my jacked-up shoulder than you do, Elliott. Hell, even skinny Miguel over there has you beat."

Miguel Estrada chucked a glove at Quinn. "Watch it. I may have dropped a few pounds, but I've got more reason than anyone here to make that shot count."

The door to the loft in the schloss a half mile away from Vlad's cottage burst open, and every last sniper reached for his weapon.

A woman with dark hair in a ponytail wedged her hands on her slim hips. "I'll make that decision when the time comes."

Quinn's jaw dropped. He'd had a vague picture of Ariel in his head, but this woman, whose face they all knew, wasn't it.

Alexei, the blunt Russian-American, voiced what was in all their heads. "You! Lauren West, the wife of Defense Secretary West."

"That's not who I am here." She crossed her arms and propped up the doorjamb with her shoulder. "I'm Ariel, and I'm still the leader of this task force."

Once they all got over the shock of Mrs. Shane West being the infamous Ariel, they dug in to discuss their plans.

They wouldn't all be stationed in this hunting lodge. They had visibility of Vlad's schloss from a few well-hidden treetops and a museum that would be closed to the public tomorrow.

Ariel instructed Austin to keep tabs on Rikki and to

notify her immediately if it looked like Rikki was not headed in their direction.

Quinn clamped a fist against the knots in his gut. He had to be right about the location of this meeting. It made too much sense. It synced up with Ariel's belief that the meeting would be in this forest.

His gaze tracked to the vibrant brunette giving orders as well as or better than her husband ever did, and Shane West was one of them—a retired navy SEAL sniper. How had she known? What connection did she have with Vlad? Her husband had come up against him a few times, but nothing like how the team in this room had.

A few hours later, after a meal and talk about the assignments that had led them all to this forest on this night, Quinn's teammates began scattering again—this time to take down a terrorist who had threatened them all and the ones they loved.

THE NEXT MORNING, Quinn peeled a banana and made it his breakfast. He had stayed in the schloss with Ariel, the only two who had buddied up, and for the hundredth time he cursed the gunshot wound in his shoulder. But if he thought his close proximity to Ariel would get her to open up, he couldn't be more wrong.

Which one of them would Ariel choose for the honor? All of them were at the top of their game, even Miguel after his time in captivity. Alexei could be a hothead, but not in a sniper situation, and Slade was laid-back enough to step away and let others take credit.

He and Josh had the most experience, but given his current condition, it might fall to Josh Elliott to take out their nemesis.

It was anyone's guess at this point, and Ariel kept her lips sealed.

The radio crackled, and Austin's cowboy twang came over the airwaves. "Our subject is on the move. Leaving the hotel."

Quinn tossed the banana peel in their makeshift trash bag and wiped his hands on his jeans. He shouldn't have eaten anything. His stomach churned.

Ariel studied him through narrowed eyes. "Don't worry about Rikki. She can handle herself."

"I know that, but if this isn't the meeting place, I screwed up royally and we'll have to scramble to catch up to them."

"You didn't screw up, Quinn. This is it."

He ran his tongue along his teeth. "How can you be so sure? How did you know it would be Grunewald forest when Rikki mentioned Berlin?"

Fire sparked from her dark eyes, and her nostrils flared, giving her a completely different appearance from the sophisticated, put-together lady of Washington. "You're not the only one who knows Vlad."

Quinn's brain whirred for the best response to get Ariel to open up, but Austin's voice interrupted him.

"They're on the autobahn, leaving the city."

The knots returned to Quinn's gut, and his shoulder throbbed. A jumbled prayer ran through his head that Rikki would head straight to the schloss, that she'd be safe, that Bella would be safe.

Austin's voice filled the room. "Headed this way. On track. The subject is on track."

The others hooted and whooped it up, but Quinn silently thanked God as his gaze met Ariel's.

Throughout the morning, strangers had wandered into the forest and along the lake, and the team had ID'd them as operatives for Vlad. They clearly had no clue that they were already surrounded by a team of navy SEAL snipers and a support group whose sole purpose over the past year had been to neutralize Vlad and his terrorist network.

None of them knew what Vlad looked like. He'd changed his appearance like a chameleon in every fuzzy, vague photo they had of him. But he'd be the one meeting with Dawson and Rikki. There would be no question about that, so they had to wait. They couldn't just start taking down people as they got out of cars or made their way to Vlad's hunting lodge, giving him a heads-up.

After the tense waiting of the morning, everything started unfolding faster than Quinn had anticipated.

Ariel started spitting out directions in the military manner she must've learned from her husband, the secretary. She had Quinn zeroing in on the car carrying Rikki and Dawson.

He'd had some painkiller injected directly into his shoulder, and the numbness prevented him from even feeling the heft of his rifle resting there. The car pulled up on the gravel drive of the schloss, and Rikki stepped out.

For the second time in less than two years, Quinn lined her up in his scope. He whispered. "C'mon, Buttercup. We're gonna do this."

Rikki threw back her head, laughing at some quip from Dawson, but Quinn could almost believe she'd heard his quiet entreaty.

Another car pulled up, and several men exited.

Quinn held his breath. The tension coming off Ariel stifled the air in the room.

She'd joined him at the window, her own rifle, a

sleek, deadly model, hoisted and ready. How long had she trained for this?

As the group began moving toward the house, Rikki paused and shook hands with a tall man, the sun glinting off his clean-shaven head.

With rapid fire, Ariel gave them their targets. Josh had the man Rikki had just greeted. He must be Vlad. Lucky bastard.

Quinn had the driver as his target, but they had to assume he was armed as well and would pose a threat to Rikki and even Dawson once the shooting ended.

Ariel gave the countdown before the group could even move inside. She must be sure of Vlad and that he wasn't waiting inside for them.

Three. Two. One.

Quinn felled his target and then swept his scope to the other fallen men. They'd left Dawson alive, and his mouth gaped in shock.

Then he reached for a weapon as Rikki backed away from him, and Quinn took his second shot.

Rikki stood amid the dead men, her face composed, her dark hair blowing in the breeze.

Slade, who'd been stationed in one of the trees, closest to the schloss, ran onto the scene and grabbed Rikki and pulled her away. Vlad could still have reinforcements nearby, but the head of the snake had been chopped off.

Josh cackled from the museum. "I got him, boys. I got that bald-headed bastard."

Ariel winked at Quinn. "No, you didn't, Elliott. Vlad was mine. He was always going to be mine."

Epilogue

Quinn held a sleeping Bella in the crook of his arm as he stood on the hotel room's balcony next to Miguel's son, Mikey, and RJ, the son of Josh's girlfriend, Gina.

RJ squirmed. "When are the fireworks?"

"Another half hour, buddy." Quinn patted his head.

Josh swept up the boy and put him on his shoulders. "You can watch from up here when they start."

Gina came up behind them and wrapped one arm around Josh's waist as she tugged on RJ's foot. "Patience. I'm going to get you and Mikey some more food."

Miguel scooped up Mikey. "You hungry?"

Jennifer, Miguel's wife, hovered next to both of them. "I think he's been stuffing his face with beignets all day. You need to eat something, too, doesn't he, Quinn?"

Miguel rolled his eyes at Quinn. "She thinks I'm gonna break."

Quinn slugged Miguel in the arm. "This guy's unbreakable."

He cuddled Bella against his shoulder and strolled into the hotel suite where the childless couples had gathered, drinking more than the parents and anticipating the fireworks less.

Austin's girlfriend, Sophia, sat on the arm of his

chair, excitedly making a point by grabbing his arm, the diamond in the side of her nose catching the light.

Austin shrugged. "I think that's a good idea, Sophia."

Quinn grinned and elbowed Slade. "The kid might be young, but he catches on quickly."

Slade winked. "I taught him everything he knows about women."

"I don't think there's enough time in the world for that." He pointed at Slade's girlfriend, Nicole, deep in discussion with Alexei. "What are those two cooking up?"

"The mad Russian has Nicole convinced that she needs to do a documentary film on the crime families of Russia."

"Do you want me to stop him?"

"Nicole will do exactly what she wants, but Alexei's girl, Britt, can keep him in line." Slade waved at Britt, and she shrugged, a smile curving her lips, as she stroked Alexei's hair. "She even has Alexei on board for adopting the orphaned baby of his worst enemy."

Slade cranked his head from side to side. "Did you invite Ariel, or should I say, Mrs. West?"

"I did invite her, but she and the secretary are at the White House for the fireworks." Quinn checked his watch. "Probably already saw them."

"Did Rikki ever tell you how or why Ariel knew Vlad?"

Rikki swooped in on them and kissed the bottom of Bella's foot. "That's Ariel's business."

Slade raised his eyebrows. "But you know."

"I'm a CIA agent, sailor." Rikki drew her fingertip across the seam of her lips.

Slade laughed and crouched beside his sleek, polished girlfriend as she grabbed his hand and began to tell him about her new project in Russia.

Rikki patted the bandage on Quinn's shoulder. "Feeling okay?"

"It aches. My doctor was not happy when I told him about that shot I got that allowed me to hoist my rifle."

"But you nailed your target...and I'm glad you did."

"Dawson was going for a gun, Rikki. He was going to kill you for betraying him."

"I know that." She kissed his shoulder. "You don't have to defend yourself. I don't think Belinda Dawson was too upset by the turn of events, either. The CIA already talked to her, and they're going light on her."

"What about my buddy Jeff? Did Ariel tell you what was going on in New Orleans?"

"Purely bad luck. That *was* the Agency on his tail. They noted his suspicious movements and were tracking him. Seems after that Rikki Taylor turned, the CIA got jumpy."

"Can you blame them?" He tugged on a lock of her red hair. "Did you know which one was Vlad before we opened fire and Ariel killed him?"

"No. I was being introduced around. David never gave away Vlad's identity. I don't think I would've ever known. Each of those men at the schloss planned to join us for the meeting, so I never would've known which one was Vlad." She shook her head. "I still can't believe David was stupid enough to put details of Vlad's hideaway in his book. I'm sure he never told Vlad about that."

"Like I said, hubris. Dawson was the only one who'd come close enough to Vlad, outside of Vlad's inner circle, who even knew he had that hunting lodge by the lake."

"Tobias Bauer. His name is not Vlad." Alexei stood up and uttered some oath in Russian. "Let's not give him that power anymore."

Nicole asked, "But who was he exactly? Can you tell us that?"

Quinn glanced at Josh and shrugged. "The intelligence agencies are still figuring that out, but we know he was a child of about ten in East Germany when the Berlin Wall fell. He and his mother moved to the more prosperous cities of West Germany during the reunification, but she died soon after and Toby, as he was called, took to the streets—stealing, hustling, getting in trouble with the authorities."

Austin's girlfriend slid into his lap and said, "He had my friend killed. How did he become a terrorist?"

"And where did he learn how to shoot?" Jennifer, Miguel's wife, shooed the kids back onto the balcony with Rikki's mother and stepfather.

Slade answered, "He learned how to shoot in the forest. He became an excellent marksman and started hiring himself out as a mercenary."

"And a master of disguise." Miguel put his arm around his wife. "I may have even seen him when I was held in those caves. Nobody really knew what he looked like."

"Except Ariel." Austin cleared his throat and glanced at Rikki.

"As more is discovered about him, his terrorist network will be dismantled." Josh raised his glass. "To the fall of Tobias Bauer and the protection of innocents everywhere."

A boom echoed from outside and RJ dashed into the room from the balcony. "The fireworks. The fireworks."

Quinn tucked his sleeping daughter into a bassinet

and took Rikki's hand. She squeezed his hand and they kissed before joining everyone on the balcony.

While holding on to the woman he loved, Quinn watched the exploding colors reflected in the faces of his teammates. One by one, he met their eyes and nodded, a silent affirmation among them all that they'd do anything to protect the people gathered here and to protect the red, white and blue.

* * * * *

DANGER ON DAKOTA RIDGE

CINDI MYERS

Chapter One

What she was planning wasn't illegal, Paige Riddell told herself as she hiked up the trail to Dakota Ridge. Her friend Deputy Gage Walker might not agree, but she hadn't asked his opinion. The mayor of Eagle Mountain, Larry Rowe, would object, but Larry always took the side of corporations and businesses over people like Paige—especially Paige. But she knew she was right. CNG Development was the one breaking the law, and she had a copy of a court order in her pocket to prove it.

The tools she carried clanked as she made her way up the forest trail. She had borrowed the hacksaw from a neighbor, telling him she needed to cut up an old folding table to put out for recycling. The bolt cutters were new, purchased at a hardware store out of town. Planning for this expedition had been exciting, she had to admit—a nice break from her routine life of managing the Bear's Den Bed and Breakfast Inn and volunteering for various causes.

She stopped to catch her breath and readjust the straps on her pack. A chill breeze sent a swirl of dried aspen leaves across her path, bringing with it the scent of pine. In another week or two, snow would dust the top of Dakota Ridge, rising in the distance on her right. In another month, people would be taking to the trail with snowshoes instead of hiking boots. Thanks to Paige, they would be able to make their way all the way up and along the top of the ridge, their progress unimpeded by CNG's illegal gate.

She set out again, walking faster as she neared her destination, a mixture of nerves and excitement humming through her. She planned to leave the copy of the court order at the gate after she cut off the locks, so that whichever CNG employee discovered the damage would know this wasn't a random act of vandalism, but an effort to enforce the court's ruling that CNG couldn't block access to a public trail that had been in use across this land since the late nineteenth century.

The trail turned and followed alongside an eight-foot fence of welded iron and fine-mesh wire. Snarls of razor wire adorned the top of the fence. Paige was sure the razor wire hadn't been there when she had last hiked up this way about ten days ago. What was so important on the other side of that fence that CNG felt the need to protect it with razor wire?

She quickened her pace. CNG had the right to protect its property however it saw fit, but if the management wanted to keep out hikers, they needed to reroute their fence. Maybe wrecking their gate would encourage them to do so. Waiting for them to comply with the court ruling hadn't worked, so it was time for action.

She had considered asking other members of the Eagle Mountain Environmental Action Group to join her. The local hiking club, which had evolved into the closest thing Rayford County had to a political action committee, had a diverse membership of active people, most of whom were already up in arms about the gate over one of the most popular trails in the area. With more people and more tools, they probably could have dismantled the obstruction. But more people involved meant a greater chance of discovery. Someone would shoot off their mouth in a bar or to the wrong friend, and the next thing Paige knew, CNG would have filed a countersuit or criminal charges or something. Better to do this by herself—less chance of getting caught. CNG might suspect her of having something to do with the messed-up gate, since she was head of the EMEAG and one of its most vocal members, but they would never be able to prove it.

She quickened her pace as the offending gate came into view. Welded of black iron, four feet wide and at least six feet tall, topped with pointed spikes, it sported a massive padlock and the kind of chain Paige associated with cargo ships, each link easily three inches across. She stopped a few feet away, slipped the pack from her back and dropped it onto the ground beside the trail, where it settled with an audible *clank*.

She moved closer, inspecting the setup. The lock was new, made of heavy brass. She had heard Gage had shot the old one off when he and his girlfriend, Maya, were up here searching for her missing niece. Paige grabbed the lock—which was bigger than her hand—and tugged. Not that she expected it to be open, but she would have felt really foolish if she went to the trouble to cut it off, then found out it hadn't even been fastened.

The lock weighed several pounds. The hasp was thick, too. She returned to her pack and fished out the cutters and the hacksaw. Some videos she had watched online had showed people slicing through locks with portable grinders, but that approach had struck her as noisy and likely to attract attention. Better to snip the lock off with the bolt cutters, or saw through the hasp.

She tried the bolt cutters first, gripping the hasp of the lock between the jaws of the cutters and bearing down with all her might.

Nothing. They didn't even make a dent in the metal. She gritted her teeth and tried again, grunting with the effort. Nothing, save for a faint scratch. A little out of breath, she straightened, scowling at the recalcitrant lock. Fine. Time to get the hacksaw. Her neighbor had assured her it would cut through metal.

Sawing the blade was hard, tiring work, but after half a dozen strong strokes, she had succeeded in making a dent in the hasp. Another half hour or so of work and she might sever the hasp—provided her arm didn't fall off first. But hey—she wasn't a quitter. She bore down and sawed faster.

She was concentrating so hard on the work she didn't hear the voices until they were almost on her. "Over here!" a man shouted, and Paige bit back a yelp and almost dropped the saw.

She recovered quickly, gathered her tools and raced into the underbrush, heart hammering painfully. She waited for the voices to come closer, for someone to notice the damage to the lock and complain. Had they seen her?

Her pack! Feeling sick to her stomach, she shifted her gaze to the dark blue backpack clearly visible by the side of the trail. Did she dare retrieve it? But moving would surely attract attention.

She held her breath as two men in forest camo parkas, watch caps pulled down low on their foreheads, emerged from the woods on CNG's side of the gate and tramped down the trail toward her. She shrank farther back into the underbrush, sharp thorns from wild roses catching on the nylon of her jacket and scratching the backs of her hands. Her eyes widened and her heart beat even faster as the men drew nearer and she could make out semiautomatic weapons slung across their backs. Since when did a real-estate development company equip their security guards with guns like that?

Talk about overkill! Anger took the place of some of her fear. If those big bullies thought they could intimidate her, they had another think coming. She had every right to be here, on a public trail, and if they didn't like it, they could take it up with the sheriff's department, but she was in the right.

She had about decided to emerge from her hiding place and tell them so when they reached the gate. But instead of stopping and opening it, or yelling out at her, the two men walked past, along the fence line. Now Paige could see they carried something between them. Something heavy, in a large wooden packing crate. She shuddered as they passed. Though the shape wasn't exactly right, the big box reminded her of a coffin. What the heck were these two doing with that out here in the middle of nowhere? After all, there was a perfectly good road leading right onto the property, which had once been planned as a luxury resort. Last she had heard, CNG wanted to turn the abandoned resort into a high-altitude research laboratory. So why sneak through the woods carrying a heavy box instead of just driving it to wherever they needed it? And why carry guns along with the box?

As soon as the men had passed her hiding place and moved out of sight, Paige emerged. She shoved the tools and the pack out of sight under some bearberry bushes, then hurried down the trail after the men. The former Eagle Mountain Resort had been the site of plenty of shady activity lately—maybe this was more of the same. It was her duty as a citizen to find out. Besides, who could resist a mystery like this?

She didn't have any trouble tracking the two men. They crashed through the underbrush like a pair of bull elk. They probably didn't expect anyone else to be up here. Word had gotten out around town that the trail was blocked, and no one lived on the abandoned mining claims that surrounded CNG's property, except Ed Roberts, who was practically a hermit and made a point of keeping to himself. Paige had counted on that same privacy to help her get away with cutting the lock off the gate. She'd have to make another attempt at that. Next time, she would bring more muscle, and maybe power tools.

Wherever the two guys with guns were headed, they weren't wasting any time. Paige had to trot to keep up with them. Fortunately, the trail paralleling the fence made movement easy, and her lightweight hiking boots made little noise on the soft ground. She stayed far enough behind that the men would have to turn all the way around to see her, but she could still keep them in her sights.

A few hundred yards from the gate, they turned away from the trail. Paige stopped and crouched down. She watched through an opening in the underbrush as they carried the box about fifty feet, then stopped and set down their burden. The man in the lead bent and felt for something in the drying grass. The sound of metal scraping against metal carried clearly in the still air. The man turned around, then descended into the ground. The second man shoved the box toward the spot where his companion had disappeared and tipped it up, then slid it in. Then he disappeared after it.

Paige straightened, her mind racing to solve this puzzle. She looked around, noting her surroundings. Gage and Maya had been trapped in an underground chamber on the resort property. Maya's niece, Casey, had climbed out and run for help. That must be the same chamber where the two men had disappeared just now. What were they doing in there? What was in that box? And why did they have to carry it through the woods instead of driving it to the storage bunker that led to the chamber?

She would definitely be paying Maya and Gage a visit to find out their take on all this. Of course, she had no proof anything at all illegal was going on, but given the property's history, it might be worth watching. She turned and made her way back down the trail and collected her pack and tools. She checked the lock again, but all her efforts had barely marked it. She would have to come up with a better plan.

Shouldering the pack once more, she started back down the trail. She needed to get back to the B and B. She had a new guest checking in this afternoon. Some government worker, Robert Allen. His secretary had made the reservation, and the credit card information she had given Paige had checked out. He had reserved her best suite for a week, a real bonus, considering this was her slow time of year—past prime summer tourist season, too late for fall leaf-peepers and too early for the Thanksgiving and Christmas holidays.

These thoughts occupied her until she reached the spot where the two men had turned away from the fence.

She couldn't resist taking another peek, to see if she could make out anything else distinctive about the site. She bent over and wormed her way into the opening in the undergrowth, a more difficult task while wearing the pack. But she managed to wedge herself in there and look through—just in time to see the second man join the first up top. He bent and slid whatever cover was over the opening back in place. Then both men started straight toward her.

Paige quickly backed out of her hiding place, fighting the branches that snagged on her clothing and tangled in her pack. She swatted a vine out of her way and a thorn pricked her thumb, a bead of bright red blood welling against her white flesh. The tools in her backpack clanged like out-of-tune wind chimes as she pushed her way back toward the trail.

"Hey!" a man yelled.

Something whistled through the air past her and struck a tree to her left, sending splinters flying. A second gunshot followed the first. Paige yelped and ran, heart racing and legs pumping. Those maniacs were shooting at her! You couldn't shoot at someone on a public trail! Gage was definitely going to hear about this.

They weren't shooting anymore. They probably couldn't get a clear view of her. The trail was downhill and Paige ran fast. The two men would have to fight through heavy underbrush and get over or around that fence to pursue her. She had left her car parked at the trailhead and she was sure she could get to it before they could.

Idiots! In what universe did they think they could get away with something like this? You could bet she would be filing charges. She'd call the papers, too. CNG would get plenty of bad publicity from this fiasco. And when the corporate lawyers came calling to apologize and persuade her to settle out of court, she'd use that leverage to have them remove that gate over the trail. In fact, she'd make sure they donated some of their high-value ridgetop property as a conservation easement. They would have to if they had any hope of recovering their precious reputation.

Buoyed by these plans, she jogged down the trail, head bent, watching for roots and other obstacles that might trip her up. She didn't see the big man in the dark coat who stepped out in front of her—didn't register his presence at all until she crashed into him and his arms wrapped around her, holding her tight.

Chapter Two

As a DEA agent for the past fifteen years, Rob Allerton had faced down his share of men and women who wanted to kill him, but none had outright tried to run him over. The sound of gunfire had sent him charging up the trail, only to be almost mowed down by a female hiker who fought like a tornado when he grabbed hold of her to steady them both. He managed to pin her on the ground, then satisfied himself that she wasn't armed—and therefore probably not the source of the shots he had heard.

"I'm not going to hurt you," he said, speaking slowly and distinctly in her ear, ignoring the alluring floral fragrance that rose from the soft skin of her neck. "I'm a law enforcement officer. I only want to help." Carefully, he eased back and released his hold on her.

She sat up and swept a fall of straight honey-blond hair out of her eyes, and he felt the angry look she lasered at him in the pit of his stomach—and farther south, to tell the truth. He hadn't seen Paige Riddell in almost two years, but she wasn't the kind of woman a man forgot easily.

"Agent Allerton." She pronounced his name as if it was a particularly distasteful disease. He had figured out the first day they met that she seldom bothered masking her feelings or suppressing her passions. Feeling the heat of her hatred only made him wonder what it would be like to be on the receiving end of her love.

"What are you doing here?" she demanded, standing and dusting dirt from the knees of her jeans.

He rose also. "I heard gunshots. Was someone shooting at you?"

"*I* certainly wasn't shooting at *them*." She adjusted her pack, which clanked as she shifted her weight.

He frowned at the dark blue backpack. "Is that a *saw* you're carrying?" He walked around her to get a better look. "And a pair of bolt cutters?" He moved back in front of her. "What have you been up to?"

"None of your business." She tried to walk past him, but he blocked her way. She glared up at him, with those clear gray eyes that still had the power to mesmerize.

"It's my business if someone was shooting at you." He touched her upper arm, wary of startling her. "Are you okay? Are you hurt?" He should have asked the questions earlier, but he was so surprised to find her here he had forgotten himself.

"I'm fine." She shrugged off his hand, but he recognized the pallor beneath her tan.

"Who fired those shots?" he asked. "It sounded like a semiautomatic."

She glanced over her shoulder, in the direction she had run from. "I'm not going to stand here, waiting for them to come back," she said. "If you want to talk, you can come with me."

He let her move past him this time, and fell into step just behind her on the narrow trail. "Did you get a look at the shooters?" he asked. "Was it anyone you know?"

"I don't know who they were—two men up at the

old Eagle Mountain Resort." She gestured toward the property to their left. The trail had turned away from the fence line and descended away from the property. "I spotted them carrying a big wooden crate through the woods. They lowered it into an underground chamber of some kind. At least, they both disappeared through some kind of trapdoor in the ground, and came out without the crate. I guess they saw me watching and fired. I took off running. They were on the other side of that big fence, so they couldn't chase me."

"Maybe they thought you were trying to break in," he said. "Were you using those bolt cutters on their fence?" He wished he could see her face, but she didn't look at him, and walked fast enough so that he had to work to keep up with her.

"No, I was not trying to break through their fence," she said.

"What were you doing? Bolt cutters and a saw aren't typical hiking gear."

"I was going to cut the illegal lock off their illegal gate over a legal public hiking trail," she said. "I have a copy of a court order instructing them to remove the lock and open the gate, which they haven't done."

"So you decided to take matters into your own hands," he said.

"The lock was too tough," she said. "I'll have to get someone up here with power tools or a torch or something." She might have been discussing her plans to build a community playground or something equally as virtuous. Then again, Paige Riddell probably saw opening up a public trail as just as worthy an enterprise. This was the Paige he remembered, absolutely certain in her definitions of right and wrong, and that she, of course, was in the right.

"You're not worried someone is going to shoot at you again?" he asked. "Next time they might not miss."

She glanced back at him. "I'm going to report this to the sheriff. I was on a public trail. They had no right to fire on me. Even if I'd been trespassing—which I was not—they had no right to try to shoot me."

"You aren't the first person who's been fired on up here," Rob said. "Someone tried to shoot the sheriff and his deputies when they visited the property months ago."

"So there's a pattern of unlawful behavior," she said. "It's time to put a stop to it."

"Except no one can ever identify the shooters," Rob said.

"I could identify these men." She bent to duck under a low-hanging branch, then glanced back once more. "What are you doing here?" she asked. "I doubt you just decided it was a nice day for a hike."

"I'm staying in town for a few days—a little vacation time." Long practice made him reluctant to share his plans with anyone, especially a woman he didn't know that well, who had made no secret of her dislike of him. "I heard a new company had taken over this property and I wanted to check out what they were doing here."

"You didn't find anything illegal when you were there last month, did you?" she asked.

"No." He had overseen an investigation into an underground laboratory that had been discovered on the property, but his team had found no signs of illegal activity.

"The new owners say they're going to use the property to build a high-altitude research facility," she said. "Did you know that?"

"I heard something to that effect," he said. "What do you think of that idea?" Paige headed up the local environmental group that had gotten the injunction that stopped development at the resort years ago.

"It's better than a resort that only gets used half the year," she said. "Depending on what they research, that kind of facility might actually do some good, and I wouldn't expect a lot of traffic or other stressors on the environment. We'll wait and see what they plan to do, and we'll definitely have some of our members at their permit hearings."

"Do you ever worry you'll get on the wrong side of the wrong person?" he asked.

She stopped so suddenly he almost collided with her. She turned to face him. "No, I'm not afraid," she said. "The kinds of people we do battle with—people or companies who want to do harmful things for their own gain, without thought for others—they want us to be afraid. They count on it, even. I'm not going to give them that satisfaction." She turned and started walking again.

"You don't think that's foolhardy sometimes?" he asked, picking up his pace and squeezing in beside her. "Not everyone plays by the rules. Some of them can be downright nasty." He had met his share of the second type in his years in drug enforcement.

"I try to be smart and careful, but I'm not going to back down when I'm in the right."

There was that passion again, practically sparking from her eyes. He couldn't help but admire that about her, even when they had been sparring on opposite sides of a battle. "Tell the sheriff what you saw," he said. "Then let him and his deputies handle this. Don't go up there by yourself again."

"I told you I try to be smart," she said. "Next time I'll go up there with other people. I might even have a reporter with me." She smiled. "Yes, I think that would be a great idea. Companies like CNG hate bad publicity."

They reached the trailhead, where his black pickup truck was parked beside her red Prius. She studied the truck. "Is that yours?" she asked.

"Yes. It's my personal vehicle. I told you, I'm on vacation."

She turned to him again. "I just realized I've never seen you when you weren't wearing a suit." Her gaze swept over his hiking boots and jeans, over the blue plaid flannel shirt, up to his hair, which he hadn't found time to get cut lately. He felt self-conscious under that piercing gaze, wondering if he measured up. Did Paige like what she saw? Was he vain, hoping the answer was yes?

But her expression was impossible to decipher. He half expected her to say something derogatory, or at least mocking. Instead, she said, "I guess the truck suits you."

What was that supposed to mean? But before he could ask her, she stashed the pack in the back seat of the Prius, climbed into the driver's seat and sped away, leaving him standing beside his truck, feeling that, once again, Paige had gotten the upper hand.

OF THE PEOPLE she might have expected to encounter on the trail that morning, Paige had to admit that DEA agent Rob Allerton was probably five hundredth on the list of possibilities. Sure, he had ended up in Eagle Mountain a month ago, leading an investigation into that underground lab, but she had managed to avoid crossing paths with him. Once he had wrapped that up and gone back to live and work in Denver, she had comforted herself that she would never have to see the man again.

Now that she was alone, and the full impact of what had happened up on Dakota Ridge was making her break out in a cold sweat, she could admit that she had been relieved to see him, once she realized he wasn't a friend of the shooters. Rob Allerton might be a coldhearted pain in the behind, but he had probably been armed, and he knew how to handle criminals. For all her talk of not letting fear make her back down, she had been relieved not to have to face those two men and their guns by herself.

She gripped the steering wheel more tightly and glanced in the rearview mirror, to see Rob's Ford pickup behind her. She might have known he would drive a truck. He had always had a bit of a cowboy swagger—something she might have admired if they hadn't been adversaries.

And they were adversaries, she reminded herself. Rob Allerton was the reason her brother, Parker, had ended up in jail, instead of in a rehab program where he belonged. She had fought like a mama bear—and spent most of her savings—to get her little brother into a program that would help him, and to get the sentence deferred if he completed all the requirements of his parole. Allerton hadn't lifted a finger to help her, and had in fact spoken out against any leniency for Parker. She was never going to forgive him for that.

Remembering how she had won that battle, and that Parker was all right now and well on his way to putting his life back together, calmed her. She rubbed her shoulder, where it ached from carrying the pack and tools, and slid her hand around to massage the back of her neck, then froze. Her fingers groped around her collar, then back to the front of her throat, under her T-shirt. Her necklace was gone—the thin gold chain from which hung the gold charm of a bird in flight. She had purchased the necklace shortly after her divorce, as a symbol that she was free as a bird. She never took it off—but it was gone now. She swore to herself. The chain must have caught in the bushes when she pushed through them to get a better look at those two men. Or maybe when she had retreated.

She would have to go back up there later and look for it. But she wouldn't go alone. She would take plenty of friends with her, and she would make sure they were armed with more than bolt cutters and saws.

By the time she parked the Prius in front of the Rayford County Sheriff's Department, she felt ready to relate her story calmly. She headed up the walkway, only to meet Rob Allerton at the front door.

He held the door open for her. "After you."

"Are you following me?" she asked.

"I needed to check in with the sheriff anyway," he said.

"Why? I thought you said you were here on vacation."

"Just professional courtesy, to let him know I'm in town." He followed her into the reception area. "Besides, I can add my account of the shooting to yours."

"Agent Allerton! What a nice surprise!" Adelaide Kinkaid, the sixtysomething administrator for the sheriff's department, greeted Rob with a wide smile. She didn't exactly flutter her eyelashes at him, but the implication was there.

"Ms. Kinkaid. Nice to see you again." Rob clasped her hand and flashed a smile of his own, and Adelaide looked as if she might swoon. Paige crossed her arms over her chest and looked away. Honestly! It wasn't as if Rob Allerton was the only good-looking man on the planet. Yes, he had that young Jake Gyllenhaal charm going on that probably appealed to Adelaide's generation, but Paige had always liked men who were a little rougher around the edges. Less glib. Less deceptive.

"I just stopped by to say hello to the sheriff," Rob said. "Ms. Riddell needs to make a report of an incident up on Dakota Ridge, though."

"Oh, hello, Paige," Adelaide said. "I didn't see you standing there."

"No, I don't imagine you did," Paige muttered.

"Did you say an incident? On Dakota Ridge?" Sheriff Travis Walker, Gage's brother, joined them in the reception area. Clean-shaven and spit polished, Travis could have been a law enforcement poster boy. The fact that he was smarter than most and full of grit had made him a local hero, and at twenty-nine, the youngest sheriff in Rayford County history.

"It's Paige's story to tell," Rob said. "I only happened upon the tail end of things."

"Come into my office." Travis led them down the hall to his office and shut the door behind them. Paige sat in the chair in front of the battered wooden desk, while Travis took the black leather chair behind it. Rob stationed himself by the door. "Tell me what happened," Travis said.

"I hiked up the Dakota Ridge Trail this morning," Paige said. "I wanted to see if CNG Development had complied with the court order to remove the gate over the trail. They hadn't."

She glanced at Rob, daring him to reveal her plans to remove the lock, but he said nothing. "While I was up there, I saw two men on the other side of the gate, on the old Eagle Mountain Resort property. They didn't see me. They were carrying a large wooden crate between them—about the size of a coffin, though I don't think it was a coffin. It looked heavy. I thought it was really odd that they would be carrying something like that through the woods, instead of driving up to wherever they needed to be. The second thing that was odd was that both of the men had semiautomatic rifles slung over their backs. I'm no expert, but I think they were AR-15s."

Travis's brow wrinkled, and he pulled a pad of paper toward him and began making notes. "Can you describe these men?"

"Muscular—big shoulders. They were wearing forest camo parkas and black knit watch caps. I didn't get a really good look at their faces through the trees, but I didn't recognize them."

"What happened next?" Travis asked.

"They continued through the woods, on the other side of the fence. I went back down the trail, but I was curious to know what they were up to, so I followed them. They stopped and one of them bent down and I heard the scrape of metal on metal. I think they opened a trapdoor or something. Then one of them climbed down into the ground. The other one pushed the box in and climbed down after it."

"So they went underground?" Travis asked. "Out of sight?"

She nodded. "I wondered if they were going into that same chamber where Gage and Maya were trapped this summer. But then I wondered again why they hadn't just driven up to it. Isn't it connected to that underground lab you found?" She looked to Rob for confirmation. "That's what Maya told me."

"It is," Rob said. "But we didn't find any sign that that chamber had been used for anything in a long time."

"That chamber is farther from the fence line," Travis said. "I don't think you could see the opening at the top from the fence."

"I don't think so, either," Rob said.

"Maybe it's just underground storage of some kind," Travis said.

"Fine, but why sneak through the woods, especially carrying something heavy?" she asked. "And why were those guys armed? And why did they shoot at me when they saw me watching them?"

"Did they say anything?" Travis asked.

"No. They just yelled 'Hey!' or something like that, and started firing. I couldn't get out of there fast enough."

"Did they try to follow you?" Travis asked.

"I don't know. I just ran." Her heart raced, remembering. "I knew they were on the other side of the fence and they'd have a hard time catching up to me. I figured I could make it to my car before they did. Then I ran into Agent Allerton." No sense elaborating on how he had pinned her to the ground. Though she had to admit that was after she did her best to knee him in the crotch.

"I heard the gunshots and came running up the trail," Rob said. "I met Paige coming down."

"What were you doing up there?" Travis asked.

Paige watched his face, not hiding her curiosity. Would he give the sheriff his story about a vacation? He shifted his weight. "I took some personal time to do a favor for my aunt."

"What kind of favor?" Travis asked.

Rob glanced at Paige. Was he going to ask her to leave the room, or suggest that he and Travis talk later? "I didn't ask you to leave while I told my story," she said. "I think I can hear yours."

"It's not exactly a secret," he said. "My aunt by marriage is Henry Hake's older sister. She asked me to look into his death a little more, see what I could find out."

"We're still investigating Henry Hake's death," Travis said. The man behind the Eagle Mountain Resort development had disappeared earlier in the summer. His body had been discovered on the property last month, but so far no one had been able to determine either how he had died or why.

"I'm not trying to step on any toes," Rob said. "But she's been worried sick since Hake disappeared early this summer. When he was found dead in that bunker on what had been his own property, it left her with more questions than answers. I told her I didn't expect to find anything you hadn't already learned, but she begged me to try." He shrugged. "I had some time off coming, and it's not exactly a hardship to spend a few days hanging around Eagle Mountain."

"Does your aunt have any ideas about what might have happened to her brother?" Travis asked.

"He had heart trouble, but she doesn't think he died of a heart attack," Rob said. "She's sure he was murdered. He was definitely afraid of someone in the weeks before he died. I'd like to find out who."

Chapter Three

Rob gave Travis credit—the sheriff didn't even blink when he learned Rob's reason for a return to Eagle Mountain. Paige, however, was gaping at him as if he had revealed a secret identity as a circus clown. "You're related to Henry Hake?" she asked.

"Not exactly," he said. "My uncle's second wife is Hake's sister. I never met the man." He turned to Travis. "And it's not my intention to interfere with your investigation. I just promised my aunt I would see what I could find out. I hiked up that trail this morning thinking I would start by getting another look at the place where his body was found—or as close as I could get, since the gates to the compound were locked up."

Travis nodded and turned back to Paige. "I'll go up to the resort property and take a look around. Do you think you could identify either of the men who shot at you if you saw them again?"

"Yes," she said.

"Good. I'll be in touch." He stood, and Paige rose also.

"While you're up there, would you look for my necklace?" she asked. "It's a gold chain, with a charm of a bird in flight. I was wearing it this morning and I don't have it now. I think it must have snagged on the bushes near where I was watching those two men."

"Sure, we can look for it," Travis said.

"Thank you, Sheriff," she said, and turned toward the door.

"Paige?"

"Yes, Sheriff?"

"Don't go up there by yourself anymore," Travis said. "At least until we get this settled. And tell the other hikers you know the same."

"All right." She turned toward Rob and acted as if she wanted to say something, then closed her mouth and left the room.

"Stay a minute," Travis said to Rob.

He nodded, and waited until they heard the front door close behind Paige before he took the seat she had vacated.

"Did you see either of the men she described?" Travis asked.

"No. I wasn't that far up the trail before she came barreling down." He chuckled. "I didn't recognize her at first, and I'm sure she didn't recognize me. When I took hold of her to try to calm her down, she fought like a tiger." He rubbed the side of his face, where she had scratched him.

"You knew each other before?" Travis asked.

Rob nodded. "Yes. And it's safe to say I am not one of her favorite people."

Travis waited, silent. He was probably a good interrogator, using silence to his benefit. "I'm the one who arrested her brother," Rob said.

"For possession of meth?" Travis asked.

"Yes. And for trying to sell stolen property. He was

part of a group of addicts who were robbing apartment complexes in Denver. I was part of a joint drug task force working that case. We had already determined the thefts were linked to drugs."

"There was no doubt of his guilt?"

"None." He sighed, all the frustration of those days coming back to him. "Paige wanted an adjudicated sentence, with her brother, Parker, allowed to go to rehab instead of prison. I didn't agree."

"From what I've seen, she can be a little protective of Parker," Travis said.

"I get it. As far as I know, he's the only family she has. But the fact that part of my job was to help see that he was punished for his crimes made me the enemy. Her opinions about right and wrong tend to be very black-and-white."

"She went up there today to cut off that lock, didn't she?" Travis asked.

Rob grinned. "I didn't see a thing. Though she was carrying a hacksaw and a pair of bolt cutters with her."

Travis shook his head. "When Paige believes she's in the right, there's no changing her mind."

"I certainly learned that." Though he would have preferred she didn't see him as the bad guy. Still, she wasn't his chief concern at the moment. "As long as I'm here, maybe I could help you out with Henry Hake's case," he said. "Is there anything you'd like me to look into? Unofficially, of course."

"Did your aunt say who her brother was afraid of?"

"No. Except she thinks it had something to do with his business."

"So not necessarily Eagle Mountain Resort. He had other real-estate holdings, didn't he?"

"A few apartment complexes and some office build-ings," Rob said. "Eagle Mountain Resort was definitely his most ambitious project. When the court ordered him to stop development, I gather it put him in a financial bind."

Travis nodded. "That's what I've learned, also."

"What can you tell me about the property's new own-ers—CNG Development?" Rob asked.

"They're another real-estate development company, out of Utah. They're much larger than Hake Develop-ment, with projects all over the United States. I wondered why they even bothered with Hake—he was pretty small potatoes, compared to them."

"Maybe they're one of these companies that special-izes in finding small firms in financial straits and buy-ing them for bargain prices," Rob said.

"Maybe so."

"Paige says they want to build a research facility up there."

"So they've said. They haven't presented anything concrete to the town for approval. The couple of times I've been up there since Hake's body was found, the place has been deserted."

"It wasn't deserted today," Rob said. "I'd sure like to know why those two were going around armed—and what was in that box. And why they reacted the way they did when they caught Paige watching them."

"Want to go up there with me to check it out?" Tra-vis asked.

"You know I'm not officially on duty," Rob said. "My boss doesn't even know where I am."

"You wouldn't be participating in any official capac-ity," Travis said. "I just want someone to watch my back."

"I can do that." And maybe he would get lucky and discover something he could tell his aunt. He couldn't bring her brother back to her, but finding out what had really happened to him might ease her suffering a little bit.

THOUGH PAIGE VOWED to put Rob Allerton firmly out of her mind and focus on work at the bed-and-breakfast where she both lived and worked, she couldn't stop thinking about the man. He was always so aggravatingly calm and sure of himself. Having him here in town annoyed her, like walking around with a pebble in her shoe. Those days following Parker's arrest had been among the worst in recent memory. Her brother had needed help and men like Rob were preventing her from helping him. Yes, Parker had broken the law, but he wasn't a bad person. His addiction had led him to do things he never would have done otherwise. Instead of punishing him, why not treat his addiction and give him another chance?

Rob Allerton had made it clear he didn't believe in second chances. No thanks to him, Parker had at least gotten a chance to get clean, though he had had to serve time, too. But he was clean now, going to school and staying out of trouble. Another year and the charges would be wiped from his record.

But he was in that position only because Paige had fought for him. Other people weren't so lucky. They had to deal with the Rob Allertons of the world without anyone on their side.

She sat down at her desk off the kitchen and tried to put Rob out of her mind. His vacation wouldn't last forever, and she had more than enough to keep her occupied in the meantime. She was working there a little later when the back door opened and Parker entered. He dropped his backpack on the bench by the door and pushed his sunglasses on top of his head. To some of the more conservative people here in Eagle Mountain, he probably looked like trouble, with his full-sleeve tattoos and often sullen expression. But Paige saw past all that to the little boy she had read stories to and made macaroni and cheese for more times than she could remember. "How was class?" she asked.

"Okay." He opened the refrigerator. "What did you do today?"

Attempted vandalism and ended up getting shot at by two thugs, she thought. "I was up on the Dakota Ridge Trail and you'll never guess who I ran into."

He took out a block of cheese and a plate of leftover ham. "I don't have to guess," he said. "You always tell me anyway."

"Rob Allerton is in town."

"Who?" He took a loaf of bread from the box on the counter and began making a sandwich.

"Rob Allerton. Agent Allerton? The DEA guy who arrested you?"

"What's he doing here?"

"He says he's on vacation." He hadn't told the sheriff about her attempt to cut the lock from the gate up on the trail, so she figured she could keep quiet about Rob's aunt and Henry Hake. Parker wouldn't care about any of that anyway.

"Maybe he wanted to see you," Parker said.

"Me?" She blew out a breath. "I'm sure I'm the last person he would ever want to see. Don't you remember how we clashed at your trial?"

"I remember sparks." He shot her a sideways look. "He thought you were hot."

"He did not!"

"You thought he was hot, too."

"You're delusional."

He turned back to his sandwich. "I'm not the one blushing."

"I'm not blushing. This room is too warm." She opened the refrigerator and began putting away the items he had removed. "Are you volunteering at the museum this afternoon?" she asked. She had talked Parker into volunteering at the local history museum. Her friend Brenda Stenson, who ran the museum, needed the help, and it was a good way for Parker to keep busy. Everything she had read had said that having too much free time could be a problem for a recovering addict.

"No." He took a bite of the sandwich.

Paige tore off a paper towel and handed it to him. "What time does your shift at Peggy's start?" She had found him the job as a delivery driver at Peggy's Pizza as another way to keep him out of trouble.

"I'm off tonight," he said, then took another bite of sandwich.

"Oh. Well, I guess you can use the time to study." He was enrolled in classes at a nearby community college. Another condition of his parole.

"I'm going out," he said.

"With who?"

"A friend."

"Do I know this friend?"

"I doubt it."

"Parker, we are not going to do this."

"Do what?" He didn't bother trying to look innocent. If anything, he was annoyed.

"Don't make me give you the third degree," she said. "Just tell me who you're going out with. I don't think that's too much to ask."

"And it's not too much for me to ask that you give me a little privacy."

A flood of words came to mind, beginning with the notion that he had violated his right to privacy when he had gotten hooked on drugs, broken the law and gone to prison. But she had vowed when she took him in that she wasn't going to throw his mistakes back in his face. Her husband had done that and she knew how miserable and degraded it made her feel. So she swallowed back most of what she wanted to say.

"Be careful, and be quiet when you come in," she said.

"I will." Carrying the rest of his sandwich, he retreated to his room off the kitchen. Paige sagged against the counter. She was exhausted and it wasn't even one o'clock yet. Big guys with guns, Rob Allerton and her troublesome baby brother—maybe what she really needed was a vacation from men.

WHEN ROB AND TRAVIS arrived at the entrance to the former Eagle Mountain Resort, Rob wasn't surprised to find the gates shut tight. "This is how they were this morning when I stopped here," he said. He peered through the iron bars at what had once been the resort's main street. Weeds sprouted in holes in the asphalt, and in places the paving had disappeared altogether, the road little more than a gravel wash. A weathered sign still proclaimed that this was the future site of Eagle Mountain Resort, a Luxury Property from Hake Development. No sign of luxury remained in the crumbling foundations and sun-bleached wood of the few structures scattered about the property. Rocks ranging from those the size of a man's head to boulders as big as small cars spilled down from the ridge above at the site of a major rock slide where two men had been killed earlier in the year.

"It doesn't look any different than it did when I was here a month ago," Rob said.

"I'm guessing if CNG does plan to develop the place—for a research facility or anything else—they'll wait until spring," Travis said. "In another few months there will be eight to ten feet of snow up here. The county doesn't plow the road up this far and there's always a danger of avalanches on the ridge. It's one reason the judge agreed with Paige's group that a housing development up here was a bad idea."

Rob looked again at the deserted street. "What do we do now?" he asked.

"Let's hike up the trail a ways," Travis said. "You can show me where you were when you heard the shots, and where you ran into Paige."

They drove back down the road to the public trail-head, then started hiking uphill. After about half a mile, the trail began to parallel the fence line for CNG's property. The black iron fence, eight feet tall and topped with curls of razor wire, was almost hidden in places by a thick growth of wild roses and scrub oak, but in other spots the undergrowth thinned enough to provide a glimpse through the bars of the fence.

"About this point is where I heard the shots," Rob said. "I thought they came from the other side of the fence. I picked up speed and I hadn't gone far when I saw Paige running down the trail toward me. I thought at first someone was pursuing her, but then I realized she was alone. She said two men had shot at her. Then my focus became getting her safely away."

"Did you stop by the entrance to the property before you went to the trailhead, the way we did just now?" Travis asked.

"Yes. The gates were locked and I didn't see anyone. No cars or anything."

"Let's see if we can figure out where Paige could have seen the shooters," Travis said.

They moved up the trail, which soon curved sharply, still following the fence line. Another hundred feet and they came to an opening in the wall of bushes and vines next to the trail. Broken branches and scuffs in the leaf litter told the tale of someone plunging into this opening—and exiting in a hurry.

Travis went first, with Rob close behind. Bending over, they had a clear view onto the resort property, but what they saw was unremarkable—a few stunted evergreens, oak brush with the last brown leaves of summer clinging to it, and some dried grasses. Travis took binoculars from his belt and scanned the area. "I don't see anything," he said.

They waited a moment, listening, but heard only the sound of their own breathing. The silence and the deserted—abandoned, really—property made Rob feel uneasy. "I don't think we're going to find anything here today," he said, keeping his voice low.

"No." They returned to the trail and started back toward the parking area. "I could try for a warrant to search the place," Travis said. "But I doubt a judge would grant the request."

"They were shooting at an unarmed woman," Rob said. "A woman who wasn't even on their property."

"That's what Paige said happened, but she wasn't hit and there weren't any witnesses."

Rob started to object, but Travis cut him off. "I know—it's not like her to make things up. I'm just telling you what CNG's lawyers are going to say."

"I heard the shots," Rob said.

"Right. People shoot guns all the time out here—at targets, at animals. It's elk season right now. Maybe they were hunting. It's not illegal to shoot off a gun."

Rob blew out a sigh of frustration. "So what do we do now?"

"We keep an eye on the place and look for a reason—any reason—to come back up here and take a closer look."

They fell silent, trudging down the trail. The sun was already disappearing behind the ridge, a chill descending in the fading light. Rob shoved his hands in the pockets of his jeans and reviewed the events of the morning in his head. Had he missed something—some clue that would help them figure out what was really going on? Had Paige's presence distracted him from noticing everything he should have noticed?

They reached the parking lot and Travis's SUV. The sheriff pulled out his keys and pressed the button to unlock the vehicle, but he froze in the act of reaching for the door handle, his gaze fixed on the door.

"What is it?" Rob, who had already opened the passenger door, asked.

"Take a look."

Rob walked around to the driver's side and stared at the thin gold chain affixed over the door handle with a piece of clear tape. A gold charm shaped like a bird dangled from the chain, stirred by a slight breeze. The sight of the delicate, feminine ornament so out of place sent a chill through him. "That looks like the necklace Paige described," he said. "The one she said she lost up here."

Chapter Four

Travis took out his phone and snapped several pictures of the necklace, then examined the ground around the vehicle. "This gravel is too hard-packed to leave prints," he said.

"We might get prints off the tape," Rob said.

Travis went to the back of the vehicle and opened it, then took out a small box. He put on gloves, then took out a paper evidence pouch and a thin-bladed knife. Carefully, he lifted the edge of the tape with the knife, then peeled it back. He transferred both tape and necklace to a plain white card, then slipped them in the pouch and labeled it. "I'll have a crime scene tech go over the car when we get back to the office," he said. "Though I doubt we're going to find much."

They both took another look around. Rob scanned the trees that surrounded the parking area. "Do you think they're watching us now?" he asked.

"The person or persons who put that necklace there?" Travis asked. He opened the door and slid into the driver's seat. "Maybe. Maybe they've been watching us the whole time."

"Why did they bother returning the necklace?" Rob

asked, as he buckled his seat belt and Travis started the SUV.

"Maybe a hiker came along behind us, found the necklace on the trail and figured it must belong to whoever was in this vehicle," Travis said. "Or they figured giving it to a cop was the right thing to do."

"And where is this hiker?" Rob scanned the empty trailhead. "Why didn't we see them? Where did they park?"

"They changed their minds about the hike?" Travis backed out of the small parking area.

"Or maybe the person or persons who left the necklace there was the same person or persons who shot at Paige," Rob said. "They left the necklace because they wanted us to know they were watching. That they could, in fact, have taken us out if they had been so inclined."

"Could be," Travis said.

They drove to the sheriff's office, where Deputy Dwight Prentice greeted them at the door. "Hello, Rob," Dwight said. "Are you here because of the report on Henry Hake?"

"What report is that?" Rob asked.

"It must have come in while we were gone," Travis said. "Because I haven't heard about it, either." He led the way into his office and settled behind his desk. "Tell us about this report."

"The medical examiner's office sent over an updated report on their findings in Henry Hake's death," Dwight said. He handed a printout to Travis, who scanned it, his face giving away nothing. He passed the papers to Rob.

"I thought the ME ruled Henry Hake probably died of a heart attack," Rob said.

"He did," Dwight said. "But one of his bright young

assistants got curious about some nasty-looking lesions on the body and did some more digging. This report is what he came up with."

Rob read quickly through it, only half listening as Dwight continued talking. His gaze shifted to the bottom section and the words *Conclusion: Death from Tularemia.*

"What is tularemia?" he asked.

"It's also called rabbit fever," Dwight said. "It's a naturally occurring bacteria that, if treated with antibiotics, is rarely fatal."

"And if untreated?" Travis asked.

"According to the Centers for Disease Control fact sheet attached to that report, a bite from an infected animal could cause skin ulcers, while inhaling the bacteria can lead to pneumonia or, in the most severe cases, typhoid-like symptoms," Dwight said.

"And the ME thinks that's what killed Henry Hake?" Travis looked skeptical. "Was he bitten by a rabbit or what?"

"Tularemia is one of the biological weapons the government experimented with in World War II," Dwight said. "It's one they were supposedly working on here in Rayford County. I remember reading about it." Recently, news about just such a secret government lab, located somewhere in the county, had come to light, causing a bit of a stir among history buffs.

Rob let out a low whistle.

"That government lab was supposedly located in an old mine somewhere near here," Travis said. "Could Henry Hake have picked it up in the soil while messing around looking for the lab?"

"Maybe," Dwight said. "But when I found his body, it

was hanging from the ceiling in that underground chamber on the resort property—Hake didn't do that himself."

"You found the body after the DEA determined that chamber didn't have anything to do with either the World War II experiments or any modern crime," Rob said. "And the ME ruled Hake died weeks ago—so someone brought his body to that location after we left, and several weeks after he died."

"Right," Dwight said. "So while it's possible Hake died in that underground chamber and someone hid his body for a while, then brought it back, I don't think it's likely. Why go to all that trouble?"

"How would the government have used tularemia as a weapon?" Travis asked.

"Apparently, the idea was to put the bacteria in an aerosol," Dwight said. "You could put it in the ventilation system of a building or simply spray it over a crowd. Not everyone would catch the disease, and of those that did, not everyone would die."

"You said antibiotics will kill it," Rob said. "So it doesn't sound like a very practical weapon today."

"Except that most people wouldn't realize they had been exposed, or that they were suffering from tularemia," Dwight said. "Anyone with a compromised immune system, or lung or heart disease, might die before anyone figured out what was wrong."

"Henry Hake had a bad heart," Travis said.

"Did whoever killed him know that?" Rob asked.

"More unanswered questions," Travis said. "Would this be enough for the DEA to go back into that underground bunker and do some testing?"

"Maybe." Rob sighed. "I'm not even supposed to be here, you know."

"Your aunt wanted to know what really happened to Hake," Travis said. "This might be your best chance to find out."

Rob glanced at the clock on the wall by the door. "It's after five in DC, where the decision would have to be made," he said. "I'll contact my boss in the morning and let him take it from there." That would give him a few more hours to come up with a better explanation for why he was in Rayford County right now. Maybe he could persuade his boss he had just come here to fly-fish.

"Let us know what he says." Travis glanced at the report once more. "I wonder what the market is for biological weapons."

"What made you think of that?" Dwight asked.

"Because so many times these things come down to money," Travis said.

"My guess is there are terrorist groups who would hand over a lot of cash to get their hands on a weapon that was easy to distribute, tough to detect and effective for mass destruction," Rob said.

"Is there a weapon like that?" Dwight asked. "Tularemia doesn't sound like it would be very effective."

"Then maybe the point of the lab is to develop something better," Travis said. "It's one angle."

"Hake had a lot of money tied up in that resort project," Dwight said. "CNG Development talks like they want to spend even more money up there."

"Yet we've had two murders there—three, if you count Hake," Travis said. "As well as two accidental deaths, three people kidnapped, and a number of unexplained discharges of firearms up there."

"Maybe we can get the county to declare the place a public nuisance," Dwight said.

"More likely, CNG will complain that local law enforcement isn't doing a good job of keeping the criminal element off their property," Travis said. He straightened. "I'll give CNG a call and see what they have to say about this latest discovery."

"Let me know what they say," Rob said.

"Don't worry," Travis said. "You're part of this now, whether you want to be or not."

PAIGE TOLD HERSELF she had to trust Parker, as she watched him drive away. He was a good kid. Or rather, a good man. She had to remind herself her little brother wasn't a child anymore, and she shouldn't treat him like one. Yes, he had made some mistakes, but he was too smart to make those mistakes again. She wanted to believe this.

She checked the clock as she passed through the kitchen on the way to her office. It was after three thirty. She had expected her new guest, Robert Allen, to check in before now. Then again, maybe he had gotten a late start from Denver, or decided to do other things before showing up at the B and B. She asked that guests notify her only if they planned to arrive after 9:00 p.m.

She switched on her computer and prepared to focus on balancing her books and updating her financial records—a task guaranteed to require all her attention. She was deep into the frustration of trying to make her numbers agree with the bank's when the doorbell rang. She started and glanced at the clock, surprised to see she had been working for almost an hour. She closed her laptop and hurried to the door, fixing a smile in place, prepared to play the gracious hostess.

A check of the security peephole wiped the smile from her face. She unlocked the door and swept it open.

"What do you think you're doing, following me around like this?" she demanded of a startled Rob Allerton.

He settled his features into his usual inscrutable expression. "I have a reservation," he said. "What are you doing here?"

"I own this place."

He glanced up at the neat white Victorian home, with its black shutters, and neatly mulched flower beds filled with lilacs and peonies fading into winter dormancy. "Nice," he said.

"You're Robert Allen?" she asked.

He had the grace to wince. "The assistant who made the reservation must have automatically used my cover name," he said. "Sorry about that."

He made a move to walk past her into the house, but she stepped forward to join him on the front porch and shut the door behind her. "You can't stay here," she said.

"Why not?"

"Parker lives here now."

"I'm not interested in your brother," he said.

"I don't want to upset him." Parker had enough to deal with without having to face over the breakfast table every morning the man who had arrested him.

"We're all adults here," Rob said. "I don't see why there should be a problem."

"It's a problem for me. You'll have to find somewhere else to stay."

"Eagle Mountain doesn't have that many choices for accommodations," he said. "I spent plenty of time at the only motel while I was part of DEA's investigation into that underground lab."

"The motel is very nice," she said.

"It's adequate, but everyone there knows I'm a DEA

agent. I prefer to keep this visit separate from that investigation. This is a personal visit and I'd like to keep to the appearance of a relaxing vacation as much as possible. When my assistant suggested a B and B I liked the idea."

Paige crossed her arms and scowled at him. She had the right to refuse service to anyone, but he could make a big stink if he wanted to. And turning away a paying customer at this slow time of year would be foolish, wouldn't it? But to have this man, who had almost ruined Parker's life, in her home—well, Rob had helped to almost ruin Parker's life, since she couldn't deny that Parker was the one who was mostly to blame. Still, it galled her to think of having Rob living here for the next week.

"What are you afraid of?" Rob asked. "If you're that worried, you can lock your door. Or should I lock mine?"

She wanted to slap the wolfish smile off his face, but before she could raise her hand, he grabbed her by the shoulders and shoved her to the ground. For the second time that day she found herself fighting him as he held her down. Then gunfire exploded very near her ear and tore into the door where she had been standing only seconds before.

Chapter Five

Paige's scream merged with the screech of tires and the roar of an engine as the black sedan raced down the street in front of the Bear's Den B and B. Rob, his weapon drawn, straightened and peered at the retreating car. There was no license plate, and the darkly tinted windows prevented him from seeing the occupants. Though there had been at least two people inside—the driver and the person who had fired the gun out the passenger window.

"What happened?" Paige asked, her voice shaky. She tried to sit up and this time he let her. He returned the gun to the holster at his hip, then reached down and pulled her to her feet.

"Was someone shooting at us?" she asked.

"Yes." He turned his attention from the street to look at her more closely. "Are you all right?" he asked.

"I'm okay." She rubbed her elbow. "Just a little banged up."

"Sorry if I was a little rough," he said. "I glimpsed the gun and had to move fast." He had acted on pure instinct, pushing her out of danger, shielding her with his own body.

"I'm okay," she said again. She straightened her

blouse. "Who was it? Was it the men from the resort property? The ones who shot at me before?"

Rob shook his head. "I don't know. I didn't get a good look at them. I saw their silhouettes and the gun." He pulled his phone from his pocket and dialed the sheriff's office—Travis's direct number.

Travis answered on the second ring. "Hello?"

"This is Rob Allerton. I'm at Paige Riddell's place. A black sedan, tinted windows, no plates, two men inside, just drove by and fired on us."

"Dwight is already on his way over," Travis said. "We had a report of gunfire in the area. Is anyone hurt?"

"No. Some damage to the front door." He surveyed the line of bullet holes across the bright red door, like a row of stitches. His roller bag sat inches from the door, but was unscathed.

"I think I need to sit down." Paige sank onto the bench beside the door, her head between her knees. Rob walked out to the street and studied the angle of the shot. He had parked his truck in the paved area between the B and B and the house to the left—which meant anyone driving by had a clear view of the front porch where he and Paige had been standing. The house was only about a hundred feet from the street, making for an easy target.

As he stood at the curb, a Rayford County Sheriff's Department SUV pulled up. Dwight rolled down the passenger window and leaned toward Rob. "I just heard from Travis. You and Paige okay?"

He glanced over his shoulder to where Paige sat, upright now, hands gripping the edge of the bench, staring at the floor between her feet. "She's a little shaken up," he said. "But she'll be okay."

"We've got a BOLO on the car you described," Dwight said. "Can you show me where the bullets hit?"

The two men walked up on the porch. "Hello, Paige," Dwight said. "You okay?"

She nodded.

"Did you get a look at the shooter?" Dwight asked.

"I never saw them. Rob pushed me out of the way before I even knew they were there."

Dwight nodded, then bent to examine the damaged door. He took some photos. "At least some of the bullets are embedded in the door," he said. "We'll get someone out here to collect them. Is there anything else you can tell me—about the car or the shooters?"

"I'm sorry," Paige said. "I can't think of anything."

"We'll do our best to patrol here more frequently," Dwight said. "But you might want to think about staying somewhere else for a while."

She stared at him. "I can't do that. I have guests. And Parker is here."

Dwight's eyes met Rob's. "It would be better if you went somewhere safer," Dwight repeated.

"How do you know I was even the target?" Paige asked, with more strength in her voice. "I imagine a DEA agent has made all kinds of enemies."

Rob looked at the door again. "Maybe so," he said. "But the shots were fired where you were standing."

Her face paled, but she set her jaw. "I'm not leaving my home and my business," she said.

"I can't force you," Dwight said.

"I'm staying here," Rob said. "I'll keep an eye on things."

"Let us know if you see anything suspicious." Dwight nodded to Paige, then left.

When they were alone again, Rob turned to Paige. "Where's Parker?" he asked.

"He's out."

"Out where?"

"None of your business."

He almost smiled. This was the Paige he was used to. "Do you know where he is?" he asked.

"He's an adult. I don't keep track of his every move."

Somehow he doubted this was a philosophy she had adopted willingly, having seen her mother-bear act in court. "Do you want me to call him?" he asked.

"No!"

"I thought maybe you would feel better with him here."

"No. There's no need to worry him."

"Did you tell him about what happened this morning? The other shooting?"

"No. He doesn't need to know."

"There's such a thing as being too independent, you know," Rob said.

She stood. "Come on. Let's get you checked in."

He could have pressed the issue, but what would be the point? Paige wasn't going to change on his say-so. He reclaimed his roller bag from beside the door and followed her inside.

The interior of the home was comfortably furnished with a mixture of antique and contemporary pieces. Art on the walls depicted local scenery. Rob saw none of the chintz and cutesiness he had feared when his admin had suggested a B and B for his stay. Instead, the decor was low-key and classy—like Paige herself.

She moved to a small desk in what must have been the home's front parlor or formal living room and unlocked an adjacent cabinet to reveal a computer. "What name is on the credit card you'll be using?" she asked, typing.

"Robert Allerton."

"Not Robert Allen?"

"As I said before, I'm not here on business." Not exactly. He had sworn his admin to secrecy. After he talked to his boss in the morning, he might be assigned to the case, but for now, he was on his own dime.

She scanned the card he handed her, then returned it, along with a set of old-fashioned keys on a brass fob. "The round one is for the front door," she said. "The other is for your room. You're in the Grizzly Suite. Turn left at the top of the stairs and go all the way to the end of the hallway. Breakfast is from seven to nine each morning."

He replaced the card in his wallet. "Dwight was right," he said. "You'd be safer if you moved to a location that was unknown to whoever is targeting you."

"I have a business to run and a life to live. I can't stop everything to go hide out in a cave somewhere until you or Dwight or whoever decides it's safe to come out. I'll be smart and take precautions, but I won't do what these men want."

"What do you think they want?" he asked.

She shut the cabinet door and locked it. "For me to keep quiet about what I saw. That has to be the reason they want me dead. They think they can frighten me into shutting up. But all they've done is make me more determined to find out what is going on up there."

She started to move from behind the desk, but Rob blocked her, one hand on her arm, near enough that when she inhaled sharply, the tips of her breasts brushed his sleeve. He fought the urge to pull her close and kiss the protest from her lips. Did she have any idea how maddening and enticing he found her? "Don't get any ideas about investigating this on your own," he said. "That could be dangerous."

"I'll be careful."

Careful might not be enough, but he wasn't going to get anywhere arguing with her about it. He moved aside and started to turn toward the stairs, but she put out a hand to stop him, then grabbed hold of the sleeve of his jacket. "Rob?"

He turned back, looking into her eyes, which were the color of storm clouds, fringed with thick brown lashes. Eyes that could make a man forget every angry word she had ever leveled at him. "Yes?"

She swallowed, color rising in her cheeks. "Thank you."

"What are you thanking me for?"

"For saving my life."

He could have dismissed this with a denial that he had done anything special. He had reacted on pure instinct, with no time to think about what he was doing or why. But he wouldn't let her off the hook that easily. "You know that old superstition," he said.

Two shallow lines formed between her eyebrows. "What old superstition?"

"When you save a person's life, then you're responsible for them."

She released her hold on him as if she had been scorched. "No man is responsible for me."

He smiled, a heated curve of his lips that had reduced more than one woman to breathlessness. "Have I ever told you I'm a very superstitious person? And I take my responsibilities very seriously." He leaned forward and kissed her cheek, feeling the heat of her skin and breathing in the herbal scent of her shampoo.

When he stepped back, he half expected her to slap him. Maybe he even deserved it, but that kiss had been worth it. Instead, she only tried to wound him with her gaze. Still smiling, he picked up his bag and headed for the stairs, taking them two at a time to the second floor. His stay at the Bear's Den was going to be very interesting, indeed.

Chapter Six

Paige lay awake for hours that night, reliving every moment of being shot at—the sound of the bullets, the fear that had threatened to choke her, the feel of Rob's weight on her, crushing and frightening and yet so reassuring. The man was maddening, one moment so tender and protective, the next knowing exactly what to say to make her angry. All that nonsense about him being responsible for her—and then he'd had the nerve to kiss her.

That the kiss hadn't been on the lips unnerved her even more. If he had insisted on kissing her mouth, she could have told herself he had practically assaulted her, and that he'd taken liberties to which he wasn't entitled. But that gentle brush of his lips against her cheek had been both tender and incredibly sensuous. She still trembled at the memory, at the intensity of her awareness of him—the scent of his aftershave, the soft cotton of his shirtsleeve, the incredible heat of his mouth.

She shouldn't have let him get away with it. She should have told him off then and there. But she couldn't find the words to do it. When he had left her, still smiling that *I'm-so-sexy* grin, she had had to bite her lip to keep from calling him back. In that moment, if he had tried to kiss her mouth, she would have pulled him to her willingly.

After that, it took a long time for her to drift into a restless sleep. She woke several hours later with a start and stared into the darkness, heart pounding. She held her breath and strained her ears to listen. Yes, that was definitely the sound of the back door opening. She turned her head to check the bedside clock. One thirty-two. She heard shuffling, then the sound of someone walking— no, tiptoeing—past her door.

She sat up and switched on the lamp. "Parker, is that you?" she called.

"Yes. Go back to sleep."

Instead, she got up and went to the bedroom door and opened it. Parker stood in the hallway, hair rumpled, shoulders slumped. Her first instinct was to demand to know where he had been, but she stifled the words. "You look tired," she said instead.

He shrugged. "I'm okay." He turned away. "Good night."

"Wait," she said. "There's something I need to tell you."

He stopped, but didn't look back at her. "What is it?"

"Rob Allerton is here," she said.

"Yeah. You already told me he's in town. So what?"

"No—he's here."

He did turn this time, and craned his neck, trying to see past her into her room. "Here?"

She flushed, even though the suggestion that Agent Rob Allerton would be in her bed was preposterous. "He's upstairs. In the Grizzly Suite. He has a reservation for a week."

"Okay."

She leaned forward, studying her brother more closely. He needed a shave, and he had the beginnings of dark circles under his eyes. Was he really just tired, or was something more going on? She pushed the thought away. She had to trust him. "You're okay with him being here?"

"I guess his money is as good as anybody else's. And it's not like I'll see him much, between work and school and stuff."

Stuff. What stuff? But she didn't ask. "It's probably a good idea if you stay out of his way as much as possible," she said.

"Don't worry. I will."

"He didn't make a reservation here because of you," she said. "He didn't even know I owned the place."

"Right." He smirked.

"He didn't," she protested.

"You can believe that if you want. I think Agent Allerton knew exactly what he was doing."

She resented everything his words—and that smirk—implied. "I actually asked him to leave, but there's another reason he needs to be here right now."

Parker leaned one shoulder against the wall, arms folded across his chest. "I'm really tired, sis. Can we make this quick?"

She wet her lips. He was probably going to find out sooner or later. Better she tell him rather than have him hear the gossip from someone else. "Someone took a shot at me while I was hiking up by Eagle Mountain Resort yesterday," she said.

He straightened. "What?"

"I saw two men on the resort property. One of them spotted me watching them and tried to shoot me. Later, a car—possibly with the same two men inside—drove by here and someone shot at me again. Rob pushed me out of the way. As it is, the front door is ruined and will have to be replaced."

"Sis! What have you done?"

"What have I done? I haven't done anything."

"You must have done something to tick off these guys enough to try to take you out."

"I didn't do anything," she said again. "But until the authorities can track down those men, I thought it wouldn't be a bad idea for Rob to stay here. He does have some experience with situations like this."

"You mean he's got a gun and he knows how to use it." Parker shook his head, as if trying to clear it, then looked at her more closely. "Are you sure you're okay?"

"I'm fine." A little shaky still, but she was determined to get past that. And her little brother's concern touched her. "I really think Rob scared them away yesterday," she said. "And now the sheriff's department and probably other law enforcement agencies are looking for them. I don't think they'll bother me again."

"I hope not." He ran one hand through his hair. "You say you were up by Eagle Mountain Resort the first time? This morning?"

"Yes. I was on the hiking trail that runs alongside the resort. You remember—we went up there right after you moved to town."

He nodded. "Why didn't you tell me about it this morning?"

"I didn't want to worry you. And I certainly didn't think they would track me down here."

"It's not hard to find anybody in a town this small," Parker said. "Maybe you should go away for a while, until this is all over."

"No!" The word came out louder than she intended. She lowered her voice. "I'll be careful, but I won't put my whole life on hold and hide."

"What were those guys doing up at the resort?" Parker asked.

"I don't know," she said. "I saw them carrying a big wooden box into a hole in the ground."

"That underground chamber where Gage and his girlfriend were trapped a couple months ago?" Parker asked.

"Maybe. I don't know. I'm going to try to find out."

"Don't go up there again," Parker said.

"If I do go, I won't go alone," she said.

"Get Rob to go with you. Or better yet, stay home."

"I don't want Rob to go with me. Maybe Gage can come."

"Rob wants to be your bodyguard, why not let him?" Parker yawned.

"Go to bed," Paige said. "And don't worry about me."

"I figure I probably owe you a little worrying." He patted her shoulder, then turned and shuffled down the hall to his room. Paige returned to her room and bed, but didn't go to sleep. She was going to end up back at the resort sooner or later, she knew. She wouldn't go alone, but she wouldn't sit here doing nothing and waiting for others to solve this mystery.

MAYA RENFRO WAS a petite dynamo whose shoulder-length black hair was streaked with blue. Even at seven thirty in the morning, she bounced into the Cake Walk Café with all the energy she displayed as coach of Eagle Mountain High's girls' basketball team. "Paige, it's so good to see you," she said. "And wow, doesn't this place look great? I haven't been here since they reopened. Gage told me a driver crashed into it this summer."

"Yes. The owner, Iris Desmet, decided as long as she was rebuilding, she would expand and add a coffee bar." She ushered her friend to a table. "How are you? And how is Casey?" Casey was Maya's five-year-old niece, who lived with Maya and Gage since her parents' murders that summer.

"She's great. Last week she asked if, when Gage and I get married, she can change her name, too, so we all match." Maya snatched a paper napkin from the dispenser on the table and dabbed at her eyes. "Sorry—I still get teary thinking about it."

"That's terrific," Paige said. "I guess she's really taken to Gage?"

"He's amazing," Maya said. "For a man who swore he was a confirmed bachelor, he's turning out to be a really great father. We don't want Casey to ever forget her real parents, but it's nice to think the three of us can be a new family together."

She pulled out a chair and sank into it. "Now you've heard all about me—what did you want to see me about so early in the morning?"

"I wanted to catch you before school." And before Rob was up, watching her and questioning her. Paige sat across from Maya. "I hate to bring up a painful subject, but I wanted to ask about the underground chamber up at Eagle Mountain Resort where you and Gage and Casey were held prisoner."

Maya's smile vanished and her shoulders slumped. "What about it?"

"Where was it on the property, exactly?"

"Paige, why would you want to know that?"

She shifted in her chair. "It's kind of a long story."

"Buy me a latte and I'll give you all the time you need."

Two vanilla soy lattes later, Paige had spilled the whole story of seeing the two men disappear into a trapdoor in the forest floor with a mysterious crate, how they had later shot at her, and the drive-by shooting at her home.

"Wow!" Maya said, when the story concluded. "It definitely sounds like you stumbled onto something big. But I don't think the trapdoor you saw was over the chamber where Gage and I were."

"No?"

"No." Maya sipped her latte, then wiped foam from above her lips. "We weren't near the fence at all. I'm surprised Travis didn't tell you that already."

"I wanted to double-check." After all, Maya was the one who had been held prisoner in that chamber.

"What I don't get is why bother going through a trapdoor when there was an exit right onto the resort's main street?" Maya asked.

"So, maybe there's another chamber?" Paige said.

"Maybe there are a bunch of them. There are a lot of mines in the mountains around here, and mine tunnels, right?"

"I guess so."

"Have you talked to Gage about any of this?" Maya asked.

"No. I thought it would be easier to talk to you. I mean, he can't really tell me anything because he's a cop."

"I might be a little prejudiced, but I think he's a good one," Maya said. "You should leave the investigating to him."

"I'm not investigating," Paige said. "I'm just curious. After all, those bullets were aimed at me. You can't blame me for wanting to know why. I wonder if I can get my hands on a map of the resort. Maybe the planning commission has something." She frowned. "Of course, they won't let me look at it."

"Why not?"

"The mayor, Larry Rowe, was head of the planning commission before he ran for mayor. He still has a grudge against me because my environmental group kept the project from going forward."

"You need to be careful," Maya said. "A lot of bad things have happened that are associated with the resort property. You couldn't pay me to go up there again."

"I understand why you feel that way," Paige said. "But if everyone avoids the property, it allows whoever is up there to get away with whatever they want. Whatever they were hiding in that space was something they didn't want me to see. I want to find out what it was and expose them."

"You need to let the sheriff's department do that."

"I will let them handle anything that turns out to be illegal," Paige said. "But that doesn't mean that, as an ordinary citizen, I can't ask questions and try to gather information. It's what I'm trained to do, as an activist."

"So who are you going to question about all of this?" Maya asked.

"I'll start with the new owners of the property, CNG Development."

"I'm sure Travis and Gage have already thought of that."

"I'm sure they have," Paige said. "But these corporate types won't tell the cops anything. They'll talk to me.

How do you think I got the scoop on Eagle Mountain Resort? I made phone calls and asked questions. There's nothing dangerous about that."

"It sounds safe enough." Maya pushed aside her empty cup. "As long as you don't ask the wrong person the wrong question."

"I'll be careful." Truth be told, she was excited about the prospect. Since they'd won the injunction against building Eagle Mountain Resort and the challenge over the gate blocking the Dakota Ridge Trail, life had felt a little stale. She looked forward to the challenge of finding out what was really happening on the former resort property. She would succeed where others had failed.

DEA SENIOR DETECTIVE Dale Foster was a busy man with no patience for time wasting, so when Rob placed his call to his supervisor the next morning, he got right to the point. "I'm here in Eagle Mountain," he said. "Sheriff Walker has requested the DEA reopen our investigation of that underground laboratory we looked into up here last month."

"What are you doing in Eagle Mountain?" Foster asked. "And why did the sheriff contact you instead of contacting our office?"

"I came to do some fly-fishing," Rob lied. "I ran into the sheriff yesterday and he relayed the request."

"Humph."

Rob's gut clenched. So much for thinking he would get away with that lame explanation.

"Why does Walker want us to reopen the investigation?" Foster asked. "You told me you didn't find anything. I trust you went over the location thoroughly."

"I did. But we were looking for any indication of illegal drug manufacturing. The sheriff suspects something else might have been going on down there."

"What?" Foster barked the word, an impatient man becoming more impatient.

"The week after we left, one of Walker's deputies found a dead man in the location," Rob said. "He had been missing about a month, and the medical examiner confirms he had been dead about that long, but someone had strung up his body in that old lab space underground. Originally, the ME was unable to determine the cause of death, but more recent tests indicate the man died from exposure to tularemia."

"What is tularemia?"

"Rabbit fever. But of more interest to us, it's something that the US government considered as a possible biological weapon in World War II. You remember in my report I mentioned that we were asked to rule out the lab's use during that time period."

"And you determined nothing in the lab was that old. So I repeat—what does this have to do with us?"

"Walker wants us to take another look, see if we can detect any tularemia in the space."

"Tell him to call the health department. That's not under our purview."

Rob had expected this answer. Like every government agency these days, the DEA was chronically underfunded and understaffed. "I'll tell him, sir."

"When are you coming back to work?" Foster asked.

"I have six days left on my vacation," Rob said.

"Humph." This time the sound was uttered with a little less ire behind it.

"Is there anything else you'd like me to tell Sheriff Walker?" Rob asked.

"Tell him I'm sorry we can't help him. And, Allerton?"

"Yes, sir?"

"Let the sheriff handle this. You stick to fish."

"Of course, sir."

They ended the conversation and Rob tucked his phone back into the pocket of his jeans. The only fish he wanted to catch right now were the two men who had fired those shots yesterday. If they led him to the real reason for Henry Hake's death, so much the better. But he'd be careful not to act in any official capacity.

He stepped out of the room, locking the door behind him. When he turned he was surprised to see Parker Riddell walking toward him. The young man looked healthier than he had the last time Rob had seen him— he had gained a few pounds and lost the sickly pallor Rob associated with addicts. "Hello, Parker," he said.

"Hey." He stopped in front of Rob, arms crossed over his chest, expression somber. "Paige told me what happened," he said. "With those guys shooting at her, up at the resort, and here in front of the house."

"I tried to persuade her to leave until this was resolved," Rob said. "She refused."

"Yeah, well, no surprise there. Look up *stubborn* in the dictionary and there's Paige's picture." He ran a hand through his close-cropped hair. "I need to ask you a favor."

"Oh?" Rob waited, wary. It wasn't as if he and this young man were on friendly terms.

"Look after her," Parker said. "I mean, I can't be here all the time, but she said you're on vacation, and you're here anyway, so maybe it wouldn't be a real hardship on you to stay close."

"Paige doesn't like me."

Parker didn't exactly smile, but his expression did lighten. "Oh, she likes you. She just doesn't want to admit it. Since that fiasco with her ex she likes to pretend she doesn't need a man in her life, but it's all bluff."

"What was the fiasco with her ex?" This was the first Rob had heard about an ex.

Parker frowned. "I don't know the whole story, but I guess he started out nice when they first married and ended up being a real jerk. I don't know if he actually hit her, or just threatened her, but they sure didn't end up on speaking terms, and ever since she's been kind of standoffish with men."

Rob supposed he could take comfort in knowing he wasn't being singled out for the cold shoulder. But the idea that a man—Paige's husband—had threatened her made him feel like finding the guy and making him regret he had ever come near her.

"I'm sorry to hear that," Rob said, his voice deceptively mild.

"Honestly, I think one of the reasons she's so hostile toward you—besides the trouble you and I had—is that she's attracted to you and fighting it," Parker said.

Was Paige attracted to him, or was Parker pouring it on thick to get him to stick around? "I'll keep an eye on her," he said. "As much as she'll let me."

"Thanks." Paige's brother shoved his hands in his pockets, apparently not ready to leave.

"Is there something else?" Rob asked.

Parker sighed. "Yeah. Last night, she talked about going back up to the resort and trying to find out what's going on. Don't let her go alone. I mean, I get that she wants to be independent, but she's not bulletproof."

"I won't let her go up there—alone or otherwise."

"Good. Well, I need to go. I have a class." He nodded and shuffled off.

Downstairs, the dining room off the kitchen was empty. A long cherry table held a single place setting, with a linen napkin, gold-trimmed china plate and polished flatware. A fruit cup in a crystal dish sat in the center of the plate, and a buffet against the wall held a silver coffee service and two covered chafing dishes.

As Rob stood surveying the scene, Paige came in from the kitchen carrying a bakery box. "Good morning," she said.

"This looks impressive," he said, indicating the table. "Am I your only guest?"

"I have an older couple staying a few nights. They were up early and are already off for a day of Jeeping on the backcountry trails." She began arranging muffins on a glass serving tray. "There's an egg casserole in the chafing dish," she said. "Help yourself."

He moved the fruit cup to one side, carried the plate to the buffet and selected a muffin from the tray. "You're up and about early."

"I like to get an early start."

"Do you have time to have coffee with me?" he asked, before she could retreat to the kitchen.

She hesitated, then sat in the chair across from him. "What are your plans for the day?" she asked, as he sat and tucked into his breakfast.

"That depends." He sipped the coffee, which was hot and strong, exactly the way he preferred it. "What are *your* plans?"

"Why are you asking?"

"Because I'm staying with you." He split the muffin—blueberry—and slid in a pat of butter.

"Rob, I—"

"Don't argue, Paige." He bit into the muffin and had to suppress a sigh. It practically melted in his mouth. He swallowed and picked up his fork. "Did you make all this? It's delicious."

"I picked them up at the Cake Walk Café earlier this morning," she said. "And don't change the subject. I don't need you to babysit me."

"We both know you'll be safer with someone to watch your back. You do what you need to do and try to forget I'm here." He savored the first bite of the egg-cheese-and-sausage casserole.

She snorted—an unladylike and at the same time endearing sound. Or maybe he was being influenced by the amazing breakfast.

She sipped her coffee, then set the cup down with a clink against the saucer. "I need to see about getting the door replaced, order some supplies and run some errands," she said.

"Consider me your chauffeur."

"I don't need—"

He set down his fork and looked her in the eye. "Maybe you don't, but I do. I need to know you're safe."

Her lips parted and her eyes widened. If the table hadn't been between them, he would have been tempted to lean across and kiss her, just to see what kind of reaction he would get. Had Parker been right when he had said she was attracted to him? Was the attraction strong enough for her to act on it?

"Why do you care?" she asked. "And don't give me that line about being responsible for me now."

He sat back, hiding his disappointment. No, she wasn't *that* attracted to him. "How about this for a reason?" he asked. "You may be our best chance of solving this case."

"How do you figure that?"

"We want to catch these guys and find out what they're up to. You're the only one who got a good look at them. They want you. If they do try to come after you again, we want to be ready."

"So you want to use me as bait?" Her voice rose on the last word, almost a squeak.

"No. I'm not going to let you wait for them out in the open. But if they do come back, I'm going to be here and I'm going to be ready to stop them."

She nodded, subdued. "All right."

She remained silent while he finished his breakfast, his attention focused on the food, though he was acutely aware of the woman across from him, close enough to brush his hand against. But she might as well have worn a sign around her neck that declared Don't Touch.

The doorbell rang and she jumped. "Are you expecting someone?" he asked.

"No." She stared toward the door, but didn't move. Deny it all she liked, she was clearly still upset by what had happened yesterday.

He pushed back his chair, wiped his mouth and dropped the napkin on his empty plate. "Let's go see who it is."

Chapter Seven

Rob had probably intended to lead the way to the front door, but Paige stepped in front of him. After all, this was her house. Whoever was there wanted to see her. She wasn't going to let what had happened yesterday keep her from answering her own door. He trailed behind her. The doorbell sounded again and her stomach fluttered as if she had swallowed live eels. She shoved her nervousness aside and focused instead on how angry it made her that two lowlifes she didn't even know had frightened her this way.

Relief flooded her when she looked through the security peephole and saw the calm face of the sheriff looking back at her. She unlocked the door and swung it open. "Have you found something?" she asked.

"We haven't found the men who shot at you," he said. He looked down at the splintered door. "Only the one burst of fire? They didn't try a second round of shots?"

"I already had Paige on the ground and returned fire." Rob stepped forward, one hand on Paige's shoulder. She should have resisted the gesture, but instead, she had to fight not to lean back into his strength. "They probably didn't want to risk sticking around," Rob said.

"I'm having the door replaced today," Paige said. "As soon as I file a claim with my insurance company."

"Adelaide can give you a case number if they need it," Travis said. "May I come in?"

"Of course." She stepped back and he moved past her. Rob shut and locked the door.

"Let's go in here," Travis said, leading the way into the dining room. He took an envelope from his pocket and emptied its contents onto the table.

"My necklace," she said, and scooped up the gold chain with the familiar bird charm.

"Is this the necklace you lost up by the resort?" Travis asked.

"Yes. Where did you find it?"

"Rob and I went up to the trail yesterday after we talked to you and took a look around," Travis said. "When we got back to my SUV, someone had taped this to the driver's-side door."

"They made sure we didn't miss it," Rob said.

"Another hiker must have found it and assumed it belonged to whoever was in your vehicle," she said. She examined the necklace. It was unharmed. "Or maybe they just wanted to turn it in to the police."

"We didn't see anyone else on the trail coming or going," Rob said. "We didn't pass any other cars or hear anyone, or see anyone on the other side of the fence at the resort. And there were no other cars in the parking area."

She looked from one man to the other. Their serious expressions were starting to worry her. "Someone must have been up there," she said. "Someone had to leave the necklace for you."

"We're thinking it was someone who didn't want us to

see them," Rob said. "Someone who wanted us to know they knew about you."

A shudder went through her at the words. "Why would they do that?" She tried to put on the necklace, fumbling with the clasp.

Rob stepped up behind her. "Let me." His fingers brushed the back of her neck as he fastened the necklace, sending heat radiating through her.

"I don't know what their motives might have been," Travis said. "Maybe it is as simple as them wanting the necklace returned to you. It's possible the person who put the necklace there didn't have anything to do with the shooting. Have you remembered anything else about the men you saw yesterday that can help us find them?"

Rob had finished hooking the necklace, but he remained standing behind her, one hand on her shoulder. She told herself she should move away from him, but couldn't make herself do it. "I'm sorry—no," she said. "Everything happened so fast."

"I've got a call in to CNG Development," Travis said. "We want permission to go up there and search. I'm waiting to hear back from them."

"I talked to my boss this morning," Rob said. "He says this really is out of our area of expertise. He suggested you contact the public health department. Maybe they can test for tularemia in that lab."

Travis nodded. "That's a good idea—if we can get permission to go back in."

Paige looked from one man to the other. "Tularemia? What the heck is that?"

"Rabbit fever," Rob said.

When he didn't offer anything more, she glared at him. "Why do you care about rabbit fever?"

"It's one of the agents the government was supposedly testing during World War II for use as a weapon," Travis said.

"And?" she asked.

"And I can't tell you anything else."

She frowned. It wasn't the answer she wanted, but about what she had expected. "Is there anything else you can tell me about this case? Any leads on the men who fired on me, or their vehicle?"

The sheriff shook his head. "We don't have anything yet, but we're going to keep looking." He turned to Rob. "Are you going to be around for a while?"

"I'm here all week, but not in an official capacity," Rob said.

"If I needed backup, could you help out?"

"Yes."

"Good. I'll keep it in mind."

"I want to go back up there," Paige said. "To the resort."

Both men looked at her as if she had sprouted an extra head. "That's a bad idea," Rob said.

"I agree," Travis said. "I'm considering closing the trail to public access until we get to the bottom of this."

"You can't close the trail unless you station someone at the trailhead to enforce the order," Paige said. "And you don't have the manpower to do that. Besides, it's not as if that many people go up there."

"You don't need to go up there," Travis said.

"I'll be fine," she said. "And I'll take my bodyguard." She looked at Rob.

"You can't go on CNG property without their permission," Travis said.

"I know. I'll stay on the public side of the fence. I just

want—I need—to take another look at the scene. Maybe being there again will trigger my memory of something that will help you find these men."

Travis gave her a hard look, but she met his gaze and didn't flinch. "All right," he said. "Then I guess that means we're all going. Together."

TRAVIS HAD A meeting he had to attend, so they agreed to meet up at the sheriff's department later that afternoon. Paige had spent her morning with Rob by her side, dealing with her insurance company and arranging to have the front door replaced. He had been quiet and unobtrusive, but there was no ignoring his presence—filling up the room. What was it about the man that he seemed to take up so much space, and use up more than his share of oxygen?

"Don't you have something else you need to be doing?" she asked.

"Not really."

"You didn't take a week's vacation to hang out with me."

"I can think of worse ways to spend my time." He sat back in his chair, regarding her with a hint of a smile, eyelids at half-mast. His expression should have come across as lazy and indolent, but instead conveyed a feline sensuality, as if he was feigning his lack of energy and at any moment might pounce. "You're almost pleasant when you aren't angry with me."

"You're making me nervous," she said.

"Interesting. You don't strike me as a woman who is easily unnerved."

She shuffled the papers on the table in front of her.

"I think having your life threatened twice in one day would upset anyone."

He sat up straight. His flirtatious mood had vanished. "You're right," he said. "I didn't mean to make light of what happened."

"I've been going over and over everything so much my head hurts." She pushed the papers—insurance forms and measurements for the new door—aside. "Let's talk about something else."

"Such as?"

"If we're going to be spending so much time together, we should get to know each other better. I really don't know much about you."

"All right," he said. "What would you like to know?"

"Have you ever been married?"

He blinked. He obviously hadn't been expecting that one. Why did it feel like such a victory to throw Mr. Cool off guard? "No," he said.

"Why not?"

He shrugged. "I never found the right woman."

"What a cliché. You can do better than that, can't you?" She leaned across the table toward him. "Are you afraid of making a commitment?"

"You're one to talk, Ms. Independent." He scooted his chair closer. "Though I understand you've been married before. What was he like?"

"How did you know that?" Had he been checking up on her?

"Parker mentioned it."

"Parker? When?"

"This morning, actually. He came to my room and asked me to look after you."

A storm of emotions swept over her—tenderness,

sadness, annoyance. "That really wasn't necessary," she said.

"Maybe not. It made me curious about your ex, though."

"My ex was not a nice person." She slid her chair back. "And that's all I'm going to say on the subject." Her marriage had been a bad time in her life, when a man she had made the mistake of trusting had used love as a weapon to break her. It had taken a long time for her to find her way back to herself after that. Like someone who had suffered a long, debilitating illness, she had had to build her strength slowly. She was determined to never again go back to that dark place.

Rob looked as if he wanted to argue, but he thought better of it. "Parker looked good," he said. "Healthy."

"He is. Good and healthy."

"He said he had a class this morning. What's he studying?"

"History. I told him there weren't many jobs in that field, but he's convinced he can make it work. And it's a subject he loves, so I'm not going to discourage him. Right now he's just taking the basics, with a couple of extra history courses thrown in. And he's working, as a delivery driver for Peggy's Pizza here in town. And he volunteers at the local history museum."

Rob nodded. "He's keeping busy. That's good."

"He is good. He's staying out of trouble."

"Has he made friends here in town? A girlfriend, maybe?"

Did Parker have a girlfriend? Why hadn't she wondered about that before? "I don't think so," she said. Though maybe that explained where he was disappearing to in his off hours. But if it was a girl, why hadn't he said so? Did he think she wouldn't approve?

Paige realized Rob had continued talking. "I'm sorry," she said. "I was thinking of something else. What did you say?"

"I asked if he planned to continue living here with you for a while."

"At least until he finishes school," she said. "Why shouldn't he? I like having him here."

"No reason," Rob said. "I just wondered. I wish him luck."

If he was so concerned about Parker's future, why had he been so dogged in sending him to jail? But that was an old argument that wasn't worth rehashing. "Why did you go into law enforcement?" she asked. "And why the DEA? Don't you get tired of arresting people and putting them in jail?"

His expression hardened. "The people I arrest need to be stopped and punished. Don't forget that I put away the people who make the drugs that ruin lives—the way Parker's life was almost ruined."

"All right. I'll concede that you probably do some good."

"So what is your problem?"

"Law enforcement sees the world in black-and-white. I see so many shades of gray."

"No, you don't," he countered. "You see the world in black-and-white, too, but your definition of black-and-white is different from mine, so that makes me wrong."

"That's not true!"

"I don't want to argue with you." He leaned toward her. "We can admit that the two of us are never going to agree on everything, but we don't have to be adversaries. People like me can sharpen your vision—and people like you can temper mine."

Where was the hard-nosed officer she had sparred with when Parker was awaiting trial and sentencing? It embarrassed her a little to remember some of the shouting matches they had had in the courthouse hallways back then. The man across from her now was smart and reasonable—and even compassionate. "I never thought of it that way before," she said. "But I guess you're right."

He sat back. "And I know how much you hate to admit that."

"I guess you're doing it already," she said. "Trying to sharpen my vision."

"And what do you see?"

She saw a man who was more nuanced than she had given him credit for. A man who tempted her to be far more vulnerable than she liked. Rob made her think about taking risks—an exhilarating feeling, but one she wasn't sure she would have the courage to act on. She stood. "Come on. It's almost time to meet Travis," she said.

She walked out of the room, aware of his gaze on her as she moved past him. It had all the force and heat of a physical caress.

ROB AND PAIGE met Travis and Gage at the sheriff's department and caravanned to the parking area for the Dakota Ridge Trail. "We can't trespass on CNG property," Travis said. "The company has referred me to their lawyers, but the legal team hasn't returned my calls."

"I checked this morning and the gate is still locked and there's no sign of anyone around the place," Gage said. "Of course, we have the authority to break the lock."

"Which I don't want to do if we don't have to," Travis said. "If no one is around, there's no point. Without a warrant, we can't search any of the buildings."

"So what's the plan?" Rob asked.

"Paige thinks retracing her steps that day might help her remember more about what happened," Travis said. "So that's what we'll do." He motioned for her to lead the way.

She shouldered the day pack she had brought and started up the trail, Rob close behind her. She walked quickly, with a sure stride, her head up, back straight. If she was nervous, she certainly didn't show it.

No one said anything for the first quarter mile of walking, until the trail began to parallel the former resort property's fence. Paige slowed, scanning the fence line, until she came to the break in the underbrush that Travis and Rob had investigated the day before. "I think about here was where I heard something and ducked to the side to look." She parted the low-growing branches of scrub oak with her hands and darted into the open space next to the fence. Rob and Travis followed, crowding in close around her. Gage stayed on the trail to keep watch.

For the second time in as many days, Rob looked through the fence to a stretch of vacant forest, at dry leaves carpeting the ground beneath the white trunks of aspens and the dark green branches of evergreens. Nothing disturbed the peacefulness of the scene, and the only sound was the soft whisper of the dry aspen leaves that still clung to the trees.

"What's that?" Travis whispered. He pointed at a spot to their right.

Rob turned his head and caught a glimpse of a figure in the distance, running away from them.

"Hey!" Travis called. "Come here!"

The figure wasn't completely visible through the trees, but Rob thought it slowed for a fraction of a second before running away even faster.

Travis grasped the iron bars of the fence. "Stop! Police!" But his shouts went unheeded.

"Let's go back," Paige said, already pushing aside the oak branches. "Whoever it was is gone."

"What's going on?" Gage asked, as they emerged onto the trail.

"We saw someone," Travis said. "Someone who ran when I ordered him to stop."

They hurried down the trail. Rob kept watch along the way for any sign of the fleeing man. It had been a man, he was sure, though not a big one—not someone who fitted the description Paige had given them. "Do you think the person we saw was either of the men who shot at you?" he asked, wanting to confirm his opinion.

"I don't know," she said. "I didn't get a good look. I don't even know that it was a man. Maybe it was a deer or elk or something."

"It was a man," Travis said. A slight man wearing dark clothes, not camouflage.

In the parking area, Travis stopped beside his SUV and scanned the small gravel lot. "Whoever that was must be parked up by the resort," he said.

"They could be behind CNG's gate," Gage said. "We wouldn't necessarily be able to see their car from the road."

"We'll go check."

Travis and Gage climbed into the SUV and left. Rob took Paige's arm. "Come on. Let's follow them," he said.

"We don't need to do that," she said. "Let's go back to town and wait there."

"They might need help," Rob said. He started the truck and followed Travis and Gage out onto the road.

The sheriff turned in at the entrance to CNG's property and stopped at the gate, his engine idling. He and Gage both climbed out of the SUV. Rob got out and followed them, though Paige remained in the truck. The three men looked through the bars of the gate, scanning the property, alert for the flash of sunlight on chrome or the metallic sheen of an automobile. "I don't see anything," Rob said after a moment.

"Me either." Travis studied the broken asphalt of the drive. "It's impossible to tell if anyone has driven over this recently." He studied the gate. "Though it doesn't look to me as if this chain and padlock have been moved in a while." He indicated the fine road dust sifted over the metal.

Gage looked around. "Maybe he parked somewhere near here and scaled the fence—or found a break and slipped through."

"How much farther does the road go?" Rob asked.

"Not far," Travis said. "It dead-ends in another fifty feet or so."

"Let's take a look," Gage said.

"Are we going back to town now?" Paige asked, when Rob returned to the car.

"In a minute. We just want to check the end of the road." He waited while Travis turned the SUV around, then followed him back down the drive. The sheriff had just started to turn onto the pavement when a dark-colored, older-model sedan came barreling toward them. Travis had to jerk the wheel sharply to the left to avoid being sideswiped.

Paige screamed and grabbed on to Rob, who had

stomped on the brakes, narrowly avoiding a collision into the rear of the SUV. Travis brought his vehicle around and lurched onto the road, in pursuit of the vehicle, which had already disappeared around a curve.

"Hold on!" Rob said, and shot after them.

"Did you see the license plate?" he asked, as they barreled down the road.

"I didn't see anything," Paige said. Her fingers dug into Rob's shoulder as they skidded around a sharp curve. "Slow down. You're going to get us killed."

"Sit back," Rob ordered.

She released her hold on him and did so, though Rob could hear her gasps and moans each time the truck skidded in gravel or rocketed over a rough spot in the pavement. They rounded yet another curve to find a straight stretch of empty road ahead. The SUV sped up even more, and Rob followed suit, but there was no sign of the sedan.

"I hope we haven't lost him," Rob said.

"He could be anywhere," Paige said. "On a side road or in a driveway—or halfway to Junction by now. And you don't even know if he had anything to do with what happened to me."

"It seems pretty suspicious if you run when a cop tells you to stop," Rob said.

"Not everyone trusts the police," she said.

Rob said nothing, but continued to follow the sheriff's SUV. By the time they reached Eagle Mountain, Travis had slowed to the speed limit. Rob's cell phone rang and he hit the button on the steering wheel to answer it.

"We lost him." Gage's voice filled the car. "Did either of you get a look at the plate?"

"No," Rob said.

"Paige?" Gage asked.

"No," she said.

"All right. You two can go on back to Paige's place. Travis and I are going to drive around a little more. Maybe we'll get lucky and spot him."

"Will do." He ended the call and drove to the Bear's Den, where he parked in the side lot.

Paige had her door open and was out of the car and headed up the walk before he could come around to her side. "Where are you going in such a hurry?" he asked, when he caught up with her in the entryway.

"I'm going to my room."

She started to turn away, but he took her arm and turned her to face him. Her skin was the color of paste and her lip trembled, as if she was fighting tears. "Hey," he said. "Are you okay?"

"I'm fine." But everything about her, from the haunted look in her eyes to the pinched sound of her voice, said that statement was a lie. Seeing that man up there and the subsequent chase had shaken her up more than he had imagined.

"It's going to be okay," he said.

He tried to pull her close, but she jerked free from his grasp. "I'm going to lie down," she said. She almost ran down the hall, and half a second later he heard a door slam.

Rob frowned after her, debating knocking on her door and demanding that she talk to him. But he had already learned that pushing Paige was never a good idea. Later, when she came out again, he would try to get her to open up about what had her so upset.

The back door opened and Parker came in. He started

when he saw Rob. "I, uh, didn't know you were still here," he said. He looked around. "Where's Paige?"

"In her room." Rob took a glass from the cabinet by the sink and filled it with water. "She's resting."

As if to prove him a liar, the door to Paige's room opened and she came down the hall to join them in the kitchen. She ignored Rob and walked straight to Parker, grabbed his arm and shook it. "What were you doing up at Eagle Mountain Resort this afternoon?" she demanded.

Chapter Eight

Paige was counting on Rob's presence to force Parker to tell the truth about what he had been up to this afternoon. Though she had caught only a fleeting glimpse of the figure running through the trees, the punched-in-the-gut feeling that glimpse had engendered had raised her worst fears. The sight of Parker's car speeding away from them had confirmed those fears.

She shook his arm again. "Don't lie to me," she said. "I saw you."

Parker's face had lost all color. He glanced at Rob, desperation in his eyes. Rob folded his arms across his chest and leaned back against the counter. "Yes, tell us what you were doing up there."

Parker slid his arms out of the straps of his backpack and let it fall to the floor with a thud. "I wasn't doing anything wrong," he said.

"You were trespassing," Rob said.

Parker jutted his chin out. "Are you going to turn me in for that?"

Paige wondered if she was the only one who recognized the fear behind her brother's defiant glare.

"That depends," Rob said.

Parker stared at the floor, the muscles of his jaw

clenching and unclenching. "I'm helping Professor Gibson with a research project," he said.

"Professor Gibson?" Paige searched her memory for the name. "The old man who helped Brenda get the grant for the history museum?"

"Yeah."

"Who's Professor Gibson?" Rob asked. "One of your instructors?"

"No, he's retired." Parker shoved his hands in the front pockets of his jeans. "But he's interested in the history of this area. He and I are trying to find the location of that World War II government research lab—the one that was developing biological and chemical weapons."

"We already determined the underground lab on the resort property isn't old enough to have been in use during the war," Rob said.

"That lab, sure," Parker said. "The professor thinks there's another one on that property."

"What makes him think that?" Paige asked.

"He's got all the declassified documents from the project, and letters and maps and stuff," Parker said. "He goes over them and finds out stuff, but he's eighty years old and it's hard for him to get up in the mountains and check stuff out. That's where I come in."

"So you were on the resort property, looking for this supposed lab?" Rob asked.

"Well, yeah," Parker said. "I told the professor about Paige seeing those two guys carrying a box into a hole in the ground, and he thought it was a good possibility. I didn't touch anything, I swear. I just walked around and looked."

"Did you find another underground chamber that could have been used as a lab?" Paige asked.

"No." His shoulders sagged again. "You came along before I could see much."

"How did you get in?" Rob asked. "The gate is chained shut."

"There's a place about two-thirds of the way along the fence line on the east side," Parker said. "Part of a big tree fell on the fence and took it down part of the way. All I had to do was shimmy up the trunk and walk right in on the fallen log."

"Why did you run from us?" Rob asked.

"Because I knew if Paige saw me, she'd have kittens," he said. "And trespassing is a violation of my parole."

Paige went ice-cold all over. She hadn't thought of that. "Promise me you won't turn him in," she said to Rob, clasping her hands together in a begging gesture. "Please." When it came to her brother, she had no shame.

He gave her a long look she found impossible to interpret. He turned back to Parker. "Did you see anyone else while you were up there?"

Parker shook his head. "Just you and Paige and the sheriff."

"Do you swear you don't know anything about the two men who fired those shots at Paige?" Rob asked.

"I swear!" Parker straightened, the color high in his cheeks. "They tried to kill my sister. If I knew anything at all, I swear I'd tell you. Why wouldn't I?"

Rob didn't answer this question. "Did you see any signs that anyone had been up there recently?" he asked. "Tire tracks or new excavation or equipment?"

"Nothing like that. But I wasn't really up there that long before y'all came around." He turned to Paige again. "You don't think the sheriff recognized my car, do you?"

"I don't think so," she said. "But Travis is really

smart. You should drive my car for a few days, until this settles down."

"What are you going to do?" Parker asked Rob.

"I won't say anything to anyone," he said. "For now." He didn't look at Paige when he spoke, which was probably just as well, because she had to fight to keep from throwing her arms around his neck in gratitude. She definitely didn't want him thinking she owed him anything for this particular favor—though maybe she did.

"Thank you," she said. Then she turned to Parker. "And you tell the professor you are not breaking any more laws in the name of research. You're not even going to jaywalk across the street on your way to the campus library."

"I'm not stupid," he said.

"Then why are you acting like you are?" Paige asked.

"You can settle that debate later," Rob said. He straightened and came to stand beside Paige, facing Parker. "What has the professor learned about this World War II project?" he asked.

"A lot, I guess," Parker said. "I mean, most of it is based on that old book he used to own—the one that was destroyed before Brenda could auction it to raise money for the museum."

Rob sent Paige a questioning look.

"It was a rare book that purported to be an insider's story about the government project here in Rayford County," she explained. "Brenda's late husband had borrowed it from Professor Gibson and it was apparently worth a lot of money to collectors. One of them paid a former sheriff's deputy to destroy the book—no one has been able to figure out why."

"Right," Parker said. "But the professor has the notes

Brenda took when she read the book, as well as government documents about the project that have been declassified."

"Do the documents say where the lab was located?" Rob asked.

"Not exactly," Parker said. "A lot of the documents are blacked out—all the names and stuff like that."

"Redacted," Paige said.

"What?" Parker frowned at her.

"It's called redacted, when they black out things in documents."

"Whatever. Anyway, the professor has been comparing topographical features described in a few reports with the terrain around here, and he's sure that the lab was on or near the Eagle Mountain Resort property."

"Why is he so interested in finding it?" Rob asked.

Parker stared at him. He didn't say "Duh!" but Paige was sure he was thinking it.

"Something like that would be a significant historical discovery," she said.

"Yeah!" Parker said. "And I'd be listed as one of the people who located it. I'd have an important research credit before I even graduated. It could really help me get a great job later on. Plus, it would really rock to be famous for something like that."

"What kind of things did they try to make in that lab, do you know?" Rob asked.

Parker made a face. "It was nasty stuff, that's for sure. I think the professor said they experimented with botulism and anthrax and something called Q fever."

"What about tularemia?" Rob asked.

"Yeah, I think that was on the list. Why?"

He shrugged. "Just curious."

Parker picked up his backpack and slung it over one shoulder. "Are we okay now?" he asked.

"For now," Rob said.

Parker nodded and shuffled out of the room. Paige waited until his door closed behind him, then turned to Rob. "What was all that about tularemia?"

"Didn't we already have this conversation?" he asked.

"You and Travis said you couldn't tell me anything, but it keeps coming up. Why is it so important?"

"I still can't tell you." He put a hand on her shoulder. "Trust me on this," he said. "If it had anything to do with you or with your brother, I would tell you."

"You'll keep quiet about him being at the resort today, won't you?" she asked. "I know it was a really bad decision on his part, but it wasn't criminal."

"I won't say anything," he said. "But you have to be prepared for Travis to figure it out. He's no dummy, and a good investigator."

"And he has a lot on his plate right now," she said. "I hope finding a random stranger he glimpsed for a few seconds is low on the list."

"Before we saw Parker, did you get anything out of today?" Rob asked. "Did the visit shake loose any new memories?"

"No."

"Do you think you'd recognize the two men if you saw them again?"

"I do."

"That's simple, then. All we have to do is find them."

ROB TOOK ADVANTAGE of Parker's presence at the B and B to check in with the sheriff. He was curious to know if

Travis had recognized Parker, and if he had heard anything from CNG Development.

Adelaide Kinkaid sat at her usual post behind her desk in the lobby of the sheriff's department. When Rob stepped through the door the normally stern expression left her face, replaced by a smile that deepened the lines around her eyes. "Good morning, Agent Allerton," she said. "What can I do for you?"

"Good morning, Ms. Kinkaid," he said. "You're looking lovely this morning. That's a beautiful blouse you're wearing." The blouse was a purple-and-turquoise paisley print that wouldn't have been out of place at Woodstock.

Adelaide brushed her shoulder. "Oh, this old thing. I've had it forever."

Rob had a sudden image of a much younger Adelaide, a flower child with a beaded headband, dancing around at some outdoor concert in this very shirt. The idea was disconcerting, to say the least. "Is the sheriff in?" he asked.

"No. Lacy dragged him along with her to interview caterers for the wedding. You know, when I got married, my mother made a big bowl of punch and we served it with little finger sandwiches and after-dinner mints and called it good. But now brides want these big fancy dinners and dances that cost a small fortune." She leaned toward him. "Have you ever been married, Agent Allerton?"

"No."

"One of those confirmed bachelors, aren't you?" She pointed a pink-polished nail at him. "I know the type. You think you're immune to love and then one day you meet the right woman and bam!" She slammed her hand down on her desk, making him jump. "You're down for the count."

She made falling in love sound like a wrestling match. "I don't know—" he began.

"I know what I'm talking about," she insisted. "Gage was that way—such a ladies' man until Maya came along."

"Is Gage in?" Rob asked.

"No. He had to go over to the other end of the county to deal with a traffic accident. Some fool ran off the road and took out a section of Herbert Kowalski's fence. Two of his llamas got loose and Gage is having to help round them up before they cause another accident. That could take a while. Llamas can be hard to handle."

"I wouldn't know." And he hoped he never would.

She fixed her smile on him again. "Is there anything I can help you with?"

Adelaide struck him as the type to keep up with local gossip. "Have you heard anything else about what's going on up at the old Eagle Mountain Resort property?" he asked. "Has CNG revealed their plans?"

"They won't return the sheriff's calls, I can tell you that," she said. "Though my neighbor, Sandra, has a brother-in-law who works for a concrete company in Junction, and she said someone she thinks was from CNG called about getting bids to pour some building foundations. Which is interesting, considering they haven't even gotten approval from the county to proceed with any building. And I'm pretty sure the injunction that Paige's group got is still in place, and it prohibits any development on the site."

"Maybe they think they can go ahead without county approval," Rob said.

Adelaide snorted. "They'd better not try it. People here

are keeping an eye on them, and if they make one wrong move, Paige and her bunch, especially, will be on them."

"They're that dogged, are they?"

"I don't always agree with her, mind you, but Paige Riddell knows how to get things done." She shook her head. "Of course, being pushy like that isn't the most attractive trait in a woman—which may explain why she's still single."

"Maybe she's choosy about who she dates," Rob said. "And I like a woman who isn't afraid to stand up for what she believes in."

"Well, I—" The phone rang, interrupting her. She held up one finger, to signal he should wait, and answered.

While Adelaide dealt with the caller, Rob wandered over to look at a series of photographs on the wall—Travis, Gage, Dwight and other officers at various community events. One photo showed Travis on horseback, leading a parade. In another, Gage was surrounded by a group of schoolchildren. Rob felt a stab of envy. DEA agents weren't normally part of a community like this. He believed what he was doing was important, but the public didn't always recognize that.

"Now, that was interesting." Adelaide had hung up the phone and looked pleased with herself. "Something you might want to know."

"Oh?" He returned to stand in front of her desk. "What is it?"

"That call was from my friend Shirley, over at the county offices. You'll never guess who is on the agenda to address the county commissioners at their meeting tonight."

He could see she wanted him to ask the question, so he did. "Who?"

"A representative from CNG Development. Apparently, he wants to present their plans for the old Eagle Mountain Resort property."

"That is interesting," Rob said. "Any idea what he's going to talk about?"

"No." She picked up her phone. "I've got to call Travis. He's definitely going to want to be there."

"Yes." Rob would make it a point to be there, too. And he was sure Paige wouldn't want to miss it.

PAIGE SURVEYED THE new front door with a critical eye. It was a darker shade of red than the old one, but she decided she liked the look. And at least she wouldn't have to explain bullet holes to her guests.

She went inside and closed and locked the door behind her. Parker was at the computer, typing away. "What are you doing?" she asked.

"While you were outside I took a call from a woman who wanted to book a room for next month," he said.

"You should have put her on hold and come and gotten me," Paige said.

"Why? I took care of it." He finished typing and looked up. "She wanted the Miner's Suite and it was available for those dates, so I took her credit card information and she's all set."

Paige came to look over his shoulder. Everything about the reservation looked right. "Thanks," she said. "How did you know what to do?" It wasn't as if she had ever shown him her system—though maybe she should have.

"It doesn't take a genius to figure out," he said.

"Even though you are smarter than the average bear."

She ruffled his hair, which he hated, but he only ducked out of the way.

"What are you doing, hanging around here this morning, anyway?" she asked. "Don't you have class?"

"Not this morning."

"You're not scheduled to do a shift at the museum?"

"I told Brenda I needed to take the day off."

He avoided her gaze, which immediately set off an internal alarm bell. "A day off for what?" she asked.

"I promised Rob I'd stick around this morning and look after you. He had to go to town to do some stuff, but he didn't want to leave you alone."

"So you're my designated babysitter?"

"Hey, I couldn't exactly tell the man no, could I? I owe him."

"I'll certainly talk to him about payback when he gets here."

"Paige, don't give him a hard time," Parker said. "He's only trying to protect you. And I would have stuck around anyway, even if he hadn't asked."

"I don't need a keeper."

"Maybe not, but until those creeps who shot at you are found, you don't need to be here alone, either."

She was sensible enough to admit he was right, but the idea chafed. She was about to tell him so when the doorbell rang.

A glance through the peephole showed an attractive, sandy-haired man in his midforties, wearing sharply creased khakis and a peach-colored polo shirt that showed off a good tan, broad shoulders and a trim waist. Paige opened the door. "May I help you?"

"Are you Paige Riddell?" He held out his hand. "I'm Bryce Reed, chief financial officer of CNG Development. We own the property up on Dakota Ridge that was formerly the proposed site for something called Eagle Mountain Resort. I understand you were instrumental in halting that development."

"Yes." She eyed him warily. He seemed friendly enough, but even the friendliest person could be bent on wholesale habitat destruction. "My organization is very serious about protecting the fragile environment at that elevation," she said.

"Which is exactly what I want to talk to you about," he said. "May I come in?"

She couldn't think of a good reason to tell him no. Parker was here with her—not that she couldn't look after herself—and she was curious to hear what Bryce Reed had to say. She held the door open wider.

"This is my brother, Parker. Parker, this is Mr. Reed, with CNG Development." The two shook hands. Then Parker stepped back and crossed his arms, tattoos and tough-guy scowl on display. Paige ignored him. "We can talk in here," she said, leading the way into the family room she used as a space for guests to hang out when they didn't want to be in their rooms.

She took a seat on a sofa and he settled into an armchair adjacent to her. Parker stood in the doorway, as if blocking Reed's escape. She scowled at her brother, hoping he would get the message that she wanted him to leave, but he ignored her and continued to glower at the CNG spokesman.

Reed either didn't notice or pretended not to. "I saw the plans Hake Development had drawn up for the property," he said. "A very ambitious project."

"A ridiculous project," Paige said. "There isn't enough water up there to support the kind of development he wanted to do, and keeping the roads clear and mitigating the avalanche danger would be a logistical nightmare. Not to mention the impact on wildlife and native trees and—"

Reed held up a hand. "You don't have to convince me, Ms. Riddell," he said. "I agree with all the points you've made. CNG has a very different use in mind for the property—one that will have much less impact."

She relaxed a little. She didn't get the impression he was trying to distract her with his charm or sell her a pack of lies. She had had enough experience with that type that she could spot them within seconds of meeting them for the first time. "I'm interested in finding out more about your plan," she said.

"I appreciate you hearing me out," he said. "What we have in mind is a small, exclusive high-altitude research facility. A few researchers and interns living on-site in the summer months in very low-profile, low-impact buildings. In the late fall we would close up the place and secure everything through the winter, and reopen when the roads are clear in late spring or early summer. No need to plow the road or worry about avalanches, no impact on elk calving season, very little traffic. We think we can use solar for much of our energy, and are looking into rainwater collection systems for our water needs, as well as compostable toilets and other green initiatives."

She let his words sink in. "It sounds almost too good to be true," she said after a moment.

He laughed—a hearty, friendly sound. "After dealing with Hake Development, I'm sure it does," he said. "I read your group's presentation of your objections against the resort development and you made some very good points. We're trying to keep them in mind as we plan this project."

"What do you want from me?" she asked.

"No wasting time with you, is there?" He smiled, fine lines popping out around his blue eyes. He really was a very attractive man. He didn't have Rob's movie-star looks, but there was something very appealing about him. Not that she trusted men in general, handsome or not. "Obviously, we'd like your support, if we can get it," he said. "I'm supposed to give a presentation about our plans to the town council this evening. I think your presence and approval of our project would carry a lot of weight with the local government."

"Now you're just trying to flatter me," she said.

"Maybe a little. But can you blame me? I think we've got a great project here—something that will make good use of the land and, incidentally, get rid of what I gather has been something of a blight on the local landscape. You've seen the property as it is now—abandoned foundations, crumbling streets, and I understand it has even attracted a criminal element. That isn't what CNG wants at all. We've already locked the gate and added additional fencing to try to keep out trespassers."

"You put a lock on a gate over the public hiking trail," she said. "I have a court order for the lock to be removed, but so far CNG has ignored it."

"This is the first I've heard about it," he said, frowning. "I wasn't aware there was a public hiking trail through the property. I'll certainly have to look into that."

"There's a public easement at one corner," she said. "The trail has been there since the late 1800s. You can't legally block it."

"I'm sure we can come to some compromise that ensures our property rights are respected as well as maintaining the public's access to the trail."

"You can either remove the gate or move the fence," Paige said. "Until you do, I can't speak out in support of this development."

She waited for his anger, but instead, he gave another smile, this one almost sheepish. "You drive a hard bargain, Ms. Riddell, but a fair one. I'll see that the gate is opened."

Paige stood, and he rose also. "I'll come to the county commissioners' meeting this evening," she said. "I'm looking forward to your presentation. And I appreciate your talking to me."

He took her hand, his grasp warm and firm. "Thanks for listening," he said.

She walked with him to the foyer, but before he could leave, the front door opened and Rob walked in. He stared at the two of them, who were still hand in hand. "Hello," he said.

Paige slipped her hand from Bryce's. "Bryce Reed, this is Rob Allerton," she said. "Rob is a guest here at the B and B. Mr. Reed is with CNG Development."

"Good to meet you." Bryce shook hands with Rob, who continued to eye him as if he suspected him of some crime.

"Are you the CNG representative who's giving the presentation to the county commissioners this evening?" he asked.

How had Rob learned that? Paige wondered. Maybe Travis had told him.

"I guess it's true what they say about word getting around fast in small towns," Bryce said. "Yes, I'm going to be talking about our plans for the property up on Dakota Ridge." He turned to Paige once more. "I'd really like to take you up to the property and show you around," he said. "I want you to see exactly what we have in mind. And I'm sure you could offer some good suggestions."

"The last time I was up there, someone tried to kill me," she said.

Maybe she had hoped to shock him a little bit with this bold statement. Clearly, she succeeded. He blinked at her, mouth half-open, eyes wide—as if he had been hit in the head with a heavy object. "Kill you? I hope you're exaggerating."

"She's not." Rob moved in closer. "Two men fired on her while she was on the hiking trail that runs alongside the fence bordering your property. Later, they came here to try to finish the job."

"Two men, you say?" He had regained some of his composure, but his affable manner of earlier was gone. "What did they look like?"

"They were big," Paige said. "They wore camouflage, almost like soldiers. But I didn't really get a good look at them."

"They drove a dark sedan and the weapon was an AR-15," Rob said.

"That is unacceptable," Bryce said. He took Paige's hand once more. "I'm so sorry you had to go through that. I had heard some criminal types had been taking advantage of what they probably saw as abandoned property. I promise you, that is going to stop now."

The fierceness of his tone—and the murderous look in his eyes—sent a shiver through her. She withdrew her hand from his. "That's good to hear."

"If you know anything about this, you need to tell the sheriff," Rob said.

"I think I know how to handle my business," Bryce said, his voice mild, but his eyes still frigid. He nodded to Paige. "I'll see you tonight."

Rob opened the door and closed it again after Bryce had exited. He locked it, then leaned back against it, arms crossed. "What was he doing here?" he asked.

"He invited me to attend his presentation tonight," she said. "And he wants my support—well, the support of Eagle Mountain environmentalists—for CNG's plans."

"He wanted to size you up," Parker said.

She turned to her brother, who leaned back against the desk, his pose strikingly similar to Rob's. "What do you mean by that?" she asked.

"He wanted to see what the opposition looked like," Parker said. "What he was up against."

"I think Parker's right," Rob said. "He may have asked you for your support, but he really wanted to gauge what kind of a fight you were likely to put up."

"Maybe so," Paige said. "But my take is that he was being smart and trying to recruit me to his side. And he made some convincing arguments for his project."

"I think he knows something about those men who shot at you," Rob said.

"You saw the look on his face when I told him about them," she said. "He was stunned—truly shocked."

"Maybe." Rob looked doubtful. "I think he bears watching."

"I agree," Paige said. "And I will be watching him. But I don't think he's dangerous."

Rob moved past her, pausing at her side to touch her

arm and look into her eyes. "Don't underestimate him," he said, in a low voice that sent a hot tremor through her. "And don't underestimate what I'll do to protect you."

Chapter Nine

Parker consulted the map the professor had given him, and compared it to the landscape around him. The map was dotted with the crossed-pickaxes symbol that indicated the site of old mines, several of which were within the dark line that represented the boundary around CNG Development's Dakota Ridge property. "There may be others that aren't marked on here," Professor Gibson had said when he gave Parker the map. "But these are a good place to start. Locate as many as you can and report back to me."

Yes, he had promised Paige he wouldn't come back up here, but that had been fear talking. Now that he had had time to think about it, he couldn't see what harm could come from him taking another look at the property. If CNG really was going to develop the place, he and the professor didn't have much time left to make their discovery. And with everyone focused on Bryce Reed's presentation to the county commissioners that evening, Parker had figured this was a good time to finish what he had intended to do before the sheriff had interrupted him the other day.

Paige would have had a fit if she knew he was back up here, of course, but the way Parker saw it, the property was unoccupied—practically abandoned. And he was engaged in important historical research, not petty vandalism. He doubted CNG or the local cops would see it that way, so he had been careful to park his car out of sight, and to come into the property through the break in the fence, where no one could see him from the road or the hiking trail.

Rob Allerton definitely wouldn't approve of what he was doing, though he had been cool about not turning Parker in to the sheriff when he'd recognized him here the other day. Parker hadn't expected that, and it made him like the cop in spite of himself.

He still couldn't decide how he felt having the DEA agent living in the same house. Paige could pretend all she wanted that Rob wasn't interested in her, but Parker knew he was right. Was that a good or a bad thing? She needed something to focus on besides Parker. He hadn't said anything to his sister yet, but he was thinking of moving to Boulder next year and enrolling in the University of Colorado. Professor Gibson had already said he would recommend Parker for admission, and even help him get a scholarship to study history.

The professor had been a surprise since Parker moved to Eagle Mountain. The old guy had really taken an interest in Parker. It was an odd friendship—a young ex-con and a staid old professor—but Gibson was supersharp, and the two had just hit it off. The research they were doing together fascinated Parker, and the professor had helped him to see a future for himself that didn't involve menial jobs and always running from the stigma of his past mistakes.

The professor had determined that the government's

secret World War II lab had been located in this area. He had unearthed accounts that mentioned a rocky ridge he thought was probably Dakota Ridge, and a nearby creek, the location of which matched up with the creek that ran along the back side of CNG's property. One letter the professor had found mentioned a view of Mount Wiley, which could be seen from where Parker was standing right now.

The problem was construction on the property had altered some of the natural terrain. Had the gully shown on the map been filled in or diverted to construct that street? Had the giant boulder indicated on the map been blasted into pieces to make room for the foundation of a house? It didn't help that Parker hadn't had much experience reading maps and orienteering, or that he had only about an hour and a half before it would be too dark to see much of anything. Where was a good GPS coordinate when you needed it?

He took a few steps toward a clearing ahead, thinking if he got out of the trees, maybe he could figure out where he was, but a loud noise startled him. Heart pounding, he hurried back into the thick undergrowth. The heavy *whump! whump! whump!* of a helicopter echoed off the rock face of the ridge behind him, growing so loud Parker wanted to cover his ears.

But he remained still, craning his neck and trying to see through the canopy of trees. He caught a glimpse of a dark shape, but that was all. Maybe just as well, since if he couldn't see the chopper through the thick undergrowth, then its occupants probably couldn't see him.

He didn't have to wait long to get a good view of the helicopter, though. A minute later, it set down in the clearing in front of him. Parker shrank farther into the underbrush as the rotors slowed, then stopped, and the roar of the engine faded. The door popped open and two men, dressed in military fatigues and carrying rifles, hopped to the ground. They scanned the area. Then a moment later, a man in a dark business suit exited the chopper. He had graying hair swept back from his forehead, and dark sunglasses perched on a crooked nose, with deep frown lines on either side of a thin-lipped mouth. He surveyed the area, then said something to the men with the guns that Parker couldn't hear.

The gunmen returned to the helicopter and unloaded a large wooden crate—about the size of a coffee table or a trunk. They set it on the ground next to the man in the suit. Stealthily, trying hard not to make a sound and scarcely daring to breathe, Parker took out his phone and began snapping photographs of the men, the box and the helicopter. He had taken half a dozen pictures when a branch cracked and a deer shot from the underbrush on the other side of the clearing.

Both men in fatigues raised their rifles and fired off a barrage of shots, peppering the deer with bullets, sending bark flying off the trunks of surrounding trees. Parker bit the inside of his cheek to keep from crying out. These guys were crazy! And he needed to get out of here as fast as he could.

The man in the suit didn't even flinch at the burst of gunfire. When the gunmen had lowered their weapons, he motioned to the crate and said something. They each took an end and headed off across the clearing, away from Parker. The man in the suit followed.

Parker waited until they were out of sight, then retraced his steps to the break in the fence, and from there to his car. His hands were still shaking as he fumbled the key into the ignition. What was going on up here?

And did he dare tell anyone about it?

WORD HAD OBVIOUSLY gotten around about that night's special guest speaker at the county commissioners' meeting, since latecomers ended up standing along the walls of the meeting room on the second floor of the Rayford County courthouse. Eagle Mountain *Examiner* reporter Tammy Patterson slid into one of the last empty seats, next to Paige, and gaped at the full house. "Most of the time Dean Eggbert and I are the only people in the audience at these things," she whispered, as she took out her tape recorder.

"Why does Dean attend?" Paige asked, picturing the short, round man whose balding head and ever-present white-shirt-with-red-suspenders combo always reminded her of the picture of Humpty Dumpty in her childhood storybook.

"His wife's book club meets at their place on Monday nights," Tammy said. "This gets him out of the house." She looked past Paige. "Hello, Agent Allerton. I heard you were back in town."

"Call me Rob," he said. "I'm here on vacation. Hoping to do some fishing."

"This meeting is called to order." The chief commissioner struck his gavel and the regular business of the commissioners proceeded, from the approval of the last meeting's minutes to authorization of funds to buy a new dump truck. Paige, who had endured her share of town meetings, struggled to keep her eyes open. Next to her, Rob sat slumped in his chair with his hands in his pockets and his chin on his chest. Paige was tempted to nudge him, to see if he was awake.

"And now, Bryce Reed with CNG Development has asked to address the commissioners."

A murmur rose from the crowd and audience members straightened in their seats as Reed, dressed as he had been that afternoon, in khaki trousers and a pastel golf shirt, strode to the microphone at the front of the room. He nodded and someone in the rear dimmed the lights, and an image appeared on the screen of a long, low building set against the familiar cliffs of Dakota Ridge.

"My company, CNG Development, wants to take a piece of land that has become an eyesore and a nuisance to this community and turn it into an important high-altitude research facility that will give back to your wonderful community rather than taking away from it," Reed said.

For the next ten minutes, he walked them through a series of before and after artist's renderings of the property, as well as bullet-pointed lists of the benefits of his proposed project—everything from green building practices to wildlife habitat protection.

"He's very persuasive," Paige whispered to Rob.

"Are you persuaded?" he asked.

"I'm reserving judgment," she said. "Companies often talk a good game, but they don't always follow through."

Reed finished his presentation and asked if anyone had questions. Seemingly everyone had a question, from Al Dawson's query about local jobs at the lab site—there would be a very small, very specialized staff, but there might be a few jobs for locals—to Merrily Rayford's concern over removing some of the dilapidated structures that were already in place on the property.

"No questions?" Rob leaned over to ask Paige.

"I'll have plenty—later. When I meet with Mr. Reed again."

Once more flashing a smile that attested to many thousand dollars of dental work, Bryce Reed closed the notebook he had brought to the podium with him. "If no one else has anything they'd like to ask—"

The door at the back of the room opened and Mayor Larry Rowe stepped in. Dressed for the office in dark slacks, white shirt and no tie, he smoothed back his graying hair and strode toward the podium. "Sorry I'm late," he muttered, as Bryce stepped aside to give the mayor access to the microphone.

"I should have known Larry wouldn't miss a chance to claim his share of the spotlight," Paige whispered to Rob.

"I just wanted to go on record as saying that the city of Eagle Mountain is one hundred percent behind CNG's proposal for their Dakota Ridge property," the mayor said. "We're pleased as can be that they're going to take something that has been a problem for the area and turn it into a facility we can all be proud of."

He looked out at the audience, as if daring anyone to contradict him.

"Thank you, Mr. Mayor," Bryce said. "I appreciate your support. And I hope in time to earn the support of many more of you."

Paige realized Bryce was looking right at her. She met his gaze with a cool look of her own.

"He thinks he's won you over," Rob said.

"As I said, I'm reserving judgment until after our meeting."

She braced herself for his argument that she shouldn't meet with Reed alone. She would let him rant for a while, then tell him she intended to take him with her. That should knock the wind from his sails. But before she had a chance to speak, a piercing siren sounded.

"That's the fire alarm." Travis, who had been seated behind them, stood. Half a dozen others in the room rose, as well. In a town with no paid fire department, the alarm was the quickest way to summon volunteers to their stations.

The room was emptying out fast when Tammy stood, her phone in her hand. "My editor just texted me," she said. "The fire is up on Dakota Ridge—at the old Eagle Mountain Resort property."

ROB STUDIED THE two bodies partially visible beneath the pile of charred timbers, illuminated by the white-hot glow of powerful LED work lights on stands on either side of the former building. The sharp scent of burning wood stung his nose, and he stood well back to avoid the rivulets of wet ash that trickled from the remains of the fire. "Any idea who they are?" he asked Travis.

"Reed says he's never seen them before—that no one was supposed to be up here." Travis glanced toward where Bryce Reed stood, talking to the assistant fire chief, Tom Reynolds.

"How did the fire start?" Rob asked. "Do we know yet?"

"Tom says he can't make an official assessment until after a formal investigation, but he's pretty sure it's arson," Travis said.

The building had been one of the few complete ones on the resort site. The eight-by-ten shed had been sided with weathered cedar and roofed with rusty metal, in an attempt to mimic an old mine shack. Rob and his team had searched the structure as part of their investigation into the underground laboratory, but found only landscaping tools and a pile of real-estate signs. The structure sat by itself, surrounded by rocky ground and broken pavement, which had kept the blaze from spreading.

"Who called in the alarm, do you know?" Rob asked.

"Jim Trotter and his wife were driving home from dinner and saw the smoke," Travis said. "They live at the end of the road here." He turned to greet the assistant fire chief, a slim, redheaded man in yellow bunker gear. "Tom, this is Agent Rob Allerton, with the DEA."

Tom shook Rob's hand.

"I was just telling Rob that the Trotters called in the fire," Travis said.

Tom nodded. "It probably hadn't been burning very long at that point, but by the time we got here, there wasn't anything we could do except keep it from spreading to the forest."

"Was the gate closed when you arrived?" Rob asked.

"Oh yeah. We had to cut the chain. The roof was caving in by the time we got the trucks over to the structure."

"And you think it was deliberately set?" Rob asked.

"We could smell the diesel fuel as soon as we got out of the truck," Tom said. "And there hasn't been any lightning. There's no electricity to the structure, so that leaves out faulty wiring."

"Any chance it was a vagrant using the shack for shelter?" Travis asked. "Maybe they had a campfire that got out of hand."

"Anything's possible," Tom said. "We'll know more after my investigation."

"Any sign of a vehicle?" Travis asked.

"A vehicle?" Tom frowned.

"The two men who died in the fire had to get up here somehow," Travis said.

Tom looked around them, but Rob already knew there was no car or truck in sight, other than the fire and rescue vehicles and the sheriff's SUV. "I guess they could have walked in," Tom said.

"It's a long way to walk," Travis said. "And they'd have to have gear—backpacks, camping equipment, stuff like that."

"We may find what's left of it when we clear away the debris and move the bodies," Tom said. "We might even find identification on the bodies."

"What did Bryce Reed tell you?" Travis asked.

"That he didn't know anything," Tom said. "That no one was supposed to be up here. He thinks they must have climbed the fence and been squatting here and set fire to the building themselves."

"Why didn't they try to get out?" Rob asked.

"How do you know they didn't?" Travis asked.

"The way the bodies are lying." Rob gestured toward the burned-out building. "They're facing away from the door. Say an explosion caused the fire—a gas stove, or maybe they had a campfire and tried to get it going bigger by dumping some diesel on it, and the fumes ignited. It might have thrown them backward, away from the fire, but then I would think they would try to get out. Yet both of them are just lying there, next to each other."

"Maybe they were asleep," Travis said. "Or they had been drinking or doing drugs and passed out."

"Maybe," Rob said.

"Sheriff. There's something you need to see." One of

the firemen, his face and yellow bunker gear streaked with soot, trotted over to them.

Travis, Rob and the chief followed the firefighter over to a rock cairn about a hundred yards from the shack, across from the remains of what had once been a paved street. "Take a look at that," the firefighter said, and pointed behind the pillar. An AR-15 was propped against the rocks. "Funny place to leave a gun like that," he said.

"Unless you wanted to make sure it wasn't destroyed in the fire," Travis said. "And you wanted it to be found." He crouched down and examined it more closely, though without touching it. "We'll leave it until the crime scene team gets up here." He turned to look back at the blackened ruins. The firefighter and the chief moved toward the fire truck parked closer to the now-open gate. "What do you think the chances are the two bodies in there belong to the two men who shot at Paige?" Travis asked.

"I didn't get a good look at them," Rob said. "And to be honest, their own mothers wouldn't know them now."

"The gun is too obvious," Travis said. "As if someone left it there to find. I'm betting when we test it, we find out it's the same gun that fired the bullets we found in Paige's front door."

The rumble of an engine and the crackle of tires on gravel announced the arrival of the crime scene van, followed by a black SUV. Two men and one woman climbed out of the van and began donning Tyvek suits and booties. The SUV parked a short distance away, and Mayor Larry Rowe got out and walked over to join Travis and Rob.

"What are you doing here?" the mayor asked Rob.

"Agent Allerton is assisting us with the investigation," Travis said.

The mayor's eyebrows rose, but he made no further comment to Rob. "What have they found out?" he asked Travis.

Rob wanted to tell the man the information was none of his business. Something about Rowe rubbed him the wrong way—though maybe that was only Paige's prejudice rubbing off on him. Clearly, she had little use for the mayor. Rob remained quiet and let Travis handle this.

"We're waiting on the investigation before we announce any results," Travis said.

A woman in white Tyvek coveralls walked over to them. "What have we got, Sheriff?" she asked.

Travis glanced at the mayor.

"You can talk in front of me," Larry said. "I know how to keep a confidence, and I think I'm entitled to be briefed about the situation."

Travis nodded, then summed up their findings for the woman—Darcy Collins, with the Colorado Bureau of Investigation. "We're going on the assumption this is arson, until we establish otherwise. If it is arson, then the two bodies could be murder victims."

She nodded. "We'll find any evidence there is to find."

Travis pointed to the cairn. "There's an AR-15 behind those rocks I want photographed and bagged for evidence," he said.

"Got it." She signaled to her team and they began setting small plastic flags on thin wire stakes to establish an entry and exit corridor. They strung crime scene tape, then began photographing the burned building and the surrounding area.

"It's pretty clear to me what happened here," the mayor said, when Darcy had left them.

"Oh?" Rob asked.

"The AR-15 belongs to the two dead guys," Larry said. "They were the ones who shot at Paige, up here and at her house. They were camping out in that shack and got careless with their fire."

"We don't know yet if this AR is the one that fired at Paige," Rob said.

"You can test it," Larry said. "I'm sure that will prove I'm right."

"Thank you for your input." Travis turned away.

"You'll let me know what you find," the mayor said.

Travis didn't answer. He and Rob walked over to Travis's SUV, where they stood in the shadowed darkness, watching the investigators move in and out of the glow of work lights.

Travis waited until the mayor had driven away before he spoke. "If the bodies belong to the shooter and his cohort, then we have the guilty parties and we don't need to look further," he said.

"Very convenient," Rob said. "Except we don't know why they tried to kill Paige, or what they were doing up here."

"She said she saw them carrying a big wooden crate into an underground chamber or hole or mine shaft or something like that," Travis said. "Maybe they were stashing stolen goods up here."

"Any burglaries in the area lately?" Rob asked.

"No. I can check surrounding areas. Maybe something will pop." He kicked at a rock, which rolled away down the small incline. "It's too neat. Too convenient."

"The mayor likes it."

"The mayor watches too much television."

"What does he do, your mayor?" Rob asked. "Or is that his full-time job?"

"He has a computer consulting company," Travis said. "They specialize in financial management firms."

"He's obviously a fan of CNG."

"He ran on a platform of bringing new businesses and jobs to the area," Travis said. "And he's the type who likes to have his name in the paper as often as possible. This is a hot story, so the mayor wants to make sure he's quoted."

"I've met the type," Rob said. He tried to stay far away from them. "Do you think Reed was telling the truth—that he didn't know the men or what they were doing?"

"I don't believe anyone I don't know well," Travis said.

"He came by the Bear's Den this afternoon to talk to Paige," Rob said. "He said he wanted to share his plans for the property with her and get her support."

"That sounds smart. Paige's group isn't that large, but they know how to make a lot of noise when they're unhappy about something."

"Are you saying they're troublemakers?" Rob asked.

"Not at all. They do a lot of good for the community, but they aren't subtle. They've made enemies."

"Reed asked Paige to come up here with him for a private tour. She told him the last time she was up here, someone tried to kill her. He seemed shocked to hear this. I don't think he was faking it."

"That's interesting."

"Something I thought was even more interesting—he told Paige that 'wasn't acceptable' and that he would put a stop to it."

"As if he had authority over the shooters?" Travis asked.

"Maybe. Or maybe he was just blowing smoke, trying to impress her with how powerful and in charge he was. Or maybe it was just a figure of speech. He could have meant he was going to make sure the property was secure and no one used it for criminal activity. CNG has held the position all along that they aren't responsible for anything that has happened while the property was essentially abandoned."

"I'm wondering if either of those two is the man we saw up here yesterday," Travis said.

"I don't think so," Rob said, keeping his tone casual. "I only got a glimpse, but the person we saw seemed smaller. Like a kid, even."

"What would a kid be doing up here?" Travis asked.

"Messing around. Seeing what he could find."

"He was old enough to drive," Travis said. "He almost ran us off the road. I'm going to have to talk to Paige again. I think she knows more than she's saying."

"Why do you think that?"

"Just a hunch. She was acting odd yesterday—evasive, even."

Rob started to defend Paige, then decided anything he said was going to make the sheriff more suspicious. Travis had a reputation as a shrewd and dogged investigator. Chances were, he was going to find out it was Parker who had fled from them when they were up here yesterday. Rob didn't know Travis well enough to predict how he would handle that information, but he hoped, for Paige's sake, that he would go easy on the young man.

A trio of firemen shifted the largest of the fallen timbers and the crime scene team moved in to get their first close look at the bodies. Rob didn't envy them the task. But they would want to establish the circumstances of the deaths, and secure any identification that was on the bodies before trying to move them.

"Sheriff!" Darcy raised her head and called to him.

Travis straightened and walked over to join her. Rob was too far away to overhear what she said, but he could see the scene clearly in the bright glow of the work lights. She gestured toward one of the bodies, then bent and rolled over the second one. Travis said something, then backed out of the building and returned to the SUV.

"What did she find?" Rob asked.

"Those two didn't die in the fire," Travis said.

"Why do you say that?"

"They were already dead. Both of them had been shot in the head."

Chapter Ten

Rob was eating breakfast in Paige's dining room the next morning when Travis called him. "I'm going to Bryce Reed's office this morning to talk to him," he said. "Want to come along?"

Rob pushed back his chair. "Let me check." He headed for the kitchen, but met Paige coming out. "What are you doing this morning?" he asked her, the phone tucked under his chin.

"Eagle Mountain environmentalists have a meeting at ten. Why?"

"I might need to be away for a couple of hours," he said.

"So go," she said. "I don't need a babysitter—certainly not now that those two men are dead. You said they were probably the ones who shot at me, right?"

"We don't know that for sure."

"I'll be fine." She set a bowl of fruit on the sideboard and turned back toward the kitchen. "Go."

Rob put the phone back to his ear. "Sure, I'll come with you. Should be interesting. Where are you meeting him?"

"CNG has an office here in town," Travis said. "Come by the sheriff's office and we'll go there together."

Travis was waiting, keys in hand, when Rob arrived. "Just to be clear, I'm not here in an official capacity," Rob reminded him as they walked to Travis's SUV.

"I know. But your law enforcement connection seemed to shake Reed a little yesterday," Travis said. "I want to take advantage of that. Besides, it's always good to have another perspective."

CNG Development's Eagle Mountain offices were located in a newer strip center on the edge of town. The front room contained an empty desk and three metal folding chairs—and nothing else. Rob would have expected a file cabinet or a plant, or even pictures on the wall. Apparently, CNG wasn't too concerned about impressing visitors.

"Hello?" Travis called when he and Rob entered.

Reed, in khaki slacks and another polo shirt—mint green this time—looked out from the doorway of the office's second room. "Sheriff!" he said. "Do you have any more news about last night's events?"

"I have some information for you," Travis said. "And some more questions." He indicated Rob. "I've asked Agent Allerton to sit in with us."

"Come sit down and we'll talk." He turned to Rob. "Agent Allerton. When I met you at Paige Riddell's yesterday afternoon, you didn't tell me you were a law enforcement officer."

Reed must have been stewing about that all night, Rob thought. "It wasn't relevant," he said.

"And now it is?" Reed asked. "What interest does the DEA have in CNG?"

"Agent Allerton is assisting us with our investigation," Travis said.

Reed looked as if he wanted to argue, but he merely

pressed his lips together and led them into a sparsely furnished office. He pulled up two folding chairs and took his place behind the cheap metal desk. He must have seen Travis's and Rob's skeptical looks at the budget accommodations. "We rented this space furnished, until we can construct a more permanent facility on the site," he said. He turned to Travis. "What have you found out about those two men?"

Travis took two photographs from the file folder he carried and handed them to Reed. "Identification taken from wallets found on the bodies identifies them as Joseph Welch and Dennis Petri," he said. "We'll be confirming that with medical and dental records as soon as we can obtain them."

Reed stared at the black-and-white mug shots. Travis handed Rob copies also. The photographs showed two men in their early thirties. Welch had thinning brown hair and Petri had close-cropped, curly black hair. Each faced the camera with a sullen look on his face, booking number across his chest.

"I've never seen either of them before," Reed said, and returned the photos to Travis.

"What were they doing on CNG property?" Travis asked.

"I already told you, I have no idea. They were trespassing."

"We searched the area and we haven't been able to locate a vehicle, or any personal belongings, like a backpack or camping equipment," Travis said. "How do you explain that?"

"I don't. That's up to you to investigate."

"Both men were shot in the head," Travis continued. "Do you have any idea who might have killed them?"

"Of course not." Reed managed to look indignant.

"Any theories about what might have happened?" Rob asked.

"No. It's not my job to come up with theories. These people were on CNG property illegally."

"What is it about that piece of property that attracts so many criminals?" Rob asked.

"I could turn that around and ask why this county has such a problem with illegal activity in general," Reed said.

Travis restored the photos to the folder and sat back in his chair. "Have you considered hiring a private security company to patrol the property?" he asked. "Cameras and some lighting might also help."

"We will be doing all of those things," Reed said.

"I'll be posting extra patrols in that area, also," Travis said.

Some of the stiffness went out of Reed's posture. "I appreciate that, Sheriff," he said. "But I know yours is a small department with limited staff. I would hate to take your deputies away from here in town, where they might be needed."

"Since most of the serious crime we've had lately has had some connection to that property or people involved with it, it makes sense to me to focus our efforts there," Travis said.

"From what little I know of the former owner, he was involved with some shady characters," Reed said. "The more I consider the situation, the more I believe those two men who died in the fire—and anyone else who might have been causing trouble up there before now—must be related to that. They haven't gotten the word yet that the property has new owners who have zero tolerance for anything untoward. That is going to change now, I assure you."

"I'm glad to hear it," Travis said.

"Hello? Bryce, are you here?"

Rob sat bolt upright at the sound of the familiar voice, and turned in time to see Paige in the doorway of Reed's office. Dressed casually, in a long denim skirt, boots and a long-sleeved red blouse, she still managed to convey an air of sophistication. "Oh!" She took a step back. "I didn't know you were with someone."

"Paige, come in!" Reed rose and greeted her heartily. "The sheriff and I were just finishing up."

"What are you doing here?" Rob asked, not caring if he sounded rude.

She scowled at him, but before she could answer, Reed said, "Paige and I have a lunch date."

Now her frown was for Reed. "We agreed to talk more about your plans for your research facility," she said.

"Over lunch." He came out from behind the desk. "Gentlemen, if you'll excuse me…"

"I was going to stop by and see you this afternoon," Travis said to Paige, standing also. "But if you have a minute, we can take care of my question now."

"Of course," she said.

Travis pulled out the mug shots of Welch and Petri. "Have you seen either of these men before?" he asked.

She studied the pictures for a long moment, then shook her head. "No. I don't think so."

"Could they have been the men who shot at you on the hiking trail the other day? Or who fired on you at your house that afternoon?" Travis asked.

She looked at the photos again. "I can't say these men weren't the ones who shot at me. But I can't say they are, either. I just didn't get a good enough look at them. I'm sorry."

Rob wasn't surprised at her answer. Despite her earlier assertion that she would recognize the men again, she had glimpsed them for only a few seconds, under tense circumstance. And looking at a two-dimensional mug shot was very different from seeing someone alive and standing nearby.

"That's all right." Travis put the photographs away.

"Are those the two men you found dead last night?" she asked Rob.

He looked to Travis. This wasn't his case, and he didn't know how much the sheriff wanted to reveal. Travis nodded. "We think so, yes."

"What about the gun you found last night?" Reed asked. "Can you connect it with the attacks on Paige?"

"We're waiting on ballistics tests," he said. "Interesting thing about that gun, though."

"Oh?" Paige and Reed spoke in chorus.

"There weren't any fingerprints on it," Travis said. "Whoever put it behind those rocks had wiped it clean."

PAIGE COULD FEEL Rob's eyes on her as she exited the office with Bryce Reed. Travis hadn't elaborated any more on the gun with no fingerprints, and Reed had hurried her out. But she couldn't get Travis's words out of her head. "What do you think it means, the gun being wiped off like that?" she asked as they walked toward their cars.

"My guess is the shooters wiped it every time they used it, in case someone found it." She had started toward her car, but Reed put a hand at her back and steered her toward his. "Come in my car," he said. "We'll have more time to talk."

She could have made an excuse about having to be somewhere else right after lunch, but it seemed both silly and paranoid. Reed had given her no reason not to trust him, and it was broad daylight, after all. Not to mention Rob and the sheriff were right behind them, she thought, glancing in the mirror as she slid into the passenger seat of the big SUV Reed drove.

"Would someone really do that?" she asked, as he started the vehicle. "Wipe down a gun every time he used it? And hide it in the rocks that way?"

"A guilty person might." Reed flashed her a smile. "But hey, I've never been a criminal, so I have no idea. What do you think about the Cake Walk for lunch?" he asked. "I know Eagle Mountain doesn't have that many choices, but I had breakfast there the other day and it was great. I figure the lunch will be good, too."

"The Cake Walk is fine," she said. "Did the fire last night do much damage to the property?"

"The truth is, there's not a lot up there to burn," he said. "Chances are we would have torn down that storage shed anyway." He glanced at her. "Not that I would be thanking those two for burning it down. We take trespassing very seriously and will prosecute anyone we catch up there who doesn't have proper authorization."

She shifted in her seat, thinking of Parker. She had half a mind to call Professor Gibson and read him the riot act for asking her brother to snoop around on CNG property. She would definitely warn Parker not to go near the place again.

Reed found a parking space in front of the café and they settled into a booth along one side of the cozy restaurant. Paige recognized most of the people in the room, and nodded to a few. No doubt the gossips would be busy speculating on why she was having lunch with the local face of CNG Development—especially since news about the fire and the discovery of two bodies up there would be all over town by now. It might be interesting to hear some of the local theories about that.

"You'll be happy to know I'm having the gate across the hiking trail removed today," Reed said, after they had placed their orders.

"I'm pleased to hear that," she said. Though the primary purpose of the EME meeting this morning had been to discuss their booth for an upcoming fall festival, several people had suggested making another try at cutting the lock off the gate blocking the trail. In the end, they had decided to wait until things had settled down on the resort site. No one wanted a repeat of what had happened to Paige.

"None of the people who use the trail are interested in trespassing on private property," Paige said. "We only want to hike a trail that's a favorite of many people around here. If you want to put a fence alongside the trail to protect your property, we have no problem with that, though most people who have public right-of-way across their land settle for posting No Trespassing signs that remind people to stay on the trail."

"We'll try the signs," Reed said. "The sheriff suggested hiring a security guard and installing cameras."

"That might not be a bad idea," Paige said.

The waitress delivered her salad and his sandwich. "I'd really like you to come up there with me," Reed said. "I want to take you around and show you where everything is going to be. I think you'll really like what we have in mind."

"I'd love to see it," she said. She was dying to know

his plans—and she had to admit she wanted to see the scene after last night.

"I can take you up there after lunch, if you have time," he said.

She hesitated. She didn't have any guests arriving this afternoon. "As long as we're back by five," she said. "And I need to call my brother and let him know not to expect me." Parker had proved he was capable of handling any reservations that came in.

"Great." Reed grinned, then took a big bite out of his sandwich.

When they were done eating, he took care of the bill while Paige went outside to make her call. "The Bear's Den Bed and Breakfast," Parker answered, sounding very professional.

"Parker, it's Paige. I called to let you know I'll be away the rest of the afternoon. Would you mind the phone while I'm gone? I'll be back before you have to leave for work."

"Where are you going?" he asked.

"Up to Eagle Mountain Resort. Bryce Reed is going to show me around."

"You can't go up there with him," Parker said. "You don't even know the guy."

"He's a perfectly respectable businessman." She glanced over her shoulder, relieved to see that Reed hadn't yet emerged from the café. "It's broad daylight. And I'm not an idiot. It'll be fine."

"What about those guys who shot at you?"

"The sheriff thinks they were the men who were found dead up there last night."

"I don't like it," Parker said.

"I don't like everything you do, either," she said. "But

we're both adults. I don't get to tell you what to do and you don't get to tell me what to do. Agreed?"

"I still don't have to like it," he said. "Just—be careful."

"I always am." She ended the call and turned to find Reed waiting behind her.

"Any trouble?" he asked.

"My brother is a little overprotective sometimes," she said. "It's sweet, really."

"I guess someone with his background knows a little too much about what the wrong kind of people will do," Reed said. He took her arm.

She stiffened. "What's that supposed to mean?" she asked. "What about Parker's background?"

"I didn't mean to offend," he said. "Someone told me he'd been in prison."

"Who told you?" she demanded.

"I don't remember—just something I heard around town. I apologize. I really didn't mean to offend you."

He looked genuinely contrite. She relaxed a little. "Parker made some foolish mistakes when he was younger, but he's working hard to get past that," she said. "I hate that some people will never let him forget his mistakes."

"Again, I'm sorry I brought it up." Reed held the door while she slid into the passenger seat, then closed it and walked around to the driver's side. "But as long as we're on the subject of the men in your life, what's your relationship to Agent Allerton?"

"He's a guest at my B and B," she said.

"I guess I read the signals wrong," Reed said. "He seemed a little overprotective of you, too."

"You must have misunderstood," she said. She was

already wishing she hadn't agreed to ride with him. She hadn't expected him to question her personal life this way.

"Sorry for the nosy questions," he said. "I've devoted the last few years to my career, so I'm a little rusty when it comes to interacting with attractive women."

And what was *that* supposed to mean? "Are you married?" she asked. If he was going to ask personal questions, she might as well, too.

"Divorced. No kids. I'm a boring workaholic, though I'd like to change that. A man gets to be my age, he starts to think about the mistakes he's made."

"You're not that old," she said.

He laughed. "Maybe not. But it feels that way sometimes." He sped up when they reached the road that started the climb toward Dakota Ridge. "This is beautiful country out here," he said. "A lot wilder and more rugged than where I'm from, back east, but definitely captivating."

"Most people who live here think it's pretty much paradise," she said.

He stopped at the gates to the resort property—she couldn't help but think of it that way, even though it would never be a resort. Maybe one day everyone would call it the research campus or something similar, but until then, it would be the resort. "The fire department destroyed the lock getting to the fire last night," he said. "We'll have to fix that." He pressed a remote device clipped to the visor and the gates swung open, smoothly and soundlessly. He drove the car over the cracking pavement and parked in front of the faded sign advertising the resort. "We're going to get people in here to take all of this out," he said, indicating the sign, the broken pavement and the foundations that had never been built on. "Come on. Let's take a walk and I'll show you around."

The air held the tang of smoke, and a short distance away Paige spotted the burned-out shed, yellow crime scene tape festooning the blackened ruins. Reed saw where she was looking and took her arm. "You don't need to concern yourself with that," he said.

She pulled away from him. "Of course I'm concerned," she said. "Two people died there—men who may have tried to kill me."

"You're right. I'm sorry." He jingled his keys in his pockets. "But there's nothing we can do about that now. Will you let me show you where we hope to put the new labs?"

She followed him away from the ruins, past a Quonset hut and more crumbling foundations to a cleared expanse near the top of the ridge that overlooked a valley filled with tall spruce and pine. "The building would have a low profile and really blend in with the environment," Reed said. "You shouldn't be able to see it from the road at all."

"Where would the people who work here live?" she asked. It was a beautiful setting. Peaceful, even, if you could ignore the scent of smoke that lingered in the air.

"Some would live in town," Reed said. "Although we would have a few houses here on the property—apartments, really, again with a low profile and very green."

"That's good." She was only half listening to him, her senses attuned to the woods around them. Not even a bird sang. It ought to have been the most peaceful setting in the world, yet she couldn't shake a sense of foreboding.

"Let me show you where we plan to build the apartments." He moved forward and a stick broke under his foot with a loud pop. Paige gasped.

"It's just a stick," Reed said. "Why are you so jumpy?"

"I guess what happened last time I was here affected me more than I realized," she said.

He moved to her side and put his arm around her. "Don't worry. I'll protect you. Here, look." He pulled back his jacket to reveal a gun tucked into an inside pocket.

She backed away. Knowing he was armed didn't make her feel safer, but there was no point saying so. Instead, she pushed down her fear and changed the subject. "Where is the underground chamber?" she asked.

He frowned. "You mean the one where the deputy and his girlfriend were held? It's over here." He led her back to the Quonset hut, through two empty rooms to one with a dirt floor and a metal grate in the roof open to the outside air. "We may use this for storage," he said. "It could be useful having a chamber like this that's fairly well insulated."

She suppressed a shudder and forced herself to look around.

"Did you know this is where they found Henry Hake's body?" Reed asked. "They said he died of tularemia. The sheriff suggested getting the health department up here to test, but it turns out tularemia is naturally occurring and even quite common in areas of the West, so testing wouldn't prove anything."

"I didn't know that." She followed him out of the building, relieved to be in the open air again. "What do you think happened to Henry?" she asked.

"I don't know," he said. "Though he was obviously hanging out with a criminal element. Didn't his former bodyguard murder some lawyer in town? And attack the sheriff's fiancée?"

"Yes." At the time, most people had thought Ian Barnes's murder of Andy Stenson had been an isolated incident, but now she wondered if that crime was somehow related to Henry Hake's death. She looked around them, getting her bearings. "Isn't there another underground chamber?" she asked.

"Another one? I don't think so."

"The day those men shot at me, I was looking through the fence. I watched them carry a crate to a trapdoor in the earth. They went down into the ground. But it wasn't here. It was farther that way." She pointed up the ridge.

Reed took her arm. "You must be turned around. This is the only underground space—and as you saw, it was empty. You know, the terrain here can be deceptive. Instead of going into the ground, maybe they just went downhill, behind some rocks or something."

She knew what she had seen, but there was no point arguing with him. "Maybe you're right." She pulled away from him again. "I'm ready to go now."

They walked silently back to where he had parked, Paige forcing herself not to hurry. As they neared the SUV, a pickup truck sped into the drive and stopped beside them. Rob got out. "Hello, Paige," he said. "Mr. Reed."

"What are you doing here?" Reed asked.

"Parker called and asked me to check on you," Rob told Paige. "He was concerned."

Paige wanted to be upset with him for thinking he needed to look after her—but all she felt was relief. "Thanks," she said. "But he had no cause to be worried."

"That's right." Reed put his arm around her again.

She could feel the gun in his jacket digging into her side. "Paige and I had a pleasant lunch, and now we're having a pleasant afternoon together."

Rob looked as if he wanted to take Reed's arm off at the elbow. "This doesn't strike me as the safest place to be, considering all that's happened up here lately," he said.

"You weren't invited here, Agent Allerton," Reed said. "You should leave now."

Paige had no desire for Rob to leave her alone with Reed again. For one thing, his insistence on continuing to touch her and hug her was giving her the creeps. She shrugged out of his grasp once more. "I need to get back to my business," she said. "Rob, could you give me a ride?" Before Reed could object, she turned her most dazzling smile on him. "Thank you so much for lunch, and for taking the time to show me your plans. I'm really pleased with what you're going to be doing with the property."

"I can take you back to town," Reed said. "I'm going there anyway."

"I don't want to keep you any longer," she said. "And Rob is going right to the B and B. Thank you again." Not waiting for a reply, she opened the passenger door of Rob's truck and climbed in.

He didn't hesitate, either, and left Reed standing alone while he climbed in the truck and backed out of the drive. He didn't say anything until they were on the road leading away from the resort property. "Are you okay?" he asked.

"Yes." She hugged her arms across her chest. "A little shaken up, maybe. I don't know what was getting to me more—remembering being shot at the other day, or the sight of all that crime scene tape around the ruins...or Bryce Reed's overly chummy manner. Did you know he was carrying a gun?"

"So am I," Rob said. "Does that freak you out?"

"No. You're a law enforcement officer. He's supposed to be a business executive."

"Maybe with everything that's happened up there, he thought he needed protection."

"Maybe. It still strikes me as odd." She shook herself, trying to dispel her dark mood. "I'm probably just being overly sensitive. There's probably nothing to worry about."

"Maybe not. But I don't trust Reed. I'm not convinced he's not part of whatever is going on up there."

She stared. "He was at the commissioners' meeting last night when those men were killed and that fire was set," she said. "And he was back east when the other crimes occurred."

"I'm not saying he pulled the trigger or lit the match," Rob said. "But I think he knows more than he's letting on." He glanced at her. "And it was very convenient to have those two out of the way, and that gun planted to link them to shooting you. A little too obvious, I think."

"I asked him about what I saw that day on the trail— the two men carrying a heavy crate and stowing it underground," she said.

"What did he say?"

"He said I must have gotten turned around. Or misunderstood what I saw."

"Maybe he really believes that," Rob said. "Or maybe he's a very practiced liar."

She fell silent, replaying everything Reed had said to her that afternoon. She couldn't point to anything in particular that rang untrue. But she couldn't shake the feeling that something was off, either.

Rob parked at the B and B. Paige checked the time on her phone—it was after five, so Parker would have left for his shift at Peggy's Pizza. She noticed Rob scanning the area around the house before he stepped out, and he followed her up the walk to the door, vigilant.

She unlocked the door and tucked her keys in her pocket. When the door was safely locked behind them, she turned to him. "I wanted to be angry with you for following me up to the resort," she said. "But I was so glad to see you."

He pulled her to him and she did what she had been wanting to do for days now, pressing her body against his and kissing him, hard. He responded in kind, his lips claiming hers in a kiss that left her dizzy, heart pounding, craving more. He caressed her waist, then slid one hand to her hip, the other one at the back of her neck, his thumb stroking the pulse at the side of her throat in a way that had her almost purring with pleasure.

She pressed him back against the wall and began fumbling with the buttons of his shirt. Her fingers brushed at the hair on his chest and he growled against her throat, sending a shiver of pleasure running through her. A button popped off the shirt and bounced on the floor at their feet, but she ignored it. He had pulled up the hem of her blouse and splayed his fingers across her ribs, tracing the underside of one breast. She moaned, eyes closed and forehead pressed against his chest.

"Any other guests here?" he mumbled into her hair.

"No. They checked out this morning."

"Good." He slid his hands beneath her thighs and

hoisted her up against him, then kissed her again. Her heart pounded so hard she imagined she could hear it.

Then she realized it wasn't her heart she was hearing—it was footsteps pounding up the walk outside. She broke the kiss and pushed at Rob. "Someone—"

But it was the only word she managed before the front window broke and flames leaped across the room.

Chapter Eleven

Rob grabbed Paige's hand and dragged her away from the spreading flames, toward the back door. He tugged his phone from his pocket as he moved and handed it to her. "Call 9-1-1," he said, and drew his gun.

Smoke was already filling the rooms, and he could hear the crackling sound of the fire spreading rapidly behind them. He eased open the back door and cautiously checked outside. No sign of anyone. Paige had reached the emergency operator and was reporting the fire, her voice surprisingly calm. He took her free hand in his and tugged her out of the house and around toward the front—in time to hear the screech of tires and catch a glimpse of a dark vehicle speeding away.

By the time they had made it into the front yard, the wail of sirens filled the air. He stared after the retreating car, swearing to himself, but a gasp from Paige made him turn around.

"My house!" she moaned, as flames leaped to the second story of the structure.

Rob pulled her close. "You're safe," he said. "Parker is safe. You can build another house."

She nodded, but he could tell she was fighting to hold back tears. She looked up at him. "What happened?"

"Someone threw a firebomb through your front window," he said. "A Molotov cocktail or something similar would be my best guess." The flames had spread so rapidly they must have been helped along by gasoline or some other fuel.

She shuddered. "Who hates me so much?"

He put away his gun so that he could wrap both arms around her. "I don't know," he said. "But I won't give up until I find out."

She fumbled at his chest, and he realized she was doing up the buttons on his shirt—the ones that were left, anyway. "You probably want to, um, straighten up before the firefighters get here," she suggested.

He took over buttoning the shirt and tucking it into his pants. "I'm sorry we were interrupted," he said.

But she didn't answer, her gaze fixed on the sheriff's department SUV pulling in across the street, followed by an Eagle Mountain Volunteer Fire Department pumper and ladder truck. The firefighters poured out of the vehicles and went to work right away. Rob and Paige walked out to meet Gage, who was just getting out of the SUV.

"What happened?" he asked. He scowled at the burning house. The flames were already licking at the roof.

"Someone threw something through the front window," Paige said. "In broad daylight."

A second SUV parked behind Gage's, and Travis climbed out. His fiancée, Lacy Milligan, got out of the passenger side. Lacy hurried to Paige and embraced her. "Travis and I were headed to his folks' place for dinner when the call came in," she said. "I'm so glad you're okay."

"Rob says this wasn't an accidental fire," Gage said,

as Travis joined the two men, a short distance away from the women.

"Paige and I were in the front hall when someone threw a firebomb through the front window," Rob said. "The flames spread immediately. We went out the back door and got to the front in time to see a car speeding away."

"You were in the front hall?" Travis asked. "Had you just come in, or were you going out?"

"We had been out and hadn't been home long." No point in mentioning they had been making out. They had been moments away from doing it up against the wall.

"Paige had lunch with Bryce Reed," Travis said.

"Right," Rob said. "And after that, he took her up to the Dakota Ridge property to show her around. Parker was worried about her and called me, so I drove up there to make sure she was all right. She elected to ride home with me."

"Why would she ride with you instead of coming back with Reed?" Gage asked.

"You'd have to ask her that."

"I'm wondering about the timing," Travis said. "Was someone watching the house, waiting for Paige to come home so they could throw that firebomb? Or did they even know she was home?"

"Reed would have had a good idea about how long it took to travel from his property to the B and B," Gage said.

"A firebomb doesn't seem like his style," Rob said. "And the car I got a glimpse of wasn't his. I'm betting if you question him, he'll have an alibi to prove he wasn't anywhere near Paige's place this afternoon."

A battered Toyota pulled in behind the sheriff's department vehicles and Parker got out. Leaving the driver's door open, he ran to them. "Paige! Peggy told me she heard there was a fire here? Are you okay? What happened?"

Paige hugged her brother. "I'm okay." She glanced over her shoulder at the fully engulfed house. "I'm sorry, but anything you had in there is gone. We didn't have time to save anything."

"I've got my laptop and most of my schoolbooks in the car," he said. "But what happened?" His arm still around Paige, he addressed this last question to Rob.

"Someone threw a firebomb in the front window," Rob said.

"Who?" Parker demanded.

"We don't know," Travis said.

"Do you have any ideas?" Gage asked. "Anybody mad at you for anything?"

"No!" Paige answered before her brother could speak. "Why would you think this has anything to do with Parker?"

"*Does* this have anything to do with you?" Travis asked, addressing Parker.

"No," he said.

"The B and B is my business," Paige said. "Whoever did this wanted to hurt me."

"Parker lives there," Gage said. "Even if he's not involved in anything illegal now, he might have friends from his past who think he betrayed them, or have some other reason to want to get back at him."

"No." Parker shook his head. "I don't even know anyone like that. I was a small-time addict and a petty thief." He looked to Rob. "You know my case. Tell them this doesn't have anything to do with me."

"He's right," Rob said. "I don't think this is connected to Parker."

Travis turned to Paige. "Then what have you done that has someone so upset?" he asked.

"I wish I knew," she said.

"What is your environmental group up to these days?" Gage asked. "Are you involved in any more lawsuits?"

"No," she said. "Nothing like that."

"None of this is Paige's fault," Lacy said. "It's the fault of whoever threw that firebomb."

"We're just trying to figure out what's going on," Travis said. "Knowing who might have a motive for wanting to harm her could help."

"I haven't done anything to anyone," she said. "I even agreed to support CNG Development's plans for the Dakota Ridge property."

"That must have made Bryce Reed happy," Rob said.

"It's not as if my support means anything," she said. "I imagine the county is thrilled to see the property put to good use. Right now it's an eyesore. The research lab CNG is proposing will at least bring in some tax money and maybe even a few jobs."

"What about your ex-husband?" Rob asked.

"What about him?" Her eyes met his, her expression defiant.

"You said he wasn't a very nice man. Would he try to hurt you this way?"

She shook her head. "I haven't talked to him in years. I was so grateful to get away from that marriage that I let him keep most of the money and property." She glanced at the burning house again. "I bought this place with money an aunt willed to me."

"You can rebuild," Lacy said. "Better than ever. You have a lot of friends here in town who will help."

Assistant fire chief Tom Reynolds crossed the lawn to join them. He removed his helmet and wiped sweat from his forehead. "I'm sorry, Paige, but we weren't able to save the house. It went up so fast, I have to think it had some help."

"Someone threw a firebomb through the front window," Rob said.

Tom nodded. "I'm sorry to hear that, but knowing that will help my investigation."

"Thank you for keeping the fire from spreading," Paige said. "I know my neighbors appreciate it."

"Second arson in twenty-four hours," Tom said. "Think we have a firebug in town, Sheriff?"

"I don't know," Travis said. "We'll be looking for any connection."

"The fire's under control," Tom said. "But we're going to be here for a while, until we're sure everything's cold. I'll give you a report when I have one from my investigator."

"Thanks, Tom," Travis said. He turned to Paige and Parker. "Do you two have somewhere to stay?" he asked.

"I can stay with Professor Gibson," Parker said. "He's already made the offer for me to stay at his place anytime, and it'll make it easier to work on our research project."

"Paige can stay with me at my parents' place," Lacy said.

"Rob was staying at the B and B, too," Paige said.

"Don't worry about me," Rob said. "I'll get a room at the motel." Their eyes met. He wanted to pull her close, to comfort her and tell her everything would be all right—but that didn't seem appropriate right now, with an audience.

She leaned forward and squeezed his hand. "Thank you for getting me out of there safely," she said. "I was in such shock, I'm not sure I could have moved."

"I'll be in touch," he said.

"I guess I'd better get back to work," Parker said. "Peggy let me come over here when we heard the news, but I don't want to leave her in the lurch."

"Go on," Paige said. "I'll be fine."

"She will be," Lacy said. "Do you have your car?"

"I left it at CNG's offices this afternoon," she said.

"We can walk over to Mom and Dad's and get my car," Lacy said. "Then I'll take you to get yours." She frowned. "That is, if you have your keys."

"My keys are in my pocket." Paige patted her skirt.

"I'll call my folks and let them know we're not going to make it to dinner," Travis said.

Paige cast a last look at Rob, then let Lacy lead her away. Parker drove off, and Gage left in his cruiser. Travis turned to Rob. "Any ideas?" he asked.

"I'm thinking Paige saw something—or someone thinks she saw something—up at the resort property the day she was shot at."

"The two men who shot her are probably dead," Travis said.

"They may have been the ones to fire at her, but maybe they were acting on the orders of someone else."

"Who?" Travis asked.

"I don't know. Maybe the same person who killed Henry Hake. I think it has something to do with that property, but I can't figure out what. I'm going to do a little deep digging of my own."

"Let us know what you find out," Travis said.

"I will." And then he was going to go after whoever was making Paige's life such hell, and make them wish they had never crossed her.

MR. AND MRS. MILLIGAN were happy to have Paige stay in their guest room. "Stay as long as you need," Jeanette Milligan said. "I'm so sorry about your home and business. I hope you'll be able to rebuild soon."

"As soon as possible," Paige said. Even so, she would lose months of business. She would probably have to find other work to pay her bills. She had money in savings, but she didn't want to exhaust that.

"Do you mind if I give you a little unsolicited advice?" Lacy asked, as she and Paige walked out to Lacy's car.

"Go ahead," Paige said.

"It's easy to get overwhelmed when something horrible happens," she said. "What has helped me is to focus on what is right in front of me at the moment—what I have to do in the next hour. You have a little control over that. Trying to think much further ahead than that can be too much."

"Is that how you survived when you were wrongfully convicted of killing your boss and sent to prison?" Paige asked. She still had a hard time imagining the sunny, stylish woman in front of her living in a women's prison.

"It is," Lacy said. "Now that I'm in a better place, I can afford to think about the future more, but back then, I stayed focused on the now. It helped."

"The future like your wedding to Travis." Paige welcomed the chance to change the subject. "How are the plans coming?"

"They're going great."

All the way to CNG's offices, the two women talked wedding gowns, wedding cakes and wedding decorations. Lacy's happiness was contagious, and life seemed less bleak by the time Paige stepped out in the parking lot of the strip center to claim her car.

The door of CNG's office opened and Bryce Reed stepped out, followed by Mayor Larry Rowe. "Hello, Paige," Reed said.

"Are we interrupting something?" Paige asked, addressing her question to the mayor.

"The mayor and I were discussing groundbreaking for the new research facility," Reed said. "We want to make it a real event, with a barbecue, balloons for the kids, maybe even some games."

"You don't have approval from the county yet, do you?" Paige asked.

"With the mayor behind us, and your support, we shouldn't have any problems," Reed said.

The mayor said nothing, merely glowered at the two women and moved past them toward his SUV. Apparently, Paige's support for his new pet project wasn't enough to make him forgive her for past sins.

When the mayor had driven away, Reed said, "I was wondering if you'd forgotten about your car. I thought it would be gone before I got here, since you left the Dakota Ridge property before I did. You know I would have been happy to give you a ride back here to your car. You didn't have to run off."

She wasn't going to defend herself to this man, who at the moment sounded more like a whiny little boy. "Someone firebombed my house this afternoon," she said. "Do you know anything about that?"

"What?"

"Someone set my house on fire," Paige said.

"Paige, that's horrible." He rushed forward to take her hand. If he was faking his shock and concern, he was doing an Emmy-worthy job of it. "Are you all right? Is the damage very bad?"

"It's gone—everything I own and my business with it." Her voice shook, and she fought hard to keep back tears—tears of both sorrow and rage. "Do you know why anyone would do something like that to me?"

He took a step back. "I'm really sorry to hear that," he said. "But why would I know anything about it?"

Was he really as innocent as he looked? "Nothing bad happened to me until that day I was hiking and looked over onto your property and saw those two men, and they saw me," she said. "Since then, it's been one horrible thing after another."

"I can see how the timing seems suspicious to you," he said. "But from what I know of you and your efforts with the Eagle Mountain environmentalists, I think it's not unreasonable to believe that you're a woman who has made enemies in her life. But I'm not one of them."

Lacy touched her arm. "Maybe we should leave," she said softly.

"Yes." Paige walked to her car. Lacy went with her.

"Maybe the best thing to do would be to avoid anyone from CNG until things cool off," Lacy said. "If they do have something to do with the threats against you, there's no sense making them angrier."

Paige nodded. "You're right. I shouldn't have taken my anger over all this out on Reed." She glanced toward the office, but the door was shut now, with no sign of Bryce Reed.

"It's understandable." Lacy rubbed her back. "When

we get back to the house, why don't you take a hot bath and try to relax? I'll find some clothes for you to change into."

Paige realized the clothes she was wearing smelled of smoke from the fire. A hot bath did sound relaxing, but she didn't want to go to Lacy's house—not yet. She pulled her keys from her pocket. "Is it all right with you if I come to the house later?" she asked. "I'd like to drive around for a while—do some thinking and clear my head."

"Of course," Lacy said. "You'll be careful, won't you?"

"I will. I promise." She got into the car and waited until Lacy had pulled out of the lot before she drove out behind her. When Lacy turned off toward her parents' home, Paige kept going, all the way to the motel out by the highway. She drove around the lot until she spotted Rob's truck; apparently, the fire hadn't spread to the parking area beside her house and reached his vehicle.

She studied the row of rooms facing the parking area, then slipped her cell phone from her pocket and dialed his number. "Can I come see you?" she asked when he answered.

"Of course," he said. "Where are you now?"

"I'm right outside."

She waited, and in a few seconds, the door to one of the rooms opened and he stood there, dressed only in jeans, the phone in one hand. She got out of the car and went to him. When he pulled her into his arms, and into the room, it felt exactly like coming home.

Chapter Twelve

Rob let Paige lead the way, letting her show him what she wanted—what she needed. If she wanted comfort, he would do his best to comfort her. But as she wrapped herself around him and her lips claimed his, he realized she was picking up where they had left off at the B and B—finally letting down her guard and giving in to the passion that had sizzled between them since he had moved in under her roof.

She broke off the kiss and leaned back a little in his arms, her gaze sweeping over him, assessing. "Nice," she said, the single word sending heat through him. She planted a kiss in the center of his chest, and smoothed her hands over his stomach, stopping at the snap of his jeans. His erection strained against the fly, and when she dragged her nails over it, he shuddered.

Her eyes met his. "I hope you have protection," she said.

"I do."

"Oh?" She looked amused. "Awfully sure of yourself, aren't you?"

He gripped her waist, pulling her tight against him. "Paige, that firebomb wasn't the only thing burning in your house and you know it." He slid his hands up to cradle her head. "I've wanted you from the first day I saw you, in the hallway at the courthouse."

She blinked. "I was terrible to you that day. I accused you of not knowing how to do your job."

"Yeah, and I didn't like that one bit. But if you could have seen yourself—so beautiful and fierce and doing everything you could to stand up for your brother. I had to admire that."

"So angry women turn you on?" She slid her hands around to cup his bottom.

"No. But you turn me on."

"That first day, sex was definitely not on my mind," she said. "But you've grown on me." She reached down and started to lower his zipper, but he stopped her, then began undoing the buttons of her blouse. He pushed the fabric off her shoulders and paused to admire the full breasts swelling above the lace of her bra before reaching around and unfastening this garment and tossing it aside also.

She gasped when his lips closed over her nipple, and squirmed against him in a way that made his vision momentarily blur. He grasped her hips, stilling her, and transferred his attention to her other breast. At the same time, he lowered the zipper of her skirt and pushed it and her underwear down, until they puddled around her ankles.

He began kissing his way down her body, her skin soft and warm beneath his lips. When he lowered himself and put his mouth over her sex, she cried out and dug her fingers into his shoulders. He closed his eyes and his senses homed in on the taste and scent of her, the feel of her hands on him and his own desire building within him. All he wanted and needed right now was to be here with her, to give her as much pleasure as he was able.

She squirmed against him, her breath coming in gasps. He looked up, transfixed by the passion playing across her face. Being able to make her forget, at least for this little while, her fear and loss made him feel ten feet tall and bulletproof. She was the most precious thing in the world to him in that moment, worth every bit of aggravation she had ever caused him.

She came with a cry of triumph, and he rose to catch her in his arms, gathering her up and carrying her across the room to the bed, where they fell together, entwined.

Paige reveled in the feel of Rob's body against hers— all warm muscle and masculine strength, his every touch both tender and insistent. They stripped each other of the last of their clothing, and then he fumbled in the plastic shopping bag on the floor beside the bed and came up with a condom packet. Watching him sheathe himself with it left her breathless and trembling, but instead of pushing her down on the bed and kneeling over her, he lay back against the pillows and beckoned to her.

"What do you want?" she asked, grinning.

"The question is, what do *you* want?" He pulled her up on top of him and looked into her eyes.

She felt stripped of more than clothing beneath that gaze. He made her want a lot of things she had told herself for years that she didn't really need—companionship, protection, even love.

She kissed him, long and hard, then positioned herself over him and let him fill both her body and her spirit. They moved together, led by instinct and pleasure. They kept their eyes open, watching each other, seeing passion and trust reflected back. Their movements grew faster and more intense, and she felt herself losing control. But instead of holding back, she gave herself up to the moment, and a second, deeper climax overwhelmed her, even as he found his release beneath her.

They clung together for a long time afterward, her head on his chest, his arms wrapped around her, his sex still inside her. Then, with a long sigh, he rolled them to their sides and slid out. He discarded the condom, then lay back down, pulling her to him once more. "I'm glad you came to find me," he said, stroking her hair. "I wanted to go after you when you left with Lacy."

"She took me to get my car. Then I told her I needed to drive around and think."

"And you drove here." His gaze held the unspoken question—*why?*

"You're the person I wanted to be with," she said. "To tell you the truth, that surprises me—and frustrates me a little, too. I've worked so hard to be independent, it's hard for me to lean on someone else."

"I'm not going to confine you, Paige," he said. "I meant it when I said I appreciated how strong you are. I don't want to change that. But even the strongest nation in the world needs allies. Let me be yours."

She rested her head on his shoulder again, in that warm hollow where she fitted so perfectly. "I'm happy to have you as my ally," she said.

His arm tightened around her. "Does it upset you to talk about what happened this afternoon?"

"I think it might help, actually," she said. "Talking, I mean. Or at least, having you listen."

"Did you run into any trouble when you went back to CNG's office?" he asked.

"Bryce Reed came out of his office when Lacy and I showed up to get my car. The mayor was with him."

"I got the impression the two were pretty cozy on this project," Rob said.

"Larry still isn't speaking to me," she said. "He's never going to forgive me for opposing the original development. Not that I'm losing sleep over it."

"What about Reed?" Rob asked. "What did he say?"

"It's not so much what he said as what I said." She winced, remembering. "I kind of went off on him. I accused him of knowing something about the fire, and about the men who shot at me. He denied it, of course, and I felt bad afterward."

Rob massaged her shoulder. "Don't be so quick to mistrust your instincts," he said. "I can't prove Reed had anything to do with what happened today, but I'm going to be watching him closely. Everything seems connected to that property on Dakota Ridge. CNG owns the land, so how could Reed not be aware of what is happening up there?"

"I think I'm going to let you worry about that, while I focus on rebuilding my business." *And my life*, she silently added. She kissed his neck and sniffed. "You smell like smoke."

He kissed the top of her head. "So do you," he said. "I was getting ready to take a shower when you showed up."

"A shower sounds good. Is it big enough for two?"

"For two people who really like each other."

"Then why don't we give it a try?"

"I like the way you think."

PAIGE LEFT ROB'S hotel room well after dark, after she had called Lacy and apologized for being absent so long.

Rob hadn't tried to persuade her to stay, sensing that she wanted a little space between them to think about what had happened. So they'd parted with a kiss and a promise to talk again the next day. He slept fitfully, the smell of her clinging to the sheets and disturbing his dreams. Paige Riddell was a complex woman who promised to complicate his life considerably. But he had been taking the easy road when it came to relationships for all his adult life. Maybe it was time he tried a different, more challenging path.

He rose early, in time to call his Denver office before his boss reported for work. As he had hoped, the admin, Stacy, answered the phone. "Are you calling to tell us you're cutting your vacation short and coming back to work early?" she asked. "Because we're swamped."

"No," he said. "I'm calling to ask if you can do me a little favor."

"I thought you were supposed to be fishing," she said.

"I am—just not always for trout."

"What do you want me to do?" There was no mistaking the suspicion in her tone.

"I want you to do a little background check on a guy named Bryce Reed. He's chief financial officer of an outfit called CNG Development."

"Is this related to a case you're working on?" she asked.

"Peripherally."

"Is that a fancy way of saying no?"

"I just want a little history on the guy, and to know if he has a record," Rob said.

"The boss won't like it."

"The boss doesn't have to know."

The silence on the other end of the line was so long,

he wondered if she had disconnected. But at last she said, "True. As long as you're on the right side of the law."

"I promise I'm one of the good guys. And I'll bring you a box of Godiva chocolates for your trouble."

She laughed. "I'm not too sure you are a good guy, but I'm not going to pass up good chocolate. I'll run this guy and let you know what I find."

"Thanks."

He ended the call and checked the time—8:45. Too early to call Paige, who had had a rough day yesterday. Too early to drive out to the CNG offices and watch Bryce Reed.

Someone knocked on his hotel room door, and his heart sped up. He hurried to check outside and felt a little foolish when he saw that his visitor wasn't Paige, but Parker. "How did you know this was my room?" he asked, after he had opened the door.

Parker shrugged. "I saw your truck and figured I'd knock on doors until I found you. It's not like the motel is that big."

"What can I do for you?" Rob asked.

"Can I come in?"

"Sure." He stepped aside and the young man moved past him. He sat in one of the two chairs at the small table in front of the window, and Rob sat across from him.

Parker was wearing the same black T-shirt he'd had on the day before, and the same jeans, though he had shaved and smelled of soap.

"Everything go okay with the professor last night?" Rob asked.

"Yeah. He's cool." He shifted in his chair and looked around the room—everywhere but at Rob.

"What can I do for you?" Rob asked again.

At last Parker's gaze met his. "I want to help find out who is doing all this stuff to Paige," he said.

"How can you help?" Rob asked.

"I don't know. But two people are better than one, right?" He ran his hand through his short hair. "I just don't want to stand around doing nothing while someone tries to hurt her again," he said.

"Any ideas who that someone might be?" Rob asked.

Parker frowned. "I was up on Dakota Ridge again the evening after that day you and Paige and the sheriff saw me." He held up his hand. "I know I promised I wouldn't trespass up there again, but this was important. If I was going to find that World War II lab, I had to do it before CNG broke ground on their new research facility. After that, the place will be crawling with construction crews."

"You were there the evening those two men were killed?" Rob asked. "And you're just now saying something?"

"I didn't see anyone killed," Parker said. "And I don't know anything about the fire, either. But I did see some strange stuff while I was up there. Maybe it doesn't have anything to do with Paige, but what if it does?"

Rob studied the younger man. Parker's shoulders were slumped, but his expression was that of a man refusing to accept defeat. "Why come to me instead of the sheriff?" he asked. "I don't have any official role in this case."

No fidgeting this time. "You heard the questions Sheriff Walker was asking me yesterday. He already thinks I might have something to do with all of this."

"I think the sheriff is trying to look at this from all angles and cover all the bases," Rob said. "He's being a good cop."

Parker's look of disdain said he didn't believe "good"

and "cop" should be used in the same sentence. "You didn't turn me in to him after you saw me up at Dakota Ridge that day," he said.

"Maybe I was just trying to impress your sister."

"I figured that was a given. But you wouldn't be the worst thing that ever happened to her."

Rob definitely hadn't expected that, and had to resist the urge to ask Parker to elaborate. But now wasn't the time. "What did you see up on Dakota Ridge?" he asked.

"A helicopter. One of those little ones, like a traffic copter or something. Only this one was very sleek and expensive looking. I heard it coming and ducked into some really deep undergrowth. I figured it was a medical chopper, or maybe military, and would fly over. Instead, it landed right there in the middle of what used to be a street. The door opened and these two guys in camo fatigues, with AR-15s, jumped out. Then a man in a business suit followed them."

Rob sat forward, alert and intrigued. "What did they do?"

"The guys with the guns unloaded a wooden crate from the helicopter, while the guy in the suit watched. There was a pilot, too, but he never got out."

Paige had mentioned seeing two men carrying a wooden crate that day on the hiking trail. "What did they do with the crate?" Rob asked.

Parker shook his head. "I don't know. About that time a deer wandered out of the woods. One of the guys with the guns whirled around and fired on it—just about cut it in half. Totally freaked me out. All I wanted to do was get out of there as fast as I could. I crept back in the woods, as quietly as I could. It was probably only five minutes, but it seemed like forever until I was over the fence, and maybe another fifteen before I got to where I had parked my car, in the woods about a quarter mile back toward town."

"What time was this?" Rob asked.

"It was early. The commissioners' meeting started at six thirty, and this was before then, but not too far ahead of time—maybe six o'clock."

"What time did you leave?"

"It was six forty when I got back to my car."

The fire had been called in at seven thirty. "The crate sounds like the one Paige saw," Rob said. "Similar, at least. Did you recognize any of the men?"

"No. But I have pictures." He took his phone from his pocket, swiped through a few screens, then turned it toward Rob. "I was back in the woods a ways, and I was so nervous I was shaking, but maybe if you blow them up or work some magic in a photo lab…"

Rob stared at the blurry photograph of two men in fatigues and one in a suit, standing by a helicopter. Their faces were too indistinct to make out.

"There's more, if you want to flip through," Parker said.

The next image was a closer shot of the man in the suit. The third picture was zoomed in even closer. Though still not distinct, the photograph did make one thing clear.

"This isn't Bryce Reed," Rob said. And he didn't think the men in fatigues were either of the ones who had been killed and left to burn in the shack.

"No," Parker agreed. "I never saw this guy before in my life."

Chapter Thirteen

Paige spent much of the next day canceling reservations, helping people find new accommodations, dealing with the insurance company and transferring money from savings to pay her ongoing bills. Later, she would need to go shopping, to replace at least a few of her necessities, and she would need to start hunting for a place to live.

She hung up the phone after yet another call and stared out the window of the guest bedroom where she was working. Lacy and her parents were warm and gracious hosts, who lent her clothes and toiletries, and didn't ask questions about where she had been until late the night before, but Paige couldn't stay here long-term. She wasn't comfortable being an unexpected guest, and though the Milligans weren't at all intrusive, she valued her privacy.

She resisted the urge to call Rob. He was probably working, and the last thing she wanted was for him to think that one night of incredible sex had turned her clingy. She had decidedly mixed feelings about getting involved with the lawman. On one hand, he had been a rock at a time when everything else in her world was unsteady. He was a lot smarter—and a lot more compassionate—than she had given him credit for. He liked—

or at least he said he liked—her independence. And yes, the sex had been pretty incredible.

But he wasn't going to stay in Eagle Mountain, and she had no intention of changing her life for the sake of a man ever again. And who was to say all these warm feelings between them hadn't been generated by her current crises situation? When life settled down again, they might turn out to hate each other. Better to not let herself get too emotionally invested until she knew for sure.

She closed the notebook she had been using to keep track of all her tasks and went downstairs. She needed to get out and clear her head, so she took a walk downtown, and ended up at the Eagle Mountain History Museum.

Brenda Stenson looked up from behind the front counter when she entered. "Paige!" Brenda came out to envelop her in a hug. "I heard about your B and B. How horrible for you."

"Yeah, well, I figured I'd see if you had any advice for me when it came to rebuilding." Brenda's own house had been destroyed by an arsonist earlier in the summer. That man had been caught, but what were the odds of two women being the victims of intentional fires in such a short period of time, in such a small town?

"I can tell you plenty of things not to do," Brenda said.

"Such as?"

"Such as don't decide to build something completely different from the original house and expect the insurance company to just hand over the check," she said. "I had to threaten to take my insurer to court, and jump through dozens of hoops, before they finally agreed I could build a triplex in place of my original single-family home."

"I drove by the site the other day and it looks as if things are coming along nicely," Paige said.

"They are—finally. And I have a waiting list of potential renters."

"I guess this means you won't be moving back into one of the units?" Paige asked.

"Dwight and I prefer his cabin on the ranch."

"I'm happy for you." Paige was telling the truth. Brenda had suffered through a lot since her husband, Andy, had been murdered, and she deserved all the happiness she had found with Deputy Dwight Prentice. But Paige wasn't in the same situation as Brenda. "Too bad your rental units aren't already finished," she said. "I'm going to need some place to live until my house can be rebuilt. From everything I heard this morning, it could be a year or more before I'm ready to open for business."

"Oh, Paige, I'm so sorry." Brenda leaned over and squeezed her hand. "What will you do in the meantime?"

"I'll have to find a job. Not a lot of those around, either."

"Maybe you could find another house to run as a B and B," Brenda said.

"I thought of that. But I'd never be able to swing the loan, not when I still have a mortgage on the Bear's Den." Those payments would have to continue to be made while the house was being rebuilt. "I've got a business degree and experience running my own business," she said. "I'll find something."

"When you're ready, I can put you in touch with my contractor," Brenda said. "And if you have any questions about permitting or zoning, I feel like I'm becoming a local expert on those topics."

"Thanks," Paige said. "That's not the only reason I

stopped by this afternoon. I wanted to ask you about Professor Gibson."

"Oh?" Brenda looked surprised. "What about him?"

"Parker is staying with him until I can find a place for both of us," she said. "And they're working together on some kind of project involving that secret World War II laboratory that was supposedly located in the county."

"That's right," Brenda said. "You can blame me for getting the two of them together. I heard the professor was interested in digging into the history of the lab and I knew Parker would be the perfect person to help him. From what Parker tells me, they've really hit it off."

"I guess so," Paige said. "I just worry about Parker getting into trouble, trespassing on private land or poking his nose where he shouldn't while trying to find this lab. And wasn't the government working on some really dangerous stuff there? What if he finds it and is exposed to some horrible disease?"

"I wonder if that's what happened to Henry Hake," Brenda said.

"I heard a rumor he died of tularemia," Paige said.

Brenda nodded. "The rumor is true. And the professor tells me tularemia is one of the things the government was working on in that lab."

"But the underground space where they found Henry Hake wasn't the World War II lab," Paige said.

"No, it wasn't." Brenda shrugged. "Maybe it's just a weird coincidence. Do you want me to put a bug in the professor's ear about making sure Parker plays it safe? He and I have gotten to be pretty good friends since he took an interest in the museum."

"I'd appreciate it," Paige said. "But make sure he

doesn't know it came from me. Parker already thinks I meddle in his life too much."

The bell on the door rang as a couple with two elementary school–age girls entered. Paige excused herself and went back outside. Her phone rang as she was crossing the street—a number she didn't recognize. When she answered, she was surprised to hear Bryce Reed's voice.

"Paige. I'm glad I caught you," he said. "How are you doing?"

"I'm coping." The best answer she could think of, considering all that had happened.

"I'm calling to invite you to a press conference at our Dakota Ridge property tomorrow morning," he said. "We're going to officially unveil our plans for the site and I'd love to have you there."

So he hadn't really been calling to see how she was doing. She couldn't decide whether to be annoyed at his lack of concern or relieved. "So the county commissioners have approved your plans?" she asked.

"Oh, they will," he said. "We've heard only good things from that quarter. This is to get the public excited about what we're going to be doing. Will you be there?"

"I'll try to make it," she said. "What time?"

"Ten o'clock. I'll save a place for you."

He disconnected before she could tell him she wasn't going to be CNG's pet environmentalist, but decided that was her bad mood talking. She would go to the press conference tomorrow, if only for a chance to have another look at the property.

PAIGE WAS WAITING on the front porch when Rob arrived to pick her up for dinner that evening. As he made his way up the walk, he felt a little like a teenager, picking up his date from her parents' house. The full-skirted, flowered dress she wore added to the retro feel of the moment. He took a chance and kissed her cheek in greeting. "How are you doing?" he asked.

"All right." She smoothed the skirt of the dress. "Lacy loaned me this. It's a little frillier than I usually go for."

"It looks good on you," he said. He glanced toward the door. "Should we go inside and say hello?"

"Lacy and her folks are having dinner at Travis's family ranch. They asked me to come, too, but I think they were relieved when I told them I had other plans. They've been great about respecting my privacy."

Maybe that was because Paige was the type of woman who gave off very clear warnings for others not to get too close. Which made him feel especially privileged that she had let down her guard with him. "Where would you like to go for dinner?" he asked.

"Would you mind if we stayed here?" she asked. "I can't go anywhere in town without people stopping me to say how sorry they are about the fire, and wanting to know exactly what happened. I appreciate their concern, but it's wearing me out, not to mention the strain of reliving everything over and over again."

"Staying in sounds good." He followed her into the house, and through to a sunny breakfast room.

"Mrs. Milligan was happy to let me use her kitchen." The table was set for two, with salads and bread already in place, and a bottle of wine chilling in a silver tub. He sat where she directed and a feeling of contentment washed over him—surprising, since he had never considered himself the domestic sort.

While they ate, she talked about her day—the telephone conversations with her guests and the insurance company, and her visit with Brenda. "Do you think Henry Hake could have stumbled upon that old lab and contracted tularemia that way?" she asked.

"It's possible, I suppose," Rob said. "Though no one has found anything to indicate that. Apparently, tularemia lives in the soil in a lot of areas—so it might have been something as simple as digging a hole and breathing in particles of dirt, and being particularly vulnerable because of his heart condition."

"It probably is something like that," she said. She refilled their wineglasses. "Oh, I almost forgot—Bryce Reed called me this afternoon and invited me to a press conference he's giving up at Dakota Ridge tomorrow, to publicly unveil CNG's plans for the research facility."

"Still trying to get your support for the project?" Rob asked.

"I suppose. I want to go to the press conference, if only to get another look at the property."

"I'll go with you. I'd like to have another look at it, too," he added, before she could protest that she didn't need a bodyguard.

"I did some digging into Bryce Reed's background today," he said.

"Oh?" Paige laid down her fork and gave him her full attention. "What did you find out?"

"He's been chief financial officer for CNG for nine months, in charge of special projects. Apparently this research lab is a special project. Before that, he worked for a couple of oil companies, a financial management firm and a manufacturing conglomerate. Pretty run-of-the-mill corporate stuff."

"So nothing juicy?" Paige picked up her fork again and resumed eating the lasagna she had prepared.

"Not in his business life. His personal life is a little more interesting."

Her mouth full, she nodded that he should continue.

"He's been married three times, divorced three times. Five children, none of whom live with him."

"None of that makes him a bad person," Paige said. "I'm divorced."

"I never said it did. No, the interesting part is how he spends his time outside of work. He's been a member of several organizations the FBI classifies as fringe groups."

Paige wrinkled her nose. "What does that mean? I imagine more than a few people here in town consider Eagle Mountain environmentalists to be a fringe group."

"In this case, these are extremist groups that have advocated for things like white supremacy and limiting voting in elections to those with a certain income level."

"Is he a member of any of those groups now?" she asked.

"No. And he's never been convicted of a crime."

"So maybe those earlier affiliations were mistakes of his youth and he's a more moderate thinker now." She pushed her plate away and sipped her wine. "Lots of people make mistakes when they're young. They shouldn't have to pay for them the rest of their lives."

Rob was sure she was thinking of Parker. "Your brother came to see me this morning," he said.

She straightened. "He didn't come to see me. I haven't even talked to him since yesterday."

"He volunteered to help in any way he could to find out who has been harassing you."

Her expression softened. "And he accuses me of worrying too much about him. What did you tell him?"

"I don't know that there's much he can do—not now, at least." He decided not to mention Parker's story about the helicopter and the men with guns. She was worried enough without that burden. "I'm not even sure where to focus our efforts. I can't figure out if CNG is legit or not—they're deliberately calling attention to themselves with this new high-altitude research facility, when they could have pretended they weren't going to do anything at all with the land, and probably gotten away with whatever they wanted for a long time. So maybe they really have nothing to do with any criminal activity and someone has simply been using land they thought was vacant. Something else interesting I found out about them."

"What's that?"

"Your mayor, Larry Rowe, is a stockholder in CNG."

"You're kidding." She paused, thinking. "That's a conflict of interest, isn't it?"

"It could be. Especially if he received the stock recently, in exchange for his support for the Dakota Ridge project. I haven't had time to dig into that yet."

"I always suspected Larry was for sale to the highest bidder," Paige said.

"Reed is the man I'm most interested in," Rob said. "I asked my admin to do some more digging."

"I think we should get to the site early tomorrow," Paige said. "I want to hike up the trail and see if he kept his promise to take down the gate over the trail."

"And if he hasn't?"

"If he hasn't, I might have to raise the question at his press conference."

"That won't make him happy."

"I'm not interested in making him happy," she said. "I'm interested in making things right."

That was the Paige Rob knew best—the crusader, ready to wage battle and defeat injustice. She ignored her vulnerability by being strong. How could he get past the toughness she wore like body armor and prove she had no need for shields with him?

Chapter Fourteen

Paige couldn't have asked for a better day for a hike when she and Rob set out on the Dakota Ridge Trail the next morning before CNG's press conference. The autumn air was so crisp it practically crackled, and the gold of aspen leaves carpeted the trails and shone bright against a Colorado blue sky. Eyes closed, she breathed in deeply of the pine-scented air, her muscles unknotting as some of her tension eased.

"It's better than a tranquilizer, isn't it?" Rob asked. He had pulled a day pack from the back seat of her car and shrugged into it. Dressed in hiking boots, jeans and a flannel shirt worn open over a black T, he didn't look like a cop today—if you ignored the pistol under that shirt, which she intended to do.

"I need the outdoors like some people need coffee," she said. She wore her own pack over a cropped denim jacket, skinny jeans and a muted gold turtleneck. "And this is one of my favorite places—which is why I was so upset when the gate was installed over the trail." She led the way up the red dirt path.

Rob fell into step beside her. "I did a lot more of this kind of thing before I moved to Denver," he said. "I used to hike in the Alleghenies almost every weekend when I lived in West Virginia."

"Why did you stop?" she asked. "It's not like Denver doesn't have hiking trails."

He shrugged. "I got busy at work. I didn't have anyone to go with. Really, I think I just got lazy. You've reminded me of what I've been missing." His eyes met hers and she wondered if he meant he had been missing more than hiking.

She looked away and he continued, "I'm still hoping to get in some fishing before I leave town."

She didn't look at him. "And when will that be?"

"The fishing? I don't know. It depends on the case."

"I meant, when will you be leaving town?"

"That depends on the case, too."

Right. But he *would* be leaving. She needed to remember that.

He took her hand in his. "I'm not going yet," he said. "Maybe I'll take you with me fishing."

Her breath had stopped at the words *maybe I'll take you with me,* and then she scolded herself for being so foolish. Since when had she wanted a man to take her anywhere? To his bed, maybe. Out to dinner occasionally. She appreciated a man who took her into his confidence, though she could admit she didn't readily return the favor. No, she didn't want Rob to take her anywhere. She didn't know what she wanted from him, really, and the idea frustrated her. She was never this indecisive about anything. Could she blame the stress she was under, with the threats on her life and the destruction of her home and livelihood?

Beside her, Rob tensed, one hand reaching for the gun beneath his shirt, the other at her back. "What is it?" she asked, fear tightening her throat and making the words come out strained.

"I thought I heard someone over there." He nodded toward the fence that marked the boundary of CNG's property.

They stood still, listening. After a long moment, Paige shook her head. "I didn't hear anything. It was probably just a bird or a deer or something."

"You're right." He took his hand from the gun, but kept his palm against her back. "As beautiful as it is up here, it spooks me."

"Me, too. And that makes me even angrier. Whoever fired those shots took away my peace of mind in the wilderness."

"The way to regain that peace is to fight back," he said.

"Yes. And that's exactly what I intend to do." She quickened her pace as they passed the place where the shots had been fired, but she couldn't resist the urge to look in that direction. There was nothing to see but an opening in the trees and part of the fence.

Rob put a hand on her back again. He didn't say anything, but he didn't have to. The warm, firm weight of his touch told her he had faith in her to fight through this—and that he would be fighting with her. "I should have brought the bolt cutters and hacksaw with me," she said, her tone teasing. "Would you have to arrest me if I cut off the lock?"

"I don't know," he said. "I might have to place you in my personal custody."

"You might have to handcuff me to keep me from escaping."

"I might have to," he said. "And do a thorough search to make sure you aren't carrying any weapons."

The slope they were climbing had little to do with her heavy breathing now. She hoped the press conference was short. She would suggest they go back to Rob's hotel room and try out some of his ideas.

He must have had the same idea, because he began to walk faster, and she hurried to keep up. They topped a rise and she could see the gate—and the section of trail where the gate wasn't supposed to be. The heavy iron structure was still in place, blocking the way, with heavy barbed wire preventing anyone from getting around it.

She stopped and swore.

"When did Reed say he was going to remove it?" Rob asked.

"Right away, I thought," she said. "Just wait until I see him. I'm going to give him a piece of my mind about this. And I'll make sure every reporter at this press conference hears. If he expects my support for this project, then he needs to keep his promises. He can't restrict public access to a historic trail. This hiking trail has been in use for over a hundred years. The easement transfers with the title and all his money and power can't make it go away. When I finish with him—"

She stopped, aware of Rob's calm gaze on her. He looked as if he was trying very hard not to smile. "What?" she demanded. "What's so funny?"

He shook his head. "Nothing's funny. I just love how you're so passionate."

Warmth spread through her body as she remembered how he had brought out another kind of passion in her—one she had kept in check for too many years. Had he deliberately chosen that word to distract her? "At least you didn't tell me I'm cute when I'm angry," she said.

"No, not cute," he said. "Beautiful, and more than a little intimidating—but not 'cute.'"

He shuddered, and she couldn't help but laugh. She took his hand. "Come on. Let's get over to the press conference."

On the way back down the trail, she stopped again at the opening where she had looked in and seen the two men with the crate. "While I'm holding Reed's feet to the fire," she said, "I'm going to ask him to walk back here with me and look for that opening where the two men I saw stowed the crate. He says he has nothing to hide—let him prove it."

"He's not going to know what hit him," Rob said.

"By the time I'm done," she said. "I have a feeling Bryce Reed is going to wish he hadn't invited me today."

They returned to the car and, after she unlocked it, stashed their packs in the back once more. Instead of then going to the passenger door, however, Rob took a slow walk around the vehicle, studying it carefully.

"What are you doing?" she asked.

"Making sure no one's tampered with it while we were gone." His eyes met hers over the top of the car, and his grave expression sent a shiver down her spine. "Just being careful."

"Do you see anything?" she asked.

He opened the passenger door. "No. I think we're fine."

Her heart sped up when she turned the key in the ignition, movie scenes of exploding cars replaying in her brain. But the engine turned over smoothly and she backed out of the parking space without incident.

The gates to the resort compound were open. The first thing she noticed was that the fading sign advertising the resort had been replaced with a new placard that proclaimed this was the Future Home of Dakota Ridge Research and Development, a project of CNG Development.

The second thing she noticed was that hers was the only car in sight. "Where is everybody?" she asked. She checked the time. Nine forty-five. "The press conference is supposed to start at ten. I would think at least some people would be here by now. Reed, at least, should be here."

"Let's take a look around," Rob said. "But do me a favor and drive back out and park on the shoulder of the road."

"Why?" she asked, even as she turned the car around.

"If someone comes along and closes that gate, you don't want to be stuck in here."

She stared at him. "Do you always think in terms of worst-case scenarios?"

"It's part of my training."

She parked on the shoulder, facing toward town, and they both got out and walked back up to CNG's property, and through the open gates. Their footsteps sounded overly loud on the gravel, and louder still as they crunched over a carpet of dried leaves that had settled in a low spot where the asphalt had worn away from what had once been the main street of the resort.

She zipped up her jacket and fought off a chill. "Maybe I got the time wrong," she said. "Maybe it's supposed to be at noon instead of ten. Though I could have sworn Reed said ten."

"The gate's open," Rob said. "Someone's been up here."

"Then where are they now?" She stopped and scanned the empty streets and abandoned buildings. Empty land-

scapes usually didn't upset her. Deserted forests and vacant mountaintops usually made her feel surrounded by
peace. But this ghost town, where people had tried and
failed to make their mark, creeped her out right down
to her toes.

Rob took her arm, breaking the eerie spell. "Come
on," he said. "Let's go find out where everyone is."

"THIS PRESS CONFERENCE will be the perfect opportunity
for us to visit CNG's Dakota Ridge property with no
worries about trespassing." Professor Gibson wore an
excited expression that made him look years younger
than the eightysomething he would admit to. "As much
as I appreciate you doing the legwork so far, I'm determined to see the place for myself."

"I doubt they're going to let people wander anywhere
they please," Parker said. "And maybe they're only going
to let in people they've invited. Paige said Bryce Reed
from CNG called to invite her."

"My guess is there will be a lot of people there," the
professor said. "You can't keep something like this quiet
in a small town. Everyone in the county who can make
the time will be there to see what's so special it has to
be protected with a big iron gate and razor wire. They
won't be able to keep track of all of us. Besides, I intend
to question this CNG executive—Reed—to try to determine how much he knows about local history. It could
be his bunch has already located the secret lab and is
keeping the find to themselves."

"If they're doing that, they won't tell you about it,"
Parker said.

"You might be surprised how persuasive I can be in
my 'teacher' guise," Gibson said. "Most people are con-

ditioned from a young age to obey that voice of authority. It's a very hard habit to break."

Parker wasn't buying it, but he kept quiet about it. The professor did have an uncanny way of getting things done. "Paige said the press conference is at ten," he said. "What time do you want to leave?"

"I want to get there a few minutes early," Gibson said. "I can introduce myself to Mr. Reed and talk to him while you have a look around. You still have the map I gave you?"

"Yes, sir." Parker grinned. He might have guessed the old man intended for him to do his dirty work. Which was fine by Parker. Working with the professor was way more exciting than delivering pizza or writing English papers.

"We'll take my car." Gibson handed Parker the keys to the late-model Nissan. "You drive. And park on the road—not on the property itself. I would rather walk than get caught in the press of people leaving."

"Okay." Parking on the road was better if they needed to make a quick getaway, too.

"I've uncovered some new material on how Russia tested tularemia as a weapon of mass destruction in some very remote populations on the steppes," Gibson said. "Fascinating stuff."

For the rest of the drive out of town and up toward Dakota Ridge, the professor retold the tales of Russian experimentation, which were both fascinating and horrifying.

"The US didn't do anything like that, did they?" Parker asked.

"Not that I have been able to determine," Gibson said. "Of course, the work they were doing in Rayford County lasted less than a decade. I think by the end, they had determined that tularemia wasn't as effective a method of infecting a large number of people as things like anthrax or Q fever."

"Not with the antibiotics we have today, right?" Parker asked.

"Antibiotics don't do any good if you don't administer them," Gibson said. "In remote areas, or on particularly vulnerable populations, I imagine it would still be quite harmful."

They fell silent for the rest of the drive, Parker remembering the last time he had been up here—the day he had watched a helicopter land and a mysterious tall man in a suit and two men in camo emerge. He hadn't told the professor about that yet. Partly because he didn't want to upset the old man, and partly because he worried Gibson would call off the search for the lab just when they were so close to finding it.

"I had expected more traffic coming up here," Gibson said, as they passed the turnout for the hiking trail and climbed toward the entrance to CNG's property. "Park anywhere in here." He motioned to the side of the road.

Parker swung the car around so that it faced back toward town, and parked on the shoulder. He got out and waited while the professor unfolded himself from the seat and stood. Then he locked the vehicle and pocketed the keys. He figured he would be driving back, so he might as well keep them.

They walked up the road a short distance and turned in at the entrance to the property. The professor stopped first, staring at the big iron gate, which was pulled over the drive and locked with a large padlock. Parker stared at the lock, then shifted his eyes to a piece of paper affixed to the gate with duct tape.

The professor moved toward the paper, and Parker followed. The note, written on what looked like a plain 8½-by-11-inch piece of copy paper, was neatly typed, and read, "Today's press conference has been canceled. It will be rescheduled for a later date. We apologize for the inconvenience."

That was it—no explanation and no signature. The professor pushed back the sleeve of his jacket and checked his watch—a big, old-fashioned nickel-colored one with an expandable metal band. "It is almost exactly ten o'clock," he said.

"There must have been other people who didn't get word about the cancellation," Parker said. "Where are they?"

"I don't know." The professor tugged at the gate. It didn't move. He looked at the fence on either side, which had wicked curls of razor wire along the top. *Prison wire*, Parker thought, then pushed the thought aside.

"Did you say there's another way in?" the professor asked.

"There is, but you have to climb a tree. It's pretty rough going."

Gibson took Parker's arm. "Show me. And don't look at me as if I've lost what mind I have left. I was quite the athlete in my day. I think I can handle a tree. And I didn't come this far not to get a look at this place."

Chapter Fifteen

"I feel like an extra in some B-grade horror movie," Rob said, as he and Paige made their way down the deserted streets. He stared hard at the few remaining buildings. "I keep expecting a badly made-up zombie to lurch out at us."

"You're not helping," she said, and took his arm. "Maybe we should leave. Obviously, no one is here."

"Someone is here," Rob said.

"What makes you say that?"

He shrugged. "It's like when you're in a room in the dark—you can tell someone else is there because the air is different."

She looked at him as if he had grown an extra head. "I have no idea what you're talking about."

"Maybe it's a cop thing."

"Or maybe you're paranoid."

"Maybe that, too."

She inhaled slowly and straightened her shoulders. "If someone else is here, that means they're watching us," she said. "So I really think we should leave."

"We'll leave in a little bit," he said. "But something is going on here, and I'd like to find out what."

She nodded. "Yeah. I would, too. But I'd like to do it without getting shot at this time."

"Me, too." He took her arm and pulled her closer. "We'll just look around a little more. If we don't find anything, we'll leave. Why don't we try to find that entrance you saw to that underground chamber?"

This idea apparently intrigued her enough to set aside her fear. "It's nearer the fence," she said. "Do you remember where I showed you?"

"I think so." He led the way across a crumbling foundation, rusting rebar jutting up from the concrete, weeds sprouting in cracks. They both jumped when a chipmunk darted in front of them.

Paige gave a nervous laugh. "Maybe that was a zombie squirrel," she said.

"Can't be," Rob said. "He wasn't badly dressed."

They relaxed a little after that. Moving into the woods, out of the open, helped, he thought. He didn't feel so exposed in the shelter of the trees. They moved slowly, studying the ground for any sign of a trapdoor or grate, or any access to an underground chamber.

"I know I didn't imagine those two men disappearing into the ground with that crate," Paige said, frustration tightening her voice. "I'm sure it was right around here. I can see the fence where I was standing." She gestured toward the iron bars, and the small opening in the trees on the other side.

"They would have hidden it well," Rob said. "Let's keep looking."

He moved forward a few more steps, scanning the ground. Behind him, Paige let out a cry. "Rob. Come here!"

When he joined her, she was kneeling in the dirt and

leaves, tugging at what he thought at first was a tree root. "I think this is the handle to the trapdoor," she said. "I remember now one of the men lifted a door out of the way before he climbed down into the hole."

Rob dropped to his knees beside her and together they raked back dirt and leaves to reveal a square piece of rusty steel, with a metal handle attached. He stood and helped Paige to her feet, then took hold of the handle and tugged. "Uh." He let out a grunt. "It's heavy."

"Let me help." She wedged her fingers next to his and together they hauled back on the door. With a groan of metal on metal, it shifted, and they managed to drag it aside.

They leaned over and stared down into a black opening. Cool air hit Rob in the face, bringing the scents of damp earth and rusting metal. He pulled his phone from his pocket and switched on the flashlight app, then shone the beam into the opening, illuminating an iron-runged ladder affixed to wooden timbers sunk into the earth. But the darkness beyond quickly swallowed up the light.

"I think it might be an old mine shaft," he said.

"Just down in the ground like this?" she asked. "Don't they usually have some kind of structure over them?"

"Maybe there was one, but it was torn down," he said. "Or the main entrance is somewhere else and this is just a side tunnel someone decided to access. The ladder looks new." He leaned over, trying to see into the darkness. "I wonder what's down there."

Paige took a step back. "I'm not going to go check."

"No." He pocketed the phone again. "Maybe we can get a warrant and come out here with a team." Someone had gone to a lot of trouble to conceal this place, and he wanted to know why. And he wanted to find out what those two men had been hiding down there that had been so important they had tried more than once to kill Paige. "I'd like—"

But he never finished his sentence, as the rapid tattoo of gunfire echoed off the ridge. Men's voices shouted, and branches popped and the ground rumbled with the pounding of running feet.

"We have to get out of here before they see us," Paige said.

But it was already too late for that. A man in forest camo emerged from the woods and raised a rifle to his shoulder. Rob shoved Paige hard toward the opening in the ground. "Get down there," he said.

He was prepared to force her out of the range of gunfire if he had to, but she didn't argue, merely descended the ladder. Rob dropped in after her, as bullets struck the dirt near his head. At the last minute, he reached up and, strengthened by fear and dire need, dragged the trapdoor back into place.

"What do we do now?" Paige's voice trembled as it came to him in the utter darkness.

Rob switched on his flashlight again to illuminate a narrow tunnel lined with rock and timbers. He took Paige's cold hand in his. "Now we run."

THE PROFESSOR NAVIGATED the fallen tree with more agility than Parker would have expected. The old man seemed energized by this adventure, striding through the woods ahead of Parker, looking around with interest. "Do you have the map?" he asked, when they were several hundred yards into the property.

"Right here." Parker took the map the professor had drawn and unfolded it.

Gibson studied the drawing, one hand rubbing his chin. "I think we're about here," he said, pointing to a spot on the map. "So we want to walk this direction." He indicated a large circle on the map. "I think the lab we're looking for is somewhere within this perimeter."

"That's a pretty big area," Parker said. Judging by the scale of the map, the circle took in half a dozen acres or more.

"Then we'd better get busy." The professor pocketed the map. "We have a lot of ground to cover."

They started walking again, but hadn't gone far when a volley of gunfire froze them in their tracks. "We'd better get out of here," Parker said, and turned to leave.

The professor grabbed his arm. "We need to see what—or who—they're shooting at."

Parker gaped at him. "Why do we need to see that? And what makes you think they won't decide to start shooting at us?"

"Come on." The old man pulled on his arm, a lot harder than Parker would have thought possible. "We won't let them see us. But we need to find out what's going on so we can report it to the sheriff."

Reluctantly, Parker let the professor lead him in the direction of the shots. After all, he couldn't run off and abandon the old guy. And despite his heart beating so hard his chest hurt, he had to admit he was curious.

They crept through the trees, keeping to the deepest shadows and moving as soundlessly as possible. They both froze when a man in forest camo ran past, cradling a rifle to his chest. He was only about five feet from them, but he never saw them, so intent was he on his destination somewhere ahead.

They stood frozen for several minutes, Parker scarcely

daring to breathe. The professor's fingers dug into his arm, but Parker didn't flinch. "We need to leave," he whispered, trying again.

"Not yet," Gibson said, and started forward, in the direction the man with the gun had run.

Parker wanted to tell the old fool that while he might have lived a full life and not care if he lost it now, Parker had a lot of good years left, and he wanted to enjoy them all. But then he remembered the professor's tales of growing up in the Great Depression and fighting in Korea, and knew the man wasn't foolhardy; he was just a lot tougher than Parker would ever be. And Parker couldn't let him walk into whatever trouble was up ahead alone. So he tried to straighten his shoulders and not think about getting killed, and walked on.

The gunshots grew louder and more frequent. The two of them reached the edge of a clearing and Parker had to bite his lip to keep from crying out. Ahead of them, Paige and Rob crouched on the ground as half a dozen men with guns ran toward them. Parker closed his eyes, not wanting to see his sister cut to pieces by bullets. Then he opened them again, unable to abandon her to her fate.

"We have to do something!" he whispered to the professor.

Gibson remained silent, though his grip on Parker tightened, as if he feared the younger man might charge into the clearing.

As they stared, Paige and Rob disappeared. Or rather, they dropped out of sight, apparently into a hole in the ground. Rob pulled some kind of trapdoor after them.

Parker's eyes met the professor's, who had pulled out his cell phone and was taking photographs—though his hand shook so badly, Parker wondered how in-focus those pictures would be. He took the phone and snapped a few more shots of the scene, amazed that his own hand was so steady. Then he passed the phone back to the professor, who pushed it into his pocket and motioned that they should head back the way they had come.

Parker glanced over his shoulder at the men with guns standing around the now-closed trapdoor. He hoped he and the professor could get help in time. Or that hole in the ground might as well be Paige's grave.

Chapter Sixteen

Paige followed Rob down the long, dark corridor. Or rather, she followed the glow of his cell phone, which reflected dirt walls braced with rocks and timbers slick with moisture. The floor they ran on was wet, too, so they occasionally slipped and caught themselves by grabbing hold of the wall. "Where are we going?" she said to Rob's back.

He stopped, one hand braced on a timber, and looked back at her. "I don't know," he said. "But the farther away we get from that trapdoor, the better."

"They know where we are," she said. "They don't have to hurry." Whoever "they" were.

He raised his hand. "Listen."

She held her breath and focused on detecting any sound. Was that the scrape of metal on metal as they opened the trapdoor—or merely her own ragged breathing?

Rob frowned. "They're not coming in after us," he said.

"Like I said, they don't have to hurry. Maybe they're waiting for more men to show up, with more guns." She shuddered, picturing the figures in military fatigues who had run out of the woods, guns blazing. The shock had been like stumbling onto a battlefield in the middle of an otherwise peaceful setting.

"Why wouldn't they come after us?" Rob asked. "They saw us climb down here."

Times like this, she wished her imagination wasn't quite so vivid. Maybe their pursuers hadn't followed them down here because they were going to flood the tunnel with gas and asphyxiate them. Maybe they'd throw explosives in after them. Maybe they intended to just seal them off and let them starve to death down here. She didn't say any of this—saying the words out loud would make them too real.

She swallowed hard, forcing back panic. "Why do you think they didn't come after us?" she asked.

He looked up and down the corridor. "I think there's another entrance," he said. "Maybe one that's easier to access." His eyes met hers, difficult to read in the dim light. "But they'll have someone—probably a couple of people—watching the trapdoor, to make sure we don't get out that way."

Paige felt light-headed and weak in the knees. She steadied herself with one hand on the clammy stone wall. "You mean we're trapped down here?"

"Maybe not," he said. "Maybe there's another way out."

"A way they don't know about?" That didn't seem likely.

He touched her arm. "Let's keep moving."

She looked around at the narrow, dark passage and tried not to think about the tons of rock over their heads, or the creepy crawlies that might lurk in the darkness. "What are we going to do?" she asked.

"Come on. Let's go."

They started forward again, walking instead of running this time. "Do you think Bryce Reed is behind all this?" Paige asked. Maybe she shouldn't talk, and instead try to move as silently as possible, but what was the point? Their pursuers knew they were down here, and so far this narrow tunnel was the only place they could be. And talking—thinking out loud about what had happened and giving her mind something to focus on besides their dire circumstances—helped her stay calm. "Was the press conference just a ploy to get me up here?"

"He has to know at least some of what's going on," Rob said. "I've never believed CNG wasn't involved somehow. But why try to lure you up here? Most likely you would have seen no one was here, turned around and gone home. I was the one who suggested staying to look around."

"And I went along with you—willingly. I'm not going to play the guilt game."

He looked at her so long without saying anything that she began to feel uneasy. "What?" she asked. "Why are you looking at me like that?"

"You're incredible, did you know that?"

You're incredible, too. But she bit back the words. They sounded so sappy, and not nearly adequate to convey all she was feeling right now. She had started out hating this man, because of what she thought he had done to her brother, and for what she thought he represented. He knew how she felt, and yet he had come through for her at every turn. "Incredible" didn't begin to express what she was feeling, and part of her—she could admit this, if only to herself—part of her was waiting for him to fail her. For him to show another, uglier side, the way her ex-husband had. The way most people had.

"Come on," she said. "I want to hurry and get out of here."

They had traveled perhaps another hundred yards when the tunnel began to widen slightly, until they were able to walk side by side. Light glowed up ahead. "Is that an exit?" she asked, and began to walk faster.

He took her arm, forcing her to slow down. "Careful," he said, and drew his gun from its holster.

She moved in behind him and let him go first. They hadn't gone much farther before she realized the light they were seeing wasn't from outside the tunnel, but the glow of electric lights. They came to an intersection. The main tunnel continued straight into darkness, while a shorter side turning led to the source of the illumination—a room whose door stood open.

"Wait here," Rob whispered, motioning for her to stand in the main tunnel, just out of sight.

She wanted to protest, to insist that she go with him. But what could she do if they ran into trouble? She didn't have a weapon. At least if she stayed here she could try to go for help if he ran into trouble. She pressed her back against the rough stone of the tunnel wall and waited, counting the seconds. "One Mississippi, two Mississippi..."

She was at fifty Mississippi when Rob called to her. "It's all right. Come look at this."

Still uneasy, she walked down the short hallway and stood in the open doorway, and gasped when she saw the concrete-floored, brightly lit chamber. Rob stood in the middle of the high-ceilinged room, next to a stainless-steel counter lined with lab equipment. Paige recognized a microscope, Bunsen burner, racks of test tubes, beakers and various glass flasks. Several crates were stacked against the wall, like the one she had seen being carried down here. There were many more items she couldn't identify, all of which looked technical and complicated. "It's a laboratory," she said.

"Yes," Rob said. He picked up a flask half filled with a dark liquid and squinted at it. "And unlike the last one we found, this one is clearly in operation." He set the flask down.

She joined him in front of the workbench. "This doesn't look like World War II–era equipment," she said. "What are they doing down here? And who is doing it? Reed didn't strike me as the scientific type."

"I don't know who." Rob looked around them. "As for what, I think it might be related to that World War II operation. Maybe this is the location of that original lab and whoever is behind this decided to update it for their own purposes."

"What purposes?" she asked.

"Henry Hake died of tularemia," he said. "That's one of the diseases the government was supposedly experimenting with back then. What if someone decided to continue that research? Maybe Henry stumbled on it and contracted the disease accidentally—or maybe he was deliberately given it."

She shuddered and wrapped her arms around herself. "Maybe we shouldn't be here," she said. "What if we've already been exposed to something horrible?"

"I don't think there's too much chance of that," he said. "They have to keep the contaminants contained, or no one could work down here." He gestured toward a locked refrigeration unit that hummed in the corner. "Anything dangerous is probably in there."

He pulled out his phone and began taking pictures

of the room. Too bad there was no cell service here. He could call for help.

Paige shook her head. No sense dwelling on what they couldn't do. She needed to focus on what they could do. "If you're right about the purpose of this lab, then it would explain a lot," she said. "The secrecy, and the armed guards."

"The willingness to kill people to keep the operation secret," he said.

"Do you think CNG's plans to build a high-altitude research facility is a cover for this underground operation?" she asked.

"It would be a good one," he said. "It would explain any orders for lab equipment, and any traffic in and out of the property."

"Where are the people who work here now?" Paige asked.

"My guess is Reed sent them away until after the press conference. After that, anyone seeing something like a person in a lab coat would think they were part of the new facility. Reed could even explain away the armed guards as necessary because of the sensitive nature of scientific research."

"The mayor is certainly going to be surprised when he learns his pet project is a big lie," she said. "That won't go well for his career. Is it wrong of me to be a little happy about that, at least?"

Rob reached out and pulled her close. "Remind me to never get on your bad side," he said.

"You've already been on my bad side," she said. She rested one hand on his chest, over the reassuring, strong beat of his heart. "Or have you forgotten already?"

He moved her hand to his lips and kissed her fingers.

"I loved that you were so fierce. And you were attracted to me even back then, though you wouldn't admit it."

She pulled her hand away and tried to muster a look of outrage, though she was afraid the most she could manage was amusement. "Just like a man—imagining that every woman he meets is falling all over herself for him."

"But you're not just any woman." He kissed her cheek.

She wanted to turn her head and capture his mouth with her own, to lean into this moment and let desire and affection obliterate the fear and worry. But that wouldn't be smart, and it wouldn't help get them to safety. So instead, she pulled away from him.

"Come on," she said. "Let's go find a way out of here."

PARKER DROVE WITH his foot to the floor, the engine in the Nissan screaming in protest. Professor Gibson gripped the dash and spoke through gritted teeth. "You're not going to help your sister if we crash before we get to town. If you slow down, I could call for help."

"There's no phone service up here. And we won't crash," Parker said over the screech of brakes, as the car fishtailed around a hairpin curve. Now wasn't the time for caution. Paige and Rob didn't stand a chance if those thugs with guns caught up with them.

The professor's only answer was a sharp intake of breath as the rear wheels of the car skidded on gravel. Five minutes later, they shot out onto the pavement of the highway that led into town. The needle on the speedometer edged up to ninety. Parker wouldn't have believed the little econobox could go that fast. As they entered the town of Eagle Mountain, a cruiser parked on the side of the road hit its lights and siren and swung in a U-turn to follow them. Parker ignored the cop and kept going, skidding to a stop in front of the sheriff's department. He left the engine running and was out of the car before the professor had unfastened the seat belt.

"Parker Riddell, what the—?" The rest of Deputy Dwight Prentice's shouted question was cut off when the door to the sheriff's department closed behind Parker.

Adelaide Kinkaid looked up from behind her desk in the lobby, then stood as Parker trotted past. "Young man, where do you think you're going?"

"I need to see the sheriff," Parker called over his shoulder.

Sheriff Travis Walker stood in the doorway of his office. "Parker? What's going on?"

"Paige and Rob are in big trouble up on Dakota Ridge."

The professor and Dwight had caught up with him, Gibson looking much paler and older than he had up on the ridge. Dwight had him by the arm and led him to a chair in front of Travis's desk. "I clocked him doing ninety as he came into town," Dwight said. "He's lucky a dog or a kid didn't run out in front of him."

"You have to get as many officers as you can up to Dakota Ridge now, before it's too late," Parker said. They had already wasted too much time.

"Calm down and tell me what's going on," Travis said. He sat behind his desk, clearly not in a hurry to go anywhere.

"We might already be too late!" Parker's voice broke on the words, and he closed his eyes, fighting for control.

Travis turned to the older man. "Professor Gibson, what happened?"

"Bryce Reed invited Paige to a press conference up at CNG's Dakota Ridge property," he said. "Agent Allerton insisted on accompanying her. Parker and I decided to go, as well."

"Why did you and Parker decide to attend the press conference?" Travis asked.

"What does that matter?" Parker asked. "The point is, when we got there, there was no press conference. There wasn't anyone there. The place looked deserted."

"We decided to take the opportunity to look around." The professor took up the story again. "As you may know, I have an interest in the World War II–era laboratory that operated somewhere in the county. My research indicated that the lab was probably in an old mine on the property now owned by CNG Development. I wanted to see if my hypothesis was correct."

"Except we heard gunshots, and then a bunch of men wearing camo came running out of the woods," Parker said. "Then we saw Paige and Rob. The men with guns were shooting at them." He swallowed, still unable to believe what he had seen.

Travis looked at the professor again. "He's telling the truth," Gibson said. "Paige and Rob managed to escape by descending into a hole in the ground, and pulled a trapdoor over them." He leaned forward, hands gripping the arms of the chair. "In thinking it over, I believe they may have found an entrance into the mine where that historic lab is probably located. I'm almost sure of it."

"What happened then?" Travis asked.

"What happened is that we got out of there and came to get you," Parker said. "You've got to do something."

Travis nodded. "How many men with guns did you see?" he asked.

"A dozen," Parker said.

"There were six," the professor said. His eyes met

Parker's. "It seemed like more, with all the shooting, but I took the time to count. There were six."

"We'll need reinforcements," Travis said. He picked up the phone.

"Who are you calling?" Parker asked.

"We'll need to get the SWAT team from Junction here."

"We don't have time for that," Parker protested.

"We can't go in without a plan and enough personnel to overwhelm them," he said. "If you want us to save your sister, we need a little time to prepare."

"We don't have time," Parker said again, though with less fervor. "They could already be dead."

"I hope not," Travis said. "But going in unprepared won't save them."

"Parker." The professor's voice, strong and steady, cut through some of his panic.

He looked at his mentor. "What?"

"Remember that Paige is with Agent Allerton," Professor Gibson said. "He's a trained law enforcement officer, and he's armed. And I believe he will do everything in his power to protect her."

Parker nodded. He wanted to believe that. He couldn't afford not to believe it. "What do we do now?" he asked.

The professor motioned to the chair beside him. "We wait. And we pray."

BEYOND THE LABORATORY, half a dozen smaller tunnels branched off from the main corridor. Paige and Rob shone the light of Rob's phone down some of these. Most of them led nowhere, either blocked by piles of debris and collapsed timbers, or simply unfinished, as if the original miners who had excavated here had found nothing worth further exploration.

"How far have we walked?" Paige asked after a while. Her feet ached from navigating the uneven, rocky tunnel, and the damp chill underground had settled in, so that she shivered every time they stopped to rest or check out a detour.

"A couple of miles, I think," Rob said. "I understand some of these old mines extend for miles."

"I can't believe no one has come after us yet," she said. "Are they going to try to starve us out?"

Rob didn't answer. Instead, he illuminated yet another niche carved out of the rock, this one starting about five feet above the level of the main tunnel. "They didn't get very far with this one," he said. "Or maybe it was supposed to hold some kind of equipment?"

"Unless it leads to a way out of here, I don't care," she said. "Did you hear what I asked? Why hasn't anyone come after us?"

"I heard you, but I don't have an answer." He must be as tired and scared and cold as she was, but he didn't show it. Though maybe what she had mistaken for calm was merely grim determination.

"I wish we'd thought to bring our backpacks from the car," she said. "Then at least we'd have water and food and a warm jacket." The pack she carried hiking was equipped with all kinds of emergency supplies.

"And if I'd brought my submachine gun maybe we could blast our way out of here."

"Do you have a submachine gun?" she asked.

"No. But as long as we're wishing for things, that's what I'd wish for." Rob took her arm and they started forward again, but had gone only a few feet before he yanked her against him, hard. She would have cried out, but he clamped his hand over her mouth. "Listen!" he hissed, so close to her ear she felt the warmth of his breath.

She listened, and heard a sound she thought at first was rain drumming on a metal roof. Her knees turned to jelly as she realized she was hearing the sound of running feet on stone—running toward them.

"This way." Rob yanked her back the way they had come. When they reached the niche in the side of the tunnel, he boosted her up into it, then crawled up beside her, then switched off his phone, plunging them into darkness.

She clung to him, dizzy with fear and disoriented, afraid if she moved she'd go sliding out of the narrow space. She could fall, and never stop falling into the bottomless blackness.

Rob gripped her just as tightly with one hand. She imagined his other hand held his gun. She wondered how many of their attackers he could kill before he was dead himself. Or maybe they would both be dead before he could fire a single shot. She hoped the end was quick, and then in the same breath, rage rose up at the very idea. She was too young to die! And how cruel that she might do so just when she had found a man she could love again.

She hadn't seen that one coming—falling in love with Rob Allerton, of all men. But here in the darkness, with his arm around her and their lives in danger, all the fears and worries that had kept her from love before seemed beyond petty. Here was a man who respected—even admired—her independence, who laughed at what he called her fierceness and who made her feel more alive than anyone she had ever been with. How cruel to find all that only to lose it.

Faint light glowed in the corridor now, and the sound of tramping feet was much louder—louder even than her pounding heart, which hammered painfully in her chest. Surely they would hear it and discover them in their hiding place.

The light grew brighter, the tramping feet louder. These people weren't even trying for stealth, they were so certain that they would find their prey. "Spread out!" one man commanded. "Search all the corridors. They won't have gone far."

She closed her eyes and rested her head on Rob's shoulder. She didn't feel fierce now—only numb and almost paralyzed with weariness. The running men grew closer, closer, the echoes of boots hitting the hard stone floor bouncing off the walls and filling up the narrow space with sound. She clenched her teeth, dug her fingers into Rob's arm and waited for the end.

Time stopped, and she didn't know how long she waited like that, until Rob shook her shoulder. "They're gone," he whispered.

She opened her eyes to darkness again, and silence. She resisted the urge to shake her head and try to unclog her ears. "They didn't see us?" she whispered.

"They didn't see us." He caressed her cheek, then kissed her, his lips strong and tasting so sweet. She returned the embrace, all the love and fear and despair that warred within her distilled into that desperate, drowning kiss. She wanted to throw her arms around him, to climb into his lap and press her body to his, but their narrow hiding place prevented that. She had to settle for the connection of that kiss, tongues twined and lips melding, a communication that went beyond words.

When they broke the kiss she was left breathless, and it was a moment before she could speak. "Maybe this really isn't the time for this," she said.

"Maybe not." He traced her lips with one finger. "But I can think of worse ways to spend my time."

"Rob, I—"

"Shhh." He pressed his finger to her lips. "We'll talk later. Right now we have to go, before they come back."

He climbed down from the niche, then helped her down, and they hurried away, in the opposite direction from where the armed men had headed. Rob kept the phone off, so they had to navigate in the darkness, but it wasn't as difficult as she would have thought. The tunnel was straight and the walls close enough that she could place a hand on either side to guide her way.

When Rob stopped abruptly, she stumbled into his back. "What is it?" she whispered.

"Another side tunnel." He switched on the cell phone and shone the light to their left, then swore under his breath.

Paige bit back a scream and stared at the body of Bryce Reed, slumped against the wall, his throat cut like an awful red grin.

Chapter Seventeen

Rob switched off the light, but he had seen enough to know that Bryce Reed hadn't been dead very long. The blood that spilled over the front of his shirt still shone wetly, and rigor hadn't yet stiffened the body.

"Does this mean Reed didn't know about what was going on, after all?" Paige asked. "He must have stumbled on the operation, the way we did, and they killed him."

"Maybe," Rob said. "Or maybe he was working with them, but had outlived his usefulness to them."

"When those men don't find us, they'll come back this way to search again," she said.

"Yes." They couldn't afford to stay here. "We know there has to be another entrance, since they came that way," he said.

"They'll have someone guarding it," she said.

"But probably only one or two people," he said. "They can't have had that big of a force. The two men you saw that first day on the trail are dead—probably killed because they had attracted too much attention to the operation. Reed is dead. That leaves whoever is in charge—the man in the suit—and half a dozen guards."

"What man in a suit?" she asked. "I never saw a man in a suit."

"Parker saw him. He was up here one day and a helicopter landed. A man in a suit and two guards in fatigues got out and unloaded a crate, like the one you described."

"He never said anything to me about that."

"He didn't want to worry you."

"But he told you. And you're a cop. He doesn't want to have anything to do with cops."

"Neither did you. I guess people can change their minds." Rob had once thought she was an overly protective, cop-hating crusader who viewed him as the devil incarnate. Now she was the dearest person in the world to him. He took her arm. "It doesn't matter now. We need to get to the entrance before they come back. Once we're there, we'll figure out how to get past whatever guards they've established."

"You make it sound so simple," she said, as they started down the tunnel once more. "I wish I had your confidence."

It was more bravado than confidence, but he'd rather go out charging into daylight than cowering in the darkness.

They moved quickly now, more confident with navigating by feel and instinct. The floor had a steady upward incline, a good indication that they were moving toward the surface.

"Do you feel that?" Paige asked. "It's cooler air. I think we're getting close."

"Not far now," he agreed.

Another fifty yards and he could discern the outline of the timbers that shored up the tunnel. "The light must be coming from the entrance," Rob said. He halted and put a hand out to stop her. "Wait here," he said. "I'm going to check things out."

For once, Paige didn't argue, though she squeezed his hand and held on, so that he had to pull away from her. He drew his gun and moved stealthily forward, ears attuned to any sound. Soon he could make out the entrance, or adit, a wooden structure that jutted out from the rock face of the ridge, heavy beams supporting a metal roof. An exit gate made of thick iron bars stood open.

Rob moved forward, staying close to the wall, as much in shadow as possible. He couldn't hear any voices, or people moving about, but he wouldn't risk his life— and he especially wouldn't risk Paige's—on the chance that their pursuers had been careless enough to leave the entrance unguarded. Most likely, one or two people were out there, their guns trained on the adit, waiting for anyone to emerge.

He moved all the way into the adit, stopping when he bumped up against a stack of crates that lined the wooden wall. The lid was partially off one of the boxes. Rob stared down at sticks of dynamite with long fuses attached. Other boxes contained metal construction fasteners and nails. A few lengths of metal pipe lay alongside. Sacks of concrete mix lined the opposite wall. It looked like someone planned to expand the operation, perhaps by opening up some of the sealed-off tunnels, or blasting new ones. They had better know what they were doing, or they could bring the whole place down.

Bring the whole place down. This thought echoing in his head, Rob snatched up a handful of dynamite sticks and retraced his steps to Paige. "Hold these," he said, shoving them at her.

"What?" She stared at the objects in her hands. "Is this dynamite? As in explosives?"

"Yes. And we're going to use it to get out of here."

"How?"

He took the dynamite sticks from her and began arranging them at the base of one wall of the tunnel. "I'm going to set up an explosion to collapse the tunnel here. That will keep the men we saw earlier from traveling back this way. Any guards out front will probably come in to investigate—or they'll head to the other entrance to help their coworkers."

"Or they'll stay put and wait for us to come out," she said.

"That's a possibility, too, but I'm betting on them running in to investigate, in which case I'll be ready to pick them off." He finished arranging the dynamite and stepped back.

"What makes you think you won't bring a ton of rock down on us?" she asked.

"Because you're going to be waiting up at the entrance. And I'm going to be standing as far away as possible when the explosion occurs."

"How are you going to light the fuses?" she asked. "We don't have any matches."

"No, but I have this." He drew his gun. "A bullet striking the dynamite will set it off."

She looked doubtful. "And you know this how?"

"Let's just say my friends and I experimented during a kegger when we were young and stupid."

She laughed—nervous, desperate laughter. "It's a crazy, dangerous idea."

"It is," he agreed. "But I can't think of a better one. Can you?"

"No."

"All right." He took another step back. "You go up to the entrance. There are a lot of boxes and stuff piled against the wall. If you crouch down behind them, anyone running past shouldn't see you. After the explosion, I'll wait here to catch whoever comes in to investigate."

"Okay…" She started to move away, then came back and grabbed his shoulders and pulled him down for a fierce kiss. "I love you," she said. "Remember that."

"I love you, too," he said, but she was already gone, hurrying up the tunnel. He hoped that wouldn't be the last time he would see her. Though he had laid out the plan for her as if it was a sure thing, there were plenty of variables he couldn't account for. If things didn't go their way, they might both be dead in a very short time.

PARKER STOOD IN the parking lot for the hiking trail, hands shoved into the pockets of his jeans, staring down the road as if he could somehow see through the trees to what was going on at the abandoned resort. Almost two hours had passed since he had seen those men go after Paige and Rob. She might very well be dead by now.

"The sheriff is doing everything he can." The professor joined him at the edge of the lot. On the other side of the gravel space, Sheriff Walker and his deputies milled about with half a dozen men and women in black pants and shirts, body armor and helmets.

"What are they waiting on?" Parker asked. "Why are they wasting time standing around?"

A sheriff's department SUV pulled into the lot and Gage climbed out. "I've been trying to locate Bryce Reed," he said. "He's not at his office. He's not answering his phone. None of the news outlets knew anything about a press conference."

"He made it up, to get Paige up here," Parker said. "If something has happened to her and he's still alive—"

"Don't say anything rash." The professor gripped Parker's shoulder. "Wait and see what happens."

All he had been doing was waiting. This was worse than being in prison. At least then he had had an idea of when the waiting would end. And he had known that he deserved to be there, to pay for the crimes he had committed. Paige had never hurt anyone. She didn't deserve to die this way.

The sound of tires on pavement made them all turn, to see a black SUV make a screeching turn into the lot. It came close to hitting some of the SWAT members, who jumped back and glared at the new arrival. The driver's-side door opened and a tall man with a crooked nose and heavy jowls stepped out, his expression thunderous.

"You don't have any business here, Larry," Travis said, walking toward him.

"Who is that?" Parker asked the professor.

"That's the mayor of Eagle Mountain, Larry Rowe," he said.

"What is going on here?" Rowe demanded. "Why are all you people here? What's happened?"

"This isn't your concern, Larry," Travis said. "You need to leave."

Parker stared at the mayor, who looked like a boxer. Where had he seen him before, very recently?

"I won't leave," Rowe said. He turned to one of the SWAT team members. "Is this some kind of training exercise? Do you have CNG's permission to be here?"

"We're not on CNG property," Travis said.

"You're adjacent to it," Rowe said. "What you do here could affect them."

"Go home, Mayor," Travis said. "As I said, this doesn't concern you."

"I won't leave until you answer my questions." Rowe folded his arms across his barrel chest. "Just because you have a gun and a badge doesn't mean you can throw your weight around."

Parker moved closer, to get a better look at the mayor. "You're the man I saw here that day," he said. "The man who was in the helicopter."

The mayor glared at him. "Who are you?"

Parker ignored him and turned to Travis. "He was here, on CNG's property," he said. "He landed in a helicopter, with two men in camo, with guns. Like the men who were after Paige and Rob." Was the sheriff believing any of this? He had such a stone face, Parker couldn't tell.

"I don't know what he's talking about," the mayor said. He glared at Parker. "What were you doing on CNG property? That's trespassing. Sheriff, you need to arrest this man for trespassing."

The sheriff stared at Parker, as if he was considering doing just that. Parker took a step back. He had made a mistake, saying anything.

The leader of the SWAT team joined them. In the black clothes with all the extra elbow, knee and shoulder pads, and the heavy helmet, he looked like something out of a cyborg movie. "We're ready to go," he said.

Travis turned to Parker. "You stay here," he said. "We'll radio when it's safe for you to join us."

Parker nodded. "All right."

A car door slammed and they turned in time to see

the mayor, tires squealing, speeding out of the parking area. "Want me to go after him?" Gage asked.

"What was that about a helicopter?" Travis asked.

Parker shook his head. "I'll tell you later. Go help Paige."

Travis turned to the others. "All right," he said. "Let's go."

PAIGE CROUCHED BEHIND the crates piled at the entrance to the mine, trying not to think about the sticks of dynamite she had seen lying in the top box like rows of Christmas crackers, but so much more deadly. She watched the entrance, while her ears strained to hear what was going on behind her, back with Rob.

He had promised to stand well away when he fired into the pile of dynamite, but what if something went wrong? What if some fault in the rock made it come down on his head? What if the explosion brought down only part of the wall and the gunmen were able to get through?

What if? What if? She had to stop thinking about all these questions that couldn't be answered and focus instead on what she could control. When the explosion happened, men were likely to come running through that entrance and she had to be ready.

She thought she was prepared for the explosion, but when it came, the shock threw her forward against the crates, and a wave of dust rolled through the tunnel and over her. Her ears rang from the concussion of the blast, so that she was only dimly aware of a deep rumble and a sound like cracking earth. Then all fell silent, so silent she wondered if she had gone deaf.

The light shifted and she looked up to see the silhouette of a man in the mine entrance, broad shouldered and holding a rifle. She ducked down lower behind the boxes, praying he couldn't see her in the haze of dust.

Then he began running, boots pounding hard against the stone as he raced past her. A few seconds more and a single shot pierced the silence. She held her breath, waiting for more, but all was still. She wanted to call out to Rob, to make sure he was safe and alive, but she knew she couldn't. She didn't know who might be listening.

So she kept silent and waited, as seconds and minutes dragged by. She had no idea how much time had passed when a shadow fell over her and she looked up to see a second man in the doorway. This man was shorter than the first, and not as burly, but he, too, carried an automatic rifle. He took a step toward her, and then another. "Jake?" he called.

Jake didn't answer. The second man shifted his rifle so that it pointed forward, his hand near the trigger guard. Would he see Rob before Rob saw him? Would he kill him?

Without moving, Paige scanned the area around her, searching for a weapon. She needed to stop this guy before he got to Rob. He took another step toward her, and another, moving faster now, his rifle at the ready. When he was even with her hiding place, Paige lunged, grabbing on to his calf just below the knee and yanking with all her might.

He went down like a tree felled in the forest. Before he hit the floor, she stood and brought a length of metal pipe down on his head as hard as she could. When the pipe made contact with his skull it sounded like a melon splitting open, and she dropped the pipe in shock. The man moaned, then didn't make another sound.

Paige hurried down the tunnel and met Rob running toward her. "What happened?" he asked, grabbing hold of her.

"Another man came in and I was afraid he was going to kill you, so I hit him with a pipe. I think I might have killed him."

"Let's get out of here," he said, and pulled her toward the entrance.

They had to step around the man she had hit. He lay very still in a pool of blood. "Don't look," Rob said, and tugged her past him.

After spending so much time in the dark tunnel, Paige found the light outside blinding. She and Rob both put up hands to shield their eyes. She expected to see yet another man there with a gun, but there was no one, and she sagged against Rob with relief. "We did it," she said, the words barely audible. "We did it."

"Let's get out of here," he repeated.

"Oh, I don't think you're going anywhere."

They turned at the words and Paige gasped as she recognized the man who had said them. "Larry?"

"Throw down your weapon, Agent Allerton," Mayor Larry Rowe said.

"Larry, what are you doing here?" Paige asked. And with a gun. Larry had always struck her as the quintessential corporate type, comfortable only behind a desk or in a boardroom. Seeing him here, threatening them, threw her off balance.

"You're the man in charge of this operation, aren't you?" Rob asked.

"The gun, Agent Allerton."

Rob tossed the gun into the dirt. Larry kicked it aside, sending it skittering into the underbrush, well out of reach.

"I don't understand," Paige said. "What are you doing here? That laboratory we saw—are you really making biological weapons down there?"

"So many questions," Larry said.

"Why not give me the answers?" Paige said. "You're going to kill me anyway." The longer she could keep him talking, the longer they would stay alive. And the longer she and Rob might have to see some way out of this dilemma.

"You always did think you were the cleverest person in the room, didn't you?" Larry's mouth twisted into a sneer. "No one dares cross Paige Riddell, because she has all the answers. And yet you had no idea what was going on up here, right under your nose."

"You found the World War II lab and decided to resume the research that was done here," Rob said. "Some foreign organizations will pay a great deal of money for what you could produce there."

"Very good, Agent Allerton," Larry said.

"Did you kill Henry Hake?" Paige asked.

"Henry was happy to lease the land to us after you stalled his plans for his resort," Larry said. "So you could say that you're the one who set all this in motion."

"Why did you kill him?" she asked.

"He discovered what we were doing and objected, so we had no choice but to eliminate him."

"Henry's bodyguard, Ian Barnes, worked for you," Rob said. "Henry told everyone Barnes came to him from one of his business partners—that was you. Barnes murdered Henry's lawyer, Andy Stenson."

"Stenson was the first to figure out what we were doing here, so I asked Ian to get rid of him." He shrugged, as if ordering a murder was no big deal.

"Were Wade Tomlinson and Brock Ryan working for you, too?" Paige asked. "The men who murdered Angela and Greg Hood and kidnapped Deputy Gage Walker and his girlfriend?"

"Tomlinson and Ryan were two of my best allies," Larry said. "But they balked at killing that kid, so they had to go, too."

"Those two men whose bodies we found in that burned-out shed—did they work for you, too?"

"Oh yes." He frowned. "I thought they'd take care of you and you'd be out of my way for good, but no such luck. After that, they weren't any use to me."

"So pretty much everyone who helped you ended up dead," Rob said.

"Not everyone," Larry said. "My brother, Garrett, played the part of a billionaire who wanted to buy that mining book from Brenda Stenson. I didn't want someone else to get their hands on it and figure out where the original laboratory was." He chuckled. "He was the 'top secret agent' who fooled Eddie Carstairs, too. That was a role he really liked." Eddie had threatened Brenda Stenson and destroyed the book about the secret World War II laboratory.

"Where is your brother now?" Paige asked.

"In Connecticut, believe it or not. Acting. I told him I'd pay him a lot more money than some two-bit dinner theater, but he wasn't interested. Go figure."

"Why did you kill Bryce Reed?" Rob asked.

"He was getting nervous about the project," Larry

said. "So few people have the courage of their convictions these days."

"But—" she began.

"Enough!" He jabbed the gun in their direction. "Back into the mine."

Paige darted her eyes to Rob's, hoping to see that he had a plan. But the only emotion she could read on his face was the same desperation she felt.

"Quit stalling!" Larry barked.

She lurched forward, stumbling on a rock near the mine entrance, and fell hard, the rough grit scraping her palms. "Get up!" Larry shouted, and fired into the ground near her head.

Rage filled her. How dare he shoot at her while she was down? She closed her fingers around a handful of grit and rose up on her knees. Larry bent toward her and she hurled the grit into his face. The gun went off again, the bullet thudding into the dirt near her feet.

Rob jumped on Larry's back and forced him to the ground, then struck a savage blow to his hand, sending the gun flying. He was kneeling on Larry's back, forcing his face into the dirt, when half a dozen figures in black pants and bulletproof vests and helmets jogged toward them.

"No!" Paige cried, and lunged toward the discarded gun. She hadn't come this far to go down without a fight.

"Paige, it's all right." One of the men raised the visor of his helmet and she recognized Travis. "Put the gun down," he said gently.

She let the weapon fall and sank to her knees. One of the other officers moved forward and secured the mayor, while another helped Rob to stand.

Rob walked over to her, pulled her to her feet and put his arm around her. "Let's get out of here," he said.

She laid her head on his shoulder. "That's the best idea I've heard all day."

Chapter Eighteen

All Paige wanted was to take a shower, have a good stiff drink, eat a steak and collapse, but first she and Rob had to reassure Parker and Professor Gibson that they really were okay. Then they had to repeat the reassurances for Lacy and Brenda and Adelaide and pretty much everyone else in town.

Then they had to tell their story to the sheriff, and tell it again for their official statement. Repeating the details made the events of the last six hours seem even more surreal. It was like recounting a movie, or a horrible dream. Those things hadn't really happened to her, had they? But she had the bruises and scrapes to prove it, and memories that would haunt her for a long time to come.

"We've contacted the authorities in Connecticut," Travis said. "They'll arrest Garrett Rowe for the part he played in all this and we'll extradite him here."

"I'm amazed that Larry persuaded so many people to work with him," Paige said. "I never thought he was particularly charismatic."

"For some people, money substitutes for personality," Rob said.

"What was in the crate you saw them carrying, that first day when you were on the trail?" Travis asked.

"I have no idea," she said. That was one question she hadn't gotten around to asking Larry.

"My guess is it was lab equipment," Rob said. "It will take weeks—maybe months—to collect and analyze everything in that lab. It's also possible one or more of the crates Paige and Parker saw contained lab cultures or samples of bacteria or germs they wanted to experiment with."

"What are you going to tell your aunt about Henry?" Paige asked Rob, remembering what had brought him back to Eagle Mountain.

"I'll tell her the truth—that he was doing business with some bad people and they killed him. That's all she wanted, to know what really happened."

"It's so sad," Paige said. "What does Larry say about all of this?"

"He isn't talking," Travis said. "But with your testimony and Rob's, and the evidence from the site, I don't think we'll have any problem putting him away for a long time."

"What about the armed guards who tried to kill us?" Paige asked.

"We found one of them dead near the mine entrance, and another one with a pretty severe concussion, but he'll live," Travis said. "We arrested four others as they emerged from the trapdoor at the other end of the mine."

"I can't believe so many people died because of this," Paige said. "Andy Stenson, Brock Ryan and Wade Tomlinson, the Hoods, Henry Hake, Bryce Reed—even those two men who tried to kill me were killed because they drew too much attention to the place."

"There were millions, probably billions, of dollars at

stake," Rob said. "That's how much some foreign powers would be willing to pay for biological weapons."

"But weapons like that are illegal," Paige said. "I mean, they're against the Geneva convention."

"Some people don't care."

That idea was too depressing to consider.

"I know you're both exhausted," Travis said. "You can go for now, but we'll have more questions for you later, and you'll probably eventually have to testify in court."

Outside, Parker and the professor waited for them. Parker wrapped Paige in a hug that squeezed the breath out of her. "Don't scare me like that again," he said, his voice husky.

She pulled away and studied him. He had dark circles under his eyes and needed a shave. When had the little boy she had loved for so long grown into such a man? "Thanks for calling in the cavalry," she said.

"I understand you told the sheriff about seeing Larry Rowe in that helicopter that landed on CNG property," Rob said.

"Yeah. He said if I agreed to testify about that, he'd overlook the parole violation for trespassing."

"Excuse me." The professor moved closer. "I understand now isn't a good time, but when you've had a chance to rest, I'd appreciate hearing more about the lab you found. Do you really think it's the space used by the government during World War II?"

"It could be," Rob said. "Larry as much as confirmed it. I think finding it gave him the idea to work on developing biological weapons in the first place."

"Then I definitely want to hear more about it. At your convenience."

"Right now I just want a shower and a drink." Paige looked down at her dirty jeans and scraped hands.

"Sure thing," Parker said. "Where do you want me to take you?"

"I'll take care of her." Rob put his arm around her.

Parker took a step back. "I guess you're in good hands, then." Parker looked at Rob. "But if you do anything to hurt her, you'll have me to answer to."

Rob nodded, his expression solemn. "Understood."

When Parker and the professor were gone, Paige looked up at Rob. "Don't worry about him," she said. "If you do anything to hurt me, you'll have *me* to answer to."

"I'm definitely more frightened of you. But you don't have to worry. I won't hurt you. Ever."

"I believe you." She smiled up at him. "Let's go back to your motel."

They didn't speak even after they were inside Rob's room. He merely drew the drapes and she began to strip off her clothes in the dim light from the bedside lamp. Rob did the same, until they stood facing each other, naked. He smoothed a hand along her shoulder, and his fingers trembled. "If anything had happened to you…" he began.

"Shhh." She silenced him with a kiss. "We're both okay," she said, her lips almost touching his. "We're going to be okay."

He nodded and tried to pull her close, but instead, she took his hand and led him into the bathroom. She turned on the shower, jets all the way up and water steaming hot. Then she stepped in and beckoned for him to follow.

She thought of all the ways water could cleanse, from removing dirt from laundry to the soul cleansing of baptism. As they took turns soaping each other's bodies, she felt the strain and fear of the past days wash away, replaced by an exultant joy that they were here now, alive and able to enjoy each other this way.

The water was still warm when Rob tossed aside the soapy washrag and pulled her closer, full against his naked body, her breasts pressed against the firm wall of his chest, her hips just under his. Salty tears mingled with the shower spray as his lips claimed hers, and when he bent his knees and slid into her she stood on tiptoe to accept him, reveling in the sensation of being united with him, yet so fully herself.

They emerged from the shower replete and renewed and ravenous. The motel didn't offer room service, but Rob ordered a large pizza and promised extra if the delivery driver—not Parker—would stop at the liquor store and purchase a bottle of wine. They ate at the table by the window, sipping wine and feeding each other pizza, half-dressed and unable to stop looking at each other.

They made love again in the bed, burrowed under warm covers, alternately giggling with delight and moaning at the depth of their need. When Paige fell asleep in Rob's arms, she didn't dream of anything.

She woke with gray light showing through the gap in the curtains, and stretched like a cat, more relaxed than she could remember being in years. She rolled over onto her side to watch Rob sleeping. He lay on his back, his hair mussed, the dark shadow of beard along his jaw. She knew how intimidating he could look, how insistent he could be on doing the right, legal thing, upholding the commitment he had made as a law enforcement officer. Where once she had bristled at his unwillingness to see gray instead of black-and-white, now she drew comfort from his steadfastness.

Her chest hurt when she thought of how close she had come to losing him. Loving someone this way was so wonderful and so terrifying.

He looked up at her, his brown eyes clear and calm. "How long have you been watching me?" he asked.

"A while." She smiled.

"What does that smile mean? What are you thinking?"

"I'm thinking that I've lost just about everything, and I'm happier than I've ever been."

He reached for her hand and pulled it to his chest. "Marry me," he said.

She tried to pull her hand away, but he held it fast. "This is your romantic proposal?" she asked. "Naked and in bed?"

"I thought you weren't a traditionalist. Do you want me to get down on my knee? I will."

She wrinkled her nose. "What if I say no?"

"I'll keep asking. Are you going to say no?"

She wanted to laugh—he looked so worried. "No. Yes. I don't know."

He shoved himself into a sitting position, forcing her to sit up also, or risk a pain in her neck from trying to look up at him. "You faced down an armed killer yesterday and defeated him with your bare hands," he said. "After that, how can you be afraid of anything?"

"When you put it like that—yes."

"Yes, what?"

"Yes, I'll marry you."

He crushed her to him and kissed her until she was dizzy. Gently, she pushed away from him. "Where will we live?" she asked.

"Where do you want to live?"

"I don't know. Eagle Mountain feels like home, but your work is in Denver. And maybe a change would be good for me."

"I have a feeling I'm going to be here in Eagle Mountain for a while yet."

"Oh?"

"Somebody has to inventory that lab. That's going to take a while, and I already have experience on the property, so I think there's a good chance I'll get the job."

"So we can live here," she said.

"For a while. And then decide what we want to do. After all, we have the rest of our lives to be together."

"Yes, and I hope that's a very, very long time." She settled against him, her head on his shoulder.

"I hope so, too." He wrapped his arm around her.

"One thing's for sure," she said.

"What's that?"

"I'll never have to worry about being bored with you."

"Not every woman would see that as an advantage," he said.

"As you've pointed out before, I'm not every woman."

"Thank God for that."

"Shut up and kiss me."

"Yes, ma'am." And he did.

* * * * *

LET'S TALK
Romance

For exclusive extracts, competitions
and special offers, find us online:

MILLS & BOON

THE HEART OF ROMANCE

A ROMANCE FOR EVERY READER

MODERN

Prepare to be swept off your feet by sophisticated, sexy and seductive heroes, in some of the world's most glamourous and romantic locations, where power and passion collide.

HISTORICAL

Escape with historical heroes from time gone by. Whether your passion is for wicked Regency Rakes, muscled Vikings or rugged Highlanders, await the romance of the past.

MEDICAL

Set your pulse racing with dedicated, delectable doctors in the high-pressure world of medicine, where emotions run high and passion, comfort and love are the best medicine.

True Love

Celebrate true love with tender stories of heartfelt romance, from the rush of falling in love to the joy a new baby can bring, and a focus on the emotional heart of a relationship.

Desire

Indulge in secrets and scandal, intense drama and plenty of sizzling hot action with powerful and passionate heroes who have it all: wealth, status, good looks…everything but the right woman.

HEROES

Experience all the excitement of a gripping thriller, with an intense romance at its heart. Resourceful, true-to-life women and strong, fearless men face danger and desire - a killer combination!

To see which titles are coming soon, please visit

millsandboon.co.uk/nextmonth